W

To produce *We Poets*, Alw[...]
novel, *Prospero's Lass*. He s[...]
write in the first place, but [...]
lovelorn enough in his life [...]

Prospero's Lass was ignored by mainstream UK publishers, and quickly went out of print with its doomed small press publisher. However, it somehow developed an international cult following, and requests for translation rights began to come in. Except for the very first one, from Germany, all translation requests were refused, for Kennedy had begun to feel he hadn't quite produced the goods. Then, in the dark summer of 1999, he says he fell more than a little in love, and for a time his unhappiness was *definitive*. Finally qualified to do the job properly, *We Poets* swiftly emerged — the funniest book about bad luck and misery ever produced.

WE POETS

a novel by

Alwyne Kennedy

Part One: *Albert's Lass*

Part Two: *Beyond the Joke*

© *Alwyne Kennedy 2000, 2004*

First published as *Prospero's Lass* by Calamity Books.
Revised in 2000 for Furious Books.

ISBN: 0-9549512-0-4

Printed and bound by
Cox & Wyman

Furious Books
PO BOX 39313
LONDON
SE13 7WF
UK
mail@furiousbooks.co.uk
www.furiousbooks.co.uk

Part One
Albert's Lass

We poets in our youth begin in gladness ...
William Wordsworth

For Maureen, who recently lent me money.
They should all be like her.

1.1
Love's Cruel Arrows

Too often when Albert Fox looked out the window, or trudged into town, or read a classic novel, he reported sinking into tragic, yearning love. Currently pre-eminent in his ever-turbulent heart was Lisa, the first big love of his twenty-fourth year on earth.

Today Albert was unwell and in bed. For much of the morning he had found comfort in fancifully picturing Lisa in the role of his devoted attendant. It had been pretence on a grand scale. Tenderly, she'd mopped his fevered brow. By dim candlelight, she'd kept nightly vigil, ready to dispense laudanum to soothe his pains and allow him sleep. Patiently, she'd coaxed him back to strength so that he could complete his great twelve-volume poetic work, *So Handsome but so Melancholy*. Now, however, his suffering had become too genuinely extreme to permit romantic imaginings. Leaning over the side of his bed, his mind was starkly blank as he stared into the dim depths of a brown plastic bucket.

Eventually, after several unproductive retching motions, Albert spewed plentifully. Spent, he rested his throbbing head on the bucket's rim, unaware that a lock of his long, dark hair was dangling in puke.

Once the vomiting storm passed, however, a sweet, merciful calm followed. After rinsing his mouth with water from a cup at hand, he returned his head to the pillow, and his eyes closed peacefully. This becalmed period he experienced in the minutes after puking was almost worth being ill for, he considered. Blessed temporary heaven. And in his imagination now, Lisa was no longer at his sickbed, rather she was a shimmering, soft-focus vision in a clover field, her white milkmaid's dress effulgent in the summer sun. Daisies adorned her silken hair. Larks ascended. Bees bumbled, legs hanging fat and heavy with pollen. The river was warm and languid.

Luxuriating in these new fantasies, Albert began to feel, for once, that life wasn't so bad after all. But no, the universe was making a fresh kind of attack on him — Peep, his female black cat, was trying to eat his hair. Investigation revealed that some of it was garnished with the former contents of his own stomach — again.

He pushed Peep away, tucked the savoury part of his hair under his pillow for protection, and closed his eyes, easily resuming his latest Lisa fantasy. Soon, other milkmaids appeared beside Lisa, to play chase. The sun rose higher over the clover field, and the farmer's old black dog lazily sought the shade of a wooden cart, where it settled sleepily down, keeping one eye half-open for any rat that might dare to venture out into the yard.

"But we did not hear you call!" say the milkmaids as the farmer's stout wife comes hurrying to the gate at the bottom of the field.

"You hear me calling you indoors well enough from twice the distance when it's raining!" the farmer's wife chides good-naturedly, her fat face glowing like a hot coal in a Christmas day fireplace. "You all knows as well as I that milk don't keep long on sultry days like these, but butter does. So just you all come along now, my twelve pretty virgins, there's much churning to be done. And after churning, I'll give you each a glass of the best lemonade I ever made."

The virgins dance!

"If Albert visits, can he have lemonade too?" they excitely plead, running to the gate, with Lisa winning the race.

"There'll be lemonade waiting for Albert on this farm so long as I, my pretty milkmaids, or any of my seven fine daughters are alive to make and pour it," vows the farmer's wife.

Wallowing in this realm of contentment, Albert began to drift into sleep while the merciful, post-puking calm lasted. But then a crashing thud jarred his eyes open. Peep had somehow toppled a bookcase, spilling volumes of science, literature and poetry over his bedroom floor.

Dust billowed from the texts.

Leaving the books fallen, Albert turned on to his side and managed a dream-packed hour's sleep before being woken by the doorbell. Lifting his head from the pillow, he winced before laying the throbbing calamity back down again. No way would he get up to answer the door. Not even if it was the blonde one from Abba, made young again.

Nausea had returned.

The bell rang a second time, more insistently. Then something puzzling: was that his flatmate's voice outside, coming up the garden path? It was only eleven o'clock — Ron should have been at work.

People were entering the flat. Coming from the hall, he could hear other, unfamiliar voices. More than once he discerned his name in the unclear dialogue.

After a single loud tap, the flaking door of his darkened bedroom opened, and Ron stuck his sandy-haired, dark-blue-eyed head into the room.

'What are you doing here?' asked Albert, viewing Ron sideways, noting that he was wearing a new, trippy-coloured waistcoat under his sombre work suit.

'Came home to sort some stuff out before I go away on Sunday,' was Ron's impatient answer. 'What happened to the bookcase?'

'Peep knocked it over. Where are you going Sunday?'

'Told you yesterday,' said Ron, 'Iceland for two weeks. Work.' As his eyes began to adjust to the gloom, Ron saw the bucket. 'Christ, puking again? Were you drinking last night?'

'King's Arms with Jackie.'

Jackie's persuasion and generosity had recently begun transforming Albert from a major bedroom recluse into a minor binge drinker. This was bad: he suffered hangovers so extreme he reckoned he must be some kind of medical freak, perhaps lacking some important alcohol-digesting enzyme. It just wasn't natural what he went through the morning after the modest night before.

Binge sessions aside, Albert spent an unnatural amount of time in his bedroom, and most of the rest of his days not very far from it. He often stayed indoors for months on end, only seeing the outside world on dole signing-on days, when he might also venture to do some shopping if it looked like rain.

Albert's life, if meted out to a convict, would be deemed an inhumane punishment.

Someone once suggested he had struck a compromise with suicide.

Knowing he was about to puke again, with a low, sick, ominous moan, Albert leaned over his bucket, arm resting on its rim.

Ron was unmoved. 'There's a couple of mates of yours out here to see you.'

'I haven't got any mates,' said Albert, which wasn't far off being true.

Then he began vomiting.

Regardless of Albert's condition, Ron brought the visitors into the dim bedroom. In stepped a young policeman and an even younger policewoman. They stood at the bottom of the bed while its shadowy, undressed occupant gulped, snorted and sniffed into a bucket like some great dying beast of the field.

The policewoman eyed the toppled bookcase, like it could be a clue.

The policeman was carrying a bulging manila envelope.

Ron spoke in a death-bed-vigil voice. 'This is him. Albert Fox.'

'Could we have some light?' the policeman asked Ron.

'Bog off,' said Albert.

'He can't tolerate light,' explained Ron immediately.

As if in deference to Albert's condition, the policeman took off his helmet, and in softened Geordie tones asked, 'What's the matter with him, like?'

Albert spoke first, groaning into his bucket, 'I've got progressive melancholia.'

'That serious, is it?' the policeman asked Ron.

'You'll be lucky if he stays lucid,' returned Ron.

'It killed Van Gogh,' groaned Albert.

The policeman now addressed Albert directly. 'You going to be all right?'

Albert, head still over the bucket, answered, 'Doubt it. I'm clinically lovelorn. You'd be this way too if you'd seen Lisa.'

'They're taking the piss,' said the policewoman, simultaneously enlightening her colleague and warning Albert and Ron.

Lifting his head, which pounded in violent protest, Albert looked at his visitors for the first time: *coppers*. With a sneering face, he reached for the cup to rinse his mouth. He could feel the emergence of another post-puking tranquillity, and if it wasn't for the coppers he'd be back in clover with Lisa.

The policeman became a stern, getting-to-the-point copper, and from the manila envelope took out a letter and a pink T-shirt. Upon the T-shirt was printed, in large letters, ALBERT'S LASS. 'Last night you handed this to a young lady. What's it all about, like? And what's all the stuff about sex and death in this letter you gave her?' Putting the T-shirt down on a chair, he took two steps back to benefit from what little light was coming through the doorway, and began reading from Albert's latest love letter — and Albert had written many love letters in his time, and had resurgent interest in the art since acquiring a computer and printer.

Listening to his own composition, Albert realised the stuff about death was the stuff about *twisting wolfsbane for its poisonous wine; suffering his forehead to be touched by nightshade.* And he deduced the stuff about sex was probably the salutation: *pale Virgin shrouded in snow.*

Albert had read a lot of poetry in his teenage years — too much, some would say.

Finished reading, the officer looked hard at Albert.

Spitting a mouthful of water into the bucket, Albert lay back on the bed and stared at the ceiling. 'It's about,' he explained in a measured, solemn voice, 'me leading the world into a new age of romanticism, with Lisa by my side. We shall be as shining icons, raining light upon the dark world of modernity.'

'Lisa says she doesn't know you,' countered the policeman.

'Then I would direct her to the finest works of Keats and Blake, then she shall know me.'

Albert continued to stare at the ceiling, while the policeman stared at him in a confusion of opinions. Handing people letters and T-shirts in a pub probably wasn't an arrestable offence, he understood, but this cocky, clever bastard had to be breaking *some* law, if only he could work out which one.

The charged, speechless impasse was ended by the policewoman shining her torch at Albert's face and issuing a firm warning. 'Look, the lady wants nothing to do with you. Give her any more letters or go anywhere near her again, you'll be in big trouble. Right?'

Albert didn't respond, or even divert his gaze from the ceiling.

'Stay away from her,' said the policeman, and he and his colleague left the room, forgetting the T-shirt.

Ron followed the officers, seeing them out, a courtesy they reluctantly accepted. 'Fucking freaks,' he heard the policeman say as he closed the door after them.

Going straight back into Albert's room, Ron switched the light on and gave Albert what he felt he deserved, in a tone that seemed appropriate.

'Moron.'

Albert sank down into his bed. 'Aw, Ron, I'm suffering. Tell me off later.'

'You need your fucking head examined,' declared Ron scathingly.

'I was only having a laugh,' protested Albert, with weary indignation.

'Lisa wasn't laughing, though, was she?'

'That's all right. I laughed enough for two.'

'Why don't you grow up?' demanded Ron.

'I've outgrown the childish pursuit of maturity,' answered Albert, a retort which secretly impressed Ron, forcing him to change his angle of attack.

'What if they'd seen a joint? Or my plant in the garden?'

Seeing the dope plant was unlikely since someone had stolen it a few days earlier. Grown out of street-sight behind a bush in their front garden, it had been Ron's pride and joy, watered and fertilised daily by him. In the six months since it had been a seed, it had become nearly as tall as Albert, with lush leaves that Ron had only recently begun plundering after his regular supply ran dry.

Ron smoked a lot of dope.

'There isn't a plant in the garden,' Albert unwisely reminded Ron.

'Yeah, like I needed to be told,' said Ron, in a voice charged with grievance. 'But there should have been. Bastard Scoones would have every excuse he needed if I ended up in court on a dope growing charge. It's all right for you, you've got nothing to lose.'

'How was I to know she'd freak?' asked Albert. 'You heard it. It was actually a bloody flattering letter. Proud of it. Stole lines from some of the finest poems ever written.' Turning over on to his side, he muttered, 'I was only playing around.'

'*You* know you were playing around. *I* know you were playing around. But how was *she* to know?'

'Because she's seen my eyes,' said Albert, and a moony expression came over him as he angled his face towards Ron, showing him those eyes. 'Observe my eyes and know tenderness. She's been insensitive to my sensitivity.'

Ron didn't agree. 'You think that everyone else alive exists just to provide amusement for you, don't you?'

Albert nodded, if only because he knew it would set Ron off.

'You're arrogant, that's what you are,' indicted Ron.

Albert agreed. 'I'm supercilious too. Often bombastic.'

'You'll get your comeuppance one day,' predicted Ron. Picking up the troublesome T-shirt, he held it aloft for dismissive examination. Shaking his head, he sneered, 'One of the most cunning minds ever devised by nature. Who would believe it? Who *would* believe it?'

Albert looked at him.

'That's what Tony said about you last night,' explained Ron. 'A consultant psychiatrist, remember. *One of the most cunning minds ever devised by nature.* But I wonder. Sometimes I really do wonder.'

'Thought Lisa would have been proud to wear it,' muttered Albert.

'Who the fuck is Lisa, anyway?' asked Ron, but before Albert could conjure some fancy reply describing her as all that's dearest in nature, he threw in a good guess. 'For fuck's sake, not that bimboish one you were ogling down the King's Arms last week?'

'The bimboish one who was ogling *me* last week,' corrected Albert.

'Yeah, only because she didn't know you're weird. She knows

now, though.'

'I'm not weird," contended Albert. 'I'm deep — possessed of one of the most cunning minds ever devised by nature.'

It was now time for Ron to pass sentence: 'If you and that crappy, cheap computer you type shite on bring any more cops around, I'll thump you.'

Albert seemed genuinely sorry. 'Okay. I promise next time I send a love letter, I'll tell you first, and I'll omit my address.'

'That's better.'

'In fact I'm going to send one now — that policewoman was lovely. Switch the computer on for me and take dictation.'

Ron cracked. Taking hold of the bottom of Albert's bed, he tipped the whole thing vertical, resting it upright against the wall, with its panicking, protesting occupant slipping head first down to the floor, coming to rest in a heap of duvet, sheet and pillow.

Being six-foot-six and naturally built to match, upending Albert's bed was no hard task for Ron. In biblical times, Ron would have gone down in the exaggerated parchments as having been a mighty giant. He made almost all men feel runty when he stood next to them.

'I knew I shouldn't have got you that thing,' complained Ron. 'You're supposed to be writing a novel on it, for fuck's sake. I want my money back for it. Get a job and give me my money back, you talentless fucker.'

He started shaking the bed.

'I've already finished a novel!' claimed Albert desperately. 'I finished it yesterday.'

Ron ceased the shaking. 'What? Don't believe you. Show me.'

'The manuscript's on the table.'

Ron looked at the table, and saw only the slimmest of documents. Three pages, to be exact, and that included a title page.

The title page read: *BEFORE THE BEGINNING (My First Novel)*.

Admittedly, upon examination, the second page revealed itself to be crammed with text, and the third was well over half utilised (counting the large *The End*), but Ron couldn't help suspecting that novels were supposed to be just a little more substantial, so he cracked again. 'Get up and get a job,' he ordered, kicking the underside of the vertical bed, raising puffs of dust.

'Stop upsetting me. It's my birthday.'

Ron stopped kicking. 'It's not, is it?'

'Fucking is. Twenty-four years ago today my unhappy heart began its labour of senseless bumping.'

Ron sat down on the rickety wooden chair near the computer he had unwisely bought for Albert. 'Why the fuck do I share a flat with him?' he wanted the gods to reveal.

'For the fashion tips,' said Albert from within the heap of duvet, sheet and pillow behind the upended bed.

Ron picked up one of the science books from the floor — *Entropy: The Leveller of the Universe*, and began looking through it. 'You ought to sell these fucking books. I haven't seen you read anything for years.'

'Why are you in such an extra twatty mood today?'

'You'd be in an extra twatty mood too if you'd had to bite your tongue while being given a pathetic warning about being too informal at work,' griped Ron indignantly. 'Then he saw my new waistcoat and told me to take it off and never come in wearing anything "psychedelic" again. He's been totally paranoid about drugs since a syringe and some burnt foil was found in the toilets. I was really fucked off, so later I told him I needed to take the rest of the day off to sort out some things for Iceland. If I'd stuck around I would have punched the ugly fucker.'

So it was that Scoones bastard again. Albert hated Scoones. Scoones, Scoones, Scoones — Albert even hated his name. Scoones was Ron's manager, and he made Albert's life a misery by frequently making Ron come home from work extra twatty and kicky.

'I wouldn't bite it,' said Albert.

'And you wouldn't get paid,' Ron pointed out after mentally rewinding the conversation to determine why biting something was relevant.

'Then I wouldn't get paid.'

'Bastard Scoones,' grumbled Ron, leaving the room, taking the entropy book with him.

Ron was twenty-five. Until he was twenty-three, he'd been "unfocussed", doing casual jobs between periods of unemployment. Then he'd started to panic, bought a suit, and did a six month computer course. After the course, he'd applied for over a hundred jobs, and got three interviews. The three interviews resulted in one offer of employment as a junior Systems Trainer for a computer company just outside town. Scoones had been off sick with psoriasis when Ron was taken on, and on his return, Ron got the impression that he'd resented an employment decision having been taken in his absence. That was the start of a constant underlying tension between them that seemed only to increase as time went on, despite the generally acknowledged fact that Ron was good at his job, and was obviously popular in the office.

Ron had heard that Scoones believed he didn't respect the company enough.

As Ron left the bedroom, switching the light off on his way out, Peep entered and investigated the new furniture lay-out. Discovering an inviting heap of warm bedding, she settled down next to Albert, purring contentedly.

Albert realised he was getting better. There would be no more puking. Slow recovery was underway, and although his head still throbbed, he reckoned he could handle standing up now. Crawling from the wreckage of his bed, he swapped the insulation of the duvet for a pair of faded black jeans and a faded black T-shirt that proclaimed *Not Long Now* in white letters.

Albert was almost permanently attired in this allusion-to-suicide T-shirt.

Taking his puke bucket for sloshing-out, Albert went to the bathroom, which was essentially a breeze-block shed with plumbing, stuck on to the house as an afterthought. It was so perennially damp it had become a place of accidental beauty, often remarked upon by visitors. So flaking was the plaster, and so prolific and variegated the mould, the place appeared ancient, weathered and quite natural. In there, particularly when stoned, Albert could imagine he was in a cave behind a forest waterfall, a fantasy aided by the presence of a lush, verdant fern in a pot on the window.

Might as well have a bath while I'm here, thought Albert.

'Oi, Aquaboy,' called Ron from the hall some time later, 'I'm off into town.'

Aquaboy was one of Ron's names for Albert, applied whenever he spent more than an hour in the bathroom, which was most days.

'It's my special day,' Albert reminded Ron, with glum stroppiness, justifying his extended immersion in water, water to which, for birthday luxury, he'd added quarter of a bottle of shampoo not belonging to him. Holding his breath, he slipped completely under the water to wash his polluted hair. When he resurfaced, he heard Ron leaving the flat.

Baths did funny things to Albert. Preparing for them, he always felt like he was on the verge of a new beginning, for once washed, he would surely storm out into the world and blind it with what he could do. Trouble is, he tended to remain in the water for so long the world was coming home again for tea by the time he was dried and dressed. "A bath isn't some kind of watershed", Ron had lectured him one day, "it's just a shed full of water".

The doorbell rang, but Albert ignored it. He had important lolling to do yet.

Two minutes later, someone was tapping on the bathroom window, but he didn't move the curtain to look.

'Albert. Albert, I know you're in, I just met Ron. Get out of the bath and open the door.'

It was Jackie.

Albert didn't have what could by any stretch of the imagination be described as a wide circle of friends. Excluding his flatmate, he really only had two: Rebecca, and, more recently, her sister, Jackie. A few acquaintances, yes, (being mainly Ron's friends) but only two proper friends, and often that figure seemed extravagant to him. There were only two people he really bothered with, and who reciprocally bothered with him. Months could go by without him exchanging so much as a single word with someone additional, excluding the odd "Thanks" and "No, I don't have a fucking Loyalty card. Do I look the loyal kind?" muttered in supermarkets. All this had not gone unnoticed by Ron, who maintained that Albert was already most of the way to being an eerie recluse, predicting complete madness one day very soon if he didn't get out into the world a bit more.

Ron had even tried to organise a sweepstake on the mental event.

Albert had never dreamily pictured Jackie by his sickbed, or in a clover field, or anywhere else, except once or twice in a circus. Jackie was an oddity. Nothing about the poor girl seemed to match. Her arms were of normal length, yet her hands were tiny – he had once joked to her that she would be better off just sharpening her wrists to useful spikes. Her eyes were different colours; one pale green, one pale grey. Her breasts were also disparate, one being the size of a fried egg, the other the size of four fried eggs. Her semi-circle of upper teeth were rotated so much to one side that her two large incisors pointed thirty degrees away from dead-ahead, and her lower teeth were badly chipped from a childhood misadventure. Her shoulders were rounded, so she always appeared to be slouching, yet she was busy and efficient. Her legs were stout, yet she was generally slim. And although she was generally slim, her face was round and large, and she looked kind of generally fat, and she had a definite second chin, but her first chin was notable only for its absence.

Actually, although he sometimes viewed Jackie as a circus freak, he had fallen in love with her once. The first time he saw her, a year or so back, she had been sat facing away from him, and her lush, long brown hair had fleetingly deceived his eye and heart.

'Albert, open the fucking door,' insisted Jackie.

'Coming,' answered Albert unenthusiastically.

Stepping out of the water, he quickly towelled himself down, put his jeans and T-shirt on, and went to let Jackie in, leading her to his bedroom.

She had a carrier bag with her.

'Why's your bed like that?' she asked upon entering the darkened room. 'Why are your books on the floor?'

'Dunno,' answered Albert while returning the bed to its proper position, causing Peep to flee in imagined fear of her life. 'Mysteries just spring up around me.' Sitting on the bed, dropping his head into his hands, he moaned, 'Oh my fucking hungover head.'

'Hangover?' queried Jackie disparagingly. 'You only drank as much as me.'

'Poet's constitution,' claimed Albert in muttered defence.

'You really are crap, aren't you, Albert?'

'Have you been talking to the neighbours?'

'No. I saw it on the news last night. Can I open the curtains?'

'I've sewn them together,' said Albert, who hated the view — the view of an evangelical church across the street and its large, inspirational notice board that found new ways to depress him each month.

Jackie switched on the room light. Delving into her carrier bag, she produced a wrapped present, proffering it to Albert, who paid it no attention.

'Maggie,' he pined in a pathetic, lovelorn voice. 'Maggie.'

Jackie withdrew the present. 'Maggie? Who's Maggie.'

'Maggie from *The Mill on the Floss*,' he pined, partly to answer Jackie, partly to indulge in further romantic suffering.

'Oh, fictional again,' realised Jackie. 'She held the present out a second time. 'Happy birthday, Albert.'

Albert briefly looked at the offering, then lay back on the bed to stare at the ceiling.

'Happy? Jackie, if I've told you once, I've told you a thousand times: if you're going to talk to me, talk sense.'

'I am talking sense,' contended Jackie. 'It's your birthday — *celebrate.*'

'Birthday? Oh, yeah — spun twenty-four times around the sun. No wonder I feel sick.'

Jackie dropped the present on to Albert's chest.

'It's wonderful,' he said, still staring at the ceiling. 'What I've always wanted.'

'You could at least open it,' complained Jackie.

'Don't rush me. I'm a poet. I need to reflect.'

'Open it now,' demanded Jackie. 'Hurry, I've got to get back to work.'

With a show of disinterest, Albert sat up and began unwrapping the gift. 'How the fuck did you know it was my birthday?' he grumbled.

'I made the effort to find out.'

'How?'

'Does it matter?'

'Yes. I've been thwarted.'

'Look, just open it,' snapped Jackie. 'I asked my sister, if you must know. Rebecca's known you for years and years. She should know your birthday.'

Presently, Albert was holding in his hands a billowing, lilac silk shirt. 'Er, thanks, Jackie. You shouldn't have.'

He got up to switch off the room light.

'If I shouldn't have, I wouldn't have,' stated Jackie.

'No, I really mean you shouldn't have,' said Albert, returning to sit on the bed. 'I can't wear it.'

'And why not?'

'It's cheerful.'

'Yeah, that's why I bought it,' explained Jackie crossly. 'Make a change from that silly T-shirt you always wear.'

'But people will think I'm shallow,' explained Albert, dropping the gift on to the floor and lying back on the bed to stare at the ceiling again. 'They'll think I don't know all happiness arises from misapprehension.'

'Why do I bother with you?' asked Jackie, picking the shirt up and hanging it over the back of the wooden chair in the room.

'Make me a coffee and I'll tell you,' promised Albert.

'Put the shirt on and I'll make you one,' promised Jackie.

Albert didn't stir.

'Please,' pleaded Jackie. 'Just once.' Albert remained motionless,

18

and Jackie gave up trying to get him to wear his present. 'Oh, suit your miserable, rude self.'

'Okay,' said Albert plainly.

When she'd stopped feeling annoyed, Jackie asked, 'What are you doing for your birthday tonight?'

'Shuffling round the flat, murmuring spirituals,' answered Albert, still staring at the ceiling.

'No, really,' pursued Jackie. 'Are you going out anywhere?'

'No.'

'Why doesn't that surprise me?' she wondered redundantly. 'I couldn't have come out with you anyway. I'm at college tonight. That's why I had to come down with the present now.' The ceiling began creaking, and Jackie looked up at it. 'What's making that noise?'

'The woman from upstairs. She's started using her front room. Sounds like she doesn't have a carpet, and the floorboards creak like fuck. She walks around or paces or something. Right through the night sometimes.'

'Doesn't it drive you nuts?'

'Hasn't yet.'

'Does it keep you awake?'

'Don't pay any attention to it.'

Jackie went to make Albert's coffee, but only, she explained, because she also wanted one herself. Once she left the bedroom, Albert picked up a hand mirror and gloomily regarded his shadowy reflection, dispiritedly pushing his damp hair around. It couldn't be put off any longer: *it was time for a haircut.* Haircuts for Albert meant once a year or so tipping his head upside-down, bundling his locks and cutting six inches off the length with a swiftness reminiscent of surgeons in pre-anaesthetic days. Some years he got partially lucky with the result, but most years he didn't and ended up looking like a dumpster-living retard for weeks.

Getting off the bed to retrieve his scissors from a drawer, he positioned himself appropriately. Returning to the bedroom with the coffees, Jackie at once saw that something reckless was about to happen.

'What are you doing?' she asked in a high voice, quickly putting the cups down on the back of the fallen bookcase.

'Cutting my hair,' answered Albert, but finding his scissors had become too blunt and loose to work easily.

'No!' shrieked Jackie, wresting the scissors from him.

Sitting on the bed, Albert gave up on the idea of cutting his hair, if only because tipping his head upside-down had greatly aggravated his headache.

Jackie sat beside him. 'Why don't you go to a hairdressers for once?'

'If I've told you once, Jackie,' said Albert, wagging his finger, 'I've told you a thousand times: if you're going to talk to me, talk sense. I'm way too deep for that kind of taking-an-interest thing.'

'Why do I bother with you?' sighed Jackie.

'Make me beans on toast and I'll tell you.'

'Shut up. Go to a hairdressers. You'd look really good with a proper cut.'

Albert's response was to lie on his bed again, stare at the ceiling, and repeat pathetically, 'Beans on toast. Beans on toast...' But his manipulative whining fell on stern ears. Jackie rushed her coffee and went back to work, leaving Albert to make his own beans on toast, most of which he threw away because he was still feeling somewhat nauseous.

A little after one o'clock, with his headache tolerably diminished, Albert was closing his flat's inner door and walking across the tiled hall toward the outer, shared door of the converted house. Harry, the occupant of the attic flat, was sitting on the bottom steps with a can of lager. An alcoholic of around sixty, with little hair, three teeth, and one dirty green jumper, as ever, Harry's door keys were dangling on a thick boot lace tied loosely around his neck.

Albert ignored Harry, and Harry ignored Albert.

Opening the outer door, Albert found himself face-to-face with a postwoman. 'This you?' she asked, showing Albert a junk mail envelope.

'Uh huh,' muttered Albert, taking the letter and tossing it into the hall. 'Anything else? Anything looking like a birthday card?'

'No, sorry.'

Albert set off walking into town. He was wearing a long black coat over his *Not Long Now* T-shirt. A charity shop find, this coat, in its youth, might have warmed some well-heeled toff, for it possessed a faded grandeur, born in some distant time when style prevailed.

Albert Fox lived in Durham City, fifteen miles south of Newcastle. He was not a native of Durham City, however. He had been born and razed — how he'd once written it on a form — in Darlington, twenty miles south of the autumnal street he now walked. For someone who'd spent his entire life in the Northeast, his accent was decidedly moderate, because television and radio had been a greater influence on him than his peers had been, and both his parents had hailed from other parts of the United Kingdom.

Ron had been born and half-raised in Surrey, and his own accent still testified to that.

Jackie's parents were middle class, sounded it, and had passed on much of their speaking manner to their children.

Thirteen minutes later, Albert had reached his destination, whereupon a young lady smiled at him, said her name was Caroline, and led him to a chair.

'How short do you want it?' asked Caroline, drawing his hair away from his face once he was sitting.

'Shorter than a bucket's deep,' answered Albert, while observing the slenderness of Caroline's wrists.

*

Just after his first ever proper haircut, Albert drifted into the estate agents where Jackie worked. She was busy totalling some figures and didn't realise he was there until he suddenly slumped facedown on to her desk, whereupon she bolted upright and emitted a small shriek.

Customers turned around.

Barry, Jackie's short, camp, middle-aged, Glaswegian manager, cast a disapproving look at Albert.

'Wrists like I've never seen before,' whined Albert. 'Such maddening wrists.'

'Albert... hello,' faltered Jackie before regaining her composure. 'You've done your hair like I suggested!'

'Coincidence.'

Jackie extended a tentative hand and began fingering his locks. 'It's curling a bit now that it's much shorter. Told you it would.'

'Each curl individually sucked into shape by a supermodel.' Sitting up, he waved a lock in front of Jackie. 'See this one? Claudia Schiffer.'

'It's cut very well. Did you go to a hairdresser's?'

'Like a conquering hero,' claimed Albert. 'Cost me twelve bastard quid, though. Only got one quid left until my giro comes on Wednesday.'

'Money well spent, though,' she declared. 'You look dead raunchy.'

'But it cost me my peace of mind, too.'

'How's that?'

'If you'd seen the hairdresser, you wouldn't need to ask. Such wrists. Such maddening wrists.' Throwing himself on to the desk had caused his headache to step up a grade, and he now made it show. 'Oh, my fucking throbbing brain misery.'

When Albert swore, Barry pursed his lips and cast a reproachful look at Jackie. Getting up from behind her desk, she flashed a smile to her manager, pretending not to have understood his expression. After quickly brushing her hair, she gathered her papers together and took them into the back room, reappearing a few moments later with a glass of water and some tablets.

'Here, Albert, for your headache. Painkillers.'

'Are they effective against the sting of love's cruel arrows?' he asked, with little hope in his voice.

Jackie smiled and held the tablets out for taking, but Albert declined the offer, explaining that no medicine ever had any effect on his hangovers. 'My suffering is immutable,' he concluded.

'Jackie, don't forget the Park Mews transaction,' said Barry.

Jackie knew this meant she should get Albert to leave. She circumvented her boss by saying she was taking a coffee break, which allowed her to keep Albert in her company for a further fifteen minutes.

When he finally set off back home, Albert took a route that passed the hairdressers. Glimpsing Caroline, he whined quietly, and resolved to write a poem about her wrists one day soon, having a hunch he could successfully rhyme *maddening wrists* with *saddening trysts*. Later, turning off the main road and into Devon Road, where he lived, he saw that the evangelical church opposite his flat was posting a new inspirational slogan. A workman was just finishing pasting a twenty-foot long sign which read, in monumental day-glo orange letters, *JESUS WILL ANSWER YOUR PRAYERS!*

Wearing a T-shirt that read *JESUS ARMY*, a young man with thin arms and born again eyes was overseeing the job.

Stopping, Albert looked grimly at the slogan.

'Jesus will answer your prayers!' grinned the young man with thin arms to Albert.

Making no concession to politeness, Albert said, 'After two thousand fucking years of fucking calamities and atrocities, you'd think that even someone as dumb looking as you would realise that praying is futile.'

Caught unprepared by the unexpected challenge to his faith, the young man with thin arms only said, 'Jesus loves you.'

'What you really mean,' returned Albert, 'is watch your step because Jesus loves *me*.'

The young man with thin arms didn't stay to agree or disagree, and went into the modern, brick-built church.

For two years now, Albert had suffered a daily diet of depressing inspirational church-notice-board slogans, fed to him through his window. The sinister progress of American-led evangelism had got personal. He'd been driven to the brink, and consequently the expression of anything remotely religious at all now reduced him to pulling his own hair out. This growing militant atheism was often looked upon as a sporting opportunity by Ron, who some days seemed intent on rendering Albert bald.

Albert's list of disdained religions didn't end with the major faiths. Astrology, reflexology, and the ludicrous ilk, were as good as religions to him – or as bad as religions. And as for the Jesus Army, Albert knew them to be a culty, fundamentalist group that preyed on lost young souls, filling their heads with nonsense about demons and devils.

Feeling like he'd struck his first major blow for the advancement of scientific thinking, Albert crossed the road to reach 17 Devon Road, the converted Victorian terrace house that was his home. Lifting the gate latch, he glanced at the hole in the overgrown garden that showed where Ron's dope plant had recently existed.

Bell buttons indicated how the house was divided. The ground floor was Ron and Albert's, and this was shown not by a name below its button, but by a childish drawing of the pair. The attic flat was the home of Harry, but no name existed to testify to this, and its bell button had been hanging off the wall since before Albert had moved in. The button for the middle flat did bear a name, but the writing was so spidery it had never been deciphered, hence the ghostly occupant was referred to as the *woman from upstairs*.

The woman from upstairs was a deathly pale wretch with a body amounting to little more than the skeleton beneath her skin. Taking into consideration how apparent famine might have prematurely aged her appearance, Albert guessed her to be in her sixties.

Her eyes seemed haunted.

No one ever came to see the woman from upstairs, or Harry. They didn't even get letters – at least Albert and Ron had never seen letters for them land in the hall.

Pushing open the street door with his foot, Albert crossed the small, tiled hall where the dustbins were kept, and slid his key into his own inner door. Closing the inner door behind him, he proceeded to the drab living room he shared with Ron.

Ron, no longer in his work suit, was sitting on the sofa, pen and notepad in hand, pondering.

'Seen the fucking new monstrosity they've stuck up over the road?' complained Albert.

'No.'

Largely ignored by Ron, Albert went over to the window to glare at the offensive sign. 'Why are people allowed to spread lies? Every school kid has the lie of religion drummed into them by law. It's crazy. It shouldn't even be legal — let alone compulsory — to promote thinking that conflicts with the evidence. Why isn't it illegal?'

'Don't know.'

'Once the American evangelical warmongers have finished exterminating the Muslims, how long do you think it'll be before they start on the atheists? You know, the free-thinking pretty people with sexy haircuts.'

'Don't know.'

Turning away from the window, Albert now realised that Ron was far more interested in doing whatever it was he was doing than in conversation, which wasn't unusual.

'What are you doing?'

'Picking my lottery numbers.'

'That fool's dream again. Put the money on the horses, idiot, at least you'll occasionally win.'

Ron ignored Albert.

'Tell you what,' Albert went on, 'why don't you do what I used to do when I was still shallow enough to take an interest in money. Select your six numbers. Write them down, but don't buy a ticket. Then watch the draw and celebrate with a whoop and a dance when they don't come up and you realise you've saved a pound. Never fails.'

For all the notice Ron took of him, Albert could have become invisible and mute.

'Fifteen's a lucky number, isn't it?' mused Ron.

'Do we have to go through a paranormal numerology ritual *every* week? Just go to church instead of doing the fucking lottery. Same thing, virtually. Comparable odds of salvation, I reckon.'

Ron looked up from his numbers, and complained, 'Jeez, you've got it bad today, haven't you?'

'Too right,' agreed Albert. 'Anyway, why should fifteen be lucky?'

'Got my first shag at fifteen.'

'Ones with your dad don't count.'

'What about nineteen?' wondered Ron, looking down to his numbers again. 'That's how many different girls I've done it with.' Throwing a sideways look at Albert, he added, 'Beats your score by a long chalk, doesn't it?'

'Never told me it was a competition,' returned Albert, taking off his heavy coat.

Ron was suddenly struck by Albert's hair: it didn't look like it belonged to a feudal peasant. Collar-length and thrown back, it looked like it really belonged to a male model with a six-pack stomach. 'I don't understand,' said Ron, gaping insultingly, 'your hair looks close to reasonable... in a non-threatening, boy band kind of way.'

'Proper haircut,' explained Albert.

'Proper hairdressers?'

'Yep.'

Ron quickly realised the likely implications of this. 'You better not have spent your rent money on it.'

'Haven't touched it.'

Ten minutes later, the pair were sitting at the table beside the front window, with the cat up there with them. Ron was still pondering lottery issues, and Albert was trying to interest Peep in a speck of his own blood that had welled up on his finger after he'd accidentally pricked himself.

Peep looked at him as if he was stupid.

'What about —,' began Ron.

'Look,' cut in Albert, 'how many times do I have to tell you? Exact knowledge of the future is specifically outlawed by Heisenberg's Uncertainty Principle. There is absolutely no way of knowing due to the inherent randomness of quantum events, therefore all so-called predictive arts are clearly bullshit.'

'So what about twelve, then?'

'Heisenberg's Uncertainty Principle,' replied Albert, who knew more than most about such things.

'Twelve's the number of signs of the zodiac.'

'Say anything astrological and I'll hit you.'

'What about twenty-two?' mused Ron innocently. 'That's the number of cards in a tarot pack.'

Albert threw a small fit. 'Natural born scientist in state of fucking anger! No truly random event can ever be predicted. The Quantum

Theory, the most successful scientific theory ever, states it so.'

When Albert had begun his fit, Ron had begun leaving. 'Going to the lottery shop,' he said when disappearing through he door. 'Pay the landlord if he comes when I'm out.'

The landlord, as it happened, was just arriving in his rusting car, wearing his usual dark suit and white shirt. Stepping on to the pavement, he encountered Ron. Albert watched from the window as they exchanged limited words at the gate — it was rent day, and he'd come to collect. Appearing to be in his late twenties, the landlord lived in a neighbouring town, and that was all Albert knew about him. Every fortnight he came for the money, marked the rent card, then left. All done with the minimum of words, little eye contact, and no cheer. Visits were never more than two minute affairs, and Albert had never once seen him extend a visit to go up the stairs to collect rent from his two other tenants.

Soon there was knocking on the flat's inner door, and Albert left the table to get the rent money from a drawer. With the rent card and cash in hand, he greeted the landlord. 'Evening. Two hundred. Two weeks' rent.'

The landlord said nothing, just made an awkward, reluctant nod as he took the money. He was being watched by the woman from upstairs. Wearing a shabby, purple, jumble sale coat, she was standing by the dustbins in the hall, standing like mental patients do, lost in some private nightmare of forlorn distress.

The landlord marked Albert's rent card and left, passing the woman from upstairs without so much as glancing.

Albert went into the kitchen for a snack, sitting at the old, rickety wooden table that was badly stained and splitting in three places. When Ron returned a short time later, that is where he found his flatmate, eating, and reading his own "novel", *Before the Beginning*.

'Paid the rent?' enquired Ron, receiving a minimal nod for an answer.

Ron sat across the table from Albert.

'That was a work of rare genius,' murmured Albert, reaching the end of the story, and turning back to the first page for another reading.

'You going out with Jackie tonight?' asked Ron.

'Why should I be?' replied Albert, not diverting his eyes from his own literature.

'It's your birthday and she's your big new friend.'

'She's in college tonight.'

'Yeah? Kept it up, did she? What's she studying for, anyway? Degree?'

'Nah, just A Levels. She wants to do a degree, though. Psychology.'

'Psychology?' mused Ron. 'Maybe she wants to find out why she fancies you?'

'Jackie couldn't fancy anyone. She'd need oestrogen to do that.'

'Yeah? So explain all those casual yet flattering remarks she makes to you about you being handsome and cute. Face it, Albert, she's after you. Do something about your manners and she could be your third shag. She mightn't get the police on to you, either.'

Albert pretended he wasn't listening. 'That was a work of rare genius,' he murmured, returning to the first page to begin yet another reading while spooning some food into his mouth.

'Reckon you fancy her too,' Ron went on.

'Fuck off.'

'Come off it,' said Ron, 'you two can't keep away from each other these days, can you? It's mutual.'

'I said fuck off,' snarled Albert, brandishing his spoon.

'Well, if it isn't mutual, you're leading her on, that's for sure.'

'No I'm not.'

Ron began humming the *Love Story* theme tune, eliciting another order to fuck off from Albert before he began reading his "novel" again.

'So what are you doing tonight?' asked Ron once he'd finished teasing.

'Welling up,' answered Albert.

'Where?'

'Bedroom.'

'Got any money left?'

'No.'

'I'll treat you tonight,' offered Ron.

'Nah, staying in. Got a couple of wanks to finish.'

'It's your birthday, for fuck's sake. Go out.'

'I'm too deep for that shallow world out there. I'm a novelist of great distinction.'

'Hah,' scoffed Ron, moving over to the sink to fill the kettle, 'that's a laugh. Some novelist. It's four months since you said you were going to write a book and I got you that computer and printer, but you still haven't written anything except weird love letters.'

'That's not exactly true now, Ronald, and you know it isn't,' corrected Albert, pointing to his "novel" with his spoon.

27

'Not even two pages long,' criticised Ron, plugging the kettle in.

'That was a work of rare genius,' murmured Albert, once more returning to the first page.

Ron had had enough. He pushed Albert's face down on to the table, and menaced, 'If you haven't written a proper novel by the end of the month, I'm going to sell that computer. That'll stop you bringing cops around.'

'I'll write one!' spluttered Albert. 'I'll write one!'

'You'd better,' threatened Ron, releasing him. 'End of the month, or else.'

'I need longer,' protested Albert indignantly. 'Writing's laborious work.'

'Yeah,' sneered Ron, 'for someone who's lazy and useless.'

'It's lonely, too,' claimed Albert, with a small sob in his voice. 'I cried four times writing this.' The sob gave way to more indignation. 'Anyway, I haven't always been lazy and useless. I had a proper job once.'

'Yeah,' said Ron, in a ridiculing tone while putting teabags into two mugs, 'a poxy newspaper delivery job years ago when you were at school. And you were sacked.'

'Unfairly dismissed,' Albert countered, 'because I cared too much.'

'Wanker,' said Ron.

Upon being handed his cup of tea, Albert took it into his bedroom, placing it on the back of the fallen bookcase while he plugged in a lamp. Then he lay on his bed and stared at the ceiling, an habitual inactivity. Ron considered Albert's capacity for ceiling staring to be something of a dark freak show, and sometimes brought his less nervous friends in to wonder and sneer. Albert's own few friends and acquaintances considered his horizontal inactivities to be evidence of some mental malaise. While conceding that he was undeniably some sort of genius, he was, they agreed, also undeniably in a big slump. 'So what?' he would say, 'I'm just one of six billion all destined to return to dust.' It was also agreed that to advance his life from horizontal standstill, he should have at least *some* part of his head examined, a suggestion he never listened to. 'You never listen to anything anyone tells you, do you?' Jackie had said to him the other night. 'Not really,' he had replied, adding, 'Try subtly implying things instead. I enjoy the thrill of the chase.'

*

The breeze that had blown throughout the day had petered out. High pressure had muscled in over the north of England, promising a clear, frosty night. Tomorrow, that high was forecast to depart, allowing a rain-laden warm front to move over the country. But for now there was no cloud in the Durham sky to obscure the evening sun, a sun which offered Ron the opportunity to polish his car one more time before the week was over. Ron's car was a collector's item — a Ford Consul that, thanks to countless hours and pounds lavished on it, appeared to be in no worse condition now than when it had rolled off the production line, one day in 1960.

Wearing a bulky, khaki jacket that owed its design to the US military, Ron was devoutly polishing invisible rust blemishes off the car's chrome bumper when Albert sauntered up.

'Nice evening,' observed Ron.

'I was going to say that, but I decided it would be too vacuous,' returned Albert.

Ron stopped polishing and drew in a breath, as if to speak... 'Nah,' he eventually decided, 'it's too vacuous.'

'What is?' inquired Albert keenly. 'Go on, tell me. Go on. Please.'

Ron would not be drawn, and resumed polishing. Presently, Albert asked, 'What kind of dickhead devotes his life to overcoming bits of rust on a piece of metal?' Ron didn't answer. Albert idly watched Ron's polishing cloth as it moved in small, quick circles over the surface of the bumper, a surface that presented Albert with his own reflection. Hell, he decided in a while, Jackie was right: he *was* raunchy. He'd often accepted that he could look passably handsome under favourable conditions, but now he'd stormed into a higher league. It was the haircut. His magical haircut was elevating *all* of him. In a fit of narcissism, he began assessing his new raunchiness. His eyes were an interesting greyish-green. His nose was sensible. His lips were surely kissable. And his body was more than adequate: not far off six-foot, and fit to run a fairly swift mile if the motivation was ever great enough, which it never had been.

'I look fucking resplendent,' he declared, loudly.

'It's deeper than you think,' said Ron, not interrupting the rhythm of his work.

'My soul's resplendent too?'

'Not about you — why I polish my car so often. The universe decays *but my car endures.*'

'I'd like to take scientific issue with that statement,' said Albert contrarily.

By gift of nature and dint of languid self-study, Albert was able to argue with reasonable authority on many scientific subjects, but seldom did, for no one ever seemed to worship him adequately for it. Especially pretty girls.

'Too late,' said Ron rapidly, 'I'm already talking again. You see, it's all to do with entropy. I'm reversing its effects. *That's* why I devote my life to overcoming bits of rust.'

'You're not really understanding that entropy book you stole from me, are you? The universe decays *faster* because of your car. You've got tunnel vision. You don't see the global picture. You only accelerate entropy by doing what you're doing. The metal on your car reacts with oxygen, releasing energy. Appalled by this local entropy, you then go and release many times more energy to counter the rusting. Coal was hewn out of the ground to provide the energy to make that chrome cleaner stuff you're using—'

'I was only on page ten,' Ron cut in, suddenly polishing harder.

'And it's not just your car that destroys the cosmos,' Albert further declared, 'it's you as a person as well. You eat compounds all day long, robbing them of energy. Then you squander that energy in twatty heat and motion. You're a selfish little pocket in space-time where entropy is neutralised at the expense of the rest of the universe, that's what you are.'

Ron looked at Albert. 'I'm confused — do you want me to give you a lift to the pub tonight or not?'

'Yes,' answered Albert baldly.

Ron got on with his work, and Albert admired his own reflection again.

'Just think, it'll look even better when it peaks,' he said.

'Peaks? When what peaks?'

'My already glorious hair. 'Haircuts always peak sometime after they've been done. Jackie told me.'

'Oh.'

Albert admired himself some more. 'If you see it starting to peak, tell me so I can nip out and impress girls with it.'

Ron stopped polishing, pointed to their flat, and commanded, 'Fuck off indoors, switch on the computer I stupidly bought you, and write a proper novel.'

As if in listless compliance, Albert shuffled away. Going to his room, as instructed he did switch on the computer, but only to design and print out a counterfeit medical chart. Securing this to a clipboard he'd recently found on the street, he attached it to the bottom of his bed before lying down and staring at the ceiling.

The chart read: *DO NOT RESUSCITATE.*

1.2
A Difficult Decision

Four weeks before Albert's birthday, all places on earth experienced a day and night of equal length, and it was said the autumnal equinox had occurred. On the eve of the equinox, as the sun was setting, forty-nine men and women with a shared purpose had ascended Glastonbury Tor, a small hill. Most of the forty-nine lived in London, and the rest not far from that city. All night they remained on the hill's summit, wearing long robes of ecclesiastical cut. Forty-five wore white robes, and stood together in a choir-like formation. In front of that group, four men wearing more elaborate red robes formed their own group. Within a ring of flaming torches, these four earnest men circled what would appear to the uninitiated to be home-made metal box with an antenna and a button, atop a wooden tripod.

These four men were the High Teachers.

A small documentary film crew was present.

All night, except for toilet and food breaks, the brethren in the group and the High Teachers within the flaming ring had chanted *Om, wallah wallah, om. Om, wallah wallah, om. Om, wallah wallah, om. Om, wallah wallah, om.* Those in the group had held their palms facing the metal box, and the High Teachers had gesticulated to it strangely and intensely. Now, the sun was about to rise on their misty hill, a hill that had perhaps once stood as an island — the island of Avalon — where legend said Joseph of Arimathea built the first British Christian church. That legend deepened to purport that Joseph of Arimathea had been the uncle of Jesus, who one time, on a trading mission, had brought his divine child nephew to Avalon, causing William Blake to muse if those sacred feet really had, in ancient times, walked upon England's mountains green. Further legends state that, after his nephew's ascent to heaven, Joseph returned to Avalon to bury the Holy Grail; and that King Arthur and Queen Guinevere lie nearby in vigilant rest, alert for England's hour of need.

A High Teacher — Simon — raised his arms high, and the chanting ceased. In silence, all looked to the east, and when the sun's first rays sparkled on the horizon, the High Teachers chorused, 'Solar equinox illuminus!' and the larger group became their echo.

Exhilarated, tired, their work considered done, three of the High

Teachers left the torch-circled ring. Removing their robes, they mingled with the disassembling larger group, exchanging congratulations and smiles and chocolate bars. Simon, however, did not move or disrobe, and his gaze remained fixed on the rising sun.

On midsummer day last, Simon had reached the age of thirty-five. Seventeen years before that, he had reached five feet eight inches, and never bettered it. Thin, narrow-shouldered, anaemic-looking, with short ginger hair and thick-framed, imitation tortoiseshell glasses, Simon, if cast as a geek in a Hollywood film, would not have to spend much time in make-up before filming, or do much work on his mannerisms.

Now standing behind Simon, Charles and Andrew, two of the other high Teachers, placed the metal box in a velvet-lined wooden case while various white-robed individuals extinguished the flaming torches. Dark-haired Charles was in his mid-thirties, and had a certain air of a policeman about him, partly afforded by his height, and partly by his plodding lack of grace. Like Simon, he was a Londoner from lower-middle class origins. Unlike Simon, he was married and went to work each day.

Once the lid was secured on the wooden case, a white-robed woman unceremoniously took it away.

Simon continued to be transfixed by the rising sun. 'Amazing,' he breathed.

'Okay, supposing your dowsing was accurate,' Charles suddenly said, 'why haven't these other places been recognised as spiritual areas before?'

Pushing his glasses up, Simon faced Charles. 'I don't know. But soon I might have access to a property in one of the areas. We could use it as a teaching centre — like that idea I proposed. We could completely relocate the Orthrium Society.'

Charles sighed in weary exasperation, and briefly closed his eyes. 'How can we just go off to the middle of nowhere? We're not unemployed like you.'

'You *can* come,' argued Simon. 'It'll be run as a business. You can all have jobs there, as spiritual teachers.'

'Simon, the society's not going anywhere,' stated Andrew before walking off.

Watching Andrew depart, Simon said to Charles, 'We should at least talk about it.'

'There's nothing to talk about, Simon,' returned Charles. 'And remember, don't say a word about any of it to the other members. We don't need divisions.'

With a look of sullen, resigned agreement, Simon faced the rising sun again, whereupon his expression quickly became one of mystery and awe.

The producer in charge of the film crew was Sally, a slim, blonde woman in her early forties who spoke with a gentle Edinburgh accent. Coddled inside a yellow ski jacket, standing with her associates, she warmed her hands on a steaming coffee. Aware of Simon's enduring transport of mystical fascination, she prompted her blasé crew, 'Come on, Simon's away with the fairies again.' Approaching him, accompanied by her cameraman and sound recordist, she said, 'So that's the prayer battery charged?'

Simon took some seconds to fully return to the here and now, marking his arrival by pushing his glasses up. 'Yes. Two hundred man-hours prayer energy.'

'How does the prayer battery work?'

'We told you before, it's a secret. Only our leader knows. He was told how to make them in a telepathic transmission from the Cosmic Masters.'

'Could we have a look inside it?'

'You know it's forbidden,' said Simon firmly. 'It's sealed. Even I'm not allowed to look inside.'

Charles joined the conversation. 'Our leader knows—'

'Your leader in California?' presumed Sally.

'That's right,' confirmed Charles. 'He knows some foreign armies are secretly experimenting with psychic energy to use it as weapon. That's why we can't open the battery to—'

Sally cut in, 'Why don't these foreign armies send a spy to steal your battery?'

Appearing temporarily stumped, Charles and Simon also seemed a little annoyed by Sally's common-sense enquiry.

'We keep them safe,' said Charles.

'Yes,' agreed Simon.

'I see,' said Sally diplomatically. 'Any ideas about what you guys are going to do with all that concentrated prayer energy?'

'Our leader tells us when to release it,' said Charles.

'What did you do with your midsummer charge?'

'We stopped a war developing in Africa,' revealed Charles.

'Really?' responded Sally, appearing impressed. 'Why is it so important to charge the battery on the equinox and solstice days?'

33

'Prayer's more powerful on those days,' explained Simon.

'I see. Just like it's more powerful here in Glastonbury?'

Simon pushed his glasses up. 'Glastonbury's one of the most spiritually energetic locations in England.'

'*The* most,' corrected Charles, with an edge.

'That's not true,' Simon told Sally. 'I've discovered other places too. Snowdonia, and the northern Pennines, east of the Lake District. Both those places are just as spiritually energetic as Glastonbury. Maybe even more energetic. I'm writing a book about it.'

Charles gave a cynical sigh and walked away, watched by Simon.

'Is there some problem between you two on this?' asked Sally.

Still watching Charles, who walked to one of the nearby support tents, Simon confided, 'The other High Teachers don't agree with me. They say the land around Glastonbury's –' He tailed off as Charles disappeared into the tent, but then turned to earnestly face Sally. 'I've spent three years dowsing the ley lines across Britain. I've discovered things no one else knows.'

'Could you explain just what you mean by ley lines?'

Becoming more animated, Simon pushed up his glasses. 'Ley lines are lines of spiritual energy linking special places around Britain's landscape, like Stonehenge and mountains. Many of them were prehistoric tracks, too, because our pagan ancestors were more attuned to the energy and built their settlements and monuments along them.'

'Really? So what have you discovered about them?'

'Their full extent,' revealed Simon. 'I'm writing a book about it.'

'So how have you been able to determine where the hidden ley lines are?'

Simon answered by rucking up his robe, delving into his trouser pocket, and taking out a two-inch, elongated crystal attached to a thin cord. He dangled the crystal from a finger, whereupon it began to swing in small circles.

'See? When the dowsing crystal moves like that, I'm over a ley line.'

'Fascinating,' said Sally.

One of the white-robed men came up to Simon as he was putting his dowsing crystal away.

'Any sightings, Phil?' Simon enquired of the newcomer.

'Two,' answered Phil, with a degree of excitement, 'but the cameraman th'oomed in and said both th'were aeroplanes.'

Glancing at Sally, Simon appeared disappointed and uneasy about the identification.

'Oh, never mind what our cameraman says,' advised Sally. 'He drinks.'

Simon now appeared preoccupied, and wandered a few paces away, briefly scanning the sky before gazing at the sunrise again.

'Th'when will we be on telly?' Phil enquired of Sally.

Although Phil was only in his late twenties, he had a gaunt, older face, like he'd recently been liberated from a concentration camp. Slightly shorter than Simon, he had a dark, closely-trimmed beard, and was thin almost to the point of being a medical worry. All in all, he looked somewhat like the puppet Punch, and even possessed a suitable — almost improbable — array of speech impediments: he lisped; he spluttered; he camped — he belonged in a Tex Avery cartoon.

'Probably late next month,' answered Sally. 'Most of the editing's already done. We just had to come back to shoot one of your big prayer outings.'

'Th'imon thinks he might be gay,' blurted Phil, as if excited by the glamour of it.

Sally suppressed a smirk, but the film crew couldn't stop themselves from sniggering aloud.

'You see?' she said to them. 'That's why I'm a producer and you lot aren't.'

*

Five hours later, Sally was waiting by a busy road in London. Charles had just rang to say they were about to arrive, and she had mobilised her crew ready to capture shots of the return of the Orthrium Society. Shuffling, tired and bored, her crew waited for the coach to appear.

'This looks like the sad fucks now,' said the middle-age cameraman, whose last job had been a documentary on nudists.

Looking down the street, Sally agreed. 'Yep, this is them. I'll go on board before they get off and speak to Simon about the tube. You shoot the rest as they traipse off to their mundane real lives.'

The coach pulled up, and after receiving acknowledgement from her crew that the shot of it arriving had gone well, Sally went on board. In a short while, the passengers disembarked under the camera's gaze, all now wearing everyday clothes and going off back to their homes after their big prayer outing. Except Simon, that is. On Sally's instruction, he had remained till last, but now he emerged, carrying a scuffed blue holdall and still wearing his ceremonial red robe.

'Great,' said Sally to Simon. 'Now we'll do the tube shots.'

Simon appeared troubled. 'I'm not sure about wearing the robe on the tube.'

'But Simon, you agreed,' Sally gently protested. 'We'd film you going home. The spiritual man among the secular.'

'I know I agreed,' said Simon, 'but I've changed my mind. I don't feel comfortable.'

Sally moved closer in, speaking softly. 'Simon, it's not a question of whether you feel comfortable or not, it's how good the shot will look in the documentary.'

Simon pushed his glasses up, and averted his gaze from Sally's soulful eyes. 'I think you just want me to look out of place and peculiar.'

'No, not at all. I just want to show the end of the night's ceremony in context.'

'No, I've decided not to do it.'

Sally sighed. 'Okay, let's compromise. We'll get you a cab home, but we'll make it look like you've flagged it yourself. You'll wear it in a cab, won't you?'

'I don't use cabs,' answered Simon. 'They cost too much.'

'Compliments of Channel Four,' offered Sally.

Five minutes later, Simon, still robed, was in the back of a London black cab, together with Sally, her cameraman, and her sound recordist. Facing forward, huddled all the way into the right corner, Simon was sitting with his knees together and his holdall on his lap. Sally, sitting on the left-side, pull-down, rear-facing seat, was talking to the driver, an angular man of average height in his early thirties who spoke with a thick London accent.

'Yeah, that's the idea,' she said, 'circuits around this area. Then when we're done in ten minutes or so, back to our van, then take this chap on to his home in Lambeth.'

'Gottcha, guv.'

The cab driver, who had said his name was Carl, had short, dark hair and a hint of the simian about him. He was wearing a *Jesus Army* T-shirt. Once the filming was over, he proceeded to take Simon home to Lambeth, just south of the Thames. Along the way, he took frequent glances at his robed passenger in his rear-view mirror

'Me cab gonna be on telly, is it?'

'Probably,' answered Simon, looking and sounding tired, even though he'd slept on the coach.

'Yeah? Magic,' grinned Carl. Moments later, they were

approaching a roundabout when a motorcycle despatch rider overtook them recklessly on the left. 'Wanka!' he shouted to the distant rider, showing a clenched fist. Turning to look at his passenger, he bitterly complained, 'You see that?'

'No.'

'Yeah? Well, 'scuse me French, anyway.' After negotiating the roundabout and glancing in his rear-view mirror once more, Carl asked, 'You some kind of priest or somefink?'

'No, I'm a High Teacher of the Orthrium Society.'

'Yeah? What's that about? A religion or somefink?'

'It's not a religion,' stated Simon. 'It's the truth. Come to our society this evening and I'll tell you all about it.'

'Yeah? What society's that again?'

'The Orthrium Society.'

'Yeah? Don't fink I've 'eard of them. So when's me cab gonna be on telly?'

'Maybe late next month.'

'Yeah? Magic.'

Before they reached his place in Lambeth, Simon removed his robe, carefully folded it and put it in his holdall. After giving Carl the address of his society and once again inviting him to attend that evening, he got out of the cab and went to the door of the four storey, terraced house that was his home. It was also home to eight other men, being divided into scuffed bedsits, with a communal kitchen and bathroom. These men he shared facilities with were a mixture of asylum seekers and low paid migrant workers who had little choice over where in London they lived.

Converted from what must have originally been a spacious town house into a privately-owned facility for housing desperate people, Simon's home address was a monument to the cynical use of plasterboard. Upon moving in, every single resident sooner or later — usually sooner — experienced the same horrified moment of realisation when party walls revealed themselves to be merely thin, plasterboard mockeries, disguised with wood-chip wallpaper. Lying in bed, each resident could not only hear his nearest fellow resident's music, he could clearly hear him opening his CD covers first. It was like having only a drum skin separating the bedrooms, a drum skin that resonated to every fart and every sigh for the homeland. Simon, alone, had reasonable quiet, as he occupied the whole of the loft. Furthermore, since, unlike the other residents, he personally enjoyed a small electric stove, a kettle and a fridge, he only ever had to go downstairs to use the bathroom. There was also a television in his room, which put him in a small minority in the impoverished household.

When sitting in his draughty loft space in winter, Simon wore more layers of clothing than he would ever need to wear walking outside — three pairs of trousers; two T-shirts, two jumpers and a jacket; gloves and a woolly hat. On icy days, when even all that proved inadequate, he might drape his coffee-stained duvet over himself, unless its bulk was an inconvenience, like when he was at his computer. On those rare occasions he would resort to small rations of an electric fire.

Other tricks of Simon's wintertime strategy included using an ancient hairdryer to periodically take the chill off his computer keyboard and mouse; rolling back his carpet to allow warmer air from the rooms below easier passage into his lofty domain; and briefly employing the hairdryer under the duvet to make his bed bearable before he turned in for the night.

After giving Carl a wave, Simon stepped into his house, into dimness that became almost total once he closed the door behind him. Even after his eyes became more accustomed to the low light, he still had to feel for the first steps of the staircase. The bulbs on the stairs needed replacing again, but were situated so high up that a ladder was required. Guided only by familiarity, he ascended the twisting, narrow flights that took him to his loft space. Entering, he placed his bag down, and closed his door. He could see now, for set into the roof were two small, sloping windows that at night gave a narrow, murky view of the stars as he lay in bed.

With his ceiling also being the roof, it sloped sharply, and had many supporting struts, but he had long ago become unconsciously mindful of the various opportunities for bumping his head this presented. So now, crossing the floor to reach his computer at the far end of the loft, Simon ducked and bobbed without hardly realising he was doing it.

Before he could plug in his computer, someone tapped on his door.

'Yes? Who is it?'

'Kiron. Could I speak with you?'

Simon went to his door, half opening it.

'Sorry to disturb you,' said Kiron, a Kosovan refugee, whose eyes showed residual fear. 'Would you kindly arrange for replacement of lights on stairs? Terrible to have such blackness. All lights dead now.'

'Yes, all right. I'll ring the maintenance man today.'

'Terrible house,' opined the Kosovan, but he received no hint of confederacy from Simon. 'Terrible house,' he shrugged, groping his way back down the stairs.

Simon was known to the other residents as being the one to whom they should bring their complaints, since he seemed to know how to deal with the shadowy letting company in such matters. He also helped the others with their Housing Benefit applications, and was treated respectfully on that count. Closing his door again, he sat at his desk to write himself a reminder to contact the maintenance man. Although he called it his desk, it was not a real desk, rather it was an old school dining table to which he was careful never to apply much lateral force, since its legs were in danger of slewing catastrophically. Despite this threatened treachery, he had enough confidence in its willingness to bear simple downward weight to place his outdated computer on it.

Above Simon's unsound desk were shelves laden with books and papers, and beside the shelves, a large map of the British Isles was fixed to the wall. This map was criss-crossed with hundreds of biro lines in various colours, each tagged with a cramped description in a tiny hand. On the desk, looking at least seven years out of date, sat his computer, which he now switched on. Waiting for it to boot up, he viewed the map and pondered all the new ley lines his dowsing had uncovered. As he had done many times before, he counted the number of lines associated with the principle convergence areas, and the arithmetic reaffirmed his conviction that he should establish his business not in Glastonbury, but in one of the even more spiritually active areas he had divined. Weardale in the west of County Durham, and Snowdonia in Wales were the clear front-runners, but they presented a difficult decision: more ley lines converged in Weardale than in Snowdonia, but convergence was tighter in the latter.

The computer was ready, and Simon logged on to the internet, calling up a UFO site. Clicking *Latest Sightings*, he learned that a woman had reported seeing three lights hovering in formation high above a field in Derbyshire.

1.3
Drunk Again

'Look at that twat over there. Who do you think he is?'

Through clusters of people, Ron was indicating a short, overweight, dark-suited individual in his early forties, one of three similarly clad men standing around briefcases.

'Your style guru?' ventured Albert.

'Scoones,' revealed Ron with a snarl. ' Never seen him here before.'

Albert and Ron had just stepped into the Arts Centre, where Ron usually went drinking. As well as having a bar, the Arts Centre also had a gallery, a dance studio, two theatres, a cinema, a small restaurant and various workshops. Tonight, the bar was crowded because a theatre performance had just come to an end. Ron, wearing his khaki jacket, and Albert, wearing his long black coat, were dismayed by the legions of people, and remained on the threshold, considering the situation. Then resignation took hold, and Ron led the way to the bar, giving his manager, Scoones, a wide birth.

Following behind Ron, Albert complained, 'What are all these bastards doing clogging up my universe? And it is my universe, by the way. Been meaning to tell you that.'

Reaching the long, L-shaped bar, Ron displayed a banknote for service attention.

'Can't be your universe. Gays wouldn't be in the minority.'

'Is my universe,' insisted Albert. 'I'm everywhere I ever go in it; and everywhere I've ever been, I was there too. As far as I've ever been able to tell, I completely pervade this universe. I'm fucking omnipresent. The earth is flying through space at thousands of miles an hour, and I'm everywhere it ever gets to.'

'Having one of your little clever days, aren't you?' said Ron, in a patronising voice.

'Can't help it. I'm a mighty volcano of red hot thought. And the longer I stay silent, the bigger the inevitable intellectual eruption. Think of me as...' he tailed off. 'Look at her,' he murmured.

'Look at who?'

'Her,' murmured Albert, pointing feebly to a young lady alone at the short side of the L-shaped bar, where no serving was ever done. Perched on a high stool, she was seemingly absorbed in the reading of a thick paperback book. 'She's the one I've been looking for all my long, lonely Friday.'

Ron peered in the direction of Albert's digit. 'Who?'

'Her.'

'Where?'

'There.'

'What, the dark-haired one with the book? Do you know her?'

'Course I do,' said Albert, with eyes devotionally affixed. 'She's Helen... she's Cleopatra... she's Juliet.' He fell into a reverie, a mesmerised silence as he realised that his list of identities for the vision he was beholding in forlorn awe had been quite remiss and quite, quite unfair to her. In a low, enchanted murmur, he proceeded to correct the identification, as much to convince himself of the possibility of it as for his companion's enlightenment. 'No, she's... she's... she's...'

'Who?' demanded Ron, now sharing Albert's fascination with the lush vision on a bar-stool.

'Can it be?' murmured Albert.

'Can it be who? Tell me.'

'Can fate have finally delivered her unto me?'

'And me,' added Ron. 'Especially me.'

'Is it true? Is it her? My greatest ever love?'

'Who?'

'My God, it *is* her,' breathed Albert. 'It's her. It's her. It's bloody her.'

'Who?'

'Only Tess of the d'Urbervilles, that's all. Only bloody Tess of the bloody d'Urbervilles.'

Ron was sceptical: this wasn't the first time Albert had claimed a person to be Tess. He studied her some more, though little of her was actually visible, just her head and shoulders, the rest of her being obscured by the bar. 'Nah, it's Catherine Zeta Jones back when she was in her prime.'

'Fuck is it Zeta Jones,' challenged Albert immediately. 'Anyway, what do you know about Tess? You haven't even read the book.'

'I saw the film, though,' countered Ron.

Albert made some retching motions to show he considered the Tess in the film to be a travesty of the Tess in the book and his imagination. 'Chalk and cheese. Chalk and cheese.'

'So you think she's the real Tess?'

'Of course she is. All the hallmarks are there. Look at her eyes — do they not bewitch and inflame the heart?'

41

Ron had to agree that they did.

'And her mouth,' Albert went on. 'Has there ever been such a maddening mouth since Eve's?'

'No, I don't think there has,' decided Ron.

'Then,' said Albert, '*ipso facto, ex silentio*, she must be Tess.'

They both continued to dream in her direction.

'Did you see that?' said Albert.

'See what?'

'She looked over. She's smitten. It's my haircut.'

Ron believed he knew better. 'Rubbish. She glanced at the clock on the wall behind us.'

'No, she looked at me — lingeringly.'

'Maybe she's an anthropologist?' suggested Ron.

The gibe glanced off. Standing up, Albert announced, 'She wants me, Ron. She wants me. And Destiny demands our souls entwine. I'm going over to her.'

Ron gripped Albert's wrist. 'For fuck's sake, Albert, get back to your bedroom where you belong. What's got into you lately?'

Twisting free from Ron's grip, Albert declared, with unprecedented fire in his eyes, 'Raunchiness.'

'Hah! Raunchy? You?'

'Yeah, raunchy, me. That's what Jackie said I was this afternoon. Honest.'

'So that's it,' derided Ron. 'One compliment from a sad, fat virgin and you imagine you're irresistible all of a sudden.'

'Jackie's not fat,' countered Albert. 'She's just got a surface area problem.'

'She's a virgin though.'

'Is she?'

'Yep. Her sister told me. She's never even had a boyfriend.'

Forgetting Jackie, Albert decided that Tess would look even better if she was wearing his *ALBERT'S LASS* T-shirt, which, unknown to Ron, he'd brought along with him. He took it out from his deep coat pocket, but Ron saw it and snatched it from him.

'Give it back,' demanded Albert.

'Not a chance,' said Ron, keeping it out of Albert's reach.

'Give me it back,' demanded Albert again, making grabs.

Successfully keeping the garment out of Albert's reach, Ron cast a worried glance across the room, fearful that Scoones might be witnessing the undignified commotion. He was happy to see that Scoones and his companions were no longer present.

'Forget the fucking T-shirt,' ordered Ron. 'Just borrow some money from me and ask her if you can buy her a drink.'

Albert stopped trying to get the T-shirt.

'What, chat her up, you mean? Proper, like? Maybe ask her for a date if we hit it off?'

'That's it,' said Ron, with happy relief, 'you're beginning to understand how the game works.'

'I could never be so audacious or presumptuous,' declared Albert before resuming his attempts to snatch the garment back.

'No, you'll get yourself arrested,' said Ron, stuffing the T-shirt away into one of his jacket's many pockets.

'Bugger the T-shirt,' said Albert. 'With my haircut, kissable lips and general overall raunchiness, I'll have my soul entwined with hers faster than she can say *contraception.*'

'Please, please, don't go over to her,' begged Ron, 'you'll get both of us arrested.' Albert didn't listen, and began to move in the lady's direction. 'Smile,' Ron called out to him. 'Remember to smile.'

Albert seldom smiled, and laughed aloud only about twice a year. For him to laugh, something *really* funny had to be said.

'Smile,' Ron called out again. 'Social skills. Develop some social skills.'

Albert was now standing next to Tess, and by a slight movement she made, he knew Tess to be aware of someone being near her, but she did not look up from her book. This time, for once, Albert could be forgiven for believing he'd really met Tess of the d'Urbervilles, for this lady was suitably clad in a long black dress of a very antiquated type — Victorian, he guessed. It looked well-worn and a little dusty, as if it might degenerate into its constituent threads at any moment. It had many folds and pleats, and a low front that revealed cleavage. Over this dress, she wore a silk-lined waistcoat of a similar design. Black stockings covered her legs and disappeared into black leather shoes which could pass as old too, but probably weren't.

Her dress was odd enough, but an even stranger thing about this anachronistic vision was her hair-slide, which appeared to be a section of human skull, incorporating the eye sockets and half an inch of forehead. It looked very old, and was cut so that it resembled a pair of thick-rimmed spectacles without the lenses. Her hair was lush and plentiful, very dark brown, almost black, and the section of skull she wore served to draw long tresses from the back, casting them forward and to the sides so that her face was amid a luxuriant, tousled mane.

Albert lifted her book slightly so that he could read the title: it was Dickens' *David Copperfield*.

Tess looked up from her literature, and her eyes briefly met Albert's. 'I think you're confusing me with someone you know. I'd like to read my book, please.'

Her discernibly Northern voice sounded uncommonly intelligent to Albert's ears.

Tess returned to her book and glass of red wine.

'I know you all right,' said Albert in a soft yet insistent voice.

In an irritated and resigned manner, she put her book down. Turning to face Albert, with a finger she swept her hair away from her eyes and looked at him, and for a chilling moment he feared she was set to display anger.

'You're mistaken,' she said plainly, picking up her book again to resume reading.

'I do know you,' Albert went on. 'You're Tess of the d'Urbervilles. Tess, Tess, Tess. You're Tess, and Alex d'Urberville was so beastly to you I feel I have to make it up to you to preserve your trust in gentlemen. I shall marry you and treat you well.'

No reaction from Tess.

'Tess, continue to vex me with indifference and I fear it shall make a miserable end of me.'

She laughed, astonishing Ron, who immediately dashed over. Placing a hand on Albert's shoudler, he said, with an innocent air, 'There's a table free over here, Albert. Why not bring your friend over too?'

Albert was already aware of Ron's purpose. Nevertheless, he followed Ron to the table, boldly taking Tess's book with him. 'Come on, Tess,' he said.

After making a small show of annoyance, Tess picked up her bag and wine glass and followed Albert.

Once seated, Ron offered Tess his hand. 'The name's Ron.'

'Sarah,' she returned.

Albert began shaking his head in broken-hearted despair. 'No. No. You're Tess. You're Tess.'

'I'm not,' she smiled, 'I'm Sarah.'

'Oh, no,' groaned Ron, 'he doesn't think you're Tess of the d'Urbervilles, does he? A couple of years back, after reading the book, he was forever pointing out Tess-a-bloody-likes in the street. Mind you, it was worse after he read *Lolita*. It was all I could manage

44

to stop him hanging around the schools all day long then. Hope the stupid fucker never reads *Watership Down.*'

Sarah laughed, but Albert appeared to be sulking like a freshly admonished child.

Ron stabbed a corrective finger into Albert's chest. 'I've told you before, just because someone's wearing an old dress doesn't mean they're Tess of the d'Urbervilles, loser.'

'Wasn't the dress,' muttered Albert, with continued sulkiness.

'What was it then?' asked Sarah.

Albert sulkily answered, 'Bewitching eyes and the most maddening mouth since Eve's.'

'Oh my God,' exclaimed Sarah softly, 'you can hang around me all day long, you silver-tongued darling.'

Abandoning his sulk, Albert tenderly brushed some wayward strands of hair from Sarah's face and gazed into those bewitching eyes. 'I fascinate you,' he breathed.

'You do,' agreed Sarah.

Ron interrupted with an inquiry concerning Sarah's skull slide. She took it from her hair, tossing her tresses back with a flick of her head. 'Do you like it?' she asked, showing it to him.

'How does it stay in?' asked Ron.

She rotated it to reveal metal prongs glued to its back.

Albert suddenly demanded, 'Why are you dressed like Tess? Why do you seek to tease my heart? Answer me, woman. And why do you adorn yourself with pagan bones? Goddamnit, who and what are you? Tell me now or I'll go home.'

Sarah began her answer slowly and deliberately, 'Well, my name's Sarah. I'm doing a Ph.D. in music at the University. I'm wearing this gear because I attended a dress rehearsal this evening for a presentation that's coming up here next week in which all the performers wear period costume. And the bone? I just took a fancy to it when I was rummaging around in the props room. It's not real. It's plaster.'

'You're a proper musician?' Ron asked her.

'If that's what you want to call me. The cello's my instrument. I play in a quartet.'

The cello revelation clinched it: Albert was now in a torment of love for Sarah. Ron, however, was spoiling the picture, so he connived to get rid of him for a while by telling Sarah that Ron wanted to buy her a drink on his behalf.

Sarah perceived that Albert might be broke, and said as much.

'Flat,' he bemoaned.

'Concave,' sniped Ron.

'I don't want a drink,' said Sarah, 'I haven't finished this one yet.'

'Doesn't matter,' said Albert, 'you can stockpile them. I just want Ron to go to the bar so he'll buy me a drink too.'

'Let me get you one,' offered Sarah, delving into her bag for her purse.

Ron stayed her hand. 'No, don't,' he urged, 'he has to limit his drinking. It sets off his mental disorder.'

'Ignore him,' said Albert, 'he's just upset because we're going to sleep together.'

Sarah gave Albert a hard look. 'Are we?'

'Maybe twice, if you keep much room in your heart for pity.'

Sarah laughed.

Ron insisted on buying the drinks, and went to the bar — Albert knew he was attempting to impress Sarah with his generosity.

Sarah took a slow sip of her wine. 'So, Albert, what do you do for a living?'

'Paper boy — retired.'

'I see,' she said, mercifully not pursuing the issue. She pointed at the slogan, visible under Albert's open coat. 'What isn't long now?'

'Release,' answered Albert.

'From what?'

'Birth.'

'Yeah? Does that mean what I think it means?'

'Weep not for me, for I shall go willingly.'

'Party on,' she said, with a suitably sarcastic tone. She took another sip of wine. 'Your friend's very sweet. What's his story?'

'Sweet? Yeah, I suppose he can appear like that now. Prison improved him a lot.'

A look of concern crossed Sarah's face. 'Prison? What was he in for?'

'Manslaughter. He killed his girlfriend because she'd constantly taunted him about the diminutive size of his penis.'

'Really?' she said, glancing across to Ron, who caught her eye and smiled.

She didn't smile back.

'Yeah,' continued Albert, 'it was murder really, but he fluked a good lawyer. We're celebrating his release tonight. I met him when I was doing charity work at the prison. I don't really like him, but

46

I'm afraid to let him know. He's got a vicious temper.'

'Has he?'

'God, yeah,' confirmed Albert, injecting a fearful look. 'But don't worry, you should be safe since he thinks you're quite sweet too.'

'Does he?'

'He does. How did he phrase it? Oh yeah, he said you're the best bit of gash he's seen since he got out the slammer.'

'Gash?' queried Sarah, with a look of suspended revulsion.

'His word for women he fancies,' explained Albert. 'Horrible, isn't it?'

'Horrible? It's the most revolting expression I've ever heard!'

'You've obviously never heard his word for little girls he fancies.'

Sarah grimaced in anticipation.

'Slit,' said Albert.

'Ugh! That's even worse!'

'I know,' agreed Albert, 'should we inform his parole officer?'

Sarah laughed. 'I don't believe any of this, by the way,' she said, touching Albert's arm.

Sarah was truly beautiful. She had long, sultry, marvellously tousled dark hair; large, intelligent brown eyes; a slender body with a generous bosom; and lips the likes of which Albert had never seen before outside his imagination. And the moment she touched his arm, he resolved to devote that arm to writing poems about her until it withered on his shoulder from ceaseless toil. Ron didn't appear at all in his romantic picture. If Ron loved her too, then that was his hard luck: he'd just have to work out his base desires on a consenting Alsatian.

Ron returned with the drinks. 'You'll be sick tomorrow,' he said in a hugely patronising way as he placed a pint in front of Albert.

'No I won't.'

'He probably will be,' said Ron to Sarah. 'He usually is. Gets the worst hangovers I've ever seen in anything over the age of twelve. Anything more than a pint and there's a good chance he'll spend the next day in bed with his head in a bucket, moaning the name of whatever unlucky female he took a shine to the night before.' Pointing a finger at her, he added, 'That'll be you this time.'

'Charmed,' said Sarah, rather doubtfully. Looking at Albert, she asked, 'Why do you drink if you always get sick the next day?'

'Been told to by doctors,' returned Albert, taking up his pint, the slur on his drinking capacity having goaded him into an unwise show of bravado. 'I'm clinically lovelorn, so have been told to drink myself into a state of emotional amnesia every night.' After quickly downing his second pint of the evening, he said, 'Ron, explain to Sarah about it being traditional to buy people drinks on their birthday.'

'It's his birthday?' asked Sarah, looking to Ron and receiving a small nod as confirmation. 'Oh, happy birthday,' she then sweetly wished Albert.

'Happy?' contested Albert. 'You expect someone as deep as me to be happy?'

'Is he always like this?' she asked Ron, beginning to talk about Albert as if he wasn't there.

'Just buy him a drink and let him get on with it,' advised Ron.

Albert did get on with it, albeit at a much slower pace, moodily pursuing a state of emotional amnesia right until the clatter of the last-orders bell. Soon after, he was drunkenly trailing Ron and Sarah to the car park, where, true to the forecast, a frost lay on the ground, the first of the year. The sky was clear and the air was still. Ghostly white emanations rose straight upwards from chimneys. Orion loomed bright and large. Sarah bade her new friends goodnight, but it didn't register with Albert, and he attempted to follow her until she disappeared from his sight, whereupon he trotted over to Ron, twice slipping on what he didn't realise was ice.

Ron shoved him into the back of his car, where he lay on his side, head spinning.

Roused by the starting of the engine, Albert sat upright.

'Where's Sarah gone?'

'Home,' answered Ron. He tapped the rear-view mirror. 'That's her car leaving now.'

The rear window was annoyingly misted, and Albert rubbed at it. Kneeling on the seat, he watched in agitated regret and frustration as the tail-lights of Sarah's car diminished in the distance. 'No, Sarah,' he intoned, 'don't leave me.' He began to whine, frantically rubbing away more condensation so that he could continue to discern the departing lights of his love. 'Shit, I'll probably never see her again. I've never met anyone like her. I don't even know her surname.'

'It's all right, I'll ask her tomorrow.'

Albert slumped down on to the seat, partly in woe and partly because Ron had put the car into reverse and set off backwards, unsettling his distraught passenger.

They pulled out of the car park, going off in the opposite direction

Sarah had taken.

Now it began to sink in, Albert sat up and leaned forward. 'What do you mean you'll ask her tomorrow?'

'We're going for lunch together.'

'Lunch? You sneaky over-sized bastard. Just when did you arrange that sordid little liaison?'

'During one of your pathetic tales of lost love. The Susan Murray one, I think. Time you forgot about her.'

When Albert was nine, he'd fallen in love for the first time. The object of his passion was Susan Murray, a girl in his class. He'd loved her from afar for weeks, but one glorious Friday he saw an opportunity to advance his romantic prospects. The teacher sometimes made naughty boys relocate their desks beside girls as punishment and to keep them subdued. On that Friday, Albert had observed that the only space available next to a girl was next to Susan. The young Albert had played hell for hours, and was eventually ordered to lug his desk next to the divine Susan. That had been less than half an hour before the end of the school day, so he hadn't had much time to woo her, but he knew he had the rest of the blessed term to establish himself in her heart. However, the following Monday, at morning assembly, it was announced that Susan had moved with her family to Gateshead, and he never saw her again.

That day could well have been the first day he had stared at a ceiling.

Albert pressed his forehead against the cold, dewy back window and looked forlornly in the direction Sarah had taken. He began a low moan, which continued until they rounded a corner, whereupon he strongly advised Ron that he was going to be sick. Ron promptly braked, and even before the car fully stopped, Albert had the back door open, puking pints into the gutter.

'Stop trying to show off,' said Ron. 'She can't see you. She's long gone.'

There was something about Albert being sick into a gutter that relaxed Ron. It made him feel kind of smugly superior. So now, while Albert was going through gastric hell, Ron put the radio on and lit a cigarette.

Lying half out of the car, after puking, Albert remained motionless for some time, his face just inches away from his own steaming vomit. This was new. He didn't normally throw up until the next day — his intense hangovers thing. Mind you, tonight he'd drunk more than at any other time in his life, not that he had much of a drinking history. All that unwise, over-indulgent teenage party stuff had mostly passed him by, since he'd gone straight from climbing trees to staring at a ceiling in a darkened room.

'Gross,' said one of a group of disgusted young women walking past.

Albert looked up at the young woman, slender and pretty. 'I'll never stop loving you,' he sadly informed her.

'Prat,' she said, walking on.

Albert pulled himself fully back into the car. He felt a little better now, but suspected the improvement would prove temporary.

'She was right, you know,' said Ron. 'Gross. Teenage stuff.'

'She was right,' sighed Albert, 'right for me. Quick, give me the Albert's Lass T-shirt.'

'Dream on,' said Ron, stretching back to pull the rear door shut.

'Come on, Ron, give me it. It'll fit her. I know it will.'

'Prat,' said Ron, setting the car in motion.

*

A mile away, Lee and Dale were laughing at gangling Paul, who had slipped and tumbled some way down the dark, misty slope.

'There's nee one coming,' decided Lee, looking back up the steep, wooded bank to the floodlit cathedral. 'You wuz imaginin' it, man.'

Dale disagreed. 'Nah, some geezers were clockin' us from a car. Tellin' y'. Copper types.'

'Nah. Won't have been reported yet, man.'

Paul now picked himself up and went back up the hill to join his colleagues, collecting dropped items along the way.

Lee, Dale and Paul were teenage burglars. At six-three, Paul was taller than his slender width would classically allow, and was always the first to run from trouble, but always the first to be caught, sometimes by the ponytail he sported. Lee's dark brown hair was close-cropped. He was not so tall as Paul, but much more sturdy in his build. He looked like Action Man's less intelligent brother. Dale was weasel-like, five-eight, with an aquiline nose, and eyes that were seldom trusted. His mid-brown hair was in a style that could have been inspired by some Jerry Springer guest.

As soon as Paul reached them, short of breath and muddied, Lee decided they should all proceed down the hill to the riverbank. Leading the way, he was at once followed by Dale.

'Howay, man, wait for me,' said Paul, briefly resting against a tree trunk.

Sitting on the river bank, concealed by bushes and shadow, they examined their booty.

'Wonder why the cunts had distress flares?' said Paul, who had found a pack of marine flares in the house they had just burgled, taking them for his own.

'Mebbee they gan oot t'sea on a boat, or summat?' suggested Dale, viewing a CD with the aid of his cigarette lighter. 'Aye, th'wuz some sea fishin' books, wunt th'?'

'This fuckin' credit card's expired,' complained Lee.

'Jesus! Ah've borgled a fuckin' hippie CD!' exclaimed Dale in Geordie horror, preparing to cast the offending music into the water. 'Twats!'

'Divvent, man, Dale,' said Paul, 'ah'll have it. Who is it, like?'

'That fuckin' auldie Yes band. Tales of Tropical sommat or utha.'

'Tales of Topographical Oceans,' said Paul fluently, drawing suspicious looks from Lee and Dale.

'Paul, you a fuckin' hippie or summat?' asked Lee, his tone suggesting more than a degree of contempt for the notion.

Paul was firm in his return. 'Am ah shite an'ippie.'

Again, Dale prepared to throw the CD into the river.

'Divvent hoy it,' said Paul. 'Giz it 'ere.'

Dale offered a deal. 'Giz uz a distress flare and y'can 'ave it.'

'Fuck off, they're mine,' stated Paul, with aggressive certainty. 'Ah robbed them, not you. Anyway, ah've already got Tales of Topographical Oceans.'

'Bet y'have, y'sad hippie,' said Lee, pushing Paul's face.

'Fuck off, Lee,' returned Paul, 'ah robbed it from me uncle's collection when ah wuz a young'un. Didn't knah worrit it wuz.'

'Let one of y'flares off,' said Lee.

'Aye, gan on, Paul,' urged Dale, 'let a flare off.'

'Y' both fuckin' mad, man, exclaimed Paul. 'If we get seen, the cops'll knah it wuz uz that robbed the hoose.'

'Divvent be so soft,' said Lee. 'Who's ganna see uz?'

'Aye, man, Paul, there's nee wun aroond.'

'Nah. Not dee'n it 'ere,' said Paul.

Lee put a headlock on Paul. 'Set wun off noo or ah'll ring y'fuckin' neck, y'soft, skinny, hippie shite.'

'All right, Lee, man,' said Paul, with choking difficulty, 'ah'll dee it. Lerr'uz gan an'ah'll dee it. Promuz.'

*

Coming out of a petrol station shop, Ron stopped short of his car.

'Albert, look!'

'Ugh,' said Albert, not lifting his head from the back seat, for his state of drunken sickness had returned.

'Sit up and look,' demanded Ron, tapping the window.

'Fuck off.'

'Look!'

'Look at what?' slurred Albert.

'A weird light over the cathedral.'

'Wanker.'

'It's a fucking UFO,' declared Ron, opening the driver door and getting into his car.

'Arse,' said Albert.

'I'm telling you,' insisted Ron, 'there's a bloody glowing spaceship hovering over the cathedral.'

Albert sat up and drunkenly focused on the contentious, distant light.

'It's a flare,' he said.

'Yeah? Wonder which planet it came from?'

Albert slumped back down again, moaned Sarah's name, and continued to moan it all the way home.

1.4
Melancholy's Guiding Hand

Waking early the morning after his birthday, Albert had a bad head. A very bad head. And nausea. And a thirst that drove him out of bed in Saturday's first light to make an unsteady crawl to the kitchen.

Naked on the cold, dirty floor, wedged in between a wall and the fridge, he downed half a pint of orange squash.

Peep was expectantly rubbing herself against the cupboard where her food was kept.

Dubious of recovery, Albert collected his usual bucket before returning to bed on all fours.

Back in bed, suffering a headache he reckoned could floor a

charging elephant, he leaned over the bucket and regretted every drink he'd had the night before, especially the last one: he was certain he would have been all right if it hadn't been for that last one.

I bet my hair'll peak while my head's in this bastard bucket, he thought.

After eternal suffering, he vomited curdled orange squash. When he felt stronger, he pulled himself fully on to his bed, and slept until the doorbell sounded. Ron answered it, and Albert heard Sarah come into the flat. Lunch: Ron and Sarah were going for lunch together, he remembered. Looking at his clock, he saw it was almost noon.

Despite his raging headache, he got out of bed, pulled on his T-shirt, and went to brush his teeth, having to do so in the kitchen because Ron was shaving.

'Morning,' said Sarah brightly when Albert entered the living room. Dressed in a white jumper and black trousers, she was sitting in the armchair near the phone.

'Ugh,' returned Albert, at once lying face-down on the sofa.

'Coming out for lunch with us?'

'Eating out's too bourgeois,' groaned Albert into a cushion. 'Why aren't you dressed like Tess today? I got out of bed to see Tess.'

'Sorry,' said Sarah. 'You look rough. Hungover?'

'Either that or Ron's been doing his thallium trick again.'

'What's thallium?'

'Ask Ron,' groaned Albert, 'he's got a bag of the stuff with your name written on.'

Sarah didn't know what he was talking about, and had learned not to worry.

'Battery's dead on my mobile,' she said, changing the subject. 'Can I quickly phone my sister before she leaves work?'

Despite his headache, Albert lifted his head. 'You've got a sister?'

'Yes, Jennifer. It's her nineteenth birthday today. Can I phone her?'

Sarah had a younger sister, and Albert was already in love with her. This was much better than being in love with Sarah, since she had said Ron was sweet. Being in love with someone who thought Ron was sweet seemed so unsanitary to Albert.

'Course you can,' said Albert, getting up and unsteadily leaving the room.

Entering his bedroom, Albert stumbled over the fallen books

and cursed Peep's name. Sitting at his computer, he ran off a love letter for Sarah's sister, based on the one he'd given Lisa. True to his promise to Ron, he omitted his address this time.

The phone rang in the living room, and Ron came out of the bathroom to answer it.

'Hello? ... Oh, yeah, hello there ... God, sorry, I'll email it before I go away ... Yeah, it's finished ... It'll be in your mailbox on Monday, promise ... Yeah, cheers, bye.'

'Work?' supposed Sarah, as Ron put the phone down.

'Yeah. My wanky manager. Nothing serious.'

'We could have gone out tonight after all.'

'How come?'

'Just phoned my sister. She said her boyfriend's coming back this evening. I'm not that keen on him, so I'll keep my distance. I'll nip over after lunch, though.'

Ron picked up his jacket. 'Ready?'

'Starving and raring,' declared Sarah, getting up from the armchair. 'Let's go.'

Ron led the way to the flat's door, but Albert, sitting on his bed, called Sarah into his darkened domain.

'What?' asked Sarah, standing just inside his room.

Albert beckoned her closer.

'Did your bookcase fall over?' she asked, stepping deeper into the room.

'No, I bought it like that.'

Sarah was now standing beside Albert's bed.

'Sarah,' began Albert earnestly, proffering a folded sheet of paper, 'I ask — nay, beg, as the lowest dog may beg at the highest table — convey a note of mine to the fair Jennifer.'

Confused, Sarah took the letter. 'You mean Jennifer my sister? You want me to give her a letter from you, even though she doesn't know you? What's it about?'

'Love,' said Albert. 'The letter declares my great interest, good prospects and honourable intentions.'

Sarah looked at Albert, as if not as completely sure about him as she would like to be.

'Come on, Sarah,' said Ron impatiently. 'Bollocks to Albert. He's not right in the head.'

'You're not right in the soul,' countered Albert.

'Come on,' urged Ron, ignoring Albert's retort.

'Coming,' said Sarah, putting the letter into her pocket. 'Bye,

Albert.'

After the front door closed, there came a tap on Albert's window. 'Weirdo,' said Ron from the garden.

Albert went back to bed, sleeping until woken by Ron's solitary return just before four o'clock.

'Weirdo,' said Ron as he passed Albert's room on his way to the living room.

As he became fully awake, Albert was pleased to discover his hangover was easing, and he got out of bed to properly face the day.

'She loves me,' boasted Ron when Albert trudged barefoot into the living room, wearing, as ever, his *Not Long Now* T-shirt. 'I can tell. All the signs are there. I'm seeing her again tonight after she gets back from disturbing her sister with your letter. We're going for a meal. A posh place you could only dream about.'

Albert made a point of ignoring Ron, and got on with facing his day – he lay on the sofa and stared at the ceiling. Not a single word passed his lips in the full two hours he remained horizontal before increasing hunger drove him to the kitchen, even though Ron had frequently goaded him about Sarah.

In the kitchen, gathering cutlery, he knew it was starting. He was slipping *out of sorts*, so to speak. His life was a waste and a monotonous bore. He was getting nowhere, yet becoming footsore along the way.

Returning to the living room with his meal, he sat by the window in the fading light of another lost day. 'Did you hear that?' he asked quietly after a minute or so, his first words for hours.

'Hear what?' replied Ron, not lifting his eyes from a television guide.

'The sigh of the dying day.'

'No.'

Albert quietly said, 'That's because your life is but a roar of coarse interests that drown out the voices of the elfin sprites that sing their low-toned lamentations in poet's ears. You're fucking lucky, you are.'

'Get a stupid job and a stupid car like me, then you won't be able to hear the little elfin bastards,' returned Ron, still reading.

'Can't,' said Albert, dispiritedly toying with his food. 'I wish I could be like you. But I'm a poet, you're not. My world belongs to Melancholy, a quiet, thoughtful, deep-eyed maiden who shuns the hurly-burly of day-to-day life.'

Ron said nothing.

A minute or more elapsed before Albert quietly resumed. 'When the light thickens, she oft comes to me, you know, Ronald, and her enchantment sinks deep into my heart. It's then that I hear the sigh of the dying day in the rustle of branches or the call of a blackbird. And as the day fades away she allows me dim visions of the Great Sea, and I fancy I hear its distant murmur in my ears. She gently takes my hand in hers. *Do not linger*, she softly whispers; *hasten down, for the shadowy ships are spreading their dark sails.*'

'Punch the miserable little bitch next time,' advised Ron.

'I could never do that,' said Albert wistfully, 'she possesses a disarming beauty.'

Weary of his food, Albert abandoned it, and moved to the threadbare armchair near the gas fire. Soon feeling bored and unsettled, he decided to take a walk outside to help clear his remaining hangover.

'Where are you going?' inquired Ron when Albert began putting on his coat.

'To the shadowy ships,' answered Albert.

Leaving the flat, he headed toward the city centre. The high pressure had indeed slipped away, and the predicted warm front was already manifesting itself, the air now many degrees pleasanter than it had been the day before. But the darkening sky was overcast, threatening rain. The woman from upstairs was approaching from the other side of the street. It was unusual for her to be out at this time of day. Lost in some painful world of her own, she didn't see Albert. Had she noticed him, an awkward attempt at a smile of recognition would have been all she would have given.

She shuffled past; a small, frail, bony figure in a shabby coat, staring at the pavement.

Albert's walk with Melancholy continued. She gently encouraged him to fantasise romantically and tragically about Sarah's younger sister, who, in his mind's eye, looked just like Sarah, except a tiny bit smaller. Thinking about Sarah's sister and his boundless love for her led Albert to think about all the other ladies for whom he'd once possessed boundless love. There must be hundreds, he thought, hundreds whom he had once loved so yearningly and hopelessly. And despite his frequent finding of new love, those old loves never quite released their sorrowful hold on him.

He'd offer to pay them to release their hold on his tender heart, but suspected that would only end up with the police coming round to see him again.

There were so many old loves it was hard for Albert to bring even a fraction of them to mind, so he decided to get his love life in order by forming an alphabetical list. Thirty minutes later, wandering through a shopping area, he was at M. Although he knew the names of only a tiny fraction of the visions he'd longed for in his life, there were still lots of M's on his mental list. There were at least seven Maureens. Eight Melanies (conservatively). A Miranda, a Mirna, and another Melanie he'd just remembered.

He gave up on his list, deciding it was the kind of thing best done on his computer.

He began musing upon how different his life would surely have turned out if he hadn't spent so much of it pining over Susan Murray and her successors. He might have achieved wonders, he reckoned, wandering through the drizzle that had begun to sift down. Maybe won the Nobel Prize for detecting gravity waves. Those chicks owed him big time, he decided for the ninety-seventh time that year, but now toying with the idea of invoicing them. No, that would be a police-coming-round thing too, he realised.

Soon the drizzle turned to rain, strangely beginning with large, well-spaced drops, like the heralds of a summer thunder storm. Crossing one of the bridges spanning the river Wear, he headed toward the floodlit cathedral, where most of his strolls seemed to culminate.

He sat on a bench below the mighty edifice and got wet.

Ten minutes later, still bored and blue, now drifting homeward, Albert began fantasising about his own death. Suicide was something he hadn't thought seriously about for days now. His first resolution to kill himself had been made at the age of eighteen, death on his nineteenth birthday being the intention. He had come to regard death as desirable because life was, as he saw it then and more so now, absurd. A *disease of matter*, as he had once heard it described. Life was a disease of matter, he had understood, and life is that thing attributed solely to organisms. What is an organism? Just the vehicle DNA uses to drive itself on into the future. And what is DNA? Just molecular cancer, that's all. So, at eighteen, he had announced that he would die by his own hand on his next birthday. In the years since that first death-date, he had made numerous other such announcements. And here he was again, mentally reliving his own death. Devising elaborate methods of committing suicide was his chief form of relaxation. Not only did it tend to cheer him, he believed he had a great and prolific talent for it. All his methods were painless, too — it was all about *escaping* pain. The painless method he was now contemplating was a complicated affair involving helium gas, electric timers, a boat and benzodiazapines. 'Another one for the noble book,' he said to himself.

Albert kept a record of all the fantastic methods of topping himself he'd ever conceived, and expected it to be published posthumously in Sweden one day.

Soon he was back home again, slightly less blue for having rehearsed his own death. Going straight into the living room, not taking off his coat, he lay on the sofa and stared at the ceiling.

Sitting in the armchair by the fire, flicking through a magazine, Ron grumbled, 'Didn't win the lottery.'

'You're confusing me with someone who listens,' returned Albert.

Ron tossed the magazine unceremoniously over to Albert. 'Here, weirdo. Bought this for you yesterday. Birthday present. Forgot to give it to you.'

Condescending to glance at it, Albert saw that it was *New Scientist.*

The doorbell rang, and Ron immediately began putting his jacket on. 'That'll be that goddess you chatted up for me last night,' he said before departing.

Albert had to think about suicide again to cope.

1.5
Strange Romance

At about the same time that Albert had been composing his love letter to Sarah's sister, in an army barracks in Aldershot, four squaddies had been playing pool. Only thirty minutes away from a six day leave, these soldiers were in high spirits. Two, Luke and Stuart, swiped the cap off a gawky new recruit, passing it between themselves, denying the awkwardly-smiling seventeen-year-old his piece of uniform.

'Leave it out, you two,' said dark-haired John. 'Give it back to him.'

The new recruit was allowed the return of his cap.

Six years earlier, fresh from a Nottingham school, John himself had been a new recruit to these barracks, but no one had ever sought to tease or bully him. Six-two, with an athletic build, he possessed a confident and self-assured manner in all aspects relating to his army life. On top of this, he was handsome enough to draw glances from the young women who frequented the soldiers' pubs around Aldershot.

But John had long had his mind set on what he considered to be a superior woman.

Taffy bent down to carefully play his shot, keeping his round, rubicund face close to the pool table surface. A blond Welshman, he had twice now been warned to improve his fitness and lose weight.

'Come on, Taffy, speed it up,' said John, 'I've got to get to Yorkshire.'

'And I've got to get to Swansea,' returned Taffy, 'but pool is pool.'

Luke, a cock-sure Londoner, made a wanker motion behind Taffy's back.

'Never rush a pot,' continued Taffy, 'bound to miss if you do. It's like sniper work.'

Taffy made his shot and missed the pot.

'Shit. All the talking made me lose my aim, it did.'

John quickly took his shot and also missed.

'Because you rushed it,' declared Taffy.

'John's got more reason to hurry than you,' said Stuart, taking his turn on the table.

Stuart was from Birmingham, and sounded it.

'More reason than you'll ever have, Taffy, y'big Welsh virgin,' added Luke.

'What reason's that then?' Taffy wanted to know.

'Never seen a photo of his bird yet?' asked Stuart.

'Bit of a looker, is she?' surmised Taffy.

Screwing his face up into a sexual grimace, Luke thrust his pelvis back and forward several times for Taffy's enlightenment.

'Leave it out, Luke,' said John, 'she's class.'

'Yeah?' returned Luke. 'What's class doing with a piss-poor squaddie like you?'

John smirked and copied Luke's shagging gesture, which met with ribald halloo.

'Likes a bit of army rough, don't she!' roared Luke excitedly, and they all concurred as to the merits of army fucks, mostly with their hips.

The pool game was soon over. Collecting their things, they made their way to meet the garrison-to-train-station bus that the army regularly laid on. They had almost left it too late, and laughed with relief as they slung their bulging service bags on to the racks above their seats. Luggage stuffed away, they each automatically cracked a beer can.

Although the bus was for army personnel only, it was civilian owned and run. The driver, sporting remnants of an Elvis haircut, leaned out of his seat to direct reproachful looks at his latest passengers. 'Hey, squaddies, no drinking on the bus.'

'Fuck you!' was the general reply from all the passengers, most of whom were already drinking, and those that weren't immediately opened cans.

The driver laughed. 'No talking, either,' he ordered, setting the bus moving.

'All right! Six days leave!' roared Luke, holding his can high before guzzling from it, beer spilling from his mouth and over his jacket.

'Yeah, but then two months solid in Kosovo,' said John.

'You love it, John,' said Taffy. 'It's why you joined up.'

'We all love it,' said Luke.

The bus passed through the garrison gates, raising the customary cheer from the passengers.

Fifteen minutes later, the bus was approaching the train station. Luke drew his comrades' attention to a young man with shaggy hair and a long coat who was walking out of the station hand-in-hand with an attractive young woman. 'Look at that poncy disgrace. How did he pull a bird like that?'

'Like to see Corporal Elliot putting him round the assault course,' wished John.

'Carnage,' predicted Stuart.

Luke tapped the window to gain the pedestrian's attention, and made a wanking gesture.

'Leave it out,' said John, arresting Luke's hand. 'We're supposed to be protecting them.'

Arriving at the station, the bus halted, and the passengers began collecting their belongings.

'Should make it back for the Arsenal match,' said Luke, pulling his bag down and slinging it over his shoulder.

'If you don't, you won't miss much,' sniped Stuart.

'You don't follow a team, do you?' said Taffy to John as they shuffled along to the front of the bus.

'Nah,' replied John, 'can't see what all the fuss is about. See enough shouting and anger in the army.'

Five minutes later, they were all on a train bound for London, and John calculated he would be at his final destination, Richmond, North Yorkshire, by seven o'clock at the latest.

*

Sitting in a cafe near to where she worked, facing away from the window, Jennifer pushed her empty plate aside and picked up her coffee. She hadn't planned to eat here today. It was Saturday, and since she only worked the morning on Saturdays, she usually went home for her midday meal. But today, perhaps because it was her birthday, she'd treated herself.

Contrary to Albert's imagination, Jennifer was a long way from being simply a large fraction of her sister. Indeed, they were not even full sisters. They shared a mother, but didn't share hair colour, or build, or much at all in the way of appearance. Sarah's hair was almost black, whereas Jennifer's — just short of shoulder-length — was almost white. Sarah had brown eyes; Jennifer, blue. Sarah was near buxom; Jennifer was not. Something they did share, however, was uncommon beauty: Sarah and Jennifer turned heads.

Bending to her bag, Jennifer retrieved a book her sister had recently given her: *The Mill on the Floss*, a work which Albert had recently read, falling in love with the central character. Jennifer flicked slowly through the pages, allowing many to escape her finger at a time. On the last page, however, she lingered, reading a little before flicking through the other pages again. Only now did she see that her sister had inscribed it. The inscription read: *To "The Poet" from her sister.* It took Jennifer back to a day when she was eleven. Sitting in the kitchen, she was reaching the end of a novel, the identity of which she couldn't now recall. Her mother was busy making food and Sarah was practising her cello. Sarah had stopped when she'd noticed that Jennifer was crying.

'Mum, Jennifer's crying. It's creepy. It's putting me off my practise.'

Finished reading, Jennifer had closed her book.

'Was it a sad ending?' her mother had asked.

Taking a moment to return to the real world, Jennifer had replied, 'All endings are sad.'

'Even happy ones?' Sarah had questioned.

Jennifer had nodded sadly, and said, 'Happy endings are like the sadness in people's smiles.'

Sarah had hammed up being slack-jawed astonished, and had said, 'Mum, did you hear that! We've got a poet in the family!'

'Well leave the poet alone and get on with your practise, Sarah.'

Sarah hadn't left the poet alone. She'd poked and tickled her with her cello bow. 'Poet. Poet. Big fat smelly drunken poet.' She'd poked and tickled until Jennifer had laughed and squealed like the eleven-year-old she was. For weeks afterwards, Jennifer now remembered, *The Poet* had been Sarah's nickname for her.

Jennifer returned *The Mill on the Floss* to her bag. Leaving the cafe and crossing the street to avoid having to wade through an oncoming party of school children clad for hill walking, she glanced at a dress in the window of a small clothes shop. This shop was a mystery to her. It had quietly appeared one day some months back, but seemed never to have had a customer. Moreover, she had never even seen it open for business, although the window display occasionally changed.

Jennifer lived in Richmond, North Yorkshire — gateway to the Dales, as it liked to remind the world. It was a small town, swelled each summer by tourists — mostly day-trippers — who came to see its wide waterfall, ruined castle and quaint market square. Now, in late October, the day-trippers were few and far between, but the more seasoned hill walkers and hikers still passed through on their way to the higher Dales.

'Hi ... Yeah, just walked in the door, pet,' said Margaret to a caller before she proffered the phone to Jennifer. 'For you, Jen.'

Margaret's was an old-fashioned house in that the phone was kept in the hall, on its own low table. Arranging herself for comfort and unnecessary seemliness, Jennifer sat on the even lower stool that had come with the telephone table.

A council property when she had first moved in, Margaret now paid a mortgage on the two-bedroom terraced house she shared with Jennifer. There was nothing out of the ordinary about Margaret. Dark-haired and in her late thirties, she dressed unremarkably; worked on the production line of a local garments factory; went to local social nights; and had recently discovered a pleasure in line dancing. She looked some years older than her true age, cigarettes, early rising, and two husbands having taken their toll. When her last husband, a lorry driver, left her for a woman in Leeds, Margaret did some sums, saw a deficit, but potentially balanced the figures by advertising her spare room for rent. She had been delighted to land a lodger who, even though still in her teens, never left any mess, never played music, and, beyond her aunt and uncle, had never had a visitor.

'Hello? ... Oh, hello ... I am glad ... I'm just tired — just got in from work. Where are you? ... How long will it take you to get here from London?'

After the phone call, Jennifer helped Margaret in the garden for a while before taking a bath, and when she came down the stairs after dressing, the phone rang for her again. 'Hello? ... Hi. Where are you now? ... Yeah? ... No, I don't feel like it. Let's stay in ... I'm bored with that pub ... I know, but ... I'm tired, anyway.'

The doorbell rang, and although Jennifer knew Margaret was coming to answer it, she cited it as a reason to end her phone conversation.

'Hi,' smiled Sarah at the door, carrying a small black canvas bag. 'I believe this is where my sister Jennifer now lives. You're Margaret?'

'That's me, love, come on in. She's just here. Been on the phone.'

Jennifer took her sister on a brief tour of the house, first showing her the living room, then the kitchen, and on into the garden. When they stepped back into the kitchen, Margaret, standing at a work surface, her fingers white with flour, was attempting a recipe she'd seen on a cookery show, adding various ingredients to a mixing bowl.

Margaret was not usually to be found cooking. Ready meals constituted much of her diet.

'Like my garden, then?' asked Margaret.

'Very nice,' said Sarah, putting her bag on the floor and sitting at the central table.

'Never really bothered with it much when me husband were here, but I've really started enjoying it now. Mebbe it's them gardening programmes I watch nowadays?'

Jennifer filled a kettle at the sink.

'The electricity bill arrived today, Jennifer,' said Margaret as Jennifer plugged the kettle in.

'Did it?'

'Ee, when I opened it I felt sick from the waist down. I thought it said five hundred and twenty pounds. But there was an ink smudge on it. It was only fifty-two. You've only been here three weeks so I reckon you only owe about ten pounds on it. It's in the hall if you want to look at it.'

'My purse is upstairs.'

'No hurry, pet. Just told you while I remembered.'

Standing beside the kettle, waiting for it to boil, Jennifer folded her arms and looked vaguely downwards.

Taking a wrapped present from her bag, Sarah tossed it to Jennifer. 'Here you go, kidda. Happy birthday.'

The present was tossed from so close Jennifer caught it almost involuntarily.

'Thanks, Sarah,' said Jennifer, unconsciously placing it to one side.

'Is it your birthday?' asked Margaret, surprised. 'You never said.'

'She's nineteen today,' revealed Sarah.

'I'll have to get you a card from somewhere later,' said Margaret.

'Don't worry about it,' said Jennifer.

'You're not much of a party animal, are you?' said Margaret gently, glancing at Jennifer.

The kettle had just boiled, and Jennifer tended to it. Making two coffees, she suggested to Sarah that they go upstairs to see her room.

On the stairs, out of earshot from Margaret, Sarah, mimicking and exaggerating Margaret's vocal style, said, 'Ee, I felt sick from the waist down.'

'I know,' responded Jennifer. 'She comes out with all kinds of funny sayings.'

'Does she make them up or are they real sayings?'

'No idea. Sometimes I think she just gets confused, but sometimes I think she's being deliberately quirky.'

'I like it,' decided Sarah. 'It could catch on.' She parodied Margaret again. 'Ee, when I saw the mess they'd left, I felt sick from the waist down.'

Entering Jennifer's room, Sarah found it to be fair-sized, containing a double bed, self-assembly wardrobe, and the white dressing-table that had belonged to their mother.

'Seen worse rooms,' said Sarah, standing with her coffee while Jennifer sat on the bed, opening her present. 'Nice and cosy.'

The present turned out to be a denim jacket and jeans. 'Thanks,' said Jennifer, placing them aside.

'Denim's really come back in.'

'Has it?' asked Jennifer vaguely.

'Haven't you noticed?' Sarah watched her sister for some seconds to see if she would do the appropriate thing. 'Well, try them on.'

'Later.'

As Jennifer picked up her coffee from the floor, Sarah asked, 'When was the last time you bought yourself something? Clothes, that is. And I don't just mean knickers and socks.'

'I don't remember,' answered Jennifer, sipping her drink.

Sarah moved to the window, taking in the view, which she found was limited to the immediate street outside. 'You're not exactly poor. Thirty thousand in your account. Has your credit card come yet?'

'Ages ago.'

'Used it yet?'

'Not yet.'

Sarah took a drink of her coffee, then asked, 'Have you read that book I gave you?'

Returning her cup to the floor, Jennifer went to her wardrobe to retrieve her bag, from which she produced the copy of *The Mill on the Floss*, proffering it to Sarah. 'You can have it back now.'

Leaving the window and sitting on the edge of the bed, Sarah looked at her sister. 'Jennifer, I don't want it back. I gave it to you — to keep. You don't have any books of your own, do you? Have you read it?'

'I wouldn't be giving it back if I hadn't read it,' returned Jennifer, placing it near Sarah.

'What happens at the end?'

Jennifer sat on her bed, and reached down for her drink. 'The end? There's a flood.'

'You used to read quite a lot when you were young,' remembered Sarah.

'Did I?'

'You always used to cry when you got to the end, too. Didn't you?'

Now gazing at her drink, appearing distracted, Jennifer offered no comment on her sister's recollections.

'I'm playing a concert on Friday evening at the Arts Centre in Durham,' revealed Sarah. 'Bit of a showcase to impress the university funding institutions. Want me to put you on the guest list?'

'I might be going to Maureen's house after work next Friday,' replied Jennifer.

Sarah suspected invention — Jennifer had never socialised with her boss before. 'Guest list or not? I need to know.'

Raising her cup to her lips, Jennifer replied, 'No, it's all right. Don't bother.'

'Over four years I've been in Durham and you've never once

come to see me. It's only forty minutes away. Don't you think that's a little weird?'

'I'll visit one day.'

'I'll only be there another six months.'

Jennifer said nothing else on the matter. Cradling her coffee, with her back turned to the room, Sarah looked at the dressing table that had once graced their mother's bedroom. Made in the 1920's, it was white, delicate, with curving legs and an ornate mirror.

'Would it upset you if I tried to trace my natural father?' asked Sarah.

'Why?' responded Jennifer immediately.

Sarah had seen Jennifer's discernibly shocked reaction in the dressing table mirror.

'I don't know,' said Sarah vaguely. 'Maybe just curiosity. Maybe because I feel there's something missing for me. Do you think dad would be upset? Or mum?'

Jennifer didn't reply, and Sarah turned to face her. 'How do you feel about it?'

'It's your decision, isn't it?' answered Jennifer, holding eye contact with her sister for longer than usual for her.

Sarah looked toward the dressing table again. 'But would you feel like I was excluding you somehow if, say, I met him one day?' In the mirror, she surreptitiously viewed her sister, who was sitting very still. Jennifer seemed to be looking at her, unaware that she herself was being observed. Receiving no reply, Sarah turned away from the mirror. 'Let's forget it.' Smiling, she said, 'It's all right for you, though. You knew everything about both your real parents.'

'I never knew them as people,' said Jennifer. 'Not like you did.'

'How do you mean?'

'I was always a little girl to them. You got to talk to them more as an adult.'

'Well, take it from me, kidda, they were diamonds. Very much in love, too. Sure of that.'

'I know,' said Jennifer quietly. 'Fate smiled and arranged adjacent tables for them.'

'Fate smiled and...? Oh, that's what mum used to say about the day they met, isn't it? In a French restaurant in London. Camden Lock.' Sarah paused, viewing her sister, whose own vague gaze was cast to some place in the direction of the carpet. 'Jennifer, I can't remember the last time I heard you laugh. When *was* the last time you laughed?'

66

Jennifer briefly looked at her sister. 'The last time I heard something funny. I'm peculiar like that.'

Sarah took a sheet of paper from her pocket. 'Here,' she said, offering it to Jennifer, 'this is funny.'

'What is it?'

The doorbell rang, and Sarah believed her sister's reaction contained an element of numbed regret.

'That'll be John,' said Jennifer.

'My cue to leave,' said Sarah, standing up. 'Suppose I'd better look in on auntie Jane before I go back to Durham. I'll put your name on the guest list anyway, just in case. Next Friday evening. Arts Centre. *Try.*'

Going with Sarah to the bedroom door, Jennifer tossed the paper she had just been given back towards her bed, but it wafted further, falling off the far side, and that is where she left it.

John had already been let in by Margaret when Sarah came downstairs, closely followed by Jennifer. A smile and a glib excuse was her only interaction with her sister's boyfriend as she passed him in the hall on her way out to her car.

*

Soon after his arrival — his first visit to the house — John had declared himself ravenously hungry. Jennifer had fixed him a meal, which he had eaten in the kitchen, chatting to her all the while. He also chatted freely — more freely — to Margaret, whenever she appeared, and quickly felt comfortable in her company. Jennifer herself had not been hungry, but now, some hours later, she was taking an omelette into the living room, where John was watching TV with Margaret.

'Mind if I put a light on?' she asked.

'Course not, pet,' answered Margaret.

When watching TV in the evening, Margaret had a habit of neglecting to switch on a light or close her curtains until some other need demanded it.

A car advert came on screen.

'That's the car I want,' said John, moving enough to allow Jennifer space on the sofa. 'Should have enough saved this time next year.'

After putting a table light on, Jennifer sat with her plate on her knees.

'It's nice,' said Margaret. 'I used to drive when me husband was here. Might get meself a little car now I've got some rent money coming in too.'

Margaret went upstairs to the bathroom.

John aimed the remote, and turned the television down.

'Come on, Jenny, let's go out. I've only got five days leave. You know I've got to go to Nottingham for a few days too. Besides, I might get shot next week.'

This was a continuation of an earlier discussion.

'I don't feel like sitting in the Shepherd tonight.'

'We don't have to go to the Shepherd, do we? What about that place on the market square we went to once? The something Arms.'

'I don't feel like going out.'

'You never do much, do you?' commented John, playing with her hair.

Jennifer made no reply, so John sat forward to put his arms around his girlfriend. 'I've got a special birthday present for you, and I want to give it to you when we're out. We don't have to stay long. Want to get an early night myself.'

Eventually, Jennifer relented. After her meal, she put on a baggy, thick, light-blue jumper ready to walk to the market square with John, who wore his black puffa jacket for the journey.

Along the way, a car tooted its horn as it passed them, the four young male passengers making gestures to Jennifer.

'Know them?' asked John.

'Course not,' answered Jennifer. 'They'll be from the garrison.'

She meant Catterick Garrison, five miles south east. It was when briefly stationed at Catterick himself that John had first met Jennifer.

The Shepherd was the only pub in the market square not to have been developed by an entertainments chain, and therefore usually offered the quietest place to drink. Tonight, however, Jennifer was displeased to discover a dreary disco in progress at one end, rope lights and a sound-to-light box providing the effects. But the music wasn't too loud where they chose to sit, and she could make herself heard without having to raise her voice too much.

John went to the bar. Waiting for him to return, Jennifer viewed the small group of excitable teenage dancers, who would all throw their arms into the air at certain points in the music. She vaguely recognised some from her old school. When John came back with drinks, placing them on the table, he too looked over to the commotion.

'How long have they had dancing here?'

'Don't know,' shrugged Jennifer.

Sitting opposite Jennifer at their small, round table, John smiled and said, 'I'll be up myself after a few drinks, you watch me. Bit of dancing might cheer you up — you look a bit glum tonight. Mind you, you always look a bit glum, don't you? Suits you, though. Very mysterious. Makes you look classy.'

Jennifer smiled a little, and John touched her hand affectionately. She was about to withdraw that hand to lift her drink, when, from his pocket, he produced a ring, placing it over the tip of her finger.

'Want to wear it?'

The diamond solitaire ring, costing over four-hundred pounds, had been the most expensive available in the catalogue shop John had visited that day in Darlington. Whether Jennifer wanted to wear it or not was not apparent on her face as she stared at it.

'Engagement?'

'Engagement,' confirmed John, gently pushing the ring further down. When it was over the knuckle, he smiled and said, 'Happy birthday,' and kissed her hand. He looked at her. 'Got the right finger, haven't I?'

'Yes,' said Jennifer, pushing the ring all the way on.

At once, John took her ringed hand and began pulling her to her feet. 'Come on, show me how you can dance. You're the best looking girl in this place. Best looker in this town.'

Jennifer resisted John's pull, and remained seated. 'No, I don't want to dance.'

'Nineteen, drop-dead gorgeous, your birthday, just got engaged to a hunk, and you don't want to dance? Come on.'

He tried to pull her up again.

With a look of anxiety, Jennifer blurted, 'I don't dance. I've never danced.'

John released her. 'What? I don't believe it.'

'It's true.'

She picked up her drink, and John sat down beside her, remarking, 'You're a funny one, you, aren't you?'

Jennifer gave no reply.

John made no further attempts to persuade his girlfriend to dance with him. He was seldom sure what was the right thing to do. She was a mystery to him, and made him feel insecure. Most everything they did together they did because he pressured her in some way, and he often suspected that if he stopped calling her when he was away, she would hardly notice. But then she wasn't like other girls, he knew. She was introverted and reserved, and insecure herself, so maybe that's all it was. He could live with that.

He adored her. Adored looking at her. He felt so proud when he was out with her, and it would be worth it even if he had to put twice the effort into maintaining the relationship. Even if she wasn't anywhere as keen on him as he was on her, at least he still had her, and that's what he wanted. Besides, she had just accepted his ring, hadn't she? She *must* think he was special, in her own unspoken way.

Even though she had just accepted his ring, John decided he wouldn't initiate any sexual activity once they were in her bedroom. Born out of his insecurities over just what it was Jennifer wanted in a boyfriend, he had a plan to box clever and show by restraint that it wasn't her body he wanted above all else. It was unlikely she'd make the first move — she never did — so tonight he would show that he didn't come all the way to see her on his army leaves on the expectation of sex. Tomorrow, Sunday, he was going to Nottingham to see his family, but he would be back in Richmond on Wednesday, and sex could wait until then.

Coming out of the Shepherd, he took her hand in his for the short walk to her new home.

'Fancy me never noticing before that you don't dance,' he said.

'We've never really been anywhere dancy.'

'Suppose not. We've never really been anywhere at all, have we?'

Jennifer offered no comment, and they walked on without conversation for a while until John said, 'Next week we'll have been seeing each other two years, so it's about time we were engaged, isn't it?'

The question had enough of a rhetorical nature and tone for it not to demand an answer, and it received none. Jennifer instead raised the subject of John's impending tour of duty, a subject upon which John was voluble.

Leaving the shopping streets behind, taking a narrow, steep turning, they were soon on the poorly-lit residential street that led most of the way home for Jennifer.

'Do you want me to leave the army, Jenny?' asked John tentatively after describing his forthcoming military tour. 'We hardly see each other, do we? The odd few days here and there. You can never make it to Nottingham to stay with my folks. They're always asking about you. I can be out next summer, with a good trade under my belt. We can settle down then. I'll have a brand new car, too.'

'You like the army.'

'Not as much as I like you. You're the most beautiful woman

70

I've ever seen.'

The conversation was dampened by the appearance, from a side-street, of two young ladies of about Jennifer's age. One was tall with dark hair, the other short, blonde, overweight, with a rage of freckles. Both were ungainly tipping forward as they hurried along on their platform shoes.

'Hello,' said Jennifer awkwardly as they passed her.

'Hello,' said one of the women, perfunctorily.

'Hiya,' said the other.

'Ooh, she speaks,' said the first to her friend, loud enough to be overheard. 'What an honour.'

'What was that all about?' asked John, presuming offence. 'Were they having a go at you? It's not those ones that used to bully you, is it?'

'No, it's Claire and Davina,' explained Jennifer. 'The sixth-form friends who were with me the day I met you when you were fishing down at the river. Remember? Claire fancied you and got us to go over to you with her.'

'Oh, them. You haven't mentioned them since I left Catterick. Did you have a falling out over me? Is that it?'

'No.'

'So what's the score? None too friendly, were they?'

'It wasn't them, it was me,' said Jennifer, with an air of weariness. 'I don't know. I just got out of the habit of seeing them.'

'Why's that?' asked John. 'Would have thought you'd like having them around since you never seem to—.' He looked at her, and although he was sure she was aware of his searching gaze, she continued to look ahead. 'You're a funny one, you. Don't you want friends?'

'It's not that. It's like... I don't know. I just stopped thinking of things to say to them. And the things they said didn't interest me. I just feel awkward when I see them now. Maybe I just outgrew them. I feel bad about it all sometimes.'

John swung Jennifer's hand, and with a light air said, 'You won't go outgrowing me, will you?'

'No,' returned Jennifer in a voice that carried no extra information. After walking on some more paces, she spoke again. 'I don't like living in such a small place. You won't know what it's like. You're from a city.'

John looked at her again. 'You're a funny one, you.' He kissed her cheek and squeezed her bottom, though she continued to walk on. 'But fucking gorgeous.'

That morning, John had risen at five to work four hours in the heavy vehicle repair shop, where he was now a qualified mechanic. So upon returning to Jennifer's home, sleep was easily made his priority. Showered within ten minutes of entering the door, with a towel wrapped around his lean waist, he went into Jennifer's room and fell back on to the bed. 'I'm knackered. Long day.'

Now Jennifer took her turn in the bathroom. In a dressing gown, sitting on the edge of the toilet, she looked at the ring encircling her finger.

An alarm sounded.

John got off the bed and parted the curtain to look out the window, but was unable to determine which parked car was making the wailing noise before it fell silent. He let the curtain close. Turning, he saw a sheet of paper lying halfway under the bed, and picked it up for idle examination. When he heard Jennifer leaving the bathroom, he replaced the paper where he'd found it, and sat on the bed, resting his back against the pastel-pink padded headboard.

Entering her bedroom, Jennifer went to the dressing table to take off and stow away her hair band.

'Is my fishing stuff here or still at your aunt's?' asked John, his dark eyes fixed on Jennifer.

'Aunt's,' said Jennifer, now brushing her hair. 'What time are you setting off for Nottingham tomorrow?'

'Before noon. Want to get there before my brother leaves in the evening. He's off on active service. Not allowed to say where. How's Albert?'

'Who?' asked Jennifer, continuing to work the hairbrush.

John leaned over and grimly produced the sheet of paper he had found. Jennifer, realising something was seriously at issue, put her brush down and went to see, sitting on the edge of the bed to read it.

No amount of genuine innocence and bewilderment seemed likely to banish John's suspicions and conclusions, although Jennifer kept trying. 'John, for the fiftieth time,' she said, standing near her dressing table, 'I don't know him, or *anyone* called Albert. Sarah gave it to me just before you rang the bell. I never even looked at it. That's the whole story.'

John was now also standing, naked since his towel had fallen away.

'Well he seems to know you, doesn't he?' he stated, voice louder than necessary for the distance it was required to travel. 'Some posh, clever student Sarah introduced you to in Durham?'

'I've never been to see Sarah in Durham,' said Jennifer, her exasperation increasing. 'Phone her up and ask her about the letter. Go on, phone her.'

'You phone her,' John shot back.

'Why should I phone her?' barked Jennifer, glaring at him. 'I already know I don't know an Albert. And would you believe me if I told you what Sarah said?'

John had never known Jennifer raise her voice, and it unsettled him. She had jumped straight from passive to almost wild. An inch away from lashing out, it seemed. He sat on the edge of the bed, looking at the curtains. 'She's never liked me. Thinks I'm not good enough for you.'

'She's never said a word against you to me,' answered Jennifer truthfully, her brief flash of temper waning.

John now looked at Jennifer, saying with sullen resentment, 'She doesn't have to say it. There's other ways of speaking. Think I never noticed?'

Margaret was in the bathroom. She suffered heavy periods, and during her worst episodes resorted to wearing a modified baby's nappy. While fixing a batch of these accessories, she had been catching curious elements of John's accusations.

Margaret suspected that the matrimonial handicap her unnaturally frequent and heavy periods had presented had been the reason for the loss of her two husbands, one to a much older woman.

Coming out of the bathroom, now ready for bed, Margaret, in diplomatic, jocular tones, said, 'Hey, cut it out you two, there's decent folk trying to sleep out here. You're acting like you're married already.'

Although the bedroom door was closed, Jennifer could easily speak to Margaret. 'John thinks I'm seeing someone else.'

'You!' exclaimed Margaret cheerily, on the way to her own room. 'You never go out. Be a strange romance.'

'Satisfied?' said Jennifer to John, which somehow prompted him to jump to his feet and rip up the contentious letter, pieces of it wafting down to speckle the wine-coloured duvet. 'Don't rip it up!' she complained, trying to save it, although it was clearly too late.

'Why not? Don't want to keep it, do you? It's all fucking weird stuff, anyway.'

'Because it's not yours to rip up,' she protested before feeling she didn't want to bother with any of it any more. 'Oh, I don't care.'

Kicking off her sandals, she petulantly climbed past John and over the scattered pieces of Albert's letter. Getting into bed, she immediately switched off the light, leaving John standing naked in the dark.

1.6
Portentous

In the weeks following the autumn equinox, the space around Simon's wall map of the British Isles became cluttered with house photographs. Most were marked with a thick black cross, signifying that Simon had eventually discounted them as suitable properties for his scheme. Of the remaining unmarked photos, four were pinned in a cluster. These were his current front-runners: two being located in the mountains of North Wales; two high up in Weardale.

It was early evening, and Phil was visiting Simon. He'd brought a potato salad to share that he'd made the day before for one of his chef exams at the college he attended in north London. Standing with a chipped plate in his hands, eating frequent but small amounts of his portion of the meal, his stiff, new blue jeans hung loose and crumpled around his bony legs.

He was looking at the four unmarked photographs on the wall.

Simon, wearing three jumpers, was sitting on the edge of his single bed, a plate balanced on his lap. Speaking through a mouthful of food, he said, 'Don't say anything to Charles or the others, but it's looking more and more likely my centre will be set up in one of those four properties.'

Phil remained perplexed. 'But it'll cost thousands. Th'where will the money come from?'

After some hesitation, Simon cautiously divulged, 'I've got a business backer.'

Excited, Phil turned around. 'Th'really? Who?'

'I can't tell you anything about him. It's a secret.'

'Do I know him?'

'I can't say anything more, Phil, so don't ask.'

'Th'why not?'

'Phil, stop it.'

'Is it our leader?'

'No.'

Phil looked at the photographs again. 'Do you mean move there forever?' There was concern in his voice now.

'Yes,' confirmed Simon. 'Permanently.'

'Th'what about the Orthrium Society?' worried Phil, turning back to Simon.

'I'll still attend the quarterly prayer sessions. Have to.'

'Th'what about me?'

'You could come with me,' answered Simon at once. 'You'll have to work, though. It'll be a business.'

'Doing what?'

'I don't know,' said Simon, but sounding hopeful. 'There'll be lots to do.'

Finished eating, Phil put his plate on Simon's desk.

'Can you put the electric fire on for a bit?'

'I'm putting the computer on in a minute,' said Simon, 'that'll heat the room.' Looking down to his food, he remarked, 'This is good. Did it cost much to make?'

'The college paid for the ingredients.'

'Yeah? That's good, isn't it?'

'Can I th'work as the cook?' proposed Phil.

'I don't see why not,' answered Simon.

'Th'brilliant! I love cooking.'

'You're very good at it too.'

Phil stepped over to the map, and studied it. 'Do th'ley lines make food taste better?'

'They may do. They're positive energy, aren't they?'

'Maybe I could th'art a rethaurant or a food business there?' proposed Phil. 'I could make th'pecial th'tuff to th'ell to th'hops and things.'

Simon looked up from his plate, and murmured, 'Spiritually balanced food for national sale.'

Phil smiled tentatively. 'Do you think it's a good idea?'

'Phil,' beamed Simon, 'it's a brilliant idea! We could make a small fortune!'

Now Phil smiled with more certainty. 'A fortune! Th'great!'

*

Saturday was not a normal meeting day for the Orthrium Society. This particular Saturday, however, their temple, a red-velvet-draped room above a betting shop in Fulham, was well attended. It was not for the purposes of meditation or spiritual discussion, though. Its doors had been thrown open only to offer its members a convenient place to assemble before moving on elsewhere, and elsewhere, it had already been decided, would first be a pub.

'Excited, Simon?' enquired Karen, sociably linking her arm with his. Karen was a petite, forty-year-old reflexologist with dark-blonde, shoulder-length, wavy hair. Her compressed, chubby face and large front teeth combined to convey a rabbit impression.

'Yes. A bit,' answered Simon, appearing uneasy.

Simon had been driven to this irregular meeting by Carl, the cab driver who'd been hired by the film crew. Having followed up Simon's invitation four weeks earlier, Carl was now a full member of the Orthrium Society. Standing beside Simon, he was clutching a large zip purse filled with coins and notes, some of the fruits of his day's cabbying. He was about the same height as Simon, but had a brawnier build, and jerkier actions.

'We should 'ave brought a big telly 'ere then we could 'ave all watched it togevver,' opined Carl.

'That's what I suggested yesterday,' said Karen, her arm still linked with Simon's. She peered around the room. 'Where's Phil tonight?'

Carl answered, 'Workin'.'

'Is he still at that fish and chip shop?'

'That's right,' confirmed Simon. 'But he'll be a qualified chef soon. He's been going to college.'

'That's good,' smiled Karen. Noticing that people were starting to leave, she made one last attempt to change Simon's mind. 'Are you sure you're not coming with us?'

'I don't like pubs.'

Karen looked at Simon. 'Never mind. After we've met Charles for a drink in the Goose and Firkin, we're splitting into groups. Some of us are taking bottles back to my place in Battersea to watch the programme. We're making a party of it. Join us later.'

'I don't like parties.'

Karen squeezed Simon's arm in good-natured exasperation. 'Oh, Simon, you are a one. Well, you know where to find me.' Unlinking her arm, she said goodbye, and went to join the departing members.

After encouraging the remaining members to leave, Simon locked up the temple and walked with Carl back to the cab, a return to Lambeth being their plan.

'Bit of a waste of time us goin' all this way, weren't it?' remarked Carl once they were in the cab, speaking to Simon through the sliding glass panel that could be employed to separate him from his passengers.

He started the cab's rattling diesel engine.

'Sorry about that,' apologised Simon as Carl swung the cab around. 'I wasn't thinking. Andrew could have opened instead.'

'Andrew a key 'older too?'

'All the High Teachers are key holders.'

'You really 'ate pubs that much, then?'

'Yes. Hate them. Hate everything about them.'

'Used to like 'em a bit too much, meself,' confessed Carl. ''Ad a bit of a drink problem, I did. Religion saved me. Jesus Army. 'Aven't touched a drop in six years. Weren't for them, I'd never've got meself togevver enough to 'ave done me taxi knowledge.'

'You did well,' said Simon, looking more preoccupied than usual.

'Couldn't fackin believe it when I stopped for that produca bird an' she asked if she could film in me cab. Magic day. Cabbying for four years, but nuffink like that ever 'appened. Can't wait t'see me cab on telly. I wuz in the Jesus Army six years, but that wuz boring compared t'this stuff.'

For reasons Carl couldn't work out, the traffic was unusually heavy for a weekend evening. The conditions made him slip into the blank, automatic state that was his life for much of his bumper-to-bumper working day. The absence of conversation seemed to suit Simon, who appeared lost in thought for much of the journey to Lambeth. Only later on, in lighter traffic along Kennington Road, did he speak, when gazing at the distant, floodlit House's of Parliament across the Thames. Even then he was speaking more to himself than Carl.

'Nice clear evening. Should be some sightings tonight.'

'Yeah?'

'Raining in the North, though. I always watch the weather forecast.'

They were now approaching a complicated, busy roundabout, which required Carl's full attention. Once it was negotiated, he said, ''Ere, Simon, I'm starved. Been thinkin' 'bout fish 'n' chips since Karen mentioned 'em. 'Ave we got time t'get some? I know you ain't got much money, so I'll treat y'.'

Simon answered in the polite but preoccupied way that constituted much of his social manner. 'Thanks. Yes, we've got over half an hour yet.'

Carl immediately swung his cab completely around, then into a side street. 'Magic chip shop down this way,' he smirked knowingly. Pulling up in front of the establishment, he turned off the engine and went to stand in the small queue for service, soon returning with two bundles. 'Eat in the cab or back at your gaff?'

Simon asked how long it would take get to his home. Carl guessed another ten minutes to reach the street and find a parking place, so it was decided they should eat in the cab. Carl finished his meal before Simon had got even halfway through his, and he resumed driving while his passenger continued to dine.

Although Carl had picked Simon up several times from outside his house in the previous weeks, he had yet to see his room, but was now about to. Climbing the narrow, zigzagging staircase that shoddily incorporated elements of a previous, more substantial staircase, he waited on a landing for Simon to catch up.

Simon was still eating.

'Ain't you finished those chips yet, slow coach?' joshed Carl. ''Ere, I could murder a cup of tea.'

Upon entering his room, Simon took his kettle downstairs to fill it. In his absence, Carl looked around. Going to investigate one of the skylights, he thrice had to duck dusty, eye-level beams. Traversing this room, he discovered, meant bobbing. And getting anywhere near the front or back walls meant stooping, since they were only three feet high. The other two walls — the walls between the house and its two terraced neighbours — were full height in the centre, and against one of these bare-brick walls Simon had placed his desk.

Bobbing back to the more habitable meridian of the loft, Carl peered at a row of similar-looking paperback books on the shelves above the desk. 'Oo's Terry Pratchett?' he asked when Simon returned.

'He's really good,' said Simon, bobbing along to the far end of the room. 'Really funny. I've got all his books. He's got an orang-utan as a librarian so it can reach things. Really funny.' After plugging the kettle in, he pulled out a book. 'This is his best one. I laugh out loud every time I read it.'

'Yeah?' Carl briefly flicked through the book before placing it on the desk. 'It's cold in 'ere. Put some 'eating on, will y'?'

'The TV will heat the room up when it's on,' returned Simon.

Carl turned the chair under the desk to face the room. Sitting down, he watched while Simon, stooping in a corner next to a small fridge, made two teas. Carl observed that the fridge looked as if it might have come from a municipal dump.

Carl was slim, but had definition. His arms, whether he sat or walked, were always held bent, so his elbows stuck out at his sides. Although he was always clearly freshly shaven, he nevertheless displayed a permanent and heavy beard shadow. Carl's face was incapable of emotional trickery. It faithfully registered his every fleeting mood. However, an underlying expression seemed always to pervade: a tense frown that persisted even when he laughed. It was as if his other expressions were merely painted over this permanent undercoat in translucent colours that could wash away in an instant.

Looking around the shoddy room, Carl's face now reflected his unease at Simon's living conditions.

"Ow much is y'rent 'ere?'

'Fifty a week,' answered Simon. 'Milk? Sugar?'

'Milk, no sugar, ta,' requested Carl, and Simon bobbed over to hand him his tea. "Ow many people share the bathroom and kitchen?'

'Nine, including me,' answered Simon, with no trace of complaint in his tone.

'Gawd, it'd drive me crazy,' said Carl. Becoming fired, he urged, 'Simon, do the fackin taxi knowledge like me, then in a couple of years you'd be making enough from cabbying to get a decent place. Love my little flat in Clapton.'

'I'm all right here,' said Simon as he switched on his large but old television. Activating his video, he reported he'd picked it up from a junk shop that week for only eight pounds — marked down because its case was broken and the remote was missing.

Very soon, a TV Continuity Announcer was saying, "And now the third part in the series, *The Elaboration of Jesus.*"

Simon sat on the edge of his bed and studiously watched the programme, which opened with slow-motion shots of him dowsing on Glastonbury Tor. Carl made dozens of remarks during the fifty-minute showing, but few elicited responses. As soon it finished, Simon switched off the television and video.

'That was all right, weren't it?' said Carl cheerily.

Simon sat on the edge of his bed again, pensive and brooding.

'Magic,' Carl proudly went on. 'T'think my cab's been on telly. Magic. Mum's gonna be right chuffed.'

'I wasn't happy with it,' said Simon quietly.

Carl's expression quickly changed from glowingly satisfied to uneasy. 'Why's that then?'

'It wasn't serious enough. I'm disappointed with them. I thought they understood.'

'It wuz all right,' said Carl, nervously attempting placation.

Simon sat in brooding silence for some seconds, then got up to switch on his computer. His manner now suggested he had already put the disappointment behind him.

'Can I have the chair?' he asked Carl.

'Course you can,' said Carl, standing up. 'What you up to now?'

Settling down at his keyboard, Simon answered, 'Checking the internet for sightings.'

'Yeah? Magic. Y'mean UFO sightings?'

'That's right.'

Standing behind Simon, Carl viewed the computer's puzzling messages. 'Never done much with computers meself. What's it doing now?'

'Just starting up,' answered Simon. 'It'll take a minute or so to get on the net.'

The enigmatic boot messages soon drove Carl's attention away, and he took to looking at the large map of Britain on the wall behind the computer. 'What's all this, Simon? What's all them lines?'

'Ley lines. I've been plotting locations for a business idea I've got.'

'Yeah? What idea's that?'

Simon hesitated before deciding it would do no harm telling Carl his plans, despite the injunction Charles had requested. 'A centre for New Age teaching and research, with courses and lectures and things like that. Run it strictly as a business, though. Guests will have to pay.'

'Yeah? Magic idea. What are all these photos?'

'Potential properties to set up in.'

'Yeah? Looks like it'll seriously cost. Where will y'get the start up from?'

'I'll raise the capital from investors.'

Carl continued to look at the photos. 'Yeah? Reckon y'can do that?'

Internet connection had now been achieved. 'We're in,' announced Simon, clicking on various menus to call up latest sightings.

'Yeah?'

Carl stood behind Simon, looking over his shoulder at the screen.

'Oh my God,' breathed Simon. 'This is amazing!'

'What is?'

Scrolling down the screen, Simon explained, 'There was a sighting over Durham cathedral last week. Wow! Thirteen different reports... and a newspaper article. *The Durham Gazette*.' He read the article aloud. '*Although police insist it was a distress flare, eye witness Ken Bentham gave this account: It was a long, thin craft, throbbing with light, that hovered over the cathedral for some time before moving off at great speed.*'

'Where's Durham?' asked Carl.

Simon's excitement increased. 'That's the amazing thing! Durham's one of the areas I plotted to best site my centre.' He went to his map, showing Carl the location of his Northern choice of Weardale in the west of County Durham, and its proximity to Durham City. 'Look, less than thirty miles from where I discovered there to be the largest known ley line convergence. And the river that rises in Weardale flows around the cathedral, almost looping it. Amazing. And look, there's a ley line direct to Durham City.'

Carl peered at the map. 'Yeah?'

Simon sat on the edge of his bed again. 'Something's going on, Carl,' he said, developing a portentous air. 'Something's going on. It's starting to come together.'

Carl, looking confused, sitting side-saddle on the chair behind the desk. 'Yeah?'

'I was right,' Simon went on, bolstering his own speculations. 'It's Durham. Durham's where it's all going to happen. It's beginning. I've got to go there.'

'Yeah?' said Carl, suddenly looking more at ease. 'Can I come wiff y'? Never been up north. I'll drive yer up in me cab if y'like. Need an 'oliday. Usually go to Brighton.'

Simon hardly heard Carl. 'It's beginning,' he murmured. 'It's definitely beginning.'

''Ow far is it?' asked Carl, getting up to look at the map again. ''Bout two-fifty miles, ain't it?' Stepping back from the map, he bumped his head on a beam. Staggering forward, holding his head, he attempted to sit on the edge of desk, but the entire thing immediately collapsed, throwing him and Simon's computer to the floor.

Simon was aghast.

'Shit. Sorry, Simon,' said Carl desperately, picking himself up while simultaneously pressing a hand to his bumped head. 'Oh Christ. Don't worry, I'll get another one for y'.'

Simon stared at the fallen machine, which was obviously broken. Its monitor was blank, and its system unit emitted an unhealthy screeching noise until it fell ominously silent.

'I'll get y' a replacement,' offered Carl in an increased panic, hopelessly trying to rescue the machine, picking up the mouse and keyboard but not knowing what to do with them.

Slowly, Simon moved over to view the catastrophe, like he was looking down upon the unexpected ruin of his whole life.

'I'll get y' a replacement,' reassured Carl.

Simon continued to stare at the wreckage.

Tentatively, Carl put down the mouse and keyboard. 'Sorry, Simon. Always was a bit clumsy. I'll get y' a replacement.'

Simon looked at Carl. 'Promise?'

'Promise,' swore Carl. 'Got to pay off some of me mortgage arrears Monday, but after that, whatever I earn, I'll put it towards a replacement.'

'Equal or better in quality?' enquired Simon firmly.

'You'll be no worse off. Swear.'

Kneeling, Simon began an attempt to reconstitute his computer, but quickly conceded that it was indeed now useless to him. Sitting on the floor, he cast Carl a look of lugubrious resentment.

'You'll be no worse off. Swear,' repeated Carl. 'Get anovver soon as I can.'

Simon stared bleakly at the floor.

Carl assessed the results of his clumsiness. ''Ow much will equal or better set me back? Second 'and, we're talking, ain't we? Looks quite old, your one.'

'I don't know,' muttered Simon sullenly. 'I bought it a while back in a bankruptcy auction. Two hundred might be enough now, second hand. Just so long as it can do everything that one did. I need to get back on the internet as soon as I can. Luckily all my data's backed up.'

Carl smiled with relief. 'Reckon I can manage two 'undred by Tuesday night if I put serious cab hours in. Won't let you down, Simon. Promise.'

Simon made no reply, just continued to stare moodily at the

floor.

Sounding upbeat, but with a detectable core of concerned timidity, Carl asked, 'Still friends, ain't we?'

Taking some seconds to respond, Simon, with a look of sullen agreement, made eye contact with Carl. 'Okay. Equal or better.'

'Magic,' smiled Carl.

With the promise of a replacement satisfactorily instituted, all outward signs of Simon's morbid meditation on the broken computer completely fell away, and he went over to view his map, and stared at Durham.

1.7
Bored

After Ron left the flat to go off with Sarah, Albert did a search of Ron's bedroom, hoping to find the *ALBERT'S LASS* T-shirt. Quickly giving up the quest, he mooched morosely around his kitchen, subject to a vague hunger, but nothing in the cupboards or fridge interested him. Besides, most of it belonged to Ron, although that had never held him back. Forgoing food, he brewed some tea and slumped down to watch whatever the television had to offer. By the time nine o'clock arrived, he was bored. Very bored. Too bored even to stare at his ceiling. Bored and unsettled. He was so bored, he began watching a programme celebrating an air show, the commentator extolling the virtues of some sleek new warplane, with bombs as smart as geeks.

Albert wondered how long it would be before someone built a warplane that could bomb babies without damaging their pushchairs.

He switched over, hoping for something more gentle. A programme called *The Elaboration of Jesus* was just starting, showing a man with light ginger hair wearing a fancy red robe, dowsing with a crystal. It was fascinatingly crackpot already, and Albert watched it all the way through, learning about a cult called the Orthrium Society. The cult's followers maintained that Jesus and Buddha were Cosmic Masters, now living on other planets in our solar system, often sending telepathic messages to the cult's spiritual leader on earth.

According to the cult's devotees, the other planets abounded with such Masters.

The devotees were shown dramatically praying into small metal boxes with aerials attached, boxes they claimed were actually spiritual energy storage batteries. They also claimed that Cosmic Masters in flying saucers were frequent but secret visitors to earth orbit, waiting for the right moment to openly introduce themselves to the general population below. The right moment, it was said, would be after a Master led the world into a Golden Millennium of peace and enlightenment.

But first the bad people would be sorted from the good.

They also said that, after many progressive reincarnations, a human who is goodly enough would be allowed to "graduate" to higher planets in the solar system.

The sun's planets are like classrooms, they said, and Earth was the dunces' class.

Although the other planets appear to our telescopes and probes to be uninhabited and uninhabitable, it was deceptive, the devotees claimed. Highly advanced beings do exist on them, they insisted, but on different energy planes, only adopting physical form when deliberately showing themselves to Earthlings, as Jesus once had.

The program ended, and Albert switched channels, seeing a news report on the increasing number of people choosing heroin overdose as a method of suicide. Due to immediate coma, they were often found slumped with syringes still in their arms.

'Fucking amateurs,' muttered Albert, switching off the television.

Still bored. Very bored. What was wrong with him tonight? Why couldn't he go to his room and stare at the ceiling like he usually did? He had to find relief. Although she now worked in Durham, Jackie lived fifteen miles away in Darlington, so he couldn't go to see her to ease his boredom. And her sister, Rebecca, was probably out, doing things he couldn't afford to do, so he couldn't wander over to see her, either. Just a walk to a shop to buy a chocolate bar would be something, but right now even that small mercy was beyond his pocket.

He turned on the gas fire, which, apart from the portable heater in Ron's room, was the only source of warmth in the flat. The gas fire drove no radiators, so the rest of the flat was at the mercy of the weather. In Albert's room, dampness undermined the wallpaper in some corners, and black mould was establishing itself in ever-enlarging patches. It was in the contract somewhere that the landlord was responsible for decorating, but neither Albert nor Ron felt concerned enough to request improvements. Ron was saving to buy a place of his own, and within Albert there existed a fuzzy, secret, never-told-to-Jackie belief that he would one day begin doing something gainful. Something really gainful. Something to elevate and free him from day-to-day considerations. Albert wanted big money, not the trifling sums paid to workers for getting out of bed early each morning for years on end. If he was going to earn money, it would have to be in sums that could work wonders, although he'd never given any thought, or even daydreams, as to what those wonders might be.

Apart from an undeveloped idea for a more energy efficient saucepan, the only morally acceptable thing Albert could realistically imagine earning big money from without leaving his flat, or even getting dressed, was writing. Indeed, one day around four months back, slumped on the sofa watching a dramatisation of *The Pickwick Papers* on television, he'd sprung up and announced he was going to become the new Dickens. Ten minutes later, when Ron went to his bedroom to use his newly-purchased, top-of-the-range computer, he'd found Albert already at the keyboard. 'Better get used to it,' Albert had responded to the ensuing complaint, 'I'm only on the second word.' A long while later, Ron still hadn't displaced Albert, so he'd bribed him with the promise of a computer of his own, then password protected his own machine.

So that's when Albert's literary aspirations had germinated. But the seedling proved to be sickly and weak — so far sprouting just one micro-novel. But he felt he could manage a full-length work if he could just knuckle down to it. Soon he would have to, he reminded himself — Ron was going to sell the computer he now typed on if he didn't hurry up. Bearing that in mind, he reckoned that this, finally, was the time to start working on a proper, full-length novel. He was certainly bored enough. Yes, now was the time, he declared to himself in thought. Now was the time.

He began thinking about a plot, but his concentration immediately dissolved. 'Come on, make a start on it,' he whispered sternly. 'Nah, tomorrow,' he said out loud.

Still bored.

He tried, for a short while, to play with his cat, but Peep was in a serious mood and would have none of it.

He sat in the armchair near the fire. Finding the science magazine Ron had given him, he read half an article about an American professor who was in trouble with his university faculty for claiming to have found solid evidence for psychic interference in electronic experiments. He also read half an article about a physicist — a Nobel prize winner — who alone, at a special Congressional hearing, had spoken out *against* the continued construction of America's finally-cancelled Superconducting Super Collider, the most ambitious particle accelerator ever proposed. His opposition was curious because he was the very same scientist who had laid the theoretical groundwork that had made other scientists believe such a grand laboratory experiment was needed.

Many scientists now shunned him. One was even rude to his wife.

Next, Albert read almost a whole article concerning evolutionary psychology. Articles about evolutionary psychology usually annoyed him. They annoyed him because whatever theory they were expounding, he felt he could have easily proposed it himself if only someone had just had the sense to ask him for his views. This territory was his *forte*, for he often looked at life from an evolutionary psychologist's point of view. It made sense of murders and wars. But it sadly cheapened poetry and romance — and anything that could soften hearts in this harsh world *had* to remain valuable. So whenever he looked at life from an evolutionary perspective, he conveniently omitted poetry and romance from his scientific scrutiny, or glibly declared them transcendent.

But suicide — that really *was* transcendent. Had to be, for it was utterly unexplainable in evolutionary terms — at least he'd never managed to explain it. How could genes predisposing people for self-destruction make it through evolution?

'The noblest deed,' he murmured.

Albert suddenly perceived a great contradiction. The growing bands of Creationists — who maintain that God created people exactly as they now are — could use the existence of suicide as a pretty decent argument against evolution. However, to such people, suicide is a rejection and denial of God's love and gift of life, so their argument would essentially reduce to this: *some people hate being alive so much it is proof that life is a sacred gift from God.*

'I name that argument *Fox's fallacy*,' he said out loud, but Peep didn't seem impressed.

Wearing his scientific hat, Albert was fond of considering the human mind to be a two-storey structure, the ground floor constituting evolution's various redundant urges: racism, mob instinct, nationalism, patriotism. From the upper floor, the ground floor could be viewed, recognised and over-ruled. Unfortunately, he saw most people as lacking the imagination or the courage to climb the stairs for the overview. If only *most* people could accept that *all* minds carry a legacy from the past, then Catholics and Protestants wouldn't hate each other in Northern Ireland, and Manchester United supporters wouldn't hate Arsenal supporters.

Football: Albert wasn't the least bit seduced by the game and its trendy contemporary acceptance by people who once claimed to know better, such as women and posh people. Whenever Albert saw eleven men get together with a common purpose, he felt that purpose just had to be wrong.

Football: now *there* was material galore for the evolutionary psychologist within him, reckoned Albert. All those feelings of reflected glory in the sporting successes of others were screaming out for examination. Why should anyone follow a team? Or celebrate a team's — or nation's — sporting success? How could people sitting in their armchairs in front of a television joyously say "*we* won a medal?" or "*we* won the cup?". That's not to say he never himself felt twinges of pride and joy when his nation's team triumphed somewhere in the world. He did, and as strongly as most everyone did, he supposed. But, he concluded, those feelings were surely the abstract equivalent of an animal pack's frenzy at a successful kill by some of its hunters. Just as in all people, the evolutionary primitive ground floor of his mind delighted in abstract pack success — gold medals; war victories — but, climbing the stairs and looking from a greater height, he recognised such joys to be only the modified leftovers of redundant behaviour programs.

He saw such leftover programs as being the initiators of conflict and the deaths of children.

Albert let the magazine drop to the floor and began wishing for that chocolate bar again. No, a kebab. An oozing kebab. A kebab could lift his spirits a precious fraction right now, but he had no cash at all. Being so hard up that he was sometimes unable to feed himself was finally beginning to get to him, he realised. The lack of material things, like hi-fi's and cars, bothered him not. Neither did his inability to fund nights out — he often suspected he *preferred* being too poor to go out. It was the never-ending *petty* miseries of his hardupishness that were finally beginning to grind him down.

Sitting in his armchair, bored and hungry, he found himself toying in a defeated, half-hearted way, with the idea of getting a normal job. People were forever telling him he had more talents than any one person deserved, saying also that he could get ahead in a dozen different directions if he could just focus and direct himself. He, however, knew it would be pointless. He was psychologically unsuited to employment and the work place. There were many things he thought he could do, but nothing he thought he could ever do seriously. The only job he could realistically envisage doing without being dismissed in the first half hour would be one offering zero scope for silly subversion. Administrative work was definitely out of the question: nothing gave him greater scope for silliness than a form to fill in. His only chance would be with a job limited to a single action, such as tightening one bolt on an assemblage as it passed before him on a conveyer-belt in a factory bereft of fellow workers.

Damn it, he wished he had the money for a kebab. Maybe the time had come to suppress, or even try to defeat, his silliness? But silliness, as far as he could tell, was his reaction to a world of absurdity and cruelty.

Boredom began to swell again. Time was slowing down, so it seemed, just to piss him off, and the minutes felt like hours.

His brain was playing with the clocks.

He began thinking about time for a time, then decided not to believe in it any more as an independent entity. Time, he knew, was just that thing measured by clocks, and clocks go as fast or as slow as the observer's mind perceives them to, especially on a cold Saturday night when the unemployed observer is too poor to buy a kebab.

Time is an illusion, he thought. Merely another facet of entropy.

Time — just that thing measured by clocks, and all clocks, from a burning marked candle to a quartz watch, operate by seeking to rate and regulate entropy. Except as a measure of the inconsequential dissolution of atomic order — order he termed *arbitrary order*, like, say, the atoms that make up a cat — time was non-existent. That's all time really was, he decided: the dissolution of arbitrary order. In time, the cat must die and decay, and it is said that time has passed. The atoms that made up the cat disperse. The order that they once formed — the arbitrary order that made up that thing once called cat — is lost. But what has really happened? Nothing, Albert realised. The matter that made up the cat is intrinsically unchanged. It continues. Some of it may have undergone nuclear decay and become energy particles, but that process is reversible. Everything in the sub-atomic world is reversible. It is a world of frictionless see-saws. And one sub-atomic particle is indistinguishable from another of the same nature and energy. Therefore, he decided, time was simply an invented human expression to commemorate ongoing atomic disorder: the march of entropy, measured *with* entropy, *against* entropy, and a measure *of* entropy. Therefore, realised Albert, when entropy has run its course, time would cease to exist as a measurable thing.

In the meantime, he was bored shitless and the seconds still dragged.

It began to rain heavily. Unseasonable rumbles of thunder could be heard. He wondered about the immense energy released in storms. Each lightning bolt could heat a room for a year, he guessed.

Standing at the window to watch the spectacle, he imagined thousands of electric fires hanging on the underside of the clouds, briefly pulsing out heat instead of lightning flashes being violently ejected.

Rain lashed against the window. How much water would fall on his roof? If a half-inch of rain fell in the storm and his roof had an area of eight hundred square feet, then that would make two hundred and eight gallons. Thus just the waste run-off from his roof could sustain two hundred and eight lives in a drought-stricken country for a day or more.

It all seemed so simple.

When the storm diminished, he drifted into his bedroom where he experienced a sudden resolve to *really* begin his full-length novel.

Yes, he would.

He *would*.

He would begin another novel. Any novel — if only to tire himself out for bed.

So he did begin another novel, a novel inspired by the articles he'd read in *New Scientist*: that engineering dean claiming to have discovered true mind over matter evidence, and that Nobel physicist who had spoken out against the building of the Superconducting Super Collider. By midnight, this second novel of his had already exceeded the word count of his first, and he was still going strong. Things were really flowing. He was saved. He would make so much money from this new novel, he would be able to buy kebabs *and* stay in bed every morning for the rest of his life.

By quarter past twelve, his left index finger had begun hurting from the typing, but he could endure such suffering. He felt quite brave.

1.8
Presence

Ron finally began daring to believe that his night out with Sarah was going well when she invited him back to her place for a beer. He knew they'd hit it off as pals, but he hadn't been at all sure if things were going even better for him. At no time had he detected anything flirty in her behaviour or speech. In fact, she spoke like they had known each other as friends for years.

For the past year, Sarah had lived in one of eight single-bedroom flats in a four storey block on a council estate two thirds out from the centre of the compact city. Before her arrival, the block had been locally notorious for disturbance and burglary. Word got around and few people would accept an offer of accommodation there. Thus the council designated the flats hard-to-let, and people with low housing priority were offered tenancies when vacancies arose. Sarah got lucky: the top floor flat she was offered had been vacated by the very person who'd been responsible for much of the notoriety, and once he and his dubious visitors were out of the picture, the block became quite tolerable. At the time, however, she had been unaware of the block's background, wrongly supposing the graffiti and vandalism on the staircase to be the cause of its unpopularity with perspective tenants.

'Nice little flat,' remarked Ron when Sarah switched on her living room light. 'Pity about the rest of the building.'

'It's cheap, that's the main thing,' replied Sarah, briefly returning to her small hall to reactivate the various alarms and bolts she had installed to make her door an assurance rather than a worry. 'Flats on the private market cost a bomb to rent. You rent yours privately, don't you?'

'Yeah. Our rent's quite low, though. Bit of a dump, as you'll have noticed. Sharing makes it even more affordable. Dole boy Albert gets his half of the rent paid for him by Housing Benefit.'

'Sit down and I'll get you that beer,' said Sarah, going to her kitchen.

Ron took off his jacket and sat on the sofa, positioned under the window. Curving at one end, this armless, green velour couch stretched almost the full width of the small room, and looked able to comfortably seat maybe six average-size people side-by-side.

In the protected space between the end of the sofa and the wall stood a cello.

When Ron stretched his legs out and saw they took up much of the available floor space, he became conscious of just how un-average in size he was, and drew his legs in again.

'Don't you get Housing Benefit too?' he called to Sarah. 'Poor student, and all?'

Looking around, Ron thought that for a student, Sarah was living in unusual material comfort. She had an expensive-looking television, video and hi-fi, and nice furniture. Along in the kitchen, he could see a microwave and large fridge-freezer.

'I've got too much money to my name to get Housing Benefit,' said Sarah, returning with two beers and sitting close to Ron, sideways to face him, one leg folded under the other.

'How come?' asked Ron as he accepted a frothing bottle from Sarah, turning a little to face her better. 'Fat cheques from daddy?'

'Sort of. Thirty grand inheritance after my parents died. I've spent half, though — that's as well as my student loans. My sister got thirty grand too when she turned eighteen, but I don't think she's spent a penny of hers. She keeps trying to give me some. Might need it soon.'

'Both your parents died? What, together?'

'Car smash,' revealed Sarah, without resorting to emotional tones. 'Mum instantly; Dad a few hours later.'

'Shit,' breathed Ron. 'Pretty heavy for you.'

'Worse for Jennifer, seeing her own parents mangled before her eyes.'

'She was in the car?'

'Yeah. Could be why she's the way she is. I mean, it's not going to help, is it?'

'Was she badly hurt?'

'Not a scratch, but she's not the kid she used to be, that's for sure. But maybe she would have turned out that way anyway.'

'What way?'

'Hard to describe,' said Sarah, pausing. 'It's not what she does, more what she doesn't do.'

'So what doesn't she do?'

After taking a swig of beer, Sarah answered, 'She doesn't seem to live, Ron. Hardly takes any interest in anything. Apart from work, she doesn't even go out except when John's on leave.'

'Who's John? Boyfriend?'

'Yeah,' confirmed Sarah, a downbeat tone being noted by Ron.

'You said he's on leave. Is he in the forces?'

'Army. She only sees him occasionally. The rest of the time she just sits in, half-watching TV. Been trying for years to get her to come to Durham for a night out, but she always makes excuses. But she never says anything's wrong if you ask her. At least she's working now — she hardly left the house for a year after she left sixth form.'

'Maybe she's just shy,' suggested Ron. 'Plenty are. Used to do a bit of shying myself. I used to have hang-ups about being so big.'

'You are big, aren't you?' said Sarah. 'You fill this room on your own.'

'Tell me about it,' said Ron, in a voice that betrayed remnants of his adolescent hang-ups.

'It's not just that you're tall,' said Sarah, looking him over, 'it's your build. How often do you work out?'

'I don't. I've never worked out. Never lifted a weight in my life.'

'Really? But you're so... I don't know... meaty.'

'I'm just naturally big,' explained Ron. 'Great big chest and tree trunks for thighs.'

'I like it,' decided Sarah, in a tone lower than her usual. 'You've got presence.'

Ron wondered if he'd just been given a hint. God, he hoped so. She was the sexiest thing he'd ever met. And she was sane, too, something his previous girlfriend had proved not to be. He could hardly believe she was where she was. This was too good to be true. Sarah belonged in Hollywood, not by his side.

'She is shy,' said Sarah. 'She was always quite shy.' Moving away from the glib to struggle with the more considered, she continued,

'But now... it's like... it's like everything she does and says now is just her going through the motions. Worse since she left sixth form — I always assumed leaving school would help. In sixth form, she just went through the motions too. Didn't even turn up for some of her exams.'

For the first time, Ron witnessed Sarah drift away into a private world. Earlier, he'd noticed how, when sitting on her own at a table, waiting for him to return with drinks or come back from the gents, she always looked very much in-the-moment, but now she was elsewhere.

'You're quite preoccupied with her, aren't you?'

'Suppose I am these days,' agreed Sarah. 'Pity I wasn't before. Can't believe it, but soon it'll be seven years since the accident. I'd just started at a music boarding school. I was going to leave, but then I thought, fuck it, that's not what they'd have wanted. Last thing. Maybe the new life made it easier for me. But Jennifer was only twelve. She only went a few miles over to Reeth to live with our aunt afterwards. It must have felt like she'd lost me too. Then I came here. Maybe if I'd been around more afterwards she —'

'Fuck, Sarah,' cut in Ron, 'don't blame yourself.'

Following his interjection, Sarah fell silent a while, causing Ron to fear he may have been misunderstood, sounding like he'd just wanted the conversation to end.

'But I should spend more time with her,' Sarah eventually resumed. 'I was going to try to get her out somewhere with me tonight, except her boyfriend turned up. When I see them together, I feel it's like... I don't know. Like she's only ended up with him because she hasn't been paying attention or something.'

'Is she really so absent-minded?'

'I wouldn't know,' confessed Sarah, 'she's a mystery to me. Maybe she loves him. Maybe that's it. Maybe I should interrogate her about him properly, but asking her things is difficult. She side-steps, and the more you ask, the more she insists things are fine.'

Ron could no longer contain his desire, and had to ask, 'Haven't got any dope, have you?'

'I was going to ask you,' answered Sarah, resting her head lightly against the back of the sofa. When Ron's eyes next met hers, she held the gaze. 'I trust you, Ron. Want to know what made me trust you so soon?'

'Tell me.'

'Albert. The way you let him pick on you.'

Ron smiled, and put his arm around Sarah, and she made herself comfortable against him.

1.9
It Takes Years

The forest greens were almost luminous, yet all was also in deep shadow. For a thousand days or more he had trekked through the eerie trees, over mosses and across dark streams. He knew many had trekked before him. Some — a few only — he met returning, old and ruined. To each he would enquire if they had seen it, and each, wearily emerging from a grave reverie, would slowly nod their head. If they spoke at all, it was only to murmur how sky-reachingly high it was, or Earth-spanningly long, or hammer-turningly hard, or tunnel-defeatingly rooted.

But Albert would not be daunted: he, the first ever, would see *behind* it, and learn the great secrets.

And then the forest fell away and he saw it, and lo, it did reach the sky; did reach the horizons; and, yes, it did turn his hammer.

The Great Stone Wall, where all knowledge ended.

His was not the only hammer trying the mighty wall's properties. People were hammering as far as his keen young eye could see. Some carefully and patiently; some wildly, as if finally desperate.

Albert put his hammer away, looked up to gauge the wall's vertical challenge, and suspected a person could spend their whole life climbing, and never reach the top. Never know the secrets on the other side. Yet he began to climb. Above him, others climbed too — dotted all the way up until they were lost to distance.

From time to time, a starved and frozen body would fall past him.

But before long, in a crevice, he found a ring. A golden ring. It looked magic. He put on the ring, and lo, great eagle's wings sprouted from his shoulders, and he took to the air with mighty whooshes.

He soared higher than any knowledge-seeker had ever climbed, until at last he settled upon the wall's chill, bleak top. First looking back down the side he had ascended, he saw specks straining their limbs and minds to reach his vantage point. Turning away, taking apprehensive steps, he approached the other side to look down upon what no one had seen before... but only saw the same as was on his side of the wall: people trying, crying and dying to see behind the great barrier. And beyond, he saw a dense forest.

'Friggin' knew it,' he muttered to Peep as he fell miserably awake, the animal's appearance on his bed being responsible for the real world emerging. He soon felt even more miserable when he remembered it was Sunday. Sunday bloody Sunday. He hated Sundays. Sundays just *dragged*. There was only one sort of day Albert hated more than a Sunday, and that was a bank holiday Monday. A Sunday followed by a bank holiday was like having two Sundays in a row, except the second was even more boring than the first — it had compound disinterest.

Looking at the clock, he saw it was well past two.

Bringing his knees up under his duvet, he knew Peep would immediately jump up and settle on the hill he was forming — she always did. Now, from her high position, a shadowy form in a darkened room, she looked down at him, her yellow eyes staring while she seemed to be deciding, by dint of keen scrutiny, whether he was friend, foe or food. He liked it when Peep sat up there. He liked lots of things Peep did. When Peep curled up to sleep, if all four of her paws were stretched out in a bundle, he liked that too, but couldn't think why. The closest he got to smiling most days was when viewing Peep out in the garden. He felt kind of proud seeing her out there, hacking it in the real world, and guessed it was a dilution of how parents must feel over their kids becoming doctors. Recently, Peep had become a shoulder cat again, jumping on him when he sat at the various tables in the flat, hanging on as best she could. When she'd first taken to doing this, he'd believed it was pure affection, but over the years he'd learnt she only did it when the weather was cold. It was under-paw heating. Still, she never sat on Ron's shoulder, he'd observed, so he'd eventually concluded there was indeed some special affection at play.

Ron had yet to come home from his date with Sarah the previous evening, something Albert was trying hard to be in denial about.

Bequeathing the warmth of the bed to Peep, Albert padded off to the bathroom, where, brushing his teeth, he realised his left index finger hurt. This was a puzzle until he realised it was because of all the typing he'd done: before turning in for the night, working into and beyond the small hours, he had finished his second novel, and this one was *long*.

'I name this condition *hurty finger syndrome*,' he announced to his reflection in the mirror above the basin.

Before making some breakfast, Albert printed his second novel for proofing over toast, and found that it covered nearly eleven sides of A4 paper — maybe enough to placate Ron, especially if he double-spaced the type and concluded it all with a large *The End*.

Over toast and coffee, this is what Albert read:-

In the city of Washington, Congressional hearings were taking place to decide the fate of the Superconducting Super Collider, the largest, most ambitious particle accelerator ever proposed. Already, many hundreds of millions of tax payers' dollars had been sunk into the project, and it was still a very long way from being operational. The *raison d'etre* of the SSC was to verify the existence of, and to explore the properties of, the Higgs boson — the particle assumed to precipitate the breaking of high energy symmetry, thus recreating the conditions of the very early universe.

Called to testify at these hearings, to justify the further expense, were many of the scientists working in the field. All American Nobel Prize winning physicists were requested as a matter of course. Also requested was the Indian Physicist, Rasheed Shankra, who, thirty years earlier, had become a Nobel laureate for work which had directly led other physicists on to the trail of the theoretical Higgs particle.

Those scientists familiar with Shankra's work were surprised and heartened to learn that he had agreed to travel to Washington, for Shankra, now white-haired and in his seventies, no longer belonged to the academic world. Not long after receiving the Nobel prize, he had unexpectedly resigned his Princeton professorship, and moved back to India. Since that day, he had not contributed a single thing to science, or involved himself in any discussion or project. He had virtually disappeared for thirty years.

The scientists supposed that, feeling so strongly that this line of fundamental research should continue, Shankra had come out of seclusion to add his considerable weight to the cause.

+++

High above the lobby of the Flamingo Astoria Hotel, Las Vegas, overlooking serried ranks of slot machines, a gaudy neon sign flashed *97.4 — THE HOTTEST SLOT PERCENTAGE IN TOWN!*

Thirty-eight-year-old Alaister Dashwood, a dean of engineering at the University of Nevada, there in Las Vegas, was in the hotel to meet with a visiting associate. He and his associate, named Johnson, were discussing their current work over breakfast: the Superconducting Super Collider. The dining area had a viewing window which overlooked the slot machines. Talking leisurely about the Congressional hearings they were due to attend, Johnson viewed the neon sign and wryly said: "97.4 percent return — *we've adjusted our machines to cream off only 2.6 cents of every dollar you give us*. God, if ever proof were needed against the existence of psychic power, this city's gambling halls is where to find it."

"Maybe you're wrong," suggested Dashwood. "These machines aren't good experiments."

Johnson was surprised by Dashwood's

response. Was Dashwood defending the paranormal influence of the human mind?

"Come now," laughed Johnson, "look at those gamblers' faces, masked in concentration. It can hardly be said that they're not exerting every psychic effort to influence the random, yet still the cash flows into the casino owners' pockets in an even, predictable stream."

Dashwood looked at Johnson. "Suppose someone *had* devised a reliable laboratory test for the existence of psychic powers?"

"You?" asked Johnson.

"The very same."

"And?"

"I believe I've found evidence."

Johnson laughed and shook his head. "Well don't go public. You'll lose your deanship faster than those guys are losing their money."

Dashwood became earnest. "I'm serious. I've been running private electronic tests, and the evidence is there. The random can be influenced."

"What about those guys?" said Johnson, indicating the gamblers.

"Bad test. My powers are vanishingly small."

"Your powers?"

"My powers. I did better than anyone else. I managed a tenth of one percent. You see? A tenth of one percent is swamped by the 2.6 percent chance of losing here."

"Don't go public," urged Johnson. "You'll be ridiculed."

+++

The hearings were in progress. Every scientist called gave effusive support to the Collider, saying how necessary it was to the quest for fundamental understanding. Then Shankra was called. Looking weary and sad-eyed, he took position on the podium. As with everyone else, he was to be questioned by advocates and objectors. Advocates were mainly particle physicists, objectors mainly politicians. The advocates had been heartened by the defence put forward by their ranks so far, but now they were in for a shock, for the very man whose work had first suggested the existence of the Higgs particle was about to reject the whole direction of fundamental science.

"Gentlemen," he began with quiet nobility, "I, as the person largely responsible for beginning the quest for the Higgs particle, have been called here to give my opinion, and I shall say things that for me have been manifestly evident for many years now: I do not believe that this proposed Collider will address issues of uniquely fundamental importance, nor will it yield anything of practical value. I urge the Congress of this powerful nation to withdraw funding and to direct the money and effort to reducing human suffering instead. Just half of this money could immunise every living person against a host of diseases which currently kill millions each year."

The other scientists were dumbfounded.

An economic advisor to the President, who was opposed to the Collider, seized his chance, asking Shankra to explain his doubts. Shankra seemed reluctant to elucidate, merely saying, "the very precepts of modern physics are wrong, that much I have learnt since I set the world looking for this particle. It exists, I am sure, but we must stop looking under the street lamp for the answers, and venture away from known territory. Please do not let me live the remainder of my days knowing

I have sent the world on a foolish errand.
The billions of dollars can and should be
better spent. I say again, just half of
the money would be sufficient to immunise
the world."

Recovering a little from the shock,
one of the advocating scientists spoke.
"What have you told this hearing that has
any substance? We need to know reasons and
facts."

Shankra answered, "Gentlemen, I have
never been one to boast, but now must.
When I was eleven, as a mere schoolboy in
Bangalore, I submitted a paper to the
scientific community which proved
Goldbach's conjecture that every positive
even number could be expressed as the sum
of two prime numbers. That proof had eluded
mathematicians for two centuries: it was
child's play to me. As an adult, I was
professor of quantum mechanics at your
Princeton University, where Einstein
taught. Like Einstein, I was awarded a
Nobel prize. I say to you now, and hope
you will value and heed my opinion: do not
waste so much on a pointless journey."

"But you haven't explained your
objections!" boomed the advocate. "Why are
the precepts of physics wrong? Tell us."

Shankra obviously wished not to
elucidate, but felt he must.
"Consciousness," he said quietly, "has a
fundamental role in the cosmos. It creates
the universe, forcing reality into being
out of a quantum mechanical haze of
possibilities. It is we who make the
microscopic world real: a little bit of
God operates in us all, and that is what
should be explored."

"What is consciousness? Who can answer
that?"

"Consciousness is many things," said Shankra. "The awareness of time, for one. Consciousness can look forward or back — when back, we call it memory; when forward, you call it impossible."

"Metaphysical claptrap," was the retort.

"Has it never once occurred to you," responded Shankra, "that human thought processes might be affecting the results of quantum events? That your machines might be measuring what is within, not what is without?"

"And now he's talking mind over matter!"

The scientists laughed mockingly. All except Dashwood, who was intrigued.

"Gentleman," said Shankra, with dignity, "I was invited to offer my opinion, and that I have done. Good day to you all."

"Traitor," said someone.

Shankra stood down and left the hall, but Dashwood had a burning desire to hear more from him, for he himself had seen solid proof of the intervention of thought processes in sensitive experiments. He trusted his own results.

Discovering where Shankra was staying, Dashwood was soon outside his hotel room, knocking on the door. Shankra, who had been reading, courteously admitted him.

The curtains were drawn, and incense was in the air.

To Dashwood's surprise, Shankra was aware that his guest was the dean of engineering at the University of Nevada. "I have not removed myself *so* far from the world I once inhabited," he explained.

Apologising, Shankra told the dean that he was hungry, and asked him to postpone telling him the object of his visit until he had eaten. Dashwood said that he was not hungry himself, but would wait until Shankra had satisfied his own appetite.

Shankra contacted room service and ordered food.

Waiting for his food to arrive, Shankra began to talk about how much America had changed since he had seen it last, thirty years before. "So much technology," he said. "So many computers talking to other computers." He explained that he had been living the simplest of lives in India, and was more given to meditation than to keeping abreast with the pace of change."

Dashwood, unable to restrain his desire for information, raised the subject of Shankra's comments at the Congressional hearing, and said he had some burning questions. Shankra smiled gently and explained that although he was hungry, he would listen to what the dean had to ask while he awaited room service.

"You said consciousness could look forward as well as back," said Dashwood.

"I believe I did," answered Shankra, "although few were listening."

"And you said that when it looks forward, *we* call it impossible."

"That I believe I also said."

"Which implies that *you* don't consider it impossible."

"I do not consider it impossible. You are correct."

The dean looked ardently at Shankra. "I *know* it's not impossible. I've done experiments, experiments which gave results I couldn't explain, but I think you can."

Dashwood described his experiments to Shankra, and Shankra offered brief explanations. "What we call the present is shaped by consciousness. Each single moment the cosmos unfolds by consensus from a chaos of possibilities. Every conscious entity works to shape the chaos. Some, however, learn to peer further into the chaos than others. They see the moments unfolding."

Dashwood thought hard. "You said that consciousness can look forward as well as back. How can you mean that awareness of the future can exist if the future unfolds from a chaos of possibilities? Chaos, by its very nature, is unpredictable."

Shankra said nothing. He didn't have to, for the dean rapidly drew his own conclusion. "Probability! That's it. The collective consciousness shapes the probability for each moment. In the distant future, all given event outcomes are possible. As the present draws closer, certain conditions become more probable, until the actual real event becomes inevitable. A person who could cast his consciousness into the chaos of the future could become aware of the seeds that might grow into firm outcomes."

Shankra looked kindly at the dean. "You have arrived, almost by chance, by the eye-opener of your experiments, at the understanding I came to many years ago through pure cerebration."

The dean was hungry for knowledge. "How far into the future can useful awareness be cast?"

"The chaos becomes total beyond half a second. The moment begins to significantly crystallise almost as soon as it is upon us."

"That would explain my results!" said the dean. "My mind was unconsciously able to occasionally view the dice of uncertainty far enough into the future for me to predict outcomes better than even chance. I've managed a tenth of a percentile above even. The electronically produced randomness of my experiments, generated in only microseconds, was sensed by me once every thousand times on average."

The dean fell silent, gazing at Shankra with growing awe. "You said a person could learn to work harder at projecting their consciousness into the future — how much harder? I can only manage microseconds with a success rate on one in a thousand. How much is possible?"

Shankra was unwilling to answer, but the dean pursued the issue. "I need to know what you know."

"I am wary of divulging such knowledge."

"If you promise to show me all you know, I promise to help stop the construction of the Super Collider. I'm a crucial engineer on the project. I can say I think it's technically impossible."

"Can you also say where the saved money will be spent?" asked Shankra. "Can you direct half of it to freeing the world's poor of disease?"

"Of course I can't."

Shankra fixed him with a look. "Would you if you could?"

"Of course I would."

"If you speak out against it, you will be vilified by the academic world. The ranks will close and you'll never get a position again. They want this toy badly."

"I need to know what you know more than anything else."

Shankra seemed to be acquiescing, and the dean leapt at the open window of opportunity. "Half a second, you mentioned. Is that *your* limit. Can you cast your awareness that far with a measurable success rate? You can, can't you?"

"Do you promise to help stop the Super Collider?" asked Shankra.

"Yes," said the dean emphatically.

"Half a second is indeed my limit," answered Shankra. Chuckling, he added, "But it is so very tiring! And I am old now, and my will fades so quickly."

"How? Tell me how."

"It arrives after many years," answered Shankra.

"What does it feel like?"

"Like being in a misty dream. You may have experienced the hallucinatory effects of LSD. I understand now that part of the LSD experience arises from having one's consciousness expanded chemically ever so slightly into the future, and glimpsing the ever-unfolding chaos overwhelms the mind. Learning not to be overwhelmed, but to recognise the probable outcomes as they unfold from chaos is the task. The majority avoid and deny the chaotic mist, instinctively fearing the uncertainty. The gurus of the East abandon themselves to the mist. I, perhaps the only person ever to have done so, comprehend the mist. To teach you my methods may take years. The gurus spent years leading me into the mist, and only then after years of gaining trust in me. It is so very sacred what we do: to have so much of God operating within us."

"That's how I began feeling when I was doing my experiments. Sometimes it was like I was half a step into a misty realm. So that's where I was — unconsciously skirting the fringes of a chaos of possibilities. If I could learn to consciously wander in that mist, who knows what I might achieve?"

"Who indeed?" said Shankra quietly.

"Don't you realise what kind of power you could wield — having an early grasp on all moments?"

"I have never contemplated the power," replied Shankra.

"And all one has to do is let one's consciousness seep forward from the moment," murmured Dashwood.

"It takes years," said Shankra.

"But I already do it," countered Dashwood.

"A little."

"Becoming aware of time unfolding before it arrives...," murmured Dashwood, taking a seat, awed by the hugeness of the notion.

Shankra moved nearer to him, and began talking in a gentle, measured voice. "Consciousness is all, and all is consciousness. And time, so long held by Western science to be inviolable, is merely consciousness condensing the foggy chaos of the microscopic world for convenient, palpable examination. To behold creation in its entirety, one must explore the fog..."

As Shankra continued speaking, Dashwood found himself unconsciously attempting to enter the fog. It seemed that now he was aware of its existence, he could allow the world to melt into a dreamy mist within which time was expanded - much more so than when performing his psychic experiments.

Then the fog suddenly cleared as he was called to a fixed moment by Shankra. "Alaister, you appear to have drifted away. Wake up and answer your telephone."

Dashwood realised that the mobile phone in his briefcase was ringing. It was Johnson. Johnson said that the Collider's chief engineer, due to address the Congress that afternoon, had taken very ill, and advised that he should return at once.

The news was very upsetting to the dean — for one thing, because of his colleague and friend's illness, for another, because he would be forced to interrupt his talk with Shankra. He told Shankra he would have to return to the hearings, but begged to talk again.

"I will avail myself," Shankra assured him.

+++

Crossing Washington by taxi, Dashwood lay his head back and contemplated Shankra's words. He tried to enter the altered state of mind again, and began to feel a dreamy sensation. Looking out of the window, things appeared not just to happen, but to quickly settle into a happening. Each moment seemed to be suspended in a weak fluid of moments. The feeling, although fleeting, was even stronger than in the hotel room. "Years?" murmured Dashwood, "I'm nearly there already."

In the Congress building, Dashwood was met by Johnson, who looked grave. "He's very ill," said Johnson. "Heart attack. This project was his life. Guess the stress of having to defend it was too much for him."

Many of the project's engineering co-ordinators and administrators were present. They were desperate, for the chief engineer had been due to speak that very afternoon. "You'll have to speak his turn, Dashwood. You know more about this project than anyone else. Guess you're chief engineer now."

When Dashwood was called to the stand to defend the project, he could not let his colleagues down. Speaking out at this moment, with his friend gravely ill, would be a monstrous thing to do, he thought.

The audience applauded when he spoke of the exciting challenge the project represented.

Afterwards, as someone was shaking his hand, Dashwood was surprised to see Shankra. Upon meeting his eye, Shankra turned and walked away. "Wait!" called Dashwood, running to catch up.

"I came to hear you speak out against the wasteful folly," said Shankra, "yet you did not."

"I couldn't," explained Dashwood. "Not now. Not with him lying ill. Besides, if the government didn't spend the money on it, they'd spend it on some other science project . Maybe even something military. It wouldn't go to help the poor, that's for sure. I couldn't dictate where the money would go."

"Would you if you could?" asked Shankra once again.

"Of course I would," replied Dashwood.

Another gushy colleague came up to Dashwood, and Shankra disappeared into the crowd.

Later, at Shankra's hotel, Dashwood was informed that Shankra was out, although a message would be conveyed.

That night, alone in his own hotel room, Dashwood began experimenting with his aptitude. On his laptop PC, he devised a program to display, at random, one of two symbols. Entering into his expanded state of consciousness, he found that, in a dreamy way, he very, very briefly saw — no, experienced — both symbols fade up on his screen together before one would fade away, leaving the remaining one to persist into solid reality.

He was seeing events under construction.

Knowing which was going to fade was the crux.

In the small hours, still at his PC, he fell into a deep sleep until the morning, when SSC officials telephoned him to say that the chief had died in the night, making him head of the engineering team now — head of the biggest technical project in the world. They also said that Congress seemed likely to continue the project's funding.

During that day, Dashwood was inundated with visitors and messages.

Late in the evening, after the last visitor had left, a knock sounded on his door. It was Shankra, there to express his dismay at the likely funding of the project and to ask that Dashwood honour his promise before it was too late. Embarrassed, Dashwood said that he would do it as soon as he could.

In Skankra's presence, an email arrived from the SSC administrators informing Dashwood that the budget had been officially secured, and that, as Chief Engineer, his salary was now almost doubled.

Although saddened to learn that Congress had finally funded the project, Shankra acknowledged the *fait accompli*.

"At least you will be able to donate half of your increased salary to the world's poor. Is not that so?" he said.

Dashwood agreed it was so.

Shankra left, saying that he had private business to attend to.

+++

Many weeks passed. Back at his university in Las Vegas, Dashwood, whenever he was free, continued to explore his abilities. More and more he was able to penetrate the future mists. He found that many seemingly random events were his to predict, and his success rate was ever increasing. Soon he was scoring success rates of five per cent above even. It was then that he knew the power could be turned to profit. *Casting his awareness into the unfolding chaos of the future, and seeing it condense into events, he could cream every casino in Las Vegas.* Knowing slightly more often than not which button to press on those fast-moving win/lose chances, on average he would win 105 times every two hundred.

Dashwood did just that, although the sustained effort exhausted him daily.

After many more weeks, although drained by the effort, he was becoming a fluent winner. With a clean edge over the casinos, he became obsessed with his power. Obsessed with the profit. He was amassing many thousands day after day.

Too obsessed to continue his SSC work, Dashwood resigned his position, becoming a permanent visitor to the city's gambling halls. The city's roulette tables, however, proved too tricky: not enough time after sensing where the ball had probably settled to place a corresponding bet. Too physical.

After some months of this activity, and now a multi-millionaire, Dashwood realised there existed a greater opportunity for enrichment: the biggest casino in the world — *the stock markets*. He knew that much trading now occurred electronically. If he could sense with reasonable accuracy half a second in advance whether a commodity was going to go up or down in price, he could hit the buy or sell button in time to make the profit. Do better than even and he'd be earning big time.

Using his gambling profits, Dashwood

set up as a financial speculator, trading electronically. Employing a small team of advisors who followed market trends and informed him of potential areas for his attention, he watched computer screens for opportunities, able to hazily predict which way figures were going to go: up or down. If he sensed they were going to go up, he hit the buy button a fraction before; down, he sold. Slightly more often than not, he was right.

But it was enough.

He began risking moderate amounts: thousands rather than millions. Months later, now able to speculate in the millions, he made his first million dollar investment... and lost a small amount of money. But he expected frequent losses. *Overall*, he expected gains. He had an edge.

His first big killing came with Magnetic Industrial, following a tip-off from his advisors. They'd heard rumours that Magnetic Industrial was on the brink of being awarded a large Government contract. He watched the company's share price like a stone hawk for hours. Then, when he sensed the share price rise on his screen, he hit a button that instantly purchased two million shares a quarter of a second before they began to jump higher and higher in value. Then he sold again after sensing the peak price had been reached, and just before a minor slide back began.

He laughed when he discovered that the large contract that Magnetic Industrial had been awarded was to supply the SSC with superconducting magnets.

A year later, locked almost permanently into a hazy semi-reality atop a New York office complex overlooking Central Park, Dashwood had advanced to operating a technically offshore, unregulated and very secretive trading business. Now dealing hundreds of millions of dollars daily, he had left stocks and shares behind to speculate mostly against currencies. Monthly profits were growing almost exponentially.

It came to pass that one day an opportunity arose to speculate against the dollar in favour of the Euro. Sinking tens of billions into the opportunity, Dashwood made billions in profit in one move. With this one transaction, he had profited at the expense of the United States by as much as the SSC was set to cost.

Dashwood was now the wealthiest person alive by a long way.

Looking up from his computer screen, he was momentarily unnerved to see Shankra right before him.

"You're a very clever man," said Shankra. "Living the simple — you might say backward — life I have lived in India this last thirty years, I had never realised how my learning could benefit me. So many computers in the world now. Seconds split up so importantly these days. I see that today you made a profit more than equal to the cost of the Collider which you promised to help me have stopped. Can you not now give half of that profit to remove so much of the world's suffering?"

Dashwood said, "You too must be a clever man to have entered this office without my permission."

"Remember your promise to me, Dashwood. I am sure that from this desk you could send billions to the World Health Organisation who would put it to good use. Do it now, Dashwood."

Dashwood said that he was weary of

Shankra's requests, and that, anyway, he had developed his abilities on his own, not under any tutelage. "Persist in importuning me and I shall have my security men throw you out, fakir that you are."

Summoned by a secret button, a security man appeared.

Shankra said that he would go, but also said this: "Much of my Nobel prize money I long ago gave to the poor, so that I also became a poor man, and the very last of my money I spent coming to your country to see you. I now have not even enough for a meal. Can you not give me enough to feed myself today?"

"Do as I did," said Dashwood. "Use your powers, if you have any."

"Maybe I am too old and slow to perform such tricks," sighed Shankra, "as you might have been too by the time you had learnt the knowledge."

"Learnt it!" exclaimed Dashwood. "I am master of it."

"You have learnt nothing," said Shankra, whereupon Dashwood perceived Shankra's face changing in a strange fashion, as was the whole room. "Since you will not give me food, it seems I shall have to have the meal I ordered earlier." And the guard — who had now become a room service man — came forward with a platter of food.

Dashwood, stunned to find himself returned to Shankra's hotel room, was taken aback with shame, and did not know what to say.

Shankra politely saw him to the door, saying that he was surely due back at the hearings.

"How?" asked Dashwood, as he shuffled in confusion. "Hypnotism? Telepathy? How?"

"It takes years," said Shankra. "Now,

113

if you will excuse me, I must eat."

After his meal, Shankra opened the *Yellow Pages* and looked under Investment Advisors.

1.10
Immortality

After reading his new story twice — both times wondering how he could possibly have written something like it considering he was so lazy and misanthropic — the rest of the daylight hours had proved interminably slow for Albert. His Sunday, like most of his Sundays, had been structured around cups of tea, stealing Ron's biscuits, and television channel hopping, even though the set in the living room had an intermittent tendency to forget that blue and red existed.

Now, sitting in thickening twilight, he couldn't believe it: he'd written two novels that week, yet still wasn't a millionaire. It was so disappointing and confusing he felt compelled to go to his room, climb over the bookcase, lie on the bed and stare at the dim ceiling.

His hair needed washing, but he rode it out.

After a motionless hour, he stirred when the telephone rang in the living room.

'All right, Albert,' said the caller, 'it's Pete. Is Ron about?'

'He's masturbating in the shed. I can hear him moaning my name even from here.'

Albert now heard Ron's key working the lock, and lights were switched on.

Pete was confused. 'You haven't got a shed.'

'We have now,' explained Albert. 'Ron built a shed especially to wank in, even though I've warned him about that habit of his. He'll only end up getting emotionally involved with himself.'

Ron appeared in the living room. 'Evening, Albert. Gone mad yet?'

'Not yet,' answered Albert, dispiritedly. 'Been busy.' He proffered the phone to Ron. 'It's for you. Pete.'

Pete was Ron's main dope supplier, and the call told that a two-week drought was over.

To Ron, dope was a way of life, but to Albert, dope was simply an occasional treat, to be enjoyed late at night as an entertainment, one which he could take or leave. Albert never bought dope himself. His infrequent highs came free of charge from Ron, although he suspected there would be no limit to the amount of dope Ron would be willing to bestow on him. Ron seemed to have a deep need to share his own supply, like a seasoned boozer generously filling his more sober-minded companion's glass. Yes, Albert knew that if Ron got his way, he would be wrecked all day long too, but he often suspected this generosity of Ron's was actually rooted in a selfish desire to sedate him: when he was stoned, he tended to be only a fraction as communicative as when he was straight, and that, perhaps, was Ron's way of engineering peace and quiet.

After putting the phone down, Ron sported a smirk. 'Fabulous news. Quantities of Moroccan Black await me at Pete's.'

Driving to Pete's was now paramount in Ron's scheme of things, and he began looking for his car keys, which he had a tendency to mislay.

'I wrote another novel last night,' said Albert, 'like you ordered me to.'

'Oh yeah?' said Ron, searching under cushions for his keys.

'This one's long.'

'How long?'

'Eleven pages.'

'Not long enough,' said Ron, forcing his hand down the back of the sofa.

'Twenty-two if it's double-spaced,' tried Albert hopefully.

Ron shook his head.

'Well how long do you want?' demanded Albert. 'Tell me. Give me some boundaries.'

'Hundred pages or I sell your computer.'

Albert looked at his left index finger and wondered if it could go that distance. 'But I've already got hurty finger syndrome from excessive typing,' he whined.

'Bless you,' said Sarah, just arriving, wearing faded, flared blue jeans and a white blouse under a black velvet jacket. She had come up the garden path with Ron, but, on the doorstep, had nipped back to her car to fetch its CD player.

'Sarah, don't look at me until I've washed my hair,' insisted Albert, holding his hands over his head and scurrying past her for the bathroom.

Ron was still hunting for his keys when Albert emerged from the bathroom, hair dripping, going straight to his bedroom to use his hairdryer. Not counting the computer — which, arguably, was morally Ron's — beyond a few clothes and his stock of fallen books, Albert had two major possessions to his name: his hairdryer and an old ghetto blaster, both things he'd found on skips and repaired. He'd never even owned a mobile phone. Everything else in the flat was either the landlord's or Ron's. If Albert's room was Chad, Ron's room was Japan. Like Japan, it was neat and clean, and it bristled with technology. It had a powerful PC hooked up to a dedicated broadband phone line; a hi-fi system that could shake the house if used in anger; a wide-screen plasma TV; a video; and — the latest purchase — a recordable DVD player.

Bored with watching Ron's search, Sarah sought out Albert, which was unusual since all Ron's previous girlfriend's had avoided being alone with him. 'Can I come in?' she asked, tapping on his open bedroom door.

Knelt on the floor, drying his hair on a gentle setting Jackie had promised would allow his natural curls a better chance, Albert replied, 'Yeah, but keep your hands to yourself.'

'I will,' said Sarah, coming into the room and finding the bookcase still fallen and spewing out titles. 'Why haven't you picked your books up yet?'

'Cat did it,' answered Albert, indicating where he believed the clean-up responsibility lay.

Sarah sat on the edge of the bed and examined some of the spilled works. 'Wow, awesome, varied reading. The classics of literature; university level quantum mechanics. What are you, some kind of Renaissance man?'

Albert was about to answer in a way that would heap glory upon himself when Sarah spoke again.

'Or a poser? Which is it, Albert?'

The wind taken out of his sails, Albert appeared stuck for words, but he did manage to say, 'Bitch.'

'Ron says you wrote a novel last night?' said Sarah.

'Too fucking right I did,' said Albert, finding his words again. 'What's it about?'

'What all novels are about: sex and death. Except I didn't bother about the sex bit. Gets in the way of the death. I didn't bother much about the death bit, either, come to think of it. Didn't have time.'

Sarah now looked around the room, finding little to impress her. 'Bit grotty in here.'

'Is it? Never noticed. I'm deep.'

'You must be deep to have written a whole novel in one night. It must have been terribly exhausting. How many pages?'

'Eleven.'

'Gosh, that's a lot.'

'For normal people it would be, but luckily I'm what we writers call *fuckin' prolific*. I'm going to write another one by the end of the month. Over a hundred pages.'

A whoop of delight came from Ron in the kitchen. 'Found them! See you soon.'

The flat door slammed.

Sarah had told Ron she'd rather remain in the flat than make the journey across town again. She began to wander around Albert's bedroom, looking at things. When over by the window, she tried to part the curtains to sample the view but discovered they were stitched together. 'Christ, you're as bad as Jennifer. She's always leaving her curtains closed.'

Albert beckoned Sarah closer, indicating that she should sit at the bottom of his bed. Switching off the hairdryer, he moved nearer to her. On his hands and knees on the floor, he looked darkly into her eyes. 'Did you give her my amazing letter?'

'I did, actually.'

'And?'

'What did you expect?' asked Sarah, realistically.

'That she should be besotted with me by now,' answered Albert, sitting back on his haunches. 'Preferably suicidally. Always dreamed of having a chick top herself over me.'

'Don't even know if she's read it.'

The wind left his sails again. 'Bugger.'

'Sorry,' said Sarah, without sounding if she particularly was.

Albert sat forward again, saying in a low, intense voice, 'Tell me about her.'

'She's nineteen.'

'Tell me something I didn't already know.'

'Oh, I don't know... she's a Veterinary Assistant.'

'More,' demanded Albert.

'She's just moved into a house with a woman in Richmond, near where we grew up.'

'Richmond down south or Richmond, North Yorkshire?'

'North Yorkshire.'

Albert leaned back in sorrowful ecstasy. 'Tess has a younger sister,' he murmured heavenward before sitting forward again. 'Describe her. How tall is she?'

'Couple of inches shorter than me. Five-four.'

Taking hold of Sarah's shoulders, Albert entreated, 'Mimic her voice for me. Ape her walk. Describe her face.' He closed his eyes and puckered his lips. 'Kiss me like she kisses.'

'For God's sake, Albert,' complained Sarah, pushing his arms away, 'Ron's right, you do need your head examined. She's just my sister. Anyway, she's already got a boyfriend.'

As if he'd received a fatal blow, Albert's eyes opened starkly wide. 'No, no, it can't be,' he said before sinking to the floor. 'Get your cello and play something plaintive,' he feebly requested.

Oh my God, he thought, now fully imagining how great it would be to have someone who looked like Sarah expressing his pain through music. Awesome. Truly *awesome*.

'Violin accompaniment would be better,' said Sarah.

Lying in a heap, thinking about it, Albert didn't agree. His suffering was more noble and solemn than the violin could reflect. Definitely of the slower but deeper kind. Like a river at dusk: dark, sombre and mysterious.

'Jennifer used to play the violin,' Sarah went on, sounding a little sad.

A cello *and* a violin, Albert now considered. Yes, that would be *perfect*. Sarah's cello to reflect the unvarying, underlying, inexorable sadness of his deep nature, full of vague longings, and a violin played by someone who was a scale model of Sarah to express his moments of wilder, romantic suffering, like just now when he'd heard Jennifer had a boyfriend. With that kind of accompaniment, his melancholy and yearning would become like the very weeping of the gods — become the very rolling of the celestial spheres.

Fuck, thought Albert, suddenly struck by the realisation that this musical accompaniment fantasy could actually come *true*. She was really here, in his dim, musty bedroom: the closest thing he'd ever seen to Tess of the d'Urbervilles. And she played cello, too, and had a musical sister. 'Any good?' he quietly asked, still slumped. She would have to be good. Bad violin would diminish and detract. Bad violin would never roll the celestial spheres. Bad violin wouldn't roll rabbit shit down a slope.

If she wasn't good, she would have to dance instead, with veils and swoons.

Sarah took some moments to respond, and her voice revealed a sense of regret. 'She certainly had professional prospects. Don't think she'd have ever stood out from the professional crowd — she didn't have flying, Pagannini fingers — but she had a good ear, and she played with good feeling for someone so young at the time. Rare feeling.'

'What's with all the past tenses?' asked Albert, sitting up. '*Used* to play? *Had* a good ear?'

'Don't think she's even picked up an instrument since the accident,' said Sarah. 'Any instrument.'

'What accident?'

'Our parents died in a car crash. She was in the car too.' Sarah went on to explain how Jennifer, apparently holding her violin in the back of the vehicle, had escaped without a scratch, yet the instrument in her hands had been smashed beyond repair. 'Afterwards, she told me she'd only really played because mum and dad had wanted her too, but I don't believe that now. Think I'd die within a week if I stopped playing. Jennifer doesn't even listen to music any more. Any music.'

'You're kidding. At all?'

'Far as I know. Never known her buy a CD, or even play one for years. Took me a long time to notice that, being away most of the time.'

Albert didn't feel comfortable with how this conversation was developing. He didn't want to appear flippant with someone who looked so much like Tess of the d'Urbervilles it was a dreamy privilege to be in her company. However, he knew he inevitably would appear flippant if he opened his mouth too often. Thankfully, he realised Sarah wasn't really talking to him now — he had become an excuse for her to talk to herself.

'She's never visited their grave, you know?' she went on, briefly meeting his eyes, although Albert knew his role in the conversation was now mostly incidental... so long as he managed to continue judiciously limiting his responses.

'Whose? Jennifer? Never?'

'Not even for the funeral,' revealed Sarah, looking vaguely at the carpet. 'She was sick on the day. Really sick. Vomiting. Since then she's said she doesn't want to go because it's just a stone, not them.'

'She's got a point there,' said Albert, momentarily distracted by the discovery of a pound coin on the floor beside him. He pocketed it, but knew it couldn't have belonged to him. If he'd lost a pound since he'd vacuumed last, he would have known about it. Losing a pound to him was like a normal person losing fifty. It had probably fallen from Ron's pocket when he'd stooped to lift the bed.

'I don't even tell her when I visit the grave now,' said Sarah when Albert looked up.

Better have another, wider look, thought Albert, doing a second scan of the carpet, doing it subtly so as not to appear like he wasn't listening.

'A tragedy she gave up her instrument,' Sarah went on. 'We used to secretly learn pieces as a duet to surprise our parents. We'd get loads of candles going, then call them in to hear us. They used to be so proud. Jennifer used to be tearful when she played sometimes, if the piece was mournful. Problem was, most pieces were mournful to her. Once she said to me that upbeat music sometimes made her want to cry too, like the sadness in people's smiles. Funny thing for an eleven-year-old.'

He had to face it, there really were no more coins to be pocketed. Still, it had been a good day financially — better than most any other he'd had in his life.

'But she had never cried when they died,' reflected Sarah. 'I took it for coping bravely at the time. She had counselling and all that, but she seemed all right to them, within the context. But there was a kind of stillness about her afterwards. Even now — more so, maybe. Or maybe I'm getting fanciful. Maybe it's how she would have turned out anyway.'

'Tell her about my new haircut. That'll get the sullen bitch animated.'

Oh God, he'd done the flippant thing when he'd been trying so hard not to. It was over. Sarah would now disdain him, like all Ron's other girlfriend's had. His melancholy had lost its chance for musical accompaniment.

Sarah looked at Albert, and held the look. 'Maybe I will introduce you to her one day. Maybe a daft bastard pining for her would do her good.'

'Thanks,' sulked Albert, as if it had been a put down and as if he really cared.

'I wasn't being sarcastic,' explained Sarah, looking vaguely at the carpet again. 'I meant having you as a mate really might be good for her... I don't know, some way, somehow. You'd make her feel shy at first, but maybe she'd loosen up around you after a while, once she

120

realised she couldn't possibly make more of a twit of herself than you make of yourself every thirty seconds.'

Blimey, this was getting weird, thought Albert. Where had his world-class powers of alienation gone? Had he become prosaic?

'Now,' he demanded, standing.

'Now what?' asked Sarah, with a frown of puzzlement.

'Take me to her now. Come on, you've got a car. Don't deny it. I saw it on Friday.'

'Yeah, like I'd ever drive anywhere with a nut like you with me.'

'Please, Sarah,' he pleaded, pride cast far aside. 'Please.'

'Don't be silly, Albert. Richmond's miles away. Besides, her boyfriend's hanging around at the moment.'

The flat door opened, and the floorboards creaked like they only ever did under Ron's weight. Sarah stood up, and was about to leave the room, but Albert fell to his knees and wrapped his arms clingingly around her legs. 'I love her. I love her,' he whined. 'Go to Richmond without me then, but bring her back here. I can pay you a pound.'

'Yeah? And what about her boyfriend? Do I bring him too? And let go of my legs.'

Albert tightened his grip. 'But my whole existence revolves around her.'

'Don't be silly, Albert, you've never even met her.'

'So what? Cliff Richard's never met God, but he still reckons to love him.'

Sarah tried to reason with him. 'My sister's not like me. She's a lot more innocent.'

'Great. She'll have nothing to compare me with.'

'I don't mean sexually. I mean she's not as confident as me. If I introduce you, it'll be under controlled conditions, little bit at a time. That's if – I'm having big second thoughts. And let go of my legs, will you?'

'No, never,' declared Albert. 'You share some of Jennifer's genes.'

'Let me go.'

'No. We've become one. Can't you feel it?'

Sarah began pulling his hair. 'Albert, will you please let go of my legs.'

'Make love to me the same way your sister would. Same noises and everything.'

'Are you mad?'

'Mad for you to do it like Jennifer does.'

Ron appeared in the doorway. Exasperated, Sarah appealed to her new lover. 'Ron, can you please stop Albert hassling me for weird sex.'

'Can't,' said Ron. 'Wouldn't know how. Just stay calm and he'll probably tire himself out in a few days.'

Still trying to free herself from Albert's grip, pulling his hair some more, Sarah insisted, 'You can. You're big enough, use violence.'

Albert looked at Ron. Ron looked at Albert, then at Sarah, then back at Albert, then began a menacing walk over to him. But before he'd managed three steps, Albert made noises of pain and submission, let go of Sarah and rolled up into a ball, whimpering.

Sarah was disgusted. 'Aw, get up. He hasn't even hit you yet.'

Albert began crawling away, insisting that it hadn't been fear of Ron that had made him whimper. 'My socks started pinching, that's all.'

Sarah laughed.

'I got the gear,' said Ron, giving Sarah a quick hug.

'Brilliant. Did you get mine?'

'Yeah,' called Ron, now on his way to the living room.

Turning to Albert, Sarah saw that he was now sitting in a corner by the window, looking sad — very sad. 'I love her,' he whined, with lame despair.

'Oh, for fuck's sake, what are you like?' she said, turning her eyes and palms to the heavens. 'Albert, you've never even met her. You don't even know what she looks like.'

'She looks like you, except more virginal.'

'No she doesn't,' stated Sarah, ignoring the insult.

'Yes she does. Lots more.'

Ignoring the further insult, Sarah delved into her jacket pocket and produced a photo to show Albert. 'See? She doesn't look anything like me.'

Albert took the photo off her for closer examination, but the examination swiftly turned into breathless worship. 'She's divine. Not of this world. A Goddess.' And then some Byron:

> *She walks in beauty, like the night*
> *Of cloudless climes and starry skies;*
> *And all that's best of dark and bright*
> *Meet in her aspect and her eyes.'*

'She's a bit of a looker, that's true,' agreed Sarah, holding her hand out for the return of the photo, which was not forthcoming.

'She's a looker all right,' declared Albert. 'She makes you look like a scrap yard dog. Don't know what I ever saw in you.'

'Thanks.'

Albert continued to gaze at Sarah's sister's likeness. 'Not much in the way of family resemblance,' he observed.

'You're not the first to notice. We're only half-sisters. I was the product of a night of passion with an American on a beach in India. Mum met and married Jennifer's father when I was two.'

'Got around a bit, your dirty mum, didn't she?'

'Good for her,' said Sarah. 'Are you going to give me that photo back or not?'

'Not,' said Albert, removing it from her reach, 'it has religious significance to me.' And then he scurried out of the room, and out of the flat, into drizzle. Scurried all the way to the late shop in just his foreboding T-shirt and spent the coin he'd found on candles. When he returned, Sarah had vacated his bedroom. In her absence, he transformed his bedside table into an effulgent shrine to Jennifer — her propped-up photo amid an arc of six flames. Then he switched off the electric light and put a tape into his old ghetto blaster, quietly playing Mike Oldfield's *Ommadawn*, which sounded suitably reverential.

Sitting on the floor before the flickering shrine, he gazed dreamily at the image of his latest love.

'Miserable, spooky twat,' said Ron when he looked into the room some minutes later.

'Oh, for fuck's sake,' exclaimed Sarah, appearing at Ron's side.

Ron came in and inspected the photo, which was a little blurred and grainy. 'Oh God, you've done it now,' he told Sarah ominously, who was still standing on the threshold.

'Done what?'

'Disturbed the peace for the rest of the week.'

'Sorry,' she said. 'Wasn't thinking.'

Continuing to gaze at the photo, Albert sighed feebly.

'Loaded a pipe for you,' said Ron, without ceremony, proffering the object.

Albert wasn't a cigarette smoker, and joints rolled with tobacco made him instantly nauseous, but dope smoked pure from a pipe was tolerable. He wordlessly accepted the offering.

Ron and Sarah went away again, and Albert lit his pipe, smoking only half the modest contents, but nevertheless quickly becoming stoned. Dope really affected him. Couple of draws and he was halfway to acid. It affected him so much he'd learnt never to get stoned anywhere other than in his flat, and preferably in his bedroom, with the door locked.

Ron never seemed any different when stoned, and Albert often wondered just what it was he got from the experience, beyond a tendency to mislay things.

Closing his eyes and leaning back against the bed, Albert began to imagine he was in a soft, fresh wind beside a mountain waterfall. Everything was light and airy.

'Going to the offy for ciggie papers,' announced Ron from the hall. 'Want anything?'

Albert didn't reply. Things had gone pleasantly milky in his head, wherein the music was playing in a space as expansive as a cathedral.

'Mind if I hang with you till Ron gets back?' asked Sarah, standing in the bedroom doorway.

Without opening his eyes, Albert granted Sarah entry with a small movement of his hand. When he eventually did open his eyes, Sarah was sitting on the floor near him, smiling.

'Stoned?' she enquired.

'Stoned? Fucking fossilised.'

Viewing her in candlelight, to Albert's stoned eye she appeared soft and dream-like.

'Why are you looking at me like that?' she asked, with gentle, amused suspicion.

'Poetic reasons,' said Albert.

'You silver-tongued charmer.'

'Are you sure you're not Tess?'

'Cross my heart,' said Sarah, although she didn't.

'Thought I'd finally found her when I saw you,' he sighed. 'I've made mistakes in the past, but I was certain you were the real deal.'

'I'm sorry,' she said sympathetically, but actually wondering if he really was mad.

'So what's your sister's phone number?' he asked.

'Albert, not a chance,' responded Sarah without a moment's consideration.

'Well tell me her address... so I can orientate my prayer mat.'

'Not a chance.'

Albert pretended to be indignant. 'You said you were going to introduce us.'

Indicating the shrine, Sarah said, 'That was before this freaky worship thing.'

'I'll tone it down,' said Albert, with sudden, quietly-desperate reasonableness. Blowing out two of the candles, he pointed to his lessened creation. 'See? The freaky worship's under my control.' Looking at Sarah, however, he could see his mitigation had failed. 'Take a moment to think how gazing upon my haircut would be an addition to her happiness,' he tried, but Sarah's aspect was still unrelenting. 'Then you condemn me to live wretched and die alone,' he predicted in a voice tinted with injustice and solemn resignation.

Ron returned, and it sounded like he had brought company.

'This is Jackie,' said Ron, as Sarah came out of Albert's room. 'Jackie, Sarah.'

Once Jackie and Sarah had exchanged greetings, Ron led the way to the living room, followed by Sarah, but Jackie went into Albert's room.

'Who is she?' she asked Albert.

'Ron's new slapper,' answered Albert, re-lighting the two candles he'd extinguished.

'Oh,' said Jackie, sitting on the edge of the bed. 'Why haven't you picked up your books yet?'

'Cat did it.'

'So?'

Jackie tipped the heavy bookcase vertical again, and began replacing the strewn texts. Glancing at her, Albert saw that she was wearing flared jeans almost identical to Sarah's. However, on Jackie they seemed to say "making an awkward effort to look trendy, despite it all".

'Who's that?' she asked when she saw the photo Albert was now dreamily admiring.

'My ruin and my hope,' answered Albert. 'My saviour and my tormentor.'

'She's very beautiful,' observed Jackie, with a tone more weary than usual for her. 'Where did you meet her?'

'He hasn't met her,' said Ron cuttingly, coming into the room and offering Jackie a joint, which she declined. Sticking the joint in his lips, holding his left hand up in a fist, he dubbed it, 'The real world.' Lifting his open right hand, he dubbed it, 'Albert.' Then he made Albert flutter everywhere except near the real world, although twice the two hands came tantalisingly close, but that may have been carelessness on his part. 'See how they never come together?'

'I do see,' said Jackie.

Ron looked at Albert, who was still gazing dreamily at the photo. 'You know, Albert, if you had a pound for every one you worship, you'd be able to afford to go out with a few of them each year.'

'Move out, Ron,' suggested Albert. 'Find a place where towering freaks are tolerated.'

'Sarah wants the photo back.'

'Give me my Albert's Lass T-shirt and you can have the photo.'

'I don't negotiate with losers,' stated Ron, snatching the photo away.

'I want my T-shirt,' demanded Albert. 'Jennifer will need it to stay warm.'

'I dumped it in a bin yesterday,' said Ron, leaving the room.

'You undisciplined twat,' shouted Albert.

Quickly becoming philosophical about losing his icon, Albert blew out all but one candle, then lay on his bed, eyes directed at some imaginary point way beyond the ceiling.

Peep jumped up and settled on his chest.

The ceiling creaked to the footsteps of the woman from upstairs, and to Albert's stoned ear it sounded unusually loud until Jackie spoke, drawing his attention away.

'I met Ron outside your house,' she explained. 'I was at my sister's, so I popped round to see if you wanted to go to Newcastle clubbing with me tonight. I'm meeting some of my new college friends.'

'Jackie,' said Albert, in a voice that was both admonishing and patronising, 'if I've told you once, I've told you a thousand times: if you're going to talk to me, talk sense.'

'Come on, Albert,' she mildly pleaded.

'Jackie, I'm a thinker, not a doer. If you want someone to do stuff with you, ask Ron. He never thinks.'

'Please, Albert. I'll pay for you. I've got Monday and Tuesday off work, and my bonus came through yesterday. I want to live it up a bit. We're all going to do an E then go back to my friend's big house in Gateshead later. I haven't done one for ages.' Her entreaty elicited no response. 'I'd love to see you on E,' she appended, in a voice little more than a murmur. 'Have you ever done an E?'

He ignored her.

'Have you ever even been clubbing?' she asked.

'Jackie, if I've told you once —'

Cutting in, Jackie sighed, 'Yeah, yeah, I know — if I'm going to talk to you, I have to talk sense. Why do I bother with you, Albert?'

'I've got nice hair and I'm kind to my cat,' he answered.

'You are kind to your cat,' she agreed at once, giving the feline a stroke. 'My mum used to say you could always trust a man who's kind to animals.'

'But you should see me with fucking horses,' snarled Albert, grimly punching his palm, causing Peep to jump off him.

Jackie got up and brought a chair over to the bedside. Sitting on it, she looked at Albert while he stared at the ceiling. The small amount of dope was affecting him so much that, if he let it, a smudge on the dim ceiling might become a subtly animated Indian squaw carrying a papoose on her back, although once it became a wild horse running across expansive grasslands. If he put the light on, or just lit more candles, he knew this product of his expanded mind's struggle to make sense of limited visual information would at once vanish. Nevertheless, Ron never reported such profound experiences on just dope, and nor had anyone else he'd quizzed. There really was something about him and dope.

'What do you think about when you lie there like that?' Jackie wanted to know.

'The world with all its sorrows, and how it all adds up to nought,' he answered, with an air of weary lamentation.

'Party on,' she commented sarcastically. 'No wonder you always look so depressed.' Sitting forward, leaning on her elbows, she looked keenly at him as he in turn looked at his ceiling.

Aware he was receiving close attention, he asked, 'Is my hair peaking? Is that it?'

Ignoring his frivolous enquiry, Jackie earnestly suggested, 'Have you ever thought that you might *be* depressed? *Clinically.*'

'I'm not depressed,' stated Albert in a level voice. 'I'm melancholic.'

'And what's the difference?'

'Ordinary people like Ron get depressed when their cars rust and stuff,' he explained, 'but poets like me are melancholic because we're haunted by ethereal longings and hopeless yearnings. It's a complete twat. I'd much rather be like Ron, but that'd take a couple of head injuries.'

Jackie leaned back in her chair. 'You've never written any poems,' she reminded him, 'so how can you say you're a poet?'

Albert's answer was easily found. 'Wordsworth said poets are people more disposed to be affected by absent things. I'm haunted by hopeless yearning, therefore I'm a poet. Thus, actually writing poetry would just be for show, and you know I've never been a showy person.'

In silence, she looked at him for some time. 'Do you ever let your guard down?'

'What guard?'

'The guard that just involved you saying "what guard?".'

'Jackie,' said Albert, in the special tone he reserved for the sentence, 'if I've told you once, I've told you a thousand times: if you're going to talk to me, talk sense.'

'All the signs are there, you know,' said Jackie enigmatically. 'We've just been studying it at college — depression.'

So that was it. That's why he was getting forced, entry-level analysis: Jackie was doing 'A' Level psychology in night school.

'Signs such as?'

'Lack of motivation,' she stated.

'Why bother being motivated?' he countered.

'You constantly allude to suicide.'

'Suicide's the only thing that keeps me going most days. The prospect makes life bearable.'

'God, that's the saddest coping mechanism I've ever heard about,' responded Jackie. 'We had a lecture the other day about depression being a failure of a coping mechanism. Normal people seem to have some thought mechanism that helps them navigate through life by over-estimating their chances of success and underestimating their failure chance. Wouldn't you like a little bit of a coping mechanism yourself? Life could be such a *buzz* for someone like you. You've got so much potential.'

It was that word again — *potential*. It had followed him through life like some knife-wielding celebrity stalker.

'According to that theory,' he deduced, 'only depressed people see life as it really is?'

'Maybe — the poor bastards,' agreed Jackie quickly. 'And maybe it's why you sit in the dark while the rest of the world goes out dancing. But getting depressed is such a pointless response.'

'I'm not depressed, I'm melancholic,' Albert reminded her.

'Okay, so getting *melancholic* is a pointless response,' corrected Jackie irascibly.

'No less pointless than getting happy, for everything comes to nought in the end. At least I can say I was never fooled by any of it.'

'More fool you,' said Jackie, to which Albert made no reply. She looked at him. Studied him. 'You're so strange. So many of the symptoms of depression, yet you always joke about everything.'

'I'm not depressed,' he reminded her again, 'I'm melancholic. The most melancholic person in Durham. There ought to be monuments.'

'Yeah, that's what the world needs more of — monuments to blokes who permanently stare at their ceiling.'

'Nothing is permanent except loss.'

Jackie continued to study him.

'Why do you turn everything into a joke, Albert?'

Sitting up to re-light the dope pipe, with a hint of bitter defiance colouring his words, he returned, 'Because I can and it is.'

'Maybe it's the opposite,' theorised Jackie as he fumbled with the pipe. 'Maybe your coping mechanism's too strong, and that's why you can live like you do without freaking out?'

'Jackie, if I've told you once,' lectured Albert, breaking off to draw on the pipe, 'I've told you a thousand times...' He wagged his finger at her. '... if you're going to talk to me, talk sense.'

He took another draw on the pipe.

Watching him sucking the candle flame into the pipe, Jackie remarked, 'Don't think I've seen you smoke before.'

'Not a big one for it,' he answered, issuing much smoke with his words.

'Why not? Thought someone like you with so much time to kill would be grateful for it.'

'Ties my tongue up,' he said between more sucking.

'And where would Albert Fox be without his tongue?' returned Jackie pointedly, but receiving and observing no response. Peep began weaving between her legs, arching, and she reached down to stroke it. 'I really love your cat. It's so sweet. It's always quietly purring.'

Finished with the pipe, Albert slumped down sideways on to the bed, while his feet remained on the floor. 'Shouldn't have done that,' he groaned ruefully. Peep jumped up on him, settling on his upper arm. The music finished, but, staring at the candle, he didn't seem to notice. 'Fuck, I'm *really* stoned now. Long time since I've been like this.'

'Tony thinks you've got a depressive illness,' revealed Jackie.

'What the fuck would Tony know?' muttered Albert, lying as if in some opium state, eyes fixed on the candle flame.

'He's a consultant psychiatrist,' she pointed out.

'I'm not depressed. I'm melancholic.'

'I'm hungry,' announced Jackie, prompted by the aroma of cooking emanating from the kitchen.

'So go and fix yourself something,' mumbled Albert.

'Think I'd better,' she said. However, viewing Albert, she ventured another exploration of his psyche. 'Is your melancholia real or just a pose?'

Not quick to respond, Albert eventually said, 'Real.'

Picking up a tone in his voice she had never heard before, a tone she fancied to be a hint of sad, honest admission, Jackie said, 'Tell me about it. Tell me why you think you're melancholic.'

Flaked out, still staring at the candle flame, his cat perched on his arm, Albert mumbled, 'Already have.'

'Have you?'

'You know,' he mumbled, 'hopeless yearning, and all that fuckin' deep stuff.'

'Tell me again,' she requested. 'My memory's bad. Tell me what you yearn for.'

Taking some time to reply, Albert said, 'I never know, Jackie. But I'm sure it's not of this world. Misty, larger wants than others seem to feel. A purer state. This world is so gross, and I'm so gross. A purer state is what I yearn for, Jackie.'

'What good will staring at your ceiling do, though? Life's for living, Albert.'

'Life's so fucking transitory it's hardly worth bothering with,' he returned, mustering a cantankerous tone.

Jackie's stomach rumbled. 'God, listen to me. I need to eat.' She stood up. 'You don't really want to die,' she said, ruffling his hair and leaving his bedside, 'you're just pissed off you're not going to live forever.' She went on into the kitchen, where Ron was preparing two elaborate hamburgers for himself and Sarah, who was waiting in the living room.

It was like his soul had been jolted. It was undeniably true. It was one of those vague longings of his — perhaps the greatest of them — but now crystallised into something tangible by Jackie's throwaway parting comment: he was pissed off he wasn't going to live forever. He was so pissed off, he was inclined to turn his nose up at the paltry life-span allotted by nature. It was the natural surliness in him. He was a maximallist. It was all or nothing for him, just like it was all or nothing for him with money — if he wasn't going to be a free-living millionaire, he didn't care to have a penny.

But shit, soon it might actually be *possible* to live for ever, or at least hundreds, maybe thousands, of years. Bio-technology was surging ahead, he knew. That very day, in *New Scientist* he'd read an article on a great advancement in embryonic stem cell research, holding out the very real hope of repairing or replacing organs. And there was telomere research, too, that might coax existing body cells to reset their clocks and go on dividing well beyond their natural span. The natural span in humans is simply set at a level that allows time for reproduction and rearing. After that, who cares? Not genes. They've got on another train. But with bio-technology's promise, cruel king Nature might be overthrown by its smartest child, and thereafter in the kingdom, old men's skin would look, *and be*, young; old women's bones would be strong; failing organs returned to health. For the first time in history, now, in Albert's own generation, people could more than dream about immortality. It could reasonably happen, he understood. Powerful secrets were being unlocked daily in labs around the world.

But those secrets and technologies wouldn't be for the likes of him, he further reflected. They would be for free-living millionaires. Most weeks, after buying cat food, he couldn't even afford aspirin, let alone immortality.

Bugger.

'Want one?' asked Ron, when he learned of Jackie's hunger.

'I'm vegetarian,' answered Jackie, quickly brushing her hair. 'I'll have a cheese sandwich or something.'

'Since fucking when are you veggie?' challenged Ron, who'd seen her eat a meat dish only days before.

'Since yesterday,' returned Jackie, searching cupboards for things she fancied. 'A guy I know from college convinced me. It's just so unnecessary eating animals.'

'Full vegetarian? Given up milk and eggs too?'

'No, I'm not vegan. I'm just not going to eat anything that would miss its mother. The little bunnies and things are safe from me now.'

'What about the little fishes?' asked Ron, turning his burgers under the grill.

'Oh, thicky fishes don't matter,' said Jackie, waving the very idea of them away, 'they look so bored and stupid.'

Walking somewhat the worse for his over-indulgence on the pipe, Albert appeared in the kitchen, collecting a pen from on top of the fridge.

131

'Well, Albert looks bored and stupid too,' observed Ron, 'but he can count and spell and all sorts. He even had a girlfriend once.'

'Twice,' corrected Albert drably before leaving.

'He's had girlfriends?' blurted Jackie before Albert was out of earshot, quickly hushing her voice. 'Real ones? Not just ones in books he's read?'

'Yeah, real flesh and blood ones.'

'But I asked my sister and she said he's never been with anyone.'

'You should have asked me instead,' advised Ron. 'I live with him.'

'Who? When?'

'There was someone years back,' detailed Ron, tending his spitting burgers. 'Fiona, that was her name. Just after we moved in here. And there was this really nice Australian student one about two years back.'

'What happened to them?'

'He ditched them both after about a month. The Australian one actually cried. Saw it with my own eyes. Weird, eh? She idolised him. She wanted him to move to Australia with her. Her mother owned a ranch, and she said that with his brains, her mother'd make him ranch manager in a couple of years.'

'And he dumped that chance?' asked Jackie incredulously.

'He did. She was good looking, too.'

'Was she?' enquired Jackie, sounding casual.

'Certainly was. Built like a porn star, too. I fancied the fuck out of her.

Ron was now placing the burgers into buns, adding various salad items.

'How did he get together with them?' chatted Jackie, standing alongside Ron, cutting a block of cheese she'd found in the fridge.

'Don't know about the first, but the Australian one just grabbed him when we were down the pub — literally.'

'Yeah?'

'Then she hung on to his arm till we got home,' Ron went on. 'And then when he wanted to go to bed, she hung on to him again. He was trying to pull her off, but she wasn't having it. Wish she'd hung on to me till I was in bed.'

'I don't believe this,' said Jackie, although she didn't actually suspect lies were being told to her. 'He tried to pull her off? And she was really nice?'

'Saw it with my own eyes.'

'Is he gay?'

'Nah, just weird. Wish he was gay. He'd be more useful around the kitchen.'

Ron's burgers, oozing mayonnaise, were growing unfeasibly tall as he added layer after layer of salad, and cheese slices he was stealing from Jackie's sandwich.

'Why did he leave her?' Jackie asked, blatantly stealing some tomato and lettuce from Ron to make amends for the cheese he had taken from her.

'Told you, he's weird,' said Ron simply, whisking the burgers away to the living room like he was suddenly up against the clock.

1.11
Before the Beginning

When Jackie returned to Albert's room, he once more had all the candles lit, and was sitting on the floor before them, back rested against the bed, apparently gazing at the flames.

'Want some of my sandwich?' she offered.

'Food is the weak person's substitute for emptiness.'

Disregarding that comment, sitting on the edge of the bed, her leg touching Albert's shoulder, Jackie announced, 'I'm a vegetarian now. Eating animals is so unnecessary. Humans have options.'

Albert didn't respond.

Observing the arc of candles, Jackie realised Albert had overcome the loss of the beautiful young woman's blurry photograph by replacing it with a bad, childish drawing of her, with the name Jennifer written underneath. However, contrary to the evidence, he wasn't at that moment thinking about Jennifer. He was inwardly noting how he felt kind of disappointed to learn that some — or perhaps much — of his melancholia was rooted in a cheap desire never to die. It was like he had been undressed and found to be not as complicated as he had believed himself to be.

It was potential social embarrassment, that's what it was.

Jackie ate without making conversation. Once finished, she put the plate to one side, brushed her hair and sat on the floor next to Albert, resting against the bed. She too looked at the candles and Jennifer's drawing.

'What are you going to do with your life, Albert?'

'Doing it right now,' he answered, meaning his future lay solely in worshipping Jennifer's drawing.

'Don't you have any ambitions?'

He shrugged.

'Don't you want more than life on the dole?' Jackie went on.

'Can't be bothered shrugging again.'

'Go to college then university,' she suggested. 'With your awesome mind you could get your A Levels in no time. Some guy there did them in six months. We could go to the same university. You could have a degree in four years.'

'The prospect of another four hours wearies me.'

Jackie released a small sigh, then fell silent awhile, until she asked, 'Have you tried on your present yet?'

'Too deep.'

'Why do I bother with you, Albert?'

'Dunno. Maybe my hair's peaking.'

Peep was getting curious about the crumbs on the plate Jackie had left on the floor, so she moved it away from the animal, but Albert moved it back again.

'I should be on my way to Newcastle,' said Jackie in a while, as if she didn't fully want to leave.

'Would you like to hear an unputdownable work of rare genius I read?' asked Albert softly.

'All right.'

'Before the beginning,' he began, reciting the story he'd read so often it had been committed to memory, 'there was a brilliant physicist called Godfrey who succeeded in producing the Equation of Everything. He was a white-haired, kindly old professor, and, like many of the people working in his field, he had grown old, weary and sad-eyed trying to develop the elusive theory that successfully unifies all the forces of nature into a single one.

'After years of work, inspiration and collaboration, one night,

134

in his study at home, Godfrey realised he was finally getting somewhere. The previously accepted unification of electricity and magnetism was wrong, he sensed. It was an erroneous and misleading theory. It had seemed to work before, but that was only coincidental, like the old belief that the sun revolved around the earth each day.

'Godfrey swept aside the old theory of electromagnetism and replaced it with one of his own. He felt full of glory and wonder, and as the night wore on, working without rest, he pulled into his new theory other forces ... gravity ... the strong nuclear force ... the weak nuclear force: they were all methodically slotted in in turn. All forces were now at the behest of Godfrey's powerful mathematics. The resulting single equation was a sprawling monstrosity, tens of dozens of pages long with hundreds of variables, but it *felt* right. The more Godfrey reflected upon his discoveries, the more phenomena he realised they explained. Matter was easily explained: it was just a special manifestation of energy. Time, he realised, was merely an illusory symptom of entropy — the decay of the universe as an ordered system. He realised that, except as a measure of the inconsequential dissolution of atomic order, order he termed "arbitrary order", like, say, the atoms that make up a cat, time was non-existent. And as for space, it became a simple function of the effect of forces upon dimensionality. Yes, he was getting close to the universal truth. All parts of the jigsaw fitted, but the picture was far too large for him to be able to see it all at once. "The equations must be simpler," he told himself, "they must reduce". Throughout the next day, he worked with wise precision on the piles of formulae — integrating; cancelling like terms; amalgamating different aspects — and as each action brought him closer to a complete understanding of the discovery, he felt a growing "oneness". He was performing a sublime, mystical act, he felt. A sacred act.

'Finally, the complexities dwindled entirely away, and he began to apperceive the whole. His last mathematical act brought him complete comprehension of all the laws of nature. Hurriedly cancelling the remaining terms of the ultimate equation, he found he was left with only $x = x$. And at that moment, the moment of understanding, His mind became one with all, all with one. And for as long as it pleased Him to behold it, all was formless and symmetrical in the mind of Godfrey. Then He said, "Let there be light!" and there *was* light, a mighty *explosion* of light, such was the power of Godfrey. And when He eventually become lonely, He simply made some friends.'

Like on Radio Three after a classical concert ends, Jackie allowed a period of respectful silence before speaking.

'That was nice.'

Albert rolled his eyes and sighed complainingly. 'Come on, Jackie, it was better than nice. It was monumental. So monumental, five-brained scholars a million generations hence shall speak of it as mankind's greatest cultural achievement.'

Jackie looked at him. 'You wrote it?'

'Last Thursday.'

'I thought you said you'd read it?'

'I did read it,' he explained. 'I wrote it first, then I read it back to check for spelling mistakes.'

'You're crazy,' she said.

'Lend me a fish.'

'Sure I would if I had one,' she said quietly, laying her head back against the bed.

'Want a cup of tea?' he asked.

Blending a sigh in with her words, Jackie replied, 'I've really got to go.' Getting up, she brushed her hair and went to the toilet. When she returned to say goodbye, Albert was lying on his bed, staring at his ceiling. He was still staring at his ceiling two hours later when Sarah and Ron came into his room, standing just inside the door Jackie had left open.

'God, you're right,' said Sarah in a hushed voice, 'it is spooky, isn't it? He looks like he's dead. How often does he lie like that?'

'Five or six hours every day. Worse at Christmas.'

'Shit,' breathed Sarah. Stepping into the candle-lit room like she was entering a chapel of rest, she stood beside Albert's bed, viewing him before asking, 'What do you think about when you stare at your ceiling like that?'

'The world with all its sorrows,' answered Albert, not diverting his gaze from its accustomed upward direction, 'and how it all adds up to nought.'

'Bullshit,' challenged Ron. Striding over to the bed and kicking it, he demanded, 'What do you really think about? Come on. I bet it's pussy.'

Albert hesitated before quietly confessing, 'I think about nothing.'

'Nothing at all?' asked Sarah. 'Is your mind really that quiet?'

'You could hear a pin drop.'

'You'll hear voices one day,' predicted Ron, before walking out of the room. 'No one can live like you do and stay sane.'

'Oh my God,' exclaimed Sarah, with a mixture of amusement and concern. She had just spotted the drawing of her sister, illuminated reverently by candles. She picked it up for examination. 'It's all getting really freaky now.'

'Damage it and I'll kill you,' said Albert in a quietly threatening voice, still staring at the ceiling, 'and not in a shy way.'

Sarah quickly put it back.

Like he was coming round after a blow to the head, Albert sat up and put his feet upon the floor. 'Thank fuck the dope's wearing off,' he mumbled, kneading his temples. 'Overdid it tonight.'

Sitting down beside Albert, brightly, as if expecting Albert to share her excitement, Sarah revealed that she was going away with Ron the next day.

'Going away where?' mumbled Albert.

'Iceland,' she beamed.

'Oh yeah, Iceland,' he said, remembering that Ron had told him he was going there to work for a few weeks.

'We're setting off early tomorrow. I've just booked a seat on the same flight over the internet. Aways wanted to see Iceland. Lucky it's my mid-term break this week. Got to come back on my own though on Friday for that performance at the Arts Centre I was all dressed up for when you first met me. Isn't it funny? If you hadn't read Tess of the d'Urbervilles, I wouldn't be going to Iceland.'

'What in the fuck is there to do in Iceland?' muttered Albert, who'd never been on any kind of holiday in his life beyond a childhood cycle ride.

'Glaciers and volcanoes enough?'

'Only if they resemble Jennifer.'

'They couldn't look any less like her than your crap drawing.'

A fresh mention of the drawing caused Albert to gaze at it and sigh.

'Got to get back to my place to pack,' announced Sarah, standing. 'I'll send you a postcard.'

'I don't want a postcard of your place,' returned Albert, still gazing at Jennifer's drawing.

'You know what I mean,' accused Sarah. Patting him patronisingly on the head, she said, 'I like you very much, even though you're a bit spooky.'

She kissed him goodbye on the cheek, and left his room.

Sarah's unexpected parting gesture surprised Albert. Things could have changed since he'd taken to the solitary life, but, as a Darlington

137

lad, he was not, and never had been, accustomed to receiving goodbye kisses, even from the closest and oldest of friends. Where Albert came from, people were more likely to punch each other goodbye. Twice, if they were family.

Then it happened again: Melancholy's hand slipped into his.

Later, Albert went to the living room, to lie on the sofa and stare at the dirty ceiling. Ron was sitting in the armchair, reading a magazine. Albert hadn't spoken since Sarah's departure, but eventually he said, 'I hear you're going away tomorrow.'

'Yep. A fortnight in Reykjavik. Work.'

'With Sarah?'

'She's coming for five days. Romantic, ain't it?'

'I may not be here when you get back,' said Albert quietly.

'Oh, is that so? Where will you be?'

Albert's answer came in the form of a dejected shuffle to his bedroom while mumbling something about tablets and how everyone would miss him when he's gone and wish they'd been nicer to him while they'd had the chance.

Having withdrawn to his room, Albert lit one candle and sat on his bed. Looking at Jennifer's drawing and vaguely remembering how beautiful she really was plunged him into some therapeutically suicidal thoughts. Yes, it was true what he'd said to Jackie: suicide was all that kept him going since he couldn't live forever. Despairing suicidally about the Jenniferlessness aspect of his life led Albert to despair suicidally about his life in general. This grim and sober life-assessment was standard despondency for the night before he had to get up early to sign on the dole. Jennifer might be a new and wild pain in Albert's life, but signing on was a chronic ache. He was now suffering routine fortnightly pre-signing-on distress, routinely marginally outweighed by Christ-I-actually-managed-to-get-up-and-do-it post-signing-on relief.

Every other Sunday night, Albert would resolve to get his life in order. To him, "order" meant being dead and lamented by thousands of beautiful young ladies. Now imagining that perfect order again, his inner eye reviewed thousands of them clad in mourning black, standing solemnly in line, awaiting their turn to weep beside his tomb. Having made the pilgrimage, each lady then went away, broken-hearted, to devote the rest of her chaste life to writing volumes of poetry bemoaning his demise and pointing out how nice he'd been to his cat and what great hair he'd had.

He pictured Sarah, half mad with grief, clad as Tess, intensely

138

and wildly playing requiem cello for her lost love beside his Gothic tomb in some lonely, time-forgotten English country churchyard. He pictured a sorrowful Jennifer, diaphanously veiled in black lace, tenderly sweeping away with her gloved hand three autumn leaves lightly kissing his eternal resting place. And as Sarah's plangent threnodies enchanted the still air, all about in the moody welkin above, wet-eyed clouds gathered in mournful solemnity to darkly veil the sky summer knew vibrant and blue.

1.12
Signing On

Morning — strictly a thing of science fiction to Albert. An eerie, weird world where an unfamiliar sun hangs low and pale in the sky, obliquely illuminating alien thralls trudging grimly to their places of soulless toil.

His clock-radio went off, cynically welcoming him to the stark planet Morning. Every night before signing day, just before slipping into bed, Albert indulged in a deluded pantomime of optimism, setting his clock to wake him early, and every time he ignored it when it did its job. Today, he did more than ignore it, he cursed it — he'd been dreaming about Tess of the d'Urbervilles, weeping at his graveside, reading from his other great un-started poetic work, the thirty-seven volume *Mine is the Voice of all Suffering.*

That counted as a sex dream, to him.

Reaching in sleepy annoyance for the flex, he yanked the clock's plug out of the socket. Despite the noise Ron was making packing for Iceland, he resolved, with grim steeliness, to return to sleep, and, hopefully, the pleasure of his own grave. Signing could wait a little while.

Six hours later, with Ron long gone on his travels, Albert got up, worshipped Jennifer's drawing a bit, and thought he might as well sign on while he was vertical. So, after a cup of tea and a bowl of cereal, and almost an hour spent in the bath, he made a special effort with his hair to make himself ready for showing himself to the sort-of-cute girl he sort-of-fancied who worked at the dole office that doubled as a Jobcentre. Collecting his signing on paraphernalia (or his "loser paraphernalia", as Ron called it), he slipped his heavy coat over his ominous T-shirt, and left the flat.

The sky was grey but not threatening, and the afternoon air was heavy, saturated with the odour of damp autumn decay. At the bottom of his street, he decided to take the longer but more picturesque riverbank route into town, and crossed a playing field to reach the water where local legend maintained a terrible monster, or "worm", lived. The story of the Lampton Worm was a song-celebrated one every child for miles around learnt in the course of their junior school lessons. *"Shush me lads, an' had y'gobs, an' ah'll tell y'boot the worm ..."* From what he could remember from his infrequent school attendance, some olden-days geezer once caught a funny-looking fish *"with git big fins an' git big goggly eyes"* and threw it down a well or something, where it grew fat on virgins. Or was it crisps? he couldn't remember. Crisps had something to do with the story, he was sure. Ah, yes, that was it, in the morning break at junior school, crisps were brought round for sale.

School: he could barely remember anything about it before the age of about twelve, and not much more after that. It seemed odd to him that so very much had faded. Walking along the riverbank, he tried to picture the faces of his junior school teachers, but couldn't. He couldn't even remember their names. Couldn't even remember walking to school, or walking back. Although he'd been a compulsive truant from the age of ten, he assumed he must have put *some* time in at the office, otherwise he'd never have learned to read. But he could remember the truancy – the glorious, educational truancy. The long, solitary, noble walks to farms and brooks and meadows that, in recollection, seemed to have been to his child's eye

Apparelled in celestial light.

The stones skimmed. The curious things found. The shy and rare creatures glimpsed. All that wonder loomed large – albeit hazily – in his memory, yet the scoldings he must have bought that freedom to wander with were gone. But memory was like that, he knew, for all the poets had told him so. And how merciful! he thought, imagining how gruesome life would be if every punishment and

140

every trapped finger were recalled as vividly as the laughter and larks.

In years to come, sat in his unknown future, if he looked back to his dole days in Durham, would he see the reluctant morning awakenings? The quiet embarrassments? The petty miseries of hardupishment? Or would he see only some gentle, autumnal stroll by a meandering river, with a majestic cathedral looming on-high across the water, twice the size he was seeing it now? Moreover, if by some horrible fate he lived to be ninety, would he talk as much nonsense about the past as the ninety year-olds of today? When *they* were young, the sky was blue all day long, except when torrents of rain fell that made today's rainstorms look like morning dew. Everything was better. People were better than the sort we get nowadays. Cats *were* cats, not the miserable things of modern times. Dogs had two mouths each for biting. And horses? Well, horses in the good ol' days lived underground in burrows and fed on unwary children, but pulling their tails was the best fun ever to be had.

Sister Shivon: yes, *there* was a name from the Catholic junior school he'd attended. Not one of his teachers, but the headmistress, and a nun. He used to regularly get hauled up in front of her, he now recalled, and she caned him at least once — for being "defiant". He couldn't picture his teachers' faces, but he could picture *that* — a towering, fucked-up bitch of an angry virgin in spooky clothes pulling him around, cursing his childish personality and making his flesh sting. He'd pay good money for that now.

Up some steps to street level, then on for five more minutes and he was at the dole office. The signing line was longer than usual, with around fifteen people ahead of him. Things seemed to be taking longer, too. Some kind of action day, probably, with extra questions and extra pressure. Today's clientele seemed to be particularly dud, he observed. All stubble and lank, unwashed hair. Joining the queue as it inched and shuffled forward, his greatest fear now was that another doley would engage him in conversation: blurted, beery words about suffering dependants with holes in their trousers and the unjust price of cigarettes.

He looked at the floor.

When nearing the head of the queue, he looked up. Unfortunately, the sort-of-cute girl wasn't one of the three signers on duty. Even worse, one of the signers was the most sour-faced, sour-minded individual Albert had ever come across outside documentary accounts of serial killers. Michelle was the name on

141

her ID badge. After his first encounter with her, he'd looked in a dictionary, convinced *michelle* must also be an adjective, synonymous with permanent sullen scornfulness. Most of the staff were pleasant and polite to the claimants, but not this trout-faced woman. She was in her early forties, Albert guessed, but maturity had not mellowed her, or if it had, she must have been one seriously bad bitch in the playground. She was fair-haired, around average height, a little dumpy, and had an ill-defined, insipid, blotchy face that resembled a mass of putty splashed with tea. That was outside. Inside, she was completely humourless, taking any witticism or goofy remark as some kind of bitter poison.

Today, for an unknown reason, Michelle had her neck supported in a plaster collar. Albert wondered if it might be because someone had tried to hang her. And why not? He knew that every doley in Durham hated her. Often, while waiting in the queue, he had therapeutic, fanciful visions of furtive, skulking groups of the more desperate, down-market doleys meeting within tumble-down derelict houses to plot the bag's assassination in hushed but vengeful voices.

Having observed the cause of the signing slowness, Albert believed that this day Michelle was being particularly haughty. The signing system had apparently been revised again, and as part of the new way of doing things, she got to ask each person if their circumstances had changed in any way since their last attendance. As claimants arrived at her desk and placed their claim cards down, after determining their name and bringing their details up on screen, she enquired, "any changes?" The answer was no each time. It was procedure — new procedure —, but Albert suspected that for Michelle it was a way to bring home to the claimant their unchanging poverty, state of joblessness, and inferiority to her.

'Any changes?' asked Michelle.

'No,' replied the gruff-voiced claimant quietly, and Michelle made some keystrokes before taking his signature.

Albert was now at the head of the queue. It was three-to-two that he'd get a normal person signing him. Please, make it a normal person, he wished.

'Next,' called Michelle.

Albert proceeded to her desk. 'Someone try to hang you?' he enquired sociably as he sat down, placing his claim card on the desk.

Michelle responded to the comment only by maintaining her usual milk-souring expression while entering his details into her terminal. 'You're late,' she admonished. 'You should have signed at nine.'

'I tried to get out of bed, but I was having this great sex dream.'

She gave him a look before proceeding.

'Any changes?'

'Of course there have been changes,' said Albert, 'nothing sublunary endures...' Producing his drawing from his coat pocket and showing it to Michelle, he went on, '... except my unchanging love for Jennifer. The pure feelings I have for this gentle lady are immutable.'

Nothing. Not a flicker of humanity crossed the sullen face of Scorn sitting opposite Albert. She hadn't even looked properly at his drawing, and that's what hurt most.

'I meant,' she said, 'have there been any changes in your circumstances?'

'I've had a haircut. But I suppose you noticed my magnificence in that department straightaway.'

She didn't look properly at his haircut, either.

'If you don't give me a straight answer this time,' she warned, 'I won't ask you again and I'll close your claim. Any changes?'

'No. No changes,' said Albert, shamefully capitulating.

After making some arcane keystrokes, Michelle retrieved his claim file from a drawer below the desk. But instead of finding his signing sheet, she found a note which she explained gave instructions to suspend all payments to him until he'd been interviewed by the inspector.

Bugger.

He was told to wait near the queue of claimants, and that is what he did, occasionally looking at his Jennifer drawing.

As Albert waited, he had a feeling that this was it. This was the day the giro payments really would cease, after years of him using every trick and feint he could muster to dodge and stay unemployed and in bed. His greatest dole fear was a forced training course, on threat of losing his Jobseekers' giros, something he'd only just managed to side-step on occasions. His second greatest dole fear was a work scheme, which he'd also evaded before. Once, during one of the routine, thirteen week reviews of his claim, it looked like he really was cornered. The stern woman dealing with him was being particularly assiduous, but he'd pulled off a masterstroke. It had been the day after he'd dumped Amanda — his short-term Australian girlfriend — so he'd had a head-start, but it still deserved

143

to be celebrated in gritty folk song, he felt. When the hard-staring, menopausal civil servant had highlighted his track record of work avoidance, he'd deliberately pictured the hurt, confused look in Amanda's eyes from the night before and recalled how sorrowful he himself had felt, knowing he would never tenderly hold her in his arms again. For good measure, he'd then pictured himself at her tear-stained deathbed; then she at his. Then he'd cast his imagination back two hundred years and pictured a bent and stooped old woman walking along a lonely, wild, sombre shoreline. With the salt water surging and receding, so that an onlooker would fear for her safety, his inner eye observed as the old woman looked down and with dim sight discovered her lost son's pallid corpse, tossed ashore by the white-foamed waves. Her son lay amid the wreckage of the same fishing boat her husband had been swept away from twenty years before, never to be seen again, though she still burned a candle for him in the window of her simple house. Picturing all that, he'd managed to weep, and his stern interrogator had fallen suddenly silent. She was a guilt-ridden, tissue-offering angel after that.

But today he just felt too weary with it all to bother weeping, and had a feeling he'd come to the barren end of Dole Road.

Eventually, the inspector appeared. He was around thirty-five, with a thin face and square, gold-rimmed glasses. A grey suit ill-fitted his thin body. He led Albert into a room that contained only a table and two chairs. The walls were painted an insipid yellow. Rushed brush strokes had set hard and visible in the emulsion. The refectory-style table was unadorned except for a trapezoidal paperweight about four inches long that bore the name *John Booth* in stick-on letters. He invited Albert to take a seat, then promptly left the room, and it felt like a long time before he returned. When he did return, carrying some papers in a green cardboard folder, he sat in the chair across the table from Albert.

Half a minute of silence passed while the inspector arranged some of his papers on the table, glancing through them. Then he looked up. 'Good morning, sir,' he began in an officious manner. 'My name's John Booth, and I'm an inspector for the DSS. The reason we've called you in is to determine what efforts you've been making to find employment. This is necessary because firstly you failed to attend a compulsory Jobsearch interview, and secondly, when you were given another interview date, you attended but were uncooperative with the interviewing officer, refusing to complete the form that helps them decide your claim eligibility.'

'I did fill in the form,' Albert contradicted.

'Yes, you did,' conceded the inspector, 'but not to their satisfaction.'

'Not my fault they're fussy cunts.'

Albert received a look before the inspector retrieved the contentious form from the cardboard folder, holding it disdainfully by one corner. He spread it out on the desktop, cast a disapproving eye over it, then spun it around with a fingertip, presenting it to Albert as conclusive evidence of his uncooperative nature. He then spun it back and began reading selected parts in a disapproving voice. 'Age: weary. How far are you prepared to travel daily to get to work? No further than the 18th century. What type of work have you usually done? Paper round. Do you have any health problems that affect your ability to work? Progressive melancholia and poet's constitution.'

'The melancholia's a lot worse today,' commented Albert.

The inspector looked up from the form to peer sternly at Albert. 'Why do you treat this as a joke?'

'Because I can and it is.'

'When you're thirty and still signing on, do you think it'll still be amusing?'

'Like I'm ever going to be thirty,' said Albert.

The inspector leaned back in his chair and regarded Albert for some seconds before sitting forward again. 'It seems,' he said, 'that you're making little effort at all to find work.'

'Fair comment,' said Albert. 'I'd stop my dole if I were in your shoes.'

'Have you made any efforts to find employment?'

'None at all.'

'Why not?'

'Pointless. I wouldn't last ten minutes in a job. I'd stop my dole if I were you.'

The inspector drew a breath and held it for longer than was physiologically necessary. 'What sort of job *would* you like? We can place you in a suitable work scheme, you know?'

Albert was silent.

'Don't you realise,' continued the inspector, 'that if you can't convince me of your willingness to work you'll have your benefit withheld?'

'Think I'm on top of that one. I've already advised you to withhold it.'

'Then why are you being so defiant?'

'Defiant? I could hardly be any more *compliant*.' A sudden weariness took hold of Albert. 'Look, just go ahead and do whatever your job requires you to do, or even whatever you personally want to do, just don't expect me to show an interest, that's all.'

The inspector again scrutinised Albert coldly before looking down at a paper on his desk. 'Are there any questions you wish to ask?' he enquired while apparently studying the document before him.

'Who stole the dope plant from my garden?'

The inspector looked up. 'You've got the biggest chip on your shoulder I've ever known.'

'It'll be gone as soon as I'm out of here.'

'I doubt that,' muttered the inspector, returning to his paper and writing on it.

'You're not allowed to hit me as well as make personal comments, are you?'

Making no reply, the inspector continued writing, then collected his papers, returning them to the cardboard folder. Pushing his chair back, he went to the door, opened it, then came back to hand Albert a folded sheet of paper. Speaking formally, he said, 'I regret to inform you that from today your benefit is suspended. You may appeal to an independent tribunal if you wish, as detailed in this letter. Do you wish to appeal?'

'No.'

'Then the interview is at a close. Good day.'

The inspector immediately left the room.

Coming out of the building, Albert felt strangely exhilarated. He felt he would not be visiting that place again so long as he lived. That chapter was over. He couldn't imagine joining that defeated queue again, though he'd never really felt part of it even when he was in its midst. He knew that he was far from being a typical claimant – did he not have one of the most cunning minds ever devised by nature? Surely he did, and surely one day he would use it, perhaps in the direction of saucepan technology.

Shit, losing his dole might also mean the cancellation of his Housing Benefit, he suddenly realised. They were administered by separate agencies, but the latter was dependent on proof of the former. Maybe that proof would now be automatically rescinded? One keystroke and he would be jerked towards homelessness via pennilessness. Fuck, this was getting serious. He'd have to check it out. But if the worse came to the worse, he could always sign on again. He wouldn't even have to grovel to the independent tribunal. He knew the dole system. He knew that if he just officially signed off for a few months, lived on beans and borrowing, he could make a fresh claim, and all the hassle would be reset to its lowest level.

No, he wouldn't do that. He never wanted to set eyes on Michelle again. Fuck her. Fuck them all. He'd had enough of signing on. Totally. He didn't think he should have to do it. What he should be able to do was sign on the sick. Incapacity Benefit. The physically disabled received acknowledgement of their plight and a state allowance. Was *he* not also disabled? According to Ron, he was — he needed his head examined, did he not? According to himself, he was simply mentally incompatible with general society, and this meant that he would never be able to do a day of work to the satisfaction of an employer. He liked to think also that it meant he would never target a bomb at a dusty third-world village because a superior officer had told him to do it. He might target the bomb for his own reasons — like if someone in the village claimed to be more melancholic than him — but never because he'd been ordered. He'd bomb the fucking officer, though.

Trudging home the un-picturesque route, Albert felt a true welfare state should make provision for people like him for whom life was a wearying struggle against seriousness, herd instincts and getting up early to arrive at work on time — especially the getting up early. A *true* welfare state would provide a generous *poet benefit*, payable to all sensitive souls.

Poet benefit didn't exist, but maybe he actually *could* sign on the sick? Signing on the sick wasn't much of a career, but he wasn't really after much. Signing on the sick might do him just fine. It had all the security and promotional opportunities that he demanded from a career, and it would pay enough for his basic needs, too, as well as attracting Housing Benefit. So fuck them again with wire brushes, he thought.

A spring entered his stride. Yes, he had glimpsed a light. It was not *the* light — he still vaguely felt he was biding his time for greater things — but it was a cushier waiting game than standing in the dole queue and facing Michelle every fortnight. Moreover, it felt like a general breath of fresh air after six stagnant years. Yes, he was reviving; coming alive; and could take on the world. Back in his flat, over a cup of tea, in a rage of self-belief and confidence, he resolved to begin a new life. A life of achievement. He would be tenacious and conquering. He would be calculating and successful. He would sign on the sick. If anyone could malinger, he could. He was sure he could malinger like a hero.

There was no time to lose. He had to strike while his iron was red hot. Incapacity Benefit was his for the taking. 'Procrastination is the thief of time,' he informed Peep, curled up on a chair. Jackie's sister's husband was crucial to the plan. Tony was a psychiatrist with the power to declare him unfit for work, and Albert knew he held a clinic at the local health centre on Tuesday mornings. That was tomorrow. First thing tomorrow morning he would see Tony to get official — hopefully lucrative — recognition of the state of his mind. If he turned up first thing, Tony would suspect right away something had gone wrong with his head, for it was common knowledge he had never ventured beyond his door before noon since he'd been in the third form at school.

Yes, action. Action until he was successfully mental, resolved Albert. He at once went to his bedroom to plug in his clock and set the alarm for 7am. He felt shot through with revolutionary zeal. He was not going to ignore the clock this time. He could suffer one early rising. After that, he might never have to set his alarm again, or sign on. He would be on Easy Street. All he had to do was convince Tony he was debilitatingly mental, and a sick note would be written. He could do it. He could qualify for mental money if he just put his mind to it. He could fake schizophrenia, or something like that. Tony wouldn't know the difference.

A smug, relaxed calm settled over Albert once he'd worked out his life plan, and he spent the rest of the day enjoying what he felt was well-earned idleness — the lull before the big day. He even treated himself to a bit of widescreen TV in Ron's room, something that had never drawn him before.

At three in the morning, before going to bed he wrote a stirring message to himself in big, vibrant letters on a large sheet of paper:

GET UP, YOU
LAZY BASTARD!

He stuck this on the ceiling above his bed to encourage him to rise early in the morning, then slipped under the duvet.

148

1.13
Wanker

Tuesday — Albert's big day of action. The alarm went off at 7am, and he fucking did it — he got up. But, sitting on the edge of the bed, groping for his clothes, he at once — instantly — mentally rearranged his plans for the rest of his life to accommodate a further three hours in his warm bed. Resetting the alarm, he returned to duvet comfort, to sleep some more. At 10am, however, he was definitely up for success — up for convincing the medical profession, represented by Tony, that he was mental.

After feeding Peep, eating a light breakfast and quickly showering rather than slowly bathing, he set off on his desperate mission, hoping he would make it before noon, the time he knew Tony knocked off.

The health centre was near the city centre. As well as being a regular GP's surgery, it was also a counselling and psychotherapy centre for patients referred by the wider area's doctors, or sometimes judges. Tony had told Albert about some of the more interesting people he saw there. As well as the regular cases of emotional breakdowns and crippling phobias, there was Wolfie, the young man who howled whenever he was left alone. There was the woman whose crusade against part of the electromagnetic spectrum had culminated in her smashing up twelve cars in a supermarket car park — all of them green. There was the man convicted of breaking into dozens of women's houses to steal only items of leatherware, ignoring money and pantyhose. There was the man who rode the town's buses all day long, surreptitiously snipping children's hair. There was the nice man who just stared too much, and thus kept getting beaten up. And there was the student obsessed with destroying his own sexuality who'd successfully removed his own testicles but was disappointed to find himself still capable of erections. So he'd read up on abdominal surgery, laced himself with barbiturates, set up some mirrors in his accommodation block room, then began to root out his own prostate gland, since he'd learnt it was instrumental in his continuing unwanted tumidity. When he'd got to the stage of moving his liver aside, the pain had become too great, and he'd screamed for help.

Thinking about those cases, Albert realised he was up against some serious opposition. So, as he walked into town, he made up an original condition for himself, one he believed worthy of Durham.

A young nurse with long, straight, flaxen hair and rampaging sky-blue eye-shadow was on reception duty at the health centre. Her face was small, so her eyes seemed to bulge, like a frog's. Despite this, or maybe even because of it, Albert thought she looked rather cute, and he almost fell in love, but the uniform turned him off.

'I have to see Dr. Sampson at once,' he informed her.

'Have you got an appointment?'

Her accent was Scottish, east coast.

'No, but he'll see me. I know him, and he said if I ever want help, mentality wise, he'll look at me.'

'Are you registered here?'

'Long time ago.'

'What name?'

'Albert Fox. It excites you tremendously, doesn't it?'

Her small red mouth dropped open ever so slightly so that it formed an almost perfect O.

'Your name excites me?'

'No, my haircut. My haircut excites you, doesn't it?'

'Er, yes. It's very nice,' she said, and warily instructed him to take a seat.

It was close to the end of the morning therapy sessions, and Albert only had to sit amid coughing, maliciously wandering children for around ten minutes until Tony appeared in the waiting room.

'Albert, hello,' said Tony, with a mix of professional compassion and personal suspicion.

'Help me,' said Albert, looking soulfully up to his friend's husband.

'Come this way,' said Tony, with even greater personal suspicion.

Albert's big black coat wafted like raven's wings as he followed the doctor. He was led through a door and into a consulting room imbued with the smell of surgical spirits.

'You're here to see me in my professional capacity?' asked Tony.

'Yes, it's professional,' said Albert in a low voice, taking the seat being offered.

Tony was a medium-sized man in his mid-thirties. He had a receding hairline, a pale complexion and a wispy, blondish-gingery beard. He raised his thin eyebrows and looked at his patient for a moment before sitting in the high-backed leather chair behind his desk. Kneading his chin thoughtfully between the fingers and thumb of his left hand, he viewed Albert's medical card. 'Well, er, Albert, what can I do for you?'

'Help me.'

Tony lowered his hand to the table and looked at his patient. 'If I can. What's the problem?'

Albert spoke in a restrained yet fearfully urgent manner. 'Tony, I think I'm going mad. Going out of my mind. Going into it, even, which is a lot worse when you have a mind like mine.'

'I see,' said Tony, kneading his chin again. 'And why do you think you're going mad?'

Albert hesitated.

'Because sometimes I don't hear voices.'

Tony returned his hand to the table. 'You *don't* hear voices?'

'That's right,' confirmed Albert, trying not to blink, 'sometimes I don't hear voices, and it worries me. I've gone into my mind, right into it, and I need help.'

'You *don't* hear voices?' repeated Tony. 'What sort of voices don't you hear?'

'Nasty cruel voices saying objectionable things about me.'

'Can you explain in more detail?'

'I used to hear people saying objectionable things about me all the time. Things like "Albert, you're a bastard," and "Albert, are you ever going to give me that fiver back?" and "Albert, you're a fool," and "Albert, you've got a chip on your shoulder," and "Albert, you've got your head in the clouds." But now when people say cruel things to me, sometimes I just don't hear them. I can hear the birds singing in the trees above them. I can hear music coming from the radio beside them. I can hear children playing in the street. But I don't hear the disparaging voices.'

'I see,' said Tony. 'And how long has this been going on?'

'Years, now that I think of it,' reflected Albert, his act of discomposure slipping a little. He sought to rescue his feign of madness with a wild-eyed plea. 'I don't hear voices, Tony. How can I be expected to sign on when I don't hear disparaging voices? Any idea how disparaged I get down that fucking Jobcentre? I don't hear voices. I'm sick. Note how sick I am. Note how sick. Sick, note.'

'You want a sick note?' surmised Tony.

Albert looked taken with the sick note notion. 'Fuck, that would help, wouldn't it? Yes, please, Dr. Sampson.'

'Because you don't hear voices?'

'Because I don't hear voices.'

'I don't believe you. You're lying.'

Albert cupped a hand behind his ear. 'Pardon? I can't hear your voice. You'll have to write any disparaging stuff down.'

Tony released a sigh and leant back in his chair. 'Why do you need a sick note?'

'Don't hear voices.'

Tony cast a checking look. 'Albert, truthfully.'

'Got kicked off the dole.'

'Why?'

'I was becoming an icon to skivers. They had to cut me down. It was political. I think the decision came from the very top. If you need any help spelling paranoid delusions, just pass the sick note over to me.'

Tony showed his disrespect, impatience and reluctant amusement with a pursed smile, and indicated with a flutter of his hand that it was time for Albert to leave. 'Albert, as I said to Ron the other day, you've got a mind as cunning as most any ever devised by nature. Use it for work instead of play and you'll go far.'

'I've already gone further than I'd ever planned,' said Albert, his eyes turning to the floor.

'If you want a sick note, you should pitch for depression. I could give you a three month sick note right now, and arrange counselling for you. Get to the bottom of why you waste your life away. There's a very good woman who works here who has a solid record in helping depressives overcome their disability.'

'I'm not depressed,' insisted Albert quietly, 'I'm melancholic.'

'I can't put melancholic down,' stated Tony, pulling a pad of sick notes out from his desk drawer, poising his pen above them.

'So just do a drawing on it of me looking wistful — people will get the idea,' suggested Albert, but seeing no promise of compromise in Tony's expression. 'I smashed up fourteen blue cars on the way down here,' he tried, but the poised pen got no nearer to the sick note. 'Cutting my knob off later.' Still no movement. 'Woof.' Nothing — the pen stayed two inches above the pad.

'Depressed?' offered Tony, one last time.

'Melancholic,' maintained Albert.

The pad went back into the drawer.

'Fucking depressed now,' muttered Albert to himself on the way home. What was he going to do? How was he going to get by? Even though, just like normal people, he'd got up before noon, his new life had come to naught. What did other people do? *Could* he get

152

a job? Was stock-market speculation *that* anathema to him? What was he going to eat? What did cat taste like? How many friends did he have who would give him food? How long would they stay his friends? How could he pay the rent? Could he write a best seller before Ron sold the computer? Was there still gold to be viably panned in the Welsh mountains? How much could he sell one of his kidneys for? Just exactly how many millions of pounds worth of space-race hardware was sitting on the moon waiting to be salvaged by the first person enterprising enough to get there with a transit van?

Maybe his Housing Benefit *would* keep coming? Some glorious bureaucratic incompetence? That would be enough. So long as he could pay the rent, he could eat Ron's leftovers and go back to cutting his own hair.

As soon as he got back to his flat, Albert phoned the Housing Benefit office to check on the status of his claim, constructing a reason for the enquiry that didn't reveal his dole disallowance. The call told that his claim had been stopped because authorisation from Social Security had been withdrawn.

Shit. It had all come to an end. This was reality day.

He went to his dark room and lay on his bed in sullen contemplation, niggled by growing feelings of inadequacy and ineffectuality. He was wanker, it was now clear to him. A wanker with a personality so crap and self-defeating he couldn't even make it to mental. Christ, that sick note had been his for the taking, but he'd still fucked it. He wouldn't even have had to go on the therapy suggested — he was sure he could have skived it, easily enough. He was a complete wanker. Wanker. Wanker. Wanker. But his mood suddenly changed. A steely resolve to succeed emerged: he had said he was going to write a novel, so he fucking would. A proper one — hundred pages at least. And he'd make it brilliant too, and a best seller, just to fuck Ron off. And Tony — Tony needed fucking off too. He lifted his head up and looked at his potentially word processing computer, and in the dimness, it murkily appeared to him like some deep, brooding power: forbidding, yet beckoning.

This was it, he resolved, this was bloody it: he was going to make a start on a proper book. A real start on a real book. A new life. A life of work. A life of success. A life of industry. A life of enterprise. This really was bloody it: no more wasting time. This really was bloody it: there was no more time left *to* waste. But was this positivity just further delusion? Fuck it: even if it was, he had no choice. A best seller was the only profitable thing he could realistically do without ever getting up early or talking to people.

He lay his head back down to think. He was going to *plan* this proper, sensible literary endeavour. First, he needed a plot. No, first he needed to think about what his market should be. He knew about science, and had already written two science fiction micro-novels, so science fiction it would be. Something for geeks. As for the plot, after much uncharacteristic dedication and application, lying on his bed he came up with this idea:

Cosmologists profess that the universe began from a single point in a nothingness vacuum. Well, not quite nothingness, for, they also profess, in the quantum world, vacuums are teeming with fleeting *somethings*. In the quantum world, there are *real* particles, electrons and such, that exist indefinitely, and there are also *virtual* particles, particles which spring into existence on *borrowed* energy. From where is this energy borrowed? From nowhere, that's where. Something from nothing.

These ghost particles constantly spring from nowhere, then return to oblivion, owing their brief existence to that phenomenon of uncertainty first uncovered by the physicist, Heisenberg. They are the products of random statistical fluctuations in energy levels. Over a period of time – the merest, shortest of time – these fluctuations – expected statistical quirks – balance out: for every plus, there's a minus, so to speak. It's like rolling a die: do it ten billion times and gross statistical anomalies become statistically unlikely – *but not impossible*.

Once, just once that we know of, the borrowed energy was not immediately paid back. The virtual entity defied the persuasion of statistics, inflated ... and lo! the universe was born.

Something from nothing.

Thus the universe is but a gross statistical anomaly, and every point in space has the frightening potential to spawn a freak universe of its own – honest.

And, in a way, although the universe seems to us to be a whole lot of something, it is still nothing, for when the energies of the whole system are considered, they are found to cancel wonderfully, leaving nothing. Thus we, the human race, are perhaps no more than opportunists in a cosmic hiccup.

Lying in bedroom dimness, Albert saw his plot unfold before his inner eye like some mighty vista. The grand theme was to do with exploiting the potential of the quantum vacuum for unlimited

154

energy production. He imagined a race of advanced creatures who had just discovered how to conjure somethings from nothings. They had become Lords of Mathematics. They had learned how to load the dice of uncertainty whichever way they chose. Now, at last, they could do great things.

So one day a group of the most brilliant creature scientists came together to see if they could apply their new mathematical powers to some practical problems. First, they designed and built a bomb that would create a staggeringly big bang — the *ultimate* big bang. Of course no one intended to use this ultimate bomb because it would destroy everything, but they built it all the same. Their planet's army loved the bomb, stored it, and soon even asked for more like it. Further ultimate bombs were duly supplied. This made a lot of the planet's creatures very uneasy, but their leaders assured them that the bombs would never be used, which, it transpired, was true.

Then the scientists looked at their noble civilisation's energy production methods, and perceived there was much room for improvement. Their existing power stations were scientifically simple but technologically sound fusion reactors. At one end they took in hydrogen, the most abundant element in the universe. Out the other end was excreted harmless helium, and all the energy these creatures needed to live blissfully comfortable lives. These reactors were so reliable that not one had failed, caused an injury or polluted their beautiful planet for nearly a thousand years.

One day they announced a plan to replace the hundreds of small fusion reactors scattered higgledy-piggledy about their planet with one enormous centralised Quantum Vacuum Exploiter. So, with much excitement, a new type of power station was duly designed, one that created a mini-universe in its reactor, sucked from that universe what energy it could practically get — which was a jaw-dropping lot — then snuffed that universe out before it ran out of control and inflated at close to the speed of light. It snuffed out the created universe by buggering about with its mathematics so that it merely faded away without so much as a fizz. A dampening equation was injected.

Then it promptly created another universe.

This cycle was repeated once every millionth of a second.

These creatures really were terribly good with numbers and symbols.

And they had great confidence in their machines.

The reactor worked admirably. It gave just as much energy to the creatures of the planet as they had enjoyed before, and it could give a lot more if they needed it, which they never did. It worked admirably, that is, until the day when some of the custom mathematics leaked out because an engineer called Upal had neglected to program one of the site computers properly. Upal's beloved creature friend had left him for another creature that day, and he was very unhappy. These creatures had life spans of thousands of years, yet it was almost unheard of for a relationship to break up. They were faithful creatures. So confused was Upal that day, he was not able to concentrate to his normally high alien standard. In fact, he was heartbroken and wanted to cry.

The computer was not a particularly intelligent one. It didn't have to be for the small part it played in the big show. Nevertheless, it tried — as its operating protocol demanded — to alert Upal to query the unusual instructions it had been given, wanting its programming corroborated. Earlier in the day, however, Upal had turned down all the warning systems because the occasional bleeps they made when everything was hunky-dory had begun to irritate him. Besides, like everyone else, Upal believed that the new reactor was as safe as houses. So the computer presented Upal with a message on a screen. Through its cameras, it could see him staring at the message, but he did not respond. The computer thought about this as best it could, even though it wasn't the kind of thinking it had been designed to do. It thought harder and harder, so hard it evolved new neural nets just to explore the meaning of this unprecedented situation, smartening itself up. Eventually, it got so smart it decided this: it felt embarrassed to have made a fuss.

Concluding that it must have been given the right instructions after all, and that Upal was just being polite in ignoring the message, the computer, with computer quickness, followed the faulty programming to the letter, number and symbol. It didn't know about creature love and how it could befuddle organic brains. It had not been told. It had not been thought necessary.

This computer had a routine but crucial role to play in the functioning of the power station. Its job was to govern the dimensional shielding that kept new universe and old universe apart. It achieved this by maintaining a ten dimensional sphere around the created universe. This sphere was forever twisting in on itself like a revolving spiral. Forever going into its own centre. Forever evaginating.

When the computer finally swung into action, because of the

156

remiss programming, it allowed a wisp of custom mathematics to leak out of the reactor core. This wisp of poisonous mathematics proceeded to corrupt and contaminate the real universe in all directions at the speed of light. No one could see this tsunami of dangerous mathematics coming, so no one was ready to try to counter and cure it with an anti-equation. And once the expanding wave of custom mathematics arrived, it was too late: it made that thing which is perceived as the electromagnetic force ten trillion, trillion times stronger in the real universe, and all atoms the wave swept over collapsed into neutrons.

All life ended, and Albert sat up.

Well, there it was, an acceptable plot for a geeky science fiction novel, and it even had a moral to it.

He looked at his deeply brooding computer.

Right: action — now.

Having seriously decided what needed to be done, and when to do it, Albert felt like half the task had already been achieved . He was so pleased with this fraction of accomplishment, he decided to give himself the rest of the day off. Lying back on the bed for a well-deserved rest, he glanced up and, in dimness, saw the notice he'd taped to the ceiling the night before:

GET UP, YOU
LAZY BASTARD!

He closed his eyes and tried to ignore it.

He quickly succeeded in ignoring it.

He felt uncomfortable about ignoring it. He was supposed to be a cunning genius, after all: he should be working.

He tried to ignore the uncomfortable feeling that came from successfully ignoring the message and his genius.

He couldn't.

Aw, fuck it, he thought, I'm too intelligent to sleep.

So, burdened by what he had often been told was genius, Albert was compelled to get back off the bed. Grasping the nettle, he strode to his computer, switched it on, and almost began writing his proper, full-length science fiction book there and then. He did actually head a page CHAPTER ONE, and he did actually plan on this first chapter being as long as the whole of his last novel, but one hundred pages quickly began to feel like a ten-year career strategy, unlike his two previous efforts which had just been distractions before bedtime. A forced marathon rather than a whimsical gambol to a fairground.

In short, it felt like a job.

He lay back on his bed.

No, he wouldn't quit. He had to do it. It was his only hope.

He returned to the keyboard.

Fifteen minutes later, he hadn't thought of a suitable sentence with which to begin his career as a proper novelist. Somehow, when it was work, it just wouldn't flow. Beginning to feel a little anxious, he wondered if he was not quite the genius some people thought he was. Luckily, he was spared further creative self-doubt by Jackie tapping on his window. He let her in. She was having a day off work, and had called to say hello — say what a good time he'd missed in Newcastle on Sunday night — and see if he wanted to accompany her on a shopping trip to Gateshead.

'I can't,' he bemoaned, now lying on the bed again, staring at the ceiling, 'I'm too busy to shop.'

'What the fuck are you talking about?' said Jackie, dragging a chair to the bedside.

Albert explained that looming homelessness decreed he had to forge a proper novel because the rent would need paying.

'I thought the dole paid your rent?'

He told her what had befallen him on the fiscal side since they'd last met — that he'd been sacked from idleness.

'Sacked from the dole?' exclaimed Jackie in stunned disbelief. 'You're kidding? Why?'

'I didn't make the grade. Not go-getting enough for the dole.'

Jackie earnestly implored, 'Albert, how are you going to live?'

'Nuts and berries and carrion and things I'll steal from Ron's plate.'

'Albert,' she exclaimed in sudden frustration, 'stop avoiding life and face the real world.'

'I'd be a fool to start doing that now.'

'You're living in denial, Albert,' she declared, as if it presented a personal injury to her.

'I've never lived in denial,' answered Albert, staring at the murky ceiling, repeating a joke he'd once heard. 'I've lived in d'Thames and d'Mississippi, but never in denial.'

Jackie drew in a deep breath and released it as a sigh. 'You *are* going to have to face the real world... and get a job.'

'I'm unemployable.'

'Bullshit. Albert, with your awesome mind there's a thousand things you could do.'

'I could never take any of that role playing shit seriously.'

'What role playing shit?' demanded Jackie.

Albert sat up, and put his feet on the floor. 'It's all fucking role playing,' he insisted, sounding close to resentful and virulent. 'Act interested at the interview and don't wear a T-shirt that alludes to suicide. Say this not that to a customer. Write this, not that on a report. Don't tell the boss to fuck himself.'

'Well you shouldn't tell the boss to fuck himself.'

'That's how the nazis held on to power,' grumbled Albert, now staring at the floor.

'Oh my God!' cried Jackie, throwing her hands in the air, 'that's so silly.'

'See, told you I can never be serious,' he said, with a minor air of victory, but still staring at the floor. 'People being serious — I find *that* so silly.'

Jackie looked at him, and her tone became gentler. 'Albert, seriously, you *are* going to have to get a job.'

He lay back on the bed and looked at the ceiling. 'Why? I'll be rich when my novel's published.'

'Denial,' she said, with exasperation that was close to tearful. 'You're living in denial.'

'But the scenery's just how I like it.'

She gave up. Gave up trying to motivate him. Gave up even trying to get him to go shopping with her, and left him with an uncertain promise to drop by later.

After Jackie left, Albert again tried to start his new novel, but it just seemed so fucking daunting, and he was in no mood to be daunted. He just couldn't think of a decent line to start it all with. Maybe he should just put a line down anyway? he thought. Maybe that's how the professionals did it?

Peep jumped up on the table and became pushy regarding her dinner, treading on the keyboard to rub her face against Albert's. Her paws typed what was nearly a swear word, which made him smile with pride. And if almost typing a swear word didn't deserve gastronomic reward, what did? he thought.

Going into the kitchen, he discovered, with dismay, that beyond a modest spoonful in an already open can, there was no more cat food in stock. Fuck, he hadn't thought about this before: how would Peep get by now that he had no income? Moreover, although he had enough food to satisfy his own needs for a few days, crunch time had *already come* for Peep — having eaten her meagre meal, she was now looking soulfully at him, wondering where the rest of her dinner was.

Viewing his cat, Albert got real and resolved to get a job at once — any job. No, fuck it, no job — he had to devote his time to his novel. The cat could eat some of Ron's hamburgers.

Burgers constituted much of Ron's diet. Ron reckoned that the way he made them, with plenty of salad in a thick bun, they were a perfectly balanced meal. Also, they were quick. Thus the freezer always contained bags of processed beef cakes. Separating one of these chilly cakes from its companions, Albert defrosted it under the grill before placing it in Peep's bowl. Peep ran to it, balked, sniffed it suspiciously, then turned away, looking bewildered and betrayed.

Try as he might, Albert couldn't make the animal regard the burger as food.

He sat at the table and fretted. Standing next to her bowl, Peep now looked at him, imploring him with her piercing yellow eyes. Then she began meowing — quiet little tremulous meows that were breaking his heart. Fuck it, he *had* to get a job, and right away.

1.14
Fucking Idiot

Albert Fox, 24, retired paper boy, education dropout, social misfit and reputed genius, had resolved to find employment after ten years absence from the job market.

A job. A job. Where did people find jobs? The Jobcentre, but that was out of the question — Michelle worked there. A newspaper — look in a newspaper. He didn't have a newspaper, and didn't have a penny with which to buy one.

Fuck.

Wait a minute: today was Tuesday. On Tuesdays, the Durham Advertiser arrived. It was the local free paper, and it had jobs in it. It might be in the letterbox now.

It was.

Bringing the paper back into the living room, part of Albert felt like he'd become an adult, or something. He was putting away the unrealistic, and accepting the yoke of reality, just like most everyone else in the world. The other, quietly nagging, part of him suspected he was just playing another delusory game with himself.

Unfolding the paper, the front page headline caught his eye: *UFO BUZZES CATHEDRAL*. According to the report, the light he'd seen on Friday had caused dozens of people to call the police. One eye-witness was quoted thus: "It was a long, thin craft that hovered for sometime before moving away at great speed."

Nowhere in the article was it stated that the "object" had obviously been a simple flare.

Albert turned to the Situations Vacant pages, and soon became demoralised. Everything looked so dull and serious — more like prison sentences than occupations — and applying for any one of them promised to involve a week's work in itself. Besides, every employer seemed to want experience, and he'd only ever delivered newspapers in his life, and that was when he'd been at school. And as for the CV's requested, he knew his wouldn't impress a chicken.

But then he saw it: *Car Cleaner wanted. £40 per day. Phone Carsparkle for immediate start.*

Bingo. No CV's. No application forms. No references. No experience. This was his big break. He could clean a car, no sweat — he'd seen Ron do it often enough, and it never made him sweat. Better than sitting behind a desk in a suit feeling like a cunt, for sure. It had to be as near to his ideal, subversion-limited job of tightening one bolt on an assemblage as he'd ever be likely to find in the post-industrial world. Car cleaner — lovely little job. Just him, a soft rag, some lightly-scented polish, and a limited, repetitive, Zen-like motion that would surely draw him into contemplation of his own essential nature to the exclusion of all else, leading to pure enlightenment. £40 a day, too.

He phoned.

'Carsparkle,' said a woman, without sparkle.

'I'm phoning about the car cleaning job.'

'Can you make it in for an interview at three o'clock?'

Albert balked. It wasn't fair. He hadn't been given enough time to brace himself for the crashing weight of the yoke of reality. 'Er, you mean three o'clock today?'

She could sense his fear, he was sure.

'Three-thirty if three's too early.'

'Okay, three-thirty.'

'Do you know where we are?'

'No idea.'

'Blackheath Rise. Directly opposite the Vauxhall dealership.'

'Think I know the road.'

'See you at three-thirty,' she presumed.

'Maybe we should make it four—'

She'd already put the phone down.

Putting his own phone down, Albert felt anxious yet increasingly... increasingly exhilarated. He'd done it! He'd got a job, as good as. A perfect, gentle little job. For Peep's sake, he was going to go to that fucking interview, say nothing goofy or smart, and do the work. Even if it was boring, how much worse could it be than staring at his ceiling all day long? And all the petty miseries of hardupishment would be alleviated, too.

Three-thirty. If he had a cup of tea, then took the picturesque route into town, it would be close to three-thirty by the time he got to Blackheath Rise.

*

Upon ascending from the riverside on to Blackheath Rise, Albert easily located the Vauxhall dealership, but directly opposite it was a tyre and exhaust business, not Carsparkle. Perhaps the two were the same? he wondered. He drew nearer to the cavernous, new-built warehouse-style garage, with its dark mouth open to the road; its cold breath rubbery and oily. Nope. Nothing carwashy going on in

162

there. So where was Carsparkle with its immaculately kept Japanese Zen garden, within which a single quietly contemplative vehicle awaited his patient attention?

Then he saw a sign:

CARSPARKLE
FULL VALETING CAR WASH
DRIVE-THROUGH
£6

The sign indicated that interested parties should proceed around to the back of the tyre business.

Albert proceeded.

Albert halted — shocked. Suddenly in view was a demonic facility for destroying souls. Carsparkle was not a gentle Zen opportunity, but rather a furious, maddening, watery hell conjured by some engineering-minded zealous descendent of Dante. Contained within a large, open-sided building was a spraying, spuming, tyrannical tunnel. Smirking, power-tripping owners drove their cars through this angry contrivance, where at various stations grim-faced, soaking-wet thralls shammied and squeegeed at a pace that suggested the Dark One himself was due any moment on a bad-tempered inspection tour.

Where he'd halted was as close as he intended to get to the frightful industry, yet he had a morbid fascination with it all. Work. That was work. They did that all day, every day. But the work wasn't the most dreadful aspect: it was the workers. Six were slaving in pairs, and each, to a lesser or greater extent, had criminal features. The pair deepest into the satanic construction — grim-faced, with close-cropped hair — looked to be in their early thirties. These two seemed to be trying to out-scare each other by way of tattoos. Theirs seemed to be the hardest job, rubbing off stubborn dirt while the car remained under a multi-directional torrent fit to disperse a drunken riot. When they stepped back and gave the signal, the driver proceeded to the next pair, who were about his own age and looked like they were having a reluctant bash at going straight after a life of harsh correction. Their job seemed to be the removal of excess water and window squeegeeing. Just outside the deafening, sibilant tunnel, two slight young lads with short, gelled-down fringes dried the cars.

163

These grinning youngsters actually seemed to enjoy it all, deriving occasional additional pleasure from flicking their cloths at each other — probably some gay thing, thought Albert.

Working here would be insufferable, Albert knew. Never mind the early starts and dragging hours. Never mind the freezing water. Never mind the hospital-green *I'm a Carsparkler!* T-shirts. It was the conversations that he dreaded most. And the fights — he'd fare better in a bear pit. Two minutes into his first day, he knew he'd be dodging the tattooed fists of outraged colleagues.

Parked nearby was a customised black hatchback car. Four young men wearing baseball caps were either admiring it or considering breaking into it. One of them began taking a worrying interest in Albert, and came over to him before Albert thought to make discretion the greater part of his valour.

'You work here?' asked Albert, having just surmised that likelihood.

The man, appearing to be in his late twenties, wore thick gold chains and heavy gold rings, and looked like a slow reader. He also looked like he could be the gym-attending older brother of the lads drying the cars.

'Aye. The manager. What y'after?'

'I've come about the car cleaner job,' Albert explained, dejectedly aware that, to avoid any possible misconception, he'd just committed himself to an interview.

It may have been Carsparkle's manager's regular way of greeting prospective employees, but upon a quick scan, he produced an expression that suggested he was about as happy to have Albert as a candidate as Albert was to be one. Nevertheless, he nodded Albert to follow him, leading him to within feet of the hissing, gushing, hair-spoiling hell.

Albert felt a surging desire to make a do-or-die bolt for it.

'Dave! Dave!' shouted the manager to the most tattooed of the workers.

Dave left the car he was working on. A line of water drops that had collected along his prominent brow ridge ran off when he tilted his head to listen to the manager shouting in his ear. The message relayed, Dave gave Albert his own disdainful scan, then nodded for him to follow him into a small office.

Some water splashed on to Albert's hair, spurring him to make a bid for dryness, freedom and life. 'Forget it, mate,' he shouted, waving his hands to indicate play was over, and making a rapid exit.

They were stunned. A candidate literally fleeing was obviously a first, and, speechless, they stood watching him pace away. Their consternation was short-lived, however, and before Albert had made twenty steps, the manager shouted, 'Go on, run home!'

And Albert nearly did. Nearly ran all the way back to his hairdryer. But once he was on the street again, heading down to the river, calm returned. That had been close. Too close. Never apply for a grown-up job again, he told himself, not while you still know how to make a noose.

Along the riverbank, he paused to sit on his favourite bench under the shadow of the cathedral. Looking across the water, he reflected upon how the day wasn't really happening for him. And he'd tried so hard, too. It was un-fucking-fair, that's what it was. Worse still, Peep would be even hungrier when he got home. This was ridiculous – he was living in one of the most affluent nations on earth, was young and able-bodied to boot, yet couldn't muster forty pence for a can of cat food (or sixty pence if he bought it from the over-priced shop near his street). Just how did other people cope? he wondered.

'Life's a never-unfolding mystery to me,' he said to a large, yellow leaf that fluttered into his lap.

Maybe it really was time to launch that Herbal Abortion Kit scam he'd recently been mentally developing, he mused. Abortion – nature's gentle way, with no chemicals and definitely no preservatives. He could throw in a dedicated astrology premium rate advice line, too, so that the buyers could find the most propitious day for New Age termination. Or maybe he should dust off that idea of his for the establishment of a whole new alternative therapy: Placebo Therapy – gently works with the body's natural healing abilities without the need for toxic drugs.

Maybe.

He set off walking again, falling in longing with three passing women before leaving the riverside. He wistfully thought that if they only knew how deep and sensitive he was, with wan, soulful looks they would wordlessly hand him money for his cat, and lightly touch his face before continuing on their mysterious way, never to be forgotten by him.

That was the trouble: he never did forget. When it came to beautiful ladies, he could painfully recall fleeting moments from ten years back as clearly as he could recall the grim face of Dave from five minutes ago.

165

Poets suffer bright, painful glimpses of the past.

Undermined by the three indelible visions, Albert felt Melancholy's chill hand slipping into his once again, and his homeward step became more of a trudge. A cheerless while later, passing the over-priced shop, he stopped to look covetously at the cat food through the window, wondering if he dared shoplift. Should he really risk a criminal record for something so pathetic as a can of Whiskas? No. It was genocide or nothing for him.

There it was again, his stupid all-or-nothing pride.

Hold on, he thought: he could massacre the shopkeeper and his family, *then* steal the cat food. Least that way his charge sheet wouldn't make him look like a sissy. And if he was really lucky, in court, the cat food theft would be completely overlooked.

His spirits suddenly soared! Deliverance! Advertised in the window was a way he could feed his cat that didn't rely on the unrealistic perspicacity of facially fortunate wandering women, or murder: paper round — evenings only.

Evenings only.

It had been the inhuman morning rounds that had tripped him up ten years back, but he was sure he could hold down an evening round. Delivering papers was a bit of a social embarrassment at his age, but for his cat, he cast his pride aside and entered the shop.

Albert's local shop was run by a balding, ruddy, fair, average-sized man in his late forties. He had been a milkman in his native Newcastle, moving to Durham when he'd married, changing his occupation to allow him more time with his wife and two daughters. As with all shops of its ilk, his made much of its money from selling things people had forgotten to buy at the supermarket, at a mark up.

As Albert approached the barricade of sweets that bolstered the counter, the shopkeeper looked up from some paperwork.

'All right. Haven't seen you in a while,' he said in his sing-songy Geordie.

'Been away,' answered Albert, falling into the rhythm of lies he reserved to ease such encounters. 'Travelling.'

'Anywhere nice?'

'Sunderland.' Damn it, he was supposed to be getting a job, not playing games. Trying to inject keenness into his diction, he immediately diverted the shopkeeper with, 'I'm interested in the job advertised in your window.'

The shopkeeper was puzzled. 'What job?'

'Paper round,' explained Albert.

'Nah, paper roonds is for school kids, man.'

Albert nearly said, "That's all right, I'm frozen in immaturity, ask anyone with no true depth perception", but he held back. Instead, he just looked at the shopkeeper, expectantly and a bit pathetically.

'You seriously want a paper roond?'

'Evenings only,' stipulated Albert, careful to ward off some ghastly misunderstanding that might eventually necessitate alarm clocks and dangerous quantities of amphetamines.

The shopkeeper was a man who seldom had ideas, but when one came along he mistrusted it. Before his wife left him for a caravan-owning gas fitter, she used to tell him he had feet of clay, which, after some hard pondering, he took as a compliment, saying that if they just kept things regular and safe, then their life would be regular and safe too. But now he was having an idea — an unusual idea, to boot — and didn't much like it.

He would think it through in more detail.

So the shopkeeper regarded Albert coolly for a moment, suspiciously comparing him with his existing oldest paperboy, who was still at school and not nearly as tall. Moreover, this applicant was older than any paperboy he'd ever heard about. Regardless, he was desperate to fill any of the four rounds that had arisen after half his work force had unexpectedly joined a junior football team that practised most evenings. Kids just didn't want part-time jobs any more, he understood. Too much pocket money being handed out. So far, some of his other, steadier, lads had done double evening rounds, and sometimes he'd even had his daughters — one fourteen, one ten — going out to do a round together. But today was a particularly bad day: none of his lads had volunteered for the extra work; the fourteen-year-old daughter was poorly; and the ten-year-old was too young to do it on her own. He'd briefly considered shutting up shop to do the round himself, but had dismissed the notion, reminding himself that the shop had priority. Besides, a stock delivery was due. Thus, he'd resigned himself to having to wait until seven, when his evening assistant arrived, then going out himself to do the round late. Now, however, strange salvation seemed to have arrived.

'Doesn't pay much money,' he cautiously said.

'Didn't think it would,' returned Albert, glancing at the cat food.

'Two poond an evening.'

'A fortune to me.'

'Student?'

'Yeah,' lied Albert. 'I really just need to supplement my student loan a bit.'

The shopkeeper weighed things up again. It was getting late. The papers would have to be delivered soon or he'd upset loyal customers, and loyal customers kept things regular and safe. He couldn't do it himself until seven. He couldn't let his ten-year-old do it on her own, if only because the bag would be too heavy for her. But this geezer couldn't do it straight off, since he didn't know the round, and the papers had not been fully marked with street names, just shorthand codes. He started having another unusual idea, and liked it even less... but why not? He knew the geezer — had served him a hundred times. Even knew where he lived — had seen him going in and out of his house a dozen times. And it wasn't as if he was some seedy old man. He was a handsome young student.

'Can y'start now?'

'Raring to go,' said Albert, suspecting he looked otherwise.

After a final, cautious appraisal, the shopkeeper readied his pencil. 'What's the name?'

'Albert Fox.'

'Devon Road, isn't it?'

'Yeah. 17.'

'Y'll have t' be shown the roond first.'

'Okay.'

The shopkeeper now took the worrying plunge. 'Ah cannat leave the shop t'day, like, so me daughter'll have t'show y' the streets.'

'Okay.'

Opening a door behind him, the shopkeeper shouted up a stairwell. 'Angel, put y'coat on and come doon, darlin'.'

'Coming,' answered a child.

Fuck! He'd got a job. A job he could countenance. Perfect little job — working on his own after today. Just him, a bag, and a gentle, Zen wander around. And by the end of the wander he'd have earned enough to feed his cat for a day. It might even be enough to feed himself, too. Two pound an evening for five, maybe six evenings a week might indeed be enough to survive on. Wouldn't pay the rent, but he could ride that one out for a good while, he was sure, until something turned up.

'She's a clever little lass,' explained the shopkeeper. 'Top of her

168

class. Loves school.'

Clomping noises suggested the child was on her way down. The shopkeeper stepped into the stairwell to intercept her, delivering some kind of hushed advice. Scant seconds later he emerged with her, arranging her red padded nylon jacket better. 'This is Albert. Could you show him the Neville's Cross roond, little angel?'

'Hi,' said little angel to Albert, in an accent that was thin compared to her father's.

'Hi,' returned Albert, even though he never felt comfortable saying "hi", or "guy", for that matter.

'She's called Grace,' said the shopkeeper soberly to Albert. 'Make sure nowt happens to her.'

Grace had blonde hair cut halfway between sweet and tomboyish; a little smudge of a nose that one day might extend to pretty; and pouting lips. Coming out from behind the counter and going to wait by the shop door, she had a distracted air about her, and seemed quite untroubled at the prospect of having to spend time in the company of an unknown man dressed somewhat like a Victorian pallbearer.

'They're in order,' explained the shopkeeper, handing Albert a heavy canvas bag of papers, 'but not fully street marked. Grace'll show y'which numbers belong t'which streets. Come back with the bag when y'finished. All the best.'

Albert slung the bag across his shoulder and immediately worried the rubbing might degenerate the fabric of his cool coat.

Grace was now standing outside the shop, waiting, and when Albert emerged with his workload, she smiled. 'This way,' she said. Soon, a twenty yard gap lay between them, and she stopped to look behind, allowing him to almost catch up before walking on again. A minute later, she was once more compelled to stop. 'Hurry up, or it'll be dark before we've finished.'

'I'm a poet. I have to dawdle.'

He was about to draw level with her when she walked on again, this time with a hint of surly impatience, and holding her hands more stiffly in her jacket pockets. Suddenly thinking of Peep's vacuous tummy, he briefly experimented with increasing his pace while Grace's back was turned, but it just didn't suit him.

'Come on,' she huffed, standing at the end of the street, where it joined a main road.

Before Albert reached where she had stood, she had already crossed the road. He followed, but ended up stuck in the middle, some traffic lights further along having changed to green.

'Come on,' urged Grace. 'Run.'

Now trapped between two fast-flowing rivers of cars, Albert looked across to Grace and bleated like a lost new-born lamb. 'Behh-eh-eh-eh-eh.' God, he never realised he could bleat so authentically and pathetically, and was quite taken with the sound. 'Behh-eh-eh-eh-eh,' he vocalised again, still stranded. This talent could change his life. Now wan ladies *would* hand him money.

Grace looked ill at ease — confused, but mostly embarrassed and annoyed.

Finally, the traffic relented, and Albert dawdled across, but Grace was already on the march again. 'Behh-eh-eh-eh-eh,' he called out to her, with added distress, but she didn't look behind once until, minutes later, she stopped outside a house, waiting for him to catch up.

'Take out the first paper and check it's got fourteen written on,' she said curtly as he lazily approached.

Albert took out the inside paper.

'Other side,' said Grace despairingly.

He now took out the correct newspaper, but couldn't resist having a little read as he followed Grace up the council house's short garden path.

'Deliver it, not read it,' instructed Grace on the doorstep.

'Oh, sorry,' said Albert, folding it in preparation. Pet smells leaked from the house when he lifted the letterbox flap. Turning to Grace, he mused, 'Where do smells go?'

Grace wasn't in a musing mood.

'What?'

'Smells. Odours have been emanating for billions of years, so where do they all go?'

If Grace had been funny, she might have answered "France" or "Old people's trousers". If she'd been a Republican, she might have answered, "the Queen's fanny". But she said, 'Take out the next one.'

The next one was a magazine — *Practical Photography*. This looked tempting too, and Albert consequently received another rebuke.

'What's written on it?' asked Grace after telling him off.

'Three C S.'

'That means three Charlton Street,' she explained, pointing across the road. 'We do Charlton Street now, then come back to do the rest of this street.'

Crossing the road, Albert was informed that three Charlton Street was on the second floor of the ten-storey tower block ahead. As Grace led the way to the entrance, he pulled out the next few papers and discovered he had to deliver to number twenty — on the top floor, he reckoned. At the entrance, Grace turned and saw Albert lying on the path, staring up at the darkening, clouded October sky. She went back and glared disapprovingly down at him.

'It's no good,' he said, 'I'll never make it to the summit. You'll have to press on without me. Best of British.'

Grace felt strong opinion welling up inside her. 'How old are you?' she asked contemptuously.

'I'm as old as hunger.'

'You act like a little kid.'

Albert got up and replaced the papers he'd prematurely taken out, and Grace went on ahead again, into the tower block. Following her, he found her waiting outside the door of number three, where she wordlessly and petulantly delved into his bag, retrieved the outermost paper and shoved it through the letterbox.

'What's the next number?' she huffed.

Albert took out the next paper and suspected some mistake. 'Er, hold on.'

The door of number three opened and a middle-age man came out, holding the paper Grace had just pushed through his letterbox. 'Not ours,' he informed Albert.

'Oh, sorry,' said Albert, handing him *Practical Photography* in exchange. 'They've got a bit mixed up.'

As soon as the man closed his door, Grace scornfully rounded on Albert. 'You fucking idiot,' she cussed, glowering and sullen. 'Show me the papers.' Delving stormily into the bag, she determined which floor they had to go to next, and went on up the stairs. 'Come on.'

What was it with him and kids? wondered Albert as he followed her. He didn't meet many, but when he did they never gave him a feather's weight of respect or often even civility. Was there some kind of playground grapevine that passed his name around as a sissy suitable for disrespectful derision? Maybe he should get a tattoo, he mused.

Suddenly thinking about Peep's poor tummy again, he thought he'd better try to straighten things with Grace. His home-made wit and charm hadn't made much headway, so he thought he'd try a store-bought joke — one of the few jokes he could ever remember. 'Grace,' he called up the stairwell, 'what side of a dog has the most hair?'

No reply, so he tried again.

No reply.

When he reached her, waiting on the seventh floor, he provided the answer: 'The outside.'

Nothing. Not a flicker of humanity crossed the sullen face of Grace. Maybe she was related to dole office Michelle? Had to be, he reckoned. There had to be a blood connection somewhere — the town wasn't big enough for two such bitchy gene lines to have arisen independently.

He took out the next paper. 'Make sure it's the right one,' ordered Grace as he was about to deliver it, so he defiantly closed his eyes before pushing it through the letterbox. He applied this blind-delivery method to each paper he delivered thereafter, although he was pretty sure the papers were now going into the right houses.

His attitude did not exactly meet with Grace's approval, and by the time they had finished the round, relations between them were as dark as the sky had become.

'Fucking idiot,' said Grace for about the fifteenth time when they began walking back.

Rolling up the now empty bag, Albert ignored her for about the fifteenth time.

'No wonder you're still a paperboy at your age.'

That did it. Directing a finger at her, he warned, 'Don't push it, titless.'

'I'll have tits soon, but you'll always be an idiot.'

Fuck, that retort was good, realised Albert. Too good. Unless it had been a fluke, he was no slanging match for her. 'Why don't you run on back to your crappy little shop?'

'Dad said I had to come back with you if it was dark. He worries.'

'Yeah, poor paedophiles,' muttered Albert.

It suddenly occurred to Albert that he was almost outpacing Grace. He was in a mood, he realised — no mood for dawdling. Pity, he thought, since a good dawdle would really piss her off now. So, instead, he further increased his speed, forcing her to sometimes ignominiously trot to keep up, which also had the happy effect of rendering her too breathless to slag him. However, by the time they reached the cathedral square, a literal stone's throw from the river and only a ten minute walk along busy pedestrian streets from the shop, he was beginning to breathe hard himself, and so eased back.

'Fucking idiot,' said Grace within seconds.

Albert immediately decided to take the longer riverbank route, turning unannounced in that steeply downward direction, trusting the mist, spooky trees and sparse lighting would dissuade Grace from following.

Although thrown off his tail a moment, Grace quickly caught up.

'Fucking idiot,' she said.

Now walking at a gentler pace beside the dark water, Albert became aware that Grace was looking up at him with a kind of disdainful curiosity. Just as she began to say something, he cut in, 'I'll hit you with a hammer if you say it again.'

'No you won't,' she defiantly asserted. 'Fucking idiot.'

As they continued on their way, the nature of Grace's disdainful scrutiny was soon revealed. 'Are you a puff?'

'I hope to be by the time you're sexually active,' returned Albert.

'Are you a puff? You talk like a puff.'

Albert didn't answer, and for some time they proceeded in silence, their windless, leaf-strewn way irregularly illuminated by weak, orange lamps that were often smothered in branches. Condensed evening mist dripped from overhanging boughs, as if the trees were weeping over some ancient sorrow, and beyond the edges of their dim path lay swallowing blackness.

'These woods are haunted, you know?' said Albert, with a touch of a fearful yet faraway air.

'Don't be stupid,' retorted Grace, with bad temper.

'It's true. They call this path the Path of Sorrow. An unhappy spirit wanders here. The Wedding Dress Lady. She threw herself into the river on her wedding day because the man she loved left her standing alone in the cathedral where they were due to be married. Once a year she appears, on the same night she died, one autumn, hundreds of years ago. That's why your dad didn't want you to walk home alone in the dark. He knows about her. All adults know about her. I saw her once when I was about your age.'

'No you didn't,' challenged Grace, but beginning to sound timid, and Albert knew he had her.

'I did see her — on a night just like this. I still have nightmares about it. She was all in white, like the day she died. Dripping wet, like she was when they pulled her cold body from the river. She came after me. Nearly caught me.'

'No she didn't,' asserted Grace unconvincingly, looking nervously around as they proceeded along the dim, shadowy path overhung with autumnal trees.

A large water drop fell on to her face, which she immediately rubbed away.

'They say the trees cry tears for her the night her ghost wanders,' murmured Albert, pretending not to have noticed the droplet event. 'When I saw her, I ran as fast as I could, but the trees seemed to stoop down and close in on me, like they were trying to help her catch me. Maybe the trees around here don't like children. Do you think trees can be evil?'

Grace didn't answer, but Albert felt her hold on to his coat, and she kept in touch thus until they were back on a regular street. She was silent, too, until back on the bright, busy street, "Fucking idiot" being her first, reproachful, utterance.

Back at the shop, Grace pushed open the door and went straight to a box of crisps. Pulling out a bag, she waved it at her father, who nodded his acknowledgement and consent. Albert entered just after her, receiving sullen looks from her as she fed herself.

'Took y'time,' remarked the shopkeeper. 'Any problems?'

'Easy-peasy,' said Albert, handing the bag over.

The shopkeeper took the bag, then wondered why Albert was still standing at the counter. 'Something up?'

'Wages,' reminded Albert.

'Nah, man, ah pay on Saturdays. Didn't ah mention that?'

'Fuck,' said Albert, realising his only strawberry had been pissed on.

The shopkeeper displayed immediate, but controlled, displeasure at Albert's utterance. 'Howay man,' he quietly urged, 'keep y'language doon in front of little angel, won't y'?'

Astonished, Albert gave little angel a look, and resolutely declared, 'Fucking won't.'

The shopkeeper came out from behind his barricade of sweets, marched to the door and held it open. 'This is private property. Y'not welcome here with unchristian language like that in front of the bairn.'

Apparently not in the least concerned to have been declared *person non grata*, Albert sauntered to a shelf and blatantly pocketed a can of Whiskas.

'Dad, he's taken some cat food,' reported Grace, through a mouthful or crisps.

'My wages,' stated Albert firmly to the shopkeeper. Proceeding to the door, passing Grace, he quietly taunted her. 'Wedding Dress Lady gets little girls in their sleep.'

'No she doesn't,' Grace blurted defiantly. 'Dad, he said he was going to hit me with a hammer.'

Dark outrage swept across the shopkeeper's face as Albert walked past him.

'He said what?'

"Unchristian" — now Albert remembered how Ron, sitting at the table in their living room one recent Sunday, had remarked that the local shopkeeper was going into the church across the street, yet the top shelf of his store was crammed with wank mags.

What a shitty Tuesday it was turning out to be, thought Albert as he walked the short journey back to his flat, and it was still only six o'clock. He couldn't remember a shittier one, except, perhaps, that day he'd sat on dog shit. But had that been a Tuesday? He couldn't remember.

From his deep coat pocket, he took out the can of cat food, and a small smile of victory came to his face. This smile persisted even after he conceded that a single can of pet food did not in any way represent a successful life, or even a successful day, in the fourth richest nation on earth. The smile did fade, however, when he further conceded that it wouldn't even represent much of a success in a third world country.

Maybe Jackie had speculated right? Maybe his coping mechanism, rather than being weak or absent, was really actually too strong for his own good?

When Albert stepped into his house's entrance hall, Harry was sitting on the lower stairs with a can of lager. As ever, Harry's door keys were hanging from his neck, occasionally clanging against his lager can. Three cigarette stubs protruded from the drooping corner of his mouth. Each was unlit and of a different length. Albert ignored him, save only to reflect that the washed-out old drunk was actually doing better in life's struggle than he was. Harry had a — presumably secure — flat. Harry also had a warm jumper, which he himself had never had.

Meowing for food, Peep loped up to him when he entered his flat. Not stopping to take his coat off first, in the kitchen he cleaned the beefburger out of the cat's bowl, and replaced it with Whiskas *Duck and Lamb in Jelly*, which met with Peep's approval.

That was half the can used already, he soberingly noted, wishing he'd pocketed his full wage's worth of cans.

Going into the living room, he picked up the Durham Advertiser, sat himself down on the edge of the table with his feet on a chair, and once again turned to the Situations Vacant pages. Five seconds later, he tossed the paper away. 'Who are you kidding?' he groaned, lying backwards on the table, his coat wings spread out around him. 'You don't belong in this world.'

Peep came and sat on his chest, licking her lips.

A few minutes later, the doorbell rang, but he ignored it. Then Jackie appeared at the window, tapping for attention.

'Get off the table and let me in,' she demanded.

Remaining sprawled, stretching back to reach the window, Albert lifted the latch, leaving Jackie to realise she was expected to enter the flat unconventionally. 'Thanks, Albert,' she grumbled, ungainly climbing into the room, struggling with some carrier bags, causing Peep to wonder if she should not make a dash for her life. 'I'll go the extra mile for you one day too.' After arranging herself, she produced a newly-purchased item from one of the bags. 'Look at this jacket I've just bought.'

Not looking away from the ceiling, Albert drably demanded, 'Quiet, Jackie, I'm thinking.'

'What about?'

'Ways I can be more like Harry.'

'Don't wash,' she suggested.

'Already working on that.'

Jackie put her new jacket back in its bag. After brushing her hair, she took her purse from her pocket, retrieved one ten and one twenty pound note and placed them on the table beside Albert's head. 'Here's some money for you until Ron gets back. Pay me back when you can.'

Albert twisted over to view the offering, further disturbing Peep, who jumped away and fled into the garden through the half-open window. Getting off the table to snatch up the money, he wordlessly followed the animal's direct course out of the house.

'Albert, where are you going?' called Jackie out the window after him, watching him leave the garden and stride purposefully down the lamp-lit, tree-lined street, banknotes in hand. Receiving no reply, she huffed, pulled the window near-closed and began to look through her new purchases.

After examining her purchases, Jackie switched on the intermittently faulty television in the living room and sat down to wait for Albert to return from wherever he had gone — shopping for food, she presumed. When the programme she had begun watching ended, she went to make herself toast. When she came back to the living room, she found the television screen had become green and white, as was its wont.

The doorbell rang. Not knowing whether to answer it or not, she opened the window wide and craned her head out to try to see who it was. It was two grim-looking constables. They saw her. 'Oh, hold on a minute,' she said, suddenly worried that something might have happened to Albert. Hurriedly going to the flat's inner door, she heard a faint tinkling noise coming from beyond it. Stepping out into the house's hall, she encountered Albert sitting on the lower stairs, in the company of a six-pack of strong lager and a full bottle of whisky, which he was cradling between his legs. Three of the lagers were already drunk, and a fourth was open in his hand.

One of his shoelaces was tied loosely around his neck, threaded through his door keys.

Practise: that's how Albert had decided he could be more like Harry.

'I've gone up in the world,' he explained to Jackie, tinkling his keys against the whisky bottle. From his coat pocket, he produced a pack of cigarettes and began unwrapping them.

Jackie glowered at him. 'You spent my money on all this shit?'

'Yeah, thanks,' said Albert, raising a can to her before gulping down much of its contents. Patting the step beside him, he said, 'Join me. Together we shall float away on a Lethe stream of blessed drink.'

The bell rang inside Albert's flat again.

'There's some coppers at the door,' Jackie now informed him, hushing her voice.

Affecting a worried look, Albert snatched up his whisky, twisted the top off and began gulping it down.

'Stop,' cried Jackie, taking the bottle away from his lips. 'You idiot.'

Albert put a fag in his mouth and lit it, looking ill from the first draw.

The policemen now began knocking trenchantly, and Jackie couldn't hold back from answering. Apprehensively opening the street door, she looked up at two uncommonly tall, mature, uniformed men, one almost as tall as Ron.

'Evening,' said the tallest officer, who was greying at the temples.

'Evening,' said Jackie, carrying a whisky bottle.

'We're looking for Albert Fox.'

Jackie hesitated before guardedly admitting, 'He lives here.'

'We know he lives here. Is he in?'

Jackie hesitated again, but behind her, Albert betrayed his presence by weakly chanting, 'Come and have a go if you think you're hard enough.'

The officers stepped past Jackie and into the hall, and saw their man, cigarette in hand, leaning on the rim of a dustbin, as if about to puke.

'Albert Fox?'

Groggily, Albert straightened up. Disdainfully, he stamped out the barely-smoked cigarette and tossed the packet away. Upon looking at the constables, he blanched. 'Fuck, Jackie, you might have let me know how big they were.' Scrambling back to the stairs and his lager can, he gulped the remainder in a panic, and then, with innocent calm, asked, 'What?'

The coppers were evidently unsure about what was going on, but remained steadfastly grim. The tallest one began the enquiry. 'Mr Carter who owns the shop on Bishop Street said you threatened his little daughter with a hammer?'

Albert shrieked, snatched up another can, whipped off its ringpull and began pouring drink down his mouth.

'Albert!' cried Jackie, putting the whisky bottle down to allow her to force the can away from him.

'Well?' pursued the officer, once the pantomime subsided.

'Show me that hammer,' said Albert, swelling with sudden defiance, 'and I'll show you a false hammer.'

'He said you took his daughter down by the river and you were talking about paedophiles. Is that true?'

Albert shrieked again, grabbed the whisky Jackie had carelessly left at hand, and began guzzling.

'Albert, no!' pleaded Jackie, putting the can down and wresting the bottle away from him again.

'Give it back,' demanded Albert. 'Let me pour the ruinous solution down my throat and feel for a brief moment that I live in an agreeable world.'

'Mr Fox,' warned the second officer, leaning over Albert, 'this is a serious enquiry into serious allegations.'

Suddenly appearing ill-humoured, Albert picked up the lager can and pushed past the officers. Coat wings flapping behind him, he strode down the hall and into his flat, slamming the door behind him.

The officers followed, rapping on the door. 'Mr Fox. Mr Fox.'

Jackie hurriedly placed the whisky bottle down on the stairs and went to try to appease the officers. 'I'm sure it's all nothing. He just says stupid things to people.'

'We've noticed that,' muttered the tallest officer, like he was uncomfortable fraternising with an associate of the enemy.

The other officer rapped on the door again, and spoke to the paint. 'Mr Fox. Mr Fox.'

'He doesn't normally drink like this,' said Jackie. 'I've never even seen him touch spirits before.'

The officers had continued to knock for a minute or two, but Albert, spread-eagled on his bed, still wearing his coat, had ignored them. Now he was ignoring Jackie, shouting to inform him the coast was clear. Ignoring her was easy: the booze he'd recklessly gulped on the stairs was fully entering his system. Slumping over to reach his lager can on the floor, his head felt like it had gained extra weight and inertia, like it was pulling ten *g's* in all directions at once. Somehow he acquired the can, but his elbows had become slippery and mutinous, refusing to obey the laws of friction when he tried to lean upon them for support so that he could take a drink. Bravely, he persevered, regardless of the drenching his floor was receiving.

Receiving no reply to her calls, Jackie remembered that the living room window should still be open, and she gained entry to Albert's flat that way. Entering his bedroom, she switched on the main light and uncompromisingly took the lager can from him, although he seemed indifferent to its loss. His drink gone, he slumped back, and at once felt that the bed was slowly, and very unpleasantly, turning. Forever turning, but forever not. Closing his eyes, he very soon wished he hadn't and opened them again, then shut them again just to confirm it really had felt that bad.

'What's all this about a paper round?' demanded Jackie, sounding like a schoolmistress.

Opening his eyes again, he stared at the starkly bright lightbulb above him. It appeared to circle nauseatingly back and forth.

'Answer me,' demanded Jackie.

Albert groaned and slurred, 'Had to get a job to buy cat food, but got sacked. Too witty for Durham.' Struggling to lift his head to look at Jackie, he found enough lucidity and strength to complain,

179

'And you wouldn't believe what a bitch of a little girl I had as a boss. Wish I had hit her with a hammer. Go and get her for me, Jackie. Smash her little face in. Careful, though, she'll be a gouger. Sure of it. I'll jump in and back you up if she starts getting the better of you.'

His head fell down, leaving him to once again stare harrowingly at the drifting lightbulb.

Jackie sat on the side of the bed.

'Oh, Albert,' she said sympathetically, viewing him with sad, helpless tenderness. 'I care so much about you.'

Reaching to take the lager from her, to which she consented, Albert slurred, 'Jackie, if I've told you once, I've...'

He tailed off to begin messily consuming his drink.

'Those policemen told me to tell you not to go near that shop again,' she reported, 'or speak to the girl. They'll be keeping and eye on you, they said.'

When the last drops of his lager were either drunk or spilled, Albert let the empty can fall.

'I need a big piss,' he ruefully complained.

Yes, he needed a big piss, but didn't think he could get up. But he had to try, otherwise there'd soon be a big drop in his self-esteem. There'd be a witness, too, and word would get around. Unknowingly acquiring advantage from the dip Jackie was making in the mattress, he rolled off his bed and on to all fours, his keys still hanging from his neck and trailing the floor. Once some semblance of stability had been achieved, he began moving in the general direction of the door, appearing like some staggering, tranquillised animal. His head felt like it had a massive gyroscope clamped inside that fought against every turn and movement it was required to make. Based on balance sensation alone, he would have been prepared to swear that some unseen prankster was moving the floor around, and that two shifting bags of cement had been tied loosely to his back. Even though he was taking short, slow, quadruped steps, he still managed to trip himself up with his coat several times before making it out of the room.

Jackie wordlessly watched Albert's exit struggle. When he didn't return in reasonable time, she went to find him, and saw his coat lying outside the closed bathroom door. 'Albert, are you in there?' No answer. She tried the door — locked. 'Albert,' she called again, becoming worried now. Then she heard torrents of puking, followed by bath taps running.

She left him to it, going to make herself a coffee.

*

Last thing he remembered was staring at a lightbulb. Now, somehow, he was hunched and shivering — and clothed — in the bath. There was evidence, however, that the lost time had not been uneventful: the plug was out; both taps were on and running cold; and the sides of the tub bore a shallow tide mark of textured stains. Tilted forward and down, his head was resting on his wrists, which, along with his hands and forearms, were submerged under swirling, ever-draining water. In addition to the noise of the taps, he could hear someone banging and shouting.

'Albert, are you all right? If you don't answer, I'm going to get help.'

Feebly, he turned off the taps.

'Albert,' called Jackie. 'Albert,'

He clambered on to the side of the bath, and rested, sick head in hands.

His shoes were soaked; one loose without its lace. His black jeans were also soaked, up to mid-thigh. He was cold, so cold, and his hands, arms and forehead were chilled numb. He couldn't have been unconscious, though, he fuzzily figured, since he'd have fallen sideways into the water and be wet all over.

Puzzlingly, his door keys were hanging from his neck.

Jackie banged again. 'Albert.'

Going down on to his knees in front of the basin, despite not being able to grip properly, he managed to brush his bitter-feeling teeth. Then he crawled to the door, clumsily unbolted it, and crawled out, only to be immediately and repeatedly hit by Jackie. 'You bastard. You stupid bastard. Why didn't you answer me?' He kept on crawling, flight from Jackie being some kind of confused aim. Finding himself in the kitchen, he slumped down in a corner where he began shivering uncontrollably, a motion soon added to by Jackie shaking him.

'Albert, get up.'

'Why?' he groaned. 'Is my hair peaking?'

'Stop joking. This is serious.'

'Don't tell me that. Don't ever tell me that.'

'It is serious.' She leant over him, and he felt her fragrant hair brush across his face. She touched his brow with her hand. 'You're as cold as a corpse.'

'I wish.'

She hit him again. 'Get up and lie in front of the fire.'

Albert wouldn't get up, or even respond now. He just closed his eyes, curled up and shivered. Realising he wasn't going anywhere, Jackie retrieved his pillow and duvet from his bedroom and made him as comfortable on the kitchen floor as she believed she could. Staying with him for another hour as he slept off the worst of his misadventure, Jackie eventually felt able to leave, and went to her car to drive the fifteen miles home, tomorrow being a working day for her.

1.15
Hesitation

As heavy as a millstone, as constricting as a noose, might have been how she would have described her feelings about the ring if she were the kind to keep a secret, melodramatic diary. But she was not. Her inner voice conjured no such melodramatic words as she looked at it, encircling her finger, which in turn encircled a mug of hot chocolate. But a hundred times this day, and a hundred times yesterday, her gaze had fallen on to it, and each time a numb unease arose within her.

It was now Wednesday. John had come on Saturday, but had gone again on Sunday morning to see his family. His mother had married again on Monday, and he had been obliged to attend, although he had misgivings about her choice of third husband, who seemed too much like the second and the first. To Jennifer's surprise and relief, he had not resumed the Albert argument with her before he'd left for Nottingham — hadn't even mentioned it — but later Margaret said he'd quizzed her about it, asking that his enquiry be kept secret.

Also to her surprise, he had not had sex with her in the morning.

He almost always woke with a hard erection, and though they both might still be sleepy, sex often happened. But it had not happened on Sunday. He had just got up, with the troubles of the night before unmentioned, though not, she had suspected, forgotten, especially with the pieces of the letter still lying on the floor.

Twice on Sunday, after he left, Jennifer had rung her sister, something she rarely did, meaning to ask her about that letter. Both times Sarah's answering machine responded, but she left no message. Yesterday, she had rung again, but the outgoing message had been changed to say Sarah had gone away for a few days, but would return on Friday.

Jennifer never rang Sarah's mobile, and had no mobile herself — one of the few teenagers in Britain not to own such a device. If she had rung Sarah's mobile, she would have found it now listed as unavailable, for it had been stolen from Sarah at Newcastle airport on her way to Iceland.

Today, John had come back. He meant to stay one night, then leave to rejoin his regiment early the next day. Upon arriving in town by bus three hours earlier, he'd rung Jennifer at work, and she had informed him that Margaret should be at home to let him in the house. He'd sounded much as usual, saying he fancied meeting her after work to treat her to tea in a cafe, promising to ring again once he was back in the house. So far only her Aunt had called, and it was now almost four o'clock, and Jennifer believed this augured bad temper.

As it always was when she was at work, Jennifer's hair was tied back. She was wearing the white medical coat expected of her, but in which she self-consciously felt a sham. Sitting in the small room they called the office, she was taking her afternoon break from assisting the vet: fifteen minutes to herself, loosely available sometime around three-thirty.

The vet, Maureen, was a mother of two in her fifties who'd moved to Richmond years back to raise her family in surroundings gentler than her native Leeds.

Maureen was calling, and Jennifer put down the remainder of her drink and went to the practice room.

'We're nearly done here,' said Maureen when Jennifer appeared, implying a companion even though she was alone save for a black-and-white cat. 'Could you check on how many doses of feline panleucopoenia vaccine we have left, and fetch me a single dose for this poor little thing.'

183

Maureen also wore a white coat — sizes larger than Jennifer's. Maureen was tall, with brown collar-length flyaway hair now thickening with advancing greyness. She quickly checked the cat's teeth, and seemed satisfied.

'*Nobi-vac?*' queried Jennifer.

'That's right,' confirmed Maureen in her terse manner, a manner that Jennifer had quickly learned did not reflect impatience, only efficiency. 'And after we've given this chap his shot you can leave if you want.'

Jennifer passed a pre-packaged syringe to her employer. 'No, I'll stay till five,' she said, thinking that being at work meant not being with John, and being with John might mean a continuation of Saturday night's contrary theme. She was certain he was secretly brooding on it, believing that was why he hadn't called again.

Without needing to be directed, when the syringe was unwrapped, Jennifer held and calmed the cat as Maureen gathered the flesh of its hindquarters and inserted the needle, though the cat seemed to feel nothing untoward.

'Well, old Mr. Green's due soon with his collie,' said Maureen, depressing the syringe, 'and we'll be putting it to sleep. Thought I'd spare you that scene. No sense us both getting lumps in our throat.'

'Oh, okay, I'll leave early.'

'I won't need you. The dog won't be any trouble. No trouble left in him, poor thing.'

Five minutes later, Jennifer was walking home. Passing the small clothes shop that was never open, she stopped briefly to look at a dress that had previously caught her eye. It was black, slinky, and sparsely embroidered with silver spiders' webs. As usual, the shop's door was showing a "closed" sign, and no lights were on inside. Turning from the window, across the road she saw the stooped, boy-sized figure of Mr. Green. Dressed like the hill farmer he had for decades been, he was shuffling two young mans' paces ahead of his spent dog, a dog that in its prime had worked fields in the higher Dales.

Maureen had once told Jennifer that Mr. Green had been as active as ever until only two years back, when a stroke suddenly took away nine-tenths of his stride, after which his son calculated the family small-holding would have to be sold to pay for his care.

When Mr. Green stopped to allow his struggling dog to catch up, even from across the road Jennifer could see that he was crying.

Jennifer took longer than usual to reach her new home after

work. Her step was weighed-down and slowed with the burden of knowing that John would be there waiting for her, possibly with some renewed Albert suspicion. As she walked, however, she was, though as yet unaware of it, beginning to galvanise herself into bringing about positive change in her life.

When she pushed open the door, Margaret flashed her a smile on her way to the kitchen. She gave a strained smile back. Not yet removing her coat, she proceeded to the living room, where she found John sitting with his feet up, watching television. 'Hello. I'm back,' she said, in as warm a voice as she could muster, standing in the doorway. 'Why didn't you call again?'

John didn't get up to greet her, or even turn his head. 'Hi,' he eventually said.

Pretending not to have noticed his simmering mood, Jennifer forced a casual inquiry about what, if anything, he'd done that day since arriving.

'Went to your aunt's to get my fishing gear,' he returned. Looking at her, he asked, 'Why didn't you tell her about our engagement when she called you at work today?'

'I wanted to tell Sarah first,' Jennifer explained, 'but she's gone away somewhere till Friday. She rang auntie Jane from the airport and said she'd had her mobile stolen, so I can't reach her.'

John looked at the television again, and Jennifer went to her room to put her things away.

In her room, still wearing her coat, she sat down wearily in front of her dressing table. Resting her elbows on the table top, she put her head into her hands, hair falling over her face. Raising her head a little, her eyes met their mirrored twins, and with the determination that can arise from confronting one's reflection thus, she resolved to break the engagement. It would be madness to let her relationship with John go any further. Yes, he had been there in the past, at times when she had needed company — or at least had been quietly glad of distraction — but, she argued internally, she had outgrown him, and now his company was not wanted or appreciated, or even tolerable any more. She was going to tell him, regardless of the scene it would provoke.

She decided that she would take a deep bath, have her evening meal and wait for Margaret to leave for her line dancing class before speaking to John about her decision. After her bath, she changed into the blue jumper she tended to wear most days, and black trousers, both fresh from the tumble dryer. Going to the kitchen,

Margaret told her that John had again quizzed her about the identity of Albert.

*

She couldn't do it. When Margaret left, not due to return until around midnight, Jennifer had been expecting some resurgence of the Albert theme from John. That, she'd vaguely hoped, would somehow give her the opportunity and incentive to raise the marriage issue and properly express her reluctance. But John had not, as yet, returned to his Albert suspicions, and she had not found the courage to begin a discourse about their engagement.

They were watching evening television together. For some time, John's arm had been loosely around her as they sat side by side, their faces lit only by the light of the TV screen. But now he began to slip his hand up her jumper. She — subtly, she hoped — deflected his progress by adjusting her position on the sofa. Half a minute later, she — casually, she hoped — left the room to go upstairs.

John soon followed her. Standing in the doorway of her bedroom, he watched as she folded some tumble-dried clothes. Ostensibly joking, he asked, 'Avoiding me or the television?'

'You know I can't stand Eastenders,' she replied, continuing with her chores. 'All that arguing.'

Coming fully into the bedroom, John put his arms around her while she was leaning over the bed to tend to her pile of clothes. Grinding his pelvis against her bottom, hands going up to her breasts, he pulled her upright and began kissing her neck. Turning her around, he manoeuvred her so that she lay on her back on the bed. Sitting over her, he began to peel off her trousers, to which she only passively consented. Seeing the look on her face, he halted, and rolled off her, disgruntled and sullen. 'Great. My last evening before two months getting shot at in fucking Kosovo. Some wife you'll be.'

Jennifer said nothing.

'You never were too passionate in the sack though, were you?' he sniped, getting off the bed and leaving the room. 'Going down the Shepherd to play pool,' he called from halfway down the stairs.

The front door opened, then closed with a thud that rattled the bedroom window.

Jennifer felt helpless. She felt she lacked the strength and the callousness to do what had to be done. Switching off the room light, she lay in darkness, berating herself for being so weak. The television was still making noise downstairs, and, eventually, she went to switch it off. The phone rang. It was her aunt, Jane, already picturing the dress she would wear for the wedding. Pastel lilac: it would be pastel lilac, she had decided. And John would wear his army uniform. And at the reception she would feed her two little poodles wedding cake crumbs.

Although born only five years before her mother, to Jennifer, her aunt had always seemed to belong more to her grandmother's generation. So much more prim and proper than her mother had been. So much more twin-set and whist drives.

She nattered incessantly.

'Well, haven't you got something to tell me? Something about a ring?' said Jane after the greetings were done.

Jennifer hesitated. 'We're engaged, auntie.'

'And to a lovely young man,' said Jane contentedly. 'Very polite, he is. Very respectful to Tom as well, he is. We're very happy for you. You know we can't help thinking about you as the child we never had. I know your mother and I were never very close — we weren't like most sisters, not that we disliked each other, we just had nothing in common, that's all — but that never came between me and you, and your mother never wanted it to either.'

After the accident, Jane and her self-employed accountant husband, Tom, had become Jennifer's guardians. They lived in a row of stone-built houses in Reeth, a large village six miles further up Swaledale from Richmond. Sarah, too, had fallen under Jane's wing, but for her Reeth had merely been a place to stay between terms at her boarding school, and once she had been accepted by her first-choice University, Durham became her permanent address.

Just as she was to Sarah, Jennifer was a mystery to Jane. The control Jennifer kept over herself was almost preternatural. Her reserve was spooky. Where was the vim of youth? But Jane's instincts to coax Jennifer into outgoing activities were always tempered by the reality that she was not her own daughter. Also, the fact that a profitable financial package had come with the guardianship gave Jennifer an independence in Jane's mind, a paradoxical independence not to have things, or do things, if she didn't care to. Thus Jennifer had even been able to avoid holiday trips, Sarah taking charge of her and the house on those occasions when she had been too young to be left on her own.

If Jane had effectively been paying for Jennifer's place on a holiday out of her own pocket, she would have brooked no reluctance or disinterest, and Jennifer would have been heated by the

Mediterranean sun, like it or not.

Jane knew Jennifer had been quieter than most children even before the accident, and witnessing her parents receive fatal injuries couldn't have helped, she knew, but things still seemed odd. Even her reaction to the violent loss had seemed odd. There seemed to have been too little hurt, yet too little healing. But it was all so vague, and like Sarah, Jane often conceded that Jennifer was the way she was because it was simply her nature. Besides, Jennifer never claimed any special unhappiness, and one time had said that the worst thing in her life was other people assuming she was somehow suffering. That was unfounded, tedious and exasperating, she had said.

John's fiancée was asleep in bed when he returned.

1.16
Keeping it Real

The phone had been ringing on and off for much of the morning, and Peep had long since turned militant in her demands for food, but Albert, still on the kitchen floor, head throbbing fit to burst, rode it all out. He could ignore the phone indefinitely, but Peep eventually pricked his face and conscience too much. At just before eleven, not once daring to raise his poorly head above waist height, blanketed by his duvet, he spooned the last of the Whiskas he'd liberated from the shop into his pet's bowl. He was still fully-clothed from the night before save for a mysteriously absent shoe, and his keys were still hanging from his neck, and this is how he remained after feeding the animal, for he immediately slumped down, drifting in and out of sleep for a further hour.

Peep slept off her meal on the lump that he constituted.

During this additional hour on the floor, Albert realised slow recovery was underway. With recovery came a bleak awareness of his various predicaments. Shit. Serious shit. Then a lifting thought: suppose something had gone wrong with the system and his giro had been sent after all? Why not? — once he'd received a duplicate by mistake, and they never asked for it back. If they had screwed up, today, Wednesday, was the day it would arrive. Temporary salvation might be on his doorstep.

Taking his duvet with him, he began a slow crawl out of his flat to the street door, ignoring another phone call along the way. Yes! — a brown envelope. Could it be? No, it was a fucking TV licence reminder. No giro. For the first time since leaving school, no giro. Under his duvet, he sat beside the door, and felt more hollow than at any other time in his life.

Peep came into the hall, and made a nest for herself in his bedding.

Staring at a dustbin opposite, Albert sat for what seemed a long time, listening to the phone occasionally ringing in his flat. Just Jackie calling to see if he was still alive, he supposed — no one else ever rang during a work day. His head still hurt, but recovery was on-going. From recent experience, he knew that if he just took it easy, within an hour or two he'd improve from floor-bound nauseous to walking wounded. But what he was going to do with that perambulatory ability, he couldn't think. Moreover, what was he going to do with his life? He couldn't even live it as well as Harry. Harry could hold his drink, but even that murky avenue of false comfort was closed to him.

He heard his gate open, and someone pace purposefully toward the door. Then a pause while the caller presumably looked at the doorbells. Then the bell in his flat rang. Reaching up, he opened the door, swinging it as far as it would go against his duvet-covered legs. Looking up to the caller, he saw a short, slightly overweight man in his early forties, wearing a dark suit and carrying a leather attaché case. Atop, there was impeccably cropped brown hair; below, a pair of slip-on black leather shoes with small gold buckles. From head to toe he suggested Mormon.

'Got your work cut out if you think you can persuade me there's a merciful god.'

The man was temporarily confused. Then he smiled in recognition of his own astuteness. 'Don't worry, I'm not a Jehovah's Witness.'

'I know,' returned Albert, 'you're a fucking Mormon.'

'I'm not a Mormon, either.'

'Well you look like a Mormon, so fuck off anyway.'

Albert pushed the door shut.

The moment the door closed, the man's mobile rang, and Albert could hear him conversing. 'Tim speaking ... Ron ... Yes, I'm outside your place now. Some guy lying on the floor just inside your door told me to fuck off ... No, I didn't get chance ... No, young. About your age ...' Now he spoke through the letter box. 'Is your name Albert?'

'Yeah,' admitted Albert.

'I've got your flatmate on the phone. He wants to speak to you.'

Albert reached up, reopened the door, and wordlessly accepted the phone.

'What's up?' said Albert to Ron, leaning his sick head against the wall.

'Wanker,' said Ron.

'Lucky guess,' returned Albert.

Ron sounded genuinely annoyed. 'That's Scoones you just told to fuck off.'

'Oops. Thought he looked a bit familiar.'

Over the previous few weeks, on his bedroom computer, Ron had been working on amendments to a training manual. He'd brought the finished file into work, but as he'd left early in a mood on Friday after his dressing-down from Scoones, he'd neglected to hand it over, and it had stayed in his pocket, a pocket which was now in Iceland. Occupied with Sarah over the weekend, he'd also neglected to email it, as he'd promised to do when Scoones had called him on Saturday afternoon. Now the work was urgently needed by his department. All morning Ron had been ringing Albert, with the intention of getting him to email it on his behalf, but his calls had not been answered, and all morning Scoones had been ringing Ron in Iceland to check on the progress. Assured by Ron that his flatmate would actually be in bed, perhaps hungover, Scoones had ventured to call round to see if he could rouse him directly.

After explaining the situation to Albert, Ron finally, and firmly, said, 'And before you let him into my room, make sure nothing druggy's lying around. Okay?'

With weariness in his voice, Albert said, 'Yeah, yeah, okay.'

He handed the phone back to Scoones, who closed the call with Ron.

Bundling his duvet under his arm, Albert stood as best he could manage under the influence of his remaining headache, and opened the door fully.

With some apprehension apparent, Scoones stepped into the hall. 'This where you sleep?' he asked, sounding as if he was serious.

'I never sleep. I just scowl in the garden overnight.'

Scoones made no reply, and Albert, with his hurting head bent down and his shoulders wincingly pulled in, led the way into his flat, miserably herding Peep in ahead of him. The activity threw his recovery back, and once inside, he lay on his sofa, head over the side, staring at the carpet, feeling that he might be about to vomit.

The keys still hanging around his neck trailed the floor.

'You look rough,' said Scoones. 'Had a drink too many?'

'Had a fucking life too many.'

'I'm sorry to hear you feel that way,' said Scoones unsurely. 'Want me to come back later?'

'I might be dead later.'

'So you want me to proceed with the business?'

'I want you to get me the bucket from under the sink in the bathroom. Very quickly.'

Scoones at once obliged, placing the bucket next to Albert, who leant on its rim, virtually embracing it.

Scoones waited the best part of a minute before asking, 'So where does Ron keep his computer?'

'In his bedroom.'

Scoones left the room, and it took Albert some moments to realise what had happened: he'd thought Scoones had been casually wondering where Ron kept his computer, when in fact he'd really been announcing that he would seek out the machine. Shit, he was supposed to be clearing Ron's room of dope paraphernalia first.

Picking up his bucket, Albert hurried to Ron's room. Scoones was sitting in Ron's high-backed swivel chair, and on the desk before him, the £2500 computer system was booting up. But Scoones wasn't looking at the screen, he was looking at a block of dope, half the size of a box of kitchen matches, which he tentatively picked up and sniffed.

Stooped, holding a hand to his sick forehead, Albert took the dope from Scoones and collected up the cigarette papers lying on the desk. 'Fuck, wondered where I'd left my gear. Don't tell Ron I've been using his room, will you? He doesn't approve of my lifestyle.'

He went back to the sofa to rest on his bucket again.

Although he had yet to reach the age of forty-five, Scoones was like a person twenty years older in that he had no experience of recreational drugs beyond a few parties he'd never really been invited to in his teenage days where joints had been smoked by others. When those joints had been passed around, he had declined to participate. His dangerous partying days soon over, his later life became focused on slowly but doggedly climbing the managerial ladder and being prudent with his money. At twenty-six, he'd married a primary school teacher he'd met at a pub quiz, and at twenty-eight they'd started a family once their combined salaries and savings allowed them to move into a new house on a new estate. Anything beyond this was alien to his mindset. Thus, in his eyes, Ron was now the number one suspect for the person who'd been injecting heroin in the company's toilets.

Having transferred everything he needed to a CD, Scoones went to the threshold of the living room. Sounding subdued and preoccupied, he said, 'All done. I'll see myself out.'

By the time Albert lifted his head, Scoones had all but left the flat. Embracing the bucket again, he cheerlessly said, 'Bucket, my miserable comforter, it's just you and me now. You and me against the world.'

It didn't look it, but it was quite a comfortable position to remain in, and Albert rested on his miserable comforter until his hangover reduced to a muddy feeling inside his skull that he believed a cup of tea might largely disperse. Going into the kitchen, he took that ameliorative drink at the table, using the last of the milk. He began wondering where his other shoe might be, and went to look for it. He found it beside his coat, which was lying just outside the bathroom. The shoe was very damp. Going back to the kitchen, he untied the keys from around his neck and returned the lace to his shoe, putting the finished article in the oven on its lowest setting and leaving the door ajar.

He sat at the table again to drink the rest of his tea.

Peep came into the kitchen. Jumping up on to the work top, she found the empty Whiskas can and began dipping her paw in for the flavour. He'd have to buy her some more food, and although he believed he had some money left from the amount Jackie had given him, there was probably only enough to last a man and a cat a couple days.

Fuck.

A solution of a kind grimly suggested itself: kill himself. *Really* do it, not just indulge in therapeutic visions of lamenting beauties, or imagine fanciful, complex methods. It was a new, bleak vision of his own death he was glimpsing now, accompanied by pangs of anguish and fear and a sense of desolate failure. But if he died now, who would look after Peep? He'd have to wait until Ron got back, at least. Ron would take on the feline responsibility, he was sure. Although Ron had never bothered playing with Peep much, or even stroking her, he was always fair with her. Maybe he should kill himself *and* Peep? No, that would look *really* weird and sad. He had *some* pride.

Shaking off the hollow reverie, swallowing the last of his tea, Albert slowly set about getting himself together. He ran a bath, and while the tub was filling, quickly washed his jeans and T-shirt in the kitchen sink. After spinning them in the washing machine, he laid the jeans out for special emergency drying. He had long ago discovered that a pair of jeans could be dried in less than half an hour by placing them on the floor, weighing down the edge of the waistband and the hem of one leg with books, and sticking a hairdryer nozzle in the other leg so that the garment inflated with hot air. And his T-shirt would be ready to wear this way in less than five minutes.

He'd melted three hairdryers so far, though.

Lying in the bath, head still slightly crook, he made a big resolution to start on his commercial novel again. He'd tried sickness and employment, but they weren't for him: the contemplative, creative life was obviously what he was cut out for. He was an artist.

After his bath, he managed some food, and felt the better for it. Moderately revived, he took a coffee into his room, and switched on his computer. Sitting at the keyboard, he waited for things to happen, but nothing did. After twenty fallow, dispiriting minutes, he put an opening line down anyway, but it was shit, so he deleted it. Five minutes later, he typed another opening line, which was also shit. So he deleted that too.

Peep stared at him. She wanted feeding again. He would have to go to a shop on her behalf right away. Checking his coat pocket, he found he had only £2.40 left from the £30 Jackie had lent him — even less than he'd hoped would be there.

Fuck.

On the way to a shop that lay in a different direction to his last place of employment, Albert pondered his troubles. Money — he'd need more money very soon. He had to get real about it. Seriously real. Yes, he'd formulated a plot for what was planned to be a seriously commercial novel, but that delusion had to end — even if he knuckled down and wrote like a God, he'd still starve to death before anything could come of it, and so would his cat.

The solution arrived: he would sell his computer. Sell his one valuable possession, despite the fact that morally it belonged to Ron.

He decided to place an advert in the Durham Advertiser. The computer and printer had cost Ron £350 new four months back, so Albert reckoned he should be able to get £200 for them now, easy.

£200! That was his life sorted! He'd never have to work again!

1.17
She Lies all the Time

Albert was waiting to submit his computer sale advert in the Durham Advertiser's office-come-drop-in-shop, located just a few doors away from where Jackie worked. The woman behind the counter appeared to be in her early forties. She was heavily made up, with an artificial tan, sternly plucked eyebrows and dyed-black hair fixed with spray. She wore a grey skirt with a white blouse, and her short, porcine legs tapered into black high-heeled shoes. With an expression of suspicious puzzlement, she quietly read the card just handed to her: 'Imminent suicide forces quick sale.' Her expression swiftly changed to something resembling scandalised anger. She was having none of this, and pushed the card across the counter, back to the man standing in front of Albert. 'You can't place an advert with those words. Sorry.'

She folded her arms and stood back, implacable and immovable.

'Please,' said the man in front of Albert.

'No. You'll have to change the wording.'

Albert surreptitiously peered around the side of the man and read his card. 'You've spelt imminent wrong,' he informed him. 'Unforgivable in this modern age of vitamins and callipers. It ends in e-n-t, not a-n-t.'

The man, who was wearing a black coat similar to Albert's, but more worn and tatty, glanced over his shoulder, but didn't acknowledge the spelling advice.

He was damp-eyed, noted Albert.

Seeming to be in his mid thirties, the man was about the same height as Albert, but more angular, with wider shoulders and disproportionately large yet nevertheless artistic hands, hands that looked equally apt for playing violin or strangling burglars. His hair was cut about the same length as Albert's, except his was black and more unkempt. He hadn't shaved for a day or two or three, and this, coupled with his heavy black eyebrows and gypsy complexion, would have made him perfect for playing the villain in some Victorian stage melodrama, were it not for his evidently weepy nature.

The man once more implored, 'Please.'

The woman shook her head resolutely. 'I've already told you, we can't accept that kind of wording for a sales advert.'

'Please,' begged the man quietly. 'Don't deny my despair a voice. You don't understand what shaped this miserable wretch you see before you. I've been wronged and wronged again, and wronged fifty-fold by the most devious spirit that ever took female form. Me. Poor me. Me, by nature pitched too high; by suffering plunged too low.'

That did it: Albert knew he was in the presence of a fellow poet, and felt instant, protective comradeship. Like he was drawing some mighty sword too long rested in ignoble sloth, Albert stepped up to the counter. 'Lady, you foe of feeling. You enemy of empathy. This man has clearly been grievously pained by some foul demon in a dress. Give him a frigging break, won't you?'

The woman shrunk back a step. This was unreal. Some kind of coalition of the insane.

'He speaks the truth,' said the man. 'It *was* a demon in a dress.' Holding his card out to the woman, he said, 'Print these words and let the world know my despair and the evil that wrought it.'

'Do it, bitch,' ordered Albert, who knew this woman. He'd met her a thousand times in a thousand guises, and she'd wearied and saddened and worn him down a further fraction on each occasion. She belonged to that great bulk of people — the ninety-nine in every hundred — who could laugh fit to burst at the latest alternative comedy show, but when such imaginative outpourings occurred in their very presence, they were viewed as, at best, idiotic or insane; at worst, seditious.

It was all to do with context recognition , believed Albert.

'Could you leave the office now,' asked the woman. Her voice was controlled but her eyes showed apprehension. 'Or do I have to call for help? Twelve men work here, you know.'

Albert menacingly punched the palm of his hand. 'Twelve dead men.'

Without letting her persecutors out of her sight, the woman banged on the door behind her. 'Dave! Gordon! Trouble!'

Dave and Gordon came out like they'd been waiting on call behind the door all along.

Albert took hold of the tearful man's sleeve and pulled him away. 'Flee!'

'Please,' implored the man, looking to the woman while simultaneously allowing himself to be pulled away.

Once outside, Albert let go of the man's sleeve. 'We could have taken those geezers,' he said. But when he looked behind, his fellow warrior was sitting on the pavement, quietly crying. 'Or maybe not.'

'She lies all the time,' said the weeping man quietly, eyes cast down to the ground. 'Will she ever end my agony? Just five minutes of honesty is all I ask.'

'Who's she?' asked Albert.

'The Antichrist,' said the man, slumping back against the facade of the gift shop behind him.

Albert began to have second thoughts about the man. 'She's a real person, right? You're not just some religious psycho out for a nutty walk?'

'She can disguise herself as human,' replied the sad man quietly, his eyes still downcast. 'Appearing to be the very essence of sweet reasonableness is her speciality deception.'

'You're mad, aren't you?' accused Albert, with amusement in his voice.

'Maybe,' murmured the man. 'I fear that may be the case. It's a terrible fear to have.' But then his aspect became dark and grim. Looking at Albert, he spoke gravely, 'No, not mad. Maddened. Maddened by communion with the Antichrist. She spun a tangled web of deceit around me. Yes, she's a real person, with a conventional name, but I've vowed never to utter it again. It's too evil for Durham.'

'Is it Grace?' asked Albert. 'Is that her name? Skinny lass. About ten.'

The sad man's damp eyes turned downwards once again, and the grimness passed away from his aspect, forlorn incomprehension occupying the vacancy.

'No, it's not Grace,' he wearily answered. Then he began crying into his hands, becoming the object of some passing public curiosity and concern. 'Scheming, plotting, lying, cunning bitch,' he painfully sobbed.

'Fuck, don't bawl like that,' urged Albert. 'People will think we're having a big gay break up.'

The man drew up his knees, hugging them tight, sobbing against them.

'For fuck's sake,' despaired Albert, 'observe me and learn manly fortitude.'

'Albert, what have you done to him?'

It was Jackie's voice. Albert turned and found her standing just behind him, holding a small, stiff paper bag from which the tops of two bread roll sandwiches protruded. She was wearing her smartest blue work dress with a white blouse, but not looking like she really suited either of them. The problem, thought Albert as he viewed her, was that she didn't have a waist. She wasn't particularly fat around the middle, it's just that she didn't go in where other woman did.

'Never touched him,' protested Albert.

'Don't lie,' said Jackie, employing her schoolmistress tone. 'You must have done something to him.'

'Not me. Some scheming, plotting, lying, cunning bitch.'

The man cast a tearful, wet-faced attempt at a censuring look. 'Don't call her a scheming, plotting, lying, cunning bitch. She's the mother of my daughter.'

'Albert!' Jackie reprimanded, slapping his arm. 'Stop provoking people all the time.'

'He called her it first,' Albert pointed out indignantly. 'Anyway, I don't provoke. I stimulate. Imagine how dreary his day was until he met me.'

The man's sobbing was now easing, although he remained a tormented sight.

'Who is he?' asked Jackie.

'Fuck knows.'

Jackie now put the question directly, but gently, to the man, and he said his name was Joe, whereupon Jackie introduced herself and Albert. Viewing Joe compassionately, she quietly commented to

Albert, 'Looks like you're not the most melancholic person in Durham after all.'

Albert felt instant pangs of outrage. 'Stuff off, Jackie. He's just a cry baby or something. There won't be nearly as much natural thoughtful depth to him as me. I'm way too deep for tears. Bet he was happy-go-lucky until that scheming, plotting, lying, cunning bitch fucked him over.'

'Oi, don't call her a bitch,' cautioned Joe, albeit feebly.

Jackie slapped Albert's arm again. 'Albert, don't talk about the mother of his daughter like that.'

Joe got up and tidied himself a bit, grumbling sullenly, 'Only I can attack her with an unsullied conscience. Only I know what really happened. Only I can call her an evil-minded, selfish, malicious, pathetic, spineless piece of shit.'

'See what I mean?' said Albert to Jackie.

Joe began walking in the same direction as Jackie's agency, and Jackie and Albert naturally walked with him, but after a few paces he wiped the wetness from his eyes and stopped to cross the road.

'Where are you going?' asked Jackie.

'Where everyone goes,' answered Joe, stepping off the kerb behind a black, London-style taxi that was pulling up.

Jackie and Albert stood and watched him walk away.

'Bit of a weirdo, wasn't he?' commented Albert.

'No worse than you,' returned Jackie. 'But much more melancholic.'

'Jackie,' said Albert, 'if I've told you once, I've told you a thousand times: if you're going to talk to me, talk sense.'

They began walking again.

'I rang you a couple of times to see if you were all right after last night,' said Jackie.

Albert arrested her with a tug on her sleeve. 'Hold on. Will you do me a favour?' He produced the advert he'd wanted to submit. 'Will you pop into the Durham Advertiser and hand this ad in?'

Before thinking, she took it from him.

'Why can't you do it?' she suddenly objected.

'I tried, but me and Joe just got kicked out.'

Jackie rolled her eyes and released a noisy breath.

'It was Joe's fault,' protested Albert. 'Honest.'

Jackie read the advert.

'You're selling your computer? Why?'

'Have to. Fucking cat keeps getting hungry. Fifty billion mice in

198

the world and my cat still can't hack it.'

Jackie rolled her eyes again, released another noisy breath, and thrust her bag of food into Albert's hands. 'Take this to Barry. Don't wind him up. And have a cup of coffee waiting for me.' Then she stomped toward the Durham Advertiser.

'I'm sorry, but I can't give you that kind of information,' the woman at the counter was adamantly saying when Jackie walked in.

Simon was in town. Carl, looking uneasy and confused, was with him.

'I'm not asking for his number,' said Simon politely, his expression one of simple bewilderment. 'I want you to give him mine.'

So recently battle-hardened, the woman reiterated her misapprehended stance. 'I told you, I can't give you that kind of information.'

Simon's bewilderment increased. Eventually, he came to some kind of understanding about the intercourse, and his expression changed to meek determination. 'Can I speak to your manager?'

For a fleeting moment, the woman looked angry, but she checked herself, and picked up the phone.

'Sharon, could you pop down to the counter a moment? A gentleman wishes to speak to you.' She put the phone down. 'Ms Ascough, the manager, will be down shortly.'

'Thank you,' said Simon, standing aside to wait.

Jackie saw her opportunity. 'Excuse me. Could I place this advert?'

The woman took it from her and irascibly read it aloud, as if expecting Jackie to be the next episode in her nightmare afternoon. 'For sale. Computer. 1.7 gig processor; 20 gig hard drive; CD-writer; 15 inch colour monitor; mouse; keyboard; 56K modem; colour inkjet printer. Two hundred pounds.'

Carl piped up. ''Ere, Simon, did you 'ear that? Computer for sale. Two 'undred.' Simon drew close, and Carl now spoke to Jackie. ''Ere, mind if me friend 'as a look? We're lookin' for a computer ourselves.'

Jackie gestured to the woman at the counter for the temporary return of Albert's advert. Receiving it, she passed it to Simon.

'Looks a good replacement for mine,' said Simon as he read. 'A bargain. Does everything I need. Printer, too.'

Carl grinned with pride at having been the bargain's discoverer. 'Yeah? Magic.'

Simon addressed Jackie. 'Can we have a look at it?'

'Actually, it's not mine. I'm putting the advert in for a friend. But why don't you write down his number and ring him?'

'Yeah, okay,' agreed Simon. Addressing the woman behind the counter, he asked, 'When will this advert come out?'

'Tuesday,' she answered, not sounding very friendly.

'That's good,' said Simon to Carl. 'Six days advance on the public.'

'Yeah? Magic.'

Simon wrote down the computer's details and Albert's number, then passed the advert back to the woman.

'This should be fine,' said the woman to Jackie.

Jackie said thank you and left, giving Simon an unreciprocated smile on her way out.

Looking uncertain yet collected, Ms Ascough appeared. She was a tall, blonde, stylish lady of around forty. She first heard her underling's explanation of the request for her presence, then Simon's. The situation comprehended, she called up some information on a screen behind the counter, then picked up a phone.

'Oh, good morning. Is that Ken Bentham? ... Oh good. Sharon Ascough from the Durham Advertiser. I've got a gentleman in the office who wants you to have his phone number. We didn't want to give your number out, but he wants you to ring him so he can speak to you about the UFO you reported to us. The one that was really a distress flare.'

Mr Bentham said he would be willing to phone Simon, and accepted his number.

'Thank you,' said Ms Ascough, with practised brightness.

She put the phone down.

'That was just the official cover-up story,' said Simon, in a tone that was part sulky, part educational. 'It wasn't a flare.'

Ms Ascough smiled. 'Really? Whatever next.'

She went away.

Simon's mobile vibrated in his pocket, and he took it out.

'Didn't know you 'ad a mobile, Simon,' remarked Carl.

Carl received no reply.

'Simon Barnes ... Yes. Hello, Mr Bentham, thanks for calling.'

*

Albert was standing just inside the door of Jackie's workplace, waiting to give her her coffee. Upon arrival, she accepted it without ceremony or thanks.

There were no customers present.

'Did you do the business?' asked Albert.

Jackie was being terse with him today. 'Advert comes out Tuesday. Some geezer I met in there saw it and might ring you about it beforehand.'

'Yeah?'

Barry came out of the back office, smiling gleefully. Although he was wearing work-smart black trousers with a plain white shirt and black tie, his belt had silver studs, and the free end was hanging long. 'It's done,' he informed Jackie jubilantly. 'Sold — three million.'

'Brilliant!' returned Jackie.

'*Absolutely* brilliant,' modified Barry, rubbing his hands together and returning to the back office.

'What's brilliant?' Albert asked Jackie.

Passing her desk to join Barry, she thrust a finger at a folder. 'We've just sold this heap.'

In Jackie's absence, Albert examined the folder's contents. The property it described, Deepdale Hall, was located high in the moors that spawned the river that flowed through Durham City. Over two miles from the nearest settlement, it was a rambling, mock Gothic creation, built by some mid-nineteenth century industrialist, all set in five acres of walled land with woods and a stream. A private residence until the early seventies, it had then become a school for children with special needs until two years back, when an attic fire had broken out, consuming sections of the roof. Closed up and unused since, with only tarpaulins to keep out the rain, it was suggested the building was suitable for restoration and conversion to a mid-sized hotel, subject to planning approval, perhaps targeted at guests wishing to enjoy the area's grouse shooting. A gatehouse cottage in the grounds was occupied by the former groundsman and caretaker, who, having been associated in one way or another with the estate for fifty years, had been allowed to stay on rent-free after the fire in exchange for watching over the larger property.

In the back room, Jackie and Barry were discussing some business matter. Albert was curious to overhear his own name crop up in the conversation, introduced by Barry, and not in his usual tone of thinly veiled disapproval.

When she came out, Jackie asked Albert what he was doing for the next couple of hours.

'Algebra,' he answered.

'Where?'

'Libya.'

'You're coming for a little drive with me instead.'

Albert was suspicious. 'Where to?'

'That house you've just been looking at.'

'Why?'

'Someone's got to explain to a man who lives in a cottage in the grounds that the estate's been sold. Barry can't go today, and company rules say I can't go alone since that estate agent woman went missing years back.'

'Phone him,' suggested Albert.

'He doesn't have a phone.'

'So write him a letter.'

Barry now came out of the back room. 'We wrote him a letter to explain that a buyer might have been found, but he didn't respond. He's an old man, and the situation's a bit sensitive. We have to make him understand that he'll have to negotiate his tenancy with the new owners. Besides, the new owners plan to have builders around tomorrow — we're scared he might try to run them off with a shotgun. He's a bit funny.'

'Come on, Albert,' said Jackie, 'it'll be like a holiday for you.'

'Holidays are the simpleton's substitute for inner voyages,' said Albert.

Barry pulled as much of a face as he dared, and returned to the back office.

'Come on, Albert,' Jackie now whined. 'Please.'

'Oh, all right,' acquiesced Albert, with a slouch in his voice. 'But don't tell my biographers.'

Jackie collected her jacket, the match for her dark blue skirt, and walked to the door. 'Come on then.'

Following her out to the street, Albert griped, 'And no weaving around in the car. I'm still hungover.'

'I'm not surprised,' said Jackie. 'You were in such a state last night.'

'Worse this morning. Least last night I was too drunk to know how bad I felt.'

'Why do you drink if you know you're going to be bad the next day?' asked Jackie, with care in her voice. 'I don't mean last night — that was exceptional, hopefully — but when we go out and just have two or three, you're ill the next day but I'm fine. Why do you do that to yourself?'

Shrugging, Albert admitted, 'It's a mystery to me, too.'

'Can't you just stick to one?'

"I have to drink. I'm a poet."

'You don't have to drink,' argued Jackie. 'Albert, please, you don't know how much you worried me last night. At least promise me you'll never drink like you did last night again.'

With a roll of his eyes and a complaining sigh, Albert stopped, put his hand to his heart and said, 'I, Albert Fox, as witnessed by Jackie Nicholson, do solemnly vow to spurn all strong liqueur from this day forth, and to never drink more than one pint of beer or lager in any one day.'

'Thank you,' said Jackie, and Albert walked on again.

The drive from Durham City to the small Weardale village of Rookhope, the nearest settlement to Deepdale Hall, would normally take Jackie forty minutes. This time it took her nearly twice as long, for Albert demanded frequent stops on account of his residual hangover.

During their stop-start journey, the views at first changed from the urban residential compactness of Durham City to ploughed arable fields. Upon reaching the undulating Pennine foothills, commercial conifer forestation dominated, which, with increasing elevation, gave way to bleak, windswept moorland.

Arriving at Rookhope, Jackie confessed she was unsure of the way, and asked an old, hardy-looking man for directions. With his shepherd's stick, he indicated what was little more than a lane, telling her to look out for a small stone cottage amid a copse on the left, which was the occupied gatehouse of Deepdale Hall. Then, as if defending the tenancy in court, he insisted, 'Cottage is Danny Thompson's place. Danny Thompson's place. Kept those squatters away from the big house last year. And those funny travelling folk. Cottage is Danny Thompson's place.'

Watching him shamble away, Jackie appeared moved and troubled.

'Let's mug him,' urged Albert.

Jackie drove on.

'No, I'm serious,' pursued Albert. 'We're townies — let's mug the mumbling country cunt. I want his stick. I could rule half of Durham with a stick like that. My brains and that stick — awesome potential. He might have some money, too. Looked like a miser. Probably carries it all on him. That's why he needs a scary stick.'

They drove along the lane the man had indicated, which soon closely followed the relatively flat course of a small beck running between two immense folds of moorland. Often the lane was so narrow that two cars could only just pass each other. So narrow that an oncoming tractor might prove a major inconvenience. On both sides, a continuous dry stone wall kept adventurous sheep at bay. Immediately beyond those walls the land was sectioned into grassed fields, but these climbed only a limited way up the hills before deferring to open moorland.

Above the moors brooded a big, big sky.

As they dipped and turned with the road's course, deciduous trees came into view on the left — the border of a dense wood, but its extent was not apparent. Proceeding along the edge of the wood, they encountered the one-storey gatehouse, and pulled up. Engulfed on three sides by encroaching, overhanging, creeping branches, and shielded by evergreen bushes in front, if it had been verdant, high summer they might have passed the small, stone-built cottage without spotting it. Furthermore, time and neglect had naturalised it, so that it no longer seemed to be a construction of man, but some insidiously transformed absorption of the forest itself.

A lane ran into the wood, leading to the estate's large, ornate wrought iron gates, chained and secured with a padlock. This forbidding barrier was supported either side by mossy stone columns that stood taller than a stretching man.

Looking apprehensively at the gatehouse, Jackie said, 'I'll toot the horn first to let him know someone's here before knocking.'

'That'll only give him time to load his gun.'

'Yeah. Maybe.'

Jackie tooted, and in response, dirty net curtains twitched in a tiny, murky window. But no one came to the door. 'You'd better wait in the car while I speak to him,' she said, getting out of the car. She knocked on the flaking green door of the gatehouse, but no one answered. 'Mr Thompson,' she called, knocking again, 'I'm from the estate agents. I've come to tell you that the estate's been sold, Mr Thompson. You should have got a letter.'

Albert wound his window down. 'Burn him out,' he urged, causing Jackie to wince and put a shushing finger to her lips.

Jackie knocked again. 'Mr Thompson, I really have to speak with you.'

A face briefly appeared in a window. Then the door slowly opened and a tall, gaunt, old, grey-bearded, incurious man in a shabby brown duffel coat stepped out. His cheeks were sunken; his were eyes watery.

He didn't speak.

Jackie explained who she was and the news she bore, and how it might affect him. He listened in unfriendly silence, and when she'd finished, with slow, long, shaky strides, he walked to the car. Stooping to peer at Albert through the open window, he muttered something. With whatever curiosity he had about Albert satisfied, he returned to Jackie, wordlessly handed her a padlock key from his pocket and pointed to the gates to indicate its area of usefulness. From another pocket, he handed her a collection of keys tied with string. Then he went back into his home and closed the door, leaving Jackie to realise that the act of relinquishing the keys had signified his understanding and resigned acceptance of the situation.

'Okay?' asked Albert as Jackie re-entered the car.

'Seems so. Bit of a character, isn't he? He smelt like old twigs.'

'Would have burnt well, then.'

'What did he say to you?'

Albert shrugged. 'Dunno. Incomprehensible.'

'Maybe he thinks you're the new owner?'

'I'd have had him flogged for insolence by now if I was, then sold as thatching material. Who is the new owner, anyway?'

'Some London solicitor bought it on behalf of some property development company,' explained Jackie, gazing at the gates. 'He came to the office today to finalise the purchase.' She continued to look at the gates. 'Fancy a peek at it?'

Albert said he did fancy a peek, and she handed him the padlock key.

Beyond the gates, the lane became increasingly leaf and twig littered as they followed its gloomy course through the wood, which at one point bridged a shallow, clear stream. Finally emerging from the trees, they received their first view of sombre, imposing Deepdale Hall. A moment later, it shone, as if specially for their arrival, illuminated by the last visible fraction of the sun as it penetrated a cloud on the skyline, sitting in a dip between two dark folds of moorland.

Jackie stopped the car. It was like they'd stumbled upon some great secret, for considering the openness of the surrounding land, Deepdale Hall, and most its grounds, had until now been quite hidden. It had not once been visible from the public road, or even the gates. It owed its seclusion to being set in a natural depression some way up the valley side, so that, seen from anywhere along the valley floor, the general landscape seemed hardly interrupted.

'What a house!' breathed Jackie. 'And look at all this land. What a garden!'

205

'Shitty roof, though,' said Albert, referring to the dark green tarpaulins stretched over part of the edifice. 'Let's go home. My roof's much better.'

Jackie ignored Albert, and drove on toward the house, parking on its gravel-strewn forecourt. Getting out of the car, they surveyed the exterior of Deepdale Hall. As dilapidated mock Gothic mansions go, disregarding the roof, seen from the outside this was not an overly moribund one. True, it must have enjoyed much sprucer days, but that was part of its charm. Sadly, it wasn't quite as Gothic in appearance as Jackie had hoped — too plain; not enough gargoyles — but she liked the look of it nevertheless. The main building was about sixty paces in width and about twenty-five in depth; at least two lofty storeys high, maybe attic rooms as well. Autumn-coloured ivy was abundant, almost completely overrunning some of the narrow, arched windows. In the centre, a vaulted entrance porch with mock fortifications opened up like the black mouth of a cave, leading to a large, wooden door with a heavy iron knocker.

Albert rapped the knocker, just to hear the sound it made.

'Should we have a quick look inside?' proposed Jackie.

'Come on then.'

Jackie chose the grandest key among the bunch she'd received from the old man in the gatehouse, and found that it was the right one to unlock the door, which creaked as she pushed it open. Inside, it was dungeon-dim, as if the night poised to descend upon the land outside was lurking there in malevolent wait.

'You go in first,' said Jackie.

Just inside the door, Albert found some light switches, but they had no effect. The electricity was unlikely to be on, Jackie explained. Three paces ahead was a pair of more ordinary doors. Pushing these open, they tentatively proceeded into the even dimmer interior, where floorboards, gritty under their feet, replaced the hard surface of the entrance porch. Enough twilight was diffusing through the narrow, ecclesiastical windows for them to see that they were now in a bare, high-ceilinged, whitewashed room, as large as all the rooms in Albert's flat combined twice over. At the far end of this room, a sootier darkness lurked, which, once their eyes began adapting to the paucity of light, they could see was actually an arched passage as wide as three plough horses abreast.

With Jackie holding gingerly on to Albert's sleeve, they went to the arch, and standing under it, looked into an even larger, even dimmer room. Almost blind, they began a shuffling exploration. A substantial but indistinct architectural feature drew them closer, whereupon it became a fireplace guarded by two stone griffins. It appeared malevolent and coldly dominant in the gloom. Keeping to walls, they continued around the room, coming across several old school desks and tables. Reaching the opposite side to the fireplace, they found themselves standing at the foot of a wide, grand, curving staircase.

'Sensational place for a party,' said Jackie.

'Bit over the top,' returned Albert. 'I've only got three friends.'

He began ascending the staircase, but Jackie called him back. 'No, Albert, it'll be all fire-damaged upstairs. It's way too dark, anyway.'

'But there might be some bodies.'

'There won't be any bodies.'

'Well maybe just some heads. It's worth a look — I need all the friends I can find.'

'No, come on, let's go now,' insisted Jackie. 'It's too dark. You'll have an accident or get lost. We're not even supposed to be here.'

'Scaredy cat,' said Albert.

Jackie got her way, and they left the house, emerging into the last of the twilight. On their way to the car, Albert stopped and turned to view the house. Now silhouetted against a fiery, brooding sky, it was sombre and darkly dominant, like something rising out of history.

Jackie stood beside Albert. 'Beautiful,' she said.

'It is,' agreed Albert. 'Evocative. Unchanging and timeless.'

'Won't be so unchanging tomorrow. Roofing contractors start work. Poor Mr Thompson. Wonder what'll happen to him?'

'Dunno,' said Albert, 'but I bet he's a hoarder. That cottage of his is probably stuffed full of treasure. Let's ram raid it.'

Jackie put her arm briefly around Albert's waist to guide him toward her car. 'No. No ram raiding. Let's go home now. It's been a long day for me.'

1.18
First Kiss

It was almost eight o'clock when they got back to Durham City. Jackie looked tired, and had hardly spoken on the journey, although her stomach had growled loudly several times. When she pulled up outside Albert's flat and was asked if she was coming in, she said she needed to eat, and was thinking about getting a take-away .

'Get one delivered here,' suggested Albert. 'Local Chinese delivers free.'

Slowed by drowsiness, Jackie took some moments to respond. 'Yeah, all right.' She switched off the engine. 'I'll buy you one too, as a thank you for going to see Mr Thompson with me.'

'Cool. I'm starving.'

'Vegetarian, mind you,' insisted Jackie before opening her door.

'Aw, Jackie,' complained Albert as they got out the car, 'I was already visualising Sweet and Sour Pork. Come on, I went all the way to see that twiggy nutter with you to shield you from his shotgun — lay down my precious life for you if I had to.'

'Albert,' she said, with fair-sounding resolution in her voice, walking behind him to the house, 'if I'm ordering, I'm not asking for meat. It makes me an accessory.'

'Aw, Jackie. Don't be a cunt to me just five days after my birthday.'

'No, Albert.'

'Well pass me the phone after you've ordered yours, and I'll add my order.'

When she'd said "ordering", she'd really meant "paying", but she accepted she'd been remiss, and reluctantly agreed to Albert's compromise.

In Albert's living room, the first thing Jackie did after phoning her food order was to take off her jacket and brush her hair while Albert placed his own order.

'Twenty-five minutes before delivery,' he informed her. 'Okay?'

'I'll survive,' said Jackie.

When Albert came off the phone, Jackie slumped on to the sofa and declared herself capable of murdering a joint.

'There's a huge slab of Moroccan in my room,' he informed her. 'Ciggie papers, too. Help yourself.'

Jackie brightened. 'Yeah? How did you get hold of that?'

Still wearing his big coat, Albert went over to squat by the gas fire, warming his hands. He could see up Jackie's skirt to her white knickers, and the red line they had engendered on her milky, soft inner thighs.

'Not mine. Ron's.'

'And it just walked into your room, did it?'

Albert told her about the episode with Ron's manager that morning — how Scoones was reputed to be on a crusade of suspicion regarding substances in the workplace, and how he'd whisked the dope away from him.

Jackie sat up. 'Shit, Albert. Have you told Ron?'

'He's in Iceland,' returned Albert, with an attitude of lazy indifference that on this particular occasion Jackie found annoying.

'So? You could ring him, couldn't you? It might affect his job. Try his mobile now.'

'Nah, he might mistake it for affection.'

'Albert, you fucker,' chastened Jackie, 'ring him.'

'Stop being so freaked,' he said. 'His dickhead manager saw some dope in his bedroom — gee friggin' whiz.'

Jackie simmered down. Looking into the incandescence of the gas fire, she divulged, 'Barry's on coke all the time. He spends a hundred a week on it.' She paused, then looked at Albert. 'Barry really hates you, you know?'

'Hadn't escaped my attention.'

With her face suddenly screwing up into an expression of incomprehension, shaking her head, she asked, 'Doesn't it get to you? People hating you all the time?'

Albert wagged his finger at her. 'Jackie, if I've told you once, I've told you a thousand times —'

Jackie finished off the sentence for him in a wearily exasperated, breathy voice.

Albert turned the fire down to a little above its minimum, and stood up to remove his coat.

'Can I make that joint now?' asked Jackie.

Indicating she should follow him, Albert went to his bedroom.

'Smells of stale beer in here,' she commented as she sat on the bed.

'And they said I'd never amount to anything,' responded Albert.

'Will Ron mind? About me smoking his dope, I mean.'

'Only when I tell him and wildly exaggerate the liberty,' answered Albert, handing her Ron's weighty stash.

Jackie sat at the computer table to roll her joint, while, behind her back, Albert re-established his shrine to Jennifer on the bedside table. Once all six candles were burning, he switched off the room light.

Jackie turned around, wondering where the continuing light was coming from.

'Oh, not that again,' she moaned.

Albert ignored her displeasure, and sat before his shrine, his back propped against the side of the bed.

Returning to her task, Jackie remarked on how easily the dope was crumbling, and that it didn't need much preparatory warming. 'Hope the stuff isn't too strong,' she said when the joint was complete. 'I might have put too much in. I'll be comatose.' She turned to Albert. 'Do you want me to fill that little pipe I saw on Sunday?'

'Don't know where it is,' he said, sounding indifferent on the matter.

'It's on the floor near my foot.'

'Go on then,' he conceded. 'Not too much, though.'

Once the pipe was ready, Jackie went over to sit on the floor beside Albert.

'Here you go,' she said, handing him the pipe.

He put it next to the candles, saying he'd smoke it after their meal.

Jackie lit her joint off one of the candles, but it absorbed some wax and became a mini-blaze. 'Urh!' she cried out, waving the thing in a frantic attempt to extinguish it. A small, flaming shred of cigarette paper landed in her lap, causing her to panic and ditch the joint so that she could tend to her endangered skirt.

The flaming joint was now on the table, too close to Jennifer's drawing.

'Oi!' rebuked Albert, diving in to rescue his drawing. 'Careful with my love life.'

'Fuck off, Albert,' snapped Jackie, brushing away the inconsequential fire from her lap. 'I'm burning.'

'Yeah, and my heart isn't?' he returned, pulling the drawing away from the riotous joint.

'Oh, give it up. Take something seriously for once.'

As the last of the absorbed candle wax burned off the end of the joint, it became perfectly sedate in its rate of combustion.

Examining her skirt, Jackie discovered it to be blackened slightly over an area the size of her fingernail, but perhaps not actually burnt. 'Think I might have got away with it,' she said. With most of her usual serenity of temper now regained, she took up the joint again, sucking on it. With her first smoky exhalation, she muttered, 'Shit, think I did make this too strong. Still, what's done is done.'

Albert replaced the drawing of Jennifer amid the candles, and gazed at it in moony adoration. 'God, she's fucking gorgeous,' he murmured. 'I'll never stop loving her.'

'She's a line drawing,' Jackie pointed out in a tone of cruel realism.

'She's the line drawing I've been waiting for all my life.'

Putting her joint down, Jackie re-examined her skirt. While experimenting with a wetted finger to see if she could remove the blackening, she asked, 'Albert, why do you get infatuated so often?'

He could tell from her tone that she was manoeuvring towards something analytical or instructional or judgmental.

'Keeps me busy and out of trouble,' he returned.

'Tony says you constantly fall in infatuation because you lost that Susan Murray girl when you were younger and —'

'What the fuck does Tony know about my mind?' interjected Albert, in a slightly raised voice.

'He should know something, he's a psychiatrist,' argued Jackie, picking up her joint again. 'Anyway, it imprinted within you the futility of love, and ever since then you've been reliving the same pattern of hopelessness. The same life script. You've been chasing the unattainable ever since.' With the tips of her fingers, she lifted up the drawing of Jennifer and dangled it in front of his eyes. 'There has to be an insatiable longing in your life, doesn't there? Otherwise you're lost. It's the chase, not the consummation that obsesses you, isn't it? And you have to fail as well, don't you?'

Ignoring Jackie's assertions, Albert reclaimed the drawing, returning it to its place.

After taking another draw on her joint, Jackie went on, 'And Tony says your deep-rooted sense of futility spills over into the rest of your life, and that's why you never do anything to help yourself — get a job, or even get out of bed some days.'

'Some years,' corrected Albert, climbing on to his bed to stare at the ceiling.

Afraid she might become too stoned to eat the awaited meal, Jackie stubbed out the remaining half of the joint, saving it for later. Still sitting on the floor, now gazing at and beyond the candles, in a softer, more intimate voice, she asked, 'What happened with those girls you were seeing a while back? Ron said you left them both after about a month.'

'So?'

Her tone became challenging again. 'Well you claim to be the world's greatest romantic. And Ron said one of them was gorgeous and she cried when you dumped her.'

No response came from Albert. Turning her head, she looked at him, and gently enquired, 'Didn't you get on with them?'

'Not really,' he said, with a shrug in his voice. 'Don't get along with hardly anyone, do I? Only you and a few others.'

The doorbell rang.

'Food's here,' said Albert, immediately getting up and going to the street door.

'I'll get the money,' said Jackie, going to the living room.

Presently, Albert had set out some plates on the living room table, and was delving into the white carrier bag the food had arrived in. 'What's in here?' he wondered out loud, retrieving a stiff brown paper bag. 'Oh, those prawn cracker things.'

Jackie sat at the table while Albert, standing, dished out her food.

'Can we have the telly on in twenty minutes?' she asked. 'There's a programme about Jung I want to watch.'

'Course you can,' answered Albert, now tipping hot, glutinous, Sweet and Sour sauce over pork balls nestled in an accommodating bed of bridal-white rice.

Peep jumped on to Albert's intended chair and began surveying the table for raiding opportunities. 'Knob off, cat,' he said, pushing her away, 'you've given me enough grief this week.' Displaced, with an air of defiant, grumbling resentment, Peep slouched over to lie in front of the gas fire. 'Sorry, Peep,' he said, 'didn't mean to be so nasty.'

Settling down to eat the most sumptuous meal he'd had in months, Albert's mouth was watering in lascivious anticipation. Cutting a pork ball in half, loading it with some rice, he brought the first taste of the feast to his lips.

'Pigs are as intelligent as cats,' said Jackie, as the fork neared his mouth.

'Not my cat,' returned Albert, speaking with his mouth full now. 'My cat's thick.'

When the second half of the pork ball was nearing his mouth, Jackie said, 'Think, Albert. Think about the story behind that fleeting, tasty spoonful. The years of stress. The enclosed cages. The fear. The isolation. The pain.'

212

'That's my story too,' said Albert, chewing, 'but you forgot the indignity and the despair and the bed-wetting.'

Throughout the meal, every time Albert was set to spoon food into his mouth, Jackie sought to advance her case for vegetarianism, insisting that since she'd paid for the meal, she had the right to put him off it. It was so nutritionally unnecessary to consume other intelligent beings, was her main thrust, with a few side stabs relating to the ludicrous environmental inefficiency of rearing animals for slaughter rather than growing crops. She also made passing reference to the contribution the farts of farm animals make to the greenhouse effect, and the much lower chances of succumbing to food poisoning, heart disease or cancer with a vegetarian diet.

Once their appetites had been sated, Albert switched on the television for Jackie, which today was prepared to operate in full colour. They both slumped down on to the sofa to watch. With some minutes to go until her programme was due on, Albert flipped channels while she smoked the remainder of her joint. A documentary of some sort was chanced upon. By unsettling coincidence, it showed a cow being stunned before slaughter, and from the corner of his eye, Albert saw that it made Jackie wince.

Putting his hand to his heart, he said, 'I, Albert Fox, as witnessed by Jackie Nicholson, do solemnly vow to spurn all meat from this day forth.'

Jackie lit up. 'Yeah? You mean it?'

'Mean it. My wrath has been kindled against animal husbandry.'

'Brilliant!'

'Can I still eat eggs?'

'Eggs don't think, so yes. I still eat them. I still eat fish as well. Fish look so stupid.'

Albert flipped channels. More animals — some nature documentary on emperor penguins, huddled against a driving, sunless, Antarctic winter storm, each improbably protecting an egg on their shuffling feet, incubated under the drooping folds of their long-empty bellies.

'Makes you wonder about eating eggs, doesn't it?' commented Albert.

'It does,' admitted Jackie, taking another draw on her joint. 'God, look at the poor, frozen, miserable bastards. See how bad animals have it?'

'That's how I feel all the time,' said Albert, 'except they've got it lucky. All their hearts desire is a tent and some sardines.'

'And what does your heart desire?' asked Jackie, looking at him with a curious intensity.

'You know, standard poet longings,' he answered glibly. 'All that's brightest and best and everlasting.'

'Sounds like religious longing,' huffed Jackie before taking another drag on her joint.

Albert wagged a languorous finger at her. 'Jackie, if I've told you once, I've told you a thousand times: if you're going to talk to me, talk sense.'

With a flimsy structure of ash about to fall from the joint's tip, Jackie asked Albert to get the ashtray she'd been using in his bedroom.

'Can't get up. Too melancholic.'

'Please,' whined Jackie, giving him a push with her shoulder. 'I'm really tired.'

'Still too melancholic. Likely to be so for quite some time.'

'You're not too melancholic,' Jackie whiningly insisted, now forced to smoke her joint upright to balance the ash.

'I know,' agreed Albert, 'I'm worse than melancholic now. I'm... there's just no word for it. I've gone beyond the mere human experience of misery. Perhaps in the desolate language of the emperor penguin there's some word that conveys my woe. Some mournful penguin word that relates to those ice-bound, forsaken months they spend nursing the forlorn hope of new life nestled perilously on their frost-mauled feet. Their word for keeping that single, fragile egg alive through the dark Antarctic winter, with their only solace being an uncertain memory of less cold days having followed on from some previous long night, though they be troubled always by gnawing, icy doubt. The word, the most plaintive word in all nature, probably sounds like this: *burrawkoo*.'

It was at times like this that Jackie didn't know whether to get on her knees and worship Albert, or run screaming from him.

'Skeel,' she said.

'What?'

'Skeel,' she repeated. 'A happy penguin word. Penguin for "I've just found a nuclear-powered hot water bottle".'

'Never validly exclaimed by any penguin in history,' declared Albert, getting up, 'but they invented it all the same, and live in dejected, misapprehended, ice-bound hope.'

'Skeel,' said Jackie defiantly.

'Burrawkoo,' said Albert, in a suitably moaning tone as he left the room. When he returned, bearing the ashtray, he was shuffling and inching rather than walking, and Jackie saw that he had an egg balanced on his feet. 'Burrawkoo,' he moaned miserably. 'Burrawkoo. Burrawkoo.'

When he sat on the sofa, the egg remained on his feet.

'Make me a coffee before the programme starts,' requested Jackie.

'Can't. Incubating an egg.'

'I'll incubate it for you,' she said, taking the egg and placing it on her own feet. 'Coffee, please.'

'Can't. Coarse labour would dull my poetic sensitivities. And what use is a dulled poet?'

Jackie sighed with exasperation. 'Albert, shut the fuck up about being a poet. You're not a poet. Poets write poems. You've never written a poem.'

'But I have the feelings of a poet, and that's what counts, lady.'

'Yeah? So how do you poet's feel?'

'Like other people, only more so.'

Albert knew he had her on that comeback, and let her dangle a while.

'Anyway,' he eventually continued, assuming a tone of indignant protest, 'so where does my fateful anticipation of loss and sorrow come from? I'm a poet, all right.'

'You're not,' said Jackie, adhering to her contradiction. 'Poets write poems.'

'Could write a poem if I wanted to.'

'Prove it. Write one now.'

'Can't. Got to make you some coffee.'

'Fuck the coffee. Write a poem. Now.'

Albert now appeared excessively evasive and panicky, but this was swept away by a sudden hurricane of noble resolve, and he stood up. 'Right, you doubting bitch, I'll write a poem moving enough to make a shark weep.'

He strode out the room.

'And make it rhyme,' Jackie called after him. 'None of that cop-out modern shit. Let's see how poetic you really are.'

Albert went to his room and switched on his computer, while Jackie went to the kitchen to put the egg back in the fridge and make coffee. He stayed in his room while she watched her programme. When it ended, sixty minutes later, she went to him, and found him illuminated by a single candle, lying on his bed, staring at the ceiling.

'How's the poem coming along,' she asked, stepping into the

bedroom.

'Finished. It's on the table. It's an epic.'

'Yeah? Can I read it?'

'If you think you can handle titanic extremes of pathos.'

Jackie collected the poem, printed over two sheets of A4, and sat on the side of the bed to read it.

THE RHYME OF THE BRAVE BRAVE MAN
by Albert Fox, aged 24. His first ever poem.

Penguin penguin tell have you seen
With your sight so keen a brave brave man
Who hatched a plan to take a flag
Inside a bag upon a sled he would pull
Indefatigable 'cross your frozen clime
In your summertime

Poet poet we cold penguins speak
In tones so bleak of such a man
Who had a plan to plant a flag
That he did drag 'cross endless snow
And of his woe when he did see
He'd brought company

Penguin penguin what company
Did brave brave he who put a flag
Inside a bag bring to your
Cold icy shore and of his woe
I need to know to write a rhyme
Of his hard time

Poet poet he put that flag
Inside a bag but mice did creep
And run and leap to make a bed
Of white and red cloth they found
Bravely bound to come our way
The very next day

Penguin penguin please tell more
I implore of this strange tale
And of his bale and what he saw
In winds so raw when he looked
For what he'd tucked inside that bag
A noble rag

Poet poet his heart did break
And such a lake of tears he cried
When he spied that mice had fed
(Who at once had fled) upon that flag
Inside that bag that he did tow
'Cross endless snow

Penguin penguin what came of him
Who on a whim took England's flag
Inside a bag then with tears did see
That mice so wee had made their dinner
As they got thinner from that fabric
Of fate so tragic

Poet poet the flag was shreds
Its whites and reds all chewed and torn
And he did mourn so bitterly
To think that he had braved so much
But now did clutch in his cold hand
Insult to his noble land

Penguin penguin such calamity
But where is he who bore that flag
Inside that bag wherein mice did feast
Not the least caring of the woe they wrought
And of how distraught he would be
All eternity

Poet poet he is there still
In icy chill at the Southern Pole
That was his goal when he brought that flag
Inside that bag from England's shore
That mice did gnaw away to shreds
First to make their beds

Penguin penguin tell does he live
So I may give his family
Those children three a hope that he
May one day come back again
Someday when skylarks shall sing
And bells shall ring

Poet poet when he did weep
Such tears did seep as he cried
He soon died for his tears then froze
Upon his clothes and held him still
Against his will and murderous cold
Killed one so bold

Penguin penguin so he did die
And now does lie on cold cold snow
Where surely no dead thing can rot
Or worms cannot spoil that man
Whose noble plan was to take a flag
Inside a bag

Poet poet true on our snow
Worms cannot grow on fallen men
And bodies when they cease to be
Last eternity for on our shore
Breeds nought to gnaw the flesh of those
In final repose

Penguin penguin then this I say
That one day by mankind's science
In bold defiance of nature's plan
That frozen man whose eyes do wait
In perfect state once more shall see
His children three

Poet poet his eyes were gnawed
His limbs were clawed by fifteen mice
Now chilled to ice who once they
All could say that he was dead
Came back and fed upon his flesh
Cold kept so fresh

Penguin penguin lonely as the ice
Cold as the mice that crept inside
And then did hide within a bag
That held a flag transported to
With derring-do your place below
All bound with snow

Poet poet you know so well
The frozen hell that is our life
Know the strife that marks our days
And the ways our spirit can fail
And why we wail as you do to
Burrawkoo Burrawkoo Burrawkoo

The end

Once she'd finished reading, with a disappointed and critical tone, Jackie muttered, 'Hmm, this the great poetry of Albert Fox we've all been waiting for? Not exactly Shakespeare, is it?'

'But wholesome and suitable for children of all ages,' countered Albert, still looking at the ceiling. 'And of a sweeping, epic nature, you'll have to agree.'

Putting the poem aside, Jackie grumbled, 'Sweeping, epic piss take. Should have expected it, coming from you.'

The woman from upstairs began moving around, her shuffling, creaking footsteps slowly crossing the ceiling, then back again, over and slowly over again.

'Did the egg hatch?' asked Albert.

'Yes, but Peep ate the chick.'

'Burrawkoo.'

Glancing upwards, Jackie remarked, 'The woman from upstairs is a bit active tonight.'

Albert offered no comment, and Jackie turned her attention to other matters. 'Will it be all right if I roll another joint before I go? I won't use so much this time.'

'Do what you like.'

Going to sit at the desk, Jackie prepared her second joint of the evening. When it was ready, she took it to the candle. 'I'll be a bit more intelligent lighting it this time,' she promised.

Seeing Albert's pipe by the candle, she reminded him that he still hadn't touched it.

'Yeah, I'll have a toot now,' he said, unenthusiastically getting off the bed to sit on the floor for his smoke.

Jackie sat beside him. 'I'd better not smoke all of this,' she said, looking at her joint. 'Got to drive home later. Smoke it next time I'm around.' She lay her head back against the bed, exposing her stretched, smooth neck while Albert sucked on his pipe. 'It's chilly in here,' she complained, sitting up straight again. 'You should get some kind of heater. You must freeze lying in here in just that T-shirt.'

'I'm used to it,' he returned, in puffs of smoke.

Within seconds, Albert felt the dope take effect, the usual milky sensation clouding his brain. His hearing mutated — he was never sure whether dope made his hearing more acute, or just more discriminatory. On many occasions when he'd been alone and stoned, listening to music or the television, he'd believed and worried that the sound was up too loud until some other noise that he knew must be little more than a whisper would drown out what he'd been fearing was a din. Like the other week, watching the news, stoned, thinking the sound was up way too loud, a strange, unaccountable hissing noise got louder and louder until he could no longer hear the newscaster. Eventually, he'd realised he was hearing the kettle boil way off in the kitchen, which he'd plugged in but forgotten about.

Now, the footfalls of the woman from upstairs seemed to fill the room for Albert. In a moment of druggy anxiety, the experience suddenly felt claustrophobic, almost threatening.

'It is a bit cold in here,' he said, putting the pipe down. 'Let's go into the living room.'

Getting up, Albert collected his ghetto blaster, and, leaving the bedroom, asked Jackie to bring the candle. Once in the living room, he plugged in the music, and Jackie placed the candle on the table before switching off the electric light. With the fire set to a gentle heat, he sat on the floor to enjoy its warmth, back rested against the sofa. Jackie sat beside him, and the fire's diffuse red glow made their faces seem flushed.

'Who's this?' she asked softly, referring to the music.

'Nick Drake. Five Leaves Left.'

'It's beautiful. Sad, though. It sounds like autumn.'

Albert closed his eyes. Stoned, each instrument could be heard above the others, existing in its own space, yet remaining deftly woven within the lush fabric of melancholy sound. The most subtle sub-rhythms could be isolated; every harmony and every counterpoint could be apperceived.

Jackie, too, seemed content to sit in quiet, thoughtful appreciation of the music.

As the songs played on, Jackie, becoming drowsy, leant lightly against Albert's shoulder, her head inclined towards his. And when the album finished and he got up, she stirred as if awakening from a long sleep.

'What time is it?' she asked.

'Nearly midnight,' he answered, scrutinising the table to see if there was any food left he could scavenge.

'Shit, I'd better be going,' she said, but without moving. 'I'm too tired to drive all the way back to Darlington. I'll nod off.'

'Sleep in Ron's room if you like,' offered Albert.

Discovering there to be some prawn crackers left, Albert began nibbling them.

'No, I'll go home,' decided Jackie wearily, her gaze cast down. 'Could stay at my sister's. No, she'll be in bed by now.'

'Got some serious munchies,' said Albert, drinking from a half glass of water to help the crackers go down.

Jackie got off the floor and brushed her hair before putting her jacket on. 'It'll be one o'clock before I get to bed. Have to get up again at seven.'

'You should have thought about that when you applied for the job,' mumbled Albert through a mouthful of crackers.

'Yeah,' conceded Jackie, with a quiet sigh, heading for the door, 'you're right.'

Carrying in one hand his bag of prawn crackers, and in the other a glass of water, Albert saw Jackie to the street door, and watched until she drove off. Returning indoors, he retrieved the pipe and block of dope from his bedroom, taking them into the living room, thinking he'd have another little amount and listen to some more music before bed.

She did mean to go home, but, two streets away, she turned her car around and headed back towards Devon Road, pulling up outside Albert's flat. Sitting in the vehicle, she tried to figure out just what in the hell she thought she was up to. If she went to him now and told him how she really felt, what good would it do? At best, he might be her reluctant lover for just this night — he'd ditched prettier faces than hers. Yes, she was being crazy, she told herself. There was absolutely no way he could be interested in her as a lover. If she had the looks of that Jennifer person she'd seen in the photo, or Sarah, or even her own sister, or even just bits of her own sister, then it might be a different story. She could make a play for him then. But she didn't have looks on her side, and knew that well enough.

She began counting her misfortunes. Her uneven, saggy breasts. Her flaccid bum. Her missing first chin. Her second chin. Her large, moon-like face. Christ, she didn't even walk like a normal person. And was it not Albert himself who'd first joked that she had the grace of a bag of putty? It was — yet how she still wanted him.

Head getting the better of heart, she put the car into gear. But with an impulsive, jerky motion she pulled out the ignition key, killing the engine. She would go to him. After all, she felt something special existed between Albert and her, something to do with implicit understanding. Maybe that's what he really needed in a relationship, she speculated, conveniently disregarding her earlier support for Tony's theories: implicit understanding. Maybe that's why his few previous relationships hadn't lasted?

She got out of the car.

Reaching Albert's gate, she stopped. But then she continued, crossing the garden to tap lightly on the living room window.

Seeing Jackie at the window, Albert put his half-smoked pipe down, and got up to go to the street door.

'Forgotten something?' he asked.

Jackie nodded slightly, and he stood aside so she could enter. Inside the flat, she went to the sofa and sat down. She had shakily resolved to risk all, not least her pride, and tell him how she felt. If only a single night's intimacy came of it, then at least she would have had the privilege of a night with the only person who'd ever made her feel weak with longing. The only person — sometimes merely upon hearing his name — who could make her heart feel like it was going to stop or burst or something glorious. And maybe the crippling spell would be broken after tonight, whatever the outcome?

Bringing his bag of crackers, Albert sat beside her, and Jackie suddenly felt in the grip of something powerfully physiological — something supra-physiological. From her tightening scalp to her strangely tingling feet, and every enfeebled inch between, she was alive to his proximity. It was like she had had the fright of her life, except there was no resolution, no relief, no exaltation of escape; the gripping fright went on and on, and she feared she was about to cry or scream or die or something unknown.

'Well?' he spluttered, stuffing half a cracker into his mouth.

Staring intensely at the fire, Jackie was beginning to tremble. 'Albert, there's something I have to tell you.'

'Yeah?' he mumbled, chewing.

Jackie's revelation was not forthcoming.

'Is my hair peaking?' he asked, taking a drink of water. 'Is that it?'

He stuffed another piece of cracker into his mouth.

Jackie's whole body had become a confused rush of anguished desire. But although she was desperate for the person sitting beside her, some part of her mind was clearly saying she should leave before any damage to their friendship was done. She held herself in check, listening to that small voice counselling refrain. 'Nothing. It'll wait,' she said, wishing she'd gone straight home instead of weakening and coming back. It was stupid of her to believe she could ever have the sort of romances others enjoyed. It would never happen. She had nothing to offer. She was unattractive and peculiar.

'No, tell me. You've got me all curious now.'

She knew she was very close to some sort of emotional deluge. Tears were welling up. She rose quickly, and hurried to the door, keeping her back to Albert, hoping she could retain control until she was alone in her car.

Albert finally began to realise something strange was going on.

With the door handle within reach, Jackie stopped, turned around, and dashed to Albert, throwing herself at him on the sofa, her lips ardently seeking his. In automatic self-defence, he raised the crackers bag to protect his face from assault, and Jackie's lips met with greasy brown paper.

He rolled off the sofa.

Wounded by the cruel rejection, crushed by the failure, Jackie hunched up into a ball on the sofa and burst into sobs. 'I love you, Albert, I really do. I've loved you for months.'

It took some seconds for Albert to work out what had happened: she'd made a frantic, clumsy pass at him, and he'd humiliated her with a paper bag. 'Fuck. Sorry,' he said, not really knowing what to do or say. In time, he sat beside her, placing an awkwardly comforting hand on her back. 'You took me by surprise. Sorry.'

Shrugging him off, Jackie went over to sit at the table, hiding her shamed face in her hands.

'Sorry,' said Albert, sheepishly.

223

Jackie's crying began to lessen. 'I'm sorry too. It won't happen again. I promise.' She stood up, wiping tears away from her cheeks. 'I'll go now. Sorry.'

She proceeded to the door, but Albert moved to block her. 'No, don't go yet. Not while you're still crying.'

Avoiding his eyes, making an initial, small show of still wanting to leave, Jackie quietly implored, 'Let me go. Please.'

'Don't cry, Jackie. Not over me.'

She looked at him. Her pale eyes were soulful, unsure and surrendering.

'Don't cry, Jackie.'

Slowly, tentatively, she drew nearer to him. Her arms became encircling, and her head rested softly against his shoulder.

He returned the gentle embrace.

'I'm sorry, Jackie.'

'I want you, Albert,' she murmured, 'I really do want you.'

'So my hair is peaking?'

She smiled crossly and softly thumped his back.

'Sorry,' he said.

Lifting her head, their eyes met: hers tearful and deeply yearning, kaleidoscoping the candle's reflection; his in shadow.

'I love you, Albert.'

Her tearful eyes closed. Tenderly, sensually, she brought her yielding, parting lips to his. And when their lips touched as lovers' lips touch, she breathed a low moan. It was blessed resolution. It was the finding of peace.

It was *wrong*.

As they kissed, it was all her, and little of him, she suddenly, starkly realised. What was she doing? He didn't want her lips against his. Of course he didn't. She should break away. This was abject. It felt like a kind of betrayal. It wasn't betrayal, she knew — he was taking pity on her —, but in the swirl of emotions she was caught up in, it *felt* like betrayal. Confused, she drew back, frantically searching his shadowed eyes.

Then the screams began.

Everything changed. The ambience instantly chilled. Leaving Jackie in the middle of the room, Albert switched on the main light, listening intently to the cries.

'It's in the house, isn't it?' she said, in a worried, hushed voice.

'Definitely.'

More screams. Strange screams. Closer to wails than screams.

Albert went to his flat's door. Jackie followed. The wails, definitely female, were reverberating in the house's entrance hall. He opened the door, and to his stoned mind the hall was a cacophony of alarming noise. Stepping out, the noise abated, but he now heard someone coming down the stairs. With Jackie behind him, he moved deeper into the hall. The woman from upstairs appeared, a frantically shuffling mismatch of gaudy jumble sale clothes. Looking more haunted, wretched and tormented than ever, she went as fast as she could to the street door and began snatching at the lock, but was too confused and distressed to work it. Catching sight of Albert and Jackie, she ceased her ineffectual efforts and stood looking at them.

'Go and find out what's going on,' whispered Jackie, encouraging Albert with a small push.

He resisted the push.

Jackie gave him another small push. 'Go on. She's your neighbour.'

'No, please,' he said, sounding distressed, 'I can't. Not when I'm stoned. You go, please. You go.'

'What is it? Why are you so scared?'

'My mother,' said Albert, briefly closing his eyes.

'Your mother?'

'She's too like my mother. You go, please.'

Puzzled by Albert's reluctance, Jackie approached the woman from upstairs, asking, 'Are you all right? Do you want someone to open the door for you? Was that you screaming?'

'Upstairs,' said the frail, nervous woman from upstairs.

'What's upstairs?'

'Legs. Upstairs.'

Jackie looked back to Albert and suggested, 'Go upstairs and look around.'

Albert shook his head firmly. 'Too stoned.'

'Go on,' urged Jackie, 'I'll wait here with her.'

'Legs,' said the woman from upstairs, pointing up the stairs. 'Harry's legs.'

Jackie and Albert exchanged looks. Relenting, he approached the stairs.

'Don't worry, my friend's going to have a look for you,' Jackie told the cadaverous woman.

The first flight of stairs brought Albert on to a short, uncarpeted, dingy landing. But he had to go higher, for he knew Harry lived on the top floor, since he'd often seen him at his window. At the far end of the landing, a second, narrower flight of stairs led to the attic flat. Approaching this second flight, unpleasant smells met his nose. Old toilet smells. These stairs were steeper than the first flight, and Albert wondered how many times Harry must have fallen drunken victim to them.

A dim light seeped down the staircase. Albert peered upwards and saw a pair of feet in shoes lying over the top steps, motionless. Stoned, it all seemed so cinematic to him, like he was the camera in a suspense movie. Moving slowly and apprehensively, each step ascended brought more of the person into view. It was surely Harry, and Albert realised he was not lying collapsed as he'd first believed, but was hanging, his thighs suspended some inches off the floor while his feet protruded over the top steps.

The smell was now strong and foul. It took Albert back to a long-abandoned railway signal box he'd explored as a truanting child, in which piles of decomposing faeces had lain in a fire-blackened corner. Halfway up the stairs, he began to see Harry's torso. Another tentative step revealed his contorted face, and Albert now figured how the alcoholic had met his undignified end. One more step brought all of Harry into view. His face was fixed in an expression of pain and surprise, reddened eyes bulging. A cigarette stub was in the corner of his dry, dead mouth. An all-but-empty whisky bottle lay by his side — Albert recognised it as his own whisky bottle, the one he'd bought with Jackie's loan.

Becoming aware that Jackie was calling his name, Albert turned and went back down.

'Are you all right? Albert? Where are you?'

He met her halfway up the lower flight of stairs.

'It's Harry. He's hung himself trying to open his door.'

'What? Hung himself trying to open his door?'

Albert sat on the bottom step.

'Hung himself — with that cord he uses to keep his keys on. The key's in the keyhole, and he's hanging from it. He must have fallen over and strangled, too drunk to get to his feet. Looks like he's been dead some time.'

'Dead?' exclaimed the woman from upstairs in a murmured, breathy gasp of bewildered, fearful astonishment that seemed to express a dozen different feelings, not least of which was annoyance — definitely some annoyance. 'He's dead?'

'Dead,' confirmed Albert, not wishing to look at her.

Passing Albert, Jackie went to the woman from upstairs. 'Do you know who we should call? Does he have any family?'

Shuffling between two dustbins to put distance between herself and Jackie, with sudden, embarrassed, agitated irritation, the woman from upstairs said, 'He's my husband.'

'Your husband?'

'Yes.'

Looking at Albert, Jackie knew him to be just as surprised and bemused at this matrimonial revelation as she was. Looking back to the woman from upstairs, Jackie saw that she was rapidly sinking into some desolate, withdrawn condition.

'Come out from there,' said Jackie gently, holding out her hand.

The woman from upstairs looked at Jackie, but it was now like she was looking from beyond her own grave. Reaching to take her bony hand, Jackie encouraged her to leave the company of the dustbins, leading her nearer to the stairs.

'I'll phone the police,' said Albert, going to his flat.

In no hurry to go back into the hall after making the 999 call, Albert sat on the end of his sofa. Things felt vaguely heavy and burdensome. It was a drag, that's what it was, a depressing drag. Allowing what he gauged to be a couple of minutes to pass, he returned to Jackie, who was now standing at the open street door, watching for the police.

The woman from upstairs was standing among the dustbins again.

'Thought I heard a siren just now,' said Jackie as Albert approached.

Faint strobing on the chimneys of some houses further down the street told Albert an emergency vehicle was close by. 'They're just round the corner.'

A police car appeared, pulling up across the street. Two youthful officers, one male, one female, trotted to the house.

'Hi. Responding to a call about a death,' said the WPC as she reached the gate.

It was a subdued, sombre Albert who took the male constable to see Harry while the WPC stayed with Jackie and the woman from upstairs. Remaining on the first landing, he directed the constable up the second stairs, answering his questions in a voice that had become low and monotonous. He offered his own theory as to the cause of death, but the constable made no comment. Soon, two more constables arrived, both going up to view the corpse.

Overhearing their jargonised conversation, Albert surmised that they deemed a forensic investigation appropriate.

Coming down with the first constable, Albert met an ambulance crew arriving. They were directed by the WPC to attend to the woman from upstairs, who nervously shrunk back from them, going deeper in between the dustbins.

'I'll need to take a statement from you and your friend,' said the constable, taking out a notepad.

'Okay,' said Albert.

Wearing a look of tired, drooping concern, Jackie was standing by the street door, watching the woman from upstairs meekly resisting capture.

Albert gestured for Jackie to come over to him. 'We have to give statements,' he said, turning so that he didn't have to look at the woman from upstairs.

'All right.'

Jackie gave her account of the night's events first, then stood by Albert's side as he began to tell his more detailed story. All the while, behind them, the woman from upstairs — Harry's wife — was being coaxed, gently talked to, and reasoned with, but she would not agree to leave the house.

'Go with them,' a new, stern voice said. 'They want to help you.'

Albert turned around. It was the landlord. He'd obviously dressed in a hurry; no socks on, no shirt under his jacket. Strands of his dark hair, long at the fringe but usually neatly combed back, were falling over his eyes. His face was like stone.

The ambulance crew and the WPC were clearly uncomfortable with his overbearing tone and manner.

'Go with them,' the landlord again ordered, pointing to the street door.

The woman from upstairs, with a haunted, nervous, yet strangely yearning look in her eyes, complied, shuffling out from behind the bins.

Seeing that that was taken care of, the landlord approached the constable taking Albert's statement, bluntly cutting into the conversation. 'Tell me what's happened.'

The constable was clearly annoyed to be disrespectfully interrupted. 'And who are you?'

'Son of the deceased,' answered the landlord tersely.

Fuck. Harry was the landlord's father, which, Albert presumed, made the woman from upstairs his mother.

His tone hardened by a perception of insolence from the son of the deceased, the constable began giving the story — as he currently understood it — to the landlord, who listened impassively.

Deferring to the landlord, Albert, looking pale and fatigued, moved away from the constable, nearer to his flat's open door.

'You okay?' asked Jackie gently, coming to stand at Albert's side.

'Yeah,' he answered, in a kind of weary sigh. 'I had to be stoned tonight, didn't I?'

In a natural action of support, Jackie slipped her right hand into his left. As if in some vague, weary dream, at first Albert didn't respond, but then he returned the comforting clasp.

'When I held her hand, it was awful,' said Jackie. 'There was no response at all. It felt like a bird's talon.'

'No, please, Jackie, don't tell me. Not when I'm stoned. That's when they can really trouble me.'

'What can?'

To the accompaniment of a jaded exhalation, Albert's eyes closed. When they opened again, it was to stare down at the floor.

'Memories, Jackie.'

'Memories? About your mother? You said the woman from upstairs was like her.'

'Too much like her. Too fucking much.'

Jackie looked at him while he continued to look leadenly down at the floor.

'I've never heard you mention her before,' said Jackie. 'Do you want to talk about it?'

'If I talked about it, you'd think I was making it up.'

'Try me.'

'Forget it, Jackie,' he said, with some firmness. 'It's not important.'

'It doesn't sound not important.'

Two men arrived, each wearing all-over white laboratory suits and gloves, and carrying aluminium equipment cases. Albert leaned against the wall behind him and watched as they opened their cases to take out strange looking cameras and instruments before going upstairs.

'I really should be going,' said Jackie. 'I'm dead on my feet.' She looked at Albert, and after some hesitation, ventured to say, 'Unless you want me to stay with you longer? You look like you need company.' She waited for some reply or response. Any at all. 'Do you want me to stay? Just tonight?'

Albert shifted his standing position, and in doing so, his hand left Jackie's. 'No, it's all right,' he said without looking at her, and sounding as if he'd hardly been listening. 'The dope's wearing off now. I'll be okay soon.'

He continued to look away from her, down the hall to the where the police were.

'Good,' said Jackie. 'Glad to hear it. You'll be back to your usual wise-cracking self then.'

She left without another word.

He showed no emotion, the landlord, as the constable spoke. When he spoke in return, it was with cold concision. But when two men appeared on the staircase, struggling to keep a weighty, covered stretcher level, he showed his first involved response. Looking like he'd suddenly suffered a twinge of pain, he turned away from the sight, moving near to where Albert was standing, safely away from the stretcher's exit line to the street door.

To keep out of the stretcher bearers' way, the constable followed the landlord.

Albert sombrely watched as the body was manoeuvred down the stairs.

Behind the stretcher bearers, someone carried a clear plastic evidence bag containing the whisky bottle.

'Don't know how he got hold of that,' the landlord remarked to the constable. 'He was allowed six cans of lager a day. I had a pre-paid arrangement with the off licence. Six cans, spread out over the day. Not a drop more, and nothing stronger.'

'It was mine,' said Albert, meant as a sorry admission, but sounding flat. 'I left it out on the stairs last night.'

The landlord sternly faced Albert. 'You gave an alcoholic a full bottle of whisky?'

This wasn't the same, gaze-averting man who collected the rent, Albert understood. This was someone bulging with pent-up anger. Swift to try to clear up the misunderstanding, Albert explained, 'I didn't give him it. I accidentally left it out. I was really pissed last night. He must have found it.'

'You fucking moron,' the landlord growled with disdain and acrimony.

'Hey,' said the constable, pointing a cautioning finger at the landlord.

'Keep out of this,' returned the landlord swiftly. 'This is between me and my tenant.' He looked at Albert again. 'Time I had a word with you about something. Something important.' He strode towards

Albert's door. 'Follow.'

Taking a moment to condescend to the landlord's command, Albert began to follow him into the flat.

'Don't forget I'll need you to finish your statement,' the constable reminded Albert.

'Yeah. Won't be long,' said Albert, his voice reflecting the drag he was finding it all. 'Just see what he wants.'

'If you need us in there, just shout.'

'It'll be all right.'

The landlord was standing in front of the fire and holding the ashtray Jackie had been using when Albert entered his living room.

'Interesting smoking habits you have,' said the landlord grimly, picking out and displaying the half-smoked joint Jackie had left.

'Just a bit of dope,' said Albert.

'A bit?' the landlord challenged sternly. Turning around, he picked up Ron's block of Moroccan from on top of the fireplace, where Albert had left it. 'Should we ask those coppers if this is just a bit? Sell the stuff, do you?'

Albert wanted to tell him to fuck himself.

'No.'

'Grow the stuff though, don't you?'

'Fuck yourself.'

The landlord glared at Albert, and Albert felt adrenaline course cold through his body. But the landlord tempered himself, and replaced the block of dope where he'd found it. 'I'm not having drug stuff going on in the house where my mother lives,' he said sternly, 'or having the stuff grown in my garden. I want you out in a week. Both of you. Out by next Wednesday evening.'

He left the flat.

Albert sat on the end of his sofa. The feeling of vague heaviness and oppression was resurgent. That had been a drag. A depressing drag.

*

Wretched tears wet Jackie's face once she was in her car. She couldn't even give herself away for one night — to the person she most wanted. The person she'd most wanted ever. She should never have tried. Those things weren't meant for her. Never had she cried like this before. Tonight, the stoicism that had marked her life finally failed, and driving along, her tears reduced the street lights to watery, impressionistic images.

On a duel carriageway just outside Durham, her distress became so intense and abject she couldn't go on any further, and, half blind, she pulled into a short, unlit lay-by. Immediately sliding her seat back, she buried her face between her knees, sobbing and convulsing, her hair spilling down to the floor. 'Why? Why?' she pitiably asked in a strangulated voice, over and over again, pouring out her years of unspoken anguish and heartache. 'Why? Someone please tell me why.' Every time she felt the agony about to lessen its grip on her, it would rise again, and the wretchedness would begin anew. Suffocating, desolate wretchedness.

But even the most violent storm blows itself out, and Jackie's sobbing eventually abated. Becoming quieter and quieter, she finally sat up, sniffling and wiping away tears. The tempestuous misery that had seemed to her like the beginning of some wild madness had all but passed, and in its wake, a spent, hollow feeling. One hour earlier she had felt like she was at the mercy of a raging torment cast upon her from above by the cruellest of the gods, but now that torment had eased to a dull, more worldly-feeling after-sorrow. Vaguely watching the cars go past, she had a sense that a key change had occurred in the music that the Fates had composed for her. A minor key now played. Her life's grand passage was over, and her symphony would never again soar or plunge.

Reaching down to slide the seat forward, her hair felt unnaturally cold falling over her face. Fingering it, she realised it was, in parts, wet with her own tears. She began to brush it, but stopped, dropping the brush on to the back seat. Putting the car in gear, she pulled out of the lay-by and joined the sparse south-bound traffic. Within forty minutes, she was in her bed in the small flat she rented cheap from her property-letting employers.

When her alarm went off less than four hours later, Jackie wasn't sure whether she'd slept well or not at all. But the very second the clock began bleeping, she pulled her duvet back and got out of bed in almost mechanical manner. From the bed, she moved over to sit at her dressing table, and regarded herself in the mirror. Her hair was a tangle this morning. Women often said they were jealous of her lush hair — the only truly feminine thing nature had given her, she used to think. She looked at her face, which she'd neglected to cleanse before bed. The make up she'd been wearing was now pillow-smudged. And there had been all that crying, too. All that crying. All that bitter crying. But it didn't matter now. Nothing like that mattered now. She knew she would never cry like that again.

With no forethought to the deed, she retrieved a pair of sharp scissors from the top drawer of the dressing table, and holding them firmly, looked hard at herself in the mirror.

Then she did it.

1.19
Stairway to 'Eaven

Wearing an old Army surplus jumper, Simon was walking slowly across the mossy, gravel forecourt of Deepdale Hall — the same mansion house that Albert had visited with Jackie only days before. He was dowsing intently with a small, clear crystal suspended from his finger by a gold thread. Occasionally, superimposed on to its minor, chaotic perturbations, the crystal would move in tiny, irregular circles. 'Amazing,' he breathed, seeing significance in some new pattern of motion. Briefly looking up from his work, he scanned the blue and billowing-white sky, the sparse ginger stubble on his chin and upper lip glinting like glass splinters in the sunlight.

Nearby, leaning up against his cab, Carl was admiring the facade of Deepdale Hall, with its autumn-coloured ivy aglow in the midday sun.

"Ow long since it wuz occupied, Simon?'

'Two years,' answered Simon, now dowsing again, his crystal refracting the sunlight into flashes of colour. 'It was a special school when the fire hit.'

'Yeah? Funny kids, y'mean?'

'That's right.'

'Fantastic, ain't it?' said Carl. 'Needs a lot of work, mind. What time did y'say those builders are comin'?'

'They're due now.'

'Be great once the roof's sorted,' predicted Carl before a look of concern took over his mutable face. 'It's all paid for? We're not trespassin'?'

'No, we're not trespassing,' assured Simon. 'The purchase was completed by my investment partner's solicitor yesterday while you

233

were waiting in the cathedral car park. He picked the keys up from the estate agent this morning while you were still asleep and brought them to me at the campsite.'

'Yeah?' smiled Carl. 'So that's what you were doing this morning? 'Ow come you do everything big like that when I'm not around?'

It had been said as a harmless observation, but, unbeknown to Carl, Simon's face had revealed a discomfort.

''Oo's this investor partner of yours, anyway?' continued Carl.

'You don't know him.'

''E must 'ave buckets of money. 'Ow much wuz the 'ouse exactly?'

'I'm not allowed to say.'

'Yeah? Where'd 'e get 'is money?'

'Property. Renting property.'

Carl wandered over to Simon, who continued to dowse.

'Yeah? Where d'you meet 'im?'

'He owns the house I live in in Lambeth.'

'Yeah? Your landlord? No offence meant, but small wonder 'e's rich — didn't spend no money on your gaff.'

Simon didn't reply. He'd become too absorbed with his crystal, which was again moving in small circles. 'Amazing,' he breathed.

'So we sleep 'ere from now on?' Carl asked for the purpose of final clarification. Until now, they had been sleeping in a tent on a camp site near Durham.

'That's right,' said Simon, still dowsing.

To take in his new circumstances, Carl slowly turned a complete circle. His gaze first swept across the undulating panorama of russet moors beyond the estate, where Nature played out her wildest moods. Then his eye lingered on the mellow copse. From there it was attracted to the babbling stream flowing into the copse. Then it returned to Deepdale Hall, which seemed as natural a part of the landscape as any tree or hill.

Suddenly beaming, he said, 'All right up North, innit?'

'Amazing,' returned Simon, 'I'm finding so much energy here.'

'Yeah? Can I 'ave a go?'

'Yes,' said Simon, willingly handing Carl the crystal. 'You should try too. But it might not work for you. Not many people can channel the energy.'

Suddenly looking anxious, even though he'd proposed the experiment himself, Carl received the crystal like he was being handed a violin for the first time and ordered to play before a public audience.

Dangling from Carl's finger, the crystal made no circular

movements.

'Walk slowly around,' advised Simon.

Keeping a keen, worried eye on the crystal, like he was transporting an egg in a teaspoon, Carl shuffled around the forecourt, but the crystal remained orthodox in its motions.

'Ain't doin' nuffink for me, is it?'

'You're not a channeler,' explained Simon. 'Don't worry about it, we're rare.'

Handing the crystal back to Simon, Carl said, 'Oh well, gave it a try.'

Now Simon took his turn to slowly view the surroundings, gazing across the land with the air of a wise and grave mountain man tenuously sensing a perhaps ominous change in the weather.

'It's all coming together, Carl,' he said quietly. 'I can feel it.'

'Yeah?'

'The Golden Millennium is about to dawn. The Expected One will soon appear.'

'Why didn't it dawn when the proper millennium 'appened, Simon? Y'know, when we hit two thousand an' all that?'

'We thought it would,' answered Simon, staring across the land. 'But when it didn't, we realised there's nothing to say the Golden Millennium should have anything to do with our calendar. It could start any time. Anyway, the exact birth year of Christ is unknown. Some historians think he was born six years later.' He paused. 'Wait a minute... if he was, then the beginning of the Golden Millennium might tally with the real calendar date for the new millennium. Amazing!'

'Yeah?'

'It's all coming together,' murmured Simon.

Carl lightly prodded Simon's arm. ''Ere, what about that computer then? We gonna phone the geezer?'

Emerging from his mystical reverie, pushing his glasses up and taking out his mobile, Simon said, 'Yes. I'll ring him now.'

*

After he'd delivered his edict to Albert the night before, the landlord had directly left the house. The final policeman had left some two hours later, at around four in the morning, informally telling Albert at the door that Harry's death was not likely to be treated as suspicious. Once alone, Albert had sat in the living room, staring blankly at the fire until his eyelids began to sink and his head began to loll. Finding then that he'd become too tired to bother with going to bed, he had lain down on the sofa, and the next thing he knew it was daylight and the phone was ringing.

Now, although he stirred, he ignored the call, and the ringing ended within a minute. Turning over on to his other side, he remembered he'd been dreaming he was on a torpedoed aircraft carrier, being tossed by a hurricane. The other passengers, all fleeing in planes from the deck, had been gravely warning him the ship was drifting towards the Bermuda triangle, and that he should take his chances in a plane too.

Seeing his eyes briefly open, Peep began her breakfast manoeuvres, pawing his face, and he was very soon forced to sit up, still picturing that drifting, storm-tossed vessel.

The Bermuda triangle — curious how all the superstition and fanciful discussion about it had fallen away in recent years, he reflected, even though it had been all the rage when he'd been a child. Unbidden, the plot for another novel popped into his head. In it, the American military had long since discovered that the Bermuda triangle was real — an occasional, freakish product of the earth's magnetic field that not only interfered with compasses, but also affected the brain activity of those within its range, engendering confusion, emotional instability, and a tendency to come a panicky cropper.

Albert knew that the American military had a real, mysterious, high-power radio transmission network known as HARP. In his novel, he would have HARP revealed as a technology that had been developed to secretly quell the Bermuda triangle. In wartime, however, HARP would be a force able to evoke and relocate the Bermuda triangle, so that it could be used as a disorientating weapon. Furthermore, the CIA would begin experimenting with the Bermuda effect within the USA itself. In his story, he would have a new political party emerge in America, one more genuinely liberal than the Democrats, and highly dependent on the black vote, which consequently was revitalising after years of indifference and non-registration. To scupper this, the CIA would embark on an operation they would code name *Voter Apathy* — focusing just enough of the Bermuda effect on black neighbourhoods on local election days to generate a malaise sufficient to keep large numbers away from the polling booths. Mildly disoriented, it was calculated they would also crash a few cars and drop a few babies, but within economically acceptable numbers.

Someone within the CIA had calculated that, for the benefit of

236

America's industrial-military complex, it was economically acceptable for a black baby to die so long as it was concomitant with at least 14,131 less votes for the new party.

Certain vocal people would be on to them, of course, making public their suspicions, but they would be dismissed by the government as lunatic conspiracy theorists. Eventually, the CIA would become so adept at tuning HARP — at tweaking different emotions — they would venture to spread the Bermuda effect over the whole nation on a presidential election day. People under its refined influence then would still feel inclined to go out to vote, but would experience just enough induced paranoia to vote right wing, no matter what their former political leanings. The novel would end by having the people all vote Republican, but also all becoming artificially paranoid enough to now believe that they really *were* being insidiously controlled by the CIA, who really *had* moved the Bermuda triangle. Then, led by rabid calls from the formerly ultra-Republican National Rifle Association, the American people would exercise its cherished right to take up arms against its own government, and all the .38's and .45's, and all the worst things in private hands across the USA, would be unleashed against every cop, every politician, every government employee, every soldier, every postman.

No, a film. Albert would write it as a film, he decided.

Scriptwriting! That's what he'd do in life. Easier than novels, surely. None of that tedious descriptive narrative to bother with. Fuck, if he started typing right now, he might have it finished by the time the advert for his computer came out on Tuesday.

Yes, that's what he'd do. He had seen the light. He would write all his stories as easy-peasy film scripts.

The phone rang again, and this time Albert answered it.

'Hello.'

'Hello,' returned the caller. 'I met a young lady in the office of the Durham Advertiser yesterday and she told me you had a computer for sale?'

'But without a computer to type on, how will I tell the world the secret things I know about the Bermuda triangle?'

Fuck, shut up, Albert admonished himself. Stay real. Just sell the frigging thing. You know you'll never get around to typing any fucking film scripts. You can't even sit through a film, let alone write one. Cat food. Cat food.

The voice on the phone became confused, yet boyishly eager.

'What about the Bermuda triangle?'

Cat food. Cat food.

'What? I never said anything about the Bermuda triangle.'

'You did.'

'I didn't. You must have heard the television on behind me.'

'It wasn't a television. It was your voice.'

'No it wasn't.'

'It was.'

'The Americans have learnt how to turn the Bermuda triangle on and off. They can move it, too. They can use it as a disorienting weapon in times of war.'

FUCK! SHUT UP, ALBERT! CAT FOOD! CAT FOOD!

Silence. Then, 'We have to talk.'

'Yeah, all right. It's a 1.7 gigahertz—'

'No, about the Bermuda triangle.'

'What? What are you on about?'

'The Bermuda triangle — how the American's can use it as a weapon.'

'You're bonkers. Where'd you get an idea like that?'

'You said it.'

'No I didn't. Do you want the computer or not?'

Silence. Then, falteringly at first, 'Yes, the computer. I'm interested. It works, does it?'

God, that was a dumb question, thought Albert, but he held his tongue. 'Works like a magician. Still under warranty. Only four months old. Got all the original boxes.'

Eventually, after several more questions that tried Albert's patience almost to the limit, the caller asked to see the computer, and a viewing at two o'clock that afternoon was agreed.

'Southern tosser,' said Albert after putting the phone down.

Going into the kitchen, Albert first fed Peep, then poured himself a bowl of cereal and a cup of coffee, taking them back to the living room. Sitting at the table, he glanced out the window and saw, in huge, day-glo letters:

JESUS LOVES YOU

This was fucking personal. It was only six days since the last one went up. Previously, messages had always stayed up a month. It was meant for him, he was sure. It was that thin-armed twat's revenge.

He closed the curtains. After finishing his cereal and coffee, he sat on the sofa, staring blankly at the fire until, compelled by a desire to piss somewhere other than on his own furniture, he went to the bathroom. Once relieved, he thought he might as well have a bath while he was there, so did not re-emerge for another ninety minutes, even though the phone rang several times.

After his bath, he went to see if he had any mail, daring to wish a delayed, mistaken giro would be lying in the hall. Approaching the doormat, he counted four letters, but from their sizes and natures, he could already tell none was a giro. Picking them up, he read that two were for Ron, and two for him. He opened his own letters sitting on the stair where Harry used to sit. One confirmed his Jobseeker's Allowance was cancelled, and the other confirmed his Housing Benefit cancellation since he was no longer receiving Jobseeker's Allowance.

'Burrawkoo,' he said before lapsing into a blank yet dismal-feeling state. 'Burr-fucking-rawkoo,' he said some minutes later when he revived. Fuck, he somehow had to find a new place to live within a week. Tricky – he had no money. Nah, it'd be okay. The landlord would chill, and Ron'd pay his share of the rent on top of his own while he got back on his feet. Anyway, they had rights as tenants, didn't they? The landlord couldn't throw them out on a whim. They were living in a mature and stable democracy, weren't they?

Jackie would know how they stood. He'd ask her about it.

The letter box opened, and a boldly printed leaflet was pushed through into the hall. Picking it up, Albert saw that on one side it read *JESUS LOVES YOU,* and on the other, *THE BIBLE IS THE WHOLE TRUTH.*

'You thin-armed wank stain,' he muttered, dropping the leaflet into a bin while picturing himself gripping that pasty-faced, Jesus Army fuckwit by his pipe-cleaner arms, lifting him off his undersized feet and stuffing him into the bin too.

Going back into his bedroom, he opened the wall cupboard and retrieved the three boxes his computer had come in, stacking them beside his desk. After erasing all his personal files from his hard drive, he lay on his bed, staring at the ceiling until the bell rang some ten minutes later. Opening the street door revealed an unfamiliar man with short, wiry, black hair who was wearing a *JESUS ARMY* T-shirt under a fawn bomber jacket.

Albert bristled with contempt.

'Awright, guv,' chirped the caller, 'come to look at y'computer. Me mate Simon spoke wiff y' earlier, but 'e couldn't come. 'Ad to stay t'deal wiff some builders oo were late. 'E rang loads of times, but there wuz never no answer.'

It took some moments for the false assumption Albert had formed about the caller to sufficiently clear away, but he retained a dull, residual moodiness, evoked by that T-shirt.

'Oh. Come, in.'

'The name's Carl,' said the caller, stepping into the house.

'Albert.'

Albert led to the way, going directly to his bedroom, where he indicated the computer. 'There you go.'

There was a Jesus freak in his bedroom. A fucking brain-dead Jesus freak.

'Smashin',' said Carl. 'Simon said all I 'ave to do is make sure I see it all workin'.'

Wordlessly, Albert switched on the computer.

'What's it doin' now?' asked Carl, appearing worried by the machine's mysterious callisthenics.

'It'll take a while to boot up and load Windows,' answered Albert, sounding bored and stand-offish.

'Yeah? That normal, is it?'

Albert didn't deign to answer that question.

Carl produced an envelope from his pocket. 'While it's doin' its thing, can I give you this?'

Albert looked suspiciously at the envelope being proffered by a Jesus Army fuckwit, and showed no inclination to accept it.

Carl explained, 'Me mate Simon wants t'speak t'y'soon 'bout what you told 'im 'bout the Bermuda triangle. So 'e put all 'is details down an' wants y' t' ring 'im.'

Snubbing the envelope, Albert went to lie on his bed. 'Carl,' he said, staring at the ceiling, 'if I've told you once, I've told you thousand times: if you're going to talk to me, talk sense.'

Carl was confounded. 'You ain't never told me nuffink before.'

Albert did not respond, and Carl, warily baffled, returned the envelope to his pocket. Looking at Albert in repose, he ventured to ask, in a sympathetic voice, 'Not sleep well last night or somefink?'

'I never sleep well.'

'Why's that?'

'I'm a poet, and poets have longings that usurp sleep.'

A poet! Carl also liked to think of himself as something of a poet. Sometimes, when waiting up in taxi ranks in the small hours, he would scribble down lines about life, and every few weeks or so he'd have enough material to cobble together a poem. He now had over thirty poems, carefully written in a special notebook he'd bought. However, with a heavy heart, he knew that nothing he wrote ever came close to matching the sonnet he'd had printed in a magazine. It had only been his school's magazine, but he was still wont to talk about it now, seventeen years later, glibly reeling off the cherished verses at the slightest hint of an invitation to do so.

Tentatively, Carl said, 'You a poet, then?'

'A professional melancholic.'

'What, you've 'ad stuff published and that?'

'An anthology of auto-epitaphs. *Here Lies Albert Fox.*'

God, that was clever, thought Albert. So clever, he indulged in explaining the various meanings to himself in thought. There was the face value meaning — an apt title for a book of tombstone inscriptions. There was the fact that as he had said it, he'd actually been lying down. And there was the fact that it was a pack of lies.

An uneasy silence suggested that Carl didn't know what an epitaph was. When his discomfort mostly passed, to the accompaniment of a nervous shift of his body, he said, 'I'm a bit of a poet too.'

No response from Albert.

'Yeah, I'm a bit of a poet,' Carl was forced to repeat, but speaking more forthrightly this time. 'Sonnets are what I do. 'Ad one published in a magazine once.'

Albert remained unresponsive, but Carl recited the poem anyway.

It was awful. Fourteen lines of poo. It made Albert's own penguin poem seem deep and skilled by comparison. For something that attempted to be a traditional-style sonnet, its lines showed a disquieting tendency to have at some times a great clamouring quantity of syllables, and at other times to be sorely lacking in them. It was an attempt to describe in rhyme his eternal love for some freakish lady named Rosalynn, who, according to the unequal lines, was a peerless beauty of a virgin endowed with a heart at least as true as Sir Galahad's and an intellect to rival Isaac Newton's.

Making no acknowledgement of the recital, in a downbeat tone, Albert said, 'Computer's ready.'

Standing in the middle of the room, uncomfortable after having been so blatantly ignored, Carl turned to look at the computer. 'Yeah? Ready now?'

'Give it a whirl.'

'Yeah?' said Carl, in an unsure voice. He stepped over to the computer, eyes roaming apprehensively over its various components. 'Got to be 'onest wiff y', don't know nuffink 'bout 'em meself. Could y'show me?'

Albert got off the bed and went to the computer.

'What's this thing 'ere?' asked Carl, pointing. 'This the printer?'

'Yeah. Inkjet. Six pages per minute.'

'Get that too, don't I?'

'Part and parcel.'

Using the mouse, Albert brought up some text and pictures to print.

'Magic,' said Carl when the paper began to churn out. 'That works, then. Can it get the internet an' stuff?'

'There's an internal 56K modem. Internet Explorer's installed.'

'Yeah? That's the gubbins, is it?'

'Trust me. It's internet ready. Just plug it into a phone line.'

'Yeah?'

Carl stood back and considered the machine a while, his expression reflecting his purchasing worries. 'Goes in all those, does it?' he asked, indicating the boxes stacked beside the desk.

'Yep. All the manuals and disks are in there too.'

'Yeah?'

With a furrowed brow, Carl considered the machine some more. 'Seems to be in workin' order. Looks lots newer than the one it's replacin'.' He suddenly beamed. 'All right, guv, I'll take it. Two hundred, yeah?' He unzipped a pocket and took out a roll of banknotes, counting out most of them into Albert's hand, who slipped them into his own pocket.

'I'll box it up for you,' said Albert, at once beginning to disassemble the computer.

'Yeah? Magic. It's not for me, actually. It's for me mate. 'E needs it so 'e can check up on UFO sightings on the internet. That's why we're in Durham. A UFO was parked over the cathedral the other week.'

Albert's eyes rolled upwards and he sighed noisily. 'That was a fucking distress flare. I saw it myself.'

Carl hesitated before arguing, 'Nah. Simon says that's the official cover-up story.'

Glancing sullenly at Carl's T-shirt, Albert asked, 'So where does your fundamentalist Jesus Army bunch fit in with UFO's? Where in the Bible does it say that God created beings ten times as smart as us?'

'I ain't in the Jesus Army no more,' explained Carl, looking down at his T-shirt. 'Just got a load of T-shirts left over, that's all. To be 'onest wiff y', I wuz in the Jesus Army more for the buzz than anyfink else. It wuz all right, but all that bangin' on 'bout the devil an' stuff wuz a bit much. In the Orthrium Society now. Mebbe y'saw me mate on telly on Saturday? Me cab wuz on too. Magic documentary. Channel Four.'

'Not that bunch of people chanting on a hill?'

'That's us. Me mate Simon's an 'igh Teacher. Picked 'im up in me cab few weeks back an' 'e 'ad a film crew wiff 'im, and 'e told me all about the Orthrium Society.'

'All about Jesus being a Cosmic Master living on Venus, sending telepathic messages to your society's leader?'

'That's right. So I left the Jesus Army.'

The computer was now separated into its components, and Albert began winding up the various leads.

'Need any 'elp, there?' asked Carl.

Ignoring Carl's offer, Albert said, 'Let me get this right. You believed the Bible was the whole truth just a few weeks ago, but now you believe the Bible got it wrong. Just like that?'

'The Bible didn't get it wrong,' objected Carl, 'it's just there's more to it. Simon explained it to me. There's spaceships and things.'

'Really? That Simon guy — what a thinker.' Lifting the monitor off the desk, Albert discovered his Godfrey novelette had slipped behind. He glanced at Carl. 'The Bible did get it wrong. The true creator of the universe was a scientist born before time began. You're the first person I've told this to.'

Albert continued boxing the computer's parts.

Apprehensively, tentatively, Carl said, 'What was that, mate?'

'What was what?' asked Albert innocently.

'That thing 'bout the creator of the universe.'

'What thing?'

'That thing you said.'

'Carl, if I've told you once, I've told you a thousand times: if you're going to talk to me, talk sense.'

Slowly, Carl sat down on the computer chair. Consternation was writ large on his face. A face that instantly revealed each mercurial change in mood and mental state he passed through. Everything Carl felt, his face showed. It was a face that would be a tremendous liability in a poker game.

When placing the printer in its box, Albert looked at Carl and asked, 'Who created the universe, Carl?'

Shifting in his chair before answering, Carl said, 'Jesus's dad.'

'And who's that?'

'God, innit?'

'Wrong,' said Albert decisively. 'Not God — Godfrey.'

Kneeling down, Albert's endeavours were now directed at packing the mouse and keyboard away.

'Godfrey?' Carl queried eventually. 'Oo's Godfrey?'

'What?' said Albert, glancing casually at Carl.

'Oo's Godfrey?'

'Godfrey who?'

Carl crossed his legs tightly and sat on his hands. 'You just said 'e created the universe. Was 'e that scientist? Why d'y'keep sayin' things then forgettin' 'em?'

Everything was now boxed, and Albert stood up. 'Do I? I don't recall saying anything about anything. Maybe it's you imagining it all.'

'It ain't me, it's you,' disputed Carl, uncrossing his legs but still sitting on his hands. 'I said oo's Godfrey, then you said—'

Albert placidly cut in, 'Before the beginning, there was a brilliant physicist called Godfrey who succeeded in producing the Equation of Everything ...' Moving to his bed, lying down and staring at the ceiling, speaking in a low but steady voice, Albert told Carl all about Godfrey by reciting his creation short story. '... and when He eventually became lonely, He simply made some friends.'

Confused. Bewildered. Awkward. Wary. Confounded. Albert's curious words had evoked all these feelings in Carl, feelings which conspired to produce a lost and troubled expression. 'Why you tellin' me all this stuff?' he asked. 'Some kind of wind up?'

Albert looked meaningfully at Carl. 'It's not a wind up, Carl. I've chosen you to be the first to receive the truth.'

Carl shook his head. 'I don't know what you're on about, mate.'

'The truth,' said Albert, now staring at the ceiling again. 'I'm on about the truth.'

'What truth? Y'mean that stuff 'bout that Godfrey thing?'

'Who's Godfrey?'

'Jesus!' exclaimed Carl in sudden agitated exasperation, pulling his hands from under his thighs, 'there y'go again, forgettin' what you said. That's what Simon said you did on the phone.'

'What did I say?'

'I dunno, do I?' raved Carl, flapping his arms. 'You said Godfrey was a scientist oo some'ow made the universe appear in 'is 'ead, or somefink.'

'I said all that?'

'You did,' insisted Carl.

'Did I? What a curiosity. I do babble sometimes.'

'You're takin' the piss, aren't y'?' accused Carl.

'Why should I wish to do that?'

''Ow should I know?' protested Carl, his voice still raised. 'This ain't normal what's 'appened 'ere.'

'Computer's yours now, Carl.'

Oblivious to the invitation to leave, Carl regarded Albert in agitated, almost seething, bewilderment.

Momentarily turning his head, Albert looked at Carl and repeated, 'Computer's yours now, Carl.'

Slowly remembering his true business, Carl calmed, and mumbled, 'Yeah. Computer.' Looking at the three large boxes, he asked, 'Couldn't give me an 'and wiff 'em to me cab, could y'? I'm parked right outside.'

Watched suspiciously by Carl, Albert got off the bed and picked up the heavy monitor box.

'Champion,' said Carl, suddenly smiling. Picking up the lighter but bulkier system unit box, he followed Albert out the room, then out of the house and into sunshine. 'Just by the cab, thanks,' he said, walking a few paces behind Albert.

Placing the box down beside Carl's cab, Albert regarded the vehicle as a minor curiosity. Durham had no black cabs, and he'd never been anywhere that did have them. It was larger than he'd imagined from seeing them on television.

'Champion,' said Carl, placing his own box down.

'I'll get the printer,' said Albert, going back into his flat. When he returned, Carl had put the other boxes into the rear of his cab and was waiting beside the open passenger door.

'Champion,' smiled Carl, taking the printer box from Albert and sliding it on to the passenger seat. Closing the door, he became serious in his aspect, and looked at Albert, hesitantly asking, 'So what are y'?'

'What do you mean?'

'What religion?'

Looking at Carl's cab, shining scuffed in the sun, Albert ignored the question. 'You a London cabby, then?'

'Four years,' answered Carl proudly. ''Ad Robert Plant from Led

245

Zeppelin in me cab last week. Wouldn't 'ave known oo 'e wuz, 'cept me next fare saw 'im gettin' out an' told me. Never forget it. It wuz this really pukka American bird, an' she kept sayin' "Awesome. I'm sittin' on the same seat where Robert Plant was just sittin'. Awesome". "Oo's Robert Plant", I said, an' she couldn't believe I'd never 'eard of 'im. Bought some of Led Zeppelin's records afterwards. *Stairway to 'Eaven* – magic song. It's all in there, if y'can understand it.' Now Carl's serious air returned. 'So what are y'?'

'A memory,' said Albert, walking back inside. Closing the street door behind him, he spoke to Peep, who had ventured out into the hall. 'Is it my imagination, cat, or has it been a really weird week? And it's still only fucking Thursday.'

With his foot, he gently and patiently shepherded Peep back into the flat. Sitting on the sofa, he counted his money – two hundred pounds. He counted it again – two hundred pounds. It was the most money he'd ever had in his hands. Even more than on that blessed day six years back when an extra giro had been sent by mistake.

Going into the kitchen, he was about to borrow two of Ron's hamburgers when he remembered that he'd taken a vow against meat. So he borrowed some cheese instead, making a sandwich, which he ate in the living room while watching the end of a documentary, which informed him the war in Kosovo had cost NATO 2.5 billion pounds.

After the documentary, the weather forecast came on. It warned of heavy rain beginning tomorrow afternoon.

Once fed, Albert felt strangely inclined to broaden his horizons. So, putting his long coat on over his *Not Long Now* T-shirt, he stepped out, at once appreciating the delightfulness of the day. Hardly a cloud was in the sky, and the air, though a little chilly, was almost completely at rest. Indeed, such was the day's gentle beauty, it fostered a sense of sympathetic serenity within him, and he felt a kind of potential smile affect his face as he proceeded to his gate.

Beyond his gate, putting the sun behind him, he turned towards the town centre. Devon Road was well endowed with trees, and in the sunlight the rich shades of the autumn leaves were as if afire. Gazing up to the varicoloured foliage as he sauntered along, he was spoken to by an old man doddering past.

'Pleasant day,' smiled the old man, baring grotesquely white and unbecoming dentures in his shrunken, dry, sallow, leathery mouth.

'Very pleasant,' returned Albert, surprising and also dismaying himself with his spontaneous sociability.

'Might prove the last completely agreeable day before winter,' sighed the old man, continuing his unsteady journey.

You miserable, moribund twat, thought Albert. Just when I nearly smiled, too. Fucking intellectuals, he nearly shouted back to the man.

Albert continued his own journey. Glancing to his left, his eyes were assaulted by the tawdry *JESUS LOVES YOU* sign. Further down the street, a disorder of young girls — six or seven in number, ten or eleven in age — was approaching, like a swarm of wasps on laughing gas and crack. They were all boasts and vociferous out-doings. All "I've got this" and "well I'm getting that". All mobile phones and garish clothes.

'Is wino Harry dead?' blurted one as they came level with Albert.

He stopped and looked at the girl who'd spoken, recognising her as one of the street's many kids. But standing beside her, sullen and glaring, was a kid from another street — Grace.

'As dead as Grace's heart,' he answered.

Beginning with a flat sound and rising through three or four semi-tones — a sort of mooing sandwiched between consonants — the girl from his street said, 'What?'

'Don't speak to him,' sneered Grace to her friend. 'My dad says he's weird.'

Oblivious to her friend's odium, the first girl tried again. 'Is he dead?'

Albert nodded gravely.

'How?' blurted another girl.

'I kicked him to death for saying I was weird,' answered Albert. He pointed a finger at Grace. 'Be sure to tell your shite dad that.'

He walked on toward the centre of town, taking the riverside route, stopping sometimes to look at leaves floating past, or minnows in the shallows. Although his coat was open and he only had his *Not Long Now* T-shirt on underneath, and although he was only dawdling, the sun was warming enough to make him feel that he might sweat if he wasn't careful. Mindful of this, he took a rest on the bench he favoured, shaded under a tree, and for a while watched the river slide past. Beyond, dull and distant, was the ever-present hum of rushing traffic. The people occasionally passing all seemed to be rushing too, outpacing the listless river.

More than ever before, he felt that he must live by his own private sense of time.

Looming above the wooded bank behind him was the one thousand-year-old cathedral.

He moved on, ascending some steps cut into the bank, and was soon outside Jackie's workplace. Through the window, he saw her, head bent down, at the desk where Barry normally sat. Pushing the door open and stepping inside, he realised it wasn't Jackie, but someone new. Dressed like Jackie; hair like Jackie; but much older. Glasses, too.

The new person smiled at him as he walked in. 'Can I help you?'

'No one can help me. I'm beyond redemption.'

Her smile became uncertain.

From the back office, the real Jackie appeared, carrying some work folders.

'Fuck, Jackie,' breathed Albert, 'what have you done?'

'Been meaning to cut it for months,' she said tersely, sitting at her desk. 'It just got in the way of things. And stop annoying the people I work with.'

It was unnerving. It was Jackie, but it wasn't Jackie. Where she once had lush, softening hair, she now had almost none — that morning, she had cut it as short as her sharp scissors could manage, then had visited a hairdressers to have it made neater.

Her new hard head attracted Albert's eye like a repulsive disfigurement.

'Pretty radical haircut,' he commented as she began to deal with some papers.

Without looking up from her work, she said, 'What are you doing here, Albert? I've got work to do.'

She was being icy with him, he was now sure, supposing it was to do with what had happened between them last night. It was something he'd almost forgotten about himself. To him, it seemed distant and almost trivial. But now feeling awkward, he answered, 'Just wanted to ask your advice on something.'

'Since when have you ever listened to advice?' she returned, continuing with her work.

'Since my landlord gave us a week to leave last night.'

'Why?' she asked, managing to make it sound accusatory. 'Were you obnoxious to him?'

'No. He's pissed off about drugs. He saw your joint in the ashtray. And it was him who pulled up Ron's dope plant. He wants us out.'

Jackie looked up. 'Have you told Ron yet?'

'No. Thought I'd see what our legal situation is first.'

'Tell Ron,' she directed with exasperation. 'What if he comes back from Iceland and he's got nowhere to live?'

'He's got his parents' place,' shrugged Albert.

'Do you ever think about other people's feelings?'

'Only about how tiny they are compared to mine.'

Jackie gave him an excoriating look. 'That's it with you, isn't it? You're in love with your own tears. Not that I could imagine you ever crying.'

God, she was giving him a hard time. He'd only been quipping, yet she was reacting as if he was for real. She'd turned into the rest of the world. 'Cried in the dole office once,' he reminded her, with uncomfortable, affected indignation.

'Only as a joke and a selfish trick,' denounced Jackie.

Chastened and saddened, Albert fell silent, and his gaze slipped down to the desk.

Maintaining her stern demeanour, Jackie looked at him until, discharging a noisy breath, she put her pen down. 'Have you got a tenancy agreement?' she asked, reluctantly relenting.

Looking up, Albert shrugged, 'Think so. Ron dealt with all that shit.'

'Was it an Assured Shorthold Tenancy under the nineteen-eighty-eight Housing Act?'

'Assured Shorthold sounds familiar.'

'When does it expire?'

'Dunno. Hold on. Think I remember Ron saying the flat was sorted until Christmas.'

'Then your landlord will probably need a court order to evict you before then,' Jackie informed him. 'Go to the Citizen's Advice Bureau and they'll help you.'

Albert knew he wouldn't be going anywhere. He'd just sit it out. The landlord could just fuck off to court if he wanted to enforce his edict.

Jackie returned to her work. After a long-feeling, silent twenty seconds or so, Albert took his money out, placing sixty pounds on to her desk.

Sitting up straight, Jackie curtly demanded, 'What's this for?'

'It's the money I owe you,' he explained. 'I've sold my computer.'

She pushed the money back to him. 'I don't want your money.'

'I owe you.'

'You owe me thirty quid from Tuesday, not sixty.'

'And dozens of pints.'

'Pints isn't money.'

'Well take the thirty,' he said, pushing half the notes to her.

The notes were returned to his side of the desk.

'No, Albert. Pay me back when you can spare it.'

'I can spare it. I got two hundred for the computer.'

'Albert, I earn two hundred every three days. Keep the money. You'll need it.'

She got up, taking a folder into the back office. Not knowing whether she intended to come out again soon, Albert's discomfort increased. Glancing across to the other desk, he caught the new member of staff looking suspiciously at him. She immediately looked away. He had to say something about last night to Jackie. Something to clear the air. It was an onerous prospect, but he had to do it. He was about to get up and venture into the back office when she reappeared, bearing two coffees, one of which she wordlessly placed in front of him, the other going to her colleague. Briefly re-entering the back office, she returned with a coffee of her own, and set about her work again.

Albert leaned forward slightly. 'Jackie,' he said, quietly and awkwardly, 'about last night.'

'Are you going to say something about the stupid pass I made at you?' she said without looking up, speaking like she was just irascibly tolerating him.

Albert didn't continue. He leaned back again, feeling himself colour a little. Feeling heat rise from his neck.

'Albert, I smoked too much dope. Things got a bit heavy in my head for a while. You weren't too normal later, either. Let's both of us forget it.' Without looking up from her paperwork, she took a sip of her drink. 'How did the business of Harry end?' she asked in a less severe voice, working her pen anew.

'With a whimper,' answered Albert, 'save for the landlord episode.'

'You have to tell Ron,' she urged, lifting her gaze.

'Nah, the landlord'll chill.'

'Then I'm going to tell him,' she said, looking back down at her work. 'Someone has to. Won't be much fun for him to come back and find he's homeless, will it? Think about that for a little while.'

'But it'll be like an annealing spiritual trial for him. He'll be grateful eventually. He might even become deep like me.'

Five seconds passed before Jackie spoke. 'Albert,' she said, with an absence of cordiality, 'if I've told you once, I've told you a thousand times: if you're going to talk to me, talk sense. Now could you hurry and finish your coffee because I've got work to do.'

Finding it was now cool enough to gulp, he did hurry his coffee. And when he said he was going, Jackie said goodbye without lifting her head, or her inflection.

1.20
Two Virgins

The sky was beginning to cloud over when Albert came out of Jackie's agency. He felt snubbed and wounded. Glancing through the window as he walked away, he thought he caught her looking at him, but wasn't sure — wherever she'd been looking, she'd immediately looked down to her work again.

He walked on, but with no destination in mind. Listlessly sauntering and dawdling, he looked in shop windows for a while. Standing outside a chip shop, he was staring at a large plastic model of a lobster when a short, bald, fifty-something, cheerful man came out, carrying a wrapped meal. Albert thought the man's florid, smooth skin looked like the lobster's shell.

'Go on, try to smile,' said the man buoyantly as he marched quickly past, grinning like he was on his way to bank a lottery fortune. 'Doesn't hurt, you know?'

He sounded Welsh.

I'll be smiling at your cheap funeral, and it might be sooner than you think, was the come-back Albert thought of but didn't utter.

Fuck. What was it about him that told people like that cheerful bastard they could get away with saying patronisingly happy things to him? Where was the fear a miserable-looking, taller-than-most, twenty-four-year-old North-easterner should engender in tiny, ageing men? It was like with all the kids who seemed to sense they needn't give him a feather's weight of respect or even civility. Maybe he

251

should grow a big, droopy Mexican moustache and dress like a bandito? he thought. Then he'd get some respect. No, that might look like a gay thing, he realised, and get him picked on even more. The tattoo he'd thought about the other day was the better idea — spend his two hundred on a huge, scary tattoo, and watch his life improve.

A little further down the street, he went into a newsagents for a *Fry's Chocolate Cream*. Two men were behind the counter. One, deeply lined and with a wiry build, was stacking cigarettes on to a display with one hand while eating chips with the other. The second man was reading a tabloid newspaper. This book-learning man was the cheerful Welshman who'd advised him to smile, except he didn't look quite so cheerful now.

When Albert picked up his chocolate bar, the Welshman nodded to his newspaper and remarked, 'Bill Gates, aye?'

'That loser,' said Albert.

'Sixty billion pounds, aye?' said the Welshman, oblivious to Albert's comment. Putting his paper down to serve his customer, he became cheerful once more. 'Imagine what you could do with that much money?'

'He could pay for another war in Kosova and still have fifty-seven-and-a-half billion left to sort out the Welsh,' said Albert as he handed over the money for his chocolate bar.

The Welshman's smile departed and his eyes narrowed. Albert played it insouciantly, wandering out of the shop like he'd not said anything unacceptable at all.

Finding that pissing off a cheerful person had improved his spirits, and possibly also his appetite, Albert thought he'd treat himself to a bag of chips. He'd eat them sitting on his favourite bench on the riverside, and have his chocolate bar afterwards. A little picnic to make amends for all his recent troubles.

In the chip shop, waiting in a short queue, Albert tried to imagine just what sixty billion pounds meant. It meant every person in the world giving him ten pounds, that's what it meant, even those tight-fisted Pygmies. Looking around, he depressingly supposed that if every person in the *chip shop* gave him ten pounds, he'd talk about it for the rest of his life.

Bill Gates. Bill fucking Gates. What a jerk, thought Albert. All that money and he still hadn't bought his own country and set himself up as ultimate ruler, to be feared and worshipped and snogged. *That's* what sixty billion meant, thought Albert as he came out of the chippy.

Turning a corner, the cathedral was suddenly directly in view. A religious procession was taking place. At the head of a long line of hair-sprayed women and freshly-shaven men, some kind of super vicar, perhaps the Bishop of Durham himself, was slowly leading the way to the cathedral's entrance. Humbly doing God's work, the arrogant bastard, thought Albert. In super vicars, he saw not a person worthy of added respect, but a person who'd taken bad ideas to even further extremes than most. And in the Pope, he saw the most entrenched, careerist idiot in all Christendom, who had taken most of his life just to grudgingly semi-acknowledge the glaring truth of evolution.

Albert felt a mischievous urge to enter Durham's greatest house of God. He'd just thought of a new religion, one that he wouldn't mind his name being associated with — *The Church of God the Total Slacker*. Instead of going to churches and cathedrals to flatter the supposed controlling force in the universe, instead followers of his new religion would go to church to have serious words with Him. No more supine acceptance of misfortune and suffering. No more tearful thanks for His mercy after disasters where His hand is claimed to have miraculously saved one child but is never suggested to have been at all implicated in the gruesome deaths of seventy thousand other children who all perished at the same time. No, now it would clearly be all His lazy fault, and they would bloody-well let Him know— every Sunday. It could really catch on, thought Albert, especially with the French. Go to church and speak your mind. Let Him know that you now know He's been goofing off all along. He could start the movement right away just by going into the cathedral and screaming at the ineffectual Lord and slapping a few statues of Christ to get His attention. Might get himself on TV, then the fame would snowball his new religious philosophy, and before he knew it he'd be on American cable telling Yanks the true source of their troubles and receiving cash donations. He could encourage them to sue the collected Christian divinities — the Holy Trinity; the angels; the saints — for corporate negligence. He could couple it all with a bit of home shopping and new diet plan and really coin it in.

He didn't go into the cathedral. Instead, he kept on toward the river. Just before the slope that would take him down to the waterside, some performance artists were busking their limited thing for the tourists — standing very still with their faces painted to make them look different. *They* were coining it in, he observed. Maybe that's what he should do for a living? Facile, cynical performance art. He'd excel at it, he was sure, so long as he could cast his integrity and dignity away. For starters, he could take one of his planned great poetic works, *Mine is the Voice of all Suffering*, beyond poetry and verse, and into the realms of performance and conceptual art. With ink made from his own tears, he could write while sitting hungry and shivering in a mock-up garret in an art gallery, where the paying public could observe his pain. Perhaps the living installation could be made interactive? For a (pretty) price, the public might be allowed to deepen his pain, and thus deepen the poetry. They could taunt him. Call him a puff, or something. But it wouldn't just be a self-indulgent, self-enriching undertaking. It would be for charity, too. He would pledge that when the thirty-seven volumes were finished, a copy would be sent free to each starving child in the world so that they could get their own petty, mere worldly misery into some perspective. Thus his suffering would help those more fortunate than him. Must send a proposal to the Saatchi Gallery, he thought, strolling down the short but steep slope to the river, passing a couple of young boys playing on a rope-swing tied to a tree branch. Twats, he thought a moment later when he saw that someone was lying on his favourite bench. Fuck, he thought a moment after thinking twats: it was that embarrassingly lachrymose bloke he'd met in the Durham Advertiser's office — Joe. Joe was lying on his back, staring at the clouding-over sky. His long, shabby black coat, worn over a faded black sweatshirt, was draping down to the muddy ground. His hands were half-fisted and tucked under his chin, as if he was in bewildered, anxious alarm. He looked about twelve long stops down the line from Happy Town.

'Come on, Joe,' said Albert, giving the bench a small kick, 'this is where I like to sit. Go and sleep in the library if you really need to look like a loser.'

'She lies all the time,' murmured Joe, in distressed bewilderment, but not otherwise stirring.

'Come on, Joe,' said Albert, giving the bench another small kick. 'I've got a bag of chips, and it's best if I look across the river when I eat. I'm trying to cultivate a Man of Destiny air about me, and gazing across a river is a real assistance.'

'She lies all the time,' Joe murmured again.

'Fuck, Joe, you've got to snap out of this,' urged Albert, displaying some passionate concern. 'You sprawling on a bench staring at the sky won't help me. Grow up and budge over. My chips are getting tepid.'

Joe didn't respond, so Albert gave his feet a shove with his own foot. 'I'm serious, buster. Give me space. Live and let live.' Joe still didn't respond. 'Come on, Joe, pull yourself to-fucking-gether. Anyway, you're not wistful-looking enough for the melancholic sky-staring lark. Leave it to younger, prettier blokes like me. You just look like a beleaguered old cunt.'

There was still no response from Joe. The only voices belonged to the squealing boys playing on the rope-swing halfway up the wooded slope.

'For fuck's sake,' grumbled Albert, starting to walk away, 'what a crap friend you've turned out to be. Had high hopes for you, I did. Thought you were a rare, deep find, like me. Only not quite so rare or deep.'

Joe now sat up, but whether it was anything to do with Albert's requests wasn't clear.

'Saints-a-fucking-live,' muttered Albert, returning and sitting down, unwrapping his chips to begin his woodland feast.

'She lies all the time,' murmured Joe. 'Or does she?'

'My friend, Jackie,' spluttered Albert boorishly through half-chewed chips, 'reckons you're more melancholic than me. What a load of dog poo. You're not that melancholic.'

'I'm worse than melancholic,' said Joe quietly. 'I'm sunk in deep wretchedness. Bound to ill-fortune with seven-fold chains of frosted iron.'

'Yeah, we all feel like that from time to time,' returned Albert, feeding his face some more, 'but my melancholia is positively Wagnarian in scale.'

'She lies all the time,' murmured Joe, now with his chin between his fists and his elbows on his knees, staring at the ground.

'Want a chip?' asked Albert, proffering the bag.

'She's a scheming spider,' said Joe, glancing at Albert, but ignoring the chips, 'that's what she is.' He paused. 'Or is she? Maybe it's me?'

Albert retracted the chip bag and looked across the water in an exaggerated, magisterial manner. 'How's my Man of Destiny air coming along?' he asked. But Joe was only interested in staring down at the ground between his feet again. 'Come on, Joe, don't hold back on me. Tell me how it's coming along. I need to know. I'm planning to lead the world into a new age of romanticism. I need to look the part. Image is everything these television days.'

Glancing at Albert, Joe said, 'Do you think someone can lie so much they grow to believe their own false words?'

'Was that your answer?' asked Albert, his magisterial look slipping away. 'Some kind of deep allegory or parable, was it? Shit, that'll take some working out. I might have to sleep on that one.' He ate some more chips. 'Bollocks, that's the view spoilt,' he complained when the top third of a thorough bruiser of a massive, bone-headed, tattooed, bouncer type man appeared above the reeds on the river's edge. Wearing a black skinhead's jacket, the hard-looking man was fishing with a rod in one hand and a can of lager in the other. Until now, he had been sitting, concealed by vegetation. He peered grimly at Albert and Joe, as if assessing them in terms of potential threat. Threat seemingly dismissed, he sat down again. 'That's better,' said Albert, once the view was restored. After another chip, he went on to muse, 'Wonder if thick people have thick dreams? I mean, my dreams are really clever and abstract. But that bloke we just saw — what could his brain muster? Someone should look into that. What do you think, Joe?'

'She lies all the time,' murmured Joe. 'All the time. A different story for everyone. All done to make her look wronged and innocent and reasonable. But there's a twisted malignancy inside her, too. I'm sure of that now.' He paused. 'Or maybe it's inside me? Maybe I'm the Antichrist? If it's me, the world would be better off without me.'

'Joe,' said Albert, with his mouth close to full, 'I think our friendship has now reached the stage where you should be lending me money.'

'Don't have any money,' said Joe, taking a rare interest in the here and now. 'Sent what little I had left to the Antichrist yesterday.'

'So how come I just heard some coins in your coat?' countered Albert.

Putting his hand into his pocket, appearing perplexed to find such riches, Joe retrieved some change, and then a tenner, which he placed on the bench for Albert.

'Excellent behaviour,' said Albert, finishing off his chips. 'I've revised my opinion of you. You are deep.'

The boys playing on the swing began a campaign of increased squealing. Joe looked over his shoulder at them.

'Wish those noisy, short-arse bastards would fuck off,' grumbled Albert, wiping his fingers on the cleanest bits of his chip wrapper before depositing it in the bin next to the bench. 'They're spoiling my quality time. Joe, go over and scare them off. Cry a bit and talk about the Antichrist, that should do it. But maim them if you have to. But don't tell anyone it was my idea. You never saw me, right?'

'The Antichrist,' murmured Joe painfully, still looking at the boys.

'She lies all the time,' Albert reminded him. 'And there's a twisted malignancy inside her. Unless it's actually inside you, that is.'

A grim and resolute expression appeared on Joe's face, and he left the bench, striding up the slope toward the boys. Joe's new expression was so singularly austere that, just in case, Albert, looking over his shoulder, said, 'I was only joking about killing them.'

The boys were around the same age as Grace, and had a look of nascent yobness about them. Each had close-cropped hair; one blonde; one ginger. Reaching them, Joe immediately snatched the rope from the hands of the blonde one, much to the child's consternation and apparent initial fear. With the rope now in his own hands, Joe began to climb the tree to which it was tied.

Albert assumed Joe was intending to put the rope out of their reach, or was going to untie it from the branch.

'Howay, fuck off off owa swing,' demanded the blonde child in undiluted Geordie, glaring up at Joe, who was now four or five feet above the earth.

'Go home, kid, this won't be pretty,' advised Joe, grimly.

The blonde child began to climb up after Joe. 'Giz owa swing back, y'cunt.'

As Joe climbed higher, the rope looped down and the ginger child made an unsuccessful grab for it.

'Get lost, virgin,' ordered Joe, pulling up the slack.

'Ah'm not a virgin,' contested the ginger child, venomously adamant.

'Yes you are,' said Joe, still being pursued up the tree by the blonde child.

'Am ah shite a virgin,' maintained the ginger child, increasingly aggrieved, his eyes becoming damp with passionate indignation.

With Joe now crawling out on the tree limb to which the rope was anchored, the blonde child retreated, jumping down to the ground. The ginger child turned in the direction of Albert and bawled, 'Dad! Help!'

Instantly, vegetation rustled on the riverbank, and Albert saw the hard man stand up like an alert Rottweiler. Looking back to Joe, Albert saw that he was now tying the rope into some kind of knot.

'Giz the fuckin' swing back, y'puff,' demanded the ginger child.

'Aye, howway, mister, giz it back,' asked the blonde child, trying a kind of whining diplomacy.

Throwing his foaming lager can spiralling away, the hard man flashed past Albert and started up the steep slope. He was almost as tall as Ron, and maybe heavier, and Albert had felt the ground shudder as he'd pounded past.

'What's gannin' on, lads?' the hard man called up the slope as he hurried to the rescue.

When the hard man arrived, pointing fifteen feet up the tree, the blonde child exclaimed, 'This puff's nicked owa swing.'

'He called uz a virgin,' reported the ginger child.

'What?' said the hard man, puzzled and incensed. Looking up at Joe, he demanded, 'Did you call mah bairn a virgin?'

'You're a virgin too,' said Joe, 'I can tell from your body language.'

Joe's aspersion provoked an instant, hateful grimace from the hard man. Flushed with anger, he began climbing the tree. 'Right, y'cunt,' he menaced, 'nee one calls me a virgin in front of me son.'

'Knack him, dad,' urged the ginger child, like he knew he would.

Fuck, thought Albert. This was serious. Fearing he could be putting himself in Accident and Emergency, he started up the slope, although with no plan of action. When he reached the base of the tree, the hard man was set to shinny out along the branch — as thick as a stout man's leg — to get at Joe. But Joe seemed unconcerned, and continued tying the rope — fashioning a noose, Albert alarmingly realised. The hard man was now almost within reach of Joe, who hastily put the noose around his own neck and pushed himself off the high branch, stopping Albert's heart. But the force of Joe's push-off, coupled with the weight of the hard man, caused the branch to catastrophically splinter close to the tree's trunk, spilling the hard man upside-down to the ground.

With the branch now angled sharply down, greatly slackening the rope, Joe landed on his feet upon the soft earth, then fell on to his bottom, jarred but unharmed save for a slight tightening of the noose around his neck.

'Argh!' screamed the hard man, whose shoulder had taken the brunt of his heavy fall. But even though he was obviously injured, apparently no longer having proper use of his right arm, he made a violent grab for Joe before either of them had made it to their feet.

Joe barely evaded the hard man, who scrambled after him. Still tethered, Joe was frantically forcing his fingers under the tightened rope around his neck, all the while keeping his distance from his large, enraged pursuer, who was now up on his feet, seething with murderous anger. It was fast and furious. Joe was dodging and scurrying, trying to work the rope loose, and the injured hard man was snatching and flailing. The boys had shrunk back, and Albert was in a momentary state of stunned fright. Grabbing for the rope instead of Joe, with his left arm, the hard man gave it an almighty yank, jolting Joe down on to his knees and elbows, with his fingers still under the noose. Instantly, the hard man kicked Joe in the side — a mighty, weighty kick that made Joe grunt in pain and enforced exhalation, turning him over on to his back. But the kick unbalanced the hard man, and he slipped and fell backwards. Now Albert moved into the battleground, but in the same moment, Joe got free of the noose and ran down the slope like a hare with a greyhound on its tail, and Albert ran after him. The hard man began to chase. 'You fuckin' bastards,' he shouted, 'you're dead.' But, injured and having to hold his right arm, he was no match for speed or agility on the wooded slope, and soon gave up the pursuit.

Down on the riverbank, Joe looked over his shoulder and, seeing he was no longer in danger, reduced his pace to an aimless, slow, panting walk. A moment later, Albert caught him up.

Supporting his injured arm, with the boys scurrying behind him, the hard man returned to his fishing tackle, glaring at Albert and Joe across the distance that separated them. Finding the money Joe had placed on the bench, the hard man picked it up in his left hand and held it high in his fist for his enemies to see — some kind of battle trophy or insult or stolen victory.

'Cunt's nicked your money,' said Albert. 'Should we go back and get him? I mean really get him — with sticks and stuff.'

Now a muddied mess, Joe sat on a log and began to cry into his hands while a nebulous cloud of late-season midges hovered above him.

'Jesus, not boo-hooing again?' complained Albert while keeping a solicitous eye on the hard man in the distance. 'Why do you always cry when we've got fighting to do?'

Joe didn't answer. Still glaring across the divide, the injured hard man was now overseeing the boys as they packed his fishing tackle away for him, his gruff, uncivil commands audible to Albert. Tugging on Joe's coat collar, Albert encouraged him to stand up. 'Come on, let's get away from here. That bloke still wants to spoil your joy-packed day. He might phone for some mates or something.'

Joe got to his feet, and although still weeping, walked with Albert.

'For fuck's sake, Joe,' urged Albert despairingly, 'stop crying. People will think we're having a little gay stroll.'

'Puffs!' shouted one of the boys.

'See?' said Albert. 'Told you. And if any girls ask, we won that fight.'

A high, narrow pedestrian bridge spans the river in the centre of Durham. Very soon, Albert and Joe were below that dizzying walkway, where Joe halted. Tipping his head back, exposing a grazed, bruised neck, his tear-damp cheeks glistened in the low, veiled sunlight as he surveyed the bridge's heights. The same grim and resolute expression that had preceded his attempted hanging swept darkly over him, and he strode toward the steep concrete stairs that led up the wooded bank to street level.

'For fuck's sake,' complained Albert, tagging alongside Joe, 'I know it's morally wrong for me to interfere in your noble purpose, but you really are a fucking self-murder amateur. You fucked up the hanging, and you could easily fuck up this bridge lark too. You'll land in the water or on soft earth and end up extremely embarrassed.'

Seemingly oblivious to Albert's criticism, Joe continued up the steep steps, but appeared to be experiencing pain.

'I know what I'm talking about,' continued Albert. 'I've studied suicide. I know the best ways. Painless, certain ways. I've researched them and written them down in a book. I'm special. Destined for greatness.'

Joe winced. Stopping, he pulled aside his coat and lifted his sweatshirt. His ribs where he had been kicked were red and already swelling.

'Nasty,' said Albert. 'Something could be broken.'

Joe sat down on a step.

Albert sat beside Joe, but took some care first not to get his coat muddied. 'Shit,' he said, once he was settled, 'I forgot to ask that bloke if he has thick dreams.'

'Tell me one,' said Joe after a silence.

'One what?'

'One of your painless, certain ways.'

'Can't. Unethical. I recognise your intentions as being admirable, and wish you luck, but you have to find your own road to salvation.'

Joe closed his eyes, as if experiencing some fresh pain. 'It's all been too much, Albert,' he admitted when his eyes opened again. Taking an envelope from his coat pocket, he stared bleakly at it.

'This was the final straw. A letter from the Antichrist.'

'That fucking demon in a dress,' said Albert, but showing no interest in the envelope. 'Don't know what you saw in her in the first place.'

'I never saw anything in her in the first place,' said Joe quietly, still staring at the envelope. 'She was just there. A mate's girlfriend. I never so much as checked out her arse in six years of knowing her. I'd never looked on any female so sexlessly.'

Albert now remembered he had a *Fry's Chocolate Cream*, and took it out. Unwrapping it, he gestured an offer to share it with Joe, but although Joe glanced in its direction, he seemed oblivious to its existence.

'One day I was in her flat,' continued Joe monotonously, staring vaguely down at the river — Albert got the horrible feeling a long and rambling story was about to be unleashed. 'Something good had happened to me that day. I felt so giddy I began comically flirting with her. Just saying daft things for a big, innocent laugh. I was a clown in those days. A big clown. After a while of me teasing her, she suddenly kissed me and told me it was serious now. I thought she'd just done it to embarrass and punish me, so pretended I was freaked and ran home.

'Next day, she turned up on my doorstep, crying, asking why I hadn't come to walk her dog like I usually did on that day. God, how she cried. She told me she loved me. Told me the only reason she'd gone out with my friend in the first place was because he knew me and it was a way for her to get closer to me. She said she'd grown to sort of love him at one time, but didn't love him any more, and hadn't for years. Said she hated him, even. Couldn't bear him touching her. And she kept on crying — tears that seemed so honest and true.' He sneered. 'Honest and true — that's a laugh. She later told me she'd deliberately not worn make-up that day so she'd look more innocent and sincere.'

'Do a bit of that myself,' said Albert, taking a second bite of his *Chocolate Cream* bar.

After a rueful, bitter pause that seemed to have nothing to do with Albert's flippancy, Joe continued his narration. 'With all that crying, she was bound to end up in my arms. Over the next weeks, things got more intimate, even though I called it off a dozen times. But she would always cry, and I always weakened when those tears were shed. She said she was going to leave my mate when she felt she could do it without hurting him. Always she reported she was on the brink of doing that. I avoided him. I was troubled by it all. So troubled. But so inexperienced. I was six years older than her, but six years younger in some ways. I lived in my own little world.'

'Do a bit of that myself, too,' said Albert, 'except my inner world isn't little. It's vast.'

'One day she told me she was pregnant,' Joe cheerlessly went on. 'It was going to be mine, she said. Couldn't be his. They'd only shagged a few times since she'd started seeing me, she said, and he always used condoms since she'd come off the pill. But I wasn't to worry, she said. She was going to get an abortion. That was a pack of lies, I found out. She'd wanted to become pregnant. I learnt she'd told her friends months earlier she thought a child of mine would be the best child possible. I even found a calendar she'd plotted her fertility on, and it matched the days she was keenest to have me round. She told me they were safe days at the time. She wanted my child, all right.

'So one day she comes round and tells me she's going ahead with the pregnancy. I was pretty stunned, but once it was clear the child was inevitable, that was it: I was going to be a dad, and I would be the best dad the world had ever seen. But the fact that I was calm and reasonable seemed to make her consider me a lesser person. "He hit the roof when I told him", she said. She'd apparently been telling my mate he was going to be the father too. Can you imagine how confusing it all was for me? But I uncovered it all. All the lies. All the strange psychology. All the pathetic, selfish, weird reasons — so weird. I found it all out. What she did and what she planned. She was livid at me for that. Livid at me for knowing her truly.'

Joe tailed off, and stared at the envelope... which was covered in witchcraft symbols.

The sky was rapidly losing the last of its light, and the frail orange lamps dotted sparsely along the riverside path grew in significance, weakly illuminating the faces of Joe and Albert. Now starting on a third square of his confectionary bar, Albert sucked more slowly, letting the chocolate and mint fondant melt sensuously in his mouth. 'Goddamnit, I love *Fry's Chocolate Creams*,' he declared.

Looking at the darkening river again, Joe quietly resumed his story. 'Eventually she did leave him, or at least she told me she had. One day she said she'd finally told him all about me, and that they were finished for good. But it wasn't quite how she'd said it was, I found out later. I found out so much about her later. Nothing had been like she'd managed to convince me it was. Nothing. So many lies, lies I think she even grew to believe herself. Looking back, Lord how she enjoyed lying. The lies brought sweet smiles to her face.'

A particularly miserable reverie now seemed to take hold of Joe as he continued to stare at the river and the eerie mist that was rising from the dark water.

Albert tapped Joe's arm. 'So exactly how is my Man of Destiny air coming along?' he asked, affecting a noble aspect, which was doomed to fail considering he had chocolate stains on his lips.

Joe had nothing to say about Albert's demeanour. After a time, in a voice sounding even more weary, he went on with his strange tale. 'Transpired she'd actually never admitted anything to my mate about me. But he'd become suspicious through a mutual friend. He was gutted, of course. I guess she got some kind of weird ego boost out of that — Lord, she'd done enough to bring it about. But she got a shock when he dropped her like a stone.

'So then she dropped me like a stone too. Her being pregnant with our child's what made it hurt so much. After weeks of her uttering sweet, wonderful stuff about how it was bound to be beautiful and gifted because I was the father, one evening she just said she couldn't ever possibly tell her folks that she'd been involved with me and that the child was mine. She laughed, too. Can you imagine how confused I was? And how hurt? And how humiliated?' Joe paused, then continued in a grimmer vein. 'Well, I did some investigating, and I soon understood all her reasons, but they were all pathetic and selfish and weird. I found it all out, and that was something she couldn't bear — someone knowing her truly. She was livid at me for that.'

'You've already said that bit,' commented Albert, popping another chocolate square into his mouth. 'So what happened with the kid?'

'Our little daughter,' murmured Joe. 'My little sorrow. We could have splashed in puddles together.'

'Yeah, so what happened? Hurry up, I'm a busy man. Places to go. People to meet. Time is money.'

Joe said, 'She began trying to persuade my mate that the baby would be his. She was desperate, absolutely desperate, that her parents didn't find out I was the father. She was just too spineless to tell the truth. I let them know myself, but she told them I was crazy — and I was crazy: *driven* crazy. She told them she'd never had anything to do with me at all. Funny, right from the start she used to tell me they'd guessed she was seeing me because they were so wise and insightful. She told me she'd told her sister all about me too, but I later discovered she hadn't. She had a different story for everyone. Still does.'

'What were her parents,' asked Albert boorishly and derisively, sucking on his chocolate, 'fucking lords or something?'

'No. Not unless lords live on council estates in council towns. From what people tell me, her mother was some kind of neurotic, and her father... You know, she actually believed him to be infallible? Probably still does. Just one of the strange, strange things I uncovered about her. Discovered she'd believed my mate to be infallible, too — her word, not mine. Read what you like into that.'

'I know this isn't the time or the place,' said Albert, 'I mean, you've obviously got your own little agenda going — but do you think I should get some highlights in my hair? Someone once said I'd look really cool if I did. Mind you, he was bald, so he might have just been trying to level the playing field by ruining me.'

If Albert had been mute and invisible, his question couldn't have registered less with Joe, whose attention was now directed to some desolate place and time that ostensibly lay in the direction of the river. In a while, he continued his miserable, lame drone. 'I didn't see her again until six months after the birth. I discovered by then she'd conceded to her parents there was a theoretical chance the child could be mine. But she was adamant to them it was actually my mate's. I discovered she'd told them I was refusing to take paternity tests, when in fact it was the other way round. She started telling mutual acquaintances I could come to see the child if I liked, so long as her parents weren't around. I was dumb enough to take up her offer a few times. I shouldn't have. She'd make a point of telling me who'd she'd slept with the night before. She'd decided to become some kind of vamp, you see, using and abusing men... or so she thought. They never seemed to feel abused. Some of her sex tales were true, I learnt, but some were make-believe. Some of the true ones were house-breakers and jailbirds. She would treat me with disdain while I was there, but as soon as I got up to leave, she would plonk the baby back into my lap and say I needn't leave just yet. I always ignored her attempts to hurt me, except one time when she told me she'd bedded some particularly scum bloke I knew about. Bedded him in the same room the baby was sleeping in. When she realised she'd finally rattled me, she laughed with giddy delight.' Joe tailed off again, resuming after an embittered silence.

'Around that time I had to go London for a couple of weeks, and I told her I'd come to see the child again when I got back. But she lied again. She told people I'd been pestering her to move to London with me.' Joe shook his head in stupefied disbelief. 'Those lies. Those relentless lies. And she sticks to her lies with pathological tenacity. She's the kind of person who'll tell a dozen lies to avoid telling a single truth. And even if she has to admit to having told a lie, she'll blurt a dozen carefully rehearsed excuses for the untruth.' He paused. 'All I ever wanted was honesty and straightforwardness.'

Albert was now on his last piece of chocolate, and suspected his attention and patience would be gone when the chocolate was, but until then, Joe's miserable moaning retained an audience.

'I did move to London eventually,' continued Joe. 'Just had to get away from her. Far away.' He gave a cynical laugh. 'When I told her I was leaving, she accused me of running away from my responsibilities. She also said she'd probably get back together with me after a few years, once she'd played the field a bit – her very words. Can you believe that?

'When I was away, I just couldn't forget the child. So I sought legal advice, and my solicitor wrote to her asking that DNA tests be done, and that should it be proved I was the father, I'd like to be able to offer maintenance payments and occasionally see the child. She went to a solicitor herself, who wrote back saying that his client denied ever having assured me I was the father, and – and I still remember the words to this day – "whilst disputing paternity, our client would be unwilling to submit the child to the trauma of blood tests". We didn't even ask for blood tests. We asked for DNA tests that could be done with a swab.' Joe paused again, then said sadly and softly, 'More lies. Always with the lies.'

His chocolate bar now finished, Albert stuffed the messy wrapper into Joe's pocket without him noticing.

'Just some honesty and straightforwardness would be enough,' murmured Joe. 'Just some honesty. Just five minutes of honesty. What will I have to do to get it? I've tried so hard. Is it selfish of me to want it so badly? I used to try to force honesty out of her by exposing her lies. I thought that if I exposed her every time, to everyone involved, her grotesque pantomime of lies would have to end, and I could be involved with the kid without lunacy surrounding it all. But no. That just made her worse. Much worse.' A sudden change in his aspect indicated that Joe's belief that he'd been the victim of diabolic deceits had suddenly collapsed. 'Maybe

I was to blame?' he murmured fearfully. 'Maybe it was me all along?' He desperately searched his forlorn soul. 'No, it wasn't me,' he eventually decided, but appearing as if he retained a thousand gnawing doubts. 'I did the right things. Once the child became a certainty, I accepted I would have to live for another person instead. I'd never been so serious about anything. But look how it turned out when it was the only episode in my life where I could honestly say I did nothing wrong.'

'Apart from the fact that she was a mate's girlfriend,' Albert pointed out, eliciting some strangulated sobbing from Joe.

'Apart from that,' conceded Joe in sobs.

'Jesus, man, get a fucking grip,' urged Albert, who was becoming extremely restless, but felt obliged to stick around. 'You're making me wish I'd never reminded you you'd shagged your mate's bird loads of times, day after day.'

Joe continued to sob and squeeze out strangulated words. 'It was ten years ago. Ten years ago,' he said, as if imploring some unseen judge for leniency. 'Ten years ago.'

A teardrop fell on to the envelope he was holding.

'Ten years?' remarked Albert with uncharacteristic surprise in his voice. 'All that grotesque pantomime stuff you've been banging on about happened a whole ten years ago?'

'Ten years,' Joe wearily confirmed, his latest sobbing beginning to abate.

'So why the sudden urge to hang yourself now?'

Joe seemed reluctant to answer.

'Well?' pursued Albert. 'Don't leave me in the dark. My cat's always doing that to me. Really pisses me off. It's got secrets, that cat, and I want to know them.'

With a weak voice, Joe said, 'Something very, very bad happened to me last month. The very worst thing that can happen to anyone.'

'You didn't get a job with a runty little girl called Grace, did you?'

'No,' said Joe quietly.

'Well? What happened to you? If you tell me, I promise to tell you about the sticky chocolate wrapper I hid in your pocket.'

'I fell in love,' said Joe.

'Pah? Is that all? I do that all the time. I fell in love with three wan ladies at once on this very riverbank just the other day. *Three* at once, Joe, top that and still appear truthful. Who did you fall in love with, anyway? Not that dark-haired one who does the weather

266

on the BBC? Elizabeth Saary? Wouldn't blame you if it was. I'm in love with her too. I'd stand more of a chance with her than you, though. I don't cry all the time. Ever, actually.'

'I fell in love,' said Joe again, lamentingly... fadingly.

'Yeah, who with? You're not just trying to impress me, are you? She's real, right?'

'She's real,' said Joe. 'As real as confusion. As real as illusion.'

'Bet she isn't real. Bet you're just tryng to big yourself up in my Man of Destiny eyes. If she's so real, what's her name, then?'

Joe winced, and lifted his sweatshirt to peer at his swollen bruise again, which was worsening.

Albert peered at it too. 'Never been one to reflect on other people's pain, Joe, but I really think you ought to get that looked at. Must really hurt.'

'Outer pain good,' said Joe, letting his sweatshirt fall, 'distracts from inner pain.' He looked at the river again. 'And the name of my newest inner pain is *Melissa*.' He suddenly bent forward to bury his face in his hands, weeping badly until improving enough to admit, 'I can't take any more inner pain, Albert. It's all been too much. Everything goes wrong for me. I've had the kind of bad luck a cursed god would get.' Presently, he regained enough equanimity to sit up straighter and show his face. 'So then, to top it all, I fell in love. With Melissa. Deeply, passionately, frantically in love with Melissa, after so many years of avoiding that danger, never daring to take it further than a stolen glance across a crowded room. Then Melissa fell into my lap. She was a strange lady, Albert. Even used to admit it herself. But I didn't run away early enough, and our confusing little affair was the last straw.'

'Thought you said that letter from the Antichrist was the last straw?' said Albert, pointing to the envelope in Joe's hands.

'My life's been a succession of last straws.'

'Yeah? Pull many birds with that line?'

Joe stared at the river, seemingly oblivious to Albert's cruel flippancy until he lamely lamented, 'Don't want to pull many. Just one. Just Melissa. Think I'll always be in love with her. But I ought to thank her, really — she's given me the strength not to go on.'

'Yeah? She can do that for people, can she? Can you introduce me to her?'

Joe ignored Albert's request. 'After Melissa, half wild with agitated despair and self-doubt, I got a friend in my home town to ring the Antichrist to tell her I wanted to talk to her — talk to her for the first time in ten years. I wanted to find out about our daughter and how she was getting on before I took my wretched life. To my astonishment, the Antichrist rang me within minutes, but I couldn't believe what she was saying. I was stunned. Confused. I had to hang up on her.' He looked bleakly at Albert, and held up the envelope, proffering it. 'A few days later, I got this. Read it, Albert. I beg you. Read it, please.'

Albert took the envelope from Joe at the same time Joe's mobile received a text message.

'It's from the Antichrist,' said Joe, staring apprehensively at the caller ID. Displaying the message, he read her words out: '*I suppose I ought to thank you for the thousand pounds you sent yesterday, but you owe twenty times that in child support.*'

Albert was puzzled. 'Thought you said you'd tried to use the courts to allow you to pay maintenance?'

'I did,' protested Joe. Suddenly collapsing into self-doubt, he looked wild-eyed at Albert. 'Or maybe I didn't? Maybe I'm crazy? Maybe it's me, not her. Read it, Albert. Tell me what you think. I beg you.'

Albert began reading the contents of the envelope in the murky light. It was a three-page, disjointed letter asserting the reverse of Joe's story, accusing him of having abandoned her, leaving her to look after the child on her own. Accusing him of being selfish. Accusing him of trying to force her to go back to the other bloke. One line read, "*The simple truth is that I don't know who the child belongs to. I hope she is yours. I love you, Joe. You are my dark side. My Heathcliff. I will always love you, no matter what you do to me (if you ever tell anyone I said I love you, I will KILL you)."* There was also a passage torn out from a book — *Wuthering Heights*, realised Albert, the passage wherein Kathy declares her love for Heathcliffe to be like the rocks beneath the soil, unseen but necessary, always there. And the letter concluded: "*I will not sign this letter. What letter? I deny all knowledge of it*".

'Fuck,' breathed Albert when he'd finished reading, 'you know how to pick 'em, don't you?'

Joe earnestly implored, 'Albert, tell me what you think.'

'It's a bit different from your version of events, isn't it?' said Albert, handing the letter back to Joe.

'So it was me all along then?' said Joe, fearfully. 'I'm mad? Mad not maddened? I've imagined it all?' He looked at the river and murmured, 'Maybe Wordsworth got it right when he wrote

We poets in our youth begin in gladness,
But come thereof in the end despondency
and madness.'

'You're a poet?' asked Albert tentatively, feeling creatively threatened and upstaged.

'Of the deepest ilk,' murmured Joe, although he was paying little attention to Albert.

'How deep?'

'I won a prize.'

'Big prize or little prize?'

'Big, I suppose.'

'Bastard,' muttered Albert. 'Just don't start writing poems about penguins. That's my territory.'

Joe suddenly buried his face in his hands. 'Is it me or her?' he implored wretchedly. 'One of us has to be crazy. Decide for me, Albert. I doubt everything I do and say and think and remember. Everything. Not like when I was younger. I was so strong then. Too strong. Too strong too soon.' He raised his head to look at Albert. 'Tell me, Albert, is it me or her?'

'Well, I'm not a psychiatrist,' said Albert, 'but the bit about killing you's a bit suspect. The wacky spelling mistakes don't do her any favours, either. Or the witchcraft symbols on the envelope.'

'She's big on the witchcraft thing these days,' Joe shot back. 'She was getting into it before the pregnancy, but I never found out till later. She'd read a loopy book, you see, and become convinced she was the embodiment of mythology's Queen of the Demons, Lilith. Lilith, who steals men's sperm to raise her avenging brood. She did the sperm stealing, all right.'

'Fuck, Joe,' breathed Albert, 'and you actually have to ask if she's bonkers?'

'I have to ask everything, Albert. It's all been too much. When I need to so much as lick a stamp I have to phone eight people before I'm sure which side the glue's on. And I don't care which eight.'

'Joe,' said Albert firmly, 'she's obviously bonkers.'

A wave of austere relief washed over Joe to hear Albert's judgement. Putting the letter and envelope away into his coat pocket, he said, 'When she phoned me, I just couldn't believe what I was hearing. Thought that I'd become insane on top of frantically wretched. I had to put the phone down on her. Then she started leaving messages on my answering machine saying I was being unreasonable in not communicating with her. When I didn't respond, she went and stuck it all down in that letter.' He paused. 'So I relented and resumed communication.'

'So she wants you back now, and involved with the kid?'

'Desperately,' answered Joe, staring down at the shadowy river again.

'She's got a cheek,' deemed Albert. 'What's happened? Have all her crap folks died or something?'

'No, they're still alive,' answered Joe, wearily. 'But the kid grew to look so much like me she couldn't go on saying I couldn't be the father to them. Besides, she's more fearful of the child's potential admonition now than her ageing parents' disapproval. The big new lie's for the child. She wants to portray herself as wronged and innocent in the child's eyes. She wants the kid to see her making an effort so she won't one day accuse her of robbing her of a father.' He paused. 'I don't even mind her doing that. I can live with that. But when she expects me to believe the lies too, that's just too surreal. Too surreal even for me. Infuriating.' His voice became darker. 'But having me involved with the kid's not what she really wants. She wants me back for herself, Albert. The kid's just the lure. She believed so long as she had that kid, she could always have me running back to her.' He paused. 'And so here I am — back in Durham.'

Albert's jaw dropped. 'You've gone back to the Antichrist?'

Joe shook his head feebly. 'No, I haven't. Not yet. I've just been wandering around Durham since I got back. I mean, how could it work? The kid's ten now, reared on a diet of lies about me. And how could I be in the same room as the Antichrist when just speaking to her on the phone makes me sick?'

'Tricky one,' agreed Albert.

'I'd have to bite my tongue all day long when she lies and lies and lies.'

'You'd bleed to death,' predicted Albert.

'But it's my duty,' argued Joe to himself. 'My paternal responsibility.'

Bollocks to all this sob-story stuff, thought Albert, and he stood up. 'Just tell her to fuck off,' he said, arranging his coat for the walk home.

Albert's intended valedictory remarks seemed not to have registered with Joe, who was staring at the dark river. 'Everything's gone wrong for me. Relentlessly. It's all been too much. I'm raw. Everything hurts so bad now. It's no way to live. No way to live.'

'Yeah, but you're not really melancholic by nature, are you?' deemed Albert, brushing some leaves and mud off his coat. 'Your suffering's worldly and commonplace compared to my noble sorrow. It's just twatty events that have made you sad. You're just depressed, and where's the charm in that? Not like my lovely pull-the-birds poetic wistfulness. Jackie was so wrong.'

Albert could have been miming in Dutch for all the notice Joe took of him.

'Maybe I wrote that letter myself?' murmured Joe in sudden fear. 'Maybe I really am mad? They say mad people never know they're mad. Is it me, Albert? Is it me? Or is it her? If it's me, I'd be better off dead.'

'Oh shut the fuck up,' said Albert, 'you're starting to drive me mad, too.'

'It must be me,' said Joe to himself. 'Those things couldn't really have happened. Not in the real world. It must be me.'

Albert was now about to leave. In an uncharacteristic act of overt humanity, he attempted to introduce some jaunty supportiveness into his voice. 'Anyway, best of luck with everything.'

In the ever-deepening darkness, Joe looked up at his companion. 'You said you'd studied suicide?'

'Like a hero.'

'Then help me, Albert. I've been trying to kill myself for days, but I keep fucking up. I can't do anything right any more. Tell me one of your certain ways.'

'I'm a lone hero, not a sharing hero.'

The disappointment showed on Joe's face. Cut into him. But then the grim and resolute expression that had preceded his thwarted hanging returned, and he rose to his feet. Although evidently in pain, he at once began speedily climbing the steps leading up to the pedestrian bridge. Before Albert could react, Joe had a good lead on him, and when he eventually caught him up, he was already on the high walkway, pacing to its centre.

'No, Joe,' ordered Albert. 'If you try it, I'll stop you.'

Joe ignored Albert. Near the middle of the bridge, he looked over the edge for a suitable place to jump, but it was mostly water or trees down below.

'Don't be such a fucking amateur in my illustrious presence, Joe,' said Albert. 'This fall won't kill you.'

That was perhaps true. They were only some sixty feet above the water, and just thirty above the tree tops. Nevertheless, Joe lifted a leg over the waist-high concrete parapet, grimly bearing the pain in his ribs the manoeuvre apparently engendered.

Albert grabbed him. 'No, Joe,' he pleaded, struggling to hold on to him.

There was no doubt about it, realised Albert: Joe meant to do it. He looked both ways along the bridge to see if anyone was about who could assist, but there was no one.

'Let me go,' ordered Joe, gradually winning the struggle, getting most of his weight over the ledgeless parapet. Only one leg now remained above safe ground.

Although he had a two-handed grip on Joe's coat lapels, Albert was preventing Joe from falling to his ruin, if not his death, mostly by pressing his own weight against Joe's trailing leg, pinning it against the concrete.

'Let me go or I'll thump you,' warned Joe.

And he did thump Albert — an awkward, hampered punch that only glanced Albert's temple.

'Okay! Okay!' cried Albert desperately. 'I'll tell you a better way to die. Just come back over.'

'Tell me first,' demanded Joe, still struggling for release.

'Okay! Okay! Have you got access to benzodiazipines and a seafaring boat?'

'You fucking impractical wanker,' Joe accused, attempting to kick Albert with his pinned leg. 'Tell me a proper way, you fucking fraud.'

'I don't know any proper ways!' cried Albert, fearing he was beginning to lose his grip on Joe.

'So let me go,' Joe demanded, struggling even harder.

'Overdose,' Albert suddenly advised. 'That'll do it.'

'What kind of overdose?'

'Heroin overdose. Buy enough smack and you'll be in a coma while the needle's still in your vein. You'll die painlessly.'

'I don't know where to get heroin from,' returned Joe, aiming another thwarted punch at Albert, but only hitting his shoulder.

'I do. I know,' jabbered Albert. 'There's a druggy squat across town. My flatmate buys dope there sometimes.'

Joe threw another difficult punch that only just caught Albert's chin. 'I haven't got any fucking money left to buy it with.'

The punch, though glancing, hurt, and Albert felt a surge of anger that fleetingly counselled him to release Joe and let him fall.

But he overcame that anger. 'I'll give you the money,' he said, suddenly fearing that a slip, or a snagged finger, might pull him over the bridge too. 'Just come back over.'

'Promise?'

'Promise.'

Joe stopped struggling.

'Now?'

'Now.'

After briefly deliberating, Joe added his own efforts to Albert's, and was soon safely back on the bridge, whereupon he immediately held out his hand.

'Money,' he demanded.

'You mad cunt,' said Albert, panting and slumping down against the parapet.

Still holding out his hand, Joe waited for Albert to reach into his pocket, but Albert was busy recovering from the drama. So Joe began to climb over the parapet again.

'No!' cried Albert, wrapping his arms around Joe's trailing leg. Managing to get a hand into his coat's inner pocket, he waved money at Joe. 'Here. Take a hundred. That should do it.'

Joe took the money, returned fully to the bridge, counted out one hundred pounds, dropped the remainder on to Albert, then demanded to know exactly where and how he could buy the heroin.

'You mad, mad cunt,' said Albert, gathering his change on all fours.

'Where?' demanded Joe again.

'Fucker,' cussed Albert, pocketing his remaining money and getting to his feet, brushing himself down.

Joe hitched a leg over the parapet, prompting Albert to blurt, 'Eleven Forest Lane.'

'Will they have a syringe and all that shit?'

'Bound to. Bound to. My flatmate said it's a one-stop-shop for junkies.'

Grim and resolute, Joe strode away, and Albert felt no inclination to follow him.

Two late-teenage females in short, tight skirts were now coming along the bridge. 'Give me a hundred pounds or I'll throw myself off this bridge,' said Albert when they were level with him.

'So?' shrugged one, without slowing.

'Go on then,' encouraged the other, furiously chewing gum.

When they were a little further along the bridge, in a

contemptuous tone deliberately pitched loud enough for Albert to catch, one of the teenagers said, 'Cheeky cunt.'

Understanding he had no future in emotional blackmail, Albert finished brushing himself down, then walked in the opposite direction to the hard-hearted ladies — the way home.

1.21
Dear John

It was done. Jennifer had posted the letter to John, addressed to him at his Army base in Aldershot.

The previous night, when John returned from the pub, Jennifer had apparently been asleep. He'd suspected she wasn't, but had not attempted to rouse her. Setting the alarm for five — an early return to Aldershot being scheduled — he'd slipped into bed beside her, and soon they were both asleep for real. She'd woken naturally before the alarm sounded, and when John first opened his eyes, it was to have breakfast presented to him. He'd been surprised, and was even more surprised when, after they'd shared breakfast, Jennifer initiated lovemaking. At the beginning of their sporadic relationship, to Jennifer, John had been a quiet fascination. The well-defined V-shape of his back, a back that could carry battle kit forty miles in a day; the solidity of his thighs; his strong hands; even the odour of his underarms and the fecund tackiness of his genitals in the morning — all had been things of wonder to her, things to be discovered and touched. Similarly, beyond a few kissing sessions with schoolboys, whose wandering hands had been checked, Jennifer had had no experience of the power of the aroused male physique; never felt at the mercy of muscular desire, yet knowing it was he who was really at her mercy.

John and Jennifer's first intimacies had taken place in a holiday caravan he had rented near Richmond for a fishing trip, a caravan he'd rented several times again until it became clear that overnight stays at Jennifer's aunt's would be permissible. However, by then the early fascination had faded. It had not been John who had enthralled her in the small way that she had been, she had come to understand, but the newness of, and her instinctual desire of, maleness. But that desire had always been more subdued and reserved than John wished, and of late could hardly be discerned as desire at all. But her uncommon beauty compensated for that. It compensated for everything.

That morning, however, certain within herself it was to be their final union, Jennifer had fucked with apparent passion. Then, on the doorstep, with the sun still unrisen over the distant hills, they had said their goodbyes. Toward the eastern horizon, the sky had been a beautiful blue; deep and moving, vibrant and promising. Venus, in the ascendant, had sparkled piercing white in that azure. But westward had still looked deep and dark.

Jennifer had held John tightly, bringing her lips to his. More than a minute elapsed before he broke away, slung his bulging service bag across his back, gently squeezed her hand and turned to go. Had he been a more discerning creature he might have suspected from the intensity of that goodbye kiss, delivered with her bare, ivory feet melting the early-morning frost on the doorstep, that it had not been just another goodbye, but a final goodbye. But he hadn't. He'd just thought she was sorry to see him leaving, his unwarranted suspicion about Albert forgiven, his engagement ring finally rewarded with the best fuck she had ever given him.

Walking away, military adventure ahead of him, a spring had entered his stride. A little way down the street, he'd looked back over his shoulder, but Jennifer had no longer been in sight and the door had already been closed.

With a sense of urgency she hadn't understood, Jennifer had at once set about writing a letter to put her asunder from the boyfriend who had known her first — known her without ever really knowing her. John would be devastated by the letter, she knew. It was short — just one page of her small, neat writing on blue vellum — explaining in no real depth that she no longer wanted him as a lover and that she felt it would be better if they never saw each other again, at least not for a very long while. She'd also included the ring, wrapped in a piece of black fabric torn from an old underskirt. As soon as it was finished, she'd dressed for outdoors to drop it in the postbox on her street. Enjoying the early morning air and relative absence of people, she'd walked around town for a while before returning to

Margaret's, discovering the clock had advanced more than she'd supposed. She'd had to hurry to make it to work, with no time to shower first.

So Jennifer had untangled herself from John, and felt in charge of her life. Now she was telling her employer that she wished to take a break to give her space in which to think about what she wanted to do with her future — whether she wanted to stay or move on.

'It's not really the conventional way of going about things, is it, Jennifer?' said Maureen, who was treating a thin dog for mange. 'It should be one or the other. If you're not available, I'll need someone else. Jobs aren't hobbies.'

Jennifer continued to enter the dog's treatment details into the surgery's computer.

'This chap's got quite a case of fleas,' observed Maureen, parting its coat. 'You'd better educate the owner about flea treatments when we're done here.'

'I'm due some holiday time soon,' said Jennifer, 'why don't I take that early? You needn't pay me.'

'Jennifer, I'll pay you whatever you've got coming to you.' With most of her attention still directed to the dog's treatment, Maureen formulated a deal. 'Okay, here's what we'll do. I'll get a temp in from an agency while you take a week or so off to think about things. But let me know what you're going to do as soon as you know yourself. Right?'

Jennifer expressed satisfaction with the proposed arrangement.

'Well then, that's settled,' said Maureen, 'and I think we can spare you as from end of play today, if you like.'

Despite having found the energy, will and courage to give her life some positive direction that day, when she returned home from work, Jennifer felt herself slipping. Lacking the enthusiasm to catch up on the shower she'd missed that morning, she lay on the sofa, staring at the television until the phone rang. It would be John, she guessed, unaware that he no longer featured in her life. Going into the hall, she disconnected the phone at the socket and returned to the sofa.

Later, when she heard Margaret returning from visiting her mother, she took her feet off the sofa even though Margaret had never complained about it and did it herself all the time.

'It's friggin' freezin' out,' moaned Margaret, entering the living room. 'Winter's come early. Did you tape Eastenders?'

'Missed the first couple of minutes. Sorry.'

Margaret turned up the gas fire, bending to warm her hands. Although she was otherwise thin, Jennifer noticed Margaret's hips were advancing in their middle-age enlargement.

'God, got to be at work in two hours,' complained Margaret. 'I friggin' hate starting a new shift pattern.' Turning so that the fire could affect the back of her legs, she properly viewed Jennifer for the first time since arriving. 'Blimey, you're looking glummer than usual.' Before Jennifer could make a return, Margaret noticed something awry. 'Why's the phone disconnected?'

She went to reconnect it.

'I don't want to speak to John,' explained Jennifer while Margaret was on her hands and knees in the hall.

'Well, you can't keep disconnecting the phone.'

'Sorry.'

'Pity I don't have an answering machine any more,' said Margaret, coming back into the living room to resume warming herself in front of the fire, 'then we'd know who's calling before we pick up. There used to be one here, but me husband took it with him.'

'Should I buy an answering machine?' proposed Jennifer.

'It would be a help, wouldn't it? Of course, if you move out, it's yours to take with you.'

'Fine,' said Jennifer. 'If John calls tonight, can you tell him I'm in bed? Tell him I've come down with the flu.'

'Ooo, like that is it? Four days after you're engaged and all — juicy. Tell me all about it.'

'There's nothing much to tell,' said Jennifer, with a small shrug.

'Are you sure you're a girl? Come on, let's have the gossip.'

'I sent him the ring back today.'

Margaret took in a sharp, scandalised breath, which she held until the reconnected telephone rang some seconds later.

Upon hearing the phone, Jennifer's expression revealed trepidation.

'Don't worry, pet,' said Margaret, going to answer the call, 'I've never seen anyone so sick with the flu.'

Jennifer closed the door after Margaret, and sat on the edge of the sofa, involuntarily catching snatches of the telephone conversation — as she'd anticipated, it was John on the line.

1.22
Starry, Starry Night

Standing hand in hand, looking to the heavens, Ron and Sarah were some ten miles outside Reykjavik, having been driven there by Ivor in his towering off-roader. They were hoping to see the Aurora Borealis.

Ivor was the Computer Operations Manager of a fish packaging firm that had purchased bespoke software from Ron's firm. Ron was part of a four-person team sent to train Ivor's staff in the use of that software. Ivor was now in his mid-fifties. For most of his twenties, he had worked and studied in London, and thus his command of English was excellent, if somewhat idiosyncratic. Away from the fish factory, he had a contagious passion for astronomy, and had insisted on taking Ron and Sarah out to see the Aurora, if it would show itself that night. Now that they were far away from any street lighting, the cold, starry sky above their heads appeared so much more intense, and Ivor was explaining how sometimes, especially during such periods of high sun-spot activity as they were experiencing now, it might become a dancing, folding panoply of iridescent light. As he spoke, a dull glow began to silhouette the northern skyline, becoming brighter before sweeping up into an arc of light that almost reached the zenith, throwing out vividly coloured streamers that twisted back to the horizon. Then the arc began to break up, sending out in all directions folding, rippling curtains of shimmering colour that finally, but for a dim afterglow, dissipated the display.

Sarah was wonder-struck. She'd never imagined it would be so impressive. It was the scale of it. Out here, the sky seemed very big and she felt very, very small. Out here, she felt, a person could easily be persuaded to believe in a god. She thought also that that person should be even more easily persuaded to believe in the complete insignificance of the human species in that god's great scheme. 'We're just specks, aren't we?' she murmured.

What they had seen, Ivor informed them, was a better than average display. 'Right time in the eleven-year sun-spot cycle,' he explained, with a broad smile. 'The more sun spots, the greater the solar wind. The greater the solar wind, the better the Aurora.'

A thread of light streaked across a constellation, and Sarah excitedly pointed.

'A meteor,' said Ivor. 'Make a wish.'

Sarah closed her eyes and made her wish.

They continued their appreciation of the northern sky, soon observing that the glow on the horizon seemed to be intensifying again. Ivor indicated a faint point of light slowly traversing the heavens: a satellite, he informed them. Sarah and Ron had never noticed such a thing before. Ivor observed that it was moving directly from north to south. 'Probably a spy satellite,' he said, explaining that such an orbit was an expensive thing to attain, and that only the military were ever that wasteful. 'Maybe it's a scientific research satellite,' he conceded, with a smile.

'Do you think we'll ever reach the stars?' asked Sarah.

'Of course!' returned Ivor at once.

'Nah,' said Ron. 'It'd take thousands of years to reach just the closest star.'

'True and not true,' said Ivor. 'The sun's our nearest star, but beyond that, yes, thousands of years to the next nearest star with today's technology. But consider this: at the rate biological science is progressing, within a hundred years easy, we will have overcome ageing. What is a ten thousand year trip to an immortal!'

'Very boring,' said Ron.

'True,' agreed Ivor, 'but consider this: you, the first to do so, go off in a rocket ship on a ten thousand year trip to Alpha Centauri. Ten thousand years? So what? You're immortal! When you return, your wife will still be young. Maybe even your dog will still be young. Two hundred years after blast off, technology on earth has advanced so very much that they can send a ship to catch you up and take you there in *one* thousand years. Then a hundred years later another, better, ship catches you up and promises to take you there in fifty years. When you get there, another ship comes and takes you home in twenty years.'

'Cool,' said Sarah.

'Yes, indeed cool,' said Ivor. 'Something for your immortal children.'

Ron heard his mobile ring from where he'd left it inside Ivor's vehicle. 'Got a call,' he said, walking the short distance back.

'I'm so amazed that Ron's mobile works in a country like Iceland,' said Sarah.

Ivor laughed. 'We have one of the highest mobile phone take-up in the world! And a standard of living higher than Britain, and virtually no crime. Our parliament, the Althing, is the oldest in the

279

world. Do you want me to go on?'

'I didn't mean it like that,' appeased Sarah. 'I meant Iceland's such a lonely, wild place.'

'Ah, yes. Coverage is not total, that's for sure. Hard to place a base station on a moving glacier.'

Sarah gazed at the vast, starlit sky again.

'Do you really think the end of ageing is near?' she asked.

'Me, I think so, yes. Technically. My brother is a molecular biologist, and he knows things.'

'But what about the sociological problems?' wondered Sarah. 'Would yobs be allowed to be immortal too?'

'Yobs? What is yobs?'

Sarah made some yob gestures and voicings.

'Ah, yes, yobs,' realised Ivor sadly. 'The famous British idiots.'

'And what about the yob children of yobs?' Sarah further wondered.

'What about anyone's children?' said Ivor. 'If we're all immortal, and our children too, the world would soon be full.'

'A choice,' Sarah quickly decided. 'People would have to choose between immortality or reproduction.'

'Reproduction is immortality anyway,' shrugged Ivor. 'You would just be swapping one kind for another.'

Ivor had left an interior light on in his vehicle. Glancing back, he saw that Ron was not inside, nor did he appear to be anywhere near the vehicle. Beyond the vehicle, all was too dark to see.

'Where is Ron?' he asked.

Sarah turned to look. 'I don't know. He went to answer his phone.' She began walking back to the vehicle, joined by Ivor, who switched on a powerful torch he was carrying. 'Ron? Where are you?' Ivor's torch soon ascertained Ron's location: he was lying on the ground beside the off-roader, staring upward with an expression close to something Ivor had once seen on a corpse, and even closer to something Sarah had once seen on Albert.

1.23
St. Andrew's

Not wishing to disturb Margaret, Jennifer spent the first morning of her vague sabbatical trying to be quiet. Margaret was in bed, sleeping off the first night-shift in her peculiar work pattern, which seemed to adhere to some alternative calendar devised when the planet perhaps had two suns and a varying rotation speed. Yesterday, after posting the ring back to John and telling her employer she was contemplating moving on, Jennifer felt her life had acquired a momentum. But then had come a dejected evening, and today her life seemed very much as it always had been, except she no longer had a job to pass the hours.

She knew the call from John she had avoided taking the previous night would have just been one of his regular calls. But this morning he should have received her letter breaking the engagement, and so she was even more keen not to speak to him. She had said what she needed to say in the letter, and wanted that to be the end of it. She didn't want to deal with any anger or pleading or resentment or emotion of any kind. Thus, as soon as Margaret had gone to bed that morning, she had unplugged the phone again.

But it was not certain John would have received his letter that morning. It could be another day or two, Jennifer knew, recalling he'd told her that the slow sorting of the mail had become an issue on his base, a base that handled letters for five thousand souls. Once the weekend was past, reasoned Jennifer, he should definitely have got it, and would have had time to accept its message. She believed she would feel more settled in herself then, but until then, she would avoid answering the phone, and ask Margaret to tell John, if she spoke to him, that she had gone to stay with her sister a while.

Coming in from the garden after doing some tidying for Margaret, Jennifer was surprised to discover that it was nearly one o'clock. The morning had dragged, but the last hour seemed to have gone quickly. With a small sense of relief, she realised she could watch the news for something to do. Half an hour later, when the news finished, she switched the TV off again. She was starting to feel hungry, but wasn't in a mood to prepare anything. If she'd been at work, she'd have already eaten by now — in a cafe, most likely.

That's what she could do: she could go out to eat.

Going to her room to get herself ready, in the paper bin beside her dressing table, Jennifer saw the pieces of the letter Sarah had given her. When she'd finished checking her face, she picked them out from among discarded tissues and other things. More as a jigsaw distraction than anything else, she reconstructed the letter, Sellotaping the parts together. Reading it once, she placed it on her dressing table to remind her to ask Sarah about it next time she called.

It was almost always Sarah who called Jennifer, very, very seldom the reverse.

Today was the anniversary of their parents' deaths, and Sarah usually came to Richmond to place flowers on the grave. Whether Sarah's visit would occur this year, and whether it would incorporate dropping in on her sister, Jennifer wasn't sure, for she remembered that Sarah was playing a concert in the evening.

Moving away from the dressing table to sit on the end of the bed, Jennifer fell into reflection. Seven years since their deaths, things were becoming different, she knew. The feelings of numb loss she'd carried were changing. Some things were fading, but others emerging. Before, she had missed them as a child would — secretly feeling lost and unprotected; missing the security, the help, the guidance, the comfort. But now, leaving childhood behind, she realised she was regretting that she would never be able to know them as people. As she had said to her sister, she had always been a child, and they had been parents. But, as Sarah had often confirmed, of some things she was sure: she had always known they were special. Kinder and more thoughtful than most; gentler and surely wiser. And they had loved each other very much, too. Theirs was a lover's story she wished she knew better: their mistakes, their dreams; how they had come to be together, and how they had remained so.

Jennifer felt that she could do it now — had to do it, otherwise there could be no real moving on — and resumed getting herself ready to go out, selecting the jeans Sarah had bought her for her birthday.

*

'So long as it's not stolen,' joked the lady florist when asked by Jennifer if she could pay by credit card.

The florist was tall, and anaemic in appearance, and Jennifer thought her skin seemed too thin, like it was only rice paper.

'I've never used it before,' explained Jennifer, passing the card over the counter.

The florist examined the card. 'Oh, I knew I should know you,' she said after reading the name. 'You were one of Doctor Lucas's daughters.'

'Still am,' said Jennifer.

'Of course. Stupid me.'

The card proved viable, and when Jennifer left the shop she was carrying a cluster of flowers valued at £25.

It was a dry, lightly overcast, windless day, but chilly. Jennifer was glad she'd chosen to wear the yellow puffa jacket she'd had since her sixteenth birthday, and not the denim jacket she'd received for her nineteenth. Her hair was drawn into a tight ponytail that left a fringe springing out. From the florist's, she walked toward the town centre. Nearing the clothes shop that never opened, she noticed someone leaving it. Realising that today it was actually open for business, she went in, finding herself in an establishment that seemed to belong to a former age, an age before brightly-lit, flashy presentation. In attendance was an expensively-presented, haughtily attractive woman in early middle-age who busied herself around the shop with an air of brisk efficiency while Jennifer browsed the small but unusual selection of garments. But Jennifer knew her browsing was perfunctory, for it was the dress in the window she would surely be taking home.

There was no pressure from the woman in attendance. Jennifer felt she could spend the whole afternoon sifting through the clothes racks without receiving so much as an impatient or suspicious glance. But within three of four minutes she ended the charade and asked to see the dress in the window.

'Certainly,' said the woman, reaching into the widow display to retrieve the dress. She sounded very received-English middle class to Jennifer. Upper class, even. 'Here you go. Do you want to try it on?'

'Maybe,' said Jennifer, holding it against herself to check its size. 'No, it'll be all right. I'll take it.'

'Are you sure?'

'It'll fit. I can tell.'

'You can always bring it back if it doesn't,' said the woman, taking the dress from Jennifer.

With a small laugh in her voice, Jennifer remarked, 'You're never open.'

'Simply too busy with other things to open more than a few afternoons a week,' returned the woman, but what those things were she didn't say.

The woman seemed to take particular pride, and indeed expense, in packaging the dress, an expense that the £49 sale price didn't seem to justify. First, she carefully folded it into a stiff, shiny black box lined with red satin. Then she slid the box into a stiff, black paper carrier bag embossed with the shop's name in gold. This bag was then almost ceremoniously handed to Jennifer, together with a credit card receipt.

From that shop, Jennifer went to an electrical retailers where she bought an answering machine that had call vetting, and from there she proceeded to one of the cafes she frequented in her lunch breaks. After first looking through the window to check that she could have a table to herself, she entered, requesting just a sandwich and coffee when the short, bearded, balding owner who never spoke unnecessarily came over to take her order. The coffee arrived almost at once. Putting it to one side, she lifted her carrier bag on to the table and retrieved the black box. Opening it, she viewed her new dress, folded neatly within, the only dress she had ever bought herself.

She took the garment out, feeling the fabric.

'Got a new dress have you, love?'

Jennifer naturally looked to see who had spoken. It was one of two tanned, fair-haired men seated at a nearby table, both too young to know they looked old in teenager's eyes.

'Bet you'll look lovely in it,' he smiled.

'Those flowers for me?' joked the other man.

Jennifer didn't answer, but returned the dress to its box, and the box to its carrier bag. Picking up her coffee, she looked out the window to the people passing. She heard the men mutter something in unkindly tones, but afterwards they ignored her, except for occasional glances.

Later, upon leaving the cafe, Jennifer inserted the gathered, bound and wrapped stems of the flowers into her carrier bag and began her journey to St. Andrew's church. A bus could have taken her, but walking felt more appropriate — more like a pilgrimage. It was such a nice day for it, too. The air, though a little short of being mild, was at rest, and she soon felt the need to unzip her jacket. It seemed more like spring than autumn, she thought, squinting lazily into the thinly-veiled sun that she could just feel warming her legs.

She saw no shadow of what was soon to come.

St. Andrew's, where her parents were buried, lay on the very edge of Richmond. A narrow, tree-lined lane brought visitors from a busy road to this secluded, ancient stone church, whose silverware had recently attracted thieves. Historically, only the walled grounds to the front of the church had received coffins. Many so curiously weathered as to appear melted during some bygone swelter, aged headstones existed there that testified to a centuries-old continuity of burial. But in more recent times, neater, white marble and stained-green gravel graves had been assigned to a field behind the church, which only a dozen years ago had fed milking cows.

Even when entering the churchyard, Jennifer felt no prescience of the trouble to come.

This was her first visit. "It's just a cold stone, not them", had always been her expressed attitude. She hadn't even been at the funeral, a sickness having afflicted her that day. In a corner, under a large tree, was where she had been told that cold stone stood. Only one corner was overhung, overhung by a chestnut tree that had surrendered many of its leaves to the recent frosts, and she began to walk that way, along a cinder path. However, with some thirty paces still remaining, and not yet having determined exactly which leaf-strewn grave marked her mother and father's resting place, her pace slowed, and then she stepped off the path to sit on a low wooden bench.

No longer walking, she now felt cold, and closed her jacket. Lifting the flowers out from the carrier bag, she looked at the glib message of love and longing she had written on the attached card while in the cafe. Reading that message now brought a tightness to her throat, a tightness she feared able to put an end to her.

She looked away from the card. Looked at the stout, square church tower — either sandstone or limestone, she thought. Looked at the yew tree beside her. Looked at a cluster of yellow fungi at the tree's base. Looked ahead — looked ahead for some time.

Jennifer knew she was avoiding looking in the direction her parents' bodies lay. Indeed, she knew she physically couldn't look. It would take a blacksmith's arm to turn her head that way. Neither could she get up to walk any closer.

She walked back the way she'd come, taking her flowers with her. Coming out of the churchyard, there was no sense of defeat felt about failing to place the flowers, or sense of relief to have escaped the paralysis. Nothing was felt, beyond a vague sense of impotence.

Not far from St. Andrew's, a bus happened to arrive as she was passing a stop, and she rode it into town.

Coming Together

Once he'd returned home after his dramatic encounter with Joe, Albert had felt extraordinarily unsettled, at a loose end, and... and something else that he'd taken some time to realise and admit was loneliness. He'd felt lonely. Jackie, the only person he'd been able to ring up at any time of the day or night without risking censure, had shunned him, and although he wouldn't have wanted to ring her normally, the fact that he no longer felt able to had weighed heavy on his spirits.

Thus, for the first time ever, in his flat he'd felt truly alone.

Sitting at the table by the window, he'd stared across the room at the telephone, with a vague but heavy feeling he would never see Jackie again. Perhaps that story was now over. Or was it just the fateful anticipation of loss and sorrow that quietly haunted his every hour? Although he was wont to make quips about deep-eyed Melancholy leading him to the shadowy ships, behind the quips he felt real pangs, and what moved him easiest to mournfulness was beauty. Not just the beauty of the latest pined-for enchantress glimpsed in some hazy bar, but all beauty: a walk beside a languid woodland stream; the beauty of a smiling friend. And the *memory* of beauty affected him even more so. Moreover, he was by nature disposed to feel mournful for beautiful moments and sights even before they had passed away from the present. In the midst of beauty he was so often beset by grief for its anticipated loss.

While staring at the phone, it had rung, giving him a secret hope that it would be Jackie, calling to apologise for being so hard.

'Hello.'

'Yes, hello,' the male caller had said. 'I spoke to you this morning about the computer, and my friend bought it from you.'

'So? Works, doesn't it?'

'Yes, it works all right. It's fine. But I want to talk to you about other things. My friend says you told him you saw the cathedral UFO?'

Unannounced, Albert had then put the phone down, and when it immediately rang again, he'd turned the ringer off. He had not been in the mood for it. Sitting on the sofa, he'd felt irritated by the caller's idiotic effrontery, and irked at how his afternoon's cheeky amusement was having tedious come-backs.

Reaching for his coat, he'd retrieved his money and counted it, knowing the arithmetic beforehand. One hundred, plus a few coppers left from the money Jackie had lent him. Wanker. How had he managed to lose the other hundred saving someone's life by paying for them to die? It had seemed funny and artistic and above-worldly-considerations at the time, but it had started to suck a bit.

Returning his reduced money to his coat pocket, he'd then gone to his room to lie on his bed. But within minutes he had been up again, mooching around the flat until deciding that getting stoned and listening to music over headphones would be the only palliative to his unsettled condition.

That had been the evening before. Now, it was three in the afternoon, and Albert, freshly emerged from his bed, had just got in the bath. After getting stoned the night before, he'd then got stoned and stoned again just to help pass the time away, succeeding in that endeavour until well into the small hours. Consequently, he'd felt particularly disinclined to get out of bed today, despite sunlight stabbing through chinks in his curtains and into his eyes throughout the late morning and early afternoon. The sky was clouding over now, as far as he could tell through the frosted window of the bathroom. Remembering yesterday's forecast for heavy rain, he toyed with the notion of getting out of the tub early to do the shopping he needed to do before the predicted downpour began, but the big idea came to nothing.

An hour later, just as he was stepping out of the bath, large, infrequent drops of rain began impacting against the window, and by the time he'd made a cup of tea and brought it into the living room, the rain had become steady. If he'd not remained in the bath so long, he could have been back from Tesco's already, perhaps with some biscuits to help make the day pass. Maybe he wouldn't bother now. But then he remembered he was low on cat food.

*

'That's 'im!' exclaimed Carl.

Carl had just turned his cab into Devon Road and spotted Albert walking along, holding an empty carrier bag above his head to keep the cold rain off.

'Pull up beside him,' said Simon, with placid eagerness alloyed with nervousness. He was dressed in a blue nylon cagoule worn over his army-surplus jumper. On his lap rested an old, bulky cassette recorder, which he now readied, picking up its microphone.

'We wuz just comin' to see you!' said Carl, lowering his electric window as he drew up alongside Albert. 'Been callin' you all day. Never no answer.'

With a face as dreary as the weather, Albert stopped and looked at Carl, who today was wearing a different *JESUS ARMY* T-shirt underneath his fawn coloured jacket.

'Me mate wants to interview you,' Carl explained, beaming, jerking a thumb behind him to indicate Simon.

Albert looked at Simon, who pulled the sliding passenger window down.

'Hi,' said Simon, pushing his glasses up. 'Could I talk to you?'

Wordlessly, Albert walked on.

Prompted by Simon, Carl kept the cab apace with Albert.

'Can we give you a lift?' offered Simon.

Albert stopped again, looked at the cab, then looked at the rainy sky that surely had worse things yet in store for him. Choosing comfort over solitude, he stepped up to the cab's driver-side passenger door, which Simon opened for him. Getting into the cab, the very moment he pulled the door shut after him, the rain suddenly began lashing down on the cab's roof with a fury that seemed malicious.

He gazed lugubriously out the partially misted side window.

Although appearing uneasy in the presence of Albert's taciturn unsociability, Simon said, 'Made it just in time, didn't you? It's pouring now.'

Carl twisted around. 'Where to, mate?'

'Tesco's,' answered Albert unenthusiastically, still looking out the window.

'That big one I saw couple of miles from 'ere? Down 'ere an' to the left, ain't it?'

'That's right.'

'That okay?' Carl asked Simon.

'Yes,' answered Simon, and at once the rattling knock of the cab's diesel engine picked up in frequency, and they moved off.

Simon began his interview.

'Is it all right if I record you?'

Albert looked at the microphone being pointed at him, then looked briefly at the person pointing it before slumping back a little and staring ahead.

'You daft fuck,' he said.

Simon had been personally insulted, but seemed oblivious. The overriding issue with him appeared to be that he had received a go-ahead of sorts to proceed with the interview.

288

'Ask him 'bout Godfrey,' said Carl.

'I will,' said Simon. 'First things first.' Looking at Albert, he asked, 'Could you tell me what you told me yesterday about the Bermuda triangle?'

'I never told you anything about the Bermuda triangle.'

'You did.'

'No I didn't.'

A dilute look of bewildered suspicion and caution appeared on Simon's face, and he paused. 'Okay,' he eventually proceeded, 'can we talk about the UFO?'

'You're mad,' said Albert. 'There's no such thing as UF—' Stopping, Albert momentarily generated a vague, far-away demeanour and tone. 'It hummed and throbbed with light.'

Simon became excited. 'What did?'

'What?'

'What hummed and throbbed with light?'

Albert looked at Simon. 'What are you talking about?'

'The UFO,' said Simon keenly, pushing his glasses up. 'Is that what hummed and throbbed with light?'

'What UFO?'

Carl briefly looked over his shoulder. 'Doin' it again, ain't 'e? Sayin' things then forgettin''

'The UFO seen over your cathedral,' said Simon.

'You two are crazy,' said Albert. 'It was a distress flare.'

'It wasn't,' returned Simon at once. 'We're not crazy. Distress flare is the official cover-up story.'

'It moved away at great speed,' murmured Albert.

'Amazing,' breathed Simon. 'You saw the UFO, but can't remember.'

'What UFO?' asked Albert, sounding and appearing mildly vexed.

'The UFO you can't remember,' explained Simon. Suddenly remembering formalities, he transferred the microphone to his left hand, earnestly offering his right for shaking. 'My name's Simon Barnes. I'm a High Teacher in the Orthrium Society.'

'Albert Fox,' returned Albert, lamely accepting the shake.

To Albert, Simon was weak and anaemic in appearance, and this, together with his thick-rimmed glasses, conferred a swotty yet dopey look. The look of the kind of person who'd built a lot of model aeroplanes as a boy and had never once skipped doing homework, but had always disappointed in exams. The look of the kind of person who would have bought his science fiction novel if he'd got around to writing it.

With Albert now staring ahead again, Simon was uncertain as to how to proceed, but it was Albert who broke the silence. 'I felt drawn there,' he murmured.

'Where?' asked Simon, with eagerness.

With a hint of the hypnotic about him, Albert pointed to the cathedral in the rain-swept distance.

'The cathedral?' presumed Simon excitedly.

'Sometimes my skin tingles when I'm there.'

'Amazing,' breathed Simon. He pushed his glasses up. 'I've dowsed there. It's a powerful local convergence point for ley lines. You must be really sensitive to them. Were you drawn there when you saw the UFO? Is that what you mean?'

'It hummed and throbbed with light,' murmured Albert. But then he spoke normally. 'Lot quicker to turn left here, Carl. Takes you into the back entrance. Avoids the main road.'

'Yeah?' said Carl, complying with the advice.

'What did it look like?' asked Simon.

'What did what look like?' returned Albert.

'The UFO.'

Carl was now pulling into Tesco's. In the spattering deluge, the black surface of its car park was lake-like.

'What UFO?'

Simon's look of suspicion returned until he breathed, 'Amazing. You've got some kind of subconscious memory that keeps coming to the surface.'

'Simon,' said Albert phlegmatically, 'if I've told you once, I've told you a thousand times: if you're going to talk to me, talk sense.'

'I am talking sense,' protested Simon, without aggression.

'This all right?' asked Carl, pulling up as close as permitted to a side entry door.

'Brilliant,' said Albert. 'Cheers.'

Putting his hand on the door lever, Albert was about to pull it open when Simon suddenly blurted, 'No! Wait! Listen.' Albert looked at Simon, who paused while tangents multiplied and linked in his mind. 'Oh my God,' he breathed, 'you've been deliberately contacted.'

Wordlessly turning away from Simon, with a pull of the lever, Albert stepped out into the rain, using his carrier bag as an umbrella for the short walk to the shop's side door, which swished open automatically as he approached.

'He's been deliberately contacted,' murmured Simon to Carl.

'Yeah? Pity 'e don't remember.'

Not having a pound coin on him, Albert couldn't rent a trolley. Taking a basket, he began his trudge around the shop. As a vegetarian now, he supposed he ought to buy lots of vegetables, but quickly dismissed that idea. He wasn't going to buy anything that he would have to learn how to cook. And he certainly wasn't going to buy anything that he would have to spend time preparing. No, he would eat like he had done before, except veggie sausages and veggie burgers would replace the meat with his chips or mash.

Putting only a bag of potatoes into his basket, he passed through the vegetable section and went to find where the eggs had been laid this week. The moving around of things in Tesco's was one of Albert's pet coming-home-after-shopping gripes, invariably ignored by Ron. Another of Albert's coming-home-after-shopping gripes invariably ignored by Ron concerned pedestrian controlled crossings, and how so many people chose to offend him by pressing the button more than once. Or pressing it even though the *WAIT* light was showing, indicating someone else had already pressed it. And then there were the people who stood wanting to cross busy roads without pressing the button at all. And then there were the worst people of all: the ones who furiously and repeatedly pressed until the lights changed — no sooner than they would have changed anyway. How could these people go through life without realising that one press is enough, and anything more is superfluous and likely to get them named 'n' shamed in his diary? It was halfway to a reversion to primitive magic belief, deemed Albert. If he'd been the engineer given the job of designing the crossings' control circuitry, provision would have been made for a lethal shock to anyone pressing the button unnecessarily. Except in the case of wan ladies that is. They would be let off by some sort of camera and face-recognition circuitry incorporated in the design. They'd have their right to vote taken away, though.

'Albert. Albert,' called Simon, hurrying to catch up with his archaic tape recorder slung over his shoulder. 'You have to listen to me. You've got a buried memory of your encounter. Don't fight it. Go with it.'

Albert was now walking through the pasta aisle. Pasta — there was something veggie he could face cooking, he thought. He'd seen other people cook it often enough. Cheap and really quick. He could have it with some of those ready-made pasta sauces. No, those sauces were too bourgeois.

'You saw the UFO, Albert,' insisted Simon, holding his microphone out. 'I think it might have selected you for contact.'

Making a show of ignoring Simon, Albert got on with his shopping. Despite them being socially anathema to him, he loaded a couple of jars of bourgeois pasta sauce into his basket, along with some pasta twists. Wandering off, he was closely tracked by Simon all the way.

'You know things, Albert,' said Simon as they reached the cat food shelf. 'You know things, but don't know you know. Let your mind go blank.'

Albert moved on to the cheese shelf, even though he thought cheese was a bit bourgeois too, especially if it had blue streaks.

'Tell me about Godfrey.'

'Godfrey who?'

'The scientist or something you told Carl about.'

'News to me,' shrugged Albert, proceeding to the checkout.

'Try to remember.'

'Memory's my enemy. I want to forget.'

'No,' ordered Simon, temporarily losing his equanimity in a small eruption of frustration, pulling Albert's coat sleeve. 'Remember.'

Albert stopped and looked at Simon, seeing a blend of fuming frustration, sheepish embarrassment, and worry about a possible punch in the mouth.

'Don't tell me what I can't forget.'

'I'm sorry,' said Simon, regaining an equanimity of the sullen kind.

At the checkout, Albert stood with his back to Simon, who eventually pulled his microphone jack from its socket, sulkily wrapping its lead into a coil. Through a window, Carl's cab could be seen taking a lashing in a resurgence of the deluge, and Albert knew that if he walked home, he would be wet through in no time.

Fuck.

After paying for his basket of goods, Albert carried them away in two bags, heading for the side door he'd entered by.

Simon moodily followed him.

Stopping just beyond the automatic door, under the shelter of a small porch, Albert stood looking at the sweeping rain.

'You know things,' muttered Simon.

Believing the interview to be a failure, Simon unzipped the tummy pocket of his cagoule, ready to accept the wound-up microphone.

'Before the beginning,' said Albert quietly, 'there was a brilliant physicist called Godfrey who succeeded in producing the Equation of Everything.'

Instantly, Simon's moodiness evaporated, and he brought his microphone out again, quickly plugging it in and setting his tape rolling. But Albert now stepped out into the rain, walking away. 'No,' called Simon after him. 'The tape'll get wet.' Albert ignored him, so Simon gestured for Carl to drive over, even though the door area was forbidden to vehicles. Getting into the cab, he told Carl to intercept Albert, now halfway across the car park. 'We'll give you a lift home,' he offered when they caught him up, opening the door invitingly.

'Yeah, all right,' said Albert, getting in the cab and sitting with his bags on his knees.

Carl swung the vehicle round toward the car park exit.

'Back to your gaff?' he asked.

'That's right,' answered Albert.

'Tell me about Godfrey,' said Simon, with his microphone held out.

'Godfrey who?' returned Albert. But then, in an affected, vaguely hypnotic manner and a murmuringly revelatory voice, he narrated his alternative creation story from start to finish.

'... and when He eventually became lonely, He simply made some friends.'

'Amazing,' breathed Simon, with more wonder and awe than he had ever breathed into the word before.

'Told y' it wuz amazin', Simon,' said Carl, as they pulled up outside Albert's flat.

'How do you know this?' Simon asked Albert. 'Who told you about Godfrey?'

'Godfrey who?'

'Godfrey, the alien scientist. He was an alien, wasn't he? From another planet?'

'What are you talking about?'

'Godfrey,' said Simon. 'A scientist you just told me created the universe.'

'Did I?' pondered Albert. 'How very curious. I've been having dreams like that recently. Sometimes when I'm awake.'

'Amazing,' breathed Simon.

Albert got out the cab and began walking to his house.

Simon at once slid along the seat to the door Albert had left open. 'Albert,' he called after him, 'we have to talk some more.'

'Fuck off, loony.'

'Amazing,' breathed Simon, watching Albert take his shopping into his flat. 'He's been contacted but doesn't believe.'

'Stroppy so and so though, ain't 'e?' said Carl.

Closing the cab door and leaning forward in concentration, Simon murmured, 'Oh my God! It's all coming together. Don't you see?'

'Yeah?'

'It's all coming together,' murmured Simon again, in slowly crystallising mystical realisation.

'They moved the fucking eggs again,' complained Albert to Peep when he entered his flat. Putting his shopping down, he went to the window to see if the cab was still outside. It was — skulking like some predatory hearse. Taking his coat off, he was hanging it over a chair near the fire to dry when the doorbell rang. Peeking through a chink in his bedroom curtain, he saw it was Simon at the door, so he took the batteries out of the bell and went to put his shopping away in the kitchen. The next time he looked, the cab was gone.

*

The belt of rain had mostly passed over now, and despite the approach of sunset, the sky was lightening rather than darkening, although many angry, spitting clouds remained.

'Amazing,' breathed Simon, standing fifty yards from the cathedral, gazing up at its architectural majesty, a majesty enhanced by the backdrop of a tumultuous sky.

'All right, innit?' said Carl, sat on a wet bench, eating fish and chips from a bag. 'Never knew the North was so pukka.'

A large, storm-straggler drop of rain splattered Simon's glasses. Taking them off for cleaning, he sat beside Carl. 'It's all coming together, Carl,' he said in a quietly portentous voice while rubbing the lenses with tissue paper taken from his cagoule pocket.

'Yeah?' said Carl, tilting his head back to drop a difficult piece of fish into his mouth.

'The Orthrium Society's been getting it wrong, Carl. They've veered off course. Just like Judao-Christianity veered off course, distorting the Truth first revealed to Adam. Everything got so messy. Our leader was supposed to clear everything up — all the world's religious diversity — but he failed. But the twists in the Truth are finally unfolding. I can feel it.'

294

'Yeah?' said Carl, seeming more interested in his meal than theology. ''Ow's that then?'

'It's Albert. I think he's been chosen. The Cosmic Masters are trying to pass on their wisdom to us, their true knowledge of Godfrey, the Creator.'

'Told you 'is Godfrey thing was amazin', didn't I? Don't see why 'e told me first, though. I ain't nuffink special.'

'You are special, Carl,' said Simon, putting his glasses back on. 'You know me, and I'm a High Teacher. It was the Cosmic Masters making sure the right people found out.'

'Yeah? So why don't they just go on telly and tell everyone at once?'

With glib ease, Simon delivered an answer: 'Because they're not sure if we're ready. Only when we all accept Godfrey on faith alone can they be sure we can be trusted with more knowledge. That's why they've chosen a prophet to speak their words. See how wise they are?'

'So why 'ave they chosen someone who don't believe 'imself?'

Simon looked pensively at the ground. 'I don't know,' he confessed. 'I don't know.' His voice tailed off. Then it returned, breathily awed, and he lifted his head, gazing large-eyed at, and dimensions beyond, the cathedral. 'Maybe they chose him *because* he's so sceptical? Amazing! That'll be it.' He turned to Carl. 'Carl, Albert's the last person who'd accept Godfrey on faith alone. If he can come to believe, then anyone can. Amazing. See how wise the Cosmic Masters are?'

'Yeah?' said Carl. 'These fish 'n' chips are all right. Sure you don't want none, Simon?'

'Oh my God,' breathed Simon, gazing at the cathedral again, 'that T-shirt! Maybe it's a message from the Cosmic Masters! *Not Long Now till the Golden Millennium.*'

Yes, it was all coming together in Simon's mind.

1.25
That Albert Cunt

The region's heavy rain began shortly after Jennifer returned home from St. Andrew's. Now, it had all but cleared, although the window behind the table in the living room remained streaked with rivulets of water. Standing next to that window, Jennifer was setting down and arranging the flowers meant for her parents.

The doorbell rang. Through the window, Jennifer saw it was her aunt Jane, dressed in a matching black skirt and jacket, with a cream blouse, and carrying a small black bag. As ever, her fawn hair was permed short but loose, and her face had its customary look of recent cosmetic attention.

'Auntie,' said Jennifer, affecting some pleasant surprise upon opening the door.

Jane immediately crossed the threshold. 'What's going on, Jennifer?' she asked. 'We've been worried. I called you at work, but they said you were taking some time off because you were thinking of leaving. Is everything all right?'

While speaking, Jane had progressed into the living room.

'Everything's all right,' assured Jennifer, entering the living room behind her aunt. 'I'd just got a bit fed up.'

'Why haven't you been answering the phone here?'

'Oh, Margaret unplugged it this morning when she went to bed,' lied Jennifer.

She went to reconnect the phone while her aunt inspected the room.

Until her late thirties, Jane had been slender, and even considered glamorous. Once middle-age began to swell her hips and limbs, in the course of just one single week she completely changed her wardrobe and hairstyle to reflect her fresh maturity. Only then, it seemed, did she find her true self, embarking on a flurry of appropriate social events that continued to gather pace to this day. Now in her early fifties, she was coping well with the menopause, so well she thought other women her age ought to pull themselves together a bit more. "They ought to try the menopause after forty years of sterility," she was fond of saying to her husband. "Like getting fined for something you didn't do."

'I really wish you'd get a mobile so I could keep track of you,' she said when Jennifer returned to the living room. 'Everyone has them these days. Five-year-olds. Don't see why you have to be so different. You can't live without them these days. Sarah says she's going to get another one the moment's she's back in England, and you know how much bad luck she's had with them.'

'Back in England?' queried Jennifer.

'You didn't know she went off on holiday to Iceland with some new boyfriend or other?'

'No.'

'Well, if you rang her more often, you'd find out these things. Anyway, she's lost — or rather had stolen, that is — more mobiles than's fair. Don't suppose you know she had her last one stolen at the airport the other day. What are you fed up about? Thought you liked working with animals.'

When Jane spoke, sentences came hard on the heels of their forerunners, and their direction changed unpredictably.

'I've been thinking about maybe going to college and doing my A Levels again,' said Jennifer, 'but I suppose I'll be back at work on Monday.'

As yet, Jane had not given any indication that she intended to sit down: standing gave her more scope for peering at Jennifer surreptitiously — efforts to divine her sister's daughter's true state of mind.

'Well, going to college can't be a bad idea, can it? If you stick at it, that is, and apply yourself for once. College might cure you of your shyness, too. Someone like you's got no business being shy. Prettiest girl in town, you are. Are you going out anywhere tonight?'

Jennifer had now moved to the window, and was leaning back against the sill. 'No, not really.'

'No surprise there,' said Jane. 'Pity. After all, you've got something to celebrate, haven't you?'

Staring at nothing in an effort to appear as if the question hadn't really registered with her, Jennifer didn't answer. She suspected her aunt was scrutinising her. Why she was reluctant to tell her aunt the engagement was off, she didn't quite know. She did feel vaguely that she was somehow letting her aunt down, or at least disappointing her. Also, it seemed easier not to at this stage. She'd tell Sarah all about it first, and Sarah could tell her aunt, that way she might escape well-meaning interrogation.

'Has John gone back yet?' Jane now wanted to know.

'Yesterday,' answered Jennifer, emerging from her fake reverie.

'Have you decided on a date yet? I'll have to know as early as possible. There's a lot of planning to do, and it'll be a pleasure to do it.'

'No, not yet. I'll let you know soon.'

Jane now paused, and looked at Jennifer. 'Well, aren't you going to show me it?'

'What?' asked Jennifer, genuinely puzzled.

'The ring, for heaven's sake!'

'Oh, I left it at work,' lied Jennifer. 'I'll pop over to collect it tomorrow.'

'Left it at work! What are you like? Forget your head if it wasn't screwed on, wouldn't you?' She paused, and her manner became less blustery. 'I suppose you know what day it is?'

'Yes. I know.'

'Doesn't seem like seven years, does it? Well, not to me. The years fly past as you get older. Don't suppose you went to see them?'

'No. It's just a stone, not them.'

'Well a stone helps with most people,' said Jane. 'Tom and I popped over this morning. Sarah rang me from Iceland this morning, with it being the anniversary and everything. She'll be back in England in an hour or two. Why don't you go and see her playing tonight?'

'It's tonight, is it?' returned Jennifer vaguely, although fully knowing it actually was tonight that her sister was playing a concert.

'Oh, what *are* you like?' sighed Jane in exasperation. 'It's quite a big thing, apparently. We can't make it. It's Tom's mother's eightieth, and probably her last, as you well know. Not that she recognises him when he visits. But that's how it goes in life sometimes. Margaret at work?'

'No, she's in bed. Night shift this week.'

'Have you worn the coat we got you for your birthday?'

'Not yet.'

'No? When I was your age, a new coat would have had me out every Friday for months. You're only young once, Jennifer.'

Jane had certain preparatory behaviours that indicated when she was about to be on her way. And so although she had not vocally announced the imminence of her departure, Jennifer went to the front door knowing that her aunt would follow, which she did.

After saying goodbye to her aunt, Jennifer took the carrier bag containing her dress upstairs, where she left it in a corner before sitting at her dressing table and gazing vaguely into the mirror. In a moment, she suspected she was doing it again: running away from her life by staying in the same place. If going to college to properly study for university entrance had been such a good idea yesterday, it should still hold water today. And she should have told her aunt about the broken engagement. It was no big deal at all. Maybe she really wanted to go ahead with the engagement? A predetermined course for her. An easy course. Maybe she was punishing herself? She didn't know, but she was prepared to give house room to such explanations.

Things had to change, she resolved. They really had to change.

To consciously distract herself from further introspection, she retrieved the carrier bag from where she'd left it, and took the dress out, which she lay flat on the bed. Her comfortable house clothes were removed, and she rummaged in a drawer for a strapless bra.

Wearing the new dress, she viewed herself in the mirror, and couldn't help but see that she really was an uncommonly attractive sight, something a dozen whistles and car horns reminded her of each week — and a dozen times each week she wondered if any woman in the entire history of human relations had ever been impressed by people who whistle and toot.

The dress, bare above the bust except for two thin straps, was a good, slinky fit. She began trying out various accessories that might match, most of which had been given to her by Sarah, or had belonged to her mother. The coat her aunt had given her for her birthday was taken out of the wardrobe and slipped on. It was long, black like the dress, with slightly padded shoulders, and the feel of the cool satin lining against her bare shoulders was sensual. Dipping her hands into its large pockets, she drew it up tight around herself.

The doorbell rang, and she went down to answer it. Opening the door revealed John on the doorstep. Deep within the hood of his black puffa jacket, his face was grim and troubled. When the fleeting surprise and anxiety passed from Jennifer's face, a look of numb resignation remained. Before she asked the obvious question, John said, 'Absent without leave. Serious offence.'

He stepped in, brushing past Jennifer, going directly to the living room, where he took off his jacket.

Jennifer wordlessly followed him.

Turning to face her, John said, 'Thanks for the letter,' and from his pocket he produced it, tossing it at her feet. He looked drawn and tired. In awkwardness and perhaps even shame, Jennifer dropped her gaze to the envelope on the floor. She didn't know what to say or do. Something was telling her to hold him close and say sorry. It would certainly be easier that way.

Lifting her eyes, she saw that John was now conspicuously holding the engagement ring she'd returned to him. She looked into his eyes, saw the hurt there, the pain she'd inflicted. 'You'll be in trouble for going AWOL.'

'Fuck that. They can do what they want to me.' He drew open her coat. 'What are you all done up for? Going out with someone tonight?'

'No,' she answered, moving a half a step back from him. 'I was just trying some new things on.'

He stared at her.

'Who is it?'

'Who is what?'

'Who is it you're seeing?'

'No one, John. There's been no one but you.'

'You never dressed like that for me.'

Jennifer looked down at her clothes. 'I'll take this stuff off now.'

She went directly to her room, where she slipped out of the coat, laying it over the bed. About to take off the dress, she hesitated when John appeared at the door.

'Go on,' he said. 'Don't mind me.'

She pulled the dress straps down over her arms while John, now sitting on the bed, sullenly watched.

'It's that Albert cunt, isn't it?'

Jennifer's eyes briefly closed in weary exasperation. Forgoing the removal of her dress, she dragged the chair from her dressing table over to the bed. Sitting side-saddle, turning to rest her elbows on the slender curve of black wood which formed its backrest, she faced John. Momentarily, her head fell into her hands. Drawing tense fingers through her hair, lifting it away from her eyes, she raised her head and spoke. 'It's over between us. I don't want to go on seeing you.'

'Who is it? Is it him?'

'There's no one. Even if I was seeing someone, it would have nothing to do with you. It's over between us. You should have known that a long time ago. It never even really started.'

'Never even started?' John shot back. 'So how did I end up spending hundreds of pounds on this?'

He thrust the ring in front of her face.

'I never loved you, John,' said Jennifer, with dulled anguish. 'Never even said I loved you. Not once. You were just there, that's all, and so was I, and sometimes we fucked.'

Jolted by such crushing frankness, he stared at her. 'So who do you love?'

'No one, John. Even if I was seeing someone, it wouldn't have anything to do with you now. You'd better get back to your base before you get into even more trouble.'

Standing and taking hold of her arms, he demanded, 'Who is it? Is it him?'

'There's no one, John,' said Jennifer desperately, but not fearfully.

'Liar!' shouted John, throwing her sideways and off her chair. She yelped in surprise before knocking her head against the floor. Immediately remorseful and frightened, he rushed to help her up. 'Oh, God, sorry.'

But Jennifer was already helping herself up, and angrily indicated that he shouldn't touch her.

Margaret, in her dressing gown, appeared at the bedroom door. 'What's going on?' she asked worriedly. 'What's all the commotion? John, what are you doing back?'

'It's all right,' said Jennifer, with deliberate dignity. 'John's back, but he's leaving again.' She pulled her dress straps back up and picked up her coat. 'I'm going out,' she coldly said to him. 'Don't be here when I get back.'

'I'm sorry,' pleaded John. 'I didn't mean to push you.'

Jennifer started toward the door, and although John reached for her, she would not be hindered. 'It's over, John.'

Margaret moved between John and Jennifer. 'Hey, John, this is my house not yours. Let her leave.'

Descending the stairs, Jennifer had the presence of mind to pick her purse up from the telephone table before leaving the house. Hearing the front door close, John went to the bedroom widow, and through dampening eyes saw a watery image of Jennifer leaving his life.

Bumping her head in the fall had made her feel a little nauseous, but that's all; no cuts, no bruising; and by the time she'd reached the end of her street, she felt completely well. She went on to the town centre, then down to the peaty waters of the Swale, intending to pass some time sitting near the wide waterfalls that drew countless tourists in summer. By the river, with the sky clearing yet darkening, she was alone, save for some squabbling boys with jam jars. Barbel swam in this river – John had told her that on the few occasions she'd accompanied him on his angling expeditions, back in the early days of their association, watching bored as he acted the wise and manly hunter possessed of arcane knowledge of nature's ways.

When four youths sharing two cans of strong lager came down to the water's edge, Jennifer moved away, up a short but steep lane that brought her to the market square. She thought about visiting a cafe, but decided instead to return home, guessing John would have left by now, encouraged by Margaret.

Careful of the route she took, Jennifer approached the house from behind, stopping when, over some gardens, she could just see into the living room back window. The curtains were open, the light was on, and John was in view. Turning away, she walked back toward the town centre, but felt a growing urge to get even further away. It was time to change. Time to take charge, not spend the evening wandering around waiting for an unwanted visitor to leave. Perhaps it was something to do with being dressed up, but, knowing her sister's home phone number was in her purse, she stopped at a call box, intending to inform Sarah, if she was back from Iceland yet, that she would, after all, be coming to see her perform that evening.

Sarah was not at home, and Jennifer declined the service of her answering machine. And she knew it would be pointless trying her mobile, for she now knew it had recently been stolen.

*

Deep regret was fermenting within John. Bitter regret. He'd gone AWOL to try to mend things between himself and Jennifer, but had lost his temper and behaved like a barbarian. He hadn't meant it to be like that. By going AWOL he'd hoped to impress her with his devotion, risking all just to be with her, but it had gone sour. Very sour. He had blown it.

Until she'd walked away, John had not believed that things were really over between them. Although the letter from her had been considered something that had to be acted upon quickly, it was not seen as the end — couldn't be. But the sight of her walking away drove home the finality, and never had he imagined he could ever feel so much pain inside.

Immediately after Jennifer left, John had sat on the floor, with his back against the bed and knees drawn up to his face — drawn up to hide the unmanly wetness in his eyes. Margaret had offered comforting words but he had ordered her to leave him alone, an order she'd obeyed. It was nearly an hour before he'd begun to regain some equanimity. In that hour he'd resolved to return to his army base. He was going to use his head. She wanted to be free, and he would submit to that want. It troubled him, however, that the last image he had of Jennifer was such an agonising one. He was scared that the memory of her leaving, with his eyes stinging and his throat feeling like it was in a noose, would be the one of her to dominate for ever. And how could he ever forget such pain? It would have been so much better had he just accepted the letter and stayed with his army unit, with all its distractions to keep him occupied. If he'd just accepted the letter, then his last memory of Jennifer would have been one of her warmly kissing him goodbye on a frosty morning after passionate sex.

'Are you going back to your garrison?' asked Margaret.

John was now in the living room, hiding his face by looking out the window. Still in her dressing gown, Margaret was sitting on the sofa, drinking a mug of tea. John felt that if he looked at her, he might resume crying. Delaying his reply, he stooped to pick his jacket up from the floor. 'Got a tour of duty coming up. Miss that and I'll really be for it.'

No longer looking out the window, but not looking at Margaret, he began putting his jacket on.

'You're doing the right thing,' she said, with solemn sympathy. 'I don't know Jennifer very well, but I know women, and I know she's not going back to you. Don't take it as a reflection on you, John, these things just happen. They've happened to me more than once. It's life.'

Zipping his jacket, John seemed set to leave when a dark look suddenly arose. 'I've got to know what's going on. Who's she seeing? Is it that Albert cunt? Where does he live? Durham?'

This was a rerun of an earlier interrogation, made when he'd first come into the living room, except that time it was delivered head-in-hands on the sofa, and more out of confusion than angry determination.

'John,' said Margaret patiently, 'I've told you, I've never heard of anyone called Albert. She's not seeing anyone. She never goes out when you're not home. No one even phones for her. I'd tell you if there was someone, but there isn't.'

John walked out the room, sneering, 'Yeah, and you told me she had flu.'

Closing the door of the house behind him, with a feeling of anguished emptiness in his chest and a tightness in his throat, John headed for the nearby bus stop. A bus caught there would take him north, through the town's centre, then on to the Darlington road. From Darlington, he would reverse the train journey he'd taken earlier that day. Along the short, darkening walk, he grimly resolved to put Jennifer out of his mind. Whatever, or whoever, had taken her away from him was no longer an issue in his life. He would move on, never complaining about his loss, even though he hurt inside and felt, at this moment, that he would surely hurt for ever. But he was strong and could shoulder that load, he told himself.

It was a merciful relief to John that his bus came into view only minutes after he arrived at the stop. He wanted to be gone, and gone quickly. Richmond had seen the last of him. Boarding the half-full single-decker, he proceeded to the back, slumping down one seat from the rear as it moved off again. With it now almost fully dark outside, the dimly-lit bus felt as solemn and intimate as a dream, and he worried he might become emotional again — worried that what he felt inside would show outside.

The bus had hardly built up a decent speed when it slowed again, hailed at a request stop. Now sitting half-sideways, with his back against the window, John gazed blankly down the aisle, toward the new passengers boarding. Suddenly, he was jolted: among the new passengers was Jennifer. At once he concealed himself behind the person sitting in front of him. Jennifer had not seen him, he knew, and he also knew she would sit near the front of the bus — she always did. There was no fear of tears now. He was certain she was going out to meet some new boyfriend — why else had she dressed up? Albert, surely. She had lied to him. Anger was returning. He would follow her; find out the truth. He had to know. Had to.

True to her habit, Jennifer chose a seat near the front, and during the journey to Darlington did not once look back, or if she had turned her head, it was done in the blink of John's vigilant eye. Thus, though they shared a fifteen mile ride, he remained sure she was unaware of his shadowing presence. Now their bus was nearing its Darlington terminus, passing the ugly, sixties town hall — floodlit in what a cynic might describe as an act of civic shame. Turning left after the concrete town hall, they entered the cavernous, dingy covered station. Alighting, Jennifer looked around, at first trying not to breathe the engine fumes in too deeply. Looking above her, she saw a sparrow flying to and fro, momentarily settling on one girder before trying another, frantic for the way out. John stayed on the bus. Undiscovered, he watched Jennifer as she studied a timetable before moving to another platform, where she joined a short queue waiting for a double-decker to open its doors. Above her was a sign that told John his ex-fiancée was about to board a bus that passed through Durham, where he had every reason to believe her denied paramour, Albert, could be found. It was all panning out as he'd suspected.

Unseen by her, he slunk off the bus and out of the station, where, concealed by medium-distance and a shop doorway, he waited for the beautiful young woman who'd worn his ring to emerge, on-route to a denied liaison. Just minutes later, her bus wallowed out, struggling with a sharp right turn, and he saw her sitting by a lower deck window. His plan was to let it get a lead, then take a mini-cab to catch it up before it reached Durham.

He went in search of a pub, and only had to journey around one corner. As soon as he stepped in, he could tell it was a rough house, or rather it would be in a few hours. The kind of stark, bleak rough he'd too frequently found in the Northeast — an ignorant, embittered, hateful rough where he knew his out-of-region accent might lead to stares, glares and mutterings. It was early, though — he had that in his favour — and for now the only troublesome-looking patrons were three young men wearing identical black skinhead jackets, grouped around a small table, apparently with nothing to say to each other until they noticed him standing at the bar. John was a new face. Seeing him, their elbows went on to the table, and their heads came closer together, and John could easily guess what kind of whispered antipathy and abusive conjecture his arrival had stirred up.

While a rough barmaid poured his pint, John was aware that he continued to be the occasional focus of speculation for the three yobs. Any other time, he would have been concerned and cautious, and saddened, but today he found he was partly welcoming the prospect of trouble. He would do nothing to provoke it, not even look their way, but would not mind at all if it started. If they gave him any hassle, he would give them the surprise of their lives. Unless they were carrying knives and were intending to use them without warning, he believed he could handle them. He was a head taller than one of them, half a head taller than the other two, surely fitter and stronger than any of them, and a trained warrior — one of the nation's brave young defenders. Every week he practised stopping the fist of an assailant and breaking the wrist, or putting that assailant on his back to swiftly kill him with a heel brought down hard to the sternum.

More people now came into the pub, and this somehow dissipated, or diluted, the yobs' focus on John. A one-arm-bandit became their new focus, their backs collectively turning on him.

John remained at the bar with his drink, guessing he'd better leave after no more than fifteen minutes to make sure of catching up the bus before it reached Durham. He wasn't planning to do anything to whoever it was Jennifer was going to meet, he just *had* to know what was going on, that's all. And surprising her with her lover would give him some kind of satisfaction. It would help put him back on top; give him some dignity. He would turn up, condemn her, show her he hadn't been fooled, then leave, all while her new lover trembled in fear.

Not once did he question the reasonableness of what he was doing.

Thirty minutes later, John was in the back of a mini-cab travelling at an illegal speed on the duel carriageway approaching Durham City. His driver — old enough by looks to be his father — had an unfit, unhealthy, thick-skinned appearance, despite having a slim frame. His was the appearance of a man overly familiar with brown ale, cigarettes and bookmakers. In the distance, John saw Jennifer's bus pulling away from a stop. 'Slow down now, mate,' he said, leaning forward. 'My girlfriend's on that bus. I want to see where she gets off. Slow right down.'

'Up t'nee good, is she?' the driver surmised, speaking in a slow, low voice of grim moral allegiance.

'Sure of it, mate,' said John dourly. 'Sure of it.'

'That's a Newcastle bus,' observed the driver. 'Long way t'drive slowly. Can't follow it f'long without chargin' y'extra. Miss out on other jobs if ah hang aroond.'

'Don't worry about the extra fare,' John assured him. 'I'm good for whatever it'll cost. Anyway, she'll get off soon. Sure of it.'

As he'd predicted, John's ride was over within a few more minutes.

*

'Next stop for the Arts Centre, pet,' said the woman sitting beside Jennifer. 'It's that building over there, love.'

Jennifer had earlier asked the woman if she knew what stop would be best for her.

'Thanks,' replied Jennifer, quickly leaving her seat. Stepping off the bus, she viewed the building that had been indicated, an imposing, dimly floodlit, three-story, brick-built Victorian edifice that looked as if it might originally have been a school or hospital.

Some way behind her, a mini-cab pulled up, and the driver accepted eighteen pounds into his nicotine-stained hands.

Walking the short distance from the bus stop, as she approached the Arts Centre, through its large windows Jennifer saw it to be teeming with well-dressed people. Her step slowed, but then picked up again, and she proceeded to the glass doors that opened to a small entrance space decorated with forthcoming events posters. Continuing, she found the wide ground floor to be open-plan. To her right was a dining area, roped off and marked *private function*, where men and women in black tie and evening dress were beginning to leave their tables. Opposite her was a reception desk attended by a relaxed, smiling woman wearing a blue blouse with a name tag. To her left was a bar fronted by a spacious drinking area with dozens of tables, where numerous groups, some with children, chatted or looked bored.

Behind her, a face peered grimly through a window.

Proceeding to some public telephones ranked beside the reception desk, Jennifer dialled her sister's home number, but received no answer. She was probably already somewhere in the Arts Centre, she thought, since a performance seemed imminent judging by the way people were beginning to drift to the far end of the room, beyond the dining area. Putting the phone down, and now beginning to feel nervous and agitated, she looked in the direction most people were wandering and saw a set of double doors, above which a faintly-glowing green sign read *THEATRE*. A family group was sauntering that way, and Jennifer tagged along behind them. Nearing the theatre doors, she read a small, printed sign informing her a private performance was due to begin, for which entrance was by ticket only, and all tickets had been sold.

Jennifer stepped in.

'Can I see your ticket, please?' asked a posh-sounding middle-aged lady sitting behind a table just inside the doors, looking up at Jennifer through glasses worn on a chain.

'I should be on a guest list, if my sister remembered. Jennifer Lucas.'

'Oh, another VIP,' said the lady, checking a list. 'And here you indeed are. Jennifer Lucas.'

Jennifer received a ticket and a photocopied programme sheet. 'Where do I sit?'

'Anywhere you care to, my dear.'

Just beyond the attendant's table was another set of double doors

307

that were wedged open, and through them Jennifer could see that the stage curtains were down. She stepped into the auditorium, which was softly humming with the murmured conversations of scattered groups. Choosing a seat, she examined her programme, and saw that the night was to be a mixture of music, verse and drama — a showcase for the university's performing arts faculties in order to impress funding bodies, she remembered her sister saying. A troop dressed as medieval minstrels would play fifteenth century music on replica fifteenth century instruments. A group would sing, act and play songs from Shakespeare plays as they would have been performed in their time. Poetry would be read to original musical accompaniment.

John had seen where she had gone. To follow her, rather than walk up and along, he took the angry hypotenuse, stepping over the plush, red rope barrier cordoning off the dining area that lay between him and the theatre doors. It was certainly not his intention to hurt whoever had replaced him in Jennifer's affections, but, nevertheless, the play rehearsing in his head had a theme of dominance and posturing. He wanted — needed — to come out on top. He had to be the one to do the final walking away. He needed to outwit her by catching her being unfaithful. He needed to watch her lover get scared as he delivered his final, caustic words to her. In his head, he rehearsed lines he might have call to say to Albert, or whoever it was. Powerful lines like "keep out of this, you", and "just you watch it, wanker, this hasn't got anything to do with you". In his mind's eye, he pictured himself dramatically going out into the night — into the rest of his life —, leaving Jennifer embarrassed and disgraced, and Albert belittled and fearful.

Overtaking a group of black-tied men, John passed through the outer doors of the theatre. From behind her table, the posh-sounding attendant peered up at him as he walked right past her to stand at the inner doors, where he looked into the auditorium, which was now more than half-full.

'Can I help you, young man?' asked the attendant, employing a schoolmistress tone.

John paid her no heed.

'Ticket only, I'm afraid,' she said.

The group of black-tied men were now held up from entering the theatre by John standing in their way.

'Young man,' said the attendant sternly, 'you're blocking the doorway.'

308

There she was. There was Jennifer. Near the back, but alone.

Stepping aside, John let the waiting men pass. 'What's the affair?' he asked, without courtesy, addressing the attendant.

Relieved to be getting at least acknowledgement of her station, the attendant showed John a programme sheet. 'Music and poetry for invited guests of the university. Presented in period context by students. No tickets available.'

'What time's it finish?'

'Half past nine, all going well.'

John walked back out of the theatre, taking the programme with him. This was a puzzle. It was conceivable that Sarah was playing some part in the night's performance, but surely Jennifer would have mentioned that she was intending to see her sister play? Looking at the programme, he saw Sarah's name. So why didn't Jennifer say where she was going? There was nothing to hide... unless she was expecting a lover to meet her. Yes, that had to be it. Only that could account for the extreme dressing up and secrecy. Maybe Sarah was playing tonight, but Jennifer's new lover — surely Albert, who'd written that letter — was due to arrive.

John resolved he would wait and find out, and seeing a bar across the other end of the long room, went to buy himself a time-killing drink.

*

The house lights dimmed, and a tight spotlight focused on the centre of the curtained stage. A barrel-chested, middle-aged man of average height walked on. His full head of mostly grey hair was so wayward that his mother, if she were standing with him, might find it hard not to spit on her hand to smooth her son's untidiness. His black dinner jacket acquired a purplish sheen when he entered the spotlight. 'Good evening, ladies and gentlemen,' he began, in a voice that was theatrical and booming, supported by mannerisms bordering on stagey. 'My great pleasure tonight is the honour of introducing the cream of Durham University's musical and dramatic student talent, performing works that span five hundred years of human creativity. As far as our props department could manage, all players shall appear as they might have when the music or verse first blessed our world. To begin the night's entertainment, let us return you to music's Romantic period.'

Before walking off, the Master of Ceremonies gestured to the stage behind him, whereupon the spotlight faded and the curtains parted to reveal an antiquated quartet, with Sarah as the cellist.

Taking their cues from each other, the quartet began to play. Nerves seemed tight at first. Elbows stiff. But not long into the piece, when the violin part came to the fore, the other players settled, and soon the violinist himself appeared to lose himself in the music.

Seeing her sister up on stage, so striking and passionate, Jennifer thought how proud and moved her mother would have been, but this thought also cast a disquieting shadow.

1.26
Repercussions

Friday. Six o'clock. Tedious six o'clock. God, he was super-bored already — his bedroom ceiling looked so dull this evening. What had he done to pass last Friday? That had been his birthday, and Ron had talked him into going to the Arts Centre. But staying in didn't feel like a spiritual act when no one was trying to drag him out, Albert now discovered. And a further irony was that he *couldn't* go out tonight, even though for once he felt like doing so. It wasn't for want of money — he still had over eighty pounds left in his pocket — it was for want of friends. Jackie had given him the cold shoulder; Ron was away; Jackie's sister, Rebecca, was always cross-sounding with him these days; and most everyone else in Durham thought he was weird. God, he thought, Durham was a town of around forty thousand souls, and at the moment probably only Rebecca would admit to being his friend, and he suspected she'd soon sing a different tune under just the threat of torture. 'God, what an *achievement*,' he breathed a moment later, remembering that, intellectually, he, like Oscar Wilde before him, worried if he found himself in agreement with people.

There was a tap on his bedroom window — Jackie: had to be. She was the only person who ever did that. A sense of relief swelled within him. He was saved from suffocating boredom.

He sat up and put his feet on the floor.

'Albert, are you in there?'

It was not Jackie's voice. It was Simon's.

'Albert, are you in there? Albert?'

Albert remained still and quiet. He faintly heard Carl say, 'Ain't
'e in? Looks like there's a light on. That's 'is bedroom. I wuz in
there.'

Albert kept still. Presently, he heard the gate closing, and assumed
they had left the garden. Sitting droopily on the side of his bed, he
knew he was more than bored now. He was fed up. He badly wanted
this evening to go away. Maybe he should get stoned again? he
thought. Yes, that's what he would do. Moreover, he would turn the
evening into a treat. He would go out to buy a bunch of sweets and
things, come back, get stoned, listen to music on Ron's headphones,
then gorge himself when the munchies set in. By then it would be
bedtime. Merciful bedtime.

He went to the living room to fetch his coat, left to dry on the
back of a chair in front of the fire, set low. Peep was luxuriating in
the warmth, stretched out on her side to absorb as much of the
radiant heat as she could. Bending to stroke her, his hair fell over
his eyes. Pushing it back again, it felt particularly soft – almost as
soft as the cat's fur –, and he attributed it to the rain-wash it had
received.

Leaving the cat in a state of purring contentment, and not having
the heart to switch the fire off, he put on his coat. Because he was
now *persona non grata* at his nearest shop, he intended to walk ten
minutes or so to the second nearest shop, a petrol station. Before
setting off, he peeked through the curtains to see if Carl's cab was
still outside. It wasn't, and he felt disappointed in a way. The game
was over.

Coming out of the house and walking down his street, Albert
believed he could sense a Friday evening atmosphere. The sun had
gone down on the working week and the town seemed to have a
buzz. Many of the passing cars were filled with high-spirited young
people on their way to some world of light. Not him. He was going
to buy sweets, alone. Was he just some kind of fuck-brained loser?
he wondered, in a moment of genuine, perturbing self-doubt.

A *thoughtless* world of light, he reminded himself.

At the bottom of his street, he crossed a litter-strewn and
vandalised children's play area, aiming for the stark, concrete
underpass that would put him on the same side of the busy main
road as the petrol station. Approaching the underpass from the
side, he could hear echoing voices. Stupid, young male voices that

briefly began chanting unintelligibly. Sense and trepidation told him to steer clear and take a longer route, but pride and defiance won over. After loping down a short but steep grassed embankment, he was at the mouth of the underpass, its cold breath tainted with the odour of stale urine. Yobs — around eight late-teenage yobs — were drinking lager from cans at the other end of the dim tunnel. One had a spray can and was writing his "tag" in a large scrawl. They were all drunk, or acting it. The neuro-toxin they'd swallowed was inhibiting the flow of electro-chemical signals in their frontal cortexes. They were running on primitive brain stem power.

The yobs began chanting again, their voices as gruff as they could manage to make them. Their brain stems wanted them to sound terrifying. Albert knew that any eye contact between himself and one of the brain-stemmers, however accidental or fleeting, could lead to a many-on-to-one brawl. Just his coat — his "foreign" coat — could trigger an incident. Or they might think he was a student. Student bashing had become a yob gang pastime locally. Hardly a week went by now without him reading reports of some student being found in a pool of blood, kicked senseless and toothless by overwhelming numbers.

He looked at the ground as he progressed through the grim tunnel, deliberately giving out the impression that he was lost in thought, but very wary of trouble arising. To his relief and surprise, he passed the yobs without drawing unruly attention. The spray can was higher on their minds. Each wanted possession of it next. He wondered why it was that the people least able to write were the people most inclined to do it in large letters on walls. What was it in human nature — the lowest human nature — that drove people to deface walls? It was the dumbest people that did it, and usually adolescent males, but what was the benefit to them?

Once reassuringly beyond the underpass, Albert looked over his shoulder at the yobs upon hearing that they had become excitably rowdy. One of them was now sitting on the shaky shoulders of another to spray his tag on the underpass's narrow lighting panel. When he succeeded, the others cheered gruffly, and Albert witnessed the answer to his question as to what benefit graffiti scrawlers derived from their acts: respect from their dumb peers. But why? It was a respect he was impervious to. Observing the yobs' antics from a distance, Albert began to feel like a detached naturalist taking notes on some squabbling, posturing baboon troop. How could Jesus Army creationists not accept the theory of evolution, he wondered despairingly, when so much of human behaviour was so obviously ape-like? Perhaps defacing walls with graffiti had an animal analogue? he mused, without really wanting to muse about anything, but not being able to help himself. This not-being-able-to-help-himself activity reminded him of something he often wondered about concerning his cat. Peep seemed keen on chasing things, such as string, that he produced for her amusement, but was she really amused? Maybe she just couldn't help herself? Maybe she was thinking, "Fuck, more bastard string that I can't help chasing because of my cat hunting instincts. I wish this bleak, foppish bastard would give me a break".

"Spraying" tags. Spraying was the key word, realised Albert. He thought it could be argued that those dumb lads were like a pack of baboons spraying their piss scent around. That could be the animal analogue — the evolutionary psychology explanation for graffiti. In many animal situations, adolescent males have to win territories for themselves, marking those territories with their scent. In daubing their tags in prominent positions, dumb adolescent graffiti grunts were simply unwittingly and abstractly obeying a primitive urge to piss their scent around.

In a dumb, confused way, they believed they were getting on in the world.

Once in the petrol station shop, Albert began making his choices. A *Mars Bar*. He hadn't had a *Mars Bar* in years. Even when he'd been a kid he'd thought them just a bit too excessive. Oh, and some *Doritos* — the ones in blue bag that Jackie had introduced him to. Bleeding hell! *Rolos!* — he hadn't had them in years, either. And, of course, a *Fry's Chocolate Cream*. No, fuck it, two *Fry's Chocolate Creams* — the world was a bitch. Oh, and a *Flake*. Absently taking his night's entertainment — no, medicine — to the service counter, a young woman in a red company T-shirt and a blue company cap scanned the sweets into her till, informed him of the total, and asked him if he wanted a bag.

'Are you soliciting?' said Albert unsmilingly while looking at the money he was counting in his hand. He hadn't said it as an insult — he'd glanced at her earlier and seen that she was nowhere close to being a bag. He'd merely said it in a moment of automatic, half-arsed wit.

'What?' she retorted, poised on the brink of being certain she'd been sexually something or othered.

Looking up to hand over his money, he perceived the belligerent expression raring to appear on her pretty face. She hadn't understood the lame joke. Because he wasn't smiling, she hadn't understood that it *was* a joke. He winced internally, and wished he could remember just to think jokes and not say them until he was back with Ron or Jackie or the tiny handful of other people he'd met in his time whom he'd felt accordant with. He was fast becoming weary of it all. He'd had enough. It was all so tiresome. When he was kidding, people took him seriously; when he was being serious, they laughed in his face; when he was being clever, they thought him a fool; when he was acting the fool, they thought they were clever. Were it not for the unrestricted, galloping badinage he enjoyed with his few friends he'd find it impossible to go on desperately comforting himself with the saving thought that he was an island of sanity in a great ocean of craziness.

Going to make an even bigger effort to stay in my bedroom from now on, he decided. Ceiling good; sky bad.

Leaving the petrol station shop with a bulging pocket, Albert slowly realised he'd fallen pointlessly in mismatched love with the cashier. But it was a leaden love. If the brief encounter had occurred any other time in the previous ten years, he would have been gloriously pining already, and trying to think of a rhyme for cashier (*dash here*, might have been it). In his mind's eye, he would have been seeing it all nobly before him: the barren desolation of his life without his favourite cashier to have and to hold for ever more – a wild tragedy apt for a suffering hero. Or, if he was in a good mood – like if it had been a giro day –, he'd be seeing dairy farms, free *Mars Bars* and embezzlement. But, for once, it wasn't like that. It was a love without even the ardour of tragic drama. It was misery without passion.

It was no fun at all, that's what it was.

Walking along the main road, instead of retracing his steps for the return journey, he continued along to cross at the traffic lights, avoiding the underpass. This added only a few minutes to his walk, and within ten minutes he was back on Devon Road. Here, he heard what he thought was a small lorry pulling up behind him, then drawing level with him and keeping to his pace as he walked on. Looking over his shoulder, squinting in the vehicle's headlights, he saw it was Carl's cab.

'Albert,' called Simon from the cab, 'listen to me. You're a prophet.'

Albert ignored his calling, and looked ahead again.

'You have to understand, Albert,' Simon went on, 'you've been

314

given a cosmic message.'

'No I haven't,' said Albert, 'I've been given cosmic hair.'

'You *have* been given a message,' insisted Simon. 'I've worked it all out. The Cosmic Masters have chosen you as their new mouthpiece. You have to believe me. They're communicating with you. Telepathically.'

Albert stopped, and so did the cab. He looked at Simon as if he was about to say something important — perhaps momentous. Upon raising a finger as if to deliver a point, and drawing a breath in, he deliberately deflated the moment by taking the *Rolos* tube out of his pocket instead, unwrapping one and popping it into his mouth.

He sauntered on again.

Simon got out the cab and trotted up to Albert's side, walking with him. 'You don't understand how important this is,' he said, in a blend of excitement, gravity and pressing urgency. 'There's more to it than you realise. It's all linked with the Orthrium Society. And that UFO you saw over the cathedral was there *because* of you. Earth wasn't the only planet Godfrey had populated once he'd become lonely. Cosmic Master emissaries from those planets, planets a million times more advanced than ours, are now letting us know the full truth about the universe, spreading the word of Godfrey. Don't you see what it all means?'

'It means you're bonkers, Simon.'

'No it doesn't. It means the Cosmic Masters are talking through you.' Simon's tone became awed, breathy and desperate to persuade. 'Albert, you've been chosen. You're a prophet. It's all coming together.'

Near his gate, Albert halted: suddenly, his heart was in his mouth. Observing him, Simon saw a change, and believed the thunderous import of his message had at last got through.

'It's you, Albert,' breathed Simon. 'You've been chosen to receive messages.'

'I'm being burgled,' murmured Albert. He'd glimpsed someone moving around inside his living room, and now trashing noises were coming from his bedroom. He rushed to the house door. Finding it slightly ajar, he pushed it, but something weighty was blocking its swing. Shoving the door open, he encountered a bewildering scene of destruction: it seemed that the entire contents of Ron's bedroom was lying broken in the hall. The computer looked as if it had been viciously disassembled and roughly dumped. The widescreen television and its linked components likewise. Even Ron's clothes were lying scattered. Before Albert could fully take in the reality of the scene, a dozen or so of his own books came flying and madly flapping out of his flat's door.

'What's going on?' asked Simon fearfully, standing behind Albert on the threshold of the house. 'Is it really burglars?'

A man in a white shirt and black trousers came out of Albert's flat, carrying Albert's skip-rescued ghetto blaster, which he threw on top of the pile of Ron's broken possessions. Seeing Albert, he glared furiously at him before returning inside. It was a look of barely bottled-up seething rage.

'Jesus,' breathed Carl, arriving and seeing the mess.

Stepping over the broken and tossed things littering the hall, Albert approached his flat's door, hearing fresh sounds of tumult coming from within. Whatever was going on now, it was going on inside the living room.

'I'll phone the police,' said Simon, taking out his mobile.

'No,' said Albert in a subdued, blown-away voice. 'It's not burglars. It's my landlord.'

Perhaps spurred by hearing its master's voice, Peep came running out of the living room. Bending quickly and using his knee as a barrier, Albert intercepted her before she could escape into the hall. Picking her up, he could feel her tiny heart racing, and he naturally cradled her in his arms to calm her. Moving in stunned incredulity toward the living room, he encountered his landlord systematically tipping the contents of the room's drawers on to a sheet spread out on the floor.

'What are you doing?' murmured Albert.

'Evicting you,' answered the landlord, sternly continuing his furious work, roughly discarding each drawer on to the floor once he'd emptied it. 'You're a cunt.'

'You said we had a week,' protested Albert, stupefied.

'Fuck you,' returned the landlord, opening a cupboard and pulling the contents out hand-over-fist — Ron's video and DVD collection.

'None of this stuff's even mine,' said Albert, coming out of his daze and moving deeper into the room. 'Stop it. It's all Ron's. Everything.'

'He's going too. Birds of a feather.'

Ashen with fear, Simon appeared in the doorway, backed by Carl.

'You all right?' Carl asked Albert, prompting the landlord to hurl a handful of videos that only narrowly missed their human targets, who responded by sinking away from sight.

'You two out there!' bellowed the landlord, charging over to the door and shooting out a directing arm, 'get out of my house.'

In a mixture of fear and sheepishness, Carl and Simon complied, scurrying worriedly out the flat.

'Jesus, pal, chill out,' said Albert, increasing his hold on Peep, who was freshly spooked by the flying videos and the bellowing. 'I'm sorry about leaving the whisky where Harry could find it. It was a bleeding accident.'

The landlord — a taller than average man in his physical prime, leanly muscular — moved back from the door and stepped up to Albert. 'Yeah? And what about all those drugs?'

'For fuck's sake, just a bit of dope. It'll be legal soon. Half the population of Britain smokes. Chill out.'

Glaring viciously at Albert, the landlord seethed, 'The bloke in the shop told me you've been boasting you kicked my dad to death.'

'What?!' gawped Albert, beginning to find the confrontation wryly ridiculous. 'No. I just told his daughter something goofy to freak her.'

'Would that be the same daughter you threatened to kill? You sick cunt.'

'Oh, for fuck's sake,' exhaled Albert, 'I didn't threaten to kill anyone, and I didn't kick Harry to death. End of story.'

The landlord was now shooting his sentences off like machine gun fire, his hands darting and pointing. 'I know you didn't kick him to death. I know it. I know it. He hanged — blind drunk because of you. Saying you beat him up one of your stupid jokes, was it? You were always taking the piss when I came round, weren't you? The police said they were sure there was no assault. I went to see them because of you.'

'So stop smashing up Ron's stuff,' said Albert, now angrily exasperated. 'It's all Ron's. He'll knock your teeth out when he comes back.'

Unexpectedly, there came a lull in the landlord's storm. Suddenly seeming to be on the brink of tears, he surveyed the room. 'I was born in this house. Used to be my grandparents'.'

With the landlord's mad anger apparently easing, Albert naturally sought to pacify him further. 'For fuck's sake, man, you're not the only soul who's been through wacky shit. Calm down and chill before you give yourself a breakdown.'

But there had been insufficient sympathy in Albert's tone: to the landlord, his words had sounded rancorous rather than soothing, and his anger swiftly returned. A colder anger now. Grimly gathering up the corners of the laden sheet, he made a sack which he swung over his left shoulder. 'You and your crony are history,' he grimaced, starting toward the door.

'Leave that stuff,' ordered Albert, stepping into the landlord's path, looking like a gunslinger in his long, open coat. But the instant he spoke the landlord reacted, and it came powering in too fast to be dodged. An explosive right-hander hit Albert's left eye square on, twisted his body round, took his legs away and left him at the mercy of gravity, his bulk crashing heavily down on to one of the drawers lying scattered on the floor.

A short, piercing screech ripped from Peep as she cushioned the fall of Albert's helpless body.

There was no loss of consciousness. He was back on his feet in what seemed to him to be no time at all, ready to defend himself – determined to defend himself. But when he looked, there was no combatant to be seen. Then Carl and Simon appeared – *two* Carls and *two* Simons.

Simon took hold of him, assuming him to be woozy, but Albert pushed him away.

'Get off me,' snarled Albert, 'I'm all right. Where's that bastard?'

'He's gone,' jabbered Carl, running to the window, attracted by a screech of car tyres. 'That's 'im leaving now. Jesus! Never seen a Mondeo move so fast.'

Simon moved in to support Albert again, only to be pushed away a second time. 'Simon, leave me alone. I'm all right.' But he was not all right, Albert was fast realising. Blood was dripping – almost streaming – from his nose, and his sight was distorted so much it was hard for him to make any sense of what he was seeing. Simon, standing no more than a step away, had a blurred twin hovering in the air by his side. And there were two Carls; one sharp, the other fuzzy. Putting a hand over his left eye and looking with the right, everything appeared normal. Moving his hand over to the right, looking with the left eye only, everything still appeared normal, though a little blurred. But with both eyes seeing together, things were dizzying: two images overlapping, one sharp, the other fuzzy. Some kind of brain injury, he vaguely, confusedly, assumed.

Peep – he'd fallen on Peep, hadn't he? She had screeched. With Carl jabbering on about something, and Simon looking pale and scared and repeatedly saying that they'd better leave in case the landlord came back, he bent his head down to look for his pet, assuming her to be hiding or lying injured somewhere. With an intellectual effort, he identified two shadowy shapes on the floor as being one cat. Bending to touch Peep, he missed. Putting a hand — now sticky with blood — over his damaged eye, he repeated the motion, making contact this time. There was no reaction to his touch. Lifting Peep's tiny, frail, limp head he perceived she was dead.

'You fell on it,' gushed Simon breathily. 'It was caught between you and the drawer. We were watching through the window. Is it dead?'

Albert knew Peep was dead all right. Ruptured. Tongue-lolling ruptured. Gently picking her up, he moved over to a corner of the room and squatted with her on his lap. Blood dripped ticklingly from the tip of his nose down on to his T-shirt. Only two minutes earlier, when he had risen to his feet after being sent spinning, he would have fought his landlord tooth and nail if he'd still been there. Fought him for having landed that damaging blow. But now that raging, primitive instinct was receding.

'Sorry, Peep,' he said, in a whispered, murmuring voice.

'You should call the police,' advised Simon, standing near Albert.

'Too right,' agreed Carl, leaving the window and joining Simon. 'You could get 'im banged up for what 'e's done.'

Albert tilted his head back against the wall, and the blood from his nose now glooped around and over his lips. 'It was my fault,' he said quietly.

'Weren't your fault,' countered Carl. "E started it. We wuz witnesses. You didn't do nuffink. 'E just walloped y'.'

'I did plenty,' said Albert, staring at the light in the centre of the ceiling, but seeing two lights.

'You didn't,' contested Simon, in the same innocuously assertive tone he employed for defending his spiritual ideas.

Carl stooped to inspect Albert's face. 'Blood's stoppin' now. Gonna be a beauty shiner, mind y'.'

Tilting his head level again, Albert felt real pain for the first time. The damaging blow hadn't really hurt in the normal sense. It had just happened — massively, but instantaneously — then the instinct to fight had taken over, oblivious to injury. But now a new set of hormones and sensations were taking hold, letting him know just how damaged he was.

'I can't see properly,' he said. 'Everything's double.'

'Yeah?' said Carl. 'Got a bashed eye meself, once. Fell off me moped when doin' the knowledge. Saw double like you. Doctor said it was somefink to do wiff the muscles that move the eye bein' bruised.'

That was it, Albert slowly realised, with muted relief. His brain wasn't injured — his eyes were out of alignment. Pressing a finger experimentally against the corner of his uninjured eye, he was even able to bring things from double to roughly single.

'You should go to a hospital,' advised Simon.

'Give y' a lift in me cab, if y'like,' offered Carl.

'I'll be all right,' said Albert.

Gently placing Peep's lifeless, limp body on the floor, Albert stood up and at once felt nauseous, unsure whether it was because of the blow or the dizzying sensation of seeing double — a confused kind of motion sickness. Woozily proceeding to the bathroom, discarding his coat along the way, he was silently followed by Simon, and behind Simon, Carl.

In the bathroom, he examined his face in the mirror he had set above the basin in quieter times. Holding a hand over his punched eye, a bloodied mess is what he first saw. But the blood made him look worse than he probably was, he suspected. Anyway, by misadventure, many times he'd bust his nose worse when he'd been a kid. Besides, he knew his nose had only caught a little of the blow, which had mostly impacted over his left eye, where there was bruising evident already. Beads of blood, now semi-congealed, had welled-up below the lid, and some of the white of the eyeball was stained red. But it was the protecting structures surrounding his eye that had absorbed most of the punch — his brow and cheekbone —, and from the puffiness, redness and tenderness, he knew he'd be black and blue in the morning, and for days to come.

Putting the plug in and turning on the hot tap, he sat on the edge of the bath while waiting for the basin to fill. The door was half open, and he now saw that Simon and Carl were standing watching him — two Simons and two Carls. What were they doing here? He didn't even know them. It was insane. As insane as what had just happened to him.

'How do you feel now?' asked Simon.

Dropping his vertiginous gaze to the floor, and appearing to any observer like a defeated, post-fight boxer, Albert was unresponsive to Simon's enquiry.

'I've got a healing crystal in my bag in the cab,' said Simon. 'If you keep it in your pocket, it'll help the natural healing process.'

Without looking up, Albert quietly said, 'Could you two please go now.'

'We can't go,' said Simon in his meekly insistent way. 'We've got too much to talk about. I've had an idea about how we can help you remember about the UFO and—'

'Please go,' cut in Albert.

Carl spoke up. 'Give it a rest, Simon. Look at the state of 'im.'

'Yes, sorry,' said Simon, pushing his glasses up, accepting the inappropriateness of his agenda.

'What wuz all that strife wiff your landlord about, anyway, Albert?' asked Carl.

'Nothing,' said Albert, with a strong undertone of bitterness. Standing up to turn off the tap, he repeated, 'Nothing. He's a nutter.' Careful to avoid knocking his face, he pulled off his T-shirt and dropped it on the floor. He now saw that blood had seeped through it, staining his chest like a robin's.

In a sympathetic tone, Simon asked, 'Do you want me to get the healing crystal, Albert?'

With a groan, Albert tipped his head back, and closed his eyes. This was insane. He'd just been battered; he was in growing pain; he felt sick; his cat was dead; his flat had been trashed; and now he was being insistently bugged by a couple of religious weirdoes who thought he was a prophet or something. Would his life *ever* be easy?

'I've got some homeopathic remedies in my bag as well,' continued Simon in a caring voice. 'There might be something for bruising.'

Albert turned to face Simon. 'Thought I'd told you to leave? Who the fuck are you, anyway? Why are you staring at me in my own bathroom?'

'Because I know you're a prophet,' answered Simon, pushing his glasses up. 'You have to be made to believe it yourself. You've been chosen because you're so sceptical yourself.'

Suddenly losing patience and equanimity, Albert bellowed, 'Go!' He shouted so loud it astonished him. It was louder than he would have thought himself capable. In the face of such a thunderous storm of authority, Simon winced and shrunk back. Stepping out of the bathroom, Albert — bloody from eyes to belly — pursued his infuriated tyranny. 'I'm not a fucking prophet. I made it all up. I was pulling your leg. A joke — one of my big fucking jokes. Now fuck off out of my flat. Both of you. Get out of my life.'

In a close repeat of their exit under the command of the landlord, Simon and Carl complied with Albert's bellowed, bloody-faced dictate, shuffling quickly out of the flat and into the hall. But that wasn't far enough for Albert, and he ordered them to leave the house completely, following them to the street door and slamming it after them.

'Godfrey loves you,' he heard Simon say outside the house.

Once the door was closed and he was alone, Albert sat on the edge of one of the dustbins. His anger had already subsided. He hadn't really been angry at Simon, he guiltily knew — he'd led Simon on all day. He wasn't even angry at his landlord. He had been angry with himself for getting into such a mess, and had just lashed out. The calamitous aftermath of that mess was scattered all around him. Ron would go berserk when he got back. But then again, Ron wouldn't be back for another week, so that didn't matter at all.

Returning to his flat, Albert shuffled along the wall since he couldn't depend on his sight with so many obstacles lying in his path. In the bathroom, he gently washed and sponged his face and chest, leaving the basin water a fascinating scarlet. Then he washed and sponged twice more with fresh water each time to remove all vestiges of the gore. Gently blowing his nose brought out thick, congealed, glutinous, mucousy globs of blood that messed a dozen sheets of tissue. And when he blew, it infuriated his eye, which throbbed and protested like a poked wasps' nest.

But looking in the mirror now — looking one-eyed to restore normality to his vision — he saw that he wasn't really so badly damaged, inasmuch as there was nothing that wouldn't soon heal, presuming his vision would come together again. He'd been lucky, in a way. That iron-hard punch, if it had struck a little more to the centre, could have easily broken his nose. If it had struck lower down, it could have fractured his cheekbone or knocked out front teeth. Or lower and from the side, smashed his jaw off its hinges, tearing his mouth and dislocating molars.

Leaving the bathroom, he went to his bedroom to see what kind of a mess had been made of it, not that there had been much in there to mess up. He discovered that any books that hadn't been thrown into the hall had been swept off the shelves, but that was about it, save for the ejected ghetto blaster. The box in which he kept his few clothes had been pulled out of the cupboard, but not otherwise disturbed.

With his usual T-shirt bloodied, about the only clean thing he had to put on was the lilac silk shirt Jackie had given him for his birthday, and he wore it now. Sitting on the edge of his bed, he stared at two book-strewn floors. He still felt nauseous — more so, like he had a combination of a small hangover and motion sickness. His face was hurting more now, too, but almost pleasantly sometimes, so long as he didn't exacerbate the injury in any way, like blinking too hard. What a day. What a crazy day. And it all felt like his own fault. But it wasn't, really, he also felt. He hadn't pissed off the landlord by growing dope in the garden. He hadn't bought a huge, dealer-size slab of Moroccan black.

Remaining listlessly on the edge of the bed for some time, that vaguely heavy and burdensome feeling visited him again. Staring at the floor, he was no longer consciously dwelling on the evening's events. He wasn't consciously dwelling on anything. Even the pain in his face fell away from his awareness. But unlike his accustomed quiescent state, this blankness had an oppressive weight to it, far removed from any softly wafting melancholia or wistfulness. Not a blue feeling, it was a dull, colourless feeling. Or at best, a grey feeling. Sadness without yearning.

This wouldn't do, he told himself after a while. He had work to do. After he'spurring himself some more times, he eventually left his bedroom for the task of burying Peep's body.

*

The spot Albert chose for his cat's grave was close to the rotting, waist-high wooden fence that separated his garden from the street, near an unruly bush where the ill-fated animal had liked to prowl and play. With two black bin liners cut open and spread out to kneel on, and with his shirt sleeves rolled up, he began the hole by leaning his weight on to the rusty trowel that had been the only digging implement he could find. Pushing it down to its hilt, he levered out a clump of wet soil that smelled richly of decaying vegetation and fecundity. The ground was easy to work, having the consistency of warm Christmas pudding, so, despite the darkness and his impaired sight, it wasn't long before the hole was sufficiently deep. But the exertion and the bending had enraged his throbbing eye and exacerbated his nausea, and now he rested on his haunches to recover. He could puke if he wanted to, he felt. Why a punch in the eye should make him nauseous, he didn't know, but it had.

He took in deep lungfulls of the chill night air to try to restore well-being.

In a few minutes, he felt able to proceed. Rolling his sleeves down, he returned indoors, closing the street door behind him and holding a hand over his bad eye so that he could negotiate the cluttered hall. Once he'd buried his cat, he'd have to try to get Ron's things back together — find out what was broken and what wasn't —, although he felt neither physically nor mentally up to the labour. Nevertheless, he'd do his best to restore Ron's bedroom, for he believed the landlord's anger was spent, and he wouldn't be back for a while. Perhaps he could even remain in the flat until... until something turned up.

Closing his flat's door behind him, he went into the living room for the first time since being punched. Bending over Peep, he saw that the lustre had already left her eyes, and wondered if his own eyes looked the same, because that is how he now felt.

With some alarm, he heard a small noise outside the room, and then the street door slam. The landlord — had to be. Putting a hand over his bad eye and venturing to investigate, he saw an envelope had been pushed under his door. The envelope was addressed to *The Tenants*, and he read its contents:-

Due to illegal use of the property, namely drug cultivation, your tenancy is cancelled. All occupants must vacate the property by 12 noon tomorrow. Your deposit will be returned within seven days if the accommodation is found to be in good order. Failure to vacate the property by 12 noon tomorrow will result in loss of deposit and forced eviction by hired agents one minute later.

Hired agents — Albert knew what that meant, all right. Before this flat, he'd lived in a squat, and four such hired agents brandishing baseball bats had burst in one day, giving him and two stoned others "five minutes to collect your shit things otherwise we'll throw you out by your dirty bollocks". He'd collected a kitten called Peep, even though it wasn't really his, but no one else in that panicky minute would take responsibility for it.

Placing the letter to one side, Albert went to get his coat, left lying near the bathroom. Putting it on, the weight of it on his shoulders and around his neck immediately increased his nausea. Going into the living room, feeling a kind of numb solemnity, he slipped his hands under Peep to lift her up. Carrying the flopping, head-lolling corpse at arm's length, he proceeded to the garden. Unable to place a hand over his eye to help him see, he first tried to close his bad eye, but found it painful to close just on its own, so he closed his good eye instead, and his way became negotiable, albeit blurred.

Kneeling on the bin liners, he began gently lowering his dead pet toward the dark hole in the earth... but then he suddenly convulsed and puked hot, bitter vomit from the pit of his stomach. Vomiting had never before happened to him without at least a few seconds warning. He dropped Peep — where, he couldn't see, and didn't care at that moment. The retching had tortured his face, and he wasn't sure if his nose hadn't started bleeding again. Crouching on his knees and palms, he knew he was about to retch again, and braced himself for the pain, which swiftly came as expected.

'One of the most cunning minds ever devised by nature,' said a low, mocking voice from above the fence as Albert puked.

It was Ron, but Albert had even worse things on his mind at that moment.

The fence creaked as Ron leant against it to look down upon his flatmate. 'Puking again,' he sardonically observed. 'You're obsessed, you.' A car drove past, briefly adding illumination to the shadowy garden: something peculiar had been glimpsed at the steaming spot where Albert had been sick. Flicking on his lighter for confirmation, Ron complained, 'For fuck's sake, Albert, you've only gone and puked on Peep.' But peering for longer, Ron realised things were even more awry. 'Shit, she's dead,' he said, bewildered. 'You've drowned her.'

Done puking, Albert slumped sideways on to the earth, missing the spread-out bin liners.

He issued a low, sick moan of despair.

Coming into the garden, carrying a large holdall slung over his back, Ron further investigated the cat's condition, flicking his lighter on again while stooping over the body. 'Shit, she's really dead. What happened to her?'

'She was in a fight,' groaned Albert, still lying on his side on the ground, staring at his cat's corpse, less than a foot from his face.

'What with?'

'Me.'

Putting his lighter away, Ron thought for a moment. The story didn't pan out, according to his understanding of the world. 'Nah. You'd be the dead one.'

'She was on my side,' groaned Albert. 'Me and Peep versus the landlord.'

'What?!' exclaimed Ron. 'Because of the eviction thing?'

'How did you know about that?' asked Albert, but making it sound more like a complaint than an enquiry.

325

'Jackie called me yesterday to tell me I had a week to move out because the landlord had found my dope plant or something.'

'Make that until noon tomorrow,' corrected Albert.

'What?' gawped Ron, stupefied. 'Fucking good job I came back today, isn't it? Were you really in a fight with the landlord?'

'Didn't get time to fight. I was on the deck before I knew it. Fell on Peep. Killed her.'

'Shit. And all because of my dope plant and Jackie's joint?'

'And your huge slab of black. He suspects we're dealers.'

'What? What a wanker.' Ron put his bag down and sat on it. 'Jesus, Albert, sorry about all this.'

'I'll never forgive you,' groaned Albert.

'Fuck,' breathed Ron. 'And your cat's dead too. Bad news.'

'Bad news,' agreed Albert, getting to his knees, looking like some exhausted, wounded, shadowy quadruped. He remained on all fours while his recovery continued.

'How comes you're puking? Been on the pop?'

'I wish.'

'Did you really have a fight with the landlord? You're not shitting me?'

'Really.'

'Fuck me,' said Ron, now lighting a cigarette.

'Thought you weren't back until next week?' said Albert after some seconds, again sounding more complaining than enquiring, although he perceived that now Ron was back, his own mood had elevated – life felt tragicomical again.

'Yeah, like I was going to leave you in charge of my things when we're being evicted or something. I was phoning like mad, but you never answered. Has the phone been disconnected?'

'Not that I know of.'

'Well I rang about a hundred times.'

'I never heard it,' said Albert, managing a small shrug that couldn't be seen.

Using his mobile, Ron rang the phone in the flat. 'Something's up. You can usually hear it out here.'

'Oh yeah, I switched the ringer off,' Albert now remembered.

Viewing the shadowy mound of excavated soil, Ron surmised, 'Burying the cat?'

'Trying to.'

Ron drew on his cigarette, and exhaled a smoky, breathy sigh. 'Fuck. It's all a bit of a mess, isn't it? I'm not moving out, though.

Matter of principle.'

'He's going to send heavies around tomorrow if we don't.'

'What?! Just over a bit of friggin' dope? It's madness.'

'Oh, I killed his dad. Forgot to mention that.'

Jackie had not said anything about Harry's death when she'd called Ron in Iceland, so Ron assumed Albert was joking about the landlord's father, and he ignored the confession.

Now that he'd puked, Albert was steadily improving, and felt well enough to continue with the funeral. So, ignoring the noises of bewilderment and ire that Ron had begun making, he sat back on his haunches and gently slid his hands under Peep's body, hoping not to touch any puke. Lifting her up, he held her over the burial hole. 'Well, Peep, you were a damned good companion. I'd like to think I was a good companion for you, too. Sorry it had to end so soon. So many trees left unclimbed.' His voice began to choke. 'Sorry, Peep, you were a good cat. So sorry. All my fault.' He lowered the corpse into the hole. 'You were a good cat, Peep, and I let you down.'

Realising that his flatmate was genuinely overcome, Ron felt irresistibly inclined to let him finish the burial alone. Albert showing real feelings was something Ron had never seen before, and never thought he would. He sometimes wondered if Albert had any real feelings at all, beyond his oft-affected woes and miseries. He'd never even heard Albert properly laugh, never mind get emotionally croaky. No, Albert was as emotionally cloaked as they came, so this voice-cracking-up thing was unsettling to witness — and it was over a cat, of all things.

Taking his bag, Ron went quietly indoors, but twenty-seven seconds later, he was very noisily back outside. 'What the fuck's happened to my stuff?' he bellowed before realising Albert was no longer present. Rushing to the gate, he looked both ways down the street, but there was no one to be seen.

1.27
Union

By the time the performance began, most of the people who'd
been in the bar area when John first stepped into the Arts Centre
had moved into the theatre. Now, a new crowd of evening drinkers
was beginning to congregate — small groups seemingly straight
from the office; trendy students in flares; older, middle-class
couples. Leaning sullenly against a silently flashing bandit
machine, John was swiftly putting away his second lager of the
evening. Almost the whole length of the wide building was
between him and the theatre doors, but he had a clear view, and
his eyes never strayed from them long enough to allow Jennifer
unseen exit. She was still in there, he was sure, and had probably
already been joined by her new lover.

Stepping up to the bar to purchase another drink, John
maintained his vigil, looking over his shoulder several times.
Returning to the gambling machine, he placed his glass on top
while he delved in his jacket for coins. Feeding the slot, his
attention now became divided between the machine's spinning
wheels and the theatre doors. When he won, he showed no
pleasure; and once he'd lost too much, he moved away to a
table. Roughly kicking a chair into position, he sat heavily down,
the disturbance causing the woman on reception to lift her head
and look his way. On the wall immediately behind him hung a
painting almost as tall as he was, and wider than he could stretch.
It was of Durham's cathedral, in moody, sombre hues and swirls,
but he had no mind for sentiment, and did not even glance at
the work.

Looking at his watch, he saw it was only twenty-past-eight —
he'd be rolling drunk by nine-thirty if he kept up his current
drinking rate. He didn't want that. He didn't want to appear
like some washed-out loser when he confronted Jennifer and
her new lover coming out of the theatre. Maybe he should take
a walk then come back? No, she might leave early. He'd come
this far — temporarily deserted the British Army to do so — and
would not risk failure. He remembered the programme sheet,
now in his pocket, and took it out for examination. Perhaps
Albert was one of the players tonight? he suddenly thought.
Sheet in his left hand, lager in his right, scanning down the page

he saw no Albert listed. So maybe Jennifer's only reason to visit to Durham *was* to see her sister play? But that was no reason for the secrecy... unless she kept it secret not because of some new lover, but merely because she didn't want him to come with her? Yes, *that* could be it. Sarah didn't approve of him, he was sure of that, so maybe, whenever this outing had been arranged, Jennifer had promised to come alone? Except for this white lie, had everything Jennifer and Margaret said been true? Could it be that there really was no new lover in her life?

He knew one way to find out right away — go and check on her.

Taking his drink with him, he went directly to the theatre. Inside the first doors, the attendant was still in position, but was now reading a book. She raised heedful eyes when John paced past her, ticketless and disregarding a sign forbidding drinks to be taken beyond that point. Going straight into the auditorium, John saw that Sarah's quartet was on stage, dressed olden-style. Their piece seemed to be reaching its climax. Jennifer, he could see, was sandwiched between two old women, with no likely lover sitting anywhere near.

Security had been breached, and the attendant followed John into the auditorium, whispering her concern to a male colleague sitting on the back row. Together, they approached John, but he walked out without them needing to question or censure him — he had seen all he needed to see. With applause now breaking out behind him, he returned to the bar. Sitting at a table, staring at his drink in his hand, he mulled over the situation. Jennifer really wasn't meeting anyone, he conceded. But that letter? There was still that letter from Albert. But maybe Jennifer had told the truth about that, too? He was acting crazy, he began to suspect. Indulging in wild, jealous speculations. Losing control — he prided himself on his control. Go now, he counselled himself. Yes, fuck it, just forget it. Tonight was a mistake. Everyone's allowed mistakes. Just catch a train from here direct to London, and maybe you'll make it back to the base before midnight. Go to your future, whatever it may be... mediocre, that's what it'll be, he starkly foresaw — Jennifer had been the best thing in his future. He felt useless and stupid all of a sudden... and irrelevant. He was a nobody, really, wasn't he? Not even officer material. Just an army private with a life of manual work ahead of him. Tears — tears of angry frustration — threatened to appear, but he refused them passage.

'Albert!' hailed Jackie, with quickly checked spontaneity.

Albert, holding a muddied hand over his bad eye, had unknowingly walked past her table, which was buried under the elbows, drinks and bags of half a dozen of her teenage college friends.

Hearing the name, John threw his head up and saw a young man wearing a long, black, muddied coat. Having been called by a close-cropped young woman, the muddied young man seemed momentarily puzzled over who could have addressed him from among the group seated around her table.

'Jackie,' returned Albert, sounding subdued, unsure and awkward. 'Hello.'

'Why are you holding your face?'

'Tell you in a minute,' he said, walking away from Jackie and toward the toilets, located next to the reception desk.

In all his school and army life, John had never met a person under sixty called Albert. The odds that a young Albert just happened to be in the same building as Jennifer were outlandish, he reckoned. It all came clear to him now: Jennifer *was* here to meet Albert, but *after* Sarah's performance. She had lied.

Dropping his hand from his bad eye, Albert's vision doubled. Reaching for the handle on the toilet door, he missed it first time, but succeeded by groping for the least blurred option. Beyond this first door was a short passageway that led to a second door. Pushing this open, he saw two floors and twice as many urinals as usual. He went to a basin where he rinsed the lingering taste of puke from his mouth. Thankfully, his nausea was lessening, but the pain was worsening. Studying his two reflections in the large, clean mirror above the taps, he saw that he was a minor mess — dirtied and dishevelled from digging. However, although his face now felt like it ought to be swelling up, it didn't seem to be, beyond a slightly puffy and bruised area the size of a man's fist centred around his left eye, an eye that no longer showed any white, it all being startlingly blood-red.

Taking off his coat, he began cleaning the mud off himself and his clothes.

In line with her nature, Jennifer's clapping was subdued. Moreover, self-conscious was how she vaguely felt, even though she was a long way from being the centre of anyone's attention. Everyone else seemed genuinely, spontaneously, appreciative, but she felt she was faking her outward response. It was not that she hadn't discerned the quality of the musical performance, it was that she felt like a fraud and a stranger amongst such a gregarious and social display. When all bows had been taken, and the applause fell away, Sarah and her fellow players left the stage, and the Master of Ceremonies returned, informing the audience that, following a ten minute interlude, there would be a reading of Lord Byron's *Darkness,* with original musical accompaniment.

With ten minutes available, Jennifer thought she'd better visit the toilet. After asking the elderly woman sitting beside her to watch over her coat, she went out the way she'd come in, following several other members of the audience whose intention she presumed to be identical to hers. Tagging behind them, she was led toward the main reception desk, beyond which were two doors marked with ladies and gents symbols. In public, she'd never before worn anything that left so much of her flesh exposed as her new dress did, and now, walking past groups of drinkers, she became conscious of what felt like near-nakedness.

When she came out of the ladies toilet, an arm suddenly blocked her way.

'You lied,' said John.

The sudden appearance of an obstacle in her way was the initial shock. When she realised that obstacle was John, Jennifer felt her shock flush cold.

'What are you doing here?' she asked, stunned and uneasy.

'I'm not the one who was supposed to be staying in tonight,' returned John, acrimoniously.

'You followed me,' realised Jennifer.

'I didn't follow you. I was already on the bus when you got on.'

Two women now wanted to leave the toilets, and they cast reproachful looks at John, whose arm was blocking their path.

'Come on,' said John, expecting Jennifer to accompany him to his table.

'No, John,' she said. 'I'm going into the theatre.'

She began to walk away but he caught her up near the reception desk, gaining the surreptitious attention of the thirty-something, dark-haired woman on duty.

'No you're not,' he declared. 'We've got to talk.' Taking her wrist, he began leading her to a table in a corner of the roped-off dining area, now under dimmed lights.

'There's nothing to talk about,' argued Jennifer wearily as she was being pulled along.

'Sit down,' ordered John.

Jennifer sat with her back to the room, and John sat opposite.

'I want to go back into the theatre, John.'

'How stupid do you think I am?' he asked bitterly.

Jennifer didn't know what to say. She didn't want to say anything. She didn't want to *have* to say anything. It was her life, and she owed explanations and excuses to no one. 'Leave me alone, John,' she implored quietly, looking down at the white tablecloth, 'it's over between us.'

'You lied to me, Jennifer.'

She lifted her gaze. 'I didn't lie to you. I've never lied to you.'

'You lied through your fucking teeth,' insisted John, leaning forward to get in her face. 'For starters, you said you weren't going out anywhere tonight.'

'I wasn't. I've told you.'

'So what are you doing here?'

'I only decided to come here after I left the house.'

'So why were you all dressed up? Think I'm stupid?'

With a quiet groan of tired exasperation, Jennifer leaned back and turned her head away. Looking at John again, she said, 'Please, just leave me alone. I'm sorry for everything, but I don't want you any more. It's as simple as that.'

He stared at her. 'Where are you sleeping tonight?'

Briefly closing her eyes, Jennifer wearily sighed, 'John, it's got nothing to do with you where I stay tonight.' She looked at him again, looked at the only person she'd ever slept with. 'I'll be staying at Sarah's if I can manage to contact her.'

'With him? You know — him. About my height. Dark hair. Black coat.'

'What?' said Jennifer, twisting her face in bewilderment. 'What are you talking about, John?' Standing up, she wearily asserted, 'I'm going back into the theatre now.'

John stood up too. 'I'm talking about Albert.'

'Albert? John, for the thousandth time, I don't know anyone called Albert.'

'Really? Tell you what, I'll ask the cunt himself. Hear his story.'

John strode resolutely and belligerently away. Mystified, Jennifer watched him until he entered the toilets. None the wiser, she started back to the theatre, hoping he wouldn't follow her.

The woman on reception had also watched John.

With the last of the mud scraped and washed from his clothes, and the consequent wet patches dried under the powerful hand blower, Albert gave his face another examination in the mirror above the basin. Despite his poor spirits and the pain he was in, he again had to agree with Jackie: he did look raunchy — more so than ever, this evening, it seemed. The bruising actually made him look even more handsome, he realised, but he wasn't sure if it was because it leant him a certain dangerous, rugged aspect, or if it was due to some questionable eyeliner effect. Whatever the reason, he figured that if wan ladies didn't stop to wordlessly touch his face and hand him money today, then they never would. 'You should be out there parading,' he said, wagging a finger at his reflection. 'Making the most of your youth and looks. You could be coining it in.'

Leaving his reflection, he stepped toward the exit. Just as he went to put a hand over his bad eye, someone violently pushed, or kicked, the door. It swung heavily into his face, catching his nose and striking his hand, which he jerked back so sharply he hit himself precisely where he'd earlier been punched. 'Argh!' he shouted in pain and surprise, staggering back. 'God, that fucking hurt,' he complained, holding his face in his hands and going over to lean against a basin.

It hadn't been a loud shout, but the woman on reception duty, alert for trouble, heard it and immediately sent a call over the public address system: 'Security to main toilets.'

About to re-enter the theatre, Jennifer turned to look when she heard the call for security, and saw the woman on reception come out from behind her desk and rush into the toilets.

John moved closer to Albert, making an acrimonious study of the person he believed had usurped him as Jennifer's lover. Striking him with the door had been an accident, but not one he was about to apologise for. 'How's your girlfriend?' he asked.

'Jesus arse-frigging Christ,' groaned Albert, still leaning on the basin and still pressing his hands to his throbbing, wincing face. He was beginning to realise that not only had his face been freshly enraged, but the back of his hand had been injured by the door, and was starting to smart badly.

'You at the sink,' pursued John.

Albert turned his head and, taking his hands from his face, looked at John, seeing blurred, overlapping images. 'Fuck,' he

333

murmured when he realised that the blow from the door had set his nose bleeding again. Quickly cupping his hand under his chin to catch the blood before it could drip on to his shirt, he looked at his reflection and saw that his face was almost as bloodied now as it had been after the landlord had punched him.

He bent over the basin, and let the blood drip freely.

'Is everything all right in here?' asked the receptionist, putting her head into the room.

John stepped away from Albert.

'No,' said Albert, bleeding into the basin, 'I'm leaking.'

'Oh my God,' she said when she saw the blood, rushing to aid him.

Blood. Blood and serious bruising. John hadn't realised so much damage had been done. Suddenly, he felt like a wanted man. Slipping out the gents, he encountered Jennifer immediately outside the door.

'John, what have you done in there?'

'It was an accident,' he said, speaking quickly and urgently, leading her away by the arm, toward the main exit.

'What was an accident?' questioned Jennifer, bewildered and alarmed, unthinkingly acquiescing to the manhandling.

'Honest, I didn't touch him.'

'What's happened?'

'Nothing. It was an accident. The door hit him.'

'Who?'

'Your fucking Albert,' he snarled as they reached the porch.

Jennifer suddenly dug her heels in and yanked her arm away. 'I don't know anyone called Albert,' she insisted, in a voice of seething defiance. A voice that jolted John. 'I came here to see my sister play. Don't make me lose my temper. Don't ever make me do that.'

Behind Jennifer, John saw two uniformed security officers running into the toilets. 'Shit,' he said. It hadn't been an assault, but he knew it would look like one. This could be his life in tatters. AWOL was bad enough, but AWOL to end up in the back of a police car was even worse. 'Come on, let's go,' he grimly urged, and was reaching for Jennifer's arm when the blow caught him. In full feminine fury, she had suddenly and viciously swung her clenched hand at him, catching him painfully on the ear, shocking him as well as hurting him. Before he understood what had happened, Jennifer followed the first strike with a mad flailing at his face that only stopped when he grabbed her wrists.

'Fuck off, John, I'm not your property,' she hissed, glaring at him.

John glared back, maliciously saying, 'Thank fuck for that, you frigid psycho.'

He pushed her away with sufficient force to put her on the floor, and angrily left the building.

Previously preoccupied with her friends, Jackie now noticed the commotion surrounding the gents toilets. She worried that Albert had gone in there... but that had been some time ago. She stood up and looked around the bar: he could not be seen.

She hurried into the gents.

'Albert, what happened?' she asked, finding him stood amid two security personnel and the receptionist, holding heavily blood-soaked tissue paper to his nose.

'I walked into the door when someone opened it,' answered Albert.

Having quickly picked herself up off the floor, Jennifer had followed Jackie into the gents, and was now lurking between the inner and outer doors, trying to find out what was going on without being discovered. She couldn't see anything, but she heard the reply to Jackie. She also heard the name used: *Albert*. John had spoken the truth: it had been an accident. But how did he know that person was Albert? Was it even the same Albert?

'Are you sure that's what happened?' questioned the receptionist, her forehead furrowed with concern as she peered at the bruising around Albert's eye. 'And who was he, anyway?'

'Don't know,' said Albert, perplexed as to why half the world was taking such a keen interest in him. 'I was stood behind the door and he pushed it open to come in and it hit me. He didn't half give it a shove, though.'

'I watched him coming in,' said the receptionist. 'He looked really angry. That's why I came in to check when I heard a shout. He'd just been having an argument with a girl.'

'Yeah? He said something about a girlfriend.'

Suddenly feeling complicit, Jennifer shrunk back, fearful of being discovered. She slipped out into foyer. John was not in view, and she presumed he'd gone. Hoped he'd gone. People were looking at her, and she felt horribly conscious of being the

335

centre of speculation. It was all starting to feel disorientatingly strange. Not real at all. The whole day had been extraordinary and, eventually, bizarre, confusing and distressing. Still possessing no clear understanding of the evening's events, she hurried back to the theatre. Finding the poetry recital to have already begun, she waited in the shadows before taking her seat, glancing behind to see if she'd been followed.

*

Fresh from cleaning up his bloodied face for the second time that evening, Albert, looking battered and crestfallen, was sitting alone at a table in a corner of the bar, staring out the window. The view was a confusion of overlapping vehicles, lights and shapes. Lifting a hand to block the sight of his damaged eye, everything snapped into easy recognition: the small car park, and beyond, across a short distance, the high pedestrian bridge Joe had wanted to jump off.

'Here you go,' said Jackie, arriving at his table and presenting him with a beer, which she had insisted on getting for him, believing him to be in too delicate a condition to run his own errands.

'Thanks,' he said, glancing at her.

'Come and join me and my friends,' she gently urged.

'Don't think that would be a good idea if you want to keep them as friends.'

'Yeah, you're probably right,' she conceded. 'How do you feel now?'

'I'll survive,' he answered, half standing to slip his coat off his shoulders, worrying that the strain would start his nose bleeding again.

'You're wearing my present,' she observed, with gentle pleasure. 'I didn't notice before.'

'What? Oh, yeah. Thanks.' Albert was now engrossed in examining the back of his left hand, which was bruised and swelling where it had been struck by the door. 'Hurts like fuck now. Wonder if something's broken in there?'

'You should go to the hospital,' advised Jackie.

'I'll go tomorrow, if it's any worse. They might give me a bed for the night. I'll need one by then.'

Jackie was suddenly moved by sympathy and compassion. 'Oh, Albert,' she said, sitting herself down on the opposite side of the table to him, 'what are you going to do?'

336

'Dunno,' he said. 'Is it a rollover week?'

'No, it's not.'

'Buggered then, aren't I?'

A short teenager who was threatening to be chubby — one of the crowd from Jackie's table — came over to speak to her, so Albert stared out the window again. Her friend had a wispy blond goatee; a nose stud; short, bleached hair; and no inhibitions about the width of his flared jeans. He put his hand on her back when he spoke. 'Jackie, they've all decided to go to the Dun Cow.'

Looking over, Jackie saw that her friends were putting on coats and jackets.

'Why? What's wrong with this place?'

'It's like a morgue,' the teenager complained.

'Are you going too?' Jackie asked him.

'Yeah. You coming, then?'

Jackie deliberated a moment. 'Think I'll stay here.'

'Sure?'

'I'll give it a miss.'

'Okay, then,' said the teenager, giving her a smile before returning to his crowd. He'd given Albert a smile too, but Albert had still been mostly looking out the window.

'My friends are all going to the Dun Cow,' explained Jackie, with regret evident in her voice.

Albert continued looking out the window. 'Remember that Joe bloke we met?'

'The eccentric one who was crying?'

'Yeah. I bumped into him yesterday and stopped him from jumping off the bridge out there. I mean really jumping.'

'Really?' said Jackie, her voice and expression sinking into surprised seriousness.

'Really. If I'd let go, he would have fallen.'

'Shit,' breathed Jackie. 'I thought he was like you. I didn't think he was really —' She was interrupted. Her decision not to go to the Dun Cow had been reported back to her friends, who were now all calling her, beckoning her to leave with them. 'I'm staying here,' she told them, but not sounding completely decided.

'Nah, come on,' called one girl in a floppy purple hat.

'Peep's dead,' said Albert.

Shocked, Jackie immediately returned her attention to Albert.

'No. How?'

He turned his head away from the window. 'I fell on her when the landlord biffed me.'

'Oh my God, that's terrible. Oh Albert, I'm so sorry.'

Jackie's friends tried one last time to gain her company before they left, but she let them know she was definitely staying with Albert, and they trooped out without her.

'She was a good cat,' said Albert.

'God, I'm so sorry.'

Jackie's friends were now waving goodbye to her through the window as they crossed the car park, and she reciprocated.

'College friends?' supposed Albert.

'Yeah.'

Albert fell into silence, staring into his overlapping, twin beers.

'Don't look so sad, Albert,' said Jackie, 'things won't seem so bad this time next week.'

'This time next week I'll have been sleeping rough for six nights,' Albert pointed out.

'Well, we'll just have to see what we can do about that, won't we?'

Albert looked up, and at first Jackie thought he was looking at her, but she quickly realised he was looking beyond her — he thought he'd heard a familiar voice.

'Is that large, khaki entity at the reception desk Ron?' he asked, not having the will to put a hand over his bad eye.

'Ron?' queried Jackie. 'He's still in Iceland, isn't he?' But upon turning her head, she saw that she was wrong. 'Oh my God, it is him.'

'Let the good times roll,' said Albert.

Jackie waved to Ron when he looked her way. Walking briskly with his hands in his jacket pockets, he crossed the room, homing in on Albert, who had resumed staring into his beer.

'Hi, Ron,' said Jackie. 'Thought you weren't coming back till next week?'

'Hi,' returned Ron cursorily, before having words with Albert. 'Five days,' he complained, looming large above his flatmate, 'I was away just five days and you caused total ruin to everything left in your charge.'

'I had help,' said Albert, without looking up.

'Who from? The Four fucking Horsemen?'

'They probably did have a hand in it. It was a real professional job.'

Albert glanced up at Ron, and when Ron saw the condition of his face, for a fleeting moment he appeared shocked.

But then he motioned as if to jab Albert's bad eye.

'Bog off,' said Albert, dodging and raising his hands to protect his face. 'That's inappropriate behaviour for an adult.'

'Ron,' chastened Jackie, grabbing the offensive hand, 'leave him alone. He's injured.'

'You've got some fucking top explaining to do,' grumbled Ron to Albert before going off to the bar.

'Oh dear,' said Jackie.

'Ditto,' said Albert.

'He wasn't happy, was he?'

'Might be something to do with all the posh stuff in his bedroom getting trashed.'

'What?!' gasped Jackie.

'Hi, Albert!' said a happy female voice. Albert looked up, and Jackie twisted around. He didn't need to put a hand over his eye to tell that it was Sarah. Her role in the presentation was over, and, after changing out of her stage clothes, she had come to keep a pre-arranged meeting with Ron. 'Oh my God!' she gasped. 'What happened to your eye?'

'Ron tried to gouge me.'

'What? Why?'

Sarah sat down beside Albert, gawping at him.

'Beats me,' said Albert, in a nonplussed, indignant voice. 'Maybe some kind of dark, repressed gay thing got the better of him. Like that time with that handicapped boy he battered.'

'Shut up, Albert,' said Jackie. 'He's lying, Sarah.'

'No I'm not. You saw it yourself, he did try to gouge me, but I was too fast for him.'

'Sarah, his landlord beat him up.'

'Huge guy,' explained Albert. 'Loads of tattoos. Big Mexican moustache.'

Being addressed by her name puzzled Sarah, for she was sure she didn't know the person with Albert. 'I'm sorry, have we met before?'

'On Sunday, around Albert's. I'm Jackie.'

Sarah was even more puzzled for a moment, briefly looking to Albert for some clarification before the cause of her confusion dawned on her. 'But you had long hair then, didn't you?'

'All gone now,' said Jackie.

'Oh my God!' gasped Sarah, slack-jawed. 'It was all action when we were away, wasn't it?'

'Okay, Fox,' said Ron grimly, arriving back at the table with a drink and sitting beside Jackie, and for the meantime ignoring Sarah, 'explain how ten grand's worth of damage was done to my possessions in my absence.'

'What!?' gasped Sarah.

'The landlord did it,' said Albert.

'Why?' demanded Ron. 'Just because of the dope?'

'A little bit,' said Albert. 'But mostly because I killed his dad.'

'What!?' gasped Sarah.

'Albert,' chastened Jackie, 'tell Ron what really happened.'

Drinking his beer as he went along, Albert related the events that had led up to Ron's possessions being hurled out the flat. Getting kicked off the dole. Tony's refusal to declare him officially melancholic and sign him on the sick. Getting a paper round to buy cat food. Getting on Grace's nerves. His argument with Grace's father, the shopkeeper. The search for solace in whisky. The police coming round to caution him about Grace. Finding Harry dead. Harry being the landlord's father, and the woman from upstairs his mother. Realising Harry had drunk the discarded whisky. The landlord's discovery of the dope plant and the slab of Moroccan, and the consequent eviction threat. Telling Grace he'd kicked Harry to death to spook her. Grace telling her father about the invented kicking and her father telling the landlord. The landlord snapping and hurling all the stuff out. The landlord thumping him. Peep dying. 'So you see,' he concluded, poised to swill down the last of his pint, 'it was all Tony's fault.'

Sarah had made several noises of sympathy during the story, but Ron had listened to Albert in dark silence. Now that Albert's defence speech was finished, Jackie and Sarah looked at Ron, expecting judgement.

'I don't fucking believe it,' groaned Ron grievously. Over Albert's shoulder, he had just spotted his manager, standing with some men a short distance away — and Scoones had simultaneously spotted him. 'For fuck's sake. This takes the biscuit.'

'What the hell are you doing here?' demanded Scoones, approaching Ron. 'You're supposed to be in Iceland.'

'Going back on Sunday,' said Ron, in a blend of sheepishness and defiance. 'Had to come back to sort out something. Only missed an afternoon's work.'

'You were supposed to be on call for them all weekend if they needed you.'

'I made an arrangement with Ivor,' explained Ron.

'*You* made an arrangement with Ivor?' retorted Scoones. 'The *company* made an arrangement with the company that employs Ivor that *you* would be available. It's called a contract.'

'I'm sorry,' said Ron. 'I know I should have—'

Scoones cut in, 'You'll be more than sorry when the MD hears about this.'

'But I really had to come back to do something. My—'

'Do what? Your drugs?'

'What? What drugs?' said Ron, but Scoones, acting like he'd delivered a decisive blow, returned to his friends.

Ron had had a dressing down, and an awkward, embarrassed silence ensued around the table until Jackie spoke. 'Didn't Albert tell you that your manager saw your dope in your bedroom when he came round?'

'What?' cried Ron, looking to Albert for confirmation.

'Yeah,' admitted Albert.

'I told you to check before you let him into my bedroom.'

'I goofed.'

Noisily exhaling, Ron looked up to the heavens in despair and incredulity.

Sarah reached across the table to hold his hand. 'Is it bad, then?'

'Bad?' said Ron heatedly. 'Of course it's bad.'

'That bloody Tony,' complained Albert.

Suddenly slapping Albert's bad eye with the back of his fingers, Ron barked, 'Just shut the fuck up, will you?'

Albert had jerked back, but not quick enough, and the strike to his eye caused him real pain. But the greatest upset for him was that he knew that for a fraction of a second, Ron had meant it this time. The others knew it, too. It was a poignant and saddening moment. Even Sarah, a newcomer, sensed it marked the end of something. Some kind of innocence had just passed away from the earth.

With his countenance falling short of impassive, Albert stood up and wordlessly lifted his coat off the back of his chair.

Ron avoided looking at him.

Slipping into his coat, Albert was set to leave the table when Sarah reached out and held his sleeve between her fingertips. 'No, Albert —'. Her voice tailed away. To her stupefaction, she thought she could see her sister standing over by the theatre doors.

Her fingers involuntarily relaxed, allowing Albert to slip away.

'Where are you going?' asked Jackie, concerned, twisting around as Albert passed behind her, a hand held over his eye.

'Where everyone goes,' answered Albert.

It was yet another thinly-veiled reference to suicide from Albert, of the sort he uttered twelve times a day, but this one had a strange resonance with Jackie, though she didn't know why. And his tone had been different this time. This time there had been a real bitterness beneath the wistfulness and affected suffering.

'Has he gone?' asked Ron in a low voice, staring at the table surface.

'Yes,' said Jackie, 'and your manager's just left as well — with those guys he was with.'

Wordlessly, Sarah left the table. Ron looked over his shoulder to see where she was going, assuming she was intending to catch Albert up, but quickly learning otherwise.

Through the window, Jackie watched Albert cross the car park and head toward the pedestrian bridge that would set him on a course for home. But he stopped halfway along the bridge, leaning over the side to look down at the river. Now she remembered who she'd first heard say "Where everyone goes". It had been Joe.

The floodlit cathedral was standing tall above the trees on the riverbank, but Albert, one eye covered, was looking down to the slow-moving, black water below. It seemed to him to be silently carrying some secret along. Something darkly submerged and mournful. Maybe Joe, he fancifully speculated. Maybe a multitude like Joe. Maybe all the Joes that have ever wept. Would this drop actually kill? he wondered. Possibly. Possibly. Stun, then drown, at least.

He pictured himself among the submerged, slowly tumbling, cold, pale corpses.

'Albert,' called Jackie, pulling him away from his reverie.

He looked up from the waters and saw her coming along the

bridge. 'Can you see them?' he asked as she approached, taking his hand away from his eye and no longer making sense of the world.

'See what?'

'The pale corpses,' he said, looking down to the water again. 'There, a bankrupt man. There, a mother clutching a child – the child for whom she had no more bread. And there, a noble youth, pined away with desire – he has my face. And the bankrupt has my purse. And the mother has my hope. And there – look, there – palest of all, a foolish poet who once dreamed of all that's brightest and best and everlasting.'

In the dim street light, Jackie viewed Albert and worried a change had come over him. There was something ominously grave in his tone and demeanour.

'Please come off the bridge,' she said.

'Give me one good reason to,' he returned, sounding wearily bitter.

Taking a moment to think, Jackie volunteered, 'Your hair's peaking.'

'Yeah?' said Albert, cautiously proud. 'Really?'

'Really,' confirmed Jackie. 'Let's find a bar with loads of mirrors.'

Beyond Jackie, another voice arose. 'Albert, I've brought someone to meet you.'

Looking up from the dark water, Albert saw a confusion of overlapping, backlit forms.

'Hello, Albert,' said yet another, quieter, unsure voice. 'I'm Jennifer.'

Putting a hand over his bad eye, Sarah became clear to Albert. And standing beside her, hands dipped into the pockets of a long black coat, was a vision of beguiling wanness. There was enchantment in the air for Albert, and the moment felt crystallised in time. A moment in which everything conspired to make him believe he'd fallen so much deeper in love than he'd ever fallen in love before: the dark of the night, the radiance of the backlighting upon her pale hair; his forsaken mood, her redemptive interest in him.

'O bring me my finest quill,' he murmured. 'Before my eyes... everlasting inspiration.'

'Everlasting Inspiration wants to say sorry for what happened in the toilets,' said Sarah, causing Albert to look puzzled.

'Sorry? Why?'

'It was her boyfriend who hit you with the door.'

'Sorry,' said Jennifer. 'Long story.'

'A voice like the gentle cooing of the very Dove of Peace itself,' murmured Albert.

'Go on,' urged Sarah, nudging her sister. 'Show him.'

Jennifer drew open her coat to show that, on top of her dress, she was wearing the *ALBERT'S LASS* T-shirt, which Albert now realised must have been in Ron's pocket ever since he'd confiscated it the previous week.

She closed her coat again.

'It was Ron's idea,' said Sarah. 'And I made her wear it to cheer you up.'

'Jackie!' shrieked one, then several, of a group of people walking along the riverbank below, on the opposite side to the Arts Centre. It was her college friends. 'We're going to Newcastle, clubbing,' shouted one. 'Come with us,' shouted another.

'I'm going, Albert,' said Jackie quickly, at once hurrying away along the bridge to join her friends.

'Bye,' called Sarah, fazed by Jackie's sudden departure.

'Bye,' Jackie called back, without turning around.

She broke into a run.

Albert knew Jackie was upset. She had come out to see if he was all right, but had been upstaged by the arrival of a pretty face. In growing unease, he watched her running away before calling her name, but it seemed she was too far away to hear him.

+++ **End of Part One** +++

Part Two

Beyond the Joke

*... But come thereof in the end
despondency and madness.*

2.1
Separation

He was tediously alone in a deathly-quiet elevator, unsure whether it was moving or not. After what could have been forever, the doors unexpectedly opened. Slow to respond, he began to step out but was arrested by the image reflected in a mirror across the corridor, which showed the doors still to be closed. Overpowered by this evidence, he remained confined within.

Thus had gone the dream that had taken Albert to noon.

As she'd suspected she would, Jennifer had not pursued her vague intentions to re-sit her A levels, but had returned to her job. Today, Saturday, she had left the house early to assist at the morning surgery. While she was conveniently out of the way, and Margaret was conveniently out of town visiting family, Albert meant to achieve a *fait accompli*. However, in keeping with the course of his life, he'd slept for longer than was wise, and now Jennifer was already back. She'd had little clue this was about to happen, and despite her expressed anguish, he continued to collect the things he had brought with him, placing them in his scuffed suitcase.

His few other possessions, including all his books, he had abandoned when leaving the flat he'd shared with Ron.

'Why?' Jennifer wearily asked again, sitting on the edge of her bed, feebly holding the flowers she'd bought that morning, their heads tipped helplessly to the floor. 'Tell me what you're feeling.'

Wearing the shirt Jackie had given him, Albert continued to collect his belongings. 'I've told you what I'm feeling — I feel I want to go. Apart from that, I don't feel anything, except a bit sad.'

His limited possessions accumulated, standing by the bedroom door, Albert looked at Jennifer, indulging in the desolate thought that it was likely to be for the last time. She was a rare creature. Rare in that her face seemed incapable of ever looking unattractive. There was no angle from which it could be viewed unfavourably; no expression it ever mustered that detracted. And Albert had quickly learned that the rarity also extended to her nature.

Her eyes were beginning to dampen, and Albert felt for her, but at the same time it seemed ridiculous to him that anyone should feel such emotion over his departure. 'I'm sorry,' he said, moving to embrace her; she, with hesitant limbs, standing to return the clasp she knew was to put them asunder. 'Don't cry. Please don't cry. Not for me. Never for me. I'm not worth it.'

Standing within his embrace, on the brink of weeping, with her flowers held against his back, she wanted him to stay so much it surprised and disconcerted her. She'd only known him for two weeks, so she wondered if it was just the being left that was hurting, not really to do with the person leaving. But as they continued to hold each other, the threat of tears from her eyes receded, and Albert was relieved: he didn't know if he'd be able to walk away if she were crying.

'Where will you go?' she asked softly. 'You've got nowhere to live.'

'I'll find somewhere.'

'You haven't even got any money.'

'I've got my bus fare back to Durham.'

'Margaret doesn't mind you being here. She said you've grown on her.' Albert didn't reply, and Jennifer went on, 'If you don't like living in Richmond, we can get a place together in Durham.'

'No, Jennifer. I'll be bad for you.'

'Will you?' she asked, in a vague, querying yet doubting voice. He didn't answer, and another, lesser, concern crossed Jennifer's mind. 'Sarah called me at work this morning. Ron's having a bonfire party and barbecue tonight. I told her we'd be there. She's coming to collect us.'

'Go without me,' he returned, a terseness evident in his tone.

Confused and saddened, Jennifer said nothing. As a mark of resignation, she allowed her eyes to close. Soon she was lost in the gently swaying, sacred embrace of their soft-dying romance. With her head rested lightly against his shoulder, and the scent of the flowers rising to her, time passed too easily before she sensed his preparation to move. Opening her eyes to stare at the floor, she said, 'Would it change things if I told you I think I'm growing to love you?'

'Don't love me. I'll be bad for you.'

She stepped back, and looked perplexedly at him. 'Albert, why have you started saying things like that? Why?'

'Because I've never been good for anyone. Maybe that's why I stay alone.'

'Don't be so bloody ridiculous,' she reproved, 'you've been good for me. You've given me two of the funniest weeks of my life.'

Five hundred times is how much easier it was for him to walk away when she was arguing and criticising than when she was

348

threatening to be tearful. He picked up his suitcase, saying, with a discernible bitterness that Jennifer wasn't sure was meant for her, 'Yeah, I'm good at making people laugh. Bye.' With no more words spoken, he left the bedroom, then the house. Once outside, a powerful sense of escape being felt, he found himself imagining the scene within. Would she have thrown herself, distraught, on to the bed? That prospect, he was ashamed to discover, gave him a secret sense of satisfaction. But he refused to dwell upon it further. Instead, he momentarily reflected upon how strong his character was: there were few, surely, who could resist such a temptation as Jennifer.

*

The night Jennifer had been introduced to Albert, they had sat alone together on his preferred bench on the riverbank, talking for a good while. Then she'd said she had to go back into the Arts Centre, since she was meaning to stay at Sarah's that night, and didn't want to become separated from her. So they had walked back, but on account of his dispute with Ron, Albert had declined to go in, but he did arrange to see her again the next afternoon. Returning to his flat, he'd stayed up late in his bedroom. Three or four hours after he'd finally gone to bed, he'd heard Ron come back and at once begin moving his stuff out, making several journeys. When he'd eventually got up in the morning, Ron was already history. An hour later, he himself had been packed — some clothes and a few personal belongings thrown into an old suitcase he'd once found on a skip. Everything else, including his books, was to be left behind. Then he'd waited, and at noon exactly, four burly men let themselves in and told him to get going, and when he complied, they handed him a cheque made out to Ron — the return of the rental deposit.

Leaving his flat for the very last time, carrying the suitcase, he had then gone into town to meet Jennifer in the Arts Centre. His vision was no less double, and his bruises had gloriously ripened in the night, and he'd presented quite a pitiable sight. Sarah had been with Jennifer, and from her he'd learned that Ron had gone to stay with his parents, who lived on the verges of a village some miles outside Durham. He also learned from Sarah that Ron was not even intending to complain to the landlord about the destruction of his property, since he'd come to the conclusion that it would be futile.

Sarah had soon left her sister alone with Albert. Three hours later, his battered condition and homeless position had led Jennifer to offer him a sofa for the night — no problem, since Margaret was away for the weekend. When Margaret came back, he'd next slept on Jennifer's bedroom floor, and the night after that, she had grown fond enough of him to invite him into her bed.

Further to Ron losing his flat tenancy and having many of his valuables ruined, to add to his troubles, he had also been sacked from his job for "dereliction of duty". Concomitant with all that, Albert believed he had caught a changed attitude in Ron on the two occasions they had met since the flat had been repossessed, occasions instigated and arranged by Sarah. It had been perceived by Albert that Ron was, at least, trying to distance himself; at most, angry and resentful. Picking up on those vibes, he'd understood that it was as if Ron had decided that the four years of flat-share silliness and trouble had come to its inevitable sticky end, and now was the time for seriously getting on with his life.

Things had changed. So many things had ended.

*

Outside a shop near the bus stop, Albert counted his coins — the last of his computer sale money — and realised he couldn't afford a sandwich, but could afford a bag of crisps. If he'd got up earlier, he could have made something to eat before Jennifer's return, but he hadn't. He went into the shop, but the bus came and left while he was waiting to be served, and he had to stand half an hour for the next one to take him to Darlington. From Darlington, he caught the Durham bus, and by three o'clock he was sitting, huddled in his coat, on his usual bench on the riverbank, overshadowed by the cathedral. His stomach was rumbling angrily, and he began to recollect all the occasions in his life when he'd been wasteful with money, and wished he had those squandered sums now. In a just world, he'd get £100 back from Joe alone.

Looking over his shoulder to the cathedral, he realised that his sight, which had been slow to improve after the blow to his eye, was now perfect again — the night before, there had still been some impairment, evident when looking at distant objects. His bruising had completely cleared up too, he had noticed in the mirror that morning.

He turned his head away from the cathedral and stared at the river. God, he was hungry. He wondered if there was any kind of soup kitchen, or something, in Durham. Pity his bruises had cleared, he thought: bruises would be an asset if he had to beg on the street, which was another thing he was beginning to wonder about.

350

It began to drizzle. Picking up his suitcase, he set off for the far side of town, to the one place he could think of where he might find succour.

'Any veggie food going?' he asked morosely as Rebecca opened the door.

For some reason he could never quite fathom, whenever he knocked upon Rebecca's door she always smiled and let him in, even though he picked on her husband. These days, though, the smiles she gave him were usually cross, impatient ones.

With her long, curly brown hair, pixy-like face, deep brown eyes and ballet dancer's physique, Rebecca was a very different sight to her younger sister, Jackie. Rebecca turned heads, and Albert had suffered more than two hundred separate episodes of pining for her. He'd never once admitted to desiring her, though. Everyone wanted Rebecca, and she had come to expect it of men — even demand it. One day, years back in her particularly flirtatious school days, she had boasted to him that she could make any male from thirteen to seventy fall in love with her without it looking like she'd tried, and he had said "except me." Since then, he'd made damn sure no one ever heard him pining her name, since he knew if it got back to her, she would cockily consider it as some kind of personal triumph and vindication, and would go on about it to him for ages, perhaps the rest of his life.

How she'd ended up marrying Tony was a mystery to Albert.

'Just doing some pasta, actually,' she said, smiling and letting him in.

'Is it veggie?'

'Yes, we're all veggie now. Jackie made sure of it.' Now she saw the suitcase. 'No! No! No!' she shrieked, quickly pushing him back and closing the door.

'Aw, Rebecca, let me in, please,' said Albert to the closed door.

'You're not moving in,' declared Rebecca from the other side of the door. 'No way.'

'Please, just for a week or two. Until it stops drizzling.'

'Why do you want to stay here?' puzzled Rebecca desperately. 'Thought you were shacked up with Ron's girlfriend's sister?'

'That was hours ago,' said Albert. 'Make an effort to keep up, won't you? Please, let me in. It's my birthday.'

'It's not your birthday. Your birthday was three weeks ago.'

Albert paused for a resentful moment. 'Okay,' he conceded, with reluctant reasonableness, 'I was wrong about the birthday. But I've been so right about so many other things. *Please*, let me in.'

'Go and live with Ron.'

'I can't,' answered Albert. 'He's moved back in with his parents and his mother hates me. Come on, Rebecca, let me in. I beg you.'

'Go and beg his mother.'

'I did,' lied Albert, 'but she told me to fuck off. No *vision thing*, you see. Not like you, you've got puddles of vision.'

'You're not coming in,' said Rebecca firmly. 'You'll get ensconced.'

'I won't get ensconced,' he promised, suspecting he was still lying. 'I just want to talk to you for a few hours, like we used to in happier times.'

'What about?' asked Rebecca, with deep suspicion.

Albert opened the letter box to speak through it. 'About the decay of hope.'

'Go and talk to Ron about it.'

'I did,' he lied, 'but he couldn't sweeten the bitterness in my soul. Only you can ever do that. You're special, you are, Rebecca.'

'Stop being nice to me just because you want to stay in my house. If you're going to be nice, be nice honestly. Tell me honestly you love me and you can come in.'

'Let me in, bitch,' demanded Albert, but then he immediately became whining, 'Come on, Rebecca, you owe me.'

'I owe you!' she exclaimed, in an astonished, affronted voice. 'What for?'

'It's your fault I flunked school .'

'No it's not.'

'Yes it is,' insisted Albert. 'You used to tease me for being so toweringly superior. That's why I underachieved so massively — I was trying to appear normal. You ruined my schooling with your cruel torments, so let me in.'

'No. Stop talking bollocks. Admit you love me or fuck off.'

'It's when my headaches started, too.'

'Fuck off.'

'Please, let me in. I'm lonely. If I...'

He fell silent.

Rebecca became suspicious. 'What are you doing?'

'Listening,' said Albert, strangely.

'What to?'

'I fancy... I fancy I heard a misty noise — from yon graveyard way,' he murmured. 'There, I heard it again. I believe it was a call, Rebecca. A far call bidding me journey thither, to the haven of the grave. It must be my time, Rebecca, for who would inhabit this bleak world alone? So long, companion of my youth.'

Rebecca knelt down to look out through the letter box.

Albert looked in.

Her large brown eyes met his greyish green eyes.

He flattered her with some customised Shelly:

> *'In those eyes, where whoso gazes*
> *Faints entangled in their mazes...*bitch.'

And then, with a feeble moan, he fainted.

Despite the "bitch" addition, Rebecca was nettled to find herself relenting. 'Oh, come on in then,' she grumbled, opening the door to him.

'A gullible bitch at that,' he said when picking himself up. 'Your eyes are crap. Everyone knows that.'

Rebecca was the Personal Assistant to someone high up in the region's Health Service. Adding her salary to Tony's made easy work of paying the mortgage on the detached house they had shared for over a year now. This matrimonial house of theirs lay on a new development on the edge of town, where every property had a fenced-off rear garden, a small front garden, a short drive, and a double garage.

Entering the living room, Albert encountered Tony, who was sitting on the sofa, reading a newspaper. Over the top of his newspaper, Tony peered at the suitcase.

'Homeless,' said Albert, putting the case down and taking off his coat.

Tony said nothing. Nothing, that is, that wasn't expressed by him lifting his newspaper higher.

Rebecca came in behind Albert. 'The minute you start to look ensconced, you're out.'

'I'll never look ensconced,' said Albert. 'I've got a homeless soul.'

'You better have,' muttered Tony.

Albert flicked Tony's newspaper. 'I heard that, psycho the rapist. Sorry, psychotherapist.'

'He's heard that one before,' said Rebecca, going through into the kitchen.

'Yeah, but not outside a criminal investigation into medical malpractice,' returned Albert. Flicking Tony's newspaper again, he asked, 'Any chance of a sick note today, Tony? I'm sure I look a bit pale.'

'It's my day off,' said Tony, his attention not straying from his newspaper.

From the kitchen, Rebecca shouted, 'Stop annoying Tony because you're jealous I married him and not you.'

'Get lost,' shouted Albert back. 'I'm only jealous he's got a newspaper and I haven't.'

'Come and help me in here,' ordered Rebecca.

Albert went into the kitchen, which — the Arts Centre toilet aside — he reckoned was the cleanest place he'd ever been.

'Take these to the living room table,' said Rebecca bossily. 'One's yours, one's Tony's.' She handed him two food-laden plates. 'Tony,' she shouted, 'go and sit at the table.'

Albert returned to the living room, and found Tony had already complied with his wife's order.

Putting the plates down, Albert also took a seat.

'Not there,' advised Tony. 'Rebecca likes to sit there.'

Albert moved chairs just before she came into the room, carrying her own plate.

'Nice shirt,' she remarked to Albert, managing to sound cross while delivering a compliment.

'Jackie gave it to me for my birthday.'

'That was nice of her,' she said as she settled into a chair to begin eating. 'Have you spoken to her recently?'

'Not for a few weeks.'

'She's in with some new crowd these days. Suppose she had to be since you moved away.'

Soon Rebecca quizzed Albert as to why he was no longer living with Jennifer.

'Just felt like leaving,' he answered, with a small shrug.

'You left her!' exclaimed Rebecca in astonishment. 'She didn't kick you out? *You* left *her*?'

'And she begged me to stay, too... in a kind of reserved, understated way.'

Rebecca was still thrown. 'I thought she was some kind of paragon of beauty?'

'You could say that.'

'But you left her? Left her to become homeless?'

Albert shrugged again. 'Just felt like leaving.'

Rebecca produced a disapproving, exasperated, eyes-rolled-upward, head-shaking look, but didn't seek to explore the conundrum further.

Instead, she raised the issue of Ron's Guy Fawkes party that evening.

'Don't know much about it,' shrugged Albert.

'He's having it at his folks' place at Croxdale,' said Tony, with his mouth half full, making a rare conversational contribution. 'Loads of big fireworks apparently, and a barbecue. You coming?'

'His folks hate me.'

Ron's folk's did hate Albert, mainly on account of Ron's mother being convinced that he had been, and probably always would be, a druggy influence on her son, although the exact opposite was the case. On account of recent events, Albert guessed the hate would have swollen into something that might involve knives and lunging if he ever set foot in their house.

'So you're not going?' fathomed Rebecca.

'Can't, can I?' said Albert, secretly glad he had an excuse not to: Jennifer was perhaps going to be there, and she was the last person he wished to encounter.

'I see,' said Rebecca, like she actually did.

Conversation gave sway to steady eating. Finishing first, Tony retreated to what he liked to call his study, citing unfinished work.

'Some last dots to join up?' guessed Albert.

Rebecca slapped Albert's arm, and told him to clear the dishes. He cleared the dishes.

In the kitchen, Albert's gaze fell upon a photograph of Jackie, taken before her radical haircut. Poor Jackie, he thought. She'd often been on his mind recently, regretting his behaviour after she'd confessed a desire for him. But, looking at the photo, he knew why it was so hard to take her desires seriously: she was so unattractive. She had no place in the game — that's the attitude that naturally emerged. And now that her hair was all off, she was even funnier looking.

Poor Jackie, he thought again.

*

The water supply had been restored, as had the gas. The electricity supply had been re-established too, but had failed just after reconnection and was awaiting further attention. Above, some roofers were finishing the roof, and the delivery of junk shop furniture had already been unloaded. Deepdale Hall was now well on its way to being habitable, in Simon's opinion.

Simon was in the main room — the room with the grand stone fireplace. Late-afternoon sunlight was streaming in through the high windows, structuring the dusty, airy, resonant interior with ethereal beams and shafts. Oblivious to the building noises coming from above, Simon pressed the play button on his cassette machine — another hearing of the Words of Truth.

Before the beginning, commenced Albert's recorded voice, *there was a brilliant physicist called Godfrey who succeeded in producing the Equation of Everything. He was a white-haired, kindly old professor, and, like many of the people working in his field, he had grown old, weary and sad-eyed trying to develop the elusive theory that successfully unifies all the forces of nature into a single one ...*

In the short time until the story ended, Simon was rendered virtually transfixed by the profundity of the Words of Truth, as told by Albert Fox, the faithless prophet of Godfrey.

The story told, as his own version of reality began to slowly re-apprehend him, Simon turned to his companions and said, in his High Teacher voice, 'And now let us complete the charging of the battery for the mission to make Albert believe in himself.'

They held hands to form a circle around a prayer battery, chanting low mystical utterances as they shuffled slowly clockwise, earnestly invoking all the powers that be.

2.2
The Sign

It was the flowers, not her body, she had thrown on to the bed after Albert's departure. Once he'd left, Jennifer had felt annoyed, not distraught; disappointed, not broken-hearted. But she wouldn't dwell on it, she had consciously decided. He'd stayed for two weeks, it had been nice, but now he was gone, had been her deliberately adopted attitude. And with a week's groceries needing to be bought and house chores demanding to be done, she'd found little time to accommodate any other philosophy.

If Albert had asked why she had brought flowers home, Jennifer would have answered that she'd wanted him to accompany her to her parents' grave that afternoon. That it was *important* he accompany her, because it was something she'd not been able to do on her own. But he had not asked, and the flowers had gone into a vase in the living room instead, and she had just got on with her day. Now, however, alone in the house, Jennifer was sitting in her bedroom while the evening darkened around her. Alone, that is, save for the company of a growing sense of abandonment that was beginning to choke with a grip she feared might soon be capable of putting an end to her.

Jennifer gave enough room to introspection to know that what she was feeling now was the choking hands of the invisible presence that seemed to have always haunted her: a preternatural tendency to feel alone, even when with people. Even before the death of her parents, this feeling of isolation-even-among-company had shadowed her. And now it could bedevil her at the slightest provocation, whereupon she would paradoxically seek to be truly alone, leaving whatever company surrounded her.

Some called her shy; others sensitive; others neurotic.

The ambience of a poem she'd studied at school revisited her, a poem that described how she often felt, even at the best of times — and today was certainly not a best time.

> I feel like one
> Who treads alone
> Some banquet-hall deserted,
> Whose lights are fled,
> Whose garlands dead,
> And all but he departed.

That was it, she had known even in her schooldays. That was how she could often sadly feel, translated into imagery. The feeling of being estranged from the laughing hubbub of life and youth.

As well as her frequent feelings of estrangement, Jennifer knew she was indeed as shy as so many people found her. She could easily feel awkward when talking to people. Moreover, when she felt awkward — which was often — she believed she was acting like a damper upon whatever social situation it happened to be. It's not that she didn't feel clever or witty remarks form in her mind, it's that her shyness held them back, never to be uttered. Hence people brought Jennifer little comfort, and if those people were all high-spirited and boisterous, then they might as well be demon tormentors. But she had never really felt shy around John, and had always put it down to how the intimacy between them had so quickly developed – he'd kissed her within two hours of their first encounter. But then again, she had never really felt anything with John. As she'd eventually revealed to him, he had just been there, that's all, just there. And so had she. And sometimes they had sex, always at his initiation, except on a few experimental, early occasions and on their last night together.

Albert had been the exception to the pattern of Jennifer's life. Never had she taken to anyone as easily as she had to him. Right from the start, she had secretly marvelled at how being with him just seemed so comfortable, like they had known each other for years. She thought that maybe it was because he was so ready to act the foolish child to amuse that she'd never felt any embarrassment when with him – she couldn't inadvertently say or do anything sillier than he was wont to do himself on purpose.

Now, finally, she was beginning to feel the loss. She missed him and wanted him back, especially this night – she really needed him tonight. He had amused her so many times. He was a perfect distraction, and she wanted him for that, if for nothing else. He was also good looking, and she knew they had made an attractive pair. The only thing she didn't know was why he had suddenly left her when it had all seemed to be going so good, so good she'd told him she was growing to love him before he left, and she was not free with expressions of affection – she had never once told John she loved him, and he had never dared to ask her if she did. Albert, however, had been gushingly free with expressions of affection for her. He had made twelve dozen effusive, silly speeches about her being the misty incarnation of his dearest dreams; about her being too sacred to even touch; and when he did touch her, which had been often, about her kisses being like summer rain. 'You seem like some ethereal spirit,' he had whispered one night in the dim light of the bedroom. 'The gentle ghost of the gentlest angel.' And love had been a word he'd used many times. But not in the last few days, she now realised. In the last few days it had been as if some killing frost had crept over his doting exuberance for her.

Maybe a few fucks with no commitment was what he'd really wanted? she speculated. Men were like that, weren't they?

The phone rang, and after some numb hesitation, Jennifer went downstairs to answer it. It was Sarah – as she'd guessed it would be

— calling for confirmation of her and Albert's attendance at Ron's bonfire party. When informed that Albert had left her, Sarah, too, wondered if he'd just wanted a few fucks.

'Maybe,' said Jennifer, making an effort to sound more upbeat than she felt. 'Maybe.'

'So where's he gone?'

'Think he's gone back to Durham, Sarah. Can't have gone far, he's only got a few pounds.'

'He didn't say anything? No reasons?'

'Nothing. Just that he wanted to go.'

'How do you feel about it?'

'A bit disappointed, that's all,' reported Jennifer, giving her tone another lift. 'I'll soon get over it.'

'Will he be going to Ron's tonight?'

'No, he said he wasn't.'

Sarah shared the disappointment her sister reported feeling. She was disappointed that someone she had promoted as a companion for her younger sister had seemingly proved to be so fickle. However, her instincts tentatively counselled differently, and so she sought to persuade Jennifer to attend Ron's party on her own, secretly hoping she would be able to use the event to bring Albert and Jennifer back together.

Jennifer demurred at first, but finally agreed.

'Do you want me to pick you up, or can you make your own way over?' asked Sarah. 'The Durham bus from Darlington stops just a few minutes from the house.'

'I'll get the bus.'

'There's only one stop in Croxdale,' Sarah informed her. 'Have you got yourself a bloody mobile yet?'

'No, not yet. I nearly got one the other day.'

'Find a phone when you get off and one of us'll come to fetch you.'

'What time's the last bus back to Darlington?'

'Don't bother going back. Stay overnight. There'll be spare rooms. His family's gone away for the weekend.'

'Maybe. I'll see.'

Sarah passed on the address details, and told her sister that the fireworks were scheduled to start at ten o'clock.

'I'll be there,' said Jennifer. 'Bye.'

*

It was done. In the field by the stream in the grounds of Deepdale

Hall, by the light of a burning torch, the final charging of the prayer battery had been achieved. A full two hundred hours of directional prayer energy had been captured.

Some days previous, leaving Carl to oversee the restoration of the house, Simon had taken a coach back to London to tell his fellow High Teachers all about how their society had veered off course, and how he could set them right again, but they had dismissed him. He had begged them to allow him use of the battery they'd charged at Glastonbury, but was refused. And later, when they discovered him preaching his notions to a gathering of the society's lesser members, they encouraged the gathering to rail against him and chase him out of the temple. They would brook nothing of his mad, seditious talk. Talk of some place in County Durham being as spiritually active as Glastonbury. Talk of moving the society there, to some building he claimed he had sole access to, where together they could work on the advancement of all things paranormal and New Age. Talk of the Creator having been a physicist. Talk of a young man — a prophet who had no faith in himself but who was undoubtedly receiving telepathic messages from extraterrestrials. Talk of how the prophet had to be brought into the fold, for humanity needed him if it were to reach the stars before destroying itself. They would brook absolutely nothing of such nonsense — telepathic messages from extraterrestrials were wholly the privilege of their established leader, and anyone else who said they got them was either a liar or crazy.

After Simon's denouncement and vilification by the other High Teachers, only Phil had been prepared to listen. When Simon was ejected, Phil went with him, and later, in Simon's bedsit, he heard the full new Truth, which had become as clear as daylight in Simon's mind.

It was a natural advancement on the Orthrium Society, Simon had explained. The Orthrium Society had veered off course, missed the message, got it too mixed up with Judao-Christianity, which itself was a distortion and a twisting of the Truth as first revealed to Adam. But now a great unfolding in the convolutions of the Universal Truth was surely set to occur, and only they, Carl and Albert knew about it. Emissaries from other planets, other children of Godfrey, with civilisations, technologies and cultures so much more advanced than ours, were tentatively seeking to pass on their wisdom; their knowledge of Godfrey, the Creator. They were testing the receptivity of the squabbling human race to the Truth, investigating to see if earth society was ready. And the telepathically communicating aliens who had once sought to use the leader of the Orthrium Society as their mouthpiece had now chosen another voice.

'So th'why have they chosen someone who doesn't believe?' Phil had asked, as Carl had asked before him.

'The Cosmic Masters chose Albert precisely *because* he's so sceptical.' Simon had explained. 'They chose him because he's the last person on earth who would accept Godfrey on faith alone. Only when we *all* accept Godfrey on faith alone can they be sure we can be trusted with their advanced knowledge. If he can come to believe then anyone can. See how wise the Cosmic Masters are?'

That had been quite enough for Phil. He was on board.

That next day, Simon had given Phil his key to the society's temple, instructing him to enter secretly at night and take the reserve prayer battery. He'd balked at acquiring the battery they'd all charged at Glastonbury, for that would be taking liberties with other people's prayers, but the empty, reserve battery was fair game. Besides, he planned to return it, hopefully with no one the wiser. Then he had taken a coach back up north. And two days later, Phil had ridden up to Deepdale Hall on his old motorbike, with the borrowed prayer battery strapped to it.

Since acquiring the prayer battery, Simon, Carl and Phil had assiduously chanted and gesticulated and prayed to it to charge it with spiritual energy. Now that was done, Simon extinguished the burning torch and looked up at the evening stars. Carl also peered upward. Until making this trip, he had never experienced the night sky away from smothering street lights. Never seen Orion dominate. Never lain on his back in dewy grass to ponder the imponderable. Never felt smaller; never felt greater. Never felt more humble; never felt more godlike.

'Never used to know the stars wuz so bright,' he remarked, gazing up at the heavens alongside Simon. 'Never looked at 'em in London. Street lights flood 'em out, don't they?'

'That's right,' said Simon.

'But they're always there, ain't they?'

'They're even in the sky in the daytime,' explained Simon. 'But the sunlight overwhelms them. During the eclipse before the millennium, when the sun was blocked by the moon, you could see the stars.'

'I didn't see nuffink during the eclipse,' complained Carl. 'Just clouds. Wuz workin' hard that day, anyway — me mortgage was due. Cornwall, y'had to go, wern't it?'

'That's right. That's where I went. It was amazing.'

'Th'ould we go in now?' suggested Phil. 'The food will be th'ready soon.'

'In a minute,' said Simon, continuing to gaze at the starry sky.

A celestial event occurred.

'Fackin 'ell!' bellowed Carl. 'Did y'see that? What was it?'

A thread of white light had streaked across the constellation of Cassiopeia — a meteor.

'Th'ee what?' asked Phil. 'Th'what?'

'Dunno,' said Carl. 'A shooting star or summat.'

'Amazing,' breathed Simon, gazing at where the meteor had fleetingly shone with the brilliance of the brightest stars.

'Did you see it, Simon?' asked Carl.

'I did,' said Simon quietly.

'What was it?'

Looking deep into infinite space, Simon answered, 'It was a sign, Carl. That's what it was, a sign. Durham City's over that way. The time is at hand.'

'Yeah?' said Carl.

'Yes,' confirmed Simon. 'We get Albert tonight.'

2.3
Wounded Hearts

As the evening light began to thicken with shadow, Albert, too, began to feel a choking presence.

'For fuck's sake, switch the light on before I top myself,' he complained to Rebecca, who, clad in lilac sportswear, was performing aerobics by a dim window.

Albert had changed from his birthday shirt into his *Not Long Now* T-shirt, and in the sullen light its white lettering was the strongest hint of him Rebecca could see as he lay on his back upon her floor.

Without interrupting her exercises, she reached out and switched on a light, whereupon Albert's gaze fell directly on to another photograph of Jackie. It made him begin to feel ashamed. Jackie was a dear friend who had come to love him, and he had treated like her desires and needs were insignificant and comical.

He was a brute, he decided.

Suddenly, Rebecca abandoned her exercises, stomped over to Albert, loomed large over him, and railed, 'You need your head examined. What right have you got to complain about feeling miserable when you went and left the cosiest little set-up you could ever have hoped for? Why did you leave her? Are you mad?'

'Felt like it,' shrugged Albert, down on the floor.

'That won't do, Albert,' she retorted. 'Tell me the real reason.'

Albert got up and began putting his coat on.

'Where are you going?' demanded Rebecca.

'Arts Centre — to get away from your incessant criticism. You're disturbing me emotionally. Dredging up painful memories. In a fair and just world, you'd lend me a fiver as compensation.'

He held out his hand.

Rebecca looked at that hand, made a disgruntled, snorting noise, and went to her bag, which was hanging up in the hall.

Albert followed her.

'Here, take a tenner,' she said, crabbily. 'And here's a door key — don't come back till late.'

'Fiver'll do,' said Albert. 'Took a vow never to drink more than one pint again.'

'I haven't got a fiver,' said Rebecca, slapping the tenner into his palm.

363

Once the money was in his hand, Albert left the house without saying another word.

It was still drizzling.

Travelling at a pace that varied between a dawdle and a stroll, Albert extended the walk into the centre of Durham from the half hour Rebecca would budget for it, to a full hour.

It was not a happy hour.

At any other time in his life, if asked, Albert would have claimed he'd never *had* a happy hour, but would have made some joke about his unvarying melancholia, and boasted about how he could endure any misfortune or inner suffering. But in the hour it took him to drift into town, he'd also drifted into a leaden, despondent state that was grimly beyond those occasional, vaguely heavy and oppressive feelings he had experienced before. It was *tangibly* heavy and oppressive, and it felt a long way from being the stuff of comedy, or something he could endure for long.

He hadn't expected this.

By the time he reached the high pedestrian bridge, forsaken is how he felt. Utterly forsaken. Yet he knew — not the least for Rebecca having just shouted it at him — that he had no real business with the condition, for that very morning he'd willingly left the manifestation of all he'd ever so dreamily yearned for. To him, Jennifer *was* all that is brightest and best. At least all that is brightest and best in the real world.

Halfway along the bridge, he stopped to peer at the dark, cold river below. Downstream, shimmering bright upon the inky water, floated the glowing reflection of the cathedral. Looking up, he stared at the timeless edifice, floodlit against the raven sky. A sense arose within him that all he needed to do was go into the cathedral and earnestly say, "Help me, Jesus", and all would be well.

He felt scared. Scared he would cop out in this moment of despair. Cop out like how many millions had copped out before him? he wondered. Copped out only to waste their remaining time alive banging tambourines to secure a foolishly imagined blissful, eternal afterlife.

He spun away and walked on, leaving the bridge and crossing the Arts Centre car park. The absurd thing was, he found himself tidying his hair, hoping to get it looking sultry in case Monica, the attractive student who occasionally worked on the reception desk — who Ron had told him was always glancing at him — might be present tonight. 'Please be there,' he whispered. 'Please.' He yearned so much for a tender companion, yet that very morning he'd abandoned the tenderest of them all. The ambiguity was not hidden from him, yet he still cast a hopeful glance toward the reception upon entering the building.

Perhaps he did need his head examined, he conceded.

Monica was not around, and his spirits sank even further. Yet he knew perfectly that if she had been there, he would have gone home alone, even if she'd thrown herself at him. For although he fell into what he called love ten times a week, longing for the companionship of the various objects of his wandering desire, he was remarkably adept at avoiding even the slightest real involvement. If someone he desired ever returned the sentiment, something compelled him to slip away. As Ron had told Jackie, the few actual, consummated relationships he'd fallen into had come about by extreme coaxing or sheer force: prior to Jennifer, his last girlfriend had physically dragged him to bed, with him trying to hold on to furniture. Even Jennifer had needed to do a little gentle coaxing herself. It seemed to him he only wanted when he was not likely to get, and if he did inadvertently get, then he quickly got out. Getting out before he could hurt them with his inevitable abandonment was a prime consideration. He could never imagine leaving someone who really needed him, someone for whom he had grown to feel empathy, someone he had allowed to make an emotional investment in him, so he stayed alone. He was frightened of committing himself because he was so steadfast in his resolutions.

He'd long believed all that to be true, and had often told it to himself, but was uncertain today, for he was feeling so terribly forsaken himself for having forsaken Jennifer.

Yes, he needed his head examined, he decided.

There was no one he knew in the Arts Centre bar — there was hardly anyone in at all — but if ever he'd needed company, he needed it now. Everything had been a joke until now, even misery and love, but the joke seemed to have ended.

He bought a pint of lager, and sat on a stool at the end of the bar. After drinking half faster than doctors would recommend and leaving the remainder, he found himself walking out with a sense of urgency, as if he had somewhere better to go. Outside the building, quickly crossing the car park, he pushed his hands deep into his pockets and drew his coat around himself. Once back on the high pedestrian bridge, halfway along, he slowed to a halt. Again, he looked down to the dark waters. He wasn't sure at first, but he believed he felt like crying. Reviewing the course of his existence, he knew he had plenty to cry about, not least that he'd felt compelled to say goodbye to Jennifer, who'd miraculously materialised in his life like some redemptive angel at this very same spot only fifteen nights earlier, when he'd been fancifully picturing himself among the pale corpses.

He seemed to be grieving. Yes, the anguish and despair was that extreme. He felt like he was in deep mourning, and realised he was mourning his own dead self. Tonight, he knew that it was all in vain. He felt like some wraith in a shadowy realm, and even the outstretched arms of an enchantress like Jennifer could not lure him into the light. He had become his own ghost, and would forever be alone in his darkened world, gazing upon the living through tear-dimmed eyes, but never able to reach out his yearning hands, hands bound to his sides with unbreakable chains.

A male voice arose to quote a couplet:

> *'As when some great painter dips*
> *His pencil in the gloom of earthquake and eclipse.'*

The voice spoke again. 'That's what you look like, Albert.'

His careering slide into despair arrested by the mysterious voice, Albert slowly looked up from the dark waters. It was Joe, wearing a faded denim jacket. But he wasn't looking depressed today, or even appearing to be capable of such a small business.

'Shouldn't you be dead?' observed Albert baldly. 'I paid good money for it. You owe me a hundred quid, you fraud.'

'I came back from the dead,' said Joe, stepping closer, his recently-shaven face oozing a curious, almost beatific, smile. 'Came back from that dark, frightening tomb of self-doubt.'

Albert was unimpressed and uninterested. 'I wish I could come back from the dead,' he muttered, looking down to the river again. 'I'm a ghost, that's what I am, haunting a dark land.'

There was no reply. Eventually, Albert looked up to see if Joe was still there, and saw that he was holding out an upturned hand, a hand bearing some pills.

'Of twelve fruits from the Tree of Life procured, seven remain,' said Joe, proffering them to a bemused Albert. 'Go on, take them — you paid for them.'

Albert still bore a bemused look.

'Those people you sent me to were out of heroin,' explained Joe.

'All they had was ecstasy, so I spent your money on twelve tabs, ignorantly hoping that twelve might kill me. I'd never taken the stuff before, so first I thought I'd take just one to see what it was like before I overdosed on the rest, but when it kicked in... You saved my life trying to kill me, Albert.'

Albert had never taken ecstasy either. He'd never even been in the presence of someone on it — he'd never been anywhere near a club, and hadn't gone to a party in years. Despite Ron's mother's conjecture, he barely had any drug experience at all, beyond the occasional bit of dope, and LSD a handful of times when he'd been an experimental teenager, before he'd taken to his bedroom big time. However, he was not entirely ignorant about ecstasy. He knew it was not addictive, and that it was supposed to confer happiness — but then again, so was whisky. However, despite the cynicism he inevitably had about its supposed effects, he was certainly not inclined to be prejudiced against the stuff because of all those popular newspaper reports concerning youngsters dropping dead. *New Scientist* informed him that such deaths were statistically much, much rarer than swimming accidents, and were for the most part preventable. He knew that those one-in-a-million-trip rarities had usually keeled over from dance-induced heat exhaustion or dehydration, or from ill-advised *over-enthusiastic* water drinking, leading to vital electrolytes being lost from the body, leading to coma and death.

'I've never done ecstasy either,' said Albert.

'So accept these,' said Joe, before enthusiastically quoting,

> *Those eat now, who never ate before;*
> *And those who always ate, now eat the more!*

Albert looked at Joe. With a cheerless what-the-hell attitude, he held his hand out. 'Go on, then.'

Joe tipped seven pills into Albert's palm.

'No, wait a minute,' he said, snatching one pill away. 'Just have six.'

Albert studied the six pills remaining in his hand. They were white, about the size of aspirins, and embossed with a kite mark.

'Go on, take one,' urged Joe. 'It's the best stuff that's been around in ages, according to reports.'

'Are you on it now?'

'I'd be far more serious about feeling happy if I was. It does that, you see — makes you take happiness seriously. Well, it did with me, at least.'

'So you've forgotten all that Antichrist stuff?' perceived Albert dubiously. 'Just like that?'

A dark look crossed Joe's face, and his voice became grave. 'No, such things could never be truly forgotten. But under the tender authority of these pills, I saw so clearly that you were right, Albert.'

'Me, right? About what?'

'You told me to tell her to fuck off.'

'Did I?'

'You did,' said Joe, 'and you were right. I wasn't to blame for it all going pear-shaped. I'm truly certain of that now. My crippling self-doubt washed away. Upon taking that angelic pill, I saw deep into my own conscience and found that corner of it to be as clear as a dew pool. So I did it: told the Antichrist to fuck off. Told her to fuck off big time. Should have done it ten years ago. She called me and started on some brand-new infuriating made-up stuff, so I just thought, no, I'm stepping out of her grotesque pantomime once and for all. Putting every thought of it behind me. Don't care how many daughters I've barely even met I have to forsake. I told her firmly that until and unless she stops being a weird, lying, crazy witch, she could just fuck right off. Then I rang off. Just like that. And I don't feel bad about it at all. I'm free from it all at long last, Albert. *Reborn*.'

Holding up his remaining E, Joe began to quote again, a passage Albert recognised from Milton's *Paradise Lost*:

> *'So deep the power of these ingredients pierced,*
> *Even to the inmost seat of mental sight*
> *That Adam, now enforced to close his eyes,*
> *Sank down, and all his spirits became entranced*
> *But him the gentle angel by the hand soon raised.'*

'Cool,' said Albert, now viewing the tablets in his hand with some wonder, awe and respect.

'Eat and re-enter Eden,' urged Joe.

'Is it anything like acid?' asked Albert, a little fearfully. His final LSD trip, a three-tabber, hadn't been such a pleasant ride, and he'd decided then to avoid bumpy excursions in future.

'It's a feather bed,' said Joe.

'Is it anything like being stoned?' worried Albert. 'I can barely handle even being stoned these days.'

'It's a blessed balm for wounded hearts.'

Putting five of the pills into his coat's inside pocket, Albert popped the sixth.

'Ugh!' he blurted. 'It tastes fucking awful! You've broken my tongue.'

'You're not supposed to chew it,' said Joe despairingly.

'I was curious,' protested Albert between grimaces.

'Wanker,' said Joe.

'Need some water,' announced Albert, loping back toward the Arts Centre. Upon entering, he saw that his abandoned half pint was still on the bar, and he chose that over water from the toilet taps. Swigging most of it down at once, he succeeded in cleansing his mouth of the bitter, pungent taste of the E and God knows what else that was also in the pill.

Scanning the bar, he couldn't see Joe anywhere. He had expected him to follow, but he evidently hadn't. Looking through a window facing the high bridge, he saw that Joe wasn't there, either.

Albert sat on his stool again. Staring into his remaining inch of beer, he began feeling just as forsaken as when before Joe had distracted him. It was still early, too, and he was at a complete loss to know what to do with the rest of his evening, let alone the rest of his life. He didn't want either of them. He couldn't even have another pint, on account of his vow to Jackie. Still, he'd taken some new drug, he reminded himself, so at least that might provide a distraction. And even if the trip was to turn out bad, the prospect of a drug-induced psychological nightmare mercifully offered hope of something better than he was feeling right now.

He glanced around the bar again. For a Saturday night, it was peculiarly poorly attended. He supposed people were attending fireworks displays. Over by the fruit machine were four local lads, and he began overhearing their philosophies.

'And what about the fucking Abos?' proposed one. 'They're supposed to be about fifty generations behind us.'

'They should be gassed,' said another. 'The black cunts.'

How any of that throwback foursome could see itself as relatively advanced staggered Albert, and listening to their theories filled him with despair. The existence of those lads, and the many thousands like them, made it all seem so hopeless. This was not a sanguine night for him, and their mindlessness made him think he really had had enough of life on planet earth. Turning to address them, he said, 'And if you do gas them, who in the fuck is there going to be left for people like you to imagine superiority over?'

'Who in the fuck asked you to open y'poncy gob?' snarled one once the shock of being challenged had passed.

They were an odious collection, and Albert was spoiling for a fight with them. A fight against all that was wrong with the world, perfectly represented by those four thickheads who for the span of their lives would be using up resources and polluting the planet, giving only their petty crime and aggression in return. But he wasn't really thinking about the justifications. He wasn't thinking at all. He was just feeling — feeling he was about to do something desperate. He'd had enough.

He could have argued eloquently, but didn't. What he did was to make the pretence of calmly replying, slipping off his seat to step innocuously toward them, but viciously headbutting the biggest and hoofing another in the midriff. An attack was the last thing they were expecting from someone like him, and they had been wide open. Both went down, the first silently, the second with an explosive groan. He was being hit. Heedlessly facing the onslaught, he brought a third yob to his knees with a furious attack. Three of the four were now down, and the fourth had disappeared — run away, it seemed.

Less than ten seconds after the first blow, Albert was rushing out of the building.

But he hadn't done or said any of that. There had been no fight. He'd wanted to smash them so badly; vividly imagined the scene; believed that with surprise on his side he could have emerged victorious; believed the attack would have been adequately brutal. But he had done nothing. Hadn't even challenged them verbally.

They were about to leave now, it seemed, not knowing how close they'd come to desperate retribution. Watching them go, Albert imagined following them until he could get one or two on their own, then... his anger suddenly deflated. What was the point in getting upset about the ruination of the world? What was the point? What was the fucking point? It was all ultimately meaningless.

'Hello, Albert, thought I might find you here,' said a subdued female voice, and Albert realised his heart had lifted for a moment, thinking it was Jennifer. Looking over his shoulder, he saw that it wasn't. It was her sister, wearing a long, black coat not too dissimilar to his own. Her face was clean of make-up, and her hair was drawn into a tight ponytail. She was looking grave, but her expression seemed to soften a degree when she saw that he himself was looking far from carefree. 'Well, it didn't take you long to make me regret introducing you to Jennifer.'

Albert felt an unwelcome sense of shame. Saying nothing, he returned to staring into his glass.

Sarah continued her criticism. 'I don't suppose she's feeling very happy tonight, Albert.'

'Nor am I,' he muttered.

'She was happy. At least she seemed happier than she has for a long time. Just wanted you to know that.'

'Are you thanking me or laying guilt?' he retorted, immediately regretting the crass, evasive, defensive gibe.

'Neither,' stated Sarah stiffly. 'Just wanted you to know she really liked you.'

Albert said nothing, other than to sullenly suggest they move to a table.

'Want to know what she said about you?' asked Sarah as Albert led her away from the bar. 'She said since meeting you she'd stopped feeling so bad about feeling bad, the way you joke about feeling melancholic. It was a small miracle she even admitted she ever felt bad.'

Not replying, Albert dropped heavily on to a chair at a small table, and Sarah sat opposite him.

'You've no idea,' continued Sarah, 'how much more spontaneous she was when she was with you.'

'Write me a letter about it,' said Albert, with a weary sullenness.

Sarah stared at him. 'So why did you leave her?'

'Because I felt I should.'

'That's no answer.'

'Too bad.'

Sarah was in a fearfully serious mood, and Albert wanted out. He felt himself about to walk away, but forced himself to stay out of strained courtesy. And besides, he couldn't think of anywhere else to go.

'Is there something about her you don't like?' Sarah wanted to know. 'Or did you just get bored with screwing her?'

'No,' said Albert quietly. 'She's a dream come true.'

'So why are you here and not with her?'

Sighing with exasperation, he realised he'd have to give a plausible reason otherwise he'd get no peace. After a struggle with contemplation, he said, 'Because I don't want to see her wasting her precious days chasing after what she thinks I am.'

'And what do you think she thinks you are?'

'Worth it,' said Albert decisively.

Upon that retort, Sarah cast a disapproving look his way, but, to his relief, her stern aspect quickly subsided. However, she remained horribly terse. 'Getting Jennifer out of her bedroom and into some company tonight seemed a pretty important thing, so I persuaded her to come this way without you for Ron's bonfire party at his parents' place. So if you want to see her, that's where she'll be later. Ten o'clock the fireworks start.' Firmly, she added, 'But don't tell her I came looking for you.'

'Ron's mother hates me.'

'His family's gone away.'

'I can't go. I really don't want to see Jennifer.'

'Fine,' said Sarah, rising from her seat, making it clear she intended to expend no more breath on the issue. 'See you around.'

She left.

Sitting with the dregs of his beer, Albert was aware of a certain feeling of satisfaction arising from her driven-away-departure. He felt in control. He felt solid and self-contained, just like he'd felt that morning when he'd left Jennifer's flat.

'Getting anything yet?' chirped a voice.

It was Joe.

'Where did you disappear to?' demanded Albert sullenly.

'The bogs, and then the bar to get a drink,' said Joe, not understanding how Albert could have imagined he'd vanished.

'Oh,' said Albert, realising it was probably only five minutes since he'd seen him last. 'I looked for you.'

'Should have looked in the bogs,' said Joe. 'Who was that young woman you were talking to?'

'My girlfriend's sister.'

Joe sat opposite Albert.

'How come you're looking so miserable tonight when you've got a girlfriend who probably looks like her?'

'I left her this morning. Her sister came to have a go at me.'

'So she's your ex-girlfriend,' corrected Joe. 'Maybe someone else's girlfriend by now?'

That speculation jarred and hurt Albert, and it must have shown.

'Sorry,' said Joe, shrugging, 'just stating the obvious.' He took a swig of his beer. 'Anyway, back to the original question: are you getting anything yet?'

Albert was momentarily puzzled, but then realised Joe was referring to what he himself had already forgotten: he'd taken some E.

'Bugger all. Take more than a pill to elevate my mood.'

Joe gave a little smile.

Albert took a sip of his drink, and Joe took a swig of his.

'So,' said Joe, placing his palms together and leaning forward a little, 'tell me why you left your girlfriend this morning.'

'Oh for fuck's sake,' protested Albert, throwing his arms up, 'not another one. Why can't people give me a break?'

Joe gave another little smile. 'Just curious, that's all. Curious why you left her when it seems you still want her. At least it seems you don't want anyone else to have her.'

'Leave out the head examination, will you?'

'Okay,' smiled Joe. 'So tell me about your childhood.'

Albert sighed with bad tempered exasperation while Joe chuckled.

'Well tell me about your adulthood then,' pursued Joe, mischievously.

Albert threw him a look which bounced off.

'Well tell me how your plans to lead the world into a new age of romanticism are coming along,' said Joe.

'They're coming along shit, and that's all you need to know about my life.'

'Okay,' smiled Joe, and he drank some more of his beer.

Mere seconds later, Albert began to realise he was feeling uneasy. Agitated, slightly. Anxious, slightly. Queasy, slightly. It was a very sudden thing, and he felt compelled to get up and use his limbs. Walk a little. It was the drug, he quickly understood. He was worried – this seemed like how he remembered coming up on acid, but even more physical. Now that it seemed imminent, he definitely didn't want a drug-induced psychological nightmare this night, of all nights. He told Joe he was going to the toilet, a facility which he felt he needed to use anyway. In there, he occupied a cubicle, taking a tiny, nervous piss before sitting on the edge of the seat, hopefully to compose himself. He became aware of visual changes. Like on acid, colours were becoming enhanced, but only subtly. His perception of space was becoming distorted too, but again only subtly. He sat for what seemed many minutes, waiting. Something big, and perhaps unbearable, seemed poised to happen. He kept examining things to test for the onset of full-blown acid effects: looking at the flesh on his hands; the door hinges; the ceiling; the patterns on the tiles on the floor. Nothing seemed to be anything more than subtly altered.

This was ridiculous, he thought, he'd have to leave soon. He'd been waiting ages.

He unbolted the cubicle door and stepped out, and it felt like some meaningful emergence. Leaving the toilets, the bar room seemed more intimate and lively than before; brighter and warmer.

'Was I in there long?' he asked Joe as he sat down, looking somewhat bewildered by it all.

'Not really. Why?'

'I'm definitely getting something now.'

'And how is it?'

Albert gauged things for a few seconds. 'I think it's going to be a feather bed.'

A *chirrup* noise came from Joe's pocket, and he took his phone out. 'Message from the Antichrist,' he said plainly. 'She says she wants to marry me.'

Joe simply dropped the phone into his beer, where it instantly died.

'Good work,' murmured Albert.

Maintaining his equanimity, Joe went off to the bar.

Albert was intrigued with the druggy effects he was experiencing. Looking around the room, the people, in an indescribable way, seemed more... more alive. Yes, there was *life* here. He seemed to be catching peoples' eyes, and they were nice people. Happy, welcoming people. And the women all looked angelic. But the most intriguing thing of all was the dawning awareness of a smile beginning to spread itself across his face.

Joe returned with a beer that didn't have a phone in it.

'So tell me why you left your girlfriend this morning,' he said, reoccupying his seat.

The ambience suddenly changed for Albert. Like the mood had been sucked in. 'I don't know,' he said quietly. 'I don't know.'

'So tell me about your childhood, then.'

'What do you want to know?'

'The usual things. Was it happy?'

'No,' returned Albert. A pause followed. 'There were times when I was happy. I suppose when I was outside, messing around.'

'So you were mostly unhappy at home?' deduced Joe.

'That's where it was all wrong.' A pause, then, barely audible, 'You wouldn't believe how wrong.'

'Abuse?'

'No, no,' Albert came back quickly. 'No sexual abuse, if that's what you mean. The existence of sex was something never ever acknowledged in my house.'

'Physical abuse?'

'Sometimes,' answered Albert. 'Violent outbursts from my father. Worst when I was small... just four or five or six.' He paused, as if sadly recalling those distant traumas. 'My mother used to plead with him not to hit me on the head when he was lashing out.' He paused again. 'Some of the stupidest things would turn him violent. Coming between him and his view of the TV could do it. There was always the chance it would suddenly happen for some reason or other — that was worse than the occasional blows themselves.'

'Did he ever hit your mother?'

'No, never.'

'So, apart from all that, what else was wrong about your childhood?'

Drugged though he was, Albert was aware that Joe was playing the analyst, but he seemed helpless not to go along with it. He was a willing volunteer of sorts, able to voice things that, at other times, he would simply dismiss as irrelevant; mutely feel; or deny feeling at all. For the first time in his life, he was not throwing a reflex blanket of evasion over awkward questions. He had the novelty of discussion without repression or fear of admission... or comedy. Moreover, he was saying what he felt, not what he'd intellectualised. He'd always known he'd had an unhappy childhood and had been shaped by it, but now he was lamenting and acknowledging the discontent, not just glibly detailing it, or cynically dismissing it.

'Love,' decided Albert.

'Love?'

'I never heard the word. Nothing even close. Never even heard a term of endearment.'

'But was love shown?' asked Joe.

'No. Never... Not normally.'

'No cuddles from your mum?'

'Fuck no. The only time she ever tried to hug me was the same day she was committed to an institution. She'd never even held my hand before, not even when we were crossing the road when I was a toddler. Before long, I'm sure I would have slapped her hand away if it had come too close.'

'That's sad,' commented Joe. 'What do you mean when you say

she'd tried to hug you? What happened?'

'She went completely mad one time,' reported Albert, slowly shaking his head with the lamentable incredulousness of it all. 'She didn't sleep for days on end. Didn't even sit down. A cut on her foot swelled up like a purple balloon. I was sixteen, but she'd become convinced I was a little boy again.' He looked at Joe. 'Wasted from self-inflicted starvation, dripping Holy Water she used to splash over herself to banish her imagined demon tormentors, desperately clutching her Rosary Beads for divine protection, she shuffled over to me, arms awkwardly outstretched, and—'

'And?' pursued Joe.

'I just side-stepped her and left the house,' Albert admitted quietly. 'Coldly side-stepped her.'

Allowing some seconds to pass, Joe asked, 'Where is she now?'

'Don't know,' confessed Albert. 'In some hospital, I suppose, if she's still alive. I used to get garbled letters till I moved to some new place and didn't tell her. Can't believe she could still be alive, she neglected herself so much. She used to think the devil kept her alive just to torment her.'

'What about your father? What was he like?'

Albert shook his head. 'You wouldn't believe any of it.'

'Try me.'

Struggling to find a way in, Albert began, 'It's difficult to... In many ways, he had the mental age of a child. When I was small, outside the house, he acted like an amiable buffoon, prepared to do anything to help people... to stop them disliking him. Inside the house, his frustrations and explosive anger held sway. But it was all so odd.' Albert fell quiet, subject to a momentary reverie. 'You know, he never once called my mother by her own name?'

'Never?'

'Only if someone official knocked on the door — I mean, like the woman who collected the milk money. And people like that were the only people to knock on our door. We never had a guest. Ever. Or a relative. I've never even met any of my relatives. I never even had a friend in the house when I was a kid. Didn't want it. They never got past the doorstep. The house was so ugly. He used to call my mother Sonia. Her name was Mary, but he called her Sonia. Sonia was the name of the woman he'd wanted to marry.'

'Shit,' breathed Joe. 'Way to depersonalise and demean.'

'Guess so,' agreed Albert, quietly. 'But in turn my mother never used his name either. She called him "you". Or pointedly "you

376

there" if she had to pull his peculiar attention away from the TV. But I don't think he ever even noticed she didn't use his name.'

'Pretty dysfunctional,' said Joe.

'You don't know half of it,' said Albert. He paused before looking at Joe, quietly stating, 'They weren't evil or calculating in the things they did.'

'You seem to have ambivalent feelings about them,' perceived Joe.

'I do,' agreed Albert. 'I do. If they'd been bad, it would have been easier to live with, maybe. But they weren't bad, just inadequate. They did their crap best.'

'Did they?' questioned Joe.

Albert fell into another reflective silence. 'She never stopped making sacrifices for me,' he sadly — guiltily — remembered. 'That was her way of showing her love. She never spent any money on herself. Hardly ever ate. What little cheap weird stuff she did eat she ate standing up in a corner of our tiny kitchen. Can you imagine it, a woman who never once sat down to eat in her own home? Year in, year out.'

'I can't imagine it,' said Joe. 'But how did you feel about that? Seeing her neglecting herself so much to make more for you?'

Albert shook his head, and spoke in a tone of regretful disbelief. 'Joe, she wasn't a real person to me.'

'How do you mean she wasn't a real person?'

'I never... never considered she had feelings of her own. Just never considered it. She was just like some odd, spectral presence.' He paused before murmuring, 'How strange. I can't believe I was like that.'

Perceiving Albert's internal trial, Joe told him, 'You were a child, not an adult. A child in an obviously hugely dysfunctional environment. A child who was never properly made to feel wanted. That's a terrible thing for a child. Why feel guilty about not feeling empathy there?'

It seemed Albert hadn't heard Joe. 'She disgusted me,' he remembered, with obvious guilt. 'Disgusted me. I'd forgotten how *much* she disgusted me. I could hardly bring myself to touch even the clothes in her wardrobe. Really couldn't. If I had to touch her stuff, I'd have to wash my hands afterwards.' He paused. 'I shut them out of my mind. Completely. Coldly. One day, when I was thirteen, she asked me if I'd be better off if she were dead. I just said yes and walked off. The next day, she overdosed. I found her unconscious when I got back from school, but I didn't even interrupt my plans for five minutes. Just went out to kick a football around and bully a few kids, as usual.' He paused, shamefully and incredulously remembering forgotten things. 'I was a bully, wasn't I? A terrible bully.'

'Were you?'

'I was. I was relentless with some of them, day in day out. I was the worst thing in some other people's childhood. How terrible. Shame on me.'

'But you're sweet now, aren't you?'

Albert was quiet a time before murmuring, 'I stole a Simon & Garfunkel album when I was fourteen and it made me too romantic and maudlin to cause any more trouble.'

Joe laughed, but Albert's humour had been inadvertent, and he was far from feeling amused himself, staring into unhappy, distant times.

'Your mother — did she die after you found her unconscious?'

'No, she survived,' said Albert after some seconds. 'She always survived.'

'Other attempts?'

'Lots. She even survived dropping an electric fire in her bath. She had no idea it would hurt. The screams were terrible before she fell unconscious. It was me who unplugged her. I thought she was dead. We didn't have a phone, so I yelled out the window to a passer-by to get the police, then just got on with my breakfast. That's all, just got on with my breakfast. Feeling nothing.'

'Albert, don't feel guilty about doing what you had to to survive it all. What had she ever done to make you love her? To *let* you love her.'

Albert stared at his empty glass. 'But she was a person too. How could I not have felt anything at all? She was dead before my eyes — so I thought — and I just ate my breakfast. It was like I'd built an impenetrable glass wall around myself. I saw what was around me, but it couldn't touch me.'

'You had to do that to protect yourself,' said Joe supportively. 'Internally isolating yourself.'

'Maybe,' said Albert quietly, continuing to stare at his empty glass. Fainter still, he repeated, 'Maybe.'

Joe did something surprising. He flicked a finger against Albert's beer glass, making it ring, and said, 'You left your girlfriend this morning — still isolating yourself?'

378

Albert glanced at Joe. 'Maybe,' he admitted.

'Together long?'

'No,' said Albert, looking at his empty glass again. 'Just a few weeks.'

'And what about the thousand other weeks?'

Albert didn't answer, until finally he succumbed to a kind of defensive sullenness. Taking a deeper breath, sitting back and looking at Joe, he stated in a voice that was a blend of a weary sigh and a boast, 'I can ignore desires for companionship, comfort, love.'

'Not something you should sound proud of,' said Joe.

'I know that,' returned Albert quickly. 'I know that. Anyway, it's a sham. It must be — at times I've felt so lonely. And I fall in love all the time.'

'No one falls in love all the time,' asserted Joe. 'Not real love.'

Albert looked at his empty glass again. 'I do. A walk to the shops can leave me sad for days.'

'So at the same time as rejecting love and companionship, you also seem to desperately crave it?'

'Seems that way,' admitted Albert, quietly.

Joe took a drink before methodically resuming his exploration of Albert's psyche. 'So, Albert, you say you fall in love all the time, but its always from a distance, isn't it? And this morning you put your actual girlfriend at a distance, didn't you? Seems you prefer the safety of distance, doesn't it?'

Albert didn't respond.

'So tell me, Albert,' pursued Joe, 'why do you reject love? Do you think it's because you've never learned to trust it?'

'Maybe,' said Albert, sullenly.

'So tell me why you left your girlfriend this morning, even though it's obvious to me you miss her.'

He couldn't escape, deny or ignore it now. Joe's probing had finally brought Albert to the admission he'd been avoiding for years. 'Because I was scared,' he confessed quietly, lifting his earnest gaze to meet Joe's. 'Scared of ever *really* loving someone. Ever depending on someone. Ever needing someone. I've got by by never needing or wanting anyone, not even my own mother.'

Sympathetically, Joe said, 'You've kept that defensive wall up around yourself for too long. You're just scared to let anyone at all inside, where they can do you harm.'

'I know,' agreed Albert, staring at his empty glass again.

'But they can also do you good,' said Joe. 'Maybe it's time you dared to let someone in. After all, you crave love. You said so yourself.'

'I do,' admitted Albert. 'But I've always turned love into a big joke. It's always a joke with me. And every other need or want in life I might have is mocked.'

'You're not mocking tonight,' observed Joe.

'No, I'm not,' realised Albert, feeling the druggy ambience changing again.

'Maybe it really is time you dared.'

'It is,' agreed Albert, becoming bolstered, and looking directly at Joe. 'It's never felt more fucking right, and if I've ever met someone worth the risk, it's Jennifer.'

'Who's Jennifer?'

'My girlfriend... the one I left this morning.'

'No scales or sulphurous smell about her, I trust?' asked Joe with mock gravity.

'No, no,' Albert came back earnestly, 'not like that demon in a dress you know. Not her. She's wonderful. Gentle. Sincere.'

'Then love her, Albert,' urged Joe.

'I will,' said Albert, seriously.

'And let her love you,' demanded Joe, 'because living without love isn't living at all in this sorry world. There's nothing else, Albert. Nothing else.'

'I will let her love me,' said Albert determinedly. 'I bloody well will.'

'Well, you'd better hurry up and find her before the drug wears off. You might slip back into your old ways.'

Hurrying was suddenly paramount in Albert's mind. Joe was right, for despite the big, brave talk, he knew he might lose his resolve once the ecstasy wore off. 'Right,' he declared, 'I'm going now.'

'Excellent behaviour,' smiled Joe.

'Come with me,' suggested Albert keenly. 'Do an E too. I'm going to a mate's fireworks party. She'll be there.'

'Can't. Got to meet someone soon. Stop wasting time talking to me, Albert, and hurry to Jennifer.'

'Yes,' agreed Albert. Standing up, he experienced a most overwhelming sensation, like a wave, or rush, of pure, warm, sweet bliss had washed through him. 'Wow,' he murmured, with a highly appreciative, far-out expression. 'Ecstasy.'

380

2.4
The Great Mission

On the steps of the Arts Centre, Albert paused to consider the perfect serenity of the night. All was well with the world, except that he very soon began to feel the cold, even though it was not a particularly cold evening. He blamed the drug. 'A small price to pay,' he laughed to the beautifully dark sky.

He was overwhelmed by another wave of sensuous bliss.

A bus. He had to get the bus that passed through Croxdale. He'd never been inside Ron's parents' house, but Ron had often pointed out the lane that led from the busy Croxdale main road to their place, so he knew the bus would drop him within an easy stroll of Jennifier tonight.

Walking across the pedestrian bridge, he felt good — *so* good. Every sorrow he'd ever embraced was dispelled; every anxiety soothed. The unredressed wrongs and unavenged insults of his lifetime were too small a business to recall. Everything was beautiful and nothing hurt.

Halfway along the bridge, he stopped to look over the side. 'Hey, miserable pale corpses,' he shouted down to the river, 'this'll sort you out.'

He dropped one of his ecstasy pills into the river.

Leaving the bridge, he set off on the shortest route to the bus station, which was across the cathedral square. Everyone and everything appeared so innocuous. Every open, lit door seemed to softly beckon him in. He was a citizen of the universe tonight, and the universe knew his joy. He felt *so* overwhelmingly good, he was compelled to lie on his back on a bench between the floodlit cathedral and its car park, simply to enjoy the novel perspective.

A vehicle was pulling up near him, but he paid it no heed. He just lay there, smiling at the sky.

'Albert,' called a nervous male voice.

Albert turned his head and saw three figures wearing *Not Long Now* T-shirts standing near him, in front of a black cab. He quickly recognised Simon and Carl, but the third was a stranger to him.

'Not long now,' said Albert derisively. 'You sorry losers. Take them off. Take them off.'

'No,' returned Simon, with meek yet steely defiance. 'Not long now until the Golden Millennium.'

'Take them off!'

Simon aimed a prayer battery at Albert — Albert remembered sneering at just such a contraption shown on that television documentary.

'Believe!' commanded Simon as he pressed the battery's button. 'Believe in yourself!'

'I do!' giggled Albert joyfully, throwing his limbs around. 'I do! I believe!'

Simon's spirit rose almost as high as Albert's. The prayer zap had worked! It had bloody-well worked! He had brought about a *bone fide* mystical miracle.

Albert jumped to his feet and into the cab, sliding to the far side of the wide seat.

'Come on!' he urged the trio.

Simon bundled himself and the prayer battery into the cab, sitting on the wide seat with Albert. The stranger to Albert, Phil, climbed in after him, squeezing up against Simon, pulling the door shut. Carl occupied the driver's seat.

'Godfrey bless you all,' said Albert.

'And you,' returned Simon, fazed yet exhilarated.

Confused and unsure, Carl looked over his shoulder to Simon for instructions.

'Quick, Carl,' said Albert, 'I need a lift somewhere. Drive.'

'Where to?'

'Onwards!' answered Albert. 'Forever onwards!'

Following a more detailed discussion, Simon sanctioned a drive to Croxdale. Along the way, Albert was in full sail. 'Waiting,' he explained, answering Simon's inquiry as to why he had been lying on his back on a bench.

'For what?' asked Simon.

'That's the weird thing,' said Albert, with an air of awed wonder. 'I'd felt strangely persuaded to remain there. I had this sort of feeling that something inescapable was going to happen. Then *whoosh!* You zapped me with belief.'

'Amazing,' breathed Simon. 'It would have been the forces working on you again, keeping you where we could find you. We'd gone to your old place first, but it was empty, so we just drove around looking for you.'

Albert felt uncomfortable. Cramped. He wanted to sprawl, and at once decided he should be the sole occupant of the cab's rear seat. Using his foot, he pulled down one of the two spring-loaded, rear-facing seats. 'Let me have the back seat to myself, Simon, I need to lounge. That was quite a blast you gave me. I'm winded.'

'Of course,' said Simon understandingly, at once moving over.

'You too,' said Albert, addressing the person unknown to him, who also moved over, occupying the second rear-facing seat.

Soon Albert was reclining across the full width of the wonderfully warm cab. Sorted, he thought.

'I've th'never met a prophet before,' lisped Phil to Albert.

Albert looked at Phil and was about to say something when his world pleasantly wobbled for a second or two, taking his attention away. It was as if his eyes had kind of shuddered, closely followed by another wave of bliss. '*Yes*,' he breathed appreciatively, sitting upright.

'What is it?' asked Simon keenly, pushing his glasses up. 'What happened to you? You went into a sort of trance.'

'I got a surge,' said Albert.

'Maybe we crossed a ley line,' suggested Simon. 'You're really sensitive to ley lines, remember. Have you had any more telepathic messages?'

'I'm getting a powerful one right now,' said Albert, producing the air of mystery that never failed to breeze Simon along with it, 'the strongest ever.'

'Amazing,' breathed Simon.

'So that's it,' murmured Albert, appearing to be in a state of profound abstraction.

'What?' implored Simon, pushing his glasses up. 'What?'

Albert looked into Simon's bespectacled eyes and said, 'Our great mission, Simon. Our great mission. The reason we've all been brought together. The greatest mission ever.'

'What mission?'

Albert leaned forward, grasped Simon by the shoulders, and proclaimed, 'To succeed where Christ failed.'

The ambience instantly changed for Albert, became chilled. That was an intense thing to have said in his druggy condition. Butterflies of apprehension fluttered in his belly.

Simon was awe-struck.

'Th'great!' said Phil in his unique, cartoon voice, as if a trip to the seaside for donkey rides had been suggested.

Releasing his grip on Simon, Albert leaned back against the seat. It was the drug, he told himself, that had made him feel so unnerved. Nevertheless, the atmosphere felt so charged he actually began thinking that maybe it was true? Maybe he *was* on a mission? He suddenly felt scared. Scared for his own sanity. This was a most unreal journey. But he quickly got over his fleeting, drug-induced megalomania crisis. Aw, fuck it, he thought: he was simply in a cab with two nutters, being driven by a third, having a laugh at their expense. And he was tripping to boot. The day he couldn't handle this sort of thing without thinking he'd been sent by the powers that be would simply be the day he'd stop doing it.

Simon murmured, 'What mission? Where did Christ fail?'

'The mission to create peace on earth, of course,' answered Albert simply.

'Th'great!' said Phil, stroking his trimmed beard.

'How?' asked Simon.

'By influencing all minds with mine,' returned Albert, with rising passion. 'You see, Simon, this very night I achieved nirvana.' He held up a clenched fist. 'I am now Buddha. I am now Christ. I am the Saviour. I am Albert Fox.'

'Amazing,' breathed Simon.

'Th'what's nirvana?' lisped Phil.

'The serenity in my soul,' answered Albert.

'Amazing,' breathed Simon.

Now the biggest wave of nirvana yet hit Albert, and he virtually swooned.

'Another ley line?' guessed Simon, in unabated awe and wonder.

For a purpose, Albert began chortling to himself.

'What is it?' asked Simon, smiling bewilderedly. 'Why are you laughing?'

'The Cosmic Masters just told me a space joke,' said Albert.

'Tell us it,' begged Phil.

'You wouldn't understand it,' said Albert. 'It has to be told telepathically.'

'Amazing,' breathed Simon.

*

Long knowing he'd have exclusive occupancy of his parents' home, with its adjoining paddock, this Guy Fawkes night, Ron had decided to organise some big pyrotechnics. Since the middle of the summer, he'd been amassing a bonfire, and had been spending nervy amounts on display-sized fireworks. But he'd kept quiet about this accumulation of explosives because he knew Albert would have been impatient to let them off straight away, or blow up a church.

Sitting in the utter tidiness of his mother's lounge, with not a crease to be found in its flowery sofa covers or a particle of dust to be found on its tables, Ron brought out some of the bigger fireworks for appreciation.

'They look like fucking mortars!' said one of his ex-work friends.

'Get them out of the room, Ron,' demanded Sarah anxiously, a request instantly backed up by several other people.

It was now almost ten o'clock, the appointed hour, so Ron took his fireworks through the patio doors and into the paddock, telling his numerous guests to follow. It was a good night for the event: dry and reasonably mild, with little wind. Down the far end of the field, Ron threw a makeshift lighted torch on to the petrol-primed bonfire, and it was quickly ablaze, churning out rising folds of dense smoke. Soon after, he lit the first firework.

*

Before the cab even came to a complete stop, Albert began clumsily manoeuvring his way out, ending his creative conversation with Simon mid-sentence, such was his hurry to see Jennifer. Passing down the long driveway leading to Ron's folks' house, in the light of the cab's headlamps, he recognised both Jackie's and Rebecca's cars among the various parked vehicles.

On the edge of the village, well away from the main road, Ron's family home, with its adjoining paddock, was a particularly secluded dwelling. Along one side of the one-acre paddock ran an overgrown disused railway line; the back and other side were bordered by a farmer's field; and the remainder was bordered by the house and its outbuildings. Some distance behind the unlit house, a smoky orange glow in the sky told Albert where he could find his friends.

'Albert, where are you going?' called Simon.

There was a loud thud. Moments later, a sphere of light burst high in the sky above Albert's head, temporarily gripping his attention.

'Th'fireworks!' he heard Phil exclaim somewhere behind him.

Nearing the front door, Albert's presence triggered a security light. He rang the bell and rapped on the knocker, but suspected no one was in the house, all surely being at the bonfire.

Carl, Simon and Phil had followed him out of the cab, and were now with him.

'Whose house'th is this?' lisped Phil.

'A friend's,' answered Albert.

'Th'why are we here?'

Albert now ignored Phil. No one had come to let him in, so he

385

had to find another way to the orange glow. He quickly began to feel anxiously defeated, until the simple solution hit him: climb the fence.

'Where are you going?' asked Simon as Albert began to clumsily scale the head-high fence, a fence defended by a daunting hedge.

'To the world of light,' answered Albert, struggling with repeated bushy entanglement.

'Are you going to the bonth'fire?' asked Phil.

'Yes.'

'Can th'we come?'

'No, fuck off, you can't. You're all mad. I'm staying the rest of the night here with my girlfriend, and I'll thump anyone who disturbs me. I mean it.'

He felt he did mean it, too. Tonight was for Jennifer. Tonight was for love. Tonight was for the rest of his life.

Shit, he was stuck — held almost horizontal at chest height. A push up would be champion now, but he'd just been rude to his companions.

The security light switched itself off, leaving only Carl's distant cab headlamps to illuminate Albert's entanglement problem.

'We're not mad,' stated Simon, disheartened that Albert seemed to have become faithless again.

Shit, he really was stuck. It was the ecstasy, he supposed — it was no good at all at helping a person climb a two-metre impediment.

'What about the mission?' asked Simon. 'When do we start?'

'What mission?' said Albert.

'The mission to create peace on earth. You received a psychic transmission about it on the way here.'

'No I didn't, Simon,' admitted Albert, gathering his strength and wits for a big effort to free himself.

'You did,' insisted Simon. 'You just can't remember. You're blocking things out again. You have to believe in yourself.'

'Th'why did you just tell me to fuck off?' asked Phil, innocently perplexed.

'Shut up, Phil,' said Albert, before beginning his big assault on the impediment.

They were nothing! The branches he was caught in were puny! He just had to steadily use his strength!

He was making it.

Phil tugged on Albert's coat. 'Albert, th'will there be more th'fireworks?'

'Fuck off, Phil,' ordered Albert, alarmed that the tugging was unbalancing him.

'Phil, don't annoy him,' rebuked Simon immediately.

'Th'orry,' lisped Phil, but he could only restrain his short tongue a moment. 'Albert, can't we th'watch the fireworks th'with you before we go?'

Phil just couldn't seem, for more than two seconds at a time, to grasp the magnitude of the situation: of being in the company of the saviour of mankind.

'Phil!' snapped Simon rebukingly, triggering Carl into action.

Carl rounded on Phil, his accent gaining strength for the job, 'Wot's the fackin maa'er wiff y'? Can't y'keep it shat?'

The viciousness of Carl's jumpy assault, verbal but almost physical, cowed Phil into silence.

The trio sensed a landing, and realised that the saviour of mankind had jumped down to the other side of the fence while they'd been squabbling.

Simon sat on the ground. 'It shouldn't be like this,' he murmured cheerlessly. 'It shouldn't be like this.'

'Worked for a bit, though, didn't it?' commented Carl. 'The prayer thing.'

That's right, thought Simon. It had worked for a bit. So all he had to do was keep firing prayer energy at Albert to overcome his recurring antipathy. 'It's okay,' he said with a calm resolve, getting up off the ground. 'I know what to do. We'll go back to Deepdale Hall and put some more charge into the battery where the ley lines are more concentrated, then we'll come back here early in the morning to get Albert.'

During the drive back to the moorland house, Simon fell deep into thought.

*

Moments after landing on the soft earth, another rush of bliss buffeted Albert. When it passed, he proceeded to the substantial bonfire down at the far end of the field. Nearing it, he discerned fewer familiar figures in the firelight than unfamiliar ones — people from Ron's ex-work place and friends of Sarah, he was to learn. But Pete — Ron's dealer — and his girlfriend, Lou, were there. So were Ron's friends, Judith and Roger, standing further back in the shadows. Rebecca, Tony and Jackie were also present.

Jackie. Poor Jackie. He hadn't seen her since the night he'd met Jennifer. She was laughing now, he could see, but he knew she was about to be hurt seeing him with Jennifer. But that just couldn't be helped, he told himself.

And there, taller than everyone else, was Ron. He had to apologise to him tonight for inadvertently messing his life up. He *would* apologise to him.

The aroma of bonfire and gunpowder reached him.

Another thud — more felt than heard —, and a dimly fizzing projectile coursed skyward. He stopped to watch it voyage awe-inspiringly high, up through the hazy smoke and beyond — deep into space to his trippy eye. Finally, it exploded into an astronomic sphere of light, and he fancifully imagined he was witnessing the very birth of the cosmos, each sparkle a galaxy of a billion stars.

Once the last lights of his imagined universe had burnt out, he continued toward the group. He was now just moments away from admitting and explaining to Jennifer that he'd been too blind, stubborn, foolish and proud to see beyond his own defences. Moments away from earnestly asking her to accept him back. Moments away from daring to accept her love for *him*. Moments away from peace of mind.

She wasn't there.

He stood still, tiny firelights flickering in his eyes. In his naive, druggy state it had not even occurred to him that she might not be waiting for him. The disappointment was jarring and deathly sobering.

The gathering noticed him standing in the dimness. A few called his name and beckoned, but he did not advance. They were puzzled. Sarah, hands dipped into coat pockets, stepped into the shadows to meet him.

'Changed your mind?' she observed approvingly.

'Is she here?' asked Albert in a quiet voice that sounded hollow to Sarah. 'Where is she?'

'Sorry. She hasn't turned up. You know what she's like. I was going to ring Margaret's after the fireworks to check on her.'

Murmuring, 'I'll ring her now,' Albert turned to walk the sixty yards or so back to the house, a wedge of weak light from an open back door being his beacon.

'Do you want to borrow my phone?' called Sarah, remembering that Albert was the only person she knew, other than her sister, who didn't possess a mobile. When she'd first contemplated the fact, she'd wondered if their involvement with each other was a spectacular coincidence or a natural coming together of like personalities.

Albert didn't reply to her call.

Nearing the house, Albert triggered another security light. The open door led into the kitchen, and the kitchen, he observed, had a telephone fixed to the wall. Sitting at a pine table, he dialled Jennifer's number and began to feel apprehensive waiting for his lover's voice. What would he say to her? That everything was going to be different from now on because he'd taken a drug? That wouldn't sound too good.

The dialling tone sounded strangely small and distant — that was the E, he supposed. He worried he might not be able to make sense of what would be said to him. The call was answered, but not by Jennifer. The answering machine that had remained in its box in Jennifer's wardrobe until he'd set it up for her a few days back received the call, but the outgoing message Margaret had recorded had been changed. It was now Jennifer's voice that greeted callers:

'Sarah, I know you'll phone worrying where I am. I'm not going to Croxdale. I've decided to go away somewhere. I'll have left by the time you ring. I know you'll worry about me, but don't. I'll be all right. I can't tell you where I'll be because I don't know myself yet. Anyway, auntie Jane might come looking for me — you know what she's like with me. Sorry for it all being so sudden, but I had to do it tonight, especially after what happened between me and Albert. If I don't do it I think I'll die tonight. Bye. Don't worry. Sorry... sorry for what happened to mum and dad. And tell Albert I'm sorry about John hurting him in the Arts Centre. Sorry for everything.'

There was no immediate emotion. He listened with unnatural impassivity until the message ended, whereupon, gradually, the receiver slipped from his fingers. Just as gradually, his head fell into his hands. Unbidden, he became egotistically conscious of the drama inherent in the scene, imagining how he must look to a sympathetic observer. He began to feel guilty and embarrassed to be glamorising his suffering and misfortune, and tried to stop the self-indulgent train of thought, but his thoughts seemed to have developed an independent, rebellious nature beyond his authority. His earlier, quirky preference for a drug-induced psychological nightmare came to mind and he began indulging in the spooky irony, running away with the notion. Then another bomb exploded above the field, jolting his thoughts to a halt. Suddenly, there was just stark, hollow grief. Lifting his head, he replaced the receiver, feeling much like he was sprinkling dirt on to a coffin, too numb to cry. It *was* like she was suddenly dead to him, except he knew it was he who was dead, cast into some other world. Walking away from the house and back over to his laughing friends in the field felt like leaving her graveside after the funeral. No more balmy waves of druggy bliss were to wash over him. All the drug had for him now was an almost palpable feeling of loss.

The fire had been in its raging, erratic youth when he'd arrived. Now it was burning uniformly but less brightly. Sarah was first to see him standing on the shadowy margins of the gathering, and wished to know about her sister. She beckoned him, and as he approached, he lied, or at least concealed the truth. 'She didn't want to come.'

'Typical of her,' said Sarah, with a sigh in her voice.

Albert stood near Sarah, but didn't look at her. He accidentally caught Jackie's eye, who smiled, but he couldn't respond. Peering at his face, Sarah could see that he appeared deeply troubled. She just didn't know what to make of him. He was a pendulum and a conundrum.

'I've lost her,' he murmured, staring at the fire.

'You haven't lost her, Albert,' contended Sarah. 'She didn't know you were going to be here, did she? What did she say to you?'

'I've lost her,' he repeated to himself, but heard by Sarah.

Continuing to peer at him, Sarah became concerned. 'Albert, are you all right?'

'I'm tripping,' he said, with a calculated air of weariness, glancing at Sarah. 'Please, I don't really want to talk to anyone.'

As another firework tore into the sky, Albert moved away into the shadows on the very fringe of the gathering, where he found a log to sit upon.

He was tripping, and didn't really want to talk: that is what went around.

As the night progressed, occasionally, amid the laughter, someone, most frequently Jackie, would remember about him, and venture away from the barbecue to ask him if he was all right. Each time he answered that he was, although having a bit of a bad time. So, although sometimes viewed with concern, he remained mostly alone on his damp log, warmed in a small way by the waning fire, saying next to nothing but dwelling upon his loss in deafening, repercussive silence, the laughter and spitting of the barbecue being like distant sea sounds to him.

He still wanted to say sorry to Ron about the flat and his belongings and his job, but felt inhibited now. Ron had not yet even acknowledged his presence, although, conceded Albert, he had been busy setting off fireworks and managing the barbecue.

As the night aged, Albert became aware of welcome, incremental lessenings of the drug's influence. Sometimes there would be a slipping back, and his thoughts would run bleak riot for a while, as if the drug had marshalled and rallied its dwindling forces for yet another rebellious uprising. But then that uprising would be quashed, and in the aftermath an even greater subjugation would emerge.

Ascending thus from the cold depths of his trip, sitting in deepening darkness as the firelight faded, he found himself looking Jackie's way more and more often. He felt so for her. She was so worthy of happiness, but she would never have what she wanted most in life: him. The next time she gave him her concerned attention he very nearly reached out and took her in his arms before she went back to the fire. Yes, he decided, he should just give himself to her. Sacrifice himself for someone else's happiness. Help make amends for the bad things he'd done in his life, not least hurting Jennifer. She could have him for the rest of his life. He was strong like that. And who knows, maybe he would grow to worship her? Jackie. Dear Jackie. Maybe she was what he *really* needed in life. Maybe that's why he'd left Jennifer, because deep down he knew he should be with Jackie, whose attractions obviously had no superficial element? Or was he just being prey to guilt and fanciful speculation? No, Joe had shown him why he'd left Jennifer, but that conversation seemed so distant now.

Suddenly annoyed with himself, he tightly squeezed his eyes. Fuck it, he wished he could stop his mind. There was turmoil in there now. The drug was rioting again.

He opened his eyes and looked at the remaining partygoers, grouped around the warming, tranquil glow of the ageing fire. He wanted to join them, but could not do it. He knew he was particularly reluctant to face Ron. Was Ron really giving him the cold shoulder tonight? Or was he simply imagining it in his drugged condition? He wasn't sure. He had asked to be left alone, after all.

After what seemed a joyless eternity, the last stranger to him departed. Only Ron, Sarah, Rebecca, Tony and Jackie now remained, all sitting on garden chairs before the fading fire, passing a joint around. Finally able to summon what seemed to be the necessary courage to approach them, he shuffled inconspicuously over to squat beside Jackie, and held on to her chair for balance.

Jackie turned gently surprised eyes to him, and despite the poor illumination, he noticed how large they appeared without their usual frame of hair.

'You all right now?' she asked. 'I kept forgetting about you when I couldn't see you by the firelight any more.'

Quietly managing to say something to make Jackie laugh, Albert soon became absorbed in gazing at the whispering, incandescent embers while his friends continued chatting and dreaming between themselves. But as the drug deserted him even more, he began to suffer an unbearable emptiness, and was disturbed to find himself picturing, almost hallucinating, Jennifer's face clear in his mind's eye. Hurt and confused, she was endlessly turning away from him. Unaware he was speaking audibly, he murmured, 'Don't leave me. Please don't leave me.'

'Who?' asked Ron.

The enquiry jolted Albert. With so little of the drug's encouragement of emotional honesty remaining, he consciously searched for cover, reluctant to admit his true fears and worries, and his shameful part in Jennifer's as-yet-undiscovered flight. 'The deep-eyed, melancholic Enchantress of the Dying Fire,' he lamented in an affected voice. 'She's stealing away now to her woodland grove, leaving my sighing heart longing for her sorrowful beauty.'

'I've shagged her,' boasted Ron, eliciting loud laughs from his stoned friends.

'I've shagged her daughter,' boasted Tony, eliciting no new laughter.

'No you haven't,' argued Tony's wife.

'Fire's just about had it,' said Ron, rising to his feet. 'Anyone coming inside?'

Albert felt he'd been deliberately excluded from the invitation.

Sarah stirred. Then the others. But as Jackie made to stand up, Albert, squatting beside her, gripped her hand. 'Please,' he whispered, returning her to her chair, 'stay here with me.'

Confused and apprehensive, Jackie sat down again while the others set off back to the house with Ron.

'You can have me, Jackie,' said Albert. 'I'm yours forever. You deserve me.'

At first, Jackie did not respond. Eventually, although Albert still held on to her hand, she stood up, saying plainly, 'Sorry, Albert, can't keep you company any longer. Told my boyfriend I'd pick him up from work when his shift finishes. I'm going to be late already.'

Albert peered up at Jackie's dimly-lit face. 'Boyfriend?' he murmured, in a state of bewildered incredulity. 'You don't have a boyfriend. You've never had a boyfriend.'

Wordlessly, Jackie extricated her hand from Albert's, and walked off. Holding on to her empty chair for balance, he watched her fade into darkness, leaving him feeling helplessly alone beneath the icy stars. Taking his hand from the chair, he sat on his coat tails on the wet earth. Pulling his knees up to his chin, he stared at the fire's remaining glow, which lay dull amid the ashes of its own bright life, as if weeping. He continued to stare long after the fire surrendered completely to the night, impassively enduring shivering solitude until the full crassness and arrogance of his offer to Jackie finally hit home, whereupon he groaned his desolate regrets, groans that quickly gave way to unrestrained, wretched sobbing.

*

In the big reception room of Deepdale Hall, candles lit the faces of the three followers of Godfrey, now arranged in their sacred Orthrium Society robes for a special Mass. Draughts dramatically flickered the flames, and distance extended their shadows to sinister, ogre proportions.

During the ride back from Croxdale, Simon had developed a new, improved understanding of the momentous events unfolding. It was all even deeper than he had first believed, and now he was explaining his profound insights to his subordinates. To conduct the portentous meeting, he had chosen to stand on a box in front of the stone fireplace to elevate his authority. In his hand he held the book that contained the teachings of the Orthrium Society, which he lifted high when he spoke.

'Albert is more than a prophet, he's the *prophecy*. He is the Expected One, the one the book foretells. The one who is to prepare the world for the great Millennium of Peace. Everything he said confirms it.'

'The Exth'pected One — th'great!' spluttered Phil, eliciting embarrassed shuffles from Carl.

Enraptured by his own conclusions, Simon read aloud from the Orthrium book: 'His magic will be greater than any ever seen on earth. Happiness will abound come the Golden Millennium that is nigh. There will be no more war, or sickness, or old age. Those who do not heed his words shall be removed from the earth, and the good will live without sinners in their midst.'

And Simon was convinced of his own role in bringing about the Golden Millennium: to zap Albert, the Expected One, whenever his belief in himself weakened. That was his task on earth. That was his hugely important role in the great cosmic scheme. Perhaps within Albert, speculated Simon, the great battle between Good and Evil, foretold in the Teachings, was being waged at this very moment, and if won by Good, the Golden Millennium would then dawn. And with concentrated prayer energy, he, High Teacher Simon, could tip the balance in favour of cosmic enlightenment whenever it was necessary.

Declaring it time to begin recharging the battery, Simon dramatically pointed to it in the centre of the bare room, atop its wooden tripod. 'No one sleeps tonight. Every man-minute of prayer will be needed to persuade the Expected One to come here to this special place, where the forces are concentrated. Then the New Age will dawn at last.'

Leaving his improvised pulpit, Simon joined hands with Carl and Phil to form a ring around the battery, and he led them in chanting the sacred words while they all turned slowly around the instrument that was crucial to world peace.

Om, wallah wallah, om. Om, wallah wallah, om. Om, wallah wallah, om. Om, wallah wallah, om. Om, wallah wallah, om. Om, wallah wallah, om. Om, wallah wallah, om. Om, wallah wallah, om. Om, wallah wallah, om. Om, wallah wallah, om. Om, wallah wallah, om. Om, wallah wallah, om. Om, wallah wallah, om. Om, wallah wallah, om. Om, wallah wallah, om ...

2.5
Anonymity

To Jennifer's dulled surprise, once she'd packed everything she'd thought would be essential for her immediate needs, the large suitcase she'd taken the liberty of borrowing from Margaret's bedroom had remained a manageable weight.

Shortly after she'd promised her sister that she would make the journey to Croxdale for the bonfire party, Jennifer had begun to get herself ready, as if keeping that promise was her intention. But a stronger, underlying intention gradually declared and asserted itself: a desire to flee. More than just a wish for a break or a change, it was a bid to escape her past — to escape *herself,* or what she'd become: draw a line under it all. As she began to pack things into the suitcase, she'd reflected that her solution might simply be avoidance — cowardly avoidance, even — but at least it was *a* solution, she had concluded. Besides, she was just a burden and a worry to the people she knew. Or at least they treated her like she was a burden. Or at least that's how she felt they felt.

That was another thing she wanted to escape: all the complication surrounding her life.

Even when she was closing the suitcase, Jennifer had not yet thought about where she was going. That had seemed appropriate: Albert had casually abandoned her, so she would casually abandon herself. Taking the case downstairs, she had left it by the door while she untied her life:-

— She wrote a cheque to cover two month's rent and left it for Margaret, together with some money for taking the suitcase.

— She left an apologetic message on her employer's answering machine.

— She changed the outgoing message on her own answering machine so that if — when — Sarah called wondering where she was, she would know she had gone away and wouldn't be worrying all night that she had got lost — or worse — somewhere between Richmond and Croxdale.

And that was it. That's all it had taken to untie her life.

Dressed in her yellow puffa jacket and black trousers, she had then taken her case to the bus stop, and less than an hour later was walking into Darlington train station. In that time, she had decided upon her final destination, and in the brightly-lit booking office had used her credit card to buy a first class, one-way ticket to London. The price of the ticket had shocked her, but she had very much wanted to be as undisturbed and alone as possible on the journey, so stuck with the luxury option.

A compulsion had driven her to leave Richmond, and that prioritising and excluding sense had remained with her until she was on the train and it was swishing through the night. The luxury option had paid off: there had been only five other people in her first class carriage when she'd boarded, and no two had been sitting together, so no conversation disturbed her.

Despite the quiet, the warmth, and the sense of being safely cocooned in the night, she was the only one in her carriage who hadn't dozed the small hours away. But it could not easily be said that mulling over her day's upset and upheaval had kept her awake, for as soon as the train began to move, she had become mentally void, passing much of the journey staring into the blackness that was the window beside her.

Only now, with the train nearing London, snaking slowly through urban sprawl, was she even beginning to think about the practicalities of her relocation. A hotel: booking into a hotel would be necessary.

She had only been to London once before, with her parents. Having been only five or six at the time, she now remembered very little of that half-day spent in the capital on-route to her father's mother's house in Guilford. But she had always remembered seeing a wonderful statue of charging horses in a fountain, but the rest of her family had no recollection of such a thing when she spoke of it some time later. She, however, even now, retained a clear picture of it, but was liable to wonder if it was a product of subsequent imagination or embellishment.

That fountain: she would try to find that fountain, she decided.

Cancer had claimed her father's mother less than a month after that childhood visit. She hadn't known her grandmother was dying. She'd just thought she'd needed watering. That's what she'd whispered to her mother: "granny looks like she needs watering." Cancer had also claimed her father's father, before she was born. An aneurysm had killed her maternal grandfather when she was nine; and a bottle of pills had taken her maternal grandmother a week later.

Jennifer's was an unusual family in that, as far as she was aware, there was hardly anyone left in it. With her parents now dead, the only blood relatives she could name were Sarah and her aunt.

'Good morning,' said the guard over the crackly intercom. 'The time is 3.56 am, and we will shortly be arriving at London, King's Cross, two minutes ahead of schedule. Please remember to take your belongings with you. Thank you.'

Jennifer had heard, or read, that King's Cross was considered a den of drug addicts and prostitutes, but if unsavoury things did indeed happen there, she saw nothing of them when she alighted and joined the flow of passengers hurrying to the platform exit. Once beyond the ticket collector, she scanned the cavernous station. It seemed a different world. It was four in the morning, yet this place was very much awake, with purposeful people dashing here and there; confused people staring at destination signs; and bored people sitting on suitcases. Yet despite all the souls, there was a haunting loneliness to be felt.

She looked around again. Nothing even vaguely suspicious was taking place. Everyone was just on their way, or waiting to be on their way, and she realised that for the first time in her life she was completely anonymous. Three hundred people she reckoned to be in her sight, but not one of them had ever seen her before, or would ever knowingly see her again.

Paradoxically, this gave her comfort.

Already, she had seen more non-white faces than she would in a whole tourist season in the Dales. Moreover, she realised that, as far as she was aware, there wasn't a single black person living in her home town, but here things were excitingly multi-racial.

As many public telephones as were surely in the whole of her home town were available to her in the station. Consulting a Yellow Pages at length, she finally chose a hotel from the hundreds listed. One that seemed neither grand nor cheap. This hotel, according to its accompanying advert, was near the famous Baker Street, and upon calling she learned it charged ninety pounds a night for a single room with an en-suite bathroom.

She booked for two nights, quoting her credit card number.

Now she had to get there. Looking around, she saw a sign for a taxi rank. Following its directions, she was soon on the street outside the station, and the notoriety of the area became a little more justified in her eyes. People were loitering here and there. Shifty people. She didn't want to look, or stand still, in case she was approached, and went straight to the black cabs waiting in line to pick up customers.

Just away from the station, she observed a young woman in a short denim skirt standing by the roadside, ducking to peer at the drivers of the passing cars. Jennifer realised she was soliciting. No such sight had she seen before.

Twenty or so people were ahead of her in the taxi queue, but cabs were taking on passengers all the time. Other lone females were boarding cabs, and this reassured her. Now it was her turn. 'Do you know the Kenton Hotel in Nottingham Place?' she asked, bending to speak through the window.

'Dunno about the 'otel, but I know where Nottingham Place is, luv.'

The driver was a small, trim, fair man with thinning hair and a bent nose. He bordered on laughter when he spoke. But men were almost always good-natured when they spoke to Jennifer. Some months back, it had occurred to her that she was never likely to see men as they really were. She only ever saw their greatest efforts at charm and friendliness. To know men properly, she would need to be ugly.

Since he didn't know the hotel, Jennifer was undecided about what to do. She formed a picture of herself being deposited in the middle of a long street, and having to walk up and down it with her case.

'Won't be 'ard to find,' added the driver, detecting her anxiety. 'Ain't a long street. I'll soon find it.'

This was enough encouragement for her to board the cab.

'New to London?' chirped the driver as they joined the fast, sparse traffic.

'Yes.'

'Just got in on a train?'

'Yes.'

Jennifer feared her weary, strained replies had sounded too unsociable, and guiltily believed herself responsible for the driver lapsing into silence. He didn't speak again until the journey's end, which came sooner than she would have liked — the ride had been a welcome distraction and postponement.

'Kenton Hotel, luv,' he announced as he pulled the cab up.

'How much do I owe you?' she asked, although fairly certain of the amount because of a large LED meter.

The driver pointed to the meter. 'Four-eighty, luv.'

After handing the driver the required money, being not at all sure of the correct paying protocol, Jennifer climbed out with her case. Only after the cab pulled away did she recall that it was customary to tip London taxi drivers, and she worried that her omission might have caused offence. Looking around, it was clear Nottingham Place specialised in hotel accommodation, most every property along its terraced, four-storey length being dedicated to the trade. Viewed from the outside, the Kenton was a little too discreet for her liking: whilst being too grand to look sleazy, it certainly looked shady.

Walking through its doors, she began to feel apprehensive and vulnerable. Pressing a silent button on the small reception desk, she waited, alone in the small foyer, unsure whether her presence had been divined by anyone.

A balding man of Middle-Eastern appearance emerged from a door behind the reception, and gave her a "yes, what is it you want?" look.

'Jennifer Lucas. I phoned about half an hour ago and booked a room.'

'Yes, we have your booking,' he said, in an accent unfamiliar to Jennifer.

Speaking little, the man presented her with a short form to fill in. Upon its completion and return, carrying her case, he led her up a staircase and along a short corridor. He was so taciturn she developed the impression that saying little and asking no questions was a job requirement for him. Opening her room and switching on the main light, he handed her the key. 'Breakfast served downstairs between seven and ten,' he said with some warmth. 'Please enjoy your stay.'

Entering, Jennifer locked the door behind her. In the room was a television with some kind of cable box connected, which she felt no inclination to investigate. There was also a teasmaid and a hairdryer. Taking off her jacket, she used the en-suite bathroom, then drew the curtains. Pulling back the bed cover, she began removing the rest of her clothes. But when only her bra and knickers remained, she stopped, and sat on the side of the bed. Now it struck, and struck deep: the realisation of being completely alone — forever, perhaps. For so long she'd experienced vague foreshadowings of such a fate, but now it was true: she *was* alone. She had fled to a new life, but had she just really fled to her old life writ large? Was it part of some kind of inexorable drift? Had she purposefully closed herself off from the few people who loved her, and who she loved in return, and the society of all the people on earth she knew by name? This much she admitted to herself now: part of her felt she would never see her sister or aunt again. The deed was done, and it felt irreversible.

No! she didn't want this kind of doubting, contradictory introspection any more, she angrily thought, reminding herself that to escape such wearying, internal exertions had been one of her justifications for fleeing. Okay, everything that had gone before had been messed up, but it was all over now, she told herself, and she just had start again, on her own this time.

With this resigned yet paradoxically positive thought, she took off her remaining clothes, turned off the light and got into bed.

2.6
The Final Irony

The house lights had long been switched off. After the fire had died, he'd sat shivering in the dark, crying until it hurt, then crying some more, then just emptily sitting, too cold to shiver. But now, submitting to a need for warmth and rest, he was unsteadily standing up. His legs were stiff and unresponsive: cold through to the bone, he realised, and numb through hours of immobility. He also realised that, psychologically at least, the drug had now all but worn off, opinions and abstractions replacing unhampered, raw emotions.

Shuffling over to the sleeping house, he felt so feeble. Occasionally, he stumbled. Near the back door, the security light blazed into operation, but was unable to startle him. Expecting to find it locked against him, he tried the door. It was open. In the kitchen, taking off his coat, he plunged his hands into warm water to wash and heat himself. A few minutes later, after towelling off, he cut open a bin liner and wrapped it around his torso to prevent the damp seat of his trousers from spoiling furniture, fixing it with adhesive tape.

He made himself a cup of tea, and found some biscuits for dunking. Sitting at the table, tea finished, he tortured himself in a way he'd known he would not be able to resist: he again dialled Jennifer's number to listen to the message. But listening was different this time, he found. The drug no longer being an issue, he was mentally more resilient. His defences were much re-established.

There was an underlying, disguised agitation in Jennifer's recorded voice that he hadn't picked up on the first time. She'd spoken faster than usual for her, in shorter, shallower-breath bursts. It was upsetting. He would never have guessed his leaving could have disturbed her so much. Had it? Whatever, he had let her down. He puzzled over why she should be asking Sarah to apologise to him for the mostly accidental knock John had given him with the door in the Arts Centre. It was odd, unnecessary, and ancient history. And he also found it odd that she should be saying sorry to Sarah about their parents.

Once the message played out, he replaced the receiver and stared into nothingness for some minutes. Eventually, more out of resignation than generosity, he murmured, 'I wish you every happiness, Jennifer.'

It all seemed so ironic to Albert. She'd left to find a new life, it seemed, and for sure would forget about him soon. He'd come of age just a few hours too late. A few hours earlier and he could have spoken to her before her disappearance.

Irony. His life was full of fucking irony. Always had been.

He began dwelling on how he believed Sarah would surely blame him for Jennifer's flight. And Ron, in sympathy with his girlfriend, would also censure him. The way things had gone lately between Ron and him, there might even be a scene, and that was something he couldn't face. He couldn't face any of his friends again. He had hurt so many of them, it seemed.

Alone in the living room was where he spent the rest of the night's dark hours. For some reason, a duvet had been left out on the sofa, and, more for the warmth it promised than for the unlikely prospect of sleep, he pulled it over himself — over his bin liner wrap.

Not once did he knowingly dip into sleep.

The wide sofa accommodated his slow-to-warm, restless body until the dawn's first light made shadowy, nebulous, swaying forms of the bare-boughed trees overhanging the paddock. Lying on his side, gazing one-eyed through the patio doors, he began to fancy that the mysterious, mighty trees had converged silently during the night. Converged inexorably, like some encircling army of most secret nature and fell power, finally but resolutely moved to vengeful action by some no-longer-to-be-suffered injustice.

Drawn by the scene, he lifted the duvet away and discarded his bin liner, slid open the cold patio doors and stepped out into the windless, pristine world of the early morning. With great whooshes of its wings, a heron beat its way into the air from the high, leafless branches of the tree nearest him. Wandering down to the far end of the dewy field, he sat on Jackie's chair, beside a depression that marked where he had spent much of the night.

He stared at the cold ashes of the bonfire that were as leaden in colour as the sky above him.

A new day was dawning, and for once he was up before the world, but this was another irony, for everything was over for him, he felt. It was closing time. He didn't know what to do or what would become of him. He'd never felt so contrary to things, and this time the contrariness had never seemed so malignant. It was all futile. Not only was there no place for him in the world, the world seemed to have been subtly devised to slowly break him. Maybe eternally break him. Everything that happened to him was part of some punishing design. And whenever he *had* been lifted by hope, it had only been to make a coming fall feel harder still.

And now he was becoming superstitious. It was surely the *final* irony.

Finding himself seriously, consciously, entertaining a "singled out for punishment" philosophy worried him — the thinking of it, not the thought. His mother used to think that way. Thought her way into mental hospital that way.

Mercifully halting him on his morbid track, Albert's attention was diverted by a rustling in nearby undergrowth, but, turning his head, he could not see the animal culprit. Turning back, he stared at the depression in the earth he'd made the night before, scarcely able to believe that only a few hours earlier he'd been sitting there. It seemed like some distant dream-time.

But last night *had* happened, and an undeniable memory of it remained. He *had* deeply expressed long-dismissed fears and wants to Joe. He *had* joyously determined to re-establish his relationship with Jennifer. He *had* been devastated when he'd failed to find her. He *had* looked penitently to Jackie for redemption. And although the drug had completely worn off now, and the intensity of the experience was much dimmed looking back along from but a short length of Time's misty road, the insights surely had to remain true.

He suspected that if he was ever to be content in this world, he would need to use that precious knowledge.

But it was too late, he reminded himself. *Too late.*

The wet depression in the shit-brown soil suddenly revolted him, and he became angry for wasting time looking at it. Going down to the very end of the field, he leaned against a post sunk into the earth beneath a sombre, looming tree. Two disagreeing forces struggled within him, each in turn gathering strength to push the other back. Finally, one prevailed, and decisions were made. Powerful decisions. Returning indoors, he set about writing a letter for Sarah to pass on to her sister. The letter was an explanation and an apology.

It began thus:

> *Dear Jennifer,*
>
> *Please excuse me the necessity of writing you this letter, but there's so much I have to say to you before I can rest tonight...*

By eight-thirty in the morning, his letter to Jennifer was complete. It told honestly of many things — the things that had happened to him since seeing her last; things which had opened his eyes to his own fears. It told of those fears — of running away from the fear of being abandoned. It told of his conversation with Joe. It told of his trip. It told of how he had soared on the expectation of a reunion with her. It told how sorry he was. It told of how much he had adored her, and how he knew he would never meet another so irresistibly right for him. It told of how quickly he had been growing to truly love her, and that was surely why he felt he had to leave.

It wished her every happiness.

He left a separate letter for Ron, expressing remorse for losing him his job and flat and prized belongings, saying that he hoped to make it up to him one day, even though he didn't much rate his chances of ever earning money.

The letters placed prominently, he took off his bin liner, put on his muddied coat, and quietly left the house. He would go back to Durham to pick up his suitcase from Rebecca's, and from there... he didn't know. Somewhere. Anywhere. A soup kitchen, probably. Whatever, he was putting himself in isolation from people he cared about from now on. He brought ruin with him everywhere. To leave was the least, and the most, he could do.

Tramping the lane leading from the house, he quoted deridingly,

> 'To humbly express
> A penitential loneliness.'

A quarter of a mile down the lane, the cinder of the unclassified road met the dual carriageway into Durham City. Here he stopped. He could turn right for the bus, or left and tramp for two hours to reach Rebecca's house. If he walked, it would save him a good fraction of whatever money he had left from the tenner Rebecca had loaned him.

On the unkempt grass verge stood a simple, low wooden bench made from a rotting old railway sleeper. He remembered Ron once pointing to it and saying it had originally been where farmers left milk churns for collection. Looking at it, he suddenly felt so very weary and spent. Dead beat. He needed some rest before he could proceed, whatever course back to Durham he chose. A short sojourn. But as soon as he sat down on the damp wood, he felt himself completely surrender. Gone was any comforting thought or hope that had ever secretly sustained him. Even the noble, self-sacrificing determination to walk and keep walking until he was far away from people he could hurt seemed hollow and inconsequential, like his whole life and frightening, solitary future. He was now in the bleakest, starkest, rawest, most despondent state he believed a person could inhabit. This was it, he knew: the desolate, ignoble end he'd first begun glimpsing only weeks earlier.

Yes, this was it.

Pushing up his coat sleeve, he stared at a blue ridge of vein, and wishing a syringe in his hand, resolutely squeezed sleep deep into his arm.

How much money *did* he have left? Exploring every pocket revealed him to be worth eight pounds plus a few pence in coppers, all borrowed from Rebecca. Eight pounds. Eight miserable pounds. Not enough to buy sleep. Not nearly enough. He had four E's left too — maybe he could trade them? And throw in his coat, too?

The Durham bus passed by, ruffling his hair with its chilly, indifferent wake. He guessed that, being a Sunday morning, it might be an hour before another bus came. He would walk, he decided. Besides, he had a ruthless need for every penny he could muster.

But he had to rest some more before he could think of beginning the journey. He was tired. So tired. Pushing his sleeve back down, despite the damp and mouldy rot, he lay sideways on the narrow bench, keeping one foot upon the ground for stability. Using his arms as a pillow, he put his head down and closed his eyes. But what was intended to be a short rest became a shivery, post-drug-trip drowsy state more akin to hypnotic chemical sedation than wholesome slumber, with the passing traffic sounding strangely remote and lulling, and extraordinary, fleeting images and coloured patterns presenting themselves to his inner eye.

Some indeterminate time later, while trying to rouse himself to make the journey into Durham, he was struggling to comprehend a chanting drone seeping into his drifting consciousness.

Om, wallah wallah, om. Om, wallah wallah, om. Om, wallah wallah, om. Om, wallah wallah, om. Om, wallah wallah, om. Om, wallah wallah, om. Om, wallah wallah, om. Om, wallah wallah, om ...

Half-opening his eyes, he deciphered an unreal sight: Simon in long, embroidered, red religious robes aiming a prayer battery at him. Behind Simon was Carl, in a plainer, white robe. Behind Carl was Carl's cab, its back door open. Inside the cab was Phil, also in a white robe, sitting on one of the rear-facing pull-down seats, guiltily gnawing a Mars Bar like he was embarrassed to show his teeth or be seen eating it at all.

'Believe,' ordered Simon. 'Believe in yourself and you will succeed where Christ failed.'

Lifting his head, Albert remembered he had promised to outdo Christ, or something like that. But he lay his head back down again — succeeding where Christ failed strongly seemed to be a kind of afternoon type thing.

Simon struck the battery's zap button.

Continuing to look at the cab, Albert realised it could represent his journey to Durham. Taking a deeper breath, he rolled off the damp bench and crawled, hands and knees, geriatric dog-like, past Simon to the vehicle. Once within, he hauled himself horizontally on to the large, wide, warm back seat.

Simon and Carl exchanged looks: not as dramatic a miracle as the previous night, but at least the Expected One was where they wanted him.

Bundling the prayer battery into the cab, Simon pulled down the second rear-facing seat and sat upon it.

Carl got in and started the engine.

Lying horizontal, looking with indifferent despair at Simon and Phil, who were looking apprehensively back at him, Albert was doubly-decided that the best thing he could do in life was to seek sleep. He closed his eyes, and almost immediately began drifting in and partly out of a strange, floaty mental state in which the movement and noise of the cab became integrated with his hypnagogic imaginings.

Eventually, Albert began to realise that they'd been travelling too long to be headed into Durham City. Opening his eyes, staring at the cab's floor, he quietly uttered, 'I don't want to go this way.'

No one responded.

Albert turned his head to look at Simon, who became troubled and nervous. 'I said I don't want to go this way.'

Again, silence.

It dawned on Albert, with merely a sense of impatient exasperation, that he was being kidnapped. Reaching forward, he gripped Simon's robe, heavily tugging out the rhythm of his sentence: 'I — said — I — don't — want — to — go — this — way.' Finished tugging, he held a stare at Simon, who was either mutely defiant though terrified, or just mutely terrified.

Slyly fumbling, Simon pressed the zap button on the prayer battery, hoping a trickle might remain. 'Believe,' he quietly, nervously implored.

'Th'we've been up all night,' lisped Phil irrelevantly.

'Shhh,' urged Simon.

Albert closed his eyes again, too tired to bother further. Besides, he realised his life had become so bad that being kidnapped was a big move up — at least he was warm now.

'Albert, have we crossth'ed one yet?' asked Phil.

Simon again urged Phil to be silent.

Slowly opening his heavy eyes to look at Phil, Albert noticed for the first time that Phil had a small piece of pink tissue paper lodged in his trimmed beard. He closed his eyes again. 'Crossed one what?' he asked, with a mixture of intolerance and weariness.

'A ley line,' explained Phil.

Albert pulled the collar of his coat up as far up as it would go, and rolled over to lie facing the rear.

'Th'imon th'ays there's lots of th'ley lines at the manthsion,' Phil went on.

'What mansion?' asked Albert eventually.

'The manthsion where we're going. Deepdale Hall. We're nearly there. A th'pecial bedroom's been prepared for you and everything. Th'imon says we have to get you back there so you can th'art the Golden Millennium.'

A strange sense of *deja vu* troubled Albert. Except it was oddly different to *deja vu*. He'd barely been listening to Phil, but something he'd said had... *Deepdale Hall*. He'd said Deepdale Hall, and Deepdale Hall was the name of the big house he'd been to with Jackie.

He sat up and saw that they were amid moorland scenery.

'Deepdale Hall? The big house near Rookhope that was once a school?'

'That's right,' answered Simon, suddenly enlivened. 'Do you know it?'

'I was there.'

'Th'really?' lisped Phil.

'Amazing,' breathed Simon. 'When?'

This really was all beginning to feel unreal, worried Albert. 'A few weeks back,' he murmured. 'I went with a friend who works for an estate agents. She had to speak to an old bloke who lives in the grounds about the place being sold. Mr Thompson.'

'Oh my God,' breathed Simon. 'It's all coming together.'

'Th'imon's the one who bought it!' blurted Phil.

Albert looked at Simon. 'Deepdale Hall? You've bought Deepdale Hall?'

Simon didn't answer straightaway, and sounded cagey when he eventually did. 'Yes. On behalf of a business. It's going to be a spiritual teaching centre.'

'And th'we might produce th'spiritually pure food there,' added Phil.

'It's right in the centre of an energy area,' said Simon.

Still fazed, and unable to think clearly through tiredness, despondency and a lingering sense of post-trippy remoteness, Albert mumbled, 'Where did the money come from? It was... it was three million pounds?'

'It th'was his own money!' blurted Phil.

'Shush, Phil,' demanded Simon quietly.

'His own money?' murmured Albert.

'He's got millionths and millionths in the bank,' revealed Phil excitedly. 'He th'never told anyone till last th'week when I found his bank th'atements.'

'Phil, be quiet,' said Simon, with a look of pleading censure.

'Albert's tired.'

'Th'orry,' said Phil.

Albert leaned back and stared ahead in a kind of daze. Millions and millions in the bank. Simon — screwball Simon — reportedly had millions and millions in the bank... and he believed that he was some kind of prophet, or something. Tired, despondent and remote though he felt, something nevertheless clicked for Albert, though he only vaguely sensed it.

Phil had spoken true: Simon did have millions in the bank — various secretive banks. It was all his. The investment partner he so often mentioned was merely a ruse. He had made an extraordinary fortune out of an ordinary fortune left to him by his deceased mother seventeen years earlier. The ordinary fortune had been a three-bedroomed house — a London house. Simon, eighteen and at polytechnic studying quantity surveying at the time, had the house cheaply converted into four shameful flats, rented them to desperate people, and using the income and some dubious accounting, acquired a mortgage on another house. That house was converted too. Before his twenty-first birthday, he owned seven converted houses. Every single time he got lucky with the locations. It seemed that as soon as he bought a property in an area, that area would become sought-after, and his property would increase in value well beyond the average London rise, which was high anyway.

Within eight years of his mother's death, he was paying mortgages on, and collecting rent on, twenty-three houses, including the house in Lambeth where he'd lived for so many years.

Then he'd begun selling up, expecting a collapse of the London property price bubble. After paying off the outstanding mortgages, on no house did he make anything less than a handsome profit. On some houses, he sold for nearly three times the original mortgage value. The one house he didn't sell was the Lambeth property he'd moved into himself. Less than a month after he off-loaded his last property, prices fantastically crashed, leaving countless home owners with negative equity, but handsome sums in Simon's various off-shore bank accounts. Then, with prices on the floor, he began buying again, and nine years after his first sell-up he owned seventy properties, each pulling in rent greater than the mortgage repayments, each skyrocketing in value as another property boom took hold. However, recently anticipating another price collapse, he had once again taken to selling, and had done well. Very well. He'd sold near the very peak of a soaring market. But now prices in London were sliding again. In two year's time, when he predicted prices would be at their lowest, he could rebuild his empire on an even grander scale, but for now he owned just two properties: the house in Lambeth, and Deepdale Hall.

Beyond a few trusted solicitors and one financial advisor with criminal convictions, no one knew about Simon's wealth, not even the Inland Revenue. He operated under the shadowy cloak of an offshore company that itself operated through here-today, gone-tomorrow property letting companies. Outside his secretive business life, no one ever even remotely guessed he was anything other than the long-term unemployed person he purported himself to be, the penny-pinching way he lived.

Presently, the cab drew up to a stop before the large, rusted, wrought iron gates that excluded the world from Simon's new house.

'We're here, Albert,' said Simon portentously. 'Where the Cosmic Masters want you to be.'

Albert gave Simon a look.

'They must want you here,' defended Simon. 'That's why they brought you here before. It would have been an experiment.'

Albert was about to say something when Phil suddenly announced, 'I need a th'wee.' Scrambling out of the cab like he'd left it to the very last second, he scurried behind some bushes growing unchecked near the gates, his robe catching on thorns and tearing at the hem.

Carl looked over his shoulder. 'Should I open the gates, then, Simon?'

'Yes,' said Simon.

Carl got out of the cab, his face developing a frown as he walked over to work the padlock, his white robe dragging a large twig with it.

For the first time that morning, the sun came out.

'Amazing,' breathed Simon, viewing the sky.

Phil returned to the cab, anxiously examining his torn robe.

Once the gates were open, Carl drove through, briefly parking up to lock them again. Soon they were proceeding slowly along the autumn-leaved wooded lane that led to the house, passing a thousand dew-laden webs shimmering in the morning sun.

'You can th'ee fish in the th'ream,' said Phil as they crossed over the bridge.

Albert looked down to the shallow, fast-running, clear water. On a stone, he saw a dipper bobbing its head in accordance with its name.

Soon they emerged from the wood and Deepdale Hall came into view. Albert observed that the extensive ivy cladding present on his first visit was now reduced to sparse patches of red and gold, radiant in the morning light. But the house had gained a complete roof. Furthermore, now that the tarpaulins were gone, a curious, turret-like construction was revealed atop the edifice. He first thought it was some kind of bell tower until he realised it had no open gaps to let sound out, only a stratum of small windows running around it to let light in.

Parked on the forecourt was a small, tatty, black and rusted-chrome motorcycle, which Carl drew level with.

'That's my motorbike,' explained Phil proudly.

As the cab's motion ceased, Simon looked at Albert with grave eagerness. 'When does it all start?'

'Where's my bedroom?' said Albert wearily, sun shining painfully in his eyes.

'The Golden Millennium,' pursued Simon. 'When do we start?'

'Bedroom,' said Albert. 'I came on the understanding I had a fucking bedroom.'

'Albert, th'you've got an amazing aura,' said Phil. 'I've never th'een such a th'rong aura on anyone. I can th'ense auras, you know?'

'Bedroom,' said Albert to Simon.

'Okay, bedroom,' agreed Simon. 'It was going to be my room, but it would be better if you have it. The energies are amazing in there.'

They all got out of the cab, and Albert stood to view the house.

'Amazing place, isn't it?' said Simon, coming to stand near Albert.

'Th'why are you alwayths th'lying on benches, Albert?' asked Phil.

Phil's question went unacknowledged. Perhaps it hadn't even registered. 'Who else is in here?' Albert asked Simon, beginning to feel apprehensive, although not as apprehensive as he knew he should be feeling. He knew he should be far more disconcerted — freaked, even — by what was happening, but he was just too tired and dispirited, he guessed. Everything seemed slow and dulled. And somehow, considering his wretched state of mind, the oddness and fearful uncertainty seemed... *appropriate*.

'No one yet,' answered Simon. 'We have to organise everything first. And it'll become the centre of the Godfrey Society, too.'

'Bedroom,' insisted Albert.

Speaking little, and being answered less, Simon took Albert into the house and up the grand — though somewhat grimy — wood-panelled curving staircase that lay opposite the stone fireplace in the main room. From there, they traversed half the length of a sunlit corridor that served several rooms. Reaching a narrow, freshly white-painted passage, they ascended a dim, cramped, short flight of stairs that led only to a single, bare wooden door which presented itself almost immediately after the last step.

'You'll have to be really careful coming out of your room,' warned Simon. 'The first step is right outside the door. But the energies are amazing.'

On the step below the designated room, Simon turned and looked set to say something historic, but Albert brushed past him, opened the door himself, entered, and shut the door behind him, excluding his guide.

The room was barely larger than the single bed it concealed, but it was *round*, and Albert realised he was in the turret-like construction he had observed growing out of the roof.

Everything was freshly painted. The walls, old-blood red; the high ceiling, white. On a table to the right, close to the single bed, was his computer, or rather his ex-computer. On the other side of the bed was a simple wooden chair. Recessed into the wall near the door was a tiny washbasin, in which was a bar of hard soap. The taps worked, he discovered, but cold water only. The soap didn't work, at least not easily. The light didn't work either when he operated the only switch he could see. Windows — twelve, in all — circled him at shoulder-height, offering a panoramic view of the surrounding hills and woods. The windows were identical, each being as long as his arm but only as high as his forearm. Above each window was a shelf bearing books: works on numerology, spiritualism and pyramid power. Most, however, dealt fancifully with crystals. Dowsing with crystals. Healing with crystals. The "Universal Energy of Crystals". Aura balancing with crystals. Aura cleansing with crystals. Releasing one's inner power with crystals. Just about everything with crystals excepting a genuine usage, despaired Albert, such as putting some on fish and chips. Crudely painted symbols akin to those on Simon's robe decorated the walls in blue and gold. Two small crystal pyramids were set on wrought iron stands at either side of the bed's wooden headboard. Pamphlets about the Orthrium Society lay on the bed, next to a folded, golden garment, which, when Albert examined it, proved to be a robe like Simon's, only much more elaborate.

There was no bedding or pillow, though, so, once his dulled sense of exploration was satisfied, Albert lay down in his T-shirt and black jeans, used his coat as a blanket, and the golden robe as a pillow.

Within minutes, he was properly asleep.

Downstairs, tired though they all were, Simon once again enrolled Phil and Carl to assist in re-energising the prayer battery.

*

Half asleep in her dressing gown, Sarah shuffled downstairs to make coffee, finding that two envelopes had been taped to the kettle. One bore her name; the other bore Ron's. Inside hers, she discovered two letters: one for her, and one she was expected to pass on to her sister. Despite it revealing that Jennifer had abruptly left for who knew where, the letter meant for her made her cry for Albert; and all the doubts and misgivings about him that had ever surfaced in her mind, she now regretted.

Even Ron cried when he read it.

Later, as she listened to her sister's recorded voice, Sarah, too, perceived an unprecedented speaking manner, and knew Jennifer had been subject to some powerful anguish. It was something she could scarcely believe could be accounted for by the pain of breaking up with a short-term boyfriend, especially since she'd sounded so okay about it when she'd spoken to her on the phone. And why she should be saying sorry about their parents was a mystery.

2.7
Their First Encounter

Daylight was diffusing through the heavy brown curtains in Jennifer's room when she awoke. Reaching up to pull a corner aside, she saw that the sky was clouded over, but it was still bright enough to narrow her eyes.

Letting the curtain return to its natural place, she lay on her side, staring at nothing earthly. Noises in the corridor had woken her several times in the night. Not loud noises, but it had taken little to open her eyes as she lay in a strange bed. Now she was properly awake, and had no idea what the time was. She never carried a watch, and there was no clock in the room other than the one on the teasmaid, which was not plugged in. She thought it could be as early as seven, or as late as ten.

She began to worry that a cleaner might come, and got out of bed. Unpacking her toiletries and taking them to the bathroom, she began her morning wash, choosing to quickly shower rather than run a bath. Finished washing, she studied a tourist's map of London, left on top of the television. Finding her present location, she realised she was within easy walking distance of Oxford Street. On the presumption some shops would be open despite it being Sunday, she decided to make it her first destination of the day. She needed to buy things she had omitted — through haste and practicality — to bring with her.

Wearing the same clothes she had arrived in, and not even considering availing herself of the provided breakfast, Jennifer left the hotel, learning from the clock in the empty lobby that it was now almost nine-thirty. Stepping out on to the street brought it home to her that she was living somewhere far removed now. Moreover, she was here for good, and had to remember that. She had absolutely no idea what she was going to do in London. She couldn't go on living in a hotel, for certain. Although thirty thousand pounds was available to her, she resolved to be frugal from the beginning: tomorrow, she would look for alternative, cheaper accommodation and a job.

But what job could she do? she anxiously wondered. She could phone up veterinary surgeries to enquire if there were vacancies for assistants, she supposed. Or perhaps she really should aim for a proper career — go to college to study for university entrance. The

413

problem with that was that she had no interest in any specific academic pursuit, and couldn't understand how some people could apply themselves to a discipline simply for its job prospects. Music had been her only passion, but she knew her playing skills would have rusted to dust in the years since she'd last picked up a violin.

Beyond Nottingham Street she encountered Marylebone High Street. Consulting her map, she knew that bearing right then continuing straight would bring her on to Oxford Street. But she decided to take an alternative route. Instead of bearing right, she would cross and walk along Devonshire Street, which would bring her on to the famous Harley Street — synonymous with lucrative private medicine. Harley Street used to be cited by her father when things weren't going well at his NHS practice in Richmond. "I could be coining it in in Harley Street", he would complain without seriousness, "but your mother dragged me oop North to minister to peasants.'

Walking toward Harley Street, she noticed that every phone box was festooned with what she discovered to be prostitutes' advertisement cards. No such thing went on in her home town.

Reaching Harley Street, Jennifer found it to be every bit as conservative, dignified and discreetly moneyed as she had expected. Walking along its terraces of high, imposing houses, at its southern end she consulted her map again, crossed Cavendish Square, exited by Holles Street, and a minute later arrived on Oxford Street. Almost every store was open, she discovered, including the large department stores. Despite it being Sunday morning, people were already out in numbers, with an over-representation of tall, self-assured, blonde, Scandinavian-sounding women shopping with their lofty daughters.

The day had acquired a momentum. She had things to do, and whenever she did slip into thinking about how she had arrived where she was, she would push the thought down, and tell herself that, for better or for worse, the deed was done. Walking along Oxford Street, she suddenly felt the energy of a person who has freshly set a course, yet not travelled nearly long enough to feel weary or daunted. The idea of gaining qualifications to permit university entry strengthened, and she resolved that by this time next week she would have decided what academic path to follow. It would be all positive action after today: she had come through the storms, been blown to strange lands, but was going to enjoy the available sunshine.

'You've paid the price,' she whispered to herself.

Following breakfast in a burger bar, she went into the nearest department store to begin making her "essential" purchases: more toiletries; hair-bands; knickers; tights; umbrella; lounging around clothes. But once these items were in her possession, the day's momentum quickly fell away. That was it, she realised with a sense of disenchantment, coming out of the store with three carrier bags. Now there was nothing to do, she supposed, but go back to her room. The sense of optimism she had developed about her future also fell away, and she thought no more about college on the return journey to her hotel. Along the way, she bought enough food to ensure she wouldn't need to leave her room again that day. Arriving back, she found the bed had been made in her absence, and the curtains opened. After sorting through and examining the things she'd bought, she began to feel tired. Taking off her shoes and closing the curtains again, she slept on the bed for an hour. Not long after waking, she began to feel anxious, anxious because the tedium was already killing, and it was only early afternoon. Would the rest of her life be like this, she bleakly wondered? Alone? Essentially as alone as a prisoner in solitary confinement? Although she had never been a gregarious person, she'd always had the *option* of company. Now there was no real option, and that seemed to make such a difference.

She turned the television on, but whichever programme she chose it was like watching something in a foreign language. Turning it off again, she sat on the bed, staring at a wall, vaguely wondering where the generous heat in the room came from, since she could see no obvious source.

No, she would go out again, she resolved. Even if she only walked the day away, it had to be better than this. Putting her shoes on, she decided to investigate Regent's Park, noting from her map that it wasn't far away. Maybe she could explore the underground system too? Between the park and the tube, she could kill plenty of time. However, within ninety minutes of leaving her room, she returned again. Regent's Park had hardly registered, and the tube remained unexplored. And she didn't feel like she'd killed time, merely that she'd outlived it.

Before long, she had a more substantial idea about what she could do with the rest of the day, and immediately began changing into the best clothes she'd brought from Richmond — the same clothes that had driven John into paroxysms of suspicion. Half an hour later, she was stepping out of the hotel. This journey was special, she told herself, so the underground system and buses could wait until tomorrow: copying a man further down the street, she put out her arm to draw a cab to her. Notwithstanding her justification of this choice of transport, and although money promised not to be a problem for a long time to come, she still felt ill at ease at the thought of paying such an unnecessary fare.

She asked the driver to take her to Camden Lock.

In her memory, it was always winter when, as a small child, she would be questioning her mother while helping her prepare food in the snug kitchen of their home. Eight or nine, she figured she must have been during that phase of curiosity about what had then seemed to her to be an event remote in history: her parents' first meeting. Whatever details those conversations disclosed to her infant ear, few she could recall now, except that a French restaurant in Camden Lock had been the place of their first encounter, one rainy autumn afternoon, when each had individually sought comfort in a coffee, and Fate had smiled and arranged adjacent tables.

Proceeding down a street named Parkway, the driver turned his head to ask, 'Awright if I drop you at the junction, or d'you wanna go all the way to the Lock?' Faltering slightly, Jennifer replied that it would be, not that she really knew one way or other. Further down the street, the junction he was presumably alluding to came into view, as did crowds of people crossing. Near the traffic lights, the cab swung left and stopped to let her out. But after a half-attempted fumble with the door handle, she sat back in her seat and asked to be taken all the way to the Lock.

The cab moved on, turning left at the lights. Beside the road they were now on, people were pouring out of a tube station. Almost all were young. Seeing how they were dressed, Jennifer began to feel out of place in the expensive but more traditional coat her auntie had bought her. These people were dressed in mismatches of colours and styles, all in what she believed fashion writers would describe as a funky retro seventies look.

Shops selling leather-wear and alternative jewellery lined the way, most pitching at least some of their contents out into the street, and competing music thumping out from all. So thick were the crowds down this street, the driver more than once had to assert his way forward, albeit slowly, through spillages of people lazily ignoring the usual demarcation between road and pavement. Not far on, the road rose slightly, and Jennifer realised they were actually passing over a bridge. Looking to the side, she saw that they were over a canal's lock system, and the hitherto mystery of the area's name was solved for her.

'This do?' asked the driver, and Jennifer said it would. Unlike on her first cab ride, she opted to pay the driver through the side window after exiting on to the pavement, like she'd now seen other people do. And she remembered to include a tip, which rounded the fare up to six pounds.

No more unnecessary cabs after today, she resolved, realising that the two short rides taken so far had cost her nearly as much as she used to earn in half a day at work.

Now she was stood beside a busy road overlooking a canal, being jostled by passers-by. Rain was beginning to fall. She saw a restaurant nearby called *L'Ecluse*, and wondered if it might not be the very one in which her parents had first met, since no other suitable candidate was within sight. But it had all been a long time ago, she acknowledged. Crossing the road to look through its windows, she saw that *L'Ecluse* was not a particularly grand affair, seeming in essence to be the Frenchified equivalent of an up-market cafe. She wasn't even sure if it had table service. She tried to imagine her mother sitting in there with baby Sarah in her arms, and her father somehow striking up a conversation with her, all those years ago. She wondered — if it was indeed the right place — which were the adjacent tables that had facilitated their first encounter.

Near the door, on display with the menu, were photocopies of newspaper and magazine articles relating to the restaurant. She noticed the date of one: twenty-three years old.

Yes, this had to be the place where her parents' romance had begun — where *she* had begun, really. But looking through the window and picturing them on that fateful day, she began to feel like some spectre, unseen by them, but one whose shadow would one day —

She turned away from the window to stop herself thinking on. What to do now? Go down to the market beside the canal? But the rain was beginning to come down harder. Also, the smell of the food was making her hungry. To escape the rain, and believing she had no need to fear cost or pompous service, and very conscious that she was perhaps retracing her mother's steps of twenty years past, she entered the restaurant. At once she was greeted in French by a waitress who only briefly looked at her. Despite the perfunctory nature of the exchange, Jennifer felt her face flush at the perceived expectation of having to converse in a language she knew only

417

poorly. But before she could muster an answer, the petite waitress, afflicted with an uncommonly narrow, sharply turned-up nose, asked, 'Table for one?'

'Yes, please,' returned Jennifer.

Shown to the nearest table, she sat and examined the menu, relieved to find it was written in English. Crepes were the speciality, indeed the mainstay, here, she observed, and decided upon a variation referred to as a *Florentine*.

She looked around the room. Red was the colour of most, if not all, the woodwork. The walls were presented as bare brickwork, hung with large photographic prints of rustic peasants. The floor was bare boards, stained black, supporting a few more tables than comfortable for the given space. The people eating, she observed, were not particularly representative of the type of people outside. There was more of a middle-classness about the diners. Even the young woman alone at the next table, whose attire and chunky jewellery tended towards, in Jennifer's belief, grunge, had a certain air of sophistication about her.

Another waitress took Jennifer's order, to which she'd added coffee. Feeling warm, she stood up to remove her coat, even though she worried that her dress was too glamorous and skimpy for the occasion. As she sat down again, the grungy young woman leaned over with a nervous, fidgety manner.

'Excuse me,' she said, in an accent stereotypically French, her speech as fidgety as her motions, 'I told a friend I'd be 'ere, could you watch for 'im while I'm in the ladies?'

Surprised, Jennifer reacted by nodding her agreement.

The young woman immediately smiled, smiled like a favoured child just handed a sweet she'd at first been refused. ''E's called Robert,' she said, and, touching her own shoulder, added, 'brown 'air this length.' And then she was off, bracelets and other metallic adornments jangling. Sitting a few tables away, a young man, short but with a powerful, gym-built body, watched her traverse the room. Jennifer noticed his brooding, resentful gaze, which turned on her once the French woman was gone.

She turned away, pretending not to have been aware of his attention.

Jennifer knew she was a looker, and was fast becoming inured to the percentage of desiring eyes that strayed her way wherever she went. Invasive eyes that two months ago might have rendered her self-conscious were now inclined to render her indifferent. But those

418

occasional sullen, resentful glares of the kind she suspected she was still receiving from the squat young man would always disturb.

Now looking with affected casualness toward the door, Jennifer witnessed a shorter than average man enter the restaurant. Looking to be in his early forties to Jennifer, he was wearing a long black coat of expensive material but cheap treatment, tight faded jeans, a paisley shirt, paisley waistcoat, and pointed brown ankle boots with Cuban heels. His face was kindly in appearance, but also a little comical, with a long, ski-jump nose jutting out from under close-set, indeed off-set, eyes.

He seemed in want of a good night's sleep.

These things Jennifer casually noticed about him as he glanced around the room, but then she noticed his hair. 'Robert?' she suddenly found herself uttering, and his subsequent look of mildly bewildered acknowledgement confirmed the accuracy of the presumption. 'A French woman asked me to watch for you. She's in the ladies.'

'Oh, er... er...,' he faltered for a moment, lampooning his own confusion. 'Okay,' he said, in a more together voice. 'Is this her table?'

Jennifer said it was.

Smiling and taking the seat where the French lady of his acquaintance had been sitting moments earlier, Robert, rather formally, introduced himself to Jennifer, offering his hand for shaking. With the exchange of names complete, tilting his head, he said, 'You're from the North, aren't you? Darlington way?'

His blue eyes held her gaze, like he was deeply interested in hearing her reply.

His apparent ease at locating her home town to within a dozen miles or so impressed Jennifer, particularly in view of her being aware that hers was not a strong Northern accent. Indeed, modulated perhaps by her having had a Southern father as an influence on her infant tongue, Jennifer's accent had been soft enough to incite the rougher elements of her school into calling her "posh cow".

Upon answering that she came from Richmond, North Yorkshire, Robert warmly returned that he himself was from Darlington, surprising Jennifer, for his accent emphatically indicated otherwise. Accentwise, Robert wouldn't have sounded out of place addressing a Conservative Party conference on business affairs.

The French woman returned, and seeing Robert, smiled broadly, opening her arms to him. Robert stood to greet her, saying, in a

419

silly, sugary voice, 'Yvette!'

They hugged, and she kissed Robert's stubbly cheeks.

'How are you doing?' asked Robert.

'Great,' returned Yvette.

Yvette was beautiful, Jennifer had already observed, and not dissimilar to her own sister. More angular than Sarah and a little taller, though, and with facial features more clearly defined. Sarah's was a softer face than Yvette's, but neither could be declared more appealing than the other, particularly with both having equally large and deep brown eyes, shadowed similarly with dark make up. In addition to a sleeveless black, low-cut top and a dark blue wrap skirt, Yvette was wearing bangles, pendants and other grungy accessories that Jennifer thought might look staged on anyone else, but they settled naturally on her.

Jennifer's food arrived. After serving it, the waitress greeted Robert by name and asked for his order. Robert requested a beer, stressing, close to apologetically, that he would be ordering food later.

'Ah'll 'ave a beer too,' added Yvette impulsively.

As Jennifer started her meal, she inadvertently caught Yvette's eye. Yvette instantly smiled, her head making small, appealing, coquettish jerks. But Yvette's attention at once returned to Robert, for she suddenly needed to confer some apparently urgent and important gossip about someone called Peter, for which her voice became wonderfully serious and low.

Overhearing snippets of the conversation, Jennifer found Yvette's voice an altogether pleasant sound. Charmingly French, it also had a childlike quality, as though she was talking with a burned tongue-tip. In the conversation, Robert responded with the same level of apparent deep interest and involvement he had shown when discussing Jennifer's Richmond roots.

Hearing Robert's voice now, in the light of the information he had given her, Jennifer could discern vestiges of his declared Northern origin. Curious to her ears were the inconsistencies in those vestiges. When pronouncing the word "so" his tongue was particularly undecided, most times giving it the Southern vowel sound, but sometimes giving it a telltale, stretched, "surr" treatment, straight from the council estates of Darlington.

'Jennifer, here, is from near where I was born,' he said to Yvette, unexpectedly pulling Jennifer into the conversation.

'Really?' said Yvette to Jennifer, expressing delight at the fact. "Ow long 'ave you lived in London?'

'This is my first day.'

Yvette and Robert responded remarkably. They straightened in their chairs, Robert making a gooey sympathetic and delighted noise, while Yvette actually held her arms out to embrace Jennifer. 'You're going to 'ave a wonderful time,' she said, jewellery jangling.

Jennifer found herself smiling a little and accepting the offered embrace.

'We'll look after you,' said Robert, before arresting the waitress as she passed, instructing her to put Jennifer's bill on to his.

2.8
The Crystal Age

Eyes opening to slits, Albert slowly awoke, and remembered he'd been dreaming about Jennifer. Distant down a street, with her back to him, she was ever walking on, as in some strange temporal Escher scene. The dream's ambience of distressed yearning lingered, which made him wonder how much more lovelorn he might be feeling had he been any *real* length of time with her before their split. What if it had been two years, not two weeks? What dreams would haunt him nightly then? But he knew that was why he'd left her so soon. He was scared of ever having such pain — Joe had shown him that. But Joe had also encouraged him to see how living with such a fear could never really be living at all.

Becoming more mundanely awake, he began to think about where he was and how he'd got there, and quickly decided it didn't actually bear thinking about. He'd been sort of kidnapped, and his life had become so generally bad he had to let people treat him like a Messiah just to get a place to sleep.

He should be dead now, he blandly realised. He should be slumped on his favourite bench by the river in Durham with a needle in his arm. But he had been kidnapped. He looked at his forearm. If he had the painless means at hand, would he do it now?

No, he decided honestly. He didn't have to, for it was as if he had *already* done it. He'd been there – to the desolate edge and beyond – and no one could tell him he hadn't. And part of him *had* died, he felt. The wildest, most ardent part. He felt, strangely, that if he ever did it now, it would not be in a state of tragic despair, it would be in a state of... wry amusement, or perhaps even serenity.

He wondered if anyone who hadn't been to the very edge and beyond could possible understand his thinking.

Turning over on to his other side, he found himself touching the folded robe he was using as a pillow, thinking of how intimately close Jennifer's soft presence had been only the day before, imagining she was lying beside him now – wishing she was beside him. He began to choke up, but fought it by making a resolution not to think about her any more: she and he were surely irrevocably split. There was nothing he could do about it now, except, perhaps, learn from the loss. But the only thing to be learnt was how not to make the same disaster with the next love, if fate were ever to throw such a treasure his way again. But that would be so unfair to Jennifer. She had not suffered just so he could perhaps get it right in his next relationship. No, he couldn't do that to her. He couldn't imagine being so mercenary and opportunistic. He was strong like that, even when he knew he was being foolish to himself and that life was for living and getting on with. But maybe he'd just found another excuse for denying himself the comfort of love?

'Oh, give yourself a frigging break,' he said, turning on to his back, annoyed to be once again slipping into introspection and self-doubt.

One thing he didn't doubt was that he could never again become transiently besotted. He couldn't imagine ever again falling in what he used to call love at first sight. Love had become too deep and too real for comedy and frivolity. He was sure he could now visit any petrol station in the land without hurting his heart, for he believed his true emotions had finally been uncovered, and assigned exclusively, perhaps permanently, to Jennifer.

'Wish they hadn't, though,' he sighed. He wished he could be more like other men. He wished he could iron out the love element from his life altogether and just shag girls picked up at parties the night before, or whatever most blokes his age did. But he could never be like that, he knew. He could never let down the romantic in him. He was cursed that way.

Now he had a thought: he would get Jennifer out of his mind by doing what he'd always found too sad to do before. *He would look upon even romance from an evolutionary psychologist's viewpoint.*

Genes. That's all life was, after all: genes blundering their way through the eons. What he perceived as *self* was just a single, over-complex link in a chain that stretched all the way back to a freak combination of molecules that had accidentally spawned a *cancerous* molecule in a warm primeval sea, or muddy pool, or cosmic gas cloud some billions of years ago. So what he experienced as love was surely just a genetically selfish desire to mate with, and thus pass on his genes with, what he perceived as being a suitable partner. Jennifer was eminently suitable because, being so intelligent, she could nurture his offspring successfully, equipping them with resources, both physical and social, that would in turn increase *their* chances of passing on the genetic material. And Jennifer's alluring beauty, too, would probably pass on to those offspring, thus further increasing their chances of attracting high-calibre mates. And their probable beauty, if they were female, would make it more likely for the natural fathers to stay with the family, adding to the protection and resources; or, if male, would make them more attractive to other females, thus helping the spread of the muddy pool genetic material.

Albert decided that, from now on, whenever he found his mind straying to Jennifer, he would conjure up an image of that muddy pool, with acrid, primeval gasses bubbling through its slimy unpleasantness.

He turned his head to the side, and stared blankly at one of the crystal pyramids set beside the bed on iron stands, mercifully thinking of nothing for a while, except to note that his hair smelled of bonfire. But then he began thinking of—

Muddy pool. Muddy pool.

It helped. It really helped. Just the comic absurdity alone helped. But it was a sham, he acknowledged. He knew that in his heart of hearts, he harboured a... a *faith* that he would one day be with Jennifer again. But perhaps that feeling was just an extension of that vague feeling he supposed everyone carried with them at all times: that one day, everything would be right; that all lost loves would return; that all one's ailments would be cured; that youth and vigour would return; that the Beatles *would* lead the world to the bright sunny uplands.

He tried to explain away that vague, all-things-will-be-perfect feeling from his now ruthlessly adopted evolutionary psychologist's viewpoint. That feeling was universal, he decided, and it kept people going. It was essential for keeping the transient vehicles of DNA rolling for their seventy summers. Having evolved such big brains — brains able, if they dare, to recognise the pointless muddy pool molecule in the baggage hold — mechanisms also evolved to enable people to beguile themselves on a grand scale. Mechanisms to make it all seem special. Mechanisms to make it all seem mystical and transcendent, even. That was religion, he realised. That was the explicit comfort of religions: that one day everything would be right, even if you have to die first. So *that's* what religion was: the expression of an *ultimate* coping mechanism; the glorified manifestation of the innate, universal belief that things will be better. Something that taps into that belief. Anything. Anything that defies the unbelievable, terrifying thought that this is all there is ever going to be in it for *you*, and that even this won't last the blink of an eye on the cosmic scale of things. That belief gone wild. That belief dangerously mixed up with the evolutionary legacy of pack social behaviour: pack greetings; common gestures to indicate same-tribeness; hierarchical thinking, with all subservient to an *ultimate* top dog — *you make the sign of the cross the same way I do, so you must be in my pack, so I will not attack you, but together we can defeat outsiders, and we all serve the toppest dog in the sky.*

Religion, realised Albert, was evolution's solution to intelligent insight.

Therein lay his own particular evolutionary flaw, he recognised. The brain programs that allow belief in the unbelievable weren't dominant enough in him to make him a successful breeder. He was mentally unbalanced. Too analytical. An evolutionary fuck up. He needed to be just a little bit more beguiled to be happy, and thus wont to get out of bed and shag his muddy pool molecule around. But cheating the muddy pool molecule by denying it continuation gave him a sense of twisted achievement, he realised. It was his self-denial streak, although he couldn't really explain that streak at all from an evolutionary point of view... so he blamed his mother.

He turned his head to face the other way and stared blankly at another crystal pyramid, then stared blankly at what used to be his own computer.

Muddy pool. Muddy pool.

He turned over and faced the first pyramid. Was this really happening? If so, what lunatic star governed his life? All he did was sell his computer to some Cockney fuckwit, tell him a story, and then this: a spooky room on top of a draughty, run-down mansion in the middle of nowhere, where he was supposed to be succeeding where Christ had failed, or something.

Footsteps approaching. Someone coming up the stairs. A quiet tap on the door.

He ignored it.

The tap was repeated, but louder. Then the door tentatively opened, and in came Simon, robed and carrying the prayer battery, without its tripod. Just behind Simon, also robed, Carl and Phil shuffled in too, awkwardly crowding into the tiny, round bedroom. They all looked tired. Pointing the battery at Albert, Simon was nervous yet resolute. 'Believe!' he commanded, pressing the zap button.

He waited for signs of some miracle of prayer.

'Morning nutters,' said Albert, with dulled disdain, regarding them sideways.

'Morning,' Carl and Phil loosely duetted, sounding uncertain.

'We're not nutters,' claimed Simon sullenly.

'Yeah? Well discuss it amongst yourselves downstairs,' said Albert, fluttering his fingers to waft his worshippers away.

Deliberating a moment, Simon turned around and ushered his underlings away before him.

'No, don't go away,' corrected Albert urgently, as the door was closing.

Simon at once returned, leaving his subordinates on the steps outside.

'I'm hungry,' said Albert. 'Is there any food here?'

Disappointment showed on Simon's face. 'Not really. But we're going to the village shop soon to get a few provisions. Tomorrow, we'll have a freezer and we'll be able to buy economically, and we'll keep a good store.'

'Can you get me something at the shop?' Albert ventured to ask. 'A sandwich or something. No meat, though. I'm vegetarian.'

'Okay,' agreed Simon. 'The robe's not a pillow,' he instructed. 'It's for you to wear. Golden, like the Golden Millennium.'

'That's nice,' said Albert.

Simon left the room, closing the door behind him.

'And get me some hair shampoo,' called out Albert. 'And a toothbrush and toothpaste. And deodorant.'

Muddy pool. Muddy pool.

'For fuck's sake, what am I doing here?' he muttered, sitting up on the bed. 'Still, better than the soup kitchen.'

He began to feel cold, and put on his coat, which had been his blanket. Looking at the computer, he wondered if he'd ever get around to writing that proper novel, or screenplay, or whatever he'd finally decided upon. He'd ought to, he thought, since there was no other obvious way he was ever likely to earn money to pay Ron back. If he was being encouraged to live here by those nutters, he should use the place to work. Yes, he should. Switch the computer on and start right now on that Bermuda Effect movie. He'd wasted quite enough of his life. Regardless of his duty to Ron, he needed to make his contribution to art. He had a duty to the world.

But why were so many people driven to create art, he wondered? He refused to believe that art was something that existed in its own right, so where did that drive for abstract achievement come from? So much human time and effort went into the creation and appreciation of art, it had to have some evolutionary advantage, he reasoned.

Then he remembered reading a theory about how art was all about impressing potential mates. The theory proposed that there was no such intrinsic thing as art, just elaborate courtship displays. If he were to write a *Hamlet*, or even devise a Unified Field Theory, it would just be a way of showing females what a clever, and therefore resourceful, father he could be, and what clever, and therefore more-likely-to-survive-in-the-jungle-of-life-and-pass-on-their-genetic-material, children he could sire. For *Hamlet*, read *Shag Me, I'm Dead Clever*. *Hamlet* was Shakespeare unwittingly displaying his peacock feathers. Just as peacocks evolved – through runaway sexual selection – huge, showy courtship feathers, so humans evolved artistic creativity. Every time he got depressed and frustrated because he felt his creativity was being wasted or stifled was just because of those pointless muddy pool molecules continuing on inside him. Nothing spiritual or mystical was really being expressed in Beethoven's *Fifth*. It was just an abstract, runaway mating call. And thinking thus, rock stars became the product of a genetic urge to show the whole world what a great mating partner they represented. For *Sgt. Pepper's*, again read, *Shag Me*.

No, he wouldn't bother creating an abstract courtship display, Albert defiantly decided, lying back on the bed to stare at the ceiling. If his muddy pool molecule needed to broadcast his sexually desirable cleverness to other muddy pool molecules, it could bloody well pick a method that didn't involve so much tedious typing.

'Muddy fucking pool,' sighed Albert. 'Muddy fucki—'

Millions in the bank, remembered Albert. During that strange ride here, Phil had said millions in the bank. Could it be true? Could Simon, the sad nutter who believed him to be some kind of Messiah, be a multi-millionaire? Well, he'd somehow bought this house — or said he'd bought it. The potential implications were finally beginning to invigorate Albert.

Epiphany.

Millions in the bank! During that strange, sleepy cab ride, Phil had said that Simon secretly had millions in the bank! And he was throwing it away on madness! Perhaps he could get a juicy piece of that madness? It was a Godfrey-given golden opportunity to... to pay Ron back. Ten grand. Ten grand would be enough to square with Ron for the smashed possessions. If Simon was a multi-millionaire, getting him to part with ten grand shouldn't be too hard, considering he believed him to be a Messiah. Paying Ron back by outwitting Simon had to be preferable — and more realistic — than endeavouring to earn money through art. And did he not, he reminded himself, have at his disposal a mind as cunning as most any ever devised by nature? This was surely the time to use it with a vengeance instead of regarding it as his worst enemy.

All of a sudden, Albert no longer felt anywhere near as despondent as he'd felt just an hour earlier, now that he had a delicious occupation to distract him: creaming Simon. Although it was mad, utterly mad, what was happening to him, it was the best job he could ever have hoped for: he wouldn't have to get up in the mornings, and he could be as silly as he liked — in fact, the sillier the better. *He had finally found suitable employment.*

He heard voices down below, out front. Peeking through a window, he saw Carl opening his cab door, but Simon and Phil were standing some distance away, doing something. No longer wearing robes, Carl was in a T-shirt — a *Not Long Now* T-shirt. Now he remembered they'd all been wearing them last night. Phil was wearing one, too, under a jacket. Albert guessed that, under his blue cagoule, Simon would be similarly clad. "Not long now until the Golden Millennium", he recalled Simon having said the previous night. Carl started the cab up, but Simon's preoccupation with some activity or other continued. What was it he was doing? wondered Albert. Dowsing for ley lines, he quickly realised, like he had been in that documentary.

And he was a millionaire — a fucking *multi*-millionaire.

427

Carl tooted the horn, whereupon Simon and Phil abandoned dowsing and went to the cab. Leaving the window, Albert picked up his shoes and saw how muddied they were. Taking them to the basin, he rinsed them clean. Removing his coat, he washed his face with the hard soap, which performed poorly. There was no towel, so he used his T-shirt to dry himself. Lifting his coat from the bed, he rubbed as much of the dried mud off it as he could, doing the same with his trousers. He caught sight of the Orthrium pamphlets, which he'd placed on the floor the night before. Putting his coat on first, he sat on the bed and read about the founder of the Orthrium Society, who claimed to have received the secret design for the prayer batteries in a psychic transmission from Cosmic Masters. He read about how it was forbidden for anyone to look inside a battery — *spiritual energy radiators*, as they were fancifully called. He read about the Golden Millennium. He read about the Expected One, who would lead the way for the arrival of the Cosmic Masters, in their unveiled glory. He read about the predicted end of all monetary systems. He read about earth's possible membership of the Interplanetary Parliament. He read about an invisible flying saucer, referred to as the Third Satellite, which often visited earth, under the command of The Karmic Lord Mars Sector 6. He read of how the saucer's presence enhances spiritual actions by a factor of three thousand. He read that the next predicted date for the saucer's return was a mere three months away.

While he read of these and many other even more unlikely things, from the back of his cunning mind, aspects of the required plan for enriching Ron began making themselves known.

It was clever. Damned clever.

It excited him.

But he began to feel guilty. What he was planning was pure deception. But then again, he argued internally, it couldn't be deception because he'd already told Simon he'd simply made Godfrey up, so it was Simon's fault for being so dumb.

Shit, was this happening? Was this loopy day really happening?

Hearing the cab return, Albert put the pamphlets back on the floor, and lay on the bed, staring at the ceiling. Presently, a tap on the door heralded Simon's moody entrance.

'Is a cheese and onion pasty all right?' asked Simon, producing one from the belly pocket of his cagoule.

Slow to respond, Albert quietly said, 'Tell me about the Golden Millennium, Simon.'

Unsure at first, Simon sat on the wooden chair beside the bed while Albert continued to stare at the ceiling. Initially hesitant, Simon quickly found his pace, and his tone became increasingly portentous as he talked of the period of bliss poised to becalm the world: -

- Of the emergence on earth of the Expected One to lead the way forward, preparing earth for the arrival of Cosmic Masters, openly intervening in human affairs once humans have learnt to control their incessant squabbling.

- Of the subsequent conquest of disease, old age and famine.

- Of the end of monetary systems.

- Of the entry of earth into the Interplanetary Parliament.

Finally, lowering his earnest voice, Simon said, 'It's you, Albert. You're the Expected One. The earth Master to usher in the Cosmic Masters. Like you told us last night, you're going to create peace on earth by influencing everyone with your mind.'

Silence befell the room.

'Cheese and onion's fine,' said Albert, sitting up and removing the pasty from Simon's hands. 'Any chance of a cup of tea?'

Mystically deflated, Simon muttered that there was indeed some tea available, and went to make it while Albert wolfed the pasty, which he wished had been two or three times as large. Laying his head back down on the robe-pillow and staring at the ceiling, he again pondered his extraordinary circumstances: he was in an isolated, barren country mansion, and was an object of religious adoration, regarded as the person who was going to change the world with his mind. How the fuck had this happened? Apparently, according to Simon, it was all to do with what he'd said last night. Thinking back, he began to recall more fully the "succeeding where Christ had failed" bullshit he'd conjured for his gullible companions.

When Simon appeared with the tea, Albert sat up a little, and added a minor spaced-out, distant look to himself.

'What is it?' asked Simon, his tired-looking eyes at once awakening. 'The ley lines? Messages?'

'I don't know,' murmured Albert, continuing to exist exotically until, lying back again, he said, 'It's passing.'

Simon pushed his glasses up. 'What was it? Tell me.'

'Strange feelings, Simon. Powerful feelings. Strange thoughts. Strange ideas. All cramming in at the same time. Like a hundred things had been said to me at once.'

'Transmissions,' decided Simon rapidly.

'Maybe,' admitted Albert quietly. Sitting up fully, he held out his hands for the tea. 'I've never experienced anything like it. It was a bit scary.'

'Definitely transmissions,' asserted Simon. 'Has to be. Please listen to them, Albert. The Cosmic Masters are using you.'

'I will, Simon,' said Albert, appearing a degree dazed, 'if that's what you advise.'

Much heartened, Simon handed the tea to Albert. Delving into his cagoule's bulging belly pocket, he retrieved a small bottle of hair shampoo, a toothbrush, and some toothpaste, placing them on the bed. Now speaking plainly, he said, 'One-eighty for the shampoo. Ninety-nine for the pasty. Ninety for the toothpaste, and one pound for the toothbrush. There wasn't any deodorant. Four sixty-nine in all. No charge for the tea — workmen left a box of teabags and some UHT milk.'

And he stood there, waiting for four pounds, sixty-nine pence.

Albert hoped it hadn't shown, but he was stunned. The man whom he had begun believing would bankroll him was so tight he was charging his own Messiah, or whatever, for basic hospitality. He would even have charged for the cup of tea if it had left him out of pocket. Simon was some kind of grotesque miser freak, and it felt like a huge cosmic joke. If he'd had any kind of home to go to, Albert knew he would have got up and gone to it there and then. But he didn't have a home, and he was desperate to pay Ron back, so he had to stay and just try to be even more cunning.

Concealing his amazement and dismay, he took a five pound note from his coat pocket, handing it to Simon.

'I should have change,' said Simon, lifting up his cagoule to reach his trouser pocket.

'You perplex me, Simon,' Albert quietly informed him.

'Why? How?' asked Simon, counting coins.

When Simon proffered the change, Albert gazed into his tea. 'You purport to wish the Golden Age upon mankind, yet you cling to the old age. Why is that, Simon?'

'I don't!' objected Simon, pushing his glasses up, his eyes kindling with innocently indignant passion, eyes that had not closed in rest for well over a day now.

'You do, Simon. You cling to your riches. Yet you know that when the Golden Age dawns, your riches will be valueless. Why is it, Simon? Is it because you don't truly believe?'

'Of course I believe,' insisted Simon, putting the change on the bed since Albert was showing no interest in receiving the coins. 'I do. I believe.'

Albert gave Simon a scrutinising look.

'I believe,' repeated Simon.

Staring at his tea again, Albert said, 'Then prove it to me, Simon. Destroy that five pound note. Rip it up.'

Mute horror. It was like Simon was a mother commanded to kill her child.

'Do it, Simon,' urged Albert, quietly but sternly. 'I need to know your strength and commitment. I — we — need to know you're greater than others.' He looked at Simon. 'Do it, Simon. Do it.'

Hesitantly, Simon tore the five pound note into two halves.

'Now let them fall,' commanded Albert.

Simon released the two pieces, watching their lurid descent as they fluttered down to the floor around Albert's feet.

'That will be all for now,' said Albert, gazing into his tea again. 'I need to be alone for a while.'

Simon continued to stare at the pieces of money until, after a few moments, he began slowly — hypnotically — bending down to reach them.

'Leave them,' said Albert. 'You must let them go.'

Simon resentfully snapped out of his trance, and wordlessly left the room, whereupon Albert collected up the fiver — a bit of Sellotape and he could spend it, he reckoned.

Yes, he was a cunning bastard all right, thought Albert, putting his feet up on the bed and sipping his tea. Not only had he saved himself some money, he knew he had won a major battle against an obvious neurosis. Simon would surely never consider charging him for future meals, for to do so would be to suggest a lack of faith. And he had been psychologically tenderised for further, bigger cooking.

Parting Simon from his money was now an absorbing mind game to Albert. From his new, ruthlessly evolutionary viewpoint, it was a battle of two muddy pool molecules fighting for resources, and the winner would be in a better position to attract mates. He would go along with it. It's what he was put together out of food and air and water to do for that pointless molecule of his. Besides, he owed it to Ron, although how that self-generated commitment could be explained in evolutionary psychology terms he didn't know... until a few seconds later when he decided that giving money and time away charitably was a way of showing potential mates how richly resourceful a person is. *Look at this girls, I can afford to give away thousands — got to be worth shagging, am I not?*

Getting off the bed with his tea, Albert picked some books to study from the shelves above the windows. They were crazy — artless, pseudo-scientific nonsense. But apparently Simon fell for it all, unable to spot the glaring holes in the logic and principles. Simon had *faith* in it all.

If anyone could invent compelling New Age mysticism wrapped up in scientific-sounding theory, Albert believed *he* could, and for Ron, he jolly well would.

Ridiculous ideas began teeming.

*

By lunch time, Sarah's concern for Jennifer had declined. Yes, she had sounded unaccountably distressed, and had said some puzzling things, but, in part, she was actually pleased that her sister had done something impulsive and bold for once, as she saw it. It was, thought Sarah, in a way more like the reaction of a normal person. If Jennifer had taken off penniless, that would have been a real worry, but she had more than enough money to buy safety, wherever she ended up, and Sarah hoped that, although inexperienced, she would soon learn to look out for herself well enough.

It would make or break her, thought Sarah, praying for the former.

To her aunt Jane, however, Sarah knew it would constitute a crisis, and she resigned herself to the necessity of going to Richmond to break the news and spend some time.

In the early afternoon, just after Sarah left for her aunt's, Ron re-read Albert's letter to Jennifer, and, to his surprise, he welled-up again. Putting the letter away, he decided to ring his friend to offer what solace and support he could. This decision did not come easy, for since he'd never known Albert directly express his true feelings, the likelihood of him doing so now was hugely scary — it had been bad enough when he'd choked up burying the cat. However, a call to Rebecca revealed that Albert had not returned there, and no one else he rang had seen or heard anything of him since the previous night. He grew concerned, and even fleetingly considered going out to look for him, but got stoned and watched a video instead.

*

His book studies over, after brushing his teeth, Albert took off his coat and slipped the stiff, golden gown — of identical ecclesiastical cut to Simon's — over himself... and felt like a pillock. He started taking it off again, but then steeled himself: he was going to give this one a shot for Ron.

By unravelling some thread from his T-shirt and tying a few knots here and there, he was able to fashion a tiny harness, in which he suspended one of the inch-high crystal pyramids, taken from the stands beside the bed. Putting this harnessed crystal into his pocket under his gown, he was now ready to take on the mantle of the Expected One, and announce the imminent coming of the Golden Millennium.

He opened his bedroom door slowly, and listened for noises. There were none. Peering above him, he saw a light fitting high up, but the switch for it didn't work. Taking care not to trip on his robe and tumble on the dim stairs that began just outside his door, with not a little trepidation, he left the room to seek out Simon. Once down on the dingy corridor, he stole looks into the rooms, all large, empty and cold. Each had had at least one fireplace removed, or boarded up, and large radiators installed below the windows. Some had fitted blackboards. All had neon strip lights, but none of the switches would bring them to life.

With his robe swishing and rustling as he walked, he proceeded to the head of the grand, curving, wooden staircase, and began to hear sounds coming from below. He listened: organised walking sounds; low chanting; made up words; then, in conclusion, a chorus of "not long low". About to descend, he was arrested by an unsettling development: *he began hearing his own voice*. For a moment, he was truly unnerved and chilled, until it dawned upon him that he was only hearing the recording of himself reciting his Godfrey story that Simon had made a few weeks earlier. Nerve sufficiently restored, he moved slowly down the staircase.

In the large reception room, wearing their *Not Long Now* T-shirts, Simon, Carl and Phil were sitting on old, cheap kitchen chairs surrounding Simon's cassette player, placed on an upturned wooden crate. When Albert reached the bottom stair, Simon saw him, and switched off the tape.

This was it: *show time*.

'All is being revealed to me, Simon,' murmured Albert, in a far-away manner. 'There is nothing but Godfrey in the cosmos. Godfrey is the essence. Godfrey is the mathematics. Godfrey is the symmetry.'

'Amazing,' breathed Simon, gazing upon a now golden Albert.

'The robe th'uits you,' remarked Phil.

At first appearing unsure as to how he was supposed to react, Carl finally adopted a reverential aspect.

'I have much to tell,' continued Albert, walking slowly across the mostly bare room. Arriving at the prayer battery, erected atop its tripod, he gazed at it, as if drawn to do so. 'Everything's become clear to me here. This is the place. It's all crystallised perfectly for me now. I know what I have to do.'

'It's the energies here,' deemed Simon, pushing his glasses up. 'All the ley lines.'

'Yes, it's the ley lines, Simon,' agreed Albert, placing his hands on the battery. 'They're the essence. They're the essence.'

Something beeped, and Simon and Carl turned disapproving eyes on to Phil.

'Th'orry,' he lisped. 'My th'watch.'

'What time is it?' asked Albert — far too normally.

Sounding a little mystically deflated, Simon answered, 'Four o'clock.'

Realising he'd fucked up in asking the worldly time, Albert quickly sought to rescue his spiritual image. Turning his back to the battery, he addressed his followers in a quiet yet revelatory tone. 'I am Albert Fox, the Expected One, and to recreate Eden with your help is my task.' He paused, then stressed, '*To recreate Eden.*'

Briefly murmuring something, Simon's mouth remained open.

Carl looked to Simon for guidance.

'The prayer battery's mine,' spouted Phil. 'I th'ole it from the Orthrium Society. Th'imon told me to.'

Carl half raised a fist to Phil, who half cowered. 'Shadup, will ya?'

Carl again looked to Simon for guidance, but Simon was in a state of profound abstraction.

'The Expected One,' murmured Simon, kneeling.

Carl also knelt.

Then Phil.

Albert continued his revelation. 'Peace. Love. The Golden Millennium. Earth's readiness for entry into the Interplanetary Parliament. The abolition of all monetary systems. The end of all want. That is what I, the Expected One, have been instructed to achieve. And it has, this afternoon, been disclosed to me how.'

'How?' spluttered Phil, eliciting more disapproving looks.

Albert answered decisively, 'By utilising extraterrestrial knowledge to construct a machine allowing all minds on earth to be influenced by mine, bringing peace, harmony and enlightenment to the four corners.'

434

'Amazing,' breathed Simon.

'I was chosen because of my knowledge of science, and last night I received knowledge of bliss from the Cosmic Masters. They filled me with their bliss. And in the Golden Millennium to come, all will experience my ecstasy.'

'Amazing,' breathed Simon.

'Th'great,' lisped Phil.

'Ley lines,' explained Albert, 'are the key. The ley lines channelled the messages from the Cosmic Masters to me, and that's what we're going to use to spread my peace: the ley lines. That's why Godfrey put them there so very long ago.' Looking directly at Simon, he revealed, 'We're going to use the ley lines to transmit my serenity around the globe.'

'Amazing,' breathed Simon.

'Th'great,' lisped Phil.

'And I have been told to have the machine — the Global Empathy Device — constructed by midnight, February the first.'

February the first! Simon took only a second to realise the significance of that date. Jumping to his feet, face beaming with boyish enthusiasm, he blurted, 'The next Spiritual Push!' He turned ecstatically to Carl, who quickly understood, or pretended to. Looking back at Albert, he saw puzzlement. 'The Spiritual Push!' he said again, expecting Albert to now show comprehension, which he did not. Pushing his glasses up, he tried, 'The return of the Third Satellite?'

Albert's confused look remained. 'I know nothing of those things.'

Simon realised he needed to furnish an explanation. 'Spiritual Pushes are times when a spacecraft called the Third Satellite orbits the earth, and —'

'It's invithsible!' blurted Phil, getting to his feet.

Carl also stood up.

'It's invisible,' confirmed Simon, 'and to radar. The Orthrium leader received a psychic transmission telling the dates of its visits. February the first's the next time. Midnight. That's why the machine has to be ready by then. Don't you see?'

'Every th'piritual action is magnified three thousthand timesth by the th'pacecraft!' spluttered Phil.

'Don't you see?' said Simon to Albert, 'the spacecraft will magnify your serenity transmissions three thousand times. Midnight, February the first is when the Golden Millennium begins.' He turned to the others, pushed his glasses up, punched the air, and cried,

'February the first!' Turning around with his arm still raised, he saw that Albert was now intently dowsing with a crystal pyramid dangling from his finger.

Simon was spellbound.

Continuing to dowse, Albert wandered out of the room, accompanied by his mystified followers. In the next room, he searched for whatever it was he was looking for, but seemed not to find it, and moved on again. To Phil's questions as to the purpose of this exploration of the house's ground floor, he gave no reply. In a fourth room, subject to a discreetly gesticulated threat from Carl, Phil refrained from further enquiry, only speaking again to remark on the size of a cobweb in a high corner.

Simon was in enthralled silence all the time.

Albert's divination trek passed through a number of unfurnished rooms that he guessed had once been small dormitories. Near to them, he discovered a large washroom and toilet facility. Along a side corridor lay three basically-furnished smaller rooms that he was told were being used as bedrooms. And down a shorter corridor, he found the kitchen area. The kitchen was equipped with a tatty washing machine; a small fridge that looked as if it had been in a fight; and an oven that looked as if it had been in four fights, losing them all. On the dusty, tiled floor, potholes marked where Albert assumed school-scaled cooking equipment had once stood.

All ground floor rooms having been visited, beginning to appear troubled, Albert paused for thought. 'It must be in the garden,' he murmured.

Following his finger, he went outside, roaming to and fro, absorbed in his task. Except for a sprinkling of splutterings from Phil about distant sheep and strangely shaped clouds, respectful silence was maintained by the group as they followed Albert.

Simon frequently scanned the skies for UFOs.

On the edge of the wood, many yards from the house, the crystal began circling, insignificantly at first, then in ever larger figures.

'Here,' said Albert, removing the thread bearing the crystal from his finger. 'This is it.'

'This is what?' inquired Simon.

'This is the place. This is the pole.'

'What pole?'

'The earth's ley pole,' revealed Albert. 'This is where we'll position the Empathy Device on February the first. This is the precise point where the earth's key ley lines originate, shooting off to the four corners.' His voice became awed. 'The most dynamic place on earth, hidden since the dawn of time, now revealed to us for our sacred purpose.'

'Amazing,' breathed Simon, kneeling to place his hands flat on the earth. 'I can feel it. I can feel the energy.'

He began taking deep, ostentatious breaths.

Looking uncertain, Carl also knelt down, emulating Simon's gestures and breathing.

'Th'what's it th'posed to feel like?' asked Phil, also copying Simon. 'Th'imon, what's it th'posed to feel like? Th'imon?'

But Simon was oblivious to Phil. 'Here,' he breathed reverentially. 'Here.'

'No other place on earth will do,' said Albert.

That's what he'd said, but what he was thinking while observing Simon pawing the ground was that he'd made a pretty good start. Simon had millions, claimed Phil, and Albert had observed in Phil a talent for indelicate frankness. At the very least, Simon had Deepdale Hall. Perhaps all he had to do from now on to secure Ron his compensation was to connive a little more, keep speaking in a self-assured, Messianic manner, bone up a bit more on Orthrium nonsense, and look a bit serene for a while. Easy money, he reckoned. He'd put on bigger acts just to get a beer in his time.

Maintaining a suitable equanimity, he began walking back to the house, crunching dark gravel underfoot. Simon caught him up, whereupon Albert halted, some paces from the front door. Appearing pensive yet tranquil, he gazed at the house, now a looming grey form against a darkening sky.

'Not long now, Simon,' he said quietly. 'The Golden Millennium is almost upon the world.'

'Not long now,' agreed Simon eagerly, pushing his glasses up. 'February the first.'

Simon did a quick UFO scan. Behind him, Carl did a scan too, while behind Carl, Phil studied an odd mushroom.

Still viewing the house, injecting an air of concern into his delivery, Albert said, 'But it's up to you as much as me, Simon. I'll do my part, but will you do yours?'

'Of course I will,' answered Simon.

Turning to Simon, Albert asked, 'Do you know what your part is?' Before Simon could answer, he earnestly explained, 'To support me, Simon. To trust me. To believe me. To give me everything I need to carry off this momentous thing without delay or hindrance. The

Cosmic Masters contacted me, but I was without faith. But they also wisely brought you in to help me. You've already helped me believe in myself again, but there's more they want you to do. You have to provide me with what I need to get the job done, now that you've helped me see things clearly.' He returned his gaze to the house. 'It's an elaborate device, Simon. And no one else on earth sees the Truth like you do, so no one else will help.'

Money: Albert was talking money, Simon knew right enough. 'What do you need?' he asked, bracing himself.

'Crystal pyramids,' answered Albert. 'Thirteen crystal pyramids.' Relief was visible on Simon's face.

Albert added, 'And a few tools and some electronic components.'

'What kind of—'

Cutting Simon off, Albert elucidated on his scheme for peace of mind. 'The Cosmic Masters transmitted powerful, secret knowledge to me, Simon; knowledge I must use to start the Golden Millennium. Crystal pyramids are the key to the working of the Empathy Device. It operates on the principle of energy resonance. It's like marching soldiers making a bridge collapse. They march in tune with the bridge's resonant frequency. A specific alignment — no, a sacred alignment — of crystal pyramids has been revealed to me that will amplify my serene mind waves to an intensity great enough to be sent around the world along the ley lines. Sympathetic bliss will be induced in all, allowing the millennium of peace to begin.' He dangled the quartz pyramid before Simon's eyes. 'Thirteen crystal pyramids — that's all I need from you, Simon.'

'Amazing,' breathed Simon. But then, pushing his glasses up, he shrewdly — suspiciously — enquired, 'What size crystal pyramids?'

'What size?' echoed Albert distractedly. 'What size? No great size. Extraterrestrial science has learned efficiency. It uses the power of nature. It uses zero point energy.'

'Amazing,' breathed Simon. A fantastic energy device of aligned crystal pyramids made wondrous sense to him. He was a person who believed that the lost city of Atlantis had been powered by a mountainous crystal pyramid. He believed that because he'd read it in one of his New Age books, and Albert had browsed that very book. He'd even heard about zero point energy in a science documentary he'd seen about various inventors claiming to have accidentally — albeit in a minuscule way — tapped the almost unlimited energy of the quantum vacuum. Most of these inventions involved cracking water into its constituent molecules in novel ways, resulting in unfounded claims of excess heat production. The excess was speculated as perhaps coming from the so-called zero point source — the energy of the frothing sea of virtual particles constantly being created and destroyed in the quantum vacuum. Watching the documentary, Simon hadn't really grasped the underlying principles, but he'd fully embraced the near mystical element of "mysterious" energy sources.

Turning to gaze at the dark hills, Albert said, 'All I need to make the world perfect is thirteen crystal pyramids.'

'And some equipment, you said,' remembered Simon, pushing his glasses up. 'What sort of budget are we looking at? The roof repairs and the up-coming renovation have really eaten into the available finance for the business. And the house might need rewiring, too, before we can reconnect the power. An electrician's coming on Tuesday. That's all costing extra.'

As if Simon's mundane considerations hadn't registered, Albert, still gazing at the hills, enquired, 'Do you know what zero point energy is, Simon?'

'I saw a documentary on it. It's natural energy. Incredible energy.'

'Yes, Simon, it is incredible. It comes from the quantum vacuum where particles are forever appearing and disappearing. They're created in opposite pairs — as matter and antimatter — that instantly annihilate each other again. There's enough zero point energy in a teaspoon of water to boil all the world's oceans. And I now know how to extract it, just like I know how to amplify my spiritual energy. Once the world has been made peaceful, I'll make zero point energy fully available. No more want. No more pollution. And all I need from you first is thirteen crystal pyramids.'

Epiphany.

In a daring, exciting, high-wire moment of glimpsed possibility, Albert changed his plan. He had been leading up to asking for ten thousand pounds to "buy" the tools and electronic components he might need — ten thousand pounds he would then run away with to give to Ron. But he suddenly realised he could— and also realised *how* he could — aim higher. Much higher — Simon was a fucking multi-millionaire, for fuck's sake.

'Amazing,' breathed Simon. 'You can have the crystal pyramids.'

'Diamond pyramids,' said Albert. 'I need diamond pyramids. The design calls for *diamond*.'

'Diamonds? Th'great!' said Phil, thrilled.

Phil might have been thrilled, but an aghast, funereal look at once shrouded Simon, and he wandered away from Albert, staring over into the distance where the sun had sunk below the high moors.

Albert took a few steps the opposite way, toward a small wall no higher than a tennis net, which seemed to serve no purpose.

Looking confused and perturbed, Carl eventually joined Simon.

Albert stood beside the wall, waiting. Phil came and stood next to him, soon appearing uncomfortable with the silence.

'Th'imon thinks he might be gay,' blurted Phil out of the blue.

'Yeah, whatever,' muttered Albert, dropping his serenity act considerably now that Simon was some distance away.

'I'm not th'saying it because I'm homophobic or anything. I like th'imon. He's my best friend.'

He'd blown it, Albert started to worry. He should have stuck at ten grand. Thirteen diamond pyramids would mean Simon giving him... a fortune, perhaps. No way. This was a man who wouldn't even give a sandwich to the new Messiah. Fuck. Absolute fuck. But what had been said had been said, and he'd have to stick with it now, he knew, and he wasn't going to throw in the towel — he owed Ron.

Simon came over, flanked by Carl. Standing near Albert, not looking him in the eyes, he said enigmatically, 'It was an investment, you know?'

Not particularly knowing what he was talking about, Albert made no reply.

'The house,' explained Simon, still reluctant to look Albert in the face. 'It was an investment.'

'A selfless investment the world will celebrate for a thousand years, Simon,' said Albert.

But Simon's ears had become deaf. 'I'm having it converted into a centre for New Age studies,' he continued, disregarding Albert's prediction. 'We'll offer courses to paying guests. Carl's going to be the caretaker.'

Carl nodded. 'Sick of cabbying.'

'I'm going to be cook,' said Phil, proudly. 'I'm cooking th'upper for us all tonight.'

'That's right,' confirmed Simon. 'And we're going to run a business providing spiritually balanced food grown on the ley lines. Anyway, no matter what, this property will at least hold its value. There's a lot of inward investment coming to the Northeast. A property like this will be sought-after soon.'

'Th'ouldn't I th'art collecting bits of wood for the fire before it'sth too dark?' suggested Phil.

'Yes, good idea,' returned Simon.

''Ere, I'll 'elp you,' offered Carl, joining Phil, who had already begun scavenging.

Simon vaguely watched their efforts as they wandered around, picking up builders' off cuts and pieces of broken school desks.

'You have to let go, Simon,' said Albert. 'You even told me yourself that in the Golden Millennium, monetary systems will be abolished. People will have what they need, and no one will want more.'

Turning to look at the darkly-distant moors, with his lips slightly parted, Simon bore the appearance of a person unconvinced and troubled.

Seeing the worry and doubt on Simon's face, Albert moved some steps closer to the house, surveying it. 'This house will become priceless to humanity, Simon. It will be more than you ever imagined. Things are being revealed to me even as we speak.' He went on to explain how here positive energy was maximum, and destructive negative energies were minimum, thus providing the most propitious surroundings in which to pioneer the New Age of science. This was where New Age science would soon be born. 'Science for the Golden Millennium. Science that works with and not against the New Age. A laboratory guided by the Aquarian shift in consciousness already overcoming the world, allowing science passage into the Golden Millennium.' A passion entering his voice, Albert went on to say, 'Once we've prepared the world with my bliss, here is where the extraterrestrial Cosmic Masters will come to teach us their great secrets. We'll have all the energy we'll need, and with their guidance, devices to eliminate pain and disease will be created here. Ageing will be conquered. The environment will be cleansed. Here is where it will all come true.' He turned to Simon. 'And it's all dependent on you, Simon.'

Simon gave Albert a sullen glance, then looked at the ground for some moments before scanning the sky.

'Simon,' asked Albert quietly, 'do you know how the Cosmic Masters power their spaceships?'

Shuffling in thrilled anticipation, Simon pushed his glasses up and faced Albert. 'No. We've never been told.'

'With mathematics, Simon. They are Lords of Mathematics — the language of Godfrey. And they've learnt how to make their mathematics real. Their mathematics doesn't just describe conditions in the universe, it *makes* conditions. It makes *magic*, Simon — they can alter the physical laws of the universe to suit their needs. To power their ships they create a localised dampening field on one side of the vessel that suppresses the creation of virtual particles, and the natural pressure of the particles bombarding the other side provides them with nearly unlimited acceleration.'

'Amazing,' breathed Simon.

'They do it with diamonds, Simon. Thirteen diamonds. They do everything with diamonds.'

Turning away to face the dark, brooding hills, Simon quietly, tentatively asked, 'How much will they cost?'

'I have no idea, Simon. Cost is a mere worldly issue. But I do know that the larger the diamonds, the more my serenity will be amplified.'

'Supposing it doesn't work?'

'I am the Expected One. It will work.'

'But supposing it doesn't?'

'Don't you believe in me, Simon?'

'It's not a question of whether I believe in you or not.'

'I think it is.'

'It's not,' said Simon, in a voice barely audible to Albert. 'It's not.'

'I think it is,' said Albert, before going into the house, watched lugubriously by Simon.

Indoors, making a weary effort to look serene in the gloom, Albert sat on the grand staircase and began thinking pessimistically. Simon had unconscious doubts about it all, he understood, otherwise he'd be opening his wallet right now, regardless of being some kind of ultimate miser. If he *truly* believed in the Empathy Device and the imminence of the Golden Millennium, miserliness wouldn't come into it. But he didn't truly believe, so even if he was somehow talked into paying for the diamonds, Albert knew he'd be breathing over his shoulder all the while. He just couldn't imagine Simon handing him a trunk of money and telling him to get on with it all. Ten thousand? — maybe. Ten hundred thousand? — no way.

Muddy pool. Muddy pool. Muddy bloody pool.

Epiphany.

In a moment of deepest cunning, Albert saw a sweet, irresistible peach of a deception. There was a way he could sweep away Simon's underlying doubts about... about the *magic* of it all. He would *demonstrate* powerful magic to him, and once convinced, Simon would surely be free with his sponsorship.

It was another five minutes before Simon came indoors, closely followed by Carl and Phil, who carried armfuls of wood.

'Th'hello, Albert,' said Phil when he saw him sitting on the dim staircase.

Albert didn't reply.

Haunting the shadows opposite Albert was the imposing stone fireplace guarded by the two griffins. Carl and Phil laid their wood beside it. Simon, subdued and pensive, sitting on what looked like an old school chair, occasionally glancing in sullen resentment at the dim, nebulous figure that was Albert.

'Can I th'light the candles?' asked Phil.

Simon's muttered consent set Phil on a round of fire raising.

Carl began lighting candles, too.

'Don't light too many,' advised Simon cheerlessly. 'They were expensive.'

Albert approached Simon, now gazing despondently at the floor. Not looking up, Simon gloomily said, 'Diamond?'

'Diamond,' confirmed Albert.

A pause.

'Why diamond?'

'It's the purest, greatest crystal in existence, Simon,' explained Albert in a calm voice. 'Thirteen pure diamond crystals correctly aligned will amplify my mind waves and transmit them at a frequency the ley lines can absorb. Only diamond oscillates at the same frequency as the ley lines. Other crystals could crudely amplify my mind waves if aligned correctly, but only diamond can achieve ultra-high amplification and transmit at the ley line frequency to spread my bliss around the world.'

'Amazing,' breathed Simon, unable to help himself, looking at Albert and pushing his glasses up. His mystical transport was fleeting, however. 'But what if it doesn't work?'

'Then you'll still have the diamonds.'

Simon began shaking his head. 'It'll be too much money. They might cost millions. It's too much of a risk. Things could... They might... They'd have to be cut to shape and that would cost thousands alone. No. I can't do it. Impossible. I've made up my mind.'

'I can change your mind,' said Albert.

'You can't,' said Simon, resolute now.

'I'm going to change everyone's mind.'

As the prayer battery emerged from deep dimness into candlelight, Albert, appearing to be absorbed in arcane thought, approached it.

Knowing he was being gloomily viewed by Simon, he placed a hand upon it.

'Can we th'light the fire as th'well?' asked Phil.

'Not yet,' returned Simon, continuing to observe Albert. 'It's not cold enough.'

With candlelights flickering in his eyes, Albert looked at Simon. 'I know how I can prove it to you, Simon.'

'Prove what?'

'Crystal energy resonance — but without the need for diamonds.'

'How?' asked Simon, pushing his glasses up.

Holding out the crystal pyramid he'd dowsed with, Albert said, 'I don't have diamond yet, but quartz should do for people *within* the resonance pattern.' He went to the fireplace, put the crystal on the hearth, lifted up one of the stone griffins, and brought it down upon the crystal, shattering it.

Carl looked uneasily at Simon.

Simon looked aghast. 'That cost me ten pounds.'

'Th'what did you do that for?' asked Phil.

Speaking with intensity, gripping Simon by the shoulders, looking vigorously into his eyes, Albert said, 'Do you want to sample my serenity, Simon? Be the first to glimpse the New Age? The Golden Millennium? Ahead of all others? This very night, Simon? *This very night?*'

Simon's stupefaction was total. Utterly stupefied. Utterly unable to muster any kind of answer to the momentous question. So long did Simon remain dumb-struck, it became awkward for Albert, gripping his shoulders, needing a reply.

'Can I be the first as th'well?' chimed Phil.

'And me?' asked Carl, after some hesitation.

Using their questions as an excuse to release Simon, Albert announced, 'You can all be first. You three worthy people, ahead of the whole world, shall glimpse the New Age.'

'But how?' lisped Phil in confusion. 'You haven't th'made the thing device th'yet.'

With his golden robe glittering in the candlelight, Albert picked up the crystal pieces. Six enchanted eyes were fixed upon him as he collected the shattered fragments. Returning to the battery, standing beside it, holding out the crystal shards, he pronounced, 'By placing these pieces of quartz around the house in accordance with the sacred alignment revealed to me, I may be able to directly bathe you all in bliss.'

444

'Amazing,' breathed Simon. He thought for a second. 'Why can't we use quartz in the Empathy Device?'

'Because quartz doesn't radiate at the right frequency for the ley lines. But that won't matter here because you'll be directly within the energy field. And only diamond can amplify to the level required to energise the whole world. All crystals have the potential to tap zero point energy, but diamond has by far the most, and pyramid shapes concentrate that energy trillions of times.'

'Amazing,' breathed Simon.

'Th'great,' lisped Phil. 'Th'what's th'ero point energy?'

Ignoring Phil, fixing Simon with a preparatory gaze, Albert said, 'Simon, tonight you'll learn the true power of crystals. We've had the stone age, the bronze age, the iron age, the steam age, the nuclear age, the computer age, soon we shall enter the final, purest age of them all, the *Crystal Age*. Do you want to be the first to experience the crystal age?'

Simon breathed, 'Yes.'

Paul McCartney

They were moving on to Robert's favourite bar. Clambering into a cab outside the restaurant where they had only just met less than three hours earlier, Jennifer squeezed herself in between her two new friends.

She had already drunk beyond her usual limit.

'You're quite a shy person, aren't you?' divined Robert as the cab set off.

Yvette's face jumped into an expression of scandalised disagreement. Stretching her French vowels, touching Jennifer's arm, she protested, 'No, she is not shy. You are not shy, are you, Jennifer?'

With her alleged — and refuted — shyness receiving such attention and scrutiny, Jennifer felt herself begin to colour. 'How long have you and Robert been going out together?' she asked, to deflect the focus away from her.

'Wee-er not love-ers!' exclaimed Yvette, strectching her vowels the furthest yet.

'Oh,' said Jennifer. 'I thought —'

'My boyfriend's called Peter. 'E's at work tonight.'

Jennifer began saying how she had broken up with her own boyfriend the night before, and that was mostly why she had come to London, but she was cut short when the cab stopped. She could hardly believe it: they were apparently already at their destination.

Yvette and Robert opened their doors, and standing on the road, Robert paid the driver.

When she stepped on to the kerb, Jennifer commented, 'We could have walked this in three minutes!'

'But I can drink a beer in three minutes,' said Robert, with a smirk, leading the way to the bar entrance, a step behind a young couple.

On door duty just inside the bar's entrance was a dark-haired young woman of masculine appearance. She had a narrow, hard face and dark features, and seemed to take her job with much grim seriousness. She stepped prohibitively in front of the couple ahead of Robert. 'Sorry, no tables free,' she said indifferently, her voice husky, her accent Italian.

The disappointed couple went away.

'Hello, Robert,' she said, standing aside so that he could enter.

'Trevor's been in looking for you.'

Robert showed great interest in this intelligence. 'Really?'

'About an hour ago,' said the woman. She began to turn Yvette and Jennifer away, when Robert intervened.

'No,' he said, 'they're with me.'

As if granting a privilege not really hers to bestow, she stood aside, allowing Yvette and Jennifer entry.

'Trevor left something for you behind the bar,' she informed Robert, in a low voice. 'Ask Danny for it.'

'Excellent,' rumbled Robert quietly, and he followed his companions inside.

It was like nothing in her home town. Jennifer had been expecting a pub, but this was like a lively restaurant for getting drunk in. Lighting was minimal. Candles burned on the tables. Latin music, in keeping with a general Mexican theme, played louder than she would have liked. There were indeed no tables free, but some standing space was available at a drinks bar, and that is where they headed, led by Robert. Reaching the bar, he explained that the licence only allowed for drinks to be served with a meal, but since he knew all the staff, it would be okay.

It wasn't long before Jennifer was holding her fourth beer of the evening.

'I used to be shy,' said Robert unexpectedly, necessarily speaking into Jennifer's ear to be heard above the music. 'Want to know how I got over it?'

'How?' shouted Jennifer.

'By telling myself that in any gathering I might be in, no one was anywhere near as clever as me. Just think of the other people as mere children compared to yourself, then you'll never feel shy again.'

'I'll try,' answered Jennifer.

It was warm, and Jennifer took off her coat when Robert told her he could have it stashed safely behind the bar. Yvette had already taken hers off, and, holding it, had begun moving to the music in the small space she had to herself. Robert took charge of Yvette's coat too, while she continued to dance, and passed it over the bar, to be left with the staff's things.

'I really like your dress,' said Yvette, leaning close to Jennifer to be heard above the music.

'Thanks.'

'So do I,' said Robert. 'Very elegant.'

Jennifer now noticed that the wall nearest her had been subject to an artist's brush. It showed a moonlit tropical beach scene, under the words: *Goa, where even the dark is something to see.*

'Have you been?' asked Robert, perceiving the direction of her gaze.

'No. I've only ever been to Turkey, and I was too small to remember much about it.'

'That's terrible!' exclaimed Robert. 'You have to go. You'll be knocked out. Not to Goa — that's too touristy now. Remote beaches on Thailand are where it's all happening now. I'll take you soon.'

Believing that earnest-sounding promise to have actually been made offhand and meaninglessly, Jennifer did not acknowledge it, and it was not repeated. Yvette noticed a table free, and informed Robert, who led the way over to it, away from the bar's loudspeakers. Once they were seated, Robert's conversation turned to relating his travelling exploits in exotic countries, which he sustained, on and off, for nearly an hour. And when his traveller's tales dried up, he suggested they move on to yet another establishment, this time in Soho.

Summoning their bill, Robert insisted on paying it in its entirety, despite Yvette's and Jennifer's expressed wish to share it. Minutes later, he was telling a cabby to drive to Greek Street. Tipsy with beer, excited to have been taken under the wing of such kind, warm people, speeding off to yet another bar, Jennifer felt like she was beginning to live life like it should be lived. Everything and everyone she had seen today had been new and different.

In-between clowning around, Robert and Yvette talked spiritedly about people and occasions unknown to Jennifer.

A partner in a publishing company: when asked by Jennifer, Robert said he was a partner in publishing company. 'Nothing interesting. Just business titles. We're based in Harley Street.'

Jennifer had earlier decided that Robert was probably a retired rock musician, and was disappointed to learn he wasn't.

'And 'e earns lots of money,' added Yvette proudly. 'And 'e's the most wonderful person I know.'

'I earn it so I can give it away,' said Robert, lighting a cigarette.

The driver turned his head around and tapped the back of the partition to draw attention to a prohibitory sign.

'No smoking, mate, if you don't mind.'

'Oh, awfully sorry,' said Robert with almost excessive courtesy, at once extinguishing his cigarette. 'I was a musician before I moved to London,' he said to Jennifer. 'I came down here about five years ago, but the music didn't really make me enough money, so I turned to publishing.'

A street sign told they were now travelling along Shaftsbury Avenue, and looking out the window, Jennifer began to see glitzy theatres boasting star performers. The cab turned left, on to narrower streets thronged with predominantly young pedestrians. Robert now informed her that they were headed for an exclusive establishment, a bar where, not long ago, Paul McCartney had held a party.

'Just over here, thanks,' Robert told the driver.

The cab pulled up, and Jennifer followed her companions out on to the pavement. With her face comically twisted, Yvette arranged herself while Robert paid the fare. Robert then led the way to the bar's entrance, which was defended by a stout doorman with short, gelled, ginger hair. Entering the establishment with lofty confidence, Robert nodded to him in passing.

If asked to sum up her first impressions in one word, Jennifer would have settled for *sophisticated.* Just inside the door was a long, glittering bar, where well-dressed men and women were sitting on high stools. Large, gilt-edged mirrors hung on the tastefully decorated walls. Deeper in, there was a candle-lit dining area. Robert led the way past the long bar and on to a wide, ornate staircase. Lagging a little behind her companions, Jennifer observed that Yvette was the reason why a number of men made discreet upward glances, glances she knew would soon be repeated in her own direction.

Twenty-one carpeted steps later and they were in a small, upstairs lounge, with its own corner bar. Only a dozen or so people were present, mostly sitting around low, rectangular tables that had two-seater sofas either side instead of chairs. As if exhausted, Yvette dropped down on to a sofa, blowing her wayward hair off her face through comically twisted lips. Smiling, she patted the cushion beside her, playfully enticing Jennifer to sit.

Jennifer dutifully sat beside Yvette. After removing his coat, which Jennifer had earlier noticed smelled strongly of stale smoke, Robert, smiling euphorically, sat opposite his companions. A waitress came to take their order, greeting Robert by name. Yvette asked for a bottled beer, echoed by Jennifer. Robert requested a double brandy, insisting it be *Remy Martin.* 'The best brandy in the world,' he explained to Jennifer. Calling to the waitress after she left, he instructed, 'Put it all on my tab.'

'Hello, Robert,' said a young man sitting at the bar, turning on his stool. His tone was cheerless. 'Hello, Yvette.'

'Hello,' said Yvette, her return tone approaching one of suspicion.

'Hello, Mark,' said Robert, sounding pleasantly surprised to see him.

'Don't sound surprised,' returned Mark, 'you know I'm here most nights.'

He turned his back to the room again.

Yvette pulled a sour face.

'Try working with him,' said Robert to Yvette, just so low as not to be heard by Mark. 'It's like having a rain cloud in the room with you all day long.' Looking at Jennifer, he explained, in a deprecating but forthright way, 'One of my partners. King of the barbed comment.'

Jennifer looked toward Mark. He was taller than Robert — but then so were the majority of men — with a saturnine face and weak chin. His straight, collar-length brown hair was swept back. He was wearing dark trousers with a flimsy, light jacket, as if he'd mixed his winter and summer clothes. Within his jacket, he seemed to be holding his shoulders in a lasting shrug.

Turning back to Robert, Jennifer watched him draw on his cigarette. Studying his face, she thought that if he wasn't so nice, she might describe him as unattractive.

The drinks arrived.

'Here's to Jennifer in London,' said Robert, raising his glass.

'Yes!' said Yvette with childlike enthusiasm, raising her beer bottle.

'To me,' agreed Jennifer, clinking her own bottle against the others and swigging a mouthful, some of which ran out over her lips.

After the toast, Jennifer observed that Mark had gone.

2.10
Maximum Cunning

Tonight, Albert was going to pull what seemed to him to be a merry prank. He *had* debated the morality of the prank with himself, but had concluded that since Simon, Carl and Phil were already bonkers, they had nothing to lose.

And anyway, it was their fault for kidnapping him.

And anyway, it was all for Ron.

He was taking a solitary, robed walk in the grounds now. Complete darkness was almost upon the local world, and he moved slowly to avoid tripping. He was beginning to comprehend just what he was on the brink of gaining, if this crucial night went well. When he'd ventured to aim high, it had been spontaneous and without any real contemplation of the rewards, but now he was relishing the potential spoils. "They might cost millions", he remembered Simon had worried, but he'd said it in a way that suggested he *had* millions. Yes, Phil had been right about Simon's wealth. Now Albert was daring to believe that millions might be handed over to *him* soon so that he could supposedly buy diamonds. Never mind the economics, the mathematics alone were staggering.

He turned to look at the house, and could see Phil and Carl moving around inside, in candlelight. He could still scarcely believe where he was and what he was doing, but, at the same time, he felt like he'd been rehearsing for a moment like this all his life. *This* was the kind of great thing he'd been biding his time for all those years in the dole office.

Feeling ready to execute his decisive stroke, he went back indoors.

'Th'we've lit the fire!' said Phil.

'That's good, Phil,' said Albert, like he was speaking to a child.

'Th'ould I th'art cooking dinner now?'

'I'm famished,' declared Carl.

'Not just yet,' said Albert. 'I'll tell you when. I want to get things ready first. Simon, I need Sellotape to secure crystal fragments in strategic places.'

'Sellotape?' queried Simon. 'I don't —'

'Got a roll in me cab,' interjected Carl helpfully, immediately going to retrieve it.

Some minutes later, Phil was lamenting Albert's instructions that his followers should leave the house while he placed the crystal

451

fragments in their positions.

'It can't be allowed,' returned Albert. 'It's the most powerful science on earth. This knowledge, if it were to fall into the hands of evil, could be used to spread hate around the world just as easily as love, or liberate enough zero point energy to destroy the whole solar system.'

'He's right,' decided Simon, sensibly judging the issue. 'That's why we're not allowed to see inside the prayer batteries. The technology's too powerful.'

'Precisely,' said Albert.

'How will you know th'where to put the crystals without measthuring?' asked Phil.

Although initially annoyed that Phil was questioning Albert's methods, Simon realised he also wanted to know that answer, and endorsed Phil's question with a noise. This would have been an awkward moment for Albert had he not anticipated it. 'I don't have to measure the angles and lengths,' he explained patiently, 'I just understand the pattern. It's like a bird building a nest: instinct. The extraterrestrials didn't tell me the figures, they infused the shape into my mind. I dimensionally comprehend the shape.'

'Amazing,' breathed Simon.

So, temporarily alone in the house, Albert, carrying a candle, walked to and fro, upstairs and downstairs, actually placing crystal fragments in various locations just in case he was being glimpsed through the windows. In ten minutes, he was done, and summoned his followers back inside from the near mine-shaft darkness of the grounds. Standing with the blazing fire behind him, he addressed his congregation. 'What happens next, favoured first-born children of the New Age, is that I shall pray at the activation point, and—'

'Th'where's that?' interrupted Phil.

'I can't tell you. If any of you were tempted to pray at that spot, you would flood the house with unbalanced energy. Only my energy is balanced enough to create New Age consciousness.'

'Amazing,' breathed Simon.

Albert continued. 'When I pray at the activation point, my spiritual energy should excite the crystals, which will slowly begin to resonate. It'll be like an echo growing louder, except there'll be nothing to hear. If it works, you'll gradually begin to feel my bliss increasing within you, until you're saturated.'

'Why mightn't it work?' asked Simon, shuffling, and pushing his glasses up.

'Quartz is a crude crystal, and the fragments aren't pyramids,' explained Albert. 'We just have to hope.' He gave Simon an earnest, entreating look. 'Please don't be deterred if it fails. It's not as precise as the proper device will be.'

But bliss was not quite yet ready to come, ordained Albert, declaring they should first eat their evening meal, a meal he said would become even more celebrated than Christ's Last Supper.

'Amazing,' breathed Simon.

'Th'great,' said Phil. 'I'll do chicken.'

'Yeah, I'm right famished,' said Carl, grinning.

Addressing Phil, Albert asked, 'How long will it take you to make the meal?'

'Th'forty minutes.'

'Then go, Phil,' urged Albert, revelling in the opportunity to be dramatic. 'Hasten into the kitchen to prepare the meal that shall never be forgotten.'

'Th'okay,' said Phil, hurrying away.

'Magic,' grinned Carl. 'I'm famished.'

'Should we wear our robes?' suggested Simon.

'Yes, Simon,' answered Albert, 'to reflect the dignity and grandeur of the occasion. And the spirituality. Be seated in this room in forty minutes, robed and glorious, and I, the Expected One, shall serve you the historic meal myself, like Jesus once washed the feet of his own dear disciples.'

'Amazing,' breathed Simon.

'Not long now,' said Albert, taking a candle and heading for the stairs.

'Not long now,' returned Simon.

'Yeah, not long now,' said Carl.

In his room, Albert disrobed and washed as much of himself as he could hold over, or dip into, the basin, using hair shampoo rather than the stubborn soap. The water was perishingly cold, but once he'd finished, he felt better for it. Then he performed a covert act — part of his plan for enrichment.

Putting his robe back on to return downstairs, Albert quietly sought out Phil in the kitchen, and was pleased to find that he was alone, standing at the cooker, which was illuminated by four candles. He was placing chicken pieces in a frying pan.

'Th'imon th'says you can have as much of our food as you want,' he said when he saw Albert.

'That's very kind of him,' said Albert, 'but I won't be eating with you.'

'Th'why not?' spluttered Phil, shocked.

'I'm not hungry. My body hasn't adjusted to my new spirituality yet. I feel a little bit queasy.'

'Th'well just have a small portion. I'm a th'reallly good cook.'

'No. Anyway, Phil, I don't eat meat.'

'Th'you're vegetarian?'

Albert confirmed that he was, and Phil gushed apologies for not having asked.

'Don't worry about it, Phil,' assuaged Albert, 'you weren't to know.'

'I can cook you th'omething without meat,' offered Phil.

'Maybe later.'

'Th'promise?'

'Promise.'

'Th'great!'

Albert leaned against a work surface, watching as Phil began frying the chicken. Another pan was simmering on the cooker — some kind of tomato-based sauce with sweetcorn and peppers, among other, unidentifiable, things. Should he do it now, or wait until the food was dished? Wait, he decided, observing that there was much more food being prepared than was likely to be consumed this night alone.

'Th'Albert, I'm going to grow my hair like yours,' announced Phil, agitating the chicken. 'I'll th'art tomorrow morning.'

'That's good, Phil.'

In a few minutes, the chicken went in with the sauce, and spaghetti was added to a pan of boiling water. 'Th'ure you don't want some?' asked Phil, arranging three large plates ready for the dishing out.

'Sure,' said Albert. 'Vegetarian, remember. And queasy.'

'Th'orry. Forgot.'

The spaghetti was soon ready. Draining it, Phil began dividing it between the three plates. Next came the sauce. When Phil deemed sufficient to have been dished — leaving a fair amount remaining in the saucepan — Albert told him he should go and quickly change into his robe, then sit with Carl and Simon. *He* would wait on them tonight — like Jesus waited on the Clarissions, he said, inventing a new tribe.

'Th'great,' said Phil.

Once Phil left the kitchen, Albert divided the powder that crushing three ecstasy tablets in his room had yielded. The powder was shared between the steaming meals, and worked in so it didn't show.

He hoped the heat wouldn't degenerate the blissful chemical.

That was it. That was fucking it. He'd fucking done it. Truly he did have one of the most cunning minds ever devised by nature. Simon, Carl and Phil would soon be tripping off their silly heads, believing they were undergoing some mystical experience. Beyond the unlikely possibility that the drug might be rendered impotent by the heat of the food, Albert reckoned the only thing that could go wrong now would be for one of them to recognise the effects of ecstasy. However, he just couldn't imagine any of them ever having done trips before. No, he was on safe ground, he reckoned. They wouldn't have a bloody clue.

Picking up a scrap sheet of plywood from the floor, sticking two candles on its edges, Albert placed the three plates on it, and had a tray. Deeming enough time to have elapsed for Phil to have put on his robe, he took the loaded tray into the big room, where his disciples, all robed, were seated at a trestle table positioned near the fire, set with four mismatched chairs.

He knew that if he tripped over his robe and dropped the tray, he dropped his own future as well.

'Once this meal has been consumed,' he announced, 'you will all experience the New Age.'

'Champion,' said Carl, as Albert carefully lay the tray down on the table.

'Why only three plates?' asked Simon.

'Albert's th'not hungry,' spouted Phil. 'He's too th'piritual.'

'That's right,' said Albert, passing each disciple a plate. 'It'll be some hours yet before my body becomes fully accustomed to my new energies. Until then I'll feel a bit queasy.'

'Can we start now?' asked Carl, a fork already poised over his plate.

'Yes, eat,' said Albert, sitting down at the end of the table, in the fire's warmth. 'Everybody eat. Eat it all up. The energies will work best if you've got full stomachs.'

'Magic,' said Carl, immediately tucking in.

'Th'why will the energies th'work better on a full th'omach, Albert?' asked Phil.

Shit, he hadn't thought that one through. 'Because... because it's the opposite of having an anaesthetic, isn't it? And you need an empty stomach for anaesthetics.'

'Yes,' agreed Simon, seeing the logic and wisdom.

God, this was so fucking easy! thought Albert. He could sell them any old piss and label it champagne.

Once the others began to eat, Phil took his own plate away from the table, preferring to sit alone in the shadows. His white robe rucked up to his waist, his plate balanced on his bony legs, he ate steadily, but without speaking. Albert observed that he approached the meal in much the same way he'd eaten the Mars Bar that morning: like he was worried to show his teeth, or be seen eating at all.

In the kitchen, Albert had noticed that Phil's teeth were unusually small, pointy and discoloured.

Carl was happily spooning — virtually wolfing — his food. Simon, however, although persevering with his own plateful, was fast looking like someone about to undergo surgery: he knew that what was about to happen to him was necessary and that it would do him good, but the sense of trepidation was huge and growing with each moment.

'Not being funny or nuffink, Phil,' said Carl, 'but this food's a bit over-salted.'

'Yes,' agreed Simon, subdued.

'It's awright, though,' assuaged Carl.

'Th'orry,' said Phil. 'I only th'used a bit, though. Maybe th'alt's th'ronger up north?'

'Nah,' said Carl. 'Salt's salt, innit? That right, Simon?'

'Salt's a crystal,' said Albert. 'It'll have more energy here. The ley lines.'

'Yes,' agreed Simon.

Grinning, Carl pushed his empty plate away. 'Magic. Cheers, Phil. I needed that.' He looked at Albert. ''Ere, Albert, when y'gonna start that energy thing?'

'Now,' answered Albert. 'I'll pray at the activation point in a moment. Then my spiritual energy should begin to build up, echoing around the house for a while before fading.'

'Yeah? Magic.'

Simon glanced anxiously at Albert.

Carrying his empty plate, Phil came out of the shadows to sit at the table. 'Th'finished,' he said, like a child expecting praise.

He stacked his plate on to Carl's.

Watched apprehensively by Simon, Albert left the room, taking a candle. On the way to his bedroom, three times he nearly lost the flame to draughts. Once in his room, he took off his robe, put on his coat, and reconstructed the torn fiver with Carl's Sellotape.

When he returned to his disciples, Simon was just finishing his meal, diligently cleaning up his plate, in accordance with Albert's ordination.

'It's done,' said Albert. 'I've prayed at the activation point. Your first glimpse of the New Age is imminent.'

'Yeah? Magic,' said Carl. ''Ere, what you taken y'robe off for?'

'I have my reasons, Carl. All shall become apparent.'

Not acknowledging Albert's return to the room, Simon sat sideways on his chair and stared into the fire.

'Th'imon, th'ould I clear the table?' asked Phil.

'Yes, Phil,' said Albert, answering for Simon, who now had the appearance of a man about to be hanged in the morning.

'I'll 'elp y',' offered Carl. 'Carry a candle for y'.'

As Phil and Carl left for the kitchen, Albert stood beside Simon, facing his palms to the fire's heat.

'What will it feel like?' asked Simon quietly, staring into the flames.

'It might be a little unpleasant at first,' admitted Albert sensitively.

'Why?' asked Simon, with a controlled panic in his voice.

'Quartz is not so pure a crystal as diamond. The energy might become a little distorted. It's like plucking a guitar string – the string mainly sounds the fundamental note, but overtones will be present that could cause some side effects, especially at first until you become accustomed to it. You might feel light-headed. Nauseous, even.'

Simon now looked even more apprehensive. 'Will it hurt?'

Albert sought to reassure him. 'No, it won't hurt. And don't worry. Eventually, you'll become sympathetically balanced to the fundamental spiritual vibration. Don't worry about the overtones, just enjoy the bliss of New Age consciousness. The bliss should last for hours – the quartz should be able to resonate that long without being primed again.'

Simon looked at Albert, and appeared no less apprehensive.

Briefly placing a hand on Simon's shoulder, Albert said, 'Peace be with you very soon.'

Carl returned, bearing a frown and a candle. In a few paces, he slowed to a halt and appeared as if he were seeing the room for the first time and didn't know how he'd got there. Then he began to approach the fire, but stopped once more when Albert spoke to him: 'Please tell me your poem again.'

'Me poem?' said Carl, as if suddenly on alert. 'What poem?'

'The one you told me when you first met me.'

'Oh, that poem.' Evidently nervous at first, standing with his candle, Carl began reciting his work:

> 'Before I woke before the dawn
> I dreamed I was in some distant clime
> Where as I lay in state forlorn
> I felt Rosalynn's gentle 'and touch mine.
>
> A maiden and she is wondrous fair
> Elegant, wise and kind,
> An angel with long, wavy 'air
> Who is always on my mind.
>
> Gazing at 'er all the time,
> I began to feel as one blest;
> But then she sighed a name that was not mine
> As she lay 'er sleepy 'ead upon my breast.
> Then I realised with un'appy light
> That she'd mistook me for 'er lover in the
> dead of the night.'

The recital seemed to have thoroughly transported Carl, who stood gently swaying, his mind apparently far away in time and place.

Phil returned, bearing one of the candles from the kitchen.

'That was beautiful,' said Albert to Carl.

'Thank you,' said Carl softly, still very much transported.

'Can I borrow your cab for the evening?'

Carl was jarred back to the here and now. 'Can't,' he blurted defensively. 'Not insured for you. It's me livelihood, innit? Would, but —'

'Okay. Understood,' cut in Albert placatingly, not about to insist or pull rank, regardless of how much he wanted to get away to a pub in case they became touchy-feely when the E kicked in, maybe trying to hug him.

'Where you going? I'll drive you,' offered Carl, putting his candle down in flustered readiness.

'You have to stay here, Carl.'

458

'You can borrow my motorbike,' spouted Phil. 'Can you ride a bike?'

'Yes, I can,' said Albert, but not sure whether he should – he was massively out of practise, and had never passed, or even taken, a test.

'Here'sth the key!' said Phil excitedly, rucking up his robe to reach a pocket.

Simon had been in an anxious reverie, and Albert's request for vehicles only now registered. 'Where are you going?' he blurted, rising to his feet. 'Please stay.'

'I can't tell you where I'm going, Simon,' answered Albert.

'The big one'sth for the gate padlock,' explained Phil, handing over two keys.

'Okay,' said Albert.

'You can't leave us,' implored Simon.

'I have to, Simon... for a meeting... at a sacred site. I'll be back later.'

Rooted to one spot, with a deepening frown, Carl began looking around the room, his habitual frown deepening.

'Please stay,' said Simon.

'Can't,' said Albert. 'I've been told to be at a special place at nine o'clock.'

'I'll get you my helmet from my room,' said Phil, taking a candle away with him.

'The extraterrestrials?' conjectured Simon, but with none of his usual awed wonder.

Albert nodded, confirming in a low, grave voice, 'Yes, Simon, the extraterrestrials.'

'Why?'

'I don't know. I don't at all know.'

'I feel strange,' admitted Simon.

Albert now realised that Simon was coming up, and probably had been for some minutes. He looked at Carl, and saw that Carl, too, seemed to be experiencing something challenging.

'It's working,' said Albert. 'Don't worry about the overtones, just enjoy the New Age.' Touching Simon's arm, he said gently, 'Tell Phil I'm outside with the bike.'

Taking a candle with him, he left the house.

Outside, even though there seemed to be scarcely a breath of wind, his candle immediately blew out. But that was of little consequence, for a full moon had risen, and he could easily see

459

Phil's motorcycle parked beside Carl's cab. Discarding the candle, he went to the bike and discovered it to be an old MZ — a bizarre, East European, two-stroke, oil burning make of bike that he remembered was notorious for producing a loud and odd noise. But what the hell: it would get him to the pub and out of his drugged disciple's way for the rest of the evening.

Some minutes of moonlit investigation was required before Albert discovered where to stick the key — under a flip-back plastic shield on top of the headlight. Much kick-starting followed, but eventually the bike was rattling away bravely. All he needed now was the helmet. Leaving the bike running, he approached a window, peering through: only Carl and Simon in the large room. Simon was wandering around, shifting his weight between legs. Carl was looking twitchy by the fire — but he was *grinning*. And Simon also seemed to be halfway to a smile. But there was no Phil — Albert figured Phil had probably been distracted by the discovery of a mouse dropping, or something.

No way was he going back into the house now. He would do without a helmet, estimating the chances of encountering a police car thereabouts as virtually nil.

Hitching his coat up, he straddled the motorbike, and, jerkily at first, set off down the lane through the moon-shadowed wood, the headlight proving to be only borderline adequate. Reaching the gates, he unlocked them and was soon zipping along the narrow, moonlit, winding road that led to the village. Unfortunately, as soon as any incline was encountered, the bike's engine proved sadly lacking, resulting in a first gear crawl. But it was still fun, and whenever he had the speed, he swerved around for the joy of it. However, he soon lamented not having Jennifer with him to share the moonlight.

2.11
Her First Line

She seemed a little changed. From the moment he arrived, Yvette seemed a little changed, and Jennifer noticed it.

In the bar in Greek Street, Yvette had sent a text to Peter, who worked late. She had said where she was, and he had replied that he would come to meet her. 'My boyfriend's coming later,' she had then said to Jennifer. Later turned out to be a little after ten o'clock, by which time Jennifer was more drunk than she had ever been. A little before ten o'clock, a member of the Rolling Stones had come upstairs, alone. Just after the hushed flurry following the Stone's appearance subsided, Robert had said he was going to the bar to get a light. Asking for a book of matches, he was then beside the illustrious gentleman, who was standing with a drink. Moments later, they had gone downstairs together, causing much excitement with Yvette, excitement she'd communicated to Jennifer.

But then Peter had arrived, and Jennifer believed Yvette changed. Some of her interactive exuberance was lost.

Peter was maybe a little older than Yvette, reckoned Jennifer. She had been surprised to learn that Yvette was only twenty-one, not because she really looked older, but because she seemed so worldly in Jennifer's eyes. Peter, a good-looking, slim six-footer, had very long, straight, dark-brown hair drawn into a tight ponytail. He was half English, half French, and spoke both with seeming fluency, his English flawed only by the occasional wrongly stressed syllable, which Jennifer first noticed with his idiosyncratic pronunciation of sca-*van*-ger.

Peter politely shook Jennifer's hand and asked her about herself, but it was Yvette who answered first.

'She's called Jennifer, and—'

Peter stopped Yvette with a look.

'I was asking *her*,' he said to his girlfriend.

'Sorry,' said Yvette, deferring.

After Jennifer divulged the required information herself, Yvette entered the conversation unchallenged, telling Peter in conspiratorial, yet excited tones that Robert had gone off somewhere with a Rolling Stone. But then Robert came up the stairs, alone, smiling easily. Seeing Peter, he opened his arms, and they hugged heartily, like soul brothers long separated by time and adventure.

They all wanted to know what Robert had been doing with the Rolling Stone.

'Just wondered if he'd like a line of coke,' smiled Robert.

'Yeah?' said Peter. 'Did he?'

'Did he?' enthused Robert discreetly. 'He was like a Hoover. Good job Trevor sorted me out today.' He looked at Jennifer. 'Do you want a line? It's really good stuff.'

Five minutes later, having been persuaded, cajoled and finally dubiously convinced, Jennifer was in the ladies with Yvette, apprehensively doing her first ever line of coke — indeed, her first ever drug. Doing it with the rolled-up fifty pound note Robert had passed to her. Although worried about snorting a powder up her nose, she felt secretly thrilled and glamorous. But surely it would hurt? Or at least make her sneeze for hours?

It did not hurt, or make her sneeze. And, back upstairs, she soon realised it had gone some way to clearing her woozy head, for which she was grateful.

It had also numbed her front teeth.

'You've gone all quiet again,' noted Robert a short time later.

She *had* gone all quiet, she knew. Distant is what she'd become. Distant and sad. She was back in the deserted banqueting hall of the poem she had recalled reading at school. She couldn't account for it: she was used to her ups and downs, but this down was deep, sudden and unprovoked. She wasn't thinking of anything sad in particular, yet an ambience of profound sadness had enveloped her. She'd become withdrawn, and was strangely irked by attempts to lure her into conversations she now found oppressive.

Minutes after taking a second line, she realised what it was. 'It's the cocaine,' she said to Robert. 'I think it's making me feel depressed.'

There was an immediate reaction of dismissive amusement from Yvette, who had overheard. 'Of course it's not the cocaine,' she said, playfully trying to coax a smile from Jennifer.

'Cocaine's a stimulant,' said Peter, wrongly stressing the last syllable. 'It activates the brain.'

Yvette did a little dancing motion with her arms in support of Peter's assertion.

Robert was more sympathetic. His eyes expressing concern, he briefly touched Jennifer's hand over the table. 'No, listen to her. Coke's a very subtle drug. It swings you whichever way you're naturally inclined to go.'

'That's right,' said Peter, now sharing Robert's concern.

'Yeah,' said Yvette, dropping the register of her voice, taking Jennifer's arm to give friendly comfort. 'Are you all right?'

'I'm all right,' said Jennifer self-consciously. 'Just tired. I think I'd better be going back to my hotel now.'

'No,' protested Yvette.

'We're going to a club later,' said Peter. 'Come along with us.'

'Yeah,' enthused Yvette.

Jennifer strongly felt the dispiriting effect she was having on her new friends, and part of the reason she wanted to leave was that she was now being a damper. She stood up, and asked, 'Will I be able to get a taxi outside?'

'Oh, you're not go-een!' cried Yvette. 'You can't.'

'Let me come along with you,' said Robert chivalrously, standing up.

Yvette also stood, putting her arms around Jennifer. 'Call me tomorrow,' she said. 'Robert will give you my number.'

Jennifer promised she would.

On the other side of the table, Peter also stood up, kissing Jennifer's cheeks. 'Nice meeting you. Very sorry the coke made you unhappy.'

Yvette kissed Robert's cheeks goodnight, and Peter embraced him even more enthusiastically than he had done earlier, then they vigorously shook hands.

Jennifer managed a smile as Robert led her down the stairs. 'Tomorrow,' she called back to Yvette. 'I promise.'

463

2.12
Hysterical Paralysis & Serene Guilt

Simon and Carl actually began coming up on the E while Albert was supposedly praying at the activation point. First to be affected was Simon, and it had initially served only to magnify his natural unease about being the subject of an experiment, especially one which he was being warned could have side effects. It was just so daunting, the house being swamped with spiritual energy. Becoming more and more anxious, he had been apprehensively waiting for the experiment to take effect, unaware that it already had.

'It might be a little unpleasant at first,' Albert had said.

Say something. Say something. Think of something.

'Why?' Simon had returned, as he'd continued to stare into the fire.

'Quartz is not so pure a crystal as diamond. The energy might ...'

As Albert had gone on talking, Simon had begun, for the first time in his life, to see things differently. He was a man who had never even been drunk, but reality was becoming strangely distant, yet he still hadn't realised that his mind was already being changed.

Worry.

'Will it hurt?'

No, it wouldn't hurt. And not to worry — Albert said it would be all right in the end. But he hadn't felt all right then. He'd felt scared and alone... then Albert had placed a welcomed hand on his arm.

Energy was zipping through him! He'd been unsure at first, but eventually Carl decided he could actually feel the crystal energy zipping through him. It was amazing. He'd wanted to laugh, but was suddenly hit hard emotionally:

'Please tell me your poem again.'

Suddenly feeling like he'd been caught doing something filthy, Carl had instantly stopped enjoying the energy. But he'd kept a grip on himself, and, after an internal debate over whether or not Albert had actually asked him to recite his poem, finally deciding he had, he'd begun the delivery. When he'd finished, he'd been emotionally transported back to school, passing Rosalynn in a corridor; she, laughing with friends, the centre of attention; he, ashamed of his cheap blazer, the cheapest in the school.

'Can I borrow your cab for the evening?'

'Can't. Not insured for you. It's me livelihood, innit?' Shit, he'd blurted things without even feeling he'd spoken them himself. Stupid things. This was the Expected One he was talking to. 'You can borrow my motorbike,' said Phil, and the drama all seemed to swing mercifully away from him.

He was going! He was going! Simon had been floored. Scared. 'Where are you going? Please stay.' But then Simon had remembered what it was all about: *the extraterrestrials*. And surely he was feeling so peculiar because the crystal resonance experiment was beginning to affect him? Extraterrestrial science was changing him. 'I feel strange.'

'It's working,' Albert had then said, touching his arm.

Then Albert was suddenly gone. But somehow, once he'd gone, it didn't matter to Simon. Everything was, or was promising to be very soon, exactly as it should be. He'd reminded himself that he was in the hands of a great scientist using extraterrestrial knowledge to give him a taste of New Age consciousness. Yes, he'd felt strange at first, but it was all levelling out, just as the Expected One had said it would.

Then, unconcerned, he'd heard the motorbike start up.

Energy. He was jazzing with energy again. 'Can you feel it?' Carl had said, unable to keep still, fidgeting and shifting by the fire. 'Never felt anyfink like this. Funny, I wuz really tired till just now. Couldn't sleep now if I tried. How you feeling?'

Simon had then looked at Carl, believing that no answer he could give in mere words would justly describe how he was feeling. Having braved the dangerous crags, he had stepped on to the pristine plateau, and all was calm and still and beautiful and untrodden. The candles glowed warmly, oozing divine, sumptuous light. The room, with its fire, was the cosiest room he had ever known. The shadows were things of wonder. Carl was smiling, and then he'd felt a smile come to his own face.

He had entered the New Age.

*

As he'd expected it would be, the motorbike was exceedingly noisy, but the noise seemed to have little to do with internal combustion. It was a rattling, clunking noise that could be felt irregularly bumping the machine. Being a two-stroke, oil burning engine, it was also smoky — very smoky. The noise alone would have accounted for the attention Albert received when he pulled up outside the village pub, but he also, by an unfortunate coincidence of wind and bike speed, arrived in his own personal, toxic cloud. It seemed that for some way along the road leading up to the pub, he had been travelling at the same speed as, and in the same direction as, the gentle wind, so the grimy blue smoke from the exhaust had accumulated around him.

When Albert pulled up outside the pub, a middle-age couple leaving the establishment coughed and cast disapproving looks. As he turned the engine off, a tall, gaunt, old man on his way in said, 'Shouldn't thou be wearing a helmet?'

'Don't need one,' returned Albert, getting off the bike. 'I've got a really strong aura.'

'Humph,' muttered the old man.

While Albert was putting the bike up on its stand, the old man reversed his steps. Peering at Albert, he said, 'You're wun that came t' look at 'ouse, aren't y'?'

Albert now recognised him. He was the gatekeeper of Deepdale Hall, minus much of his beard.

'That's right.'

'Was't you that bought it, then?'

'Not me.'

'One of those other wuns up there now then?'

'That's right. Simon.'

'Never even had decency t' knock on me door,' complained the gatekeeper, before going into the pub, ahead of Albert.

*

'I feel fackin great,' grinned Carl maniacally. But that's as far as it went with him. No reported deep thoughts about thoughts. No reported introspective insights. Simon, however, was filled with the true glory of it all. He was in the New Age, and the New Age was beautiful, and it was Albert Fox's magic that had made it all happen. Albert Fox truly was the Expected One, and all the Expected One needed to spread his bliss around the world was a few diamonds.

'Imagine,' he said in awed tones to Carl, 'this is what it'll be like all the time in the New Age. Everyone will feel like this.'

'I feel fackin great,' said Carl again.

Struggling in a sincere, internal attempt to describe how he himself felt, Simon finally settled for the word *hallowed.* And then his eyes juddered, and a wave of bliss washed over him. 'Amazing,' he breathed. He knelt down near the fire and fancied he could actually see Albert's spiritual energy streaming through the room. It was dark pink, but so tenuous as to be barely visible. Wispy. Ethereal.

'Amazing,' he breathed again.

He closed his eyes and began to drift away with the expanded wonder of it all.

''Ere, where's Phil?' said Carl. 'Ain't 'e s'posed to be getting 'is 'elmet for Albert?'

That was a point — where *was* Phil? And how long had he been gone? Simon looked out of a window and, in the moonlight, saw that the bike was gone. But Phil definitely hadn't come back from his excursion to his room. Or had he?

After a muddled discussion, Carl and Simon went to investigate Phil's whereabouts. Each taking a candle that oozed wonderful light, they left the big room and went down the corridor leading to Phil's bedroom, the dusty floorboards creaking beneath their feet.

A wedge of candlelight was seeping mellifluously through Phil's half open door.

'Phil,' called Carl, 'where are ya?'

There was no return call.

Reaching Phil's door, they looked in and saw him sitting hunched on his scuffed, black motorcycle helmet, fingers gripping the hem of his robe. His bony legs were drawn up to his waist, but turned to the side, so that he appeared to be riding the helmet side-saddle.

He looked scared. Very scared.

Phil turned wide-open, haunted, hunted eyes towards the doorway. 'It's not th'working,' he blurted, attempting to sound untroubled.

'What's not working?' asked Simon, perplexed.

'The energy. It's not th'working.'

'What's the fackin matter wiv ya?' asked Carl harshly, stepping into the room.

Simon followed Carl.

Phil's desperate, tracking eyes seemed to show that he was torn between seeing Simon and Carl as comforting friends and seeing them as people about to do him some great harm.

'Look at his fackin eyes!' exclaimed Carl.

'It's not th'working,' said Phil, still clutching his robe's hem.

Phil had not yet moved, or even relaxed, a muscle.

'Why didn't you bring Albert the helmet?' asked Simon. 'He's gone without one now.'

'It's not th'working,' said Phil again.

'It is working. I'm in the New Age. So is Carl.'

'I feel fackin great,' said Carl.

There was no improvement in Phil's countenance. Someone about to be disembowelled alive might have appeared more sanguine. Viewing him sympathetically, Simon reasoned, 'It must be the overtones. Maybe the energy's purer in the big room?'

'Yeah?' said Carl.

'Come into the big room,' advised Simon.

Phil did not respond.

'Come on,' encouraged Carl.

Phil confessed he couldn't move.

'Whad y' mean?' asked Carl.

'I can't th'and up,' said Phil quietly. Ashamedly. 'My legs th'won't work.'

'Why not?' asked Carl.

'Don't know.'

'We have to get him into the main room,' said Simon.

'Let's carry him,' said Carl. ''E ain't no weight.'

'No!' pleaded Phil. 'Leave me here.'

But they didn't leave him, and he remained rigid all the way, like a twisted spastic. He was put down on an old wooden chair near the fire.

'You should be all right here,' said Simon. 'The energy's purer in here.'

'It's not th'working,' said Phil again.

'It is,' said Simon. 'We're in the New Age.'

'I feel fackin great,' said Carl, who now had the idea of getting his battery-powered portable hi-fi from his room so they could have music. ''Ere, Simon, mind if I get some music going in 'ere?'

'Okay. Not loud though. Something nice.'

Beaming, Carl hurried away to his room.

Turning a chair to the fire, Simon sat on it, meditatively closed his eyes, and began softly chanting.

Om, wallah wallah, om. Om, wallah wallah, om. Om, wallah wallah, om. Om, wallah wallah, om. Om, wallah wallah, om …

Carl returned with his portable system and a shoe box full of CDs, which he rummaged through. Continuing to chant, Simon's eyes remained closed while CD cases clattered, but Phil's remained starkly open, tracking Carl's movements.

'You any better, Phil?' asked Carl, without looking at him.

'It's not th'working,' said Phil.

'Fackin workin' for me an' Simon.'

A CD having been chosen and loaded, Carl pressed the play button, and the *A minor* opening strains of Led Zeppelin's *Stairway to Heaven* began. Never had the music sounded so... so *meaningful*. Meaningful and enveloping. He began swaying, then dancing. He closed his eyes and danced, ever more vigorously as the song progressed from gentle to thunderous. Danced with lurching movements that began to worry Phil, who could not let Carl out of his already petrified sight.

After the song climaxed, Carl became still, hanging his head down while the quiet vocal coda played out.

Simon stirred from his murmured chanting, breathed deeply a number of times and opened his eyes. 'That was good music, Carl,' he said, standing up. 'But maybe not so loud next time.'

'Sorry, Simon,' said Carl, grinning. 'Feel the better for it, though. 'Ope the batteries last.'

Perceiving he was about to leave the room, Phil looked at Simon, and pathetically said, 'Th'where are you going?'

'The toilet,' answered Simon, viewing Phil as if he'd forgotten about him and his strange paralysis.

'Don't be long,' Phil pathetically requested.

'I won't be,' said Simon, who now seemed to be looking upon Phil as a dubious curiosity.

When Simon left the room, Carl put *Stairway to Heaven* on again, at a lesser volume. Nevertheless, the sound seemed equally able to fill his senses, surprising him considering how low he had set the dial. He closed his eyes and danced again, dancing that sometimes took him to the brink of stumbling.

'I missed you,' said Phil when Simon returned from the toilet.

Simon looked at Phil; looked at him as if he were some kind of suspicious anomaly, scrutiny which only worsened Phil's countenance of anxiety. Turning away from Phil, Simon reoccupied his chair by the fire, staring pensively into the flames but occasionally glancing doubtfully at his paralysed companion.

A finger moved. Phil definitely felt one of his fingers move. Then it moved again, under his control this time. The sense of relief was colossal. He was waking from the nightmare, and believed he could lift his whole arm if he really tried. He began concentrating on doing that great thing when, dancing awkwardly, Carl tripped on his own robe and stumbled forwards. Phil watched, rigid and frightened, as Carl lurched at him, almost displacing him from his seat while Jimmy Page bent a vibrato note up a tone to begin the lead guitar break.

Carl opened his eyes and looked sharply and defensively at Phil, as if, at first, believing Phil had been the one to bump *him*. But then he relaxed and was about to say sorry when Phil blurted, 'It's not th'working.'

'Of course it's working,' said Simon, turning around on his chair. 'Albert said it would, didn't he? He's the Expected One.'

'It's not th'working. It's not.'

'Course it's fackin working,' bellowed Carl insensitively. 'I feel fackin great.' Then he could hardly believe what he was seeing. 'He's pissin' 'imself!'

Simon saw that Phil was indeed pissing himself. Urine was draining off his chair on to the floor, mirroring the candle lights.

'It's not th'working,' said Phil, persevering in his attempts to sound untroubled.

With deepening insight, Simon conjectured, 'He must be evil.'

Phil instantly looked terrified.

'Evil?' questioned Carl, in an unsure voice.

But Simon was becoming ever more sure: Phil must be evil, otherwise the goodly energy would not have reacted badly with him. Was it not written that evil would try to stop the New Age from coming? It *was* so written, Simon remembered from the scriptures he poured over each day. He stood up, coldly surveying Phil.

'It's not th'working,' said Phil, his desperate attempt to sound casual hardly managing to modulate a fundamental tone of stark fear.

Simon recalled more of the scriptures: *All who do not heed his words must be removed from the earth.*

'Kill him,' he ordered, chilling the room.

Carl looked at Simon.

'We have to kill him,' justified Simon. 'He's evil. He'll try to stop the New Age, like our scriptures say. Kill him now. Quickly.'

And as we wind on down the road, went the song as Phil turned incredulous, terrified eyes to Carl, squealing like a slit pig to see a fist raised against him. Carl rained a frenzy of blows down on to Phil's head and body, knocking him off the chair. Lying sideways on the floor in a pool of his own urine, still twisted with hysterical paralysis, still gripping his robe, Phil squealed and squealed, wilder and wilder. Now Carl began stomping his victim, who cried, wailed and whimpered, but would not die. Exhausted, but about stomp again, Carl slipped on Phil's blood and urine and finished up on all fours beside him, panting like a dog.

470

Phil's wails, groans and whimperings fell away. Blood seeped from all over his smashed face. His nostrils bubbled red with each laboured breath. One glancing stomp had ripped flesh from his dislocated jaw so that it lay as a bloodied, bearded flap for his own astonished eyes to see. When those astonished eyes looked up to Simon, as if searching for an explanation, they saw him again say, 'Kill him.'

And she's buying a stairway to heaven, ended the song as Carl finished the job with a climactic stomp.

2.13
Big Trouble

The *Lorimer's Arms* was a farmer's pub. Everyone looked like they owned at least one shotgun, and Albert felt like a target walking in, but he failed to generate even the smallest stir from the shabby old men and shabby young men dressed like shabby old men. He glanced around. Polished brass and black leather horse tackle hung on the ancient, whitewashed, undulating plaster walls. Two dogs with greying muzzles lay bored and arthritic under scuffed, torn chairs. At the far end, curiously ignored by all, was a log fire. And sitting disconsolately on a stool at the side of the bar was the gatekeeper.

Prevailing over the suspicion his reconstructed five pound note had raised, Albert bought a hand-drawn pint and took it to a chair by the fire, where he began reading an Orthrium Society booklet he'd smuggled out of his mystical bedroom.

Ten minutes later, he was bored, and fell into reflection.

Twenty-five hours, that's all it was. Twenty-five hours since he'd taken his first E. He could scarcely believe it. And strictly speaking, it was still the same day in which he'd sat, hunched and tearful, by the dying fire. The same day he'd listened a second time to Jennifer's message, desolate and guilt-ridden. The same day he'd set off, heavy of heart and light of pocket, to redeem himself somehow in the eyes of those he felt he'd hurt or even ruined.

He remembered how *enthusiastic* he'd felt at the beginning of his E trip, before his Jennifer grief. Life had felt so good for that brief time.

He still had one tablet of enthusiasm left, he reminded himself.

Taking an E now might be a beautiful thing to do, he thought. He could sit peacefully by the fire in the pub until closing time, and then maybe afterwards he could buzz around the lanes on the bike. He felt sure he could handle the machine tripping. And sod the lack of a helmet: this was frontier land as far as he was concerned. The ordinary rules of the highway didn't matter up here where so little traffic moved around. No one would see him on the side roads. And he couldn't imagine getting down again like he had at Ron's bonfire party — he could hardly be destroyed over losing Jennifer again, since he'd already come to terms with that. Besides, he was in a much repaired state of mind compared to that morning — *he was on his way to riches*. Things were going right for him for once. He just *knew* his scam was going to work.

Should he really take the remaining ecstasy?

Did he dare?

He did.

There was no turning back now, he realised with fatalistic apprehension once he'd swilled the pill down with a mouthful of beer. And soon after, during a listless attempt to resume reading the booklet, he seriously wished he could cancel the E. It had been an ill-considered, rash thing to do. With increasing distress, he understood that keeping his wits about him over the next few hours might be crucial to the rest of his life, yet he had gone and undermined his wits. His capacity for self-sabotage was colossal, he recognised with pangs of anguish.

No, it wasn't all blown, he resolved, getting a grip on himself. If the E affected him too much, all he had to do was keep away from Deepdale Hall until it wore off. That's all. Just keep away until his wits returned. Sit all night in a barn if he had too.

Yes, crisis sorted, he thought with relief.

He sipped some beer.

Scant minutes later, in a small panic, Albert sensed he might already be coming up. But was his sudden tummy-fluttering excitement because of the E, or because of his apprehension *over* the E? He didn't know, but soon his panic was replaced with fleeting, sometimes almost comical, anxieties, followed by an elusive nausea, then, finally, hallowed clarity and stillness. Everything became peaceful and just as it should be, and he knew he was smiling. He was all right. He'd done a good thing after all, taking the E. Buggered if he could read his booklet, though. He just couldn't focus his eyes that near. But he didn't care: he was happy just sitting sipping his drink, the conversations reaching him from the bar being like a lulling murmur. Thoughts drifted through his mind, but they didn't hurt. Even thoughts of Jennifer didn't hurt too much.

Thirty-four hours, that's all, he calculated — it was about thirty-four hours since he'd seen her last.

He wished so much she were with him.

He wondered where she was, and who, if anyone, she was with. But she wasn't gone forever, he still dared to hope, even though he understood this feeling to be just an aspect of the inherent, necessary, universal, religious belief that all will be right in the end. Nevertheless, it bloody helped. He wished he could have more of that help. Now, he wished he could turn off his stark reasoning and just praise the Lord, or reincarnation, or Allah, or Golden Millenniums, or whatever else people praised. That would be such an escape. Be more like Simon — beguiled into contentment. Ignorance *was* bliss.

Poor Simon, he thought, just carried away with the innate comfort that things will be better, that's all. And he, Albert Fox, with a mind unfairly cunning, was going to exploit it. That wasn't nice, really. Wasn't nice at all, really. Thinking about it now, he could hardly believe what he'd done: fucked with some harmless peoples' minds just for laughs and the chance of some money.

Swiftly, it stopped being a silly game and became a callous crime. He had been a bastard. Simon's foolishness wasn't hurting anyone. If people wanted to believe rubbish, then let them — why ruin their comfort? In fact, as far as he could tell from reading the Orthrium literature, the founder of the society might perhaps only have intended to unify the disparate religions, borrowing a bit from each, with an extra-strong karma element, all done to make for a better world. It was nonsense, but was it not laudable nonsense? It was certainly more laudable than exploiting religious longing to steal a fortune.

Now he began imagining how Jennifer would react to knowing he was planning to break someone's heart and take their money.

Annoyed and angry, that's what he decided she'd be. Annoyed that he was being such a fraud. And in his mind's eye, he could see her reproving him.

Anyone viewing Albert at this juncture would have seen his face become awfully serious.

The gatekeeper loped unsteadily over to him, and said, 'You're with wuns that bought it, though?'

Albert looked up, into eyes that appeared watery and spent. 'I know them,' he admitted, in a pale voice.

'Humph,' reacted the gatekeeper, loping disconsolately away. But he came back with more vigour. 'What's going t' come of me, then, lad?' he said, making it sound like an accusation.

'Pardon?'

'Six weeks,' muttered the old man in simmering, bewildered resentment. 'Six weeks t' leave. Forty-three years lived there. Fifty years worked there, as groundsman and gatekeeper. Six weeks t' leave. No bloody where to go at my age.'

He went away again, watched by Albert as he returned to his stool at the side of the bar.

He looked so unhappy, so very unhappy to Albert.

Rent free is how Albert now remembered being told the gatekeeper had been living, in exchange for watching over the big house and maintaining the grounds. His status under Simon had evidently changed for the worse. Albert wanted to help him. Christ! the man had probably fought nazis in the war — why should he lose his home because of a silly story some cocky youngster had written about an alien physicist?

Sod evolutionary psychology. That was how he would live from now on: like a saint.

This hit him like a true afflatus.

Yes, that was the way forward: never do anything that might add to his not inconsiderable guilt baggage. Guilt was beginning to poison his life, he feared. Living like a saint was what was *needed*. A guilt-free conscience seemed a highly desirable, life-enhancing asset. It certainly seemed desirable at this druggy juncture.

Simon: he wanted to help Simon, too. It was so wrong what he'd done to him. And how could he be conceiving of stealing another person's money? He owed Ron ten thousand, but what had that to do with Simon? Nothing. Nothing at all. He was going to pay Ron back out of his fucking *own* pocket — deliver newspapers for a decade if he had to. He should return Phil's bike then hitch, or walk if he had to, back to Durham. No: if he just buggered off, Simon would spend the rest of his misguided life looking for him. The best thing would be to tell Simon the truth, especially about putting ecstasy in the food. That might convince him that he was not the Expected One. Yes, that's what he'd do. The cruel fraud had gone far enough. He would bring it to an end now while he was in a proper frame of mind.

Forgoing the last quarter of his pint – which didn't sit well on the E, anyway – Albert left the pub, proud of himself for listening to his conscience and not his haughty logic, hugely amplified by drugs though that conscience was. It was just like when he'd left the Arts Centre to join Jennifer at Ron's party. It was the same feeling of a weight having been lifted from him.

He felt exhilarated.

Outside, the moonlit motorbike looked strangely cartoonish, like it had its own quirky but innocuous personality. Straddling it and hitching up his coat, he got the engine started with one kick, and was soon on the lane back to Deepdale Hall. On an empty road, it was no big deal riding a powerless motorbike on E, or so he felt. It was certainly easier than climbing that fence at Ron's mother's place had been. He naturally slowed for the twisting corners, braked when he should and accelerated when it was wise.

However, even though he frequently checked the speedo, he was never quite sure whether he was racing or crawling.

A thought assailed him. A powerful thought. He should go and see his mother soon. As far as he was aware, she was languishing mentally ill in some institution – that's if she was still alive. He felt strong now. Felt he could do it. Felt he could countenance the disturbing sight of her. He might even be able to touch her. Hold her bony, cold hand to offer comfort, pointless for her though he knew it would be. He should do it for *himself*, if not for her.

Yes, he would go to see her soon.

Engrossed in the two-wheel experience, Albert didn't stop when he reached the gates of Deepdale Hall, but purposefully rode straight past, staying loyal to the twisting road as it snaked upward, discovering that, after passing a few farm entrances, it turned from tarmac to rutted earth.

Now he stopped.

The air was beautiful and fresh. The night, magical.

He felt reborn.

Looking back the way he'd come, in the moonlight he could see

Deepdale Hall down in the valley, amid its shielding woods. Behind him, nebulous sheep faintly speckled the higher moors.

But he really had to be getting back.

*

It was still where it had been left yesterday afternoon, on the floor of Rebecca's living room, except Albert's scuffed suitcase had now ceased being an obstacle and had become like a vague magic symbol. It was as if it were looked at long enough, the mystery of where he was would be revealed, or he would somehow be lured back.

Ron and Sarah had been searching for Albert since she'd returned from her aunt's, two hours earlier, where she'd heard Albert's name cursed several times. No one had seen anything of him all day. He didn't exactly have a wide circle of acquaintances, and that circle had been contacted, but no Albert, only a heart-rending, desperate letter. And Rebecca had confirmed that he had little money, as Ron had suspected.

Now at Rebecca's, Ron was being pressured by Sarah to contact the police.

'Maybe he's got into some kind of trouble?' feared Sarah.

'Such as?' asked Ron.

No one could think of any kind of trouble Albert might be in, so Ron rolled another joint.

*

The ride down the moor to the valley floor was a thoughtless joy. Only when he was in the grounds of Deepdale Hall did Albert begin thinking again about what he was about to do: confess. Doubts were arising, which lived on after he'd parked the bike. But he had seen so *clearly* earlier that it was a good idea to confess, he *had* to do it.

Upon lifting the large, cold, dewy iron latch on the heavy front door, he was met by Simon, robed and bearing a candle.

'What did the extraterrestrials want?' asked Simon, aglow with emotion.

'What?' said Albert, forgetting the yarn he'd spun to excuse his visit to the pub.

He was surprised to hear music coming from within.

'The extraterrestrials,' repeated Simon.

Not responding, Albert stepped past Simon and entered the main room. He sat down on the first available chair, beside a wooden crate, on top of which a system quietly played music. Turning to look at Simon, who had followed him in, he was about to speak but was pre-empted.

'I'm in the New Age,' breathed Simon. 'Master, your magic *is* greater than all others.' Adopting a more pragmatic attitude, he eagerly said, 'How much money will you need for the diamonds? You said the bigger the diamonds, the better, didn't you? I've got over seven million pounds available.'

Albert switched off the music and viewed Simon, who was beaming. Fuck: it had all worked. The crazy plan had worked. He could take him for seven million if he wanted. What a waste of an opportunity. It would be a crime to waste such an opportunity.

'Where's Carl and Phil?' he asked, downbeat. 'I need to tell you all something.'

'Carl's in the kitchen, and Phil's over by the fire. He's dead.'

'Dead?' queried Albert, utterly failing to grasp the magnitude of the revelation.

'He was evil.'

'That's right,' confirmed Carl, entering the room, feeding a sausage roll into his mouth, flakes of pastry adhering to his robe. 'I feel fackin great, Albert. Still want to lend me cab? Keys are under the driver's seat if y'want it.'

But Albert wasn't listening. He was looking toward the glowing fire, before which lay Phil, whose white robe was stained with darkness. Curled almost foetal-like, Phil wasn't moving. He wasn't moving at all.

The ability to react appropriately was disturbingly absent. Albert knew he should be rushing over to Phil, or screaming "What happened? Who did it?", but everything seemed muted, seemed to happen silently in his head, and only there. A long time seemed to have passed. Or had it? He didn't know. Now he thought how strange it was that he should be wondering about subjective time frames when a bloodied corpse lay in the room. There *was* a body in the room, wasn't there? Or was this some crazy, druggy hallucination? Or had he gone mad?

'We'll never grow old,' realised Simon in awe as Albert stared at the bloodied corpse.

It was a living nightmare. A druggy, living nightmare so unsettling Albert considered it might be a *real* nightmare. He'd had dreams before where he'd been fully aware he was dreaming — lucid dreams — and this felt like one now. But no, it wasn't. This *was* happening. Phil *was* lying on the floor, his dead hands gripping the hem of his stained robe.

Albert slowly approached the corpse.

'Fackin 'ell, you're right,' realised Carl.

'Or get sick,' added Simon, tagging along beside Albert.

A spill of dark, viscous, congealed blood surrounded Phil's head, a head that had clearly been brutally battered. His jaw was greatly dislocated. Bearded flesh was hanging from his face, attached only by a thread of tissue. His teeth, some half out their sockets, had cut through his own lips and cheeks, glistening amid red pulp.

Only Phil's bewildered, betrayed eyes seemed unscathed.

'Who did this?' murmured Albert.

'Carl,' said Simon.

'That's right,' confirmed Carl.

Turning in mute astonishment to look at Carl, Albert saw that the lower parts of his robe were stained with evidence.

'It's all right,' assured Simon. 'We discovered he was evil.'

'That's right,' said Carl. 'We 'ad to do it.'

Albert consciously wondered if he ought not to collapse to the floor, and strangely imagined himself doing so. But he remained standing within the living nightmare, not knowing at all what to do. What could he do? Call the police? Maybe Phil was still alive? No, surely not — his face was smashed in, and his eyes were staring, accusing, dead man's eyes.

'Don't worry,' said Simon, 'there's some spades in the outbuilding. We'll bury him now. No one'll find him. We didn't want to do it earlier because the crystal energy doesn't extend beyond the house, does it?'

'That's right,' chirped Carl. 'Pukka stuff, ain't it?'

Before Albert's eyes, they began pulling Phil by his feet to the door. His battered head left a dark trail, and his loose flap of skin snagged on the floorboards, coming away.

Simon picked up the hairy skin flap in his hand. 'Won't be long,' he said. 'And don't worry.'

Alone. Albert was now alone in the room. The vast, empty, silent, candlelit room with its lofty ceiling, flaking plaster, gothic adornments and sinister shadows. The stillness was killing. He should be doing something, but could now only think of sitting down. Moving to a chair, his feet seemed to stick.

Murder. There had been a gruesome murder. It was unbelievable. It was staggering. It was crazy. It was surreal. Most of all, it was numbing.

He sat down. Minutes, maybe, passed without a single formed

thought arising. He was just blown away, gazing brain-dead at his hands. Looking to where the corpse had lain, as if still unconvinced about the reality of the event, he saw a set of bloody footprints leading directly to him. He stared in awakening horror at the testimony. Yes, he had killed Phil himself, or as good as. And not only that, he was in trouble. Big trouble.

His drugged mind began a sudden riot of self-defence and panic. And that's when it started: a gripping, empty feeling in the pit of his stomach. A contained panic. An inhibited anxiety. And it didn't go even a little bit away when he tried to reason his way out of trouble.

He couldn't tell the police. Couldn't. He might go to prison for his part in the murder. No, he *would* go to prison. He'd be charged with supplying a controlled drug, at least. Supplying a Class A hard drug could mean years in prison, he knew. And he hadn't just supplied, he'd *secretly poisoned*, a poisoning that had led to a murder. He'd receive no mercy.

He had to get away. Far away. Run. But where could he go? Not back to Durham — nowhere to stay there. Should he go? Maybe he could conceal everything? Nobody knew he was here. Nobody at all... except Simon and Carl. Maybe he should kill and bury *them*, *then* run away? No, the gatekeeper had seen him. The gatekeeper would tell the police, who would identify him through Jackie's estate agency. Maybe he should kill the gatekeeper too?

No, he was being crazy. He wasn't going to kill anyone, besides, the more disappearances, the more investigations.

He had to stay calm. Use his cunning. This was happening. This was *really* happening. What he had to do was think of a way to make sure the *one* murder never came to light. That's what he had to do: use his cunning.

'It's done,' said Simon upon returning. 'He's three feet down in the woods. No one will ever find him.'

'No way,' said Carl, walking in behind Simon. 'Gawd, I feel fackin great.'

'You shouldn't swear,' said Simon to Carl. 'Not here. Not in front of the Master.'

'You're right,' agreed Carl sensibly. 'Sorry.'

Albert looked at them in stupefied bewilderment. It was bizarre: they seemed to have no sense of horror or guilt.

'Why?' he mouthed.

'We had to,' said Simon. 'It's in the scriptures.'

''E went all weird in your energy,' reported Carl. 'Should've seen it.'

'That proved it,' said Simon.

'Proved what?' implored Albert, in muted distress.

'That he was evil,' explained Simon. 'If you'd been here, you would have seen it too.'

Carl gave a demonstration of how Phil had been.

'For ages he was like that,' said Simon. 'So I asked Carl to eliminate him.' Picking up a book that was open on a chair, he read a passage that Albert could see had been underlined. '*And all who do not heed his words must be removed from the earth.*'

'Whose words?' asked Albert, in anguished incredulity.

'The Expected One's,' said Simon, as if the fact were obvious. 'Your words.'

Albert sank his face into his hands.

'Don't worry,' said Simon sympathetically. 'No one will know. And once you start the Golden Millennium everything will be different.'

Mumbling through his hands, Albert said, 'He'll be reported missing by friends before that.'

He felt immediate shame to be discussing a cover up.

'He doesn't have any friends,' answered Simon.

'Family,' muttered Albert. 'His family will look for him.'

'I'm his only family,' said Simon. 'He was my brother.'

'It's wearing off now,' said Carl, disappointedly.

After gauging things for a few seconds, Simon decided that Carl was right. 'You said it would, though, didn't you, Master? You said that the crystals would stop echoing after a while. Should we see about getting the diamonds tomorrow?'

'Can you get the energy going again?' asked Carl.

Albert was still sitting with his face in his hands, drowning in the sheer incredulity of it all. Thirty minutes earlier, he had been high on the resolution to divest himself of guilt, now he had killed someone. Could he ever win? Could he ever fucking win? Once more, he began thinking that he was in the hands of some sinister supernatural agent bent on breaking him with irony, disappointment and frustration. He forced the pernicious thought away; was angry at himself for even thinking it. He would overcome this. It was a test, that's what it was. A spiritual trial. No, don't be stupid. Don't be fucking stupid. How could it be a test? Who could be doing the testing? God? No, it wasn't a test. It just was, that's all. It just was.

Simon sat next to him. 'Don't worry, Master. We had to do it. But everything's going to be all right.'

'Work colleagues,' mumbled Albert distressfully. 'They'll report him missing.'

'He quit work last week.'

'What about the energy?' asked Carl again. 'Can we 'ave some more?'

Slow to respond, Albert eventually lifted his head, and with strong undertones of resentment and anger, said, 'No more energy. Clean all the blood away. Clean everything – the floor; the spades; your clothes. Everything. Don't leave a trace. I'm going to bed.'

Taking a candle with him, Albert walked toward the grand staircase, somehow thinking the grotesque nightmare would end once he was alone in his room.

'See you tomorrow, Master,' said Simon.

'G'night, guv,' said Carl.

'Don't worry,' called Simon when Albert began ascending the stairs. 'We'll start cleaning now.'

Albert's long, slow, creaking walk to his bedroom very soon began to seem like some perilous journey through the darkest, innermost lair of Madness. He alone preserved sanity, and only by the gift of a single candle's flickering light. He wanted to hurry, but truly felt that if he lost the flame, the shadows would close in and his mind would be lost. There was a whole box of candles in his bedroom, he remembered. As soon as he reached it, he would brightly illuminate the room. The shadows would not take him.

On the steep steps that led to his turret room, a cold draught nearly defeated his flame, but he cupped a hand around it in time. Once in his bedroom, he closed the door behind him as if closing out madness – as if it would be all right once he were hidden away.

He discovered that a sleeping bag had been left for him, rolled up on the bed.

Snatching the box of candles from one of the bookshelves, he lit four, placing them equidistant around the room. After taking a sputtering piss in the basin, he lay on the bed in his coat, and stared at the ceiling. Alone, shut away, he felt less chaotic, despite there being no let-up in the feeling of tightness in his stomach. Continuing to stare at the ceiling in growing mental remoteness, the night's events began to fall away from his consciousness. Escaping to some pathologically quiescent state, he remained on his back, inert as a mortuary inhabitant. But eventually, with the candles half gone, as

481

the E began to wear off, he mentally enlivened, although he also, paradoxically, began to feel drowsy. Sleep: he wished he could, but suspected it would be hours yet before the drug would finally release him. Many hours. Many lonely hours shut into a strange little room that was beginning to feel like a penitential cell.

Phil had been murdered. Phil really had been fucking murdered. And he was complicit. Very complicit.

Fuck: if he was coming down, then Simon and Carl might already be completely back to normal. And when back to normal, wouldn't they realise the horror of their deed? Earlier, they had been buoyed and deceived by drug-induced religious delusion, but now they might be freaking out downstairs. They might be considering killing *him*, like he had briefly considered killing them.

He got up and moved the bed over to prevent the door being opened without noise or force.

Sitting on the edge of the bed, he stared at the bare, wooden floor. How had it all gone so helter-skelter wrong? Twelve hours earlier he had been on this very bed, wondering how he had come to be regarded as a saviour, now he was wondering how he had become a killer.

He suddenly became angry with himself. No, he wasn't a killer. *Wasn't*. He'd been unlucky, that's all. Fuck it, he wasn't going to let this pull him down. It wasn't going to end *this* way. He wasn't going to be defeated by irony. He'd been right downstairs: he had to *think* his way out of this. *Had* to. He would get out of this somehow. He didn't have to wonder how it had gone wrong, he had to *analyse* it. Working out what had gone wrong might be some of the problem of how to throw a smoke-screen over the event solved.

He hadn't been the killer, the delusion of religion had been the killer. He'd unwittingly stirred up some kind of religious mania, that's all, and Phil had copped for a vicious death because of Simon's warped interpretation of some passage in some scripture.

Scriptures were the big problem with religion, Albert realised. Rambling scriptures that give people all the scope for interpretation they need to carry out their personal agendas. If only all the bibles and korans and everything elses in the world could be replaced with some simple thing too short ever to be twisted, he wished, then peace and goodwill might stand a chance. Something like: *Forget all gods and Messiahs, they can't really be hurt or angered by insults or denouncements. Worship mankind instead, then heaven shall be on earth.*

Albert's determination to elude culpability continued. He had to think and plot. Every available second he had to think and plot. He lay back on the bed and stared at the ceiling, but this time his mind churned. There had to be a way out for him. Had to be. If he could fool people into believing he was Christ's successor, he could surely cover up a murder. He had to put his sleeplessness, and set his cunning, to use.

The decision to live a guilt-free life that had taken over his thoughts earlier, he now considered to have been some insubstantial trippy obsession. It had fallen far, far away. Besides, Simon had ordered a murder, argued Albert to himself, so no compassion for him. Moreover, if he could still get his hands on the money, he bloody well would. Fuck them. Fuck those two freaks downstairs.

For much of the rest of the night, Albert became desperately saturated in the problem, methodically detailing the circumstances of the crime. If Phil really had no friends, and only Simon as family, then that was a big asset, since only Simon and Carl would ever be likely to report his death, unless the body was found. But he was buried in a private wood, and hopefully, before their trips had worn off, Simon and Carl would have cleaned enough of the blood away to avoid casual discovery. He knew that the police used a chemical spray that fluoresced when in contact with even invisible quantities of blood, but if it got to that stage, the game would be as good as up anyway. What he had to do was make sure the authorities never came looking for Phil in the first place, and they wouldn't, unless Simon or Carl, intentionally or accidentally, spilled the beans. But they'd done the murder, not him, so they would be unlikely to blab about it. But fuck, if the full facts emerged in a court of law, they might be found innocent on account of chemically diminished responsibility — an incentive to confess. And Phil was Simon's brother — an emotional wild card.

As he cogitated desperately, Albert illuminated a grotesque failing in his cunning: he'd overlooked something absolutely fundamental in his original plan to run off with millions of Simon's pounds. What he'd overlooked was simply that Simon would have been enraged and would have *wanted his money back,* and would surely have tried to *get* it back, whether via the police through deception and theft allegations, or through more sinister private means. Previously, stealing any money entrusted to him to supposedly purchase diamonds had seemed like a game; to be played, or not played. It was not a game, he now starkly understood. It would have been prison or hit men once Simon had discovered he'd been taken. To have kept the money, he would have had to live as a fugitive from the law, and possibly outlaws too.

But, Albert dared to think, what if Simon and Carl continued to be wholly indifferent about their murderous deed? Then the money would still be his for the taking. But stealing the money would illuminate Simon as to the deception, and then he would have extra reason to track him down: his deception was the thing that had led him to kill his own brother. To get his money back, Simon might confess the murder to the police, knowing he'd be found largely blameless due to the drugging.

Perhaps he could dupe Simon into believing the diamonds had actually been bought and placed within the Empathy Device? But no, on Midnight, February the first, when the world failed to become serene, Simon would know shenanigans had been afoot.

Shit, it was all so complicated and contradictory, despaired Albert, realising he could spend a lifetime posing "what if?" scenarios. He had to reduce it to simplicity, and strike at the core. He had to prevent the disease developing, rather than wonder how to deal with the rash of sores. What were the fundamentals of the problem? he asked himself. They were simply this, he eventually began to see: the authorities must never become aware of the murder, and, if he was still to make off with the money, Simon must never understand that he had been deceived and robbed.

That was it. All he had to do was concentrate on that one, or those two, criteria.

Throughout the remainder of the night, he thought and thought. Apparent solutions sometimes surfaced, only to be sunk by immediately perceived flaws. At other times, solutions were tantalisingly half-glimpsed, never to reappear. But think and think though he did, by the time the grey dawn finally crept into his strange room, no real solution had emerged, and he resigned himself to failure, conceding flight to be his only real option. Flight would just be escaping the punishment, though, he knew. What he needed was a way to escape the *crime* – or *crimes*, if he added a multi-million pound deception to it. But he felt too weary to consider fleeing. Now that he had admitted defeat, all he wanted to do was sleep. If the police burst in, then he would just have to go to jail. If Simon and Carl burst in, there would be a fight to the death.

He wondered what Simon and Carl were doing now, speculating

that perhaps they had simply fallen asleep, not to realise the horror of their deeds until refreshed.

Whatever, sleep was his own priority now. Or was he, he wondered, unconsciously but deliberately waiting at the scene of the crime to give himself up? Was he so determined to live without guilt that he was prepared to face prison? Or might it be his capacity for self-sabotage at work? Was he again undermining his own chances of success? Nothing about himself seemed definite, or even knowable, upon introspection any more. All he unearthed was a mess of self doubt.

Fuck it: he was too exhausted to entertain any more self-doubt.

He extinguished the candle stubs, took off his coat and shoes, unrolled the sleeping bag, and slipped inside. Using his coat as a pillow, he lay his head down, closed his eyes and arranged his limbs for comfort. Despite his predicament, settling down for sleep remained a gentle pleasure.

But there was no let up in the gripping sensation of anxiety in the pit of his stomach.

2.14
The Curious Mutuality

It was lightly raining when Jennifer, followed closely by Robert, stepped out on to Greek Street. He raised his arm to stop an oncoming black cab. 'Nottingham Street,' he said to the driver while simultaneously opening the door for Jennifer. She shuffled along the cab's back seat, and Robert sat on her left. Across the road, she noticed a small, illuminated red sign just inside a seedy open doorway that promised a busty, eighteen-year-old model upstairs, and couldn't understand why the authorities had not noticed it too.

'How are you feeling?' asked Robert gently, once the cab was moving.

'Sorry about tonight,' said Jennifer, glancing at him and smiling as best she could, a smile that didn't live long.

'Don't be sorry. Do you often get sad like this? Tell me exactly how you feel.'

Looking downwards, in a tone of quiet self-contempt, Jennifer said, 'How I feel doesn't matter.'

Robert admonished her in a voice that was stern yet caring. 'That's not the kind of thing I ever want to hear you say to me.'

Again she glanced at him, once more smiling as best she could. 'Sorry.'

'Are you sure you want to be alone?' he asked, in a less solemn voice. 'My Harley Street flat's just around the corner from your hotel. Why don't you come in for a while until you feel better? I don't want to be alone just yet either.'

Jennifer looked at him. 'The Harley Street where all the doctors are?'

'That's right. The floors below mine are consulting rooms for private doctors. Costs a fortune to rent. Exclusive area. It's only a five minute walk from Nottingham Street.'

'I know,' said Jennifer. 'I walked along it yesterday.' She paused, and admitted to herself that she didn't really want to be completely alone just yet. Robert was sensitive and kind, and although she was in no mood for the company of a crowd, she was not averse to the continuing company of a friend. And she harboured no fear and only minor suspicions concerning any ulterior motives he might have. 'Yeah, all right. I'll pop in.'

'Could you make that Harley Street, please,' Robert immediately said to the driver, who responded with a small, benumbed-by-boredom, nod of his head.

'You said your publishing business is based in Harley Street too, didn't you?' Jennifer now remembered.

'Yeah,' said Robert, employing a rare downbeat. The beat picked up again. 'The Harley Street flat's actually my publishing office. I'm actually between proper flats at the moment. I used to live in Maida Vale until a few weeks back.'

'You're living in your office?'

'Have to for a while. And I'm still late for work. Our publishing office is in the front room, and the big back room is my private room. It's nearly big enough to play tennis in. I should know, we tried on Thursday. Only broke three things.'

Jennifer remained much in her withdrawn state. As Robert continued to talk, it required conscious efforts from her to make

486

even small returns to his utterances, and she condemned herself for being dispiriting.

When they arrived in Harley Street, it was virtually traffic free, and completely pedestrian free. Following Robert's instructions, the driver pulled up adjacent to an imposing, highly-polished black door with brass fittings, where they got out. Stout black railings fronted the house Robert part-occupied, close to the north end of the long, straight street. Concrete stairs led down from the pavement to a smaller basement door, also painted black. Behind that basement door, Jennifer was informed, lay a dental technician's workshop.

Off the pavement, two wide steps led to Robert's grand front door, beside which were set brass plaques bearing the names of several doctors.

'Doesn't your company have a plaque?' asked Jennifer.

'Can't,' said Robert. 'Every business in the street has to be medical by law. The Queen's the landlord. Crown Estates. They don't know we run a publishing business from the address.'

Before he slid a key into the door, for possible future use, he showed Jennifer which intercom button was for him.

'You're on the second floor?' she surmised. She looked up and saw that the second floor windows were veiled by net curtains. Even by streetlight, she could see they needed a wash.

'Before you say it,' said Robert, 'I know our curtains lower the tone of the street.'

'You beat me to it.'

'You sound like you've cheered up a bit,' observed Robert.

'Think I have,' agreed Jennifer. 'Think that coke must have worn off.'

Robert opened the door, and Jennifer followed him into a lofty hall with red carpeting. A number of grand, glossy-white doors were spaced along a corridor. A world-famous gynaecologist had his consulting rooms on this floor, related Robert, and royalty sometimes visited, often entering the building through the basement to avoid scandal. 'They're not all shy, though. Three limos turned up the other day and some African ruler or something piled about ten women in for servicing.'

Pressing a timer light first, Robert led the way up a wide, deeply-carpeted flights of stairs which brought them to a landing that serviced more consulting rooms. Then up two, narrower, brown-carpeted flights, which brought them to two slightly scuffed matt-white doors.

'This one's our office,' he explained while working the lock of one door. 'The other door's for Betty — a really sweet, posh old dear who's lived in the upper rooms since before the war. It's like a museum up there.'

Following Robert into his office, Jennifer met the unexpected. What she'd assumed to see behind the door was an organised, modern work place. What she actually saw was a messy, littered, poorly-furnished living room. The walls were decorated in unappealing, faded hessian. An old, sunken, cheap brown sofa was against one wall. Half-eaten, shrivelled pizzas in boxes competed with sweet wrappers for floor space. In the centre of the room, a tubular, white Formica kitchen table supported two telephones and the dried-hard remnants of some take-away meal in an aluminium carton. The only things that really looked like business items to her eye were a computer, a laser printer and a fax machine. These rested on what appeared to be a school dining table, in the room's far corner, next to one of the net-curtained windows she had viewed from the street.

There was a faint smell of old socks.

'Sorry about the mess,' said Robert, taking his coat off and draping it over one of the four dining chairs surrounding the central table. 'Mark doesn't tidy up any more.'

Jennifer didn't know whether he was joking or not. Going to the window to sample the view while he lit a cigarette, she asked, 'How many people work here?'

Between sucking on his cigarette to establish combustion, Robert answered, 'Just three. Me, Jeremy and Mark.'

Looking at the computer, Jennifer remarked that it was the same make and apparent model as the one she used at the veterinary surgery for invoices and letters.

Robert seemed oddly interested in that intelligence. 'Really?' he said, stretching the vowel sound.

A single door separated the office room from Robert's personal room. Entering, he switched on a dimmed light, and invited Jennifer to walk through. Stepping in, she found his own room to be much more comfortable, tidy and well decorated. It was rectangular, with the door at a corner of one of the shorter walls, and a low bed in the adjacent corner. A large, uncluttered expanse of deep-piled, pale-green carpet extended to two bay windows, side by side at the far end. Below each window were identical two-seater sofas, with green covers and cushions. These sofas were sandwiched between two

488

substantial black hi-fi speakers on black metal stands. The walls were emulsioned white with a hint of pink. Along one long wall ran a series of fitted closets and mirrors, and the opposite wall was decorated with two large impressionist paintings. A black television; a white chest of drawers; a crammed, black bookshelf; and two small, very low, black, square tables positioned in front of the sofas completed the furnishing, save for a multitude of candles set on wrought iron stands.

Jennifer noticed some spirit bottles lying under the stylish tables, tables which had faint dustings of white powder.

'So how are you feeling now?' asked Robert, lighting some candles. Before Jennifer could answer, he burnt his finger, reacting in a comical, childish way, screeching and dancing around the room in pain. 'Bastards!' he laughed excruciatingly, showing her his inconsequential wound. 'Look, mum.'

'Oh, you'll live.'

'Yeah, in agony, though,' he responded returning to the candles. Suddenly, in a comically exasperated voice, he demanded, 'Take your coat off, for Christ's sake!'

Jennifer began removing her coat, placing it out of the way on the floor by the bookshelf. She caught the titles of some books. *Healing the Inner Child,* was one. Moving away from the bookcase, she sat on the floor, her back supported by a sofa. Viewing Robert now, she was strangely reminded of Albert, but couldn't think why. Maybe the similarity came from their tendencies to clown around? she thought. Like Albert, Robert could have a tongue-in-cheek, comically child-like manner that she found easy to get along with. Also like Albert, he had a capacity to say things to deliberately make himself look daft. But their styles in those endeavours were different, Jennifer had discerned. Albert's was a cerebral silliness born of his well-developed sense of the absurd, a silliness that she had observed often went over people's heads. But Robert's was an endearing, warm silliness. He made people smile when he played the fool. Robert had charm. Robert had oodles of charm.

Now Jennifer realised what it was: it was femininity. That was it. That was the curious mutuality. They were both a little feminine in their motions, longish hair adding to the impression. Not camp. Not at all camp. Just not particularly keen to appear tough and manly in their movements or postures.

'I feel drunk again,' lamented Jennifer as Robert turned off the electric light before returning to her side of the room.

'You should do another line,' advised Robert while putting on a CD which Jennifer immediately recognised as Vivaldi. 'Coke's great for sobering you up. You'll be all right here.'

'I don't think I should.'

'No, really,' argued Robert kindly. 'It'll be different here. Drugs are all to do with setting and how comfortable you feel. Anyway, if you get depressed, just have a cry. I'll join in, if my finger's still hurting.'

Placing the CD cover on one of the low tables, Robert immediately began setting out two lines on it, carefully chopping the crystals with a razor blade that Jennifer had earlier noticed on top of the television.

She shuffled over on her knees to the other side of the table. 'How much does coke cost?'

'Not as much as it used to. The riffraff can afford it now. About forty a gram now.'

'A gram? A gram can't be much.'

Robert passed Jennifer his coke, contained in a tiny paper wrap, folded to form an envelope. 'About three quarters of a gram there.'

While she assessed the envelope's quantity, Robert rolled a banknote into a tube. When she looked up to hand the coke packet back to him, he was staring at her body.

'The sparkly spiders' webs in your dress look really good in the candlelight,' he remarked.

'Do they?' she responded, looking down to the fabric.

Leaning over the low table to take his line, Robert drew back and asked, in a solemn and sincere tone, 'Why do you think you got depressed on the coke? Are you unhappy about something?' He was looking into her eyes, his expression showing sympathy and offering support.

'I've always been a bit morose,' answered Jennifer, looking away.

'Really,' said Robert, bending over the table again. 'There has to be a reason for it.'

After fluently snorting his line, he proffered the rolled-up note to Jennifer, who deliberated before accepting. Making himself comfortable on the floor while she took her line, he said, 'Describe how you felt when you went all quiet and withdrawn.'

Finished with the banknote, Jennifer placed it on the table before shuffling back to lean against the sofa again. She glanced casually around the room, and it seemed Robert's question had not registered.

He looked steadily at her. 'I'm a stranger. You can tell me

anything.'

'Alone,' admitted Jennifer, briefly looking at Robert.

'But you weren't alone. We were with you, and we all like you.'

Jennifer looked at the carpet. 'You were part of the problem. You wanted me to be fun like you all were. That's why I wanted to leave, because I was bringing you all down. And I ended up feeling irked with you all for trying to get me involved.'

'Jennifer, you weren't bringing us down,' Robert gently insisted.

She briefly looked at him again.

'What made you decide to move to London?' he asked.

'I just needed to make a fresh start, Robert. I had to get away. Nothing seemed to be under my own control.'

'Problems with your parents?'

'No, they're dead.'

'Really?' said Robert, sounding like he'd found great significance in the intelligence. Retrieving a brandy bottle and a used glass from under one of the tables, he poured himself a quantity. 'Want some?'

'Definitely not.'

Over his drink, and several more, throughout the small hours, Robert steadily encouraged Jennifer to talk about herself. She was drawn into saying things about her reserve and almost perpetual sense of aloneness that she had never even fully said to herself, let alone another person. Eventually, she talked about how she knew she had changed since the death of her parents: how she often felt numb and distant.

Always Robert was sympathetic and encouraging. In turn, he confided how he had come from a broken home and had long struggled to overcome its legacy. There had been nights when he'd cried like a child in a former girlfriend's arms, he said, pouring out locked-up pain.

But Jennifer never once mentioned John, or Albert. John was as good as forgotten, but to talk about Albert seemed both discourteous to him and annoyingly pointless to her, for she was coming to the opinion that Albert had been a strange mistake. An aberration. An insensitive person who merely played at being poetically sensitive. A person whose heart contained a chip of ice. And also, after a time, she realised that she didn't want Robert to know that just two nights earlier she had been sleeping with someone, even though she did not find him physically attractive and had no intention or expectation of ever becoming intimate with him – he looked too old and roughened by drink and cigarettes.

491

She guessed him to be at least forty.

Soon after they had begun talking, Jennifer had risked yet another line of coke, mostly because it seemed to please Robert to have his generosity accepted. But thereafter she'd automatically accepted a line each time Robert laid a pair out, finding a strange solace in the routine. Beyond taking her unwelcome sense of drunkenness away and numbing her teeth, whatever effect the coke was having on her now, she found it hard to fathom. The room felt more intimate and cosy, perhaps, and the candlelight seemed particularly rich, but that was it as far as she could tell. It wasn't the elated experience she'd associated with cocaine from things she'd read, but neither was it the depression — the anguished loneliness — she'd experienced earlier.

'Jennifer, moving to London's going to be the best thing you've ever done,' said Robert, pouring himself another brandy.

Jennifer couldn't guess at how much Robert had to drink that day. At least twice as many beers as she'd had, and many brandies. But as yet he showed no sign of drunkenness.

'I've said things to you tonight I've never even said to myself,' she admitted.

'That's good,' said Robert, chopping more coke crystals, obtained from a new packet.

Jennifer's voice sank to little more than a murmur. 'I went to see their grave for the first time the other week. But I couldn't go through with it. I turned around.'

'Really?' said Robert, still chopping the coke. 'How long is it since they died?'

'Seven years. Seven years last Friday. They died together in a road accident.'

Robert looked up from his work. 'You've never visited the grave? Weren't you at the funeral?'

'I was ill. Puking all day.'

'Really?' said Robert, again sounding as if he'd found a significant association.

Robert continued to chop the coke crystals into powder before dividing it into two lines. He snorted one, then passed the banknote he'd used to Jennifer, who took care of the remaining line.

When handing the banknote back to Robert, out of the blue, Jennifer asked, 'Why did Mark leave tonight?'

'What? Mark? He just gets weird sometimes,' said Robert. Sounding like he was only half joking, he added, 'Come to think of it, he's weird most times.'

'Was it to do with Yvette?'

For a moment, it seemed to Jennifer that Robert, in a small way, was reacting like he'd been put on the spot.

'Why d'you ask that?'

'It was the way they spoke to each other.'

'He's wild about her,' revealed Robert, 'in his own sulky, dismal, adolescent way, that is.' He drank some of his brandy. 'What were you doing in Camden today, anyway?'

After a moment of pensive hesitation, Jennifer explained how she had wanted to visit the place her parents had first met, and the French restaurant had probably been it.

'Really?' said Robert with deep interest. 'It's good that you did that. You have to explore who you are and know where you came from. We're all on a journey to find ourselves.'

As the hour approached four, Jennifer was suddenly overwhelmed by an upswelling of emotion. Hiding her face in her hands, she began sobbing. Robert moved to sit beside her, comforting her in his arms.

'This is healthy,' he said. 'You need to grieve for them. You haven't let yourself grieve yet. You haven't really accepted that they're gone. That's been your problem. That's why you can't visit their grave, because unconsciously you haven't admitted their death. That might even be why you were sick on the day of the funeral. You've been clinging to something that's not there any more. Grieve for them now, then get on with your life. It's what they'd want you to do.'

But Jennifer hardly heard him. With tearful eyes, drawing back to look desperately at Robert, she confessed, 'I killed them. It was me. I made the accident happen. I lied to everyone.'

2.15
Melanie Brown

Although not a dazzling technical prodigy, Jennifer's nevertheless uncommon musicality was recognised at her school, and, as far as could be managed by a state-run comprehensive, it was nurtured. However, although she'd only recently turned twelve, she had already surpassed the school's regular teaching capacity, so a weekly Monday lunch-time visit by a special teacher had been arranged to help advance her through the higher levels of the national grade examination system. This was in addition to the private tutelage she received at her parents' expense.

Today, being Monday, Jennifer was waiting for her special teacher to arrive. Wearing her usual white blouse and black skirt, she was alone in one of the music rooms, standing with her violin under her chin. As always when she played, her nearly waist-length hair was tied loosely back. The lively piece she was practising was the most ambitious of the works she had chosen to demonstrate for her next examination, and she believed her determination to persevere with it until she could play it with her eyes closed was near to bearing fruit. Her private tutor — described by her father as "a bit precious" — had last week assured her that playing pieces blindfold would lead her to play "from feeling, not from seeing, and perhaps, one day, from the soul".

But Jennifer believed she had already played from the soul. Two months earlier, duetting with Sarah at home, an extraordinary, exalted state had affected her. Never in all her efforts to convey emotion through her violin had she felt so oblivious to its physical involvement. Her instrument had seemed to shrink in size, fall away from her sight, become immaterial as she filled the room — no, the whole of creation — with plaintive music. That once, just that once, it had seemed that every aching feeling that had ever touched her had been hers to evoke and give voice to. It had seemed that she, through her music, was the very source of all human sorrow and all human passion. And when she'd finished playing, to her mind, a spookiness had lingered in the room.

'Transcendent,' Sarah had murmured.

Jennifer's tormentors had been to McDonald's, bringing their dinners back to school. Coming along the corridor that passed the music rooms, eating their food indoors regardless of school rules, one of them, Melanie Brown, suddenly became excited. 'Here's Patrick!'

Frequent goal-scorer for the lower school team, and widely considered among the chattering classes to be the best looker in the second form, Patrick was a dreamy god to narrow-faced, frizzy-brown-haired, first-form Melanie and her three cohorts.

Carrying a sports bag, sandy-haired, clear-skinned Patrick stopped to look into a room through the glass panel in its door, then continued on.

'Are you off to football practise?' asked Melanie when Patrick came near.

'What do you think?' returned Patrick uncivilly, continuing on his way.

Melanie and her friends had a collective swoon after he passed.

'Absolutely fuckin' gorgeous,' declared Melanie, and the others agreed.

Swaying slightly as she played, Jennifer turned slowly toward the windows, and bright sunlight streamed in upon her face. Now her closed eyes looked into a featureless, glowing red and yellow universe that seemed sometimes — some tantalising times — poised to somehow inflate to accommodate her music. Her music could *become* this inner universe, she felt.

Hearing noises at the door, she opened her eyes and turned to look while continuing her practise. Through the glass panel she witnessed Melanie Brown mimicking her playing.

First scanning the room to make sure Jennifer was alone, Melanie opened the door and entered. Her gang followed, all continuing to feed themselves.

'Is this where y'spend y'dinner time?' asked ginger Gemma, ranked second in the gang.

Jennifer stopped playing.

'Let's play y'violin,' demanded blonde Amy, ranked fourth.

'I'm not allowed to let anyone touch it,' returned Jennifer, 'it was expensive.'

In mocking posh tones, in close unison, all ranks said, 'I'm not allowed to let anyone touch it, it was expensive.'

'Y'dad's a doctor,' said Melanie, 'he can afford another one.'

'How much pocket money d'y'get?' demanded Gemma. 'Bet y'get loads, y'jammy bitch.'

'None of your business,' answered Jennifer huffily.

Melanie reached out and twanged the violin's top string. 'Y'sister goes to a special music school, doesn't she? Why don't you?'

'I might go when I'm older, if I'm good enough,' answered Jennifer crossly.

All ranks mimicked, 'I might go when I'm older, if I'm good enough.'

'The teacher's coming soon,' said Jennifer.

'She's not a proper teacher,' returned Melanie belligerently.

'I started my periods last week,' Gemma saw fit to inform Jennifer.

'So?' shrugged Jennifer.

'She's a woman now,' said Amy. 'Have you started yours?'

Mrs. Bailes, the travelling music teacher, now arrived. 'All right, you lot,' she said to Melanie's gang, 'let's have you out. This is a private lesson. Jennifer, you have the rest of the day to gossip with your friends, please don't bring them in here.'

With defiant slouches, Melanie and her troop left the room.

Although it had never been admitted to the pupils, the classes in Jennifer's school were graded according to ability. In her year, there were five classes: A, B, C, D, E. A and B were known to contain the brightest children, and often shared lessons. C, D and E shared lessons too, but only with each other. Thus, during regular lesson time, Jennifer was never thrown into the company of Melanie Brown, or her cohorts, for they had been deemed slower learners. However, between lessons was different, and she often had to pass her tormentors in corridors or sit near them in morning assembly. On such occasions she would usually suffer some insult or petty interference, but would act as if it were only a temporary irritation to her, one beneath her dignity to react to.

In the early evening of the following Thursday, Jennifer was at home, reading, sitting alone in the kitchen. The faint sounds of the television coming from the living room briefly became louder as someone opened a door. A moment later, Jennifer's mousy-haired mother came into the kitchen to check on the cooking progress of her reduced family's dinner — reduced because Sarah was away at boarding school. Next week, however, her family would be reunited during the mid-term school recess.

If Jennifer looked up from her book, through the window and across a small sheep field she would be able to see the river Swale in rare October languor. Just beyond the river, running parallel to it, lay the B road that led into Richmond and her school. And behind the road, climbed the lower hills of the North Yorkshire Dales.

When Jennifer did next look up, she was wet-eyed. She had reached the story's end. Closing her book and putting it aside, she went to her mother, who was standing at the sink. She wrapped her arms around her and pressed her face against her body. Her mother, Rachael, was taller than most women, and had begun her middle-age enlargement. In some ways, Jennifer regarded her mother as an even greater protective physical presence than her father, for she had more than once seen that her mother could summon a vanquishing temper.

'Oh sweetheart,' said Rachael, 'have you finished your book?'

Jennifer nodded sadly to confirm she had.

'You always cry, don't you?' remarked Rachael, stroking her daughter's hair. 'Was it a happy or a sad ending?'

'All endings are sad.'

That evening, Jennifer began her first period.

*

If Jennifer had any feelings of new womanhood, she kept them to herself the next day at school. On that day, to mark the mid-term break, the three lowest years had the option of staying back to attend what the teachers anachronistically billed a disco, which was to run until six o'clock. At seven o'clock, the higher years would begin their own celebration, but, unlike the lower years, they would not be expected to wear uniform.

Although she'd had misgivings, under pressure from friends Jennifer chose to attend the disco. Her misgivings proved prescient, for, as she'd assumed it somehow would, it brought her into conflict with Melanie Brown.

At a little past five o'clock, a song Jennifer had often heard being sung around the school was playing in the hall, luring most of the children on to the dance floor. She didn't know who it was by, but would have guessed Oasis, since she'd noticed they were the flavour of the month with her contemporaries — Melanie had recently bragged to her that she was going to Manchester to see Oasis. Earlier, Jennifer had received threatening looks from Melanie, but now, with her frizzy hair gelled back for the evening's event, Melanie was dancing with her friends and seemed to have forgotten about her.

Standing with Jennifer were her own friends: slender, dark-haired Claire, who couldn't dance because of asthma, and short, blonde Davina, who was too fat to dare try.

Patrick was dancing in the centre of the room, where some balloons were providing additional entertainment, punched and kicked between the children. Jennifer was aware that he often glanced her way. She was also aware that Melanie and her three subordinates were using the balloon game to get closer to him, but he proved an elusive object, and when the music next stopped, he walked away.

'All right,' said Patrick, smiling, catching his breath. 'You're Jennifer, aren't you? 1A.'

Only briefly meeting his eyes, and feeling her face flush, Jennifer answered, 'Yeah.'

'Why aren't y'dancing?'

Not looking at him, Jennifer said, 'I don't want to. I'd feel stupid.'

'Bollocks. It's a laugh, man,' replied Patrick, stepping back and beckoning her to follow. 'Come and dance with me.'

Claire was thrilled for Jennifer, and urged her on.

Jennifer looked at Patrick, and he gave her more encouragement. But then he was called by friends. 'Hold on,' he said before dashing away, 'back in a minute. Might be a party later.'

'Did that boy ask you to dance?' demanded Melanie a moment later, poking a finger into Jennifer's back.

'Speak to him again and we'll get you,' promised Gemma when Jennifer turned around.

Jennifer huffily retorted, 'I'm going home.'

'Good,' said Melanie, bearing that look of malicious disdain that only children can muster.

Claire and Davina had been too fearful of becoming targets themselves to intervene. Even now, as Jennifer went to a table to collect her jacket, they were reluctant to be seen going over to her to offer comfort.

Leaving the dance room, from the payphone in the school foyer, Jennifer called her mother. She asked to be picked up earlier than arranged, and when questioned why, answered that she simply wanted to come back to spend time with Sarah.

*

When the half-term holiday was over, Sarah went back to her boarding school, and Jennifer went back to her own school. Geography was the first lesson of the week for Jennifer, and it was the one she dreaded most. It was not difficulties in understanding glaciation or coastal erosion that caused her dread: it was Melanie Brown and her gang. They had a lesson at the same time in the classroom next door.

On her way to geography, Jennifer had hoped that at least one of their respective classroom doors would be open, but neither was: the academic cream and academic dregs of the first form got to mix in the corridor before a teacher with a key arrived.

Carrying her violin in addition to her school bag, Jennifer positioned herself so that most of her class stood between her and Melanie, and made sure never to glance Melanie's way or draw attention to herself in anyway.

She overheard someone saying that a slide projector was set up in the geography room, which she figured meant an easy lesson ahead.

'What happened to you on Friday?'

Jennifer turned to the voice behind her. It was Patrick, and she could see that Melanie was watching.

'I had to go home,' she said, only briefly looking at him.

'We all went to a party afterwards,' said Patrick, speaking quickly and earnestly. 'There was beer. I heard you playing your violin the other day. You're really good.'

Jennifer saw that Melanie had come nearer, accompanied by her three friends.

'Thanks,' she said, turning her shoulder to Patrick and looking away.

Patrick flicked her long, straight hair and lifted it away from her back. 'You've got gorgeous hair. Best in the school.'

'1D, come inside now,' called greying Mrs. Coulson, the teacher for Melanie's class, who had just arrived and unlocked the door to their classroom.

Dutifully, 1D began filing into their room, although Melanie and her friends tarried.

Mr. Siddel, Jennifer's teacher, now arrived, so tall he had to stoop to work the lock of the geography room. 'Okay, 1A, let's have you in now. A projector's set up, so no messing around.'

With Melanie still hanging back in the corridor, 1A began to fill the geography room, and Jennifer shuffled forward with her classmates.

Patrick stayed by her side.

'Do you want to come to the Youth Centre with me on Friday?' he asked cheerfully and confidently. 'There's a band on.'

'No thanks,' returned Jennifer at once, deliberately looking straight ahead as she passed close to Melanie and her gang.

'Come on, my lot,' said Mrs. Coulson, standing impatiently in the doorway of her classroom.

To hurry-on Mrs. Coulson's stragglers, Mr. Siddel placed his hand on Melanie's shoulder to usher her away. 'Melanie Brown, since when have you been in 1A? To your own classroom, please.'

Melanie swiped his hand away, spitting, 'Get y'pervy hands off me, y'dirty old bastard.'

Mr. Siddel, thirty-five and with a daughter Melanie's age, flared with anger, anger immediately tempered with fear.

'Melanie Brown,' barked Mrs. Coulson, 'get in that classroom, now.'

With her usual defiant slouch and dawdle, Melanie went from corridor to classroom.

'Don't worry,' said Mrs. Coulson to Mr. Siddel. 'I saw it all.'

'Times have changed,' said Mr. Siddel, shaking his head as he went to his class. 'Times have changed.'

Double geography for Jennifer this day was an effortless, enjoyable slide-show depicting the River Swale's course from its source in the Yorkshire Dales, through Richmond, to its confluence with the Nidd to form the Ouse, through York, then on to its tidal reaches and confluence with the Trent to form the Humber. After geography, Jennifer had double P.E., which she always hated. Fortunately, a happy arrangement of her timetable placed her music lesson with Mrs. Bailes directly after P.E., and due to this, she was allowed to leave P.E. fifteen minutes early to make sure she had time to eat beforehand.

Daydreaming by the window in his maths class, Patrick saw Jennifer hurrying across the yard to the first year dining room, blue jumper over white blouse, red bag on back, violin case in hand. The dining room was a sanctuary for Jennifer: Melanie and her friends always went out for their food. Today, as usual for Mondays, Jennifer was first in the dinner queue, and by the time the rest of her class arrived from P.E., she had finished her meal and was leaving again.

In her lesson with Mrs. Bailes, Jennifer was told that she was more than ready for her next grade examination.

*

'I'd let him do anything he wants to me,' declared Melanie wantonly, through ketchup and grease smeared lips.

'So would I,' said Amy, almost dropping her burger.

'Would you let him fuck you?' blurted Gemma, spluttering food out with her words.

'Course I would,' returned Melanie at once. 'I let David fuck me. Patrick's much better than David.'

'What if you got pregnant? asked small, black-haired Julie before taking the last mouthful of her burger.

500

'He'd have to marry me then, wouldn't he?'

Julie discarded her burger's Styrofoam container the moment it was no longer of use to her. 'Shit,' she immediately said, seeing an adult emerge from a classroom along the corridor.

'She can't tell you off,' advised Melanie, recognising Jennifer's personal music tutor. 'She's not a proper teacher. It's that one that comes to teach Posh Cow.'

Mrs. Bailes walked past without even a look of reproach for the littering and food consumption.

'Told you,' said Melanie.

'Bet Posh Cow's in that music room,' said Julie disdainfully as she unwrapped a gum stick.

'Giz some gum,' demanded Melanie.

Alone in the music room, sitting at the teacher's desk, Jennifer was sorting her sheet music, which was spread out before her. Her violin was also on the desk. Hearing the door open, she turned her head to look and saw Melanie and her three friends cautiously peering in.

She looked back to her sheet music again, as if unconcerned and uninterested.

Wordlessly entering the room, Melanie dropped her Styrofoam container on the floor. Sauntering over to sit on the desk upon which Jennifer's violin case was resting, she fed a stick of gum into her burger-greasy mouth. Her friends followed, and loitered around her, all watching Jennifer at the teacher's desk as she put her music scores away into her backpack. After buckling the bag, Jennifer stood up and swung her hair around to take off the band she wore when playing her instrument, and while doing so went over to put her violin away. Avoiding eye contact with her visitors, she was lifting the lid of the case when Melanie's greasy fingers reached out and messed with her hair.

'Oo! You've got gorgeous hair. Best in the school.'

Swiping her hair away from Melanie, Jennifer snapped, 'Get off me.'

'Gonna make me?'

Gemma picked up Jennifer's violin and pretended to play it, pulling mocking faces.

'Give me that back,' demanded Jennifer, but not being obeyed.

'Give me that back,' mimicked Julie, with her nose in the air.

Jennifer snatched her violin away from Gemma and put it in its case. She was closing the latches when Melanie used her hair to wipe her fingers clean. Suddenly turning, she slapped Melanie hard. Melanie instantly retaliated, quickly wrestling Jennifer face-down on to the ground, sitting on the small of her back to helplessly pin her.

Melanie's friends were electrified, and gathered around the fighting pair, squealing excitedly, urging Melanie on. Jennifer was writhing, kicking and bucking, but she couldn't unseat Melanie, who grabbed a fistful of her hair, violently shaking her head.

'You filthy, brainy bitch,' hissed Melanie, momentarily pulling Jennifer's head up before resuming the shaking.

Jennifer flailed her arms, catching Melanie on the side of her face, but Melanie immediately returned the violence five-fold, leaving Jennifer covering her head for protection. Taking the chewing gum from her mouth, Melanie pressed it into the hair she was holding, and Julie impulsively stooped to add her own gum. Inspired, Gemma smeared the remainder of her burger over Jennifer's violin, and Amy stuffed the last of her own meal into the instrument's sound holes.

Gemma closed the instrument case, knowing Jennifer had not seen the crime.

'Bitch,' hissed Melanie. 'Posh, brainy bitch.'

'Slut,' said Gemma.

Jennifer was now sobbing, and it induced a lull upon her tormentors as the gravity of their deeds became apparent.

'Let her up, Melanie,' said Amy apprehensively. 'She's had enough.'

With a snarling face, Melanie got off Jennifer.

'Piss off,' bawled Jennifer, getting to her feet, tasting the salt tears that were running down her face. 'All of you, piss off.'

Sheepish is how Melanie's friends now appeared; sheepish and close to apologetic.

'Come on,' Julie quietly urged Melanie, 'let's go.'

Before leading her troops away, Melanie prodded Jennifer's shoulder. 'You better not squeal,' she warned gravely.

Once they'd left, Jennifer closed the latches on her violin case and took her hairbrush out from her backpack. Running it through her disarranged hair, it stuck just past her collar. Pulling her hair around to examine the problem, she discovered clumps matted with chewing gum.

Throwing her brush away before snatching her bag and violin case, she ran out the room, crying fresh tears of distress. Although

502

she had an afternoon's lessons ahead of her, she kept running until she was well beyond the school boundaries, crying all the way. She cried until she was on the road out of town that led to her home, the road she was forbidden to walk alone. Here, as the town diminished behind her, she began to settle. Enough of the small child remained in her for her to feel, in a faded way, that she had entered some untrodden realm as she tramped the two miles to her home. Child enough to feel that, although many cars passed her, she somehow went unseen. Safer now, is how she felt in her imagined remoteness.

In time, she became aware that her violin case had bumped the side of her knee so often when she'd been running that she had a bruise, a graze and a pain.

A bus she could have taken went past, holding up three cars behind it on the hilly, winding road. But she hadn't wanted to catch a bus with her hair so matted and dirtied, although her messed state became an irrelevance to her during her solitary walk, for there was no one to see her embarrassing condition.

Only three miles separated the outskirts of Richmond from the loosely-associated five-house hamlet that was her destination. However, along that short distance the land began to show a true upland nature, with the valley sides beginning to rise and close in. Fields became divided by dry-stone walls, not wire. Side roads gave warnings of steep gradients ahead.

In wintertime, on the hill behind her house, her neighbour liked to prove that skiing was possible.

By the time she could see her bedroom window, over the river and across a sheep field, Jennifer, in her stiff school shoes, felt she'd been walking an age, and had a blister starting. Nevertheless, her pace now quickened, then became a laboured run as, burdened with her violin and backpack, she took on the steep rise in the road, over which lay the junction that served only her hamlet and two farms higher up the valley side. Once over the rise, she was on the bend leading to the junction. Turning off the main road, she was soon on the narrow stone bridge over the river, and was only a minute away from the first of the five houses that constituted her neighbourhood.

Now, running faster with her front door in sight, she began crying again, and her violin case resumed bumping her leg. Clive, a retired solicitor, whose kitchen gave a view of Jennifer's front garden, noticed her frantic homecoming and immediately called her father at his Richmond surgery.

'Oh hello, Bill, sorry to bother you at work. It's Clive from next door ... Oh, not too bad. Probably nothing in it, but I just saw your youngest run into your house, crying quite badly, and I know you're both out because your cars aren't there.'

Letting the front door slam behind her, in the living room, Jennifer dropped her violin case and bag on to the sofa, then hurried to a mirror. The phone rang, but it hardly registered with her as she distressfully viewed the matted mess that was her hair below her collar. The phone stopped ringing, but then rang again, but she wouldn't answer it — she wasn't supposed to be at home, and was too upset to speak to anyone.

Rejecting the sight in the mirror, she threw herself on to the sofa, inadvertently bouncing her violin case on to the floor. Hunched, with her face reddened from running and bawling, she wailed abjectly into a cushion, gasping air between sobs. The phone stopped ringing, then began yet again. Impulsively, she scrambled over to disconnect it at the wall. Running into the kitchen, she withdrew a knife from a wooden block, a knife that for twelve years she'd been warned could so easily take off a finger. Angrily gripping her hair behind her neck and lifting it up, slicing and sawing upwards and away, she cut off everything below the collar, throwing the gum-matted tresses on to the floor.

Then, crazed deed done, she sat on a chair to cry more tears.

Like his daughter, Bill was very fair-haired, although thinning now. A little less than average height, there was a small element of the bulldog to his appearance, but a bulldog with intelligent blue eyes and an almost permanent expression of gentle amusement. That expression was absent now, however, as he opened his front door and called his daughter's name.

Still crying, Jennifer started to go to her father, but stopped before leaving the kitchen, suddenly worried about what she'd done to her hair and that she'd ran out of school.

Her crying ceased.

About to go upstairs to Jennifer's room, Bill heard a noise in the kitchen and went to investigate. He found his daughter, with roughly shorn hair and cheeks wet with tears, standing looking at him. All the worry and trouble she'd had that day, and the worry and trouble she'd had for months before, told in her eyes, and he fell to his knees and opened his arms wide. 'What's happened, my child?'

Jennifer ran to him, tightly wrapping her arms around his neck, crying again, crying with relief now.

Bill lifted his daughter up and carried her to the living room.

On the sofa, comforted by her father's arms, crying tears that eventually abated, Jennifer told what had happened to her that day, and on all the other days when she'd been singled out for torment.

'Darling,' he said, stroking her shorn hair as she pressed her head against his body, 'you should have told us the very first time it happened. Your mother and I will go to see the head and get this sorted.'

'No, it'll only make it worse,' advised Jennifer emotionally. 'That won't stop them. You don't know what they're like. They don't care.'

The front door opened, and Rachael hastened into the room. Jennifer ran to her and held her tight, but her mother spoke over her head.

'I got the message,' she said to her husband. 'What's happened?'

'She's been bullied. Bad. For months. They attacked her and messed her hair today.'

Jennifer began crying again.

'Oh my God,' murmured Rachael when she saw her daughter's hacked hair, hair she'd proudly brushed a thousand times.

Hearing the story from her husband, growing angrier and angrier but not outwardly showing it, Rachael stood with her daughter in her arms, who pressed her head against her bosom. 'We'll make them sorry for this,' she grimly promised.

'Mum, there's nothing you can do,' said Jennifer.

'We'll see about that,' contradicted Rachael, a woman whose husband suspected she could plunge a knife into a man given just quarter of a good reason to do it.

'No, mum,' said Jennifer, beginning to sound pleading.

Picking Jennifer's violin case up off the floor, meaning to put it out of the way, Bill noticed, as Jennifer had not, something exuding. He opened it and saw that the instrument he and his wife had paid over two thousand pounds for, and had given to Jennifer just a few weeks earlier on her birthday, had been desecrated — stuffed and smeared with greasy foods.

'Did they do this?'

Jennifer looked at her violin, and sobbed anew.

'Right, that's it,' declared Rachael as Jennifer distressfully examined her violin, 'we're all going to see the head now. Jennifer, put it back in its case, take it out to the car and wait for us.'

'It won't do any good, mum,' argued Jennifer tearfully.

'Now, Jennifer,' ordered Rachael, putting the violin into its case herself and pushing her daughter toward the door.

With distraught reluctance, Jennifer left the house and waited in the back of her father's car. When her parents appeared, she pleaded with them to forget it all. 'Dad, it won't do any good,' she said when he got into the driver's seat. 'They'll just pick on me more.'

Controlling smouldering rage as she got into the passenger seat, Rachael insisted, 'Jennifer, we *are* going to see the head, and when he sees what they did to your hair and your violin, they'll get expelled.'

'They won't,' argued Jennifer as her father started the engine. 'Please. I don't care about my hair, or the violin. I hate playing.'

'Jennifer,' said her father, sharing his wife's smouldering rage, 'we know best.'

He set the car moving.

'You don't,' pleaded Jennifer. 'You don't. You'll make it worse. I don't care about my hair, or the violin.'

As the car passed over the stone bridge, Rachael turned sharply in her seat to face her daughter. 'Jennifer, you are not giving up playing because some little brats are picking on you. We'll go and see their parents afterwards. They've ruined that violin.'

Nothing could do more harm, believed Jennifer. She'd seen Melanie's parents. Seen her hard-faced mother shouting and bawling. Seen her criminally-mannered father in his baseball cap and jogging pants. 'No!' she protested, suddenly jumping from distraught to crazed. Snatching the violin out of its case, she cried, 'I don't care about the violin. I hate it.' Leaning forward, in a tempestuous fury she began smashing her instrument on the dashboard. 'I hate it. I hate it.' On the second or third rapid stroke, the violin shattered just as Bill turned to face his frenzied daughter, catching a backstroke across his face that temporarily inserted a wooden shard as thick as a pencil into his eye. Maddened though she was, Jennifer immediately realised what she'd done — terrifyingly realised that the clear liquid that had sprayed the car had been the contents of her own father's eye.

Although grievously injured, Bill only lost control of the vehicle for moment, overshooting the junction with the Richmond road by just a car's length, and stopping perpendicular across the nearside lane.

But it was enough.

From the left, a glaring, twin-headlighted 1200cc bike being ridden

506

for sport by a man in red racing leathers was accelerating out of a blind bend when a car lurched out to strangely block the oncoming lane. His own lane was still clear, though, and with insufficient time to brake, he instinctively accelerated instead, meaning to squirt past the uncertain car as quickly as possible. But the driver of a hatchback coming over the rise from the opposite direction also hadn't enough time to stop when she saw a car stall across her lane, and had to swerve around it while braking hard.

In another split-second instinctive move, the rider of the powerful bike threw it right to avoid the vehicle suddenly coming head-on through the gap he'd hoped to slip through. A blink later, he struck the stalled car, smashing into the front passenger door, knocking the whole vehicle yards back along the road. Already half off his bike before the impact, he was thrown clean over the bonnet, rolling and tumbling for what seemed an age to him before finding himself motionless on the grass verge.

Sitting up, before even checking for injury, he looked to see where his bike had landed, but was puzzled by its apparent absence.

Unreal. Everything seemed unreal to him. Quiet.

For what seemed too long, the unreal sense of the scene continued. Taking off his helmet and looking back to the cars, thirty or forty yards distant, he realised that the on-coming vehicle was leaving the scene, continuing off in the direction it'd been travelling before the collison. But where was his bike?

Now he saw that the driver of the car he'd collided with was somehow pressed against the side window, and that the window was reddened.

Help. This needed help. He had a mobile on him. Would it still work? Pulling his gloves off, he took his phone from his chest pocket. It seemed undamaged. Hearing a noise, he looked and saw the smashed car's rear door open. A young girl carrying a broken violin got out and backed slowly away from the vehicle.

He stood up, discovering at once that his lower right leg was damaged, but not too bad — he could still hobble. Dialling while limping to the car, he found there was no phone signal to be had. The young girl — uninjured, it seemed — backed away to the grass verge, looking with eerie stillness at the wreck. Now he saw his bike — it was mostly inside the car, bodywork twisted, crumpled and ripped to accommodate it. It had battered through the passenger door, tearing up the roof and running roughshod across a passenger, then on into the driver. The passenger was as good as decapitated, her head dangling upside-down over the back of her seat. The man was stabbed and crushed in a dozen places. Both their bodies were subject to the weight of the bike, and mixed in with all the metal and glass and flesh and blood and steaming water and dripping petrol, two small air bags added more pressure in the suffocating confinement.

The whine of a car reversing hard broke the impotent silence — the hatchback was returning. Stopping next to the wreck, the middle-aged female driver stepped out, ashen and tremulous.

'Can't get a signal,' said the biker, showing her his phone.

'I've already called them,' she said, pausing in her uncertain dash to the wreck to consider the silent child. 'That's why I kept going. Signal comes back just over the hill. Oh shit. Oh shit. What a mess.'

'I didn't stand a chance,' said the biker, now realising he was hurt more than he'd first thought. Painfully, he sat on the grass verge near where Jennifer was standing with her splintered violin. 'Something's really wrong inside my boot. My ankle. And my knee. I can't stand any more. My back feels weird, too.'

'Oh shit,' murmured the woman, looking into the wrecked vehicle. 'I don't know anything about first aid.'

'Think they're past that,' said the biker. 'They've got to be dead.'

The woman looked at Jennifer, uncertain about her. 'Are you hurt, darling?'

Jennifer did not respond.

'They're coming,' said the biker. 'I can hear a siren.'

'I'll move my car aside,' said the woman, hurrying to her vehicle.

Within seconds, a police car that must have already been on route to Richmond slew round the corner, pulling up close to the wreck. Two officers dashed out, going to opposite sides of the smashed vehicle. 'It's doctor Lucas,' said one officer. 'Still alive. Bleeding's still pulsing.'

'This one's a gonner,' said the other officer. 'No chance. Jesus, that bike must have been shifting.'

'Who else is hurt?' asked the first officer as the woman returned from moving her car.

'My leg's bust,' said the biker.

'What about you, pet?' said the officer to Jennifer.

Oblivious to him, Jennifer continued to stare impassively at the twisted wreck while a chill breeze rolling down from the hill behind wafted strands of her badly-cut hair across her gore-spattered face.

2.16
Ghosts

Harry was hanging gruesomely before his eyes. Then the woman from upstairs loomed into view, clutching unnaturally large rosary beads. Except it wasn't the woman from upstairs, it was his own mother. With a priest looking on in the background, she shambled forward in a desperate attempt to hug him.

A tap on the door, and Albert awoke bolt-upright, dispelling the image. He was confused, yet instantly pin-sharp alert.

'I've made you some breakfast, Master.'

It was Simon's voice behind the door.

'Down soon,' blurted Albert instinctively. Nervously. The door was tried, but the bed blocked it. 'The bed's in the way. I'll be down soon.'

'I've brought it up,' said Simon. 'I'll leave it outside the door.'

'Okay.'

'Eat it before it gets cold. It's two o'clock, by the way.'

Footsteps retreated down the steep stairs.

Albert lay his head back down and realised it was just the same: the gnawing tenseness in his stomach was still there, unchanged. And Phil was still dead. Yes, Phil was still dead, and he was still an accessory to his murder. But Simon had sounded no different, and was still calling him "Master". That was astonishing. That was utterly astonishing. The E would have long worn off for him, yet he was apparently still unperturbed regarding the murderous events of the night before. Could it be a trick? No — why should they need to trick him? Besides, Simon lacked guile. This was good, although beyond all reasonable understanding, Simon *still* didn't realise he'd been deceived. Perhaps, Albert dared to think, he might even remain deceived until midnight, February the first?

Getting out of the sleeping bag, Albert put on his shoes. He quietly pushed the bed aside and tentatively opened the door. On the step outside, he found his breakfast on an improvised tray — toast with fried eggs and mushrooms, and a cup of tea. There was also a weighty manila envelope.

He brought everything into his room, and pushed the bed back against the door. Despite his anxious state and no awareness of an appetite, his body seemed to have a ravenous, independent need for food, and he ate the meal in the manner of an escaped convict.

He needed a bath. His clothes needed washing, too – he calculated he hadn't been out of them for almost fifty hours straight. He would either have to go back to Durham to collect his stuff from Rebecca's, or somehow acquire a change of clothing. He didn't want to go back to Durham. He was in an even worse position than when he'd left: his reasons for leaving were now compounded with accessory to a murder.

There was a washing machine in the kitchen, he remembered. He could wash the clothes he had on, wearing only his coat while he waited for them to dry. Put them in front of the fire, maybe. Yes, that's what he'd do.

Finished eating, while drinking the tea he opened the envelope, discovering it to contain a quantity of money – slim bundles of fifty pound notes, each wrapped in a paper band marked £1,000. There were twenty bundles in all, together with a hand-written note, which read: *For the engineering equipment you will need. Let me know if you need more.* Twenty grand – double what he'd originally been aiming for. A bank receipt fell out the envelope. It bore the day's date, and had been stamped by a Bishop Auckland branch. Sitting on the bed, he stared at the money, realising that with twenty thousand pounds he could reimburse Ron then flee to another country – India, or some other place where ten thousand pounds might last him years. But that's not what he wanted. He wanted most of all to escape the crime, not just the punishment.

Placing the money aside, he washed his face in the basin and brushed his teeth. Putting his coat on for warmth, he sat on the floor with his back against the bed, bleakly considering his position. He still felt trapped in the room, despite now having the funds to escape far from it. What should he do? Go downstairs and find out how things stood, that's what he had to do. Fuck it, this was unbelievable. This was all so fucking unbelievable. He wanted his old life back, his old life of restless stagnation.

But, while sitting in unabating anguish, Albert felt some other part of his mind becoming *excited*. Curiously excited, for no clear reason at first. Then the reason began to become known. It was not something he was consciously calculating, it was just *emerging*. Was this the pay-off for all the desperate thinking he'd done before sleeping? Once he'd read a definition of the creative process as being one of *saturation, incubation, illumination*. He'd so often found that to be the case himself. So many times he'd thought about a problem for hours, or even days, only to give up on it. But some time later, the solution might just pop into his head. It was evidence, he believed, that without being aware of it, the brain undeniably continues working on problems that have defeated conscious abilities. Thus, he tended to regard conscious thoughts as being like the visible surface motions of a vast, deep sea of mental activity. The entire sea conspires to produce the surface swells, but people only ever hear the crashing of their inner waves, never the vast, undulating, unfathomably deep, relentless, dark body of computations that powers them.

Last night had been the saturation period, he understood, and the incubation had been his sleep time. And now he had true *illumination*. He was able to see a clear escape from the nightmare. For every problem, a cunning solution effortlessly arose to make sure the murder would never come to light.

Religion would save him.

Furthermore, he could see how he could walk clean away from the crime a much, much richer man, and Simon would never be any the wiser.

He took off his coat, and put on the golden robe. First, he would tell Simon he had seen Phil in the night — Simon had books on spiritualism on his shelves, so surely he believed in ghosts.

2.17
Thanking Nature

Robert's penis was pressing hard and insistent against the back of Jennifer's thigh when the sound of someone coming into the next room woke her. Lying beside her, deeply asleep, Robert was snoring badly, as he had done throughout much of the night, often waking her.

Now someone was tapping on the slightly ajar bedroom door.

'Robert,' said a displeased male voice. 'It's past eleven.'

Turning over, distancing herself from his erection, Jennifer gently shook Robert. 'Robert, wake up. Someone's calling you.'

Robert would not awaken. Hearing someone else arrive next door, Jennifer sat up. Peering across the dim room, she located her clothes. Wearing her knickers and the long T-shirt Robert had given her for the night, she scurried to dress and arrange herself. Finished dressing, she again tried to wake Robert, but he would not stir. She could scarcely believe someone could slumber so deeply. Leaving him, she peeped through the gap in the door. Sitting at the computer by the window, wearing a white shirt and black trousers, she recognised Mark from last night. Another man, wearing a thick Navy-blue jumper and brown trousers, was eating a pastry item on the dingy sofa. She assumed this person to be Jeremy, and guessed him to be in his early thirties. He was quite tall, with an athletic build and collar-length sandy hair which often fell over his eyes as he ate, seeming to bemuse him equally each time.

Steeling herself to enter the office, Jennifer was very conscious that it would look like she and Robert had had sex. They had not. Last night, once she'd blurted her confession, in an almost trance-like state she had gone on to tell the story of the accident — never truthfully told to anyone before. Then, it having become very late, and with her being upset and tearful, Robert had offered her a share of his bed, and that had been it — he had slept naked, and she had slept in the T-shirt she had been given.

'Morning,' said the person eating the pastry.

'Morning,' returned Jennifer, standing half in one room, half in the other.

Hearing her voice, Mark glanced over his shoulder. 'Morning,' he also said, but, thought Jennifer, with a sullen cynicism attached to it.

'I'm Jeremy,' said the eater.

'Jennifer.'

Apparently engrossed in typing, Mark said nothing more.

'Is Robert up yet?' asked Jeremy. His speaking manner was decisive but plodding; cultured, but lacking any mercurial element — like an army officer fresh from Sandhurst.

'I can't wake him,' admitted Jennifer.

Jeremy sprang to his feet. Striding to where Jennifer was standing, he tapped vigorously upon the half-open door. 'Robert,' he called, attempting an authoritative, stern voice. 'Robert.'

A groan came from within.

'We're supposed to be starting the new sales campaign today,' said Jeremy firmly.

Another groan, a groan that with one syllable said: *I'm doing my bloody best, aren't I?*

Stepping past Jeremy into the office, Jennifer asked, 'Mind if I use the bathroom?'

'Go ahead,' answered Mark, with no detectable cordiality in his voice.

'Come on, Robert,' said Jeremy, 'I'll make a you a cappuccino.'

As Jennifer had discovered the night before, the cramped bathroom was a small mess. Resembling lichen on rocks, patches of dried shaving foam speckled with stubble coloured the basin and poorly-fitted linoleum floor. The tub was grey with scum; the basin was predominantly brown with a different scum; and the toilet bowl was becoming a foul lime scale stalagmite. The fact that the room was windowless added to the dismal impression, as did the fact that all the towels were dimmed and smelly.

'Would you like a cappuccino, Jennifer?' asked Jeremy, passing by the bathroom on his way to the kitchen.

'If it's no trouble.'

Just as she was about to leave the bathroom, above the noise of draining water, she heard Robert's raised, heated voice, but the words weren't clear. Opening the door, she heard him complain, 'That bastard owes us two grand.' A quieter reply came from Mark: 'He's not the bastard, we are.'

Entering the office, with her face now freshened, Jennifer found Robert sitting at the table with his legs crossed, smoking a cigarette. He had an annoyed, preoccupied look about him. Barefoot, he was wearing the same paisley shirt and jeans he'd worn the day before.

Mark, still at the computer, had his back to the room.

'Here's your cappuccino,' said Jeremy kindly, coming into the room.

Taking her cup, Jennifer drew a chair up to the table. Easily losing his preoccupied look, Robert smiled at her, and in a tone deeper than his usual, asked, 'How are you today?'

'Better,' returned Jennifer, smiling a little. 'Got a bit of a hangover, though.'

'It's just starting,' muttered Mark.

Robert and Jeremy reacted to Mark's comment by exchanging looks of restrained annoyance.

'Jennifer was very emotional about something last night, Jeremy,' announced Robert, his words obviously intended for Mark, 'so I suggested she stay here instead of being alone in her hotel.'

Leaving his cappuccino barely touched, Robert went to the bathroom. In his absence, Jeremy made polite, gentle conversation with Jennifer. When Robert returned, his stubbly face was looking fresher.

'Should we go out for some breakfast, Jennifer?' suggested Robert, smiling as usual, 'and let Mark think his negative thoughts alone?'

'No, you can't,' reacted Jeremy, losing some of his composure. 'We have to start the new campaign today.'

Robert seemed to be coming to life now. Going sprightly back into his room, he called out, 'We'll start in the afternoon, Jeremy. One o'clock. Big push at one. Promise.'

Jennifer observed that Jeremy remained unhappy.

Very soon, Robert came out of his room, wearing his coat. Over his arm, he was carrying Jennifer's own coat.

'Coming?' he asked Jennifer, smiling.

'Okay,' she answered, accepting her coat.

'See you at one,' said Robert, leaving the room.

'One o'clock,' stated Jeremy firmly, but Robert, it seemed, was already out of earshot.

Jennifer said a quick goodbye and hurried after Robert.

The sky was clear as Robert and Jennifer emerged on to Harley Street, but puddles showed that it had rained much in the night. It was colder than yesterday, with a strong breeze, and Jennifer was glad of her full-length coat.

'What did you think of Jeremy?' asked Robert.

'Very courteous,' said Jennifer, not sure what opinion Robert would have liked her to have formed.

'Jeremy's the most fantastic person I know,' declared Robert easily.

'He's so honest and loyal. Really in touch with people's feelings and energy. I really love him.'

Five minutes of walking brought them to what Robert described as a "tapas bar and restaurant" in Paddington Street. It was in a cellar, accessed directly from the pavement, and as they descended to its door, Robert pointed out that they were right opposite Nottingham Street, where she'd said her hotel was. Inside, the ceiling was low, and the space limited. The walls were finished in a dark wood veneer, and the lighting was moody and minimal. There was a small bar, but it appeared unstaffed. Two extraordinarily pretty young women that Jennifer figured must only be around her own age were in attendance as table waitresses. Both had long, black hair, pale complexions and deep eyes. One was tall and slim, the other shorter and more rounded. Both wore identical black skirts and white blouses.

They smiled at Robert.

'Hello, Robert, how are you?' asked the shorter girl in slow foreign tones.

'Thirsty,' answered Robert, kissing her cheek before she showed him to one of the free tables.

Taking his coat off and hanging it up on a peg near him, Robert prompted Jennifer to do likewise.

'Beer or brandy?' asked the taller waitress.

'Beer, please,' said Robert, sitting down.

The girls smiled at Jennifer as they placed cutlery and menus before her.

'Anna and Denise,' said Robert, introducing the waitresses to Jennifer, Denise being the shorter of the two.

'Jennifer,' said Jennifer.

'I like your dress,' said Anna.

'Thanks,' returned Jennifer.

When they left, Robert informed her that Denise was Brazilian, and Anna, Portuguese. Watching Denise across the room, Jennifer observed that she wore a permanent, gentle smile.

Anna placed a basket of sliced French bread on the table, along with a small tub of butter, but the first thing to pass Robert's lips was a beer brought by Denise.

'What exactly do you do at work?' Jennifer asked Robert while they were waiting for the food to arrive.

'We publish business reviews,' answered Robert.

'I don't know what that means.'

Robert explained slickly, 'We work on behalf of various organisations — like, say, the Confederation of British Industry, or the Regional Health Authorities — and we publish factual and advisory yearbooks for them. The books are distributed free to industry decision-makers, and we make our profits from the advertising they contain.'

'Oh.'

A short, anachronistically denim-clad, ageing man with long, curly blonde hair that looked like a perm to Jennifer entered the restaurant. Seeing Robert, he came over. 'All right, Robert?'

He had a strong Geordie accent.

'All right, Colin,' beamed Robert, standing up to shake his hand.

Colin explained he was looking for someone, and left after Denise told him the person had already been and gone.

Jennifer remarked to Robert that when talking to Colin, his accent had become more Northern, and Robert at once agreed that it had. He was, he explained, inclined to slip back into his native accent whenever it was being spoken around him. This seemed curious to Jennifer, for, to her ear, Robert's accent had temporarily become like that of a true, albeit moderated, Geordie, and not like that of someone from Darlington, thirty or more miles south of Newcastle.

Robert explained that Colin was a tour manager in the music business, and had just done a David Bowie gig.

Anna brought their food, but Robert lost interest in his meal after a few spoonfuls and ordered another beer by waving to Denise and pointing to his glass.

'How are you feeling today?' he asked Jennifer as Denise brought him his second beer, a service he acknowledged with a smile.

'Okay,' returned Jennifer, with a deliberate upbeat.

She looked at her food.

'It was an accident, Jennifer,' said Robert, detecting evasion. 'Let yourself accept that.'

'I know it was an accident,' returned Jennifer, continuing to look at her food, moving parts of it around with her fork. 'I've always known it was an accident. But if I hadn't —'

Robert cut in. 'If you knew it was an accident, why have you been hiding the truth all these years?' Jennifer made no reply, so Robert continued. 'Here's what we'll do. We'll go to Richmond together and visit the grave. I'll carry you across the graveyard if that's what it'll take. You'll stay until you've said everything to your parents you need to say. Then we'll go and see your sister and tell her what's been bothering you. Okay?'

'Not my sister,' reacted Jennifer, acquiring an ability to look up from her plate and into Robert's eyes. 'I can't. I've tried. I just can't make the words come out.'

Robert sat back a little, and allowed Jennifer's reaction to subside. 'Would she be angry?'

Jennifer also sat back a little. 'No, she wouldn't,' she said, now looking at the tablecloth.

Robert allowed a period to pass before advising, 'Jennifer, take some time to get your balance back. A few months here away from it all will do you wonders. Then we'll seriously look at how we can sort you out. Okay?'

'Yeah, okay,' said Jennifer, in subdued agreement.

'And contact your family soon to tell them you're all right.'

'I will. Soon as I'm settled.'

'Promise?'

'Promise.'

'Really promise?'

'Really promise.'

Conscious that Robert was still looking at her, Jennifer began eating again but soon decided she had now had as much as she could stomach. 'I can't manage any more of this,' she said, pushing her plate away. 'I'm still hungover. Think I could order a coffee?'

'Could we have a coffee, please?' Robert asked Anna, who was passing their table.

Anna gave an acknowledging smile.

'Thanks,' said Jennifer to Robert.

'My pleasure,' said Robert. He looked pensive a moment. 'Did those kids at your school go on bullying you?'

Jennifer shook her head. 'No. Nothing after they died. None of them even spoke to me again. It was like they were spooked by me afterwards. It was strange. Lots of the other kids acted differently too.'

Jennifer's coffee arrived. While she sipped it, Robert quizzed her regarding what she planned to do in London. With some awkwardness, she admitted that she had no real plans at all, other than an uncertain one to go to college, and eventually university.

'You can never be too educated,' said Robert knowingly, in a lower register than usual. He paused, and when he spoke again, the pitch of his voice was raised in tentative speculation. 'Am I right in

517

guessing you've split with a boyfriend recently?'

Jennifer hesitated before saying, 'Saturday.'

'Really? That recently?'

'How did you know?'

'I didn't know,' said Robert. 'I just sensed it from the way you are. I can tell you've had a lot of relationship energy drained from you recently. Why did you leave him?'

'I didn't. He left me.'

'Really? What happened, if you don't mind me asking?'

'I've no idea what happened,' confessed Jennifer.

'What sort of person was he?'

'Don't know that, either. We weren't together long.'

Their conversation was cut short by the arrival of Jeremy.

'It's one-thirty,' said Jeremy, standing behind Jennifer. 'You said you'd be back at one.'

'I was coming soon,' claimed Robert earnestly, with no hint of indignation in his voice.

'Mark wants to know if you've got the cheque book. He needs to pay some bills.'

Patting various pockets, Robert speculated that he might indeed have the cheque book. He found it in an inside pocket, dog-eared and folded tightly, and handed it to Jeremy. 'I'll be along as soon as I've finished this beer.'

'Robert,' said Jeremy, 'it's really important we make a start on the new campaign.'

'Don't worry. I'll be back soon. Big push when I get back.'

Jeremy took the cheque book and went away, looking no less sanguine than when he'd arrived.

'He can be a bit of a mother hen at times,' said Robert, with a kindly smile.

A few minutes later, a man came over, and Robert introduced him as Mike, the restaurant owner. To Jennifer, Mike appeared to be struggling with a chronic unhappiness, and she imagined it might be that he was dissatisfied with the way he looked. In early middle-age, he had short, black, curly hair and a harried, pig-like face. He was quite tall, she noted, but his heavy body appeared lazy and shiftless, and he wore glasses with lenses so thick that without them he would surely be reduced to groping his way around the world.

Mike spoke in Robert's ear about something he obviously did not wish to have overheard — some kind of earnest business matter, Jennifer believed. After some nods and quiet agreements from Robert, he went away again, disappearing through a door behind the bar.

Once Mike left, Robert smiled and asked, 'Ready?'

'Okay,' said Jennifer. 'You have to let me pay the bill, though.'

'No, it's on me. Money's for giving.'

'Please,' said Jennifer. 'I've got money to give, too.'

'All right,' agreed Robert, appearing to understand it was important to her.

He beckoned Anna with a flutter of his fingers.

When Anna supplied the bill, it came to less than Jennifer had guessed it would. After she paid it, Robert led the way out. On the street, before they parted company, he took a pen from his pocket, writing two telephone numbers on a piece of card torn from his cigarette packet. 'Top one's for the phone in my room,' he explained, 'the other's the office number. Call me later if you need some company. And don't forget to ring Yvette.' After consulting scraps of paper retrieved from various pockets, he wrote out three numbers for Yvette, explaining that one was for her home, one for her mobile, one for a shop in Camden where he said she worked making silk prints.

'Thanks for everything,' said Jennifer, receiving the piece of card.

'Absolutely my pleasure,' said Robert.

'Sorry for getting all emotional last night.'

'Don't worry about it,' he said, and kissed her lightly on the lips in a parting gesture before walking away, smiling at the world. 'Make sure you ring Yvette,' he called back after ten or so steps. 'She really likes you.'

'I will,' returned Jennifer.

Jennifer smiled a little at the world too as she walked the short distance to her hotel. Smiled for having landed on her feet after her wild jump into the unknown. Meeting Robert and Yvette was a wonderful thing to have happened to her. She was finally beginning to live, and the past was finally beginning to feel like the past.

Upon returning to her hotel room, she slept for an hour or so. When she awoke, her hangover was gone. Plucking up the little courage she needed, she rang Yvette at her workplace, and found her to be just as friendly as she'd been the day before.

Yvette enthusiastically suggested they could rendezvous in Camden when her work finished that evening. 'Ask Robert, too,' she said.

'I will,' said Jennifer. 'I'll ring him.'

After taking a shower and washing her hair, Jennifer chose some clothes to wear from the limited selection she'd brought with her: a cream jumper and black trousers, to be worn under her yellow puffa jacket. Now she rang Robert, who said he'd definitely meet her in Camden.

By six o'clock, having taken her first ever tube ride, Jennifer was once again in Camden, at a table in the French restaurant, but this time waiting for friends. Yvette arrived a little late, for which she earnestly apologised, citing a problem at work. After they ordered food, Yvette, in the endearing, burnt-tongue-tip way she had of finding and delivering her English words, asked Jennifer how she had got on with Robert the previous night, as if expecting a romance to have developed in the cab.

'I don't like him that way,' said Jennifer, not mentioning that they had shared a bed.

'Oh, but 'e's a wonderful person!' protested Yvette.

'I know,' agreed Jennifer, 'but he's too old for me. He must be at least forty.'

'No, 'e's only thirty-two.'

'Really?'

'Really.'

'It doesn't make any difference, though. I'm not looking for a relationship with anyone at the moment.'

''Ow long is it since you separated from your boyfriend? The one you mentioned last night?'

'Did I mention him last night?'

'Yes,' stated Yvette. 'In the cab going to the Mexican bar.'

'I did, didn't I?' remembered Jennifer. 'We split just a few days ago, but we weren't together long. I don't really want to think about him any more. He's history now.'

'Listen,' said Yvette, whose thoughts had obviously galloped on, 'why don't you stay in my flat until you find a place of your own? There's no bedroom for you, but you can sleep on the big couch.'

Jennifer wasn't sure.

'You merst!' insisted Yvette, her vowels becoming even more Frenchified. 'You can't pay for the 'otel all the time.'

'Well, if you don't mind.'

That was a good as a yes to Yvette. Beaming, she embraced Jennifer. Drawing back, she said, 'Ah 'ope you like cats. Ah've got one this big!' And she flung her arms out wide to show its enormity, her bracelets jangling wildly.

Jennifer smiled.

*

After their meal, Jennifer and Yvette waited in the restaurant, stretching out cups of coffee, but Robert did not arrive. Using her mobile, Yvette left four messages on his office answering machine, but she failed to ring back.

"'E 'as so many friends 'e sometimes forgets where 'e as to be,' explained Yvette in a way that sounded as if she were feeling personally embarrassed over it. 'Don't worry, you'll see 'im soon.'

'Doesn't he have a mobile?' asked Jennifer.

'No. He says 'e keeps losing them.'

Presently, with the time approaching nine o'clock, they left the restaurant. Their plan was to make their way by tube to Yvette's flat on Holloway Road so that Jennifer could decide if she'd like to stay there. Walking out the restaurant, Yvette linked her arm with Jennifer's. She asked about Jennifer's family, and Jennifer told her story not as she'd told it to Robert, but as she'd always told it: simply and vaguely that her parents had died when she was young.

Yvette's story was that she was the daughter of a designer, well known in France, who had split from her mother when she was fourteen, and she'd seldom seen him since, but he sent money each month.

Coming out of Holloway Road tube station, it was a five minute walk to Yvette's flat, which was above a laundrette. Even at this late hour, shops were open, and the street was busy – a novel nocturnal sight for Jennifer. Entry from the street was via an inconspicuous, plain, black door which opened to an untidy, dingy staircase. Climbing two flights brought them to Yvette's inner door, which opened directly into her living room. The room, although quite spacious, had a cosseting feel, conveyed by the printed fabrics and rugs hanging from walls and across corners. As Jennifer had earlier been informed, the flat had only one bedroom, but the sofa was large and comfortable enough for her to sleep on until she found her own place.

The woman who lived upstairs was mad, said Yvette, and would jump up and down on the ceiling if she heard too much noise, or sometimes any at all.

'I have to pay you, though,' said Jennifer.

'Of course,' returned Yvette. 'But no way as much as the 'otel. We'll settle it later.'

'Can I phone my sister?' asked Jennifer.

'Of course you can. You live 'ere now.'

A big black and white tom cat appeared from the kitchen. 'Baby!' cried Yvette, picking up and cuddling the animal. She presented it to Jennifer, who stoked it. 'You 'ave to make sure 'e never gets outside. Too many cars.'

'I'll be careful,' promised Jennifer, accepting the cat into her own arms. 'What's his name?'

''E doesn't 'ave a name.'

Jennifer took the cat with her to the phone, sitting on the floor with it on her lap as she dialled her sister's number.

'Sarah, it's Jennifer ... I'm fine. I'm in London ... No, I'm all right. I'm settled with new friends.'

Once Jennifer had convinced Sarah of her security and peace of mind, and once she had apologised for taking off so abruptly, her sister said, 'Albert's disappeared. He's got no money and he's left all his things at Rebecca's. Everything. He hasn't got anything with him.'

'When?' asked Jennifer.

'The morning after the bonfire party. He was really upset that you weren't there. No one's seen him since.'

'Albert was upset? Why? He just walked away.'

'He left a letter for you,' said Sarah. 'Do you want me to read it to you?'

'No,' said Jennifer quietly. 'I don't want to hear it. It's over. I don't want to think about things past.'

'I think you should hear it.'

'No,' said Jennifer, and Sarah didn't mention Albert again.

When Jennifer was drawing the conversation with her sister to a close, Yvette came over. 'Let me speak to 'er,' she said, and Jennifer passed her the phone. Yvette promptly reassured Sarah that Jennifer was in safe hands and enjoying herself very much, and that she would be staying with her for a while.

She volunteered her address and number before returning the receiver to Jennifer.

When Jennifer eventually put the phone down, she felt relieved; exhilarated, even, in her reserved way. All that fear, prediction and reasoning that she would never see her sister again had evaporated, like the insubstantial nonsense it had surely been. Everything was going to be all right after all.

'Who is Albert?' asked Yvette.

'Oh,' said Jennifer, losing some of her upbeat feelings, 'my last boyfriend.'

Yvette looked at Jennifer, seeming to understand that she had been upset by some news or other concerning this Albert. 'I think we should go out. There's a good club near 'ere. Do you want to go? Do 'alf an E each. Just enough to get relaxed.'

Jennifer reacted with concern. 'E? You mean ecstasy? Take some ecstasy?'

'I forgot, you've never 'ad drugs before! Oh you merst 'ave some E. You *merst*! Don't worry, it's not like coke. You won't feel bad. I'll be with you. We can come back 'ere if you don't like it. But you will like it.'

'What sort of club do you mean?'

Jennifer's question was hard for Yvette to comprehend, and she answered with a gangling arms dance. 'A club!'

'Dancing?'

'Of course. Do 'alf an E and dance.'

Although apprehensive, Jennifer agreed to go to the club. The fact that she had never danced before worried her more than the prospect of taking a drug. She had never even danced alone in her locked bedroom, at least not properly.

'You can't wear that top,' pronounced Yvette. 'You'll be too 'ot. It gets really 'ot there. You'll 'ave to wear something looser.'

Taking Jennifer into her bedroom, which was also hung with fabrics and rugs, Yvette began finding things for her to wear, rummaging happily through drawers. When suitable garments had been decided on, they both began changing.

Jennifer noticed a two-inch long scar on Yvette's hip.

'How did you do that?'

Twisting round to look at it herself, Yvette made a slashing motion. 'My boyfriend did it with glass.'

'You mean Peter?'

'Yes, Peter.'

'Why?'

'Why? We were so much in love when we met. We cut each other and mixed our blood.'

Jennifer found the idea insane and disturbing. It was such a deep cut, for one thing. 'Jesus, how could he do it to you?'

Yvette responded to the criticism curiously. She didn't argue, rather she became almost sullen in her aspect. 'It's just Peter,' she muttered, ''E as a thing about glass and knives.'

Yvette's mobile rang. It was Robert, and he particularly wished to speak with Jennifer.

'I'm sorry. I'm so sorry,' he immediately gushed when Jennifer said hello. 'I was delayed. I went to the restaurant, but you'd already left.'

'That's all right,' said Jennifer.

'We're going to a club soon,' shouted Yvette.

Asking for the details, Robert promised he would meet them at the club.

*

She hated it. The moment Jennifer walked into the club, she hated it. It was hot. She could barely hear herself talking. The thumping music was repetitive, oppressive and spiritless, and it was already driving her to the end of her tolerance by the time Yvette had scored an E from a dealer. She wanted to leave. Wanted to get her coat straightaway, but stayed because she didn't want to let Yvette down.

After acquiring the E, Yvette led Jennifer up to a circular balcony overlooking the chaotic dance floor, where it was a little quieter. There were dozens of sofas and easy chairs, most with people sprawled over them. Finding an unoccupied sofa, Yvette told Jennifer to wait while she went to get some beers.

Jennifer had never been to such a place before, and none existed in her home town. Below her was a heaving, pulsing mass of young people, many with faces as if hypnotised – drugged senseless on E, she figured, although all she really knew about ecstasy were the warnings her aunt had imparted to her over Sunday lunches, and the occasional sensationalist tabloid story she'd bothered to read. People in her school had dabbled in it, she knew, but not the few people she'd associated with.

Smiling, Yvette returned with two bottled beers. She was wearing a sleeveless, loose black top and black leather trousers. A large rectangular, rough metal jewellery piece hung from her neck by a thin leather strap, so that when she leaned back its weight pressed down the fabric of her top, divulging the shape of her breasts. But Yvette was leaning forward now, breaking a small white tablet. Swallowing half with a gulp of beer, she offered Jennifer the other half. 'Go on,' she shouted above the music, 'it's beautiful.'

Jennifer swallowed her half too, whereupon Yvette applauded her with an immediate smile. What would happen now, Jennifer didn't know, and as the minutes passed, she became increasingly apprehensive, but tried not to let it show as she drank her beer.

While cheerily waiting for the E to take effect, Yvette decided to tie Jennifer's hair back, hair almost the same pale colour as the baggy silk blouse she had loaned Jennifer for the night.

A short time later, Yvette grinned and did the same little gangling arms dance that she had done the previous night to portray the effects of cocaine. 'I'm coming up now,' she announced.

Something was happening with Jennifer, too. She had begun to feel anxious. But looking nervously at the people near her, she saw that everyone was smiling. No one seemed concerned to avoid eye contact, and very soon she was equally casual with her own glances. And things were becoming brighter and fresher. Then, in an almost magical moment of discovery of transubstantiation, she realised the music had ceased being an annoyance and had become perfectly complementary to the new experience. Perfectly part of it. Enhancing it. Taking her deeper into it all.

"'Ow do you feel?' asked Yvette.

Gauging her state with misty surprise, Jennifer returned, 'Beautiful.'

'I told you,' said Yvette, pleased. 'I told you.' She stood up. 'Let's dance now.'

'No, not yet.'

'Yes, now,' insisted Yvette, taking Jennifer's hand, trying to pull her up.

'No, not yet,' repeated Jennifer, remaining rooted.

Yvette affected a chiding, sulky expression, but returned to the sofa, quickly smiling and squeezing Jennifer's arm to show her forgiveness.

Once Yvette had stopped demanding they dance, Jennifer felt that everything was... just perfect. So perfect she would have been happy just to sit until it was time to leave had she not begun to become conscious of being a disappointment to Yvette.

'Yvette!' called someone in a sugary voice from nearby. 'Jennifer!' It was Robert.

Springing to her feet, Yvette flung her arms around Robert, and Jennifer found herself doing the same thing.

'Come on, let's dance!' he demanded in a screeching, comedy voice.

'Jennifer doesn't want to,' said Yvette, sounding both sympathetic and displeased. 'She's shy.'

'What!' screeched Robert. 'She bloody well will!'

Brooking no resistance, affecting a determined expression and stance, Robert gripped Jennifer's wrist and pulled her up off the sofa, toward the stairs leading down to the dance floor. Any struggle that Jennifer might have contemplated was abandoned once Yvette began pushing from behind, and she proceeded as an apparent volunteer. Once on the dance floor, she — very self-consciously — danced alongside Robert and Yvette. She felt utterly awkward, utterly awkward until another magical moment of discovery of transubstantiation: some vague time later, she realised she'd stopped caring what she must look like. She wasn't even thinking about it any longer. The music and lights had overwhelmed and directed her, and now she consciously thanked nature for the use of her limbs.

Two hours later, they had to pull her away.

Coming off the dance floor, Jennifer was damp with perspiration, and her silk blouse, now transparent in places, was adhering to her contours. 'You have a very beautiful body,' said Robert into her ear as they went to collect their coats. But the way he'd said it had been as a statement of congratulation and fact, and Jennifer thought so little of it she didn't even feel the need to respond or even amend her smile.

'Did you enjoy yourself?' asked Yvette, once they were in a quieter part of the club.

Still in a kind of misty daze, still not quite able to believe it all, Jennifer earnestly and breathily said, 'I did. I had a wonderful time.'

Yvette was manifestly pleased, and at once linked Jennifer's arm with her own.

Someone New

As had happened the day before, Jennifer was woken by the sound of someone entering the office room. Twelve o'clock: she had to clear her things from the hotel by noon or she would be charged for another day.

The clock beside the bed gave her just over an hour.

She felt grubby. She was in the middle of her period, but she had had sex regardless: Robert's sofa and carpet, and no doubt his bed too, were stained with her menstrual blood.

It had been unexpected and not especially desired. After the club, she'd shared a cab with Robert. During the journey, he'd spoken about a self-hypnosis therapy tape in his possession, and recommended it as a way she could gain confidence and defeat shyness. He'd suggested that, rather than going to her hotel, she could pop into his place first, pick up the tape, and after he'd walk her to Nottingham Street.

Entering his room, Jennifer had encountered surprises, each with a note attached:

— Various boxes of expensive-looking French chocolates.

— A teddy bear, which he said he'd bought in Harrods.

— Four bouquets of flowers, which he said had also come from Harrods.

For an amusing hour or so, he'd gone on to lightheartedly communicate his admiration and appreciation, saying how amazingly in love with her he had fallen. 'You're the sweetest, most wonderful person I've ever met,' he'd declared. And later, after they'd both done a line — which he'd promised would reactivate her waning E — he had taken her hand and placed it on his crotch. That is how it began for Jennifer.

Robert hadn't snored as badly as he had the previous night, and consequently, once the drugs wore off, Jennifer had slept quite soundly. Now awake, she did not try to wake him too. Instead, she dressed and went into the office.

It was as it had been the day before: Jeremy eating a croissant; Mark at the computer.

'Morning,' said Jeremy.

'Morning,' returned Jennifer. 'Robert's still asleep.'

Mark glanced at her. 'Second night lucky?'

The remark puzzled and irritated Jennifer. Was he referring to the sex? she wondered, going to the bathroom.

Since she had to get back to the hotel, Jennifer didn't remain long in the office. She left before Robert woke, taking her presents with her, but not the flowers, which would be too much of an encumbrance. She walked to Nottingham Street, and after checking out from her room, took her belongings by cab to Yvette's flat. Yvette would be at work, she knew, but she had been given a key the previous night and told to let herself in. But Yvette was not at work, Jennifer found: she was huddled undressed under a duvet on the sofa, and it was evident she had been crying.

'What's the matter?' asked Jennifer as the cat snaked around her legs.

'Peter didn't come back last night,' said Yvette, with hurt eyes. 'It's the third time.'

'You mean he's seeing... God, I'm sorry.'

Jennifer put her bags down and sat beside Yvette. The cat at once jumped up and began to cuddle itself in between them, causing Yvette to smile despite her tearfulness.

They talked the matter over. Peter, it transpired, was having an affair, and had first slept with the other woman when Yvette had been in hospital. Eventually, carefully encouraged by Jennifer, Yvette said she would ask Peter to move out and end the relationship.

With that irresolute conclusion, Yvette wrapped the duvet around herself and waddled off to her bedroom, reappearing twenty minutes later clothed and moderately made up.

'I'm going out for something to eat,' she said, still sounding subdued and looking downcast. 'Do you want to come?'

The phone rang before Jennifer could respond. Yvette took the call, but quickly passed it to Jennifer, saying Robert needed to speak with her.

'Mark's left the company,' Robert immediately said to Jennifer. 'You've got to come and help us.'

'Me?'

'You know how to work computers.'

'Barely.'

Not at all knowing how she could help, Jennifer nevertheless promised to go directly to Robert's office. Offering her excuses to Yvette, and taking a cab for presumed speed, she was in Harley Street within thirty-five minutes. Announcing her arrival at the intercom, the door buzzed open, and she made her own way upstairs, finding that Robert's office door had been left ajar for her. Jeremy was sitting at the table, a picture of controlled distress, raking fingers through his hair. Robert was stood in the middle of the room, dressed in his usual clothes. He smiled and thanked her for coming, and lightly kissed her on the lips, but she could tell that beneath a mask of composure, he was troubled; perhaps even scared.

Standing beside him, Jennifer received a strong smell of spirits and cigarettes.

'Why did Mark leave?' she asked.

She'd posed the question to Robert, but it was Jeremy who answered. 'He had an argument with Robert about you.'

'About me?'

'Apparently,' said Jeremy. 'I wasn't here. I was out getting a croissant.'

Jennifer turned to Robert. 'What about me?'

Robert cleared his throat. 'It was nothing. He's just weird and jealous. It freaked him that you stayed with me overnight. Forget it.'

Jeremy looked at Jennifer, saying in his gentle, sincere way, 'Do you think you'll be able to help us?'

Jennifer was still bewildered. 'I don't know what you think I can do. I don't know anything about business or publishing.'

'You know how to work the computer though,' said Jeremy, pointing to it. 'Can you show us so that we can do it ourselves?'

Jeremy went over to the enigmatic machine, which was turned off. Robert followed him. Neither, however, seemed confident enough to occupy the seat in front of it.

Jennifer stood with them, and they all stared at the blank screen.

Robert spoke in an uncomfortable voice. 'Ideally, that's what would happen. I'm useless with computers, but Jeremy could learn what needs to be learned.'

'That's right,' said Jeremy, now sounding more upbeat. 'How does it switch on?'

'The on button,' said Jennifer, astonished at their helplessness.

'We're making progress already,' said Robert, tongue bravely in cheek.

'You'll have to excuse us,' said Jeremy, 'we were just a bit too old to have learned much about computers at school.'

'I didn't learn anything at all,' said Robert.

'I learned a bit,' said Jeremy, 'but I was more interested in the humanities. We didn't grow up using them like you would have, Jennifer.'

'I've never really bothered with them myself,' said Jennifer. 'I don't even use email. Only at work.' She switched the machine on and sat behind it. Waiting for it to boot up, she suggested, 'Why don't you employ someone from an agency or something to come in and train you? Or just do Mark's work for you?'

Robert cleared his throat before answering, 'It's not as easy as that.'

'Why not?'

After a pause, he said, 'We need someone we can trust.'

'Trust?'

'We exaggerate some of the things we say to get companies to advertise in our publications, that's all,' explained Robert.

'No we don't,' countered Jeremy.

'Yes we do,' said Robert, like he was telling him the truth for the very first time.

'But no worse than other publishers, like you always say.'

'Oh, no worse than other publishers, for sure,' agreed Robert. 'It's a very competitive market, and you've got to do what it takes to keep in the game.'

The computer was ready, but Jennifer wasn't. 'I don't know where to start,' she confessed. 'What do you want me to try to do?'

Neither Jeremy nor Robert could think of how she should proceed.

'Well, what does Mark use the computer for?' asked Jennifer.

'He keeps advertiser records in a database,' said Jeremy.

'That's right,' said Robert, dragging a chair over and sitting next to Jennifer. 'And he creates our books on a publishing system.'

'Desktop publishing,' said Jeremy. 'And there's some sort of link to the factoring company and the bank.'

But Jennifer was still no wiser about what to do. At the veterinary surgery, she'd had a software routine explained to her and had never had either the inclination or permission to venture further afield, and at her aunt's, the computer was just something her uncle used in his study for his accounting business. Neither had she ever bothered much about the internet, having soon learnt that internet bulletin boards were usually just places where screwballs and idiots gathered to take each other seriously. 'I can't even find your advertiser database,' she admitted, after working the mouse for a time.

'I thought you used a computer at work?' said Robert, lighting a cigarette.

'Robert, all I did at work was write letters and update client records. You've got Microsoft Word — I can use that for letters. But I don't recognise anything else you're using. Why can't you just ask Mark to show you what's what?'

'Because he won't want to help,' said Robert. He stared at the screen for some seconds. 'Can you find out how much money we can draw out of the bank today?'

Jeremy seemed vexed. 'We agreed we wouldn't draw any more out this week,' he said — a comment ignored by Robert.

After a discussion and several attempts, Jennifer conceded that she couldn't find out anything about bank balances. 'You're going to have to get someone else to help you.' Then she added, 'If other publishing companies can trust employees, so can yours, can't it?'

Robert wandered over to the other side of the room. After a deep draw on his cigarette, he cleared his throat and said, 'The problem is that Mark did a number of jobs, really. We'd have to get two or three people in to cover for him. And we'd have to be able to trust them all. And pay them all. Cash flow's tight at the moment.'

Jeremy also drifted away from the computer, going to sit at the table again, where he resumed drawing his fingers through his fringe.

Feeling she'd done all she could, Jennifer switched off the computer and turned on her chair to face the room. A pall hung over Jeremy and Robert, and she felt awkward and obtrusive in its presence, but she also felt duty-bound to remain in the office. Finishing his first cigarette, Robert immediately lit another, sucking hard and frequently on it. No one spoke until Jeremy had a thought: 'Penny might be able to learn how to do all the things Mark did.'

'Penny who?' asked Robert tentatively.

'Penny, my ex-girlfriend. She's got a business qualification. And she's done web design so she'll know about computers.'

'Shit! Yes, *Penny*,' said Robert, suddenly ruthlessly decided. 'And she knows about *our* business, doesn't she?. Ring her. Ring her now.'

Jeremy dialled Penny's number, but was informed by her flatmate that she was away on a trip. However, she was expected back any day now, Jeremy was further informed, and the prospect of enlisting her help continued to buttress his spirits a degree after the call. Robert, however, returned much to his brooding state.

'Don't worry, Robert,' said Jeremy, 'we'll survive. We can start the new sales campaign when Penny's back. And we'll be all right for wages once the prepayments start coming in.'

Robert had put on his coat and was now leaving the office,

failing to say where he was going or inviting Jennifer to accompany him.

His departure was watched with concern by Jeremy.

'He's under a lot of stress at the moment,' said Jeremy after the door closed.

'Where's he gone?' asked Jennifer, unsure what she should do now.

'I don't know. Maybe to the off licence.'

'He doesn't have a mobile, does he?'

'Not currently, no. He lost his last one the other week. He's always leaving them in bars. I seldom carry mine myself. I think they're unnecessary and obtrusive. They're bad for your energies, too. So are computers, I'm sure.'

To Jennifer's initial bewilderment and lasting embarrassment, Jeremy now began performing slow martial arts exercises while sitting at the table. He soon extended these controlled motions by standing up to work his way around the room, gently but firmly counteracting imaginary assailants.

He suddenly ceased his unexplained exercises, announcing, 'I've got some important phone calls to make, but you can wait in Robert's room if you like. You can have the television on quietly.'

Jennifer decided she would wait. As far as she could make out through the slightly ajar door of Robert's room, all the telephone calls Jeremy made during the remainder of that afternoon involved him speaking to accounts departments in sincere-sounding attempts to defer or reschedule bill payments.

If Robert had gone to an off licence, it was one a very long way away, for she waited in his room until past five o'clock, when Jeremy tapped on the door to say he was about to go home and needed to lock the office. Returning to Holloway by tube, she found Yvette subdued and quietly tearful again: Peter was present, collecting his things. An awkward, sombre period ensued, with Peter and Yvette saying little that wasn't related to mundane considerations as to who owned what, and where various things could be located.

Although she didn't probe, Jennifer gleaned that Peter had already decided to leave, and had not been ordered out.

After closing the door behind Peter, Yvette remained subdued and damp-eyed, but presently asked Jennifer if she wanted to go to Camden. Jennifer agreed, and less than an hour after Peter's departure, they were in an uncrowded pub near the French restaurant.

Sitting opposite Yvette, across a small table, Jennifer related the story of her afternoon visit to Harley Street. Yvette's attention, however, often slipped away, apparently to something behind Jennifer. It was natural that she should be so distracted, thought Jennifer, considering her recent emotional upheaval.

'I really 'ate Mark,' said Yvette, when Jennifer finished.

'How long were you and Peter together?' asked Jennifer, unsure whether it was wise to bring up the subject. Yvette didn't respond, for whatever had been distracting her earlier now seemed to have acquired extra fascination.

'You don't mind me asking, do you?' said Jennifer.

'Asking what?' said Yvette, briefly returning some of her attention to Jennifer. 'Oh, Peter. Two years.'

Yvette looked up and smiled, just as Jennifer heard someone say, 'Hi, they call me Steven.'

2.19
A Changed Person

The report of Phil's ghost, delivered impassively by Albert, had caused fear. Subtly led by his Master, Simon had arrived at the conclusion that Phil was intent on preventing the Golden Millennium even from beyond the grave. But Albert had assured Simon he could keep Phil's evil spirit at bay while he was building the Empathy Device. He'd explained that by taking the prayer battery and altering its extraterrestrial insides, he could make it radiate an energy field powerful enough to destroy any negative spiritual energies within — and only within — his bedroom, which he would use as the workshop.

If Phil's evil and otherwise immortal spirit were to appear in the workshop, it would wither and die, Albert had said.

But as well as safeguarding against Phil's ghost, Albert had warned that this necessarily-constrained protective energy field would be harmful to Simon and Carl — or any other person. Their own energies were not completely pure, and would not be until the Empathy Device changed them and the world. Only he, Albert Fox, the Expected One, could remain unaffected within this local energy field.

'Evil has at least a toehold in everyone,' Albert had said, 'except me. But within spiritually feeble Phil, evil gained complete control, but was hiding unseen in him, waiting for the most propitious time to act and prevent the Golden Millennium emerging. If you hadn't ordered him to be killed while he was vulnerable and disabled, Simon, I'm sure he would have killed us instead, once the crystal energy subsided. Phil was a spiritually undefended vessel, easily occupied and subjugated, and evil worked through him, and continues to work through his ghost.'

Thus it had been established that Albert's bedroom would be conveniently out of bounds during the Empathy Device construction period. And once the device was finished, he had said, it would have its own internal energy field to annihilate evil, negative spirituality. Once operating, it would be spiritually unassailable: Phil's ghost could do it no harm.

And Simon had accepted every word as Gospel.

Wearing his golden robe, Albert was walking in the estate's woods now, knowing for almost certain he was soon to become fantastically wealthy, but he wasn't excited by it, or occupied much by it in any way. Everything he did now felt like he was just going through the motions. It was like some reserve, automatic part of his mind had taken over, and the clamouring, freaked-out remainder had been quelled. When he thought, it was without personal involvement. When he ate, it was without relish. When he walked, it was without vigour.

But the gnawing, tight sensation in his stomach was still there, unchanged.

Wandering through the woods in the last of the day's light, he came upon what he straightaway knew to be Phil's grave. Some earth had recently been turned, and formed a bulge. Footprints surrounded it. He flattened the bulge as best he could with his feet, then dragged and rolled a large, decaying broken branch over it. Then he piled and scattered leaves over the whole area, so that to any unsuspecting eye, nothing would seem curious.

It was Wednesday today — he had to work that out by counting. Yesterday morning, a small team of electricians had managed to reconnect the power to most of the property. And yesterday afternoon, Simon had set off for London to inspect and collect the diamond pyramids he had been instructed to order. Prepared to spend his seven million pound fortune, Albert had advised him to spend only five million, since, he had said, diamonds to the value of five million would be more than adequate to make the world peaceful. Two million should be kept in reserve, Albert had said, in case something came up before February the first: the world needed him to continue his prudence.

Natural diamonds, Albert had said before Simon had ordered the cutting of the stones. Not cheap artificial ones. Artificial ones would be incompatible with the natural ley lines.

The cutting need not be precise, Albert had deemed, just so long as they were recognisable pyramids, and they need not be exactly equal in size. Rough pyramids would work almost as well as exact, polished pyramids: Nature was not snooty.

Utmost secrecy about the Empathy Device had to be observed, he had reminded Simon before he'd left for London. Not a word about Deepdale Hall, the Expected One, Phil, crystal resonance, Cosmic Masters, or anything.

Pushing his glasses up, Simon had agreed.

Albert had left the Deepdale Hall estate only once since the death of Phil. Yesterday, when Carl returned from dropping Simon at Durham railway station, he had asked to be taken into Darlington, where he'd bought spare clothes and all the tools and materials necessary for the great project. He'd also bought a reliable car, driving it back himself, albeit without proper legal coverage.

Now barely able to see where he was walking, Albert left the dim woods to return to the house and continue his work.

'Awright, Master,' said Carl, who was painting a chair in the main room. 'Wuz getting worried 'bout you out there in the dark. Wouldn't get me going in those woods near where we buried 'im, never mind at night. Never worried 'bout ghosts an' stuff before, but this is different, ain't it?'

'That's right, Carl. This is different. Very different.'

Albert continued up to his bedroom, where he switched on an electric fire Simon had provided and sat on the floor in front of it to warm himself before resuming his work on the Empathy Device, which was already shaping up well. Toiling in his out-of-bounds bedroom, acquiring adequate welding skills along the way, he had already done the basic construction: the bending; the hammering; the joining. He was no artisan, but stylishness was of secondary importance to robustness. Robustness was *essential*, and in his choice of materials and components, Albert believed the great secret would be safely housed for a long lifetime.

2.20
Out To Lunch

The young man who'd introduced himself as Steven had been with a friend who'd introduced himself as John. Like the John Jennifer had recently left, this John also possessed cropped dark hair and strong limbs: no slacker in the gym, it was apparent. While Steven had easily amused Yvette, John's attempts to impress Jennifer had been less successful, and that night he'd gone home alone. Steven, however, had gone home with Yvette, and, trying to sleep on the sofa, Jennifer had heard them fucking throughout the small hours.

Presumably taking another day off work, Yvette was still in bed with Steven when Jennifer left the flat in the late morning. Jennifer's intentions were to call on Robert, then go shopping for clothes in Camden. She'd telephoned him several times, but his private line was now giving an unavailable tone, and the number she'd been given for the office was always engaged. Thus she had become even more concerned for him and the fate of his business. He had been such a help to her, she wanted to help him in return, and that seemed to extend to sleeping with him, although she didn't actually think of him as a boyfriend.

In Harley Street, upon announcing her presence to Jeremy via the intercom, the door buzzed open for her. Proceeding up the stairs and into the office, she found Robert standing barefoot with a cigarette. It was apparent he had not long left his bed. He smiled when she entered the room, and Jeremy, sitting at the table, dressed for autumn comfort, said polite greetings.

She could sense right away that, despite the smiles for her arrival, the office atmosphere had sunk back to the lowest ebb of the previous

536

day: an oppressive, fretful stagnation.

'How are you?' asked Robert, briefly putting his arm around her.

'Fine,' answered Jennifer. 'Has the phone in your room been disconnected?'

''Fraid so.'

Jennifer now noticed that the telephone beside the computer — the only one she'd ever heard ring in the office — was off the hook, and she assumed it was the one she'd tried but found engaged.

'I tried ringing the other number you gave me. Why's it off the hook?'

'To give us a break while we plan what to do,' answered Jeremy.

Standing beside Robert, Jennifer began to tell him about Yvette and Peter, but Robert didn't seem interested. What did interest him was how "the company", as he called it, was going to survive financially until prepayments from the next sales campaign started to come through. It was agreed in an earnest discussion between him and Jeremy that twenty thousand pounds would be needed.

'It's not as if we haven't been here before,' Robert pointed out. 'We've needed more than twenty grand loads of times. We always cope.'

'I've told you, Robert,' said Jeremy, 'it's different this time.'

'What would you normally do?' asked Jennifer.

'We'd arrange a bigger overdraft,' answered Jeremy.

'Well, do that again.'

'I don't think there'd be much point trying,' said Jeremy. 'The bank's been getting difficult recently. We're already thirty thousand overdrawn. But they never really grasp how we operate, do they, Robert? We go for long periods without any income at all, then we get lots of money all at once.'

'That's right,' agreed Robert, after drawing on his cigarette. 'We've been fifty grand overdrawn before.'

'So there's no harm in trying,' said Jennifer.

Robert cleared his throat. 'Mark did all that stuff with the bank.'

'They'd want to see business plans and cashflow projections,' said Jeremy.

'Think Penny would be able to do all that stuff?' wondered Robert.

'I don't see why not,' said Jeremy. 'She's got a business qualification.'

'But that won't alter the fact that the bank's turned so shitty on us recently.'

'I know,' agreed Jeremy. 'It's ridiculous, really. When the sales campaign starts, we'll pull in at least enough in prepayments to clear our overdraft, and five times more from the factoring company when the book's out, but we can't do that unless we get some more money first.'

'What's a factoring company?' Jennifer asked Robert, but her question didn't appear to have registered with him.

'A factoring company collects revenue for other companies and pays a percentage in advance,' explained Jeremy in his usual earnest, plodding tones. 'If you owed us a hundred pounds, our factoring company would invoice you on our behalf and pay us sixty up front, and a further thirty-six after you'd paid them the hundred. They keep four percent for themselves.'

'Is that how it works?' remarked Robert.

'Didn't you know?' said Jeremy.

'Mark's department,' said Robert, with a dismissive tone, taking another draw on his cigarette.

For a time, Jennifer observed Robert and Jeremy continue in their depression, then said, 'I can lend you enough money to see you through.'

Jeremy sat up straight. 'Twenty thousand pounds?'

Robert cleared his throat. 'You've got access to twenty grand?'

'It's in my bank account,' said Jennifer. 'I inherited it.'

'This is amazing!' said Robert, suddenly becoming the very essence of motivation. 'We'll be able to start the new sales campaign as soon as Penny starts working for us, and we'll make a killing, like we did on the first one. Hundred and fifty grand target.'

In his own restrained, slower way, Jeremy was sharing Robert's positivity. 'And it'll be so much better not having Mark in the room. He was such a negative influence.'

'Listen,' said Robert earnestly and intensely to Jennifer, gripping her shoulders and looking fixedly into her eyes, 'we'll pay you back thirty grand within three months. It can't fail. We've been doing this for three years now, and we've made over half a million so far.'

'That's right,' said Jeremy.

'Great,' said Jennifer simply. 'Lets go to a bank now and I'll see if I can transfer the money.'

At the nearest branch of Jennifer's bank, on Baker Street, transferring the money proved to be no problem. Afterwards, Jeremy and Robert insisted on taking her to lunch, a nearby Japanese restaurant being suggested. In the restaurant, she ate with chopsticks for the first time, and Robert proposed a champagne toast to her and business success.

After the champagne, they had saki, and after the saki, Robert said he'd try some of the imported beers the restaurant was promoting.

'No,' advised Jeremy firmly. 'We should get back to the office.'

Robert grinned. 'Jeremy,' he said in a mock authoritarian voice, 'today has been declared a holiday. Saint Jennifer's day.'

'Okay,' agreed Jeremy reluctantly, 'but we really have to get cracking tomorrow.'

'Tomorrow there will be whirlwinds,' promised Robert.

'So will you come to Camden with me, then?' Jennifer asked him.

'Jennifer, I would go to hell and back with you,' returned Robert, 'just as soon as I've tried some beers.'

Since they had agreed to write the day off regarding work, Jeremy decided to use the time to sort out some things he needed to do. Thanking Jennifer again for the business loan, he went on his way, but it was another hour before Robert's alcoholic curiosity had been satisfied enough for him to leave the restaurant too. Out on Baker Street, he yelled for a cab to stop. Fifteen minutes later, at a Camden market stall, Jennifer was buying clothes more similar to the things Yvette wore, Robert offering opinions on each item.

'What do you think of this one?' asked Jennifer, holding a garish top against her.

'It'll go well with the rose,' said Robert.

'What rose?'

Producing a flower from behind his back, Robert said, 'This rose.'

With a smile, Jennifer accepted the gift. 'Thank you so much.' She kissed him.

'Jenny,' said Robert after the kiss, 'I have to see someone on business.'

'Oh, no. I wanted you to help me buy a mobile.'

'I'm the last person you should ask for help there,' said Robert. 'Can't work them when I've got them, and never had one more than a couple of months without losing it.' He squeezed her hand. 'I'm already seriously late. Ring me around seven. We'll meet up. Okay?'

'Okay,' said Jennifer, and Robert left.

Dismissing a sense of abandonment, Jennifer continued to shop alone, but didn't attempt to buy a phone. Afterwards, although laden with bags, she went to take the Underground back to Holloway Road rather than pay for a cab. Outside Camden station, the sorriest-looking, black-toothed, sore-faced wino she had ever seen was passively begging in the cold drizzle, holding a cap half out as he shuffled along. Beggars were still a fascination to her. Until Sunday, she had never in her life seen anyone ask strangers for money in the street. She'd turned her eyes away from everyone who'd approached her so far, partly out of shyness, but the sight of this man moved her, and she gave him five pounds, for which he gruffly blessed her.

As a way of travel, Jennifer had decided she liked the Underground, and couldn't understand why Robert had stated an aversion to it. It was cheaper than cabs, and she was pretty certain it was faster too. There was a station just around the corner from Robert's office, but he claimed never to have used it — never to have "sunk to its depths".

Twenty minutes later, walking along Holloway Road, nearing the entrance to her new home, Jennifer saw Yvette's cat by the door on the busy, darkening street. It was nervous, crouching whenever anyone passed by, which was every few seconds. As the flat was on the first floor, it had no hope of getting in. She couldn't imagine how it had come to be there, since Yvette had told her it was never allowed out.

Although jumpy and uncertain at first, it came to Jennifer when she bent to stroke it, and when she opened the door, it bolted inside and up the stairs ahead of her. It was waiting at Yvette's private door when Jennifer caught it up, letting herself into the flat.

'No!' cried Yvette. 'It can't come in!'

The cat hid inside.

'Why not?' puzzled Jennifer.

'Because I'm sick of it.'

Seeing Jennifer's look of incredulity and reproach, Yvette sulkily relented, and the cat was allowed peace.

'Did you see Robert?' asked Yvette.

Jennifer put down her bags and quickly recounted what had happened. Yvette praised and thanked her for lending Robert and Jeremy the money. 'Don't worry, you'll get it back. They earn lots of money. Lots and lots.'

Jennifer began taking the clothes she had bought out of their bags.

'Listen,' said Yvette excitedly, 'I 'ave to tell you about Steven.'

As Jennifer continued to unpack her new clothes, Yvette went on

540

to say that Steven was the man for her, and that she was seeing him again later that evening. Jennifer suggested to Yvette that she hadn't known Steven long enough to tell if he really was the man for her, whereupon Yvette displayed a reduced version of the sulk she had produced when her blood-swapping story had met with disapproval. But Yvette's sulk was short-lived, and she quickly turned to examining Jennifer's purchases, expressing approval for all but one garment.

Jennifer suddenly realised it was approaching seven o'clock. Calling Robert's office number, she discovered him to be in very good spirits, and he proposed she come over, saying they could go to see a film or something, if there was time.

Quickly putting on some of her new things and making up her face, Jennifer was ready to leave in only fifteen minutes, but before setting off, she took the time to feed the cat, since it appeared Yvette wasn't going to bother.

That night, she again slept with Robert.

2.21
Parliament

Each one worth nearly four hundred thousand pounds... and Albert had just been handed thirteen of them.

Simon had returned to Deepdale Hall, having done the business — at a jewellers in London's Hatton Garden, he had collected the diamond pyramids he had ordered to be cut, an order valued at over five million pounds, paid by banker's draft.

Full secrecy had been maintained, he'd solemnly claimed.

Wearing his golden robe, Albert was alone in his turret room, standing on the bed to study the roughly cut gems at a window. He felt no sense of accomplishment or excitement. Each diamond was about the size of a fingernail, and eerily cool to the touch. He tested one against the window glass, easily succeeding in making a scratch, yet no mark was to be seen on the jewel. Remembering some science article he'd read, he knew that what he had in his hand was the hardest substance known; thermal conductivity six times greater than copper; lighter but much stronger than steel. It really would be the substance of the future, he knew, once its artificial creation and manipulation was perfected. The true crystal age might see engines made from diamond. Even saucepans.

He knew that nanotechnology vaguely promised to deliver that perfection.

As well as needing to be kept in his room to shield them from Phil's malignant ghost, the diamonds, or so Simon was told, had to be decontaminated of all the negative spiritual energies they would have picked up when being handled by others. No one was allowed near them now. Only Albert's spiritual energy was pure enough. Simon already understood that, once constructed, the Empathy Device would generate a spiritual shield to protect the pyramids from any ghostly interference after they were inserted and sealed within. But Albert had also told him that opening the device for any reason would instantly contaminate the pyramids with impure ambient energy. This would render the device dangerous to use, for it would then amplify unbalanced energy, inducing imperfect mind waves in the population, which might lead to evil's final triumph in the world.

So it was forbidden, Albert had decreed, strictly forbidden, ever to force the box open, even if Phil's ghost were laid to rest.

'I understand, Master,' Simon had replied.

Now that it was almost finished, the Empathy Device looked better than Albert had expected it would. Plain metal sheeting had been cut by hacksaw and welded to create a vessel the size of a large shoe box, but all exposed surfaces had been smoothed, and would soon be enamelled black. Moreover, he believed it was solidly constructed, internally and externally.

A small antenna was fixed to the rear of the device to receive his spiritual energy for its initial charging. Albert had explained to Simon that the advanced extraterrestrial circuitry within could capture and store enough of his unique, perfectly balanced spiritual energy in a one-hour prayer session to allow its operation for a full thousand years. Drawing vast energy from the zero point source, the device's crystal circuitry would massively amplify his spiritual energy input trickle, and the second antennae on the front would broadcast the intense, blissful output. Once he inserted the diamonds, he had told Simon, the Golden Millennium would depend only on the device being prayer-charged then left working over the ley pole in the grounds, where he had built a small stone and cement shelter to house it for its proposed millennium of use.

At random angles, thirteen numbered, short, stout metal rods protruded from the device, like swords running through a magician's box. Each rod was free to move in and out, but only to click into thirteen positions marked along its length, supposedly moving a pyramid inside with it. This, he would explain to Simon, was so that only someone who knew the right positions could operate it. If any one rod were incorrectly set, then so would be the diamonds, and the device would be inert — the geometry would not be sacred. And if someone *were* to break it open before the world was made peaceful, unless the rods were already set correctly, they could not learn the powerful secret crystal geometry. All thirteen positions had to be *exactly* known, he would instil into Simon.

On the back was a three-position switch that allowed supposed connection, or irreversible disconnection, of the receiving antenna. He would explain to Simon that he would flick the switch in his shielded bedroom, pray towards the antenna, then flick it again for permanent disconnection, so that once charged by him, the device would not be at risk of accepting further spiritual energy from tainted sources.

A *real* electrical circuit was built into the device. This battery-operated circuit made a pyramid pattern of light-emitting diodes on the top activate when one rod was in a certain position. But Albert would tell Simon that the diodes would only light up when all thirteen rods were in their correct positions. It was Albert's intention that Simon would see these lights operate only once, and fleetingly at that. After that, he would secretly disconnect the battery.

Now all Albert had to do was the enamelling, then it would be ready for presenting to Simon.

*

It was becoming dark. Somewhere in the drizzly, murky distance a blackbird was singing, out of season. Albert had told Simon that he needed to walk alone with nature for a little while, but had only gone to his car. Meeting Simon and Carl just inside the door upon his return to the house, he told them to put on their robes and wait for him in the main room, for he had something sacred to tell.

Ten minutes later, Simon and Carl, robed, were stood by the fire, on the very spot where Phil had been slain. Regardless of the electricity having been reconnected, the room was lit by candles, and in the soft yellow light they watched in reverent awe as Albert, robed in gold and bearing the Empathy Device, descended the wide staircase.

He stopped halfway between the staircase and Simon.

'Amazing,' breathed Simon, moving closer to Albert.

'It's fantastic,' said Carl. 'What are all those rods?'

Albert said what the rods were: that they were effectively a combination lock disallowing others to operate it, or know its secret internal geometry.

'What's the combination, Master?' asked Simon.

'I'll reveal it to you later,' said Albert, speaking in a drab, almost monotonous voice. 'Remember, it's not to be activated until the return of the Third Satellite. And as you know, the next date for that is February the first.'

Simon pushed his glasses up. 'Why don't we activate it today? Make the world peaceful as soon as possible?'

'Because it wouldn't work unless the Third Satellite was orbiting,' answered Albert. 'The spaceship will give the extra boost needed to set the ley lines resonating. But afterwards, the device alone will be powerful enough to maintain the resonance.'

'Amazing,' breathed Simon.

'Y'could still set it goin' though, couldn't y'?' suggested Carl. 'And it'd like kick in when the Third Satellite comes?'

'No, Carl,' said Albert, 'I couldn't. I know certain foreign armies would be able to detect the output, and would come looking for it, and might use it as a weapon.'

Simon pushed his glasses up. 'Just like they want our prayer batteries.'

'Exactly,' said Albert. 'Except they would be able to home in on the Empathy Device, so it can't be activated until and unless the Third Satellite is in orbit, after which all armies will become peaceful.'

'Amazing,' breathed Simon.

Albert continued to explain the intricacies of the device. 'When the right combination is selected on the rods, these lights will glow to show that it's working. It's empty now — I haven't charged it with my prayer energy yet, and the receiving antenna's disconnected — but this is what it will look like when correctly set.'

Albert set the first twelve rods to what he pretended was their correct positions. And when he moved the remaining rod into position, a triangle of red lit up on top of the box as the secret internal battery became connected, powering the lights.

'Amazing,' breathed Simon.

544

Albert immediately reset all the rods to their base positions, starting with the rod that actually had some effect, cancelling the red lights. Sternly, he reiterated the warning he had issued earlier: 'No one must ever try to open it.'

'We understand,' said Simon, pushing his glasses up. 'Doing that would let unbalanced energy inside.'

'Too right,' said Carl, shuffling his feet with the gravity and import of it all. 'When it works proper, will it feel like the energy on Sunday?'

'Purer,' answered Albert. 'There'll be no side effects. No physical effects at all. Just peace and bliss for a thousand years.'

'Amazing,' breathed Simon.

'All you need to know, Simon,' said Albert, 'is the right combination for the rods and then it will work. When the time comes, that's all you'll have to do — place the device over the ley pole, then set the rods.'

Simon pushed his glasses up as an expression of concern appeared on his face. 'But you'll be doing it yourself, won't you, Master?'

'No, Simon, I won't. I'm going away. Forever. Tonight.'

Simon's expression of concern gave way to one of anxiety. 'Where are you going?'

Albert looked at Simon, and answered, 'Far away, Simon. On Sunday, when I went out alone to meet the extraterrestrials, I went aboard their ship, and they asked me if I would represent earth at the Interplanetary Parliament.' He paused, observing awe and dismay coexisting in Simon's eyes. 'I agreed, Simon. They're picking me up from their secret landing site tonight to take me to another planet. I will never return. I am no longer of this world. I have changed.'

'No, Master,' murmured Simon, fretfully.

'Yeah, don't leave us,' said Carl. 'Won't be the same wiffout you.'

Emotionally unaltered, Albert said, 'I have to go my room now, to charge the device with my prayer energy in a spiritually clean environment. When it's full, this switch will permanently disconnect the receiving antenna. As you know, you may not accompany me.'

In the dim candlelight, Simon watched Albert ascend the staircase, and a tear ran down his cheek.

In his room, after opening the Empathy Device to remove the real battery so that the lights would never come on again, Albert lay on the bed and pulled the sleeping bag over him. Soon he was dozing, but he dreamed of Phil, holding out the patch of flesh torn from his cheek, imploring him with a look never to be forgotten to return it to his bloodied face. Unaccountably finding the flesh in his own hand, he realised he needed the assistance of a facial surgeon, but the Yellow Pages he frantically thumbed had no listing for such a person.

He had dreamed a similar horror the night before.

And the night before that, too.

2.22
Employment

Thursday began badly for Robert.

'Robert,' called Jeremy, tapping on the bedroom door.

Jennifer, already mostly awake, sat up. 'Robert,' she said, shaking him, 'Jeremy wants you.'

'Yeah, in a minute,' he mumbled.

'Robert,' insisted Jeremy, tapping more firmly.

'I'm awake,' returned Robert, but not fully sounding as if he was.

Robert's small LCD clock was on top of a low table beside the bed, but it was facing away. Reaching sleepily over Jennifer to read the time, his fumbling hand accidentally dragged an open coke packet back with it.

The door opened, and Jeremy put his head into the dim room. Realising her breasts were bare, Jennifer pulled the duvet up, but at the same moment, Robert dropped the best part of a gram of coke over her chest.

'Aw fuck,' he complained, attempting to peel the duvet off Jennifer, but meeting with resistance. 'No!' he said in a desperate voice, 'you'll lose it.'

'Penny's turned us down,' said Jeremy, with palpable dismay, ignoring Robert's crisis and Jennifer's partial exposure.

Frantically attempting to rescue what coke he could, Robert was oblivious to Jeremy.

'Robert!' remonstrated Jennifer. 'Wait till Jeremy's gone.' Annoyed, she pulled the duvet down herself and began sweeping the powder off her chest and breasts, into Robert's instantly cupped hands.

'Careful!' he cried.

With her chest still gritty, she got out of bed, brushing herself down as she walked naked to her clothes while Robert continued to gather what coke he could from the bed.

Stepping fully into the room, Jeremy, wearing a thick, off-yellow cardigan, repeated his news. 'She's turned us down, Robert.'

'Who?'

'Penny.'

'Did you tell her how much we'd pay her?'

'Yes,' said Jeremy. 'She said she's not interested at any price. I don't understand it. She was really sardonic as well.'

'We'll think of something,' said Robert, now chopping a line of the rescued coke on a CD cover placed on what had been Jennifer's pillow. 'D'you want a line, Jen?'

'Course I don't,' said Jennifer curtly, pulling on her top. 'It's morning. Can't you go five minutes without that stuff?'

'I'd rather not.'

Walking past Jeremy, giving him a difficult smile, Jennifer went to the bathroom. Ten minutes later, she was sitting at the table in the fusty office, drinking coffee while Jeremy and barefoot Robert pondered the day's batch of enigmatic letters, less than half of which they opened before their attentions were defeated. Observing them, she began to worry about the money she had invested in their business.

Robert lit a cigarette and went to stand restlessly by the window, looking down to the street through a dirty net curtain. Jeremy remained at the table, drawing fingers through his hair, as had become his habit.

'Robert,' said Jeremy eventually, 'I think we should try Jennifer's idea about using an employment agency.'

'It'd be opening ourselves up to potential legal trouble, Jeremy,' advised Robert gravely, smoking his cigarette in frequent, snatched, deep draws. 'Lots of trouble.'

Jennifer uncharitably reflected on how Robert was smoking like a drama student would if asked to portray stress.

'We're already in lots of trouble,' Jeremy pointed out, 'financial trouble. And we're personally liable for the debts, remember. We're a partnership, not a limited company.'

'Fuck! Of course!' exclaimed Robert, turning to face the room in a moment of thrilled eureka. 'Mark's a partner too. He's liable for a third of the debts. We could sue him.'

Jeremy didn't share Robert's enthusiasm. 'He's not a partner any more,' he revealed.

'What?' shot back Robert, in a state of suspended, anguished, angry dismay.

'The bank called this morning about our overdraft and wanting to discuss the new partnership situation. They've received instructions signed by all of us removing Mark as a partner.'

'What?!' exclaimed Robert. 'We never signed anything removing him as a partner.'

'I think we might have,' said Jeremy, with a touch of sheepishness. 'A couple of weeks ago, remember?'

'Remember what? What are you talking about?'

'I was eating a croissant and you were on the phone to Trevor when Mark needed our signatures on some documents. I remember I asked him what they were and he said something about the factoring company and a partnership renewal mandate for the bank. I just thought it was something routine.'

'The fucking bastard,' growled Robert, angrily realising he'd been so easily outmanoeuvred. He faced the window again, and took a noisy suck on his cigarette. 'What did you say to the bank?'

'I confirmed he wasn't a partner any more.'

'What!?' exclaimed Robert, in a high voice, spinning around. 'You idiot.'

'I had to,' argued Jeremy, without losing his beleaguered composure. 'I could hardly say we signed something like that without even looking at it. And he had left us, anyway.'

'Jeremy, we could have had him for deception,' bemoaned Robert, grievously disappointed.

Jeremy stood up and put a decisive foot on his chair. 'Never mind about Mark. Forget him. We have to start on the new sales campaign.'

'We could have had him,' brooded Robert, drawing on his cigarette, turning back to the window.

'If Penny's not interested, we'll have to find someone else,' pronounced Jeremy, 'so I think we should call an employment agency, like Jennifer suggested.'

Jeremy waited for Robert's reply.

Not turning away from the window, Robert conceded, 'We'll have to, won't we?'

Jeremy went to a bookshelf that was a mess of unsorted papers and faxes and found a business directory. He dialled an employment agency, and answered questions as best he could, answers which to Jennifer's ear seemed nevertheless vague. When he finally put the phone down, he related the outcome to Robert, who was still by the window, staring down at the street. 'Right,' he began, standing with a foot on his chair again, studying the notes he'd taken, 'she said there were really at least four different jobs involved, but maybe not all of them at the same time. We'd probably need a bookkeeper, secretary, desktop publisher and administrator. Rates would begin at fifteen pounds an hour.'

'It's out of the question, Jeremy,' said Robert plainly.

'Why?' countered Jeremy, taking his foot off the chair. 'It would just be till we got someone permanent who could do it all.'

'And the tax and stuff would have to be legal,' said Robert.

'I could be your secretary,' offered Jennifer. 'I could do that.'

'There you go,' said Jeremy to Robert. 'We'll pull through.'

Jennifer sensed Robert's lack of conviction remained largely unchanged.

'We'll see,' he said, going to his bedroom. 'We'll see.'

While Robert was in his room, Jeremy began to discuss with Jennifer the practicalities of her working for them. She said she'd be happy to do what she could, writing letters or answering the phone, and she wouldn't want payment.

'We'd have to pay you,' insisted Jeremy. 'At least when the cashflow allows it. But it would be silly paying you now because we'd be paying you your own money, wouldn't we? But we could defer payment — pay you a lump sum on top of your loan repayment when the next book's out.'

'Fine. Okay.'

The telephone beside the computer rang, and Jeremy answered it. Finishing her coffee, Jennifer went to Robert's room, but met him on his way out. Now wearing his coat, he smiled and said he was going to buy cigarettes.

'Can I take a bath?' she asked.

'Of course,' answered Robert. 'Going for cigarettes,' he announced for Jeremy's benefit, although Jeremy was still talking on the phone and seemed quite oblivious to the rest of creation.

After her quick bath, Jennifer discovered Robert had still not returned. Jeremy was sitting on the sofa in the office room, reading a dog-eared paperback novel. She asked how much longer Robert was likely to be.

'I've no idea,' said Jeremy, looking up from the musty pages of his book.

'He can't have just gone for cigarettes, can he?'

'No, he would have been back long ago. I don't know where he's gone.'

Jennifer sat at the table. Sensitive to her frustration and disappointment, Jeremy said, 'You have to excuse him. He's under so much stress and worry.'

'I suppose he is,' agreed Jennifer.

Jeremy returned to his book, whereupon, to Jennifer, the high-ceilinged room at once became as quiet as some fusty, Victorian gentleman's club. A forbidding, creaking quiet. She didn't know whether to wait a while longer or go, but soon had her mind temporarily made up for her by the offer of a cappuccino when Jeremy reached the end of a chapter.

Drinking her cappuccino at the table, Jennifer was struck by how nothing ever seemed to happen in the office. Occasionally, the phone would ring, but the call was usually about some outstanding debt that Jeremy would earnestly say would soon be paid. And between these infrequent calls, now that he'd put his novel down, Jeremy would merely potter around, randomly picking up documents and letters, looking vaguely at them before replacing them. How this was ever going to translate into her getting her money back, she couldn't imagine.

Finishing her cappuccino, she decided not to wait any longer for Robert. Besides, she was becoming hungry. Saying goodbye to Jeremy, she put on the thick jacket with a hood she'd bought in Camden the day before — handmade by Peruvian Indians from unbleached Llama wool, she had been persuaded — and left the office. Once out on Harley Street, she revised her plan to go directly to Yvette's flat, deciding instead to eat before making the journey.

For central London, this was an odd area, Jennifer had discovered: along the whole serious and dignified length of Harley Street there wasn't an eatery, or even a shop, of any kind. She could understand this if what Robert had said about all businesses on Harley Street having to be medical was true, but this absence of small trade extended to the side streets and major criss-crossing roads too. The nearest place to Robert's office that sold even crisps was Marylebone

High Street, a good five minute walk away. Heading in that direction, she thought she might as well eat in the tapas place she had visited with Robert, just beyond Marylebone High Street. But, she worried within a few minutes, if Robert was there it might appear she'd come looking for him. So, instead, she bought a large sandwich and a milk drink, deciding to take them to Regent's Park, which she knew from her walk last weekend was only a few minutes away, across a major road. Darting across that road while traffic lights further along held most of the vehicles back, she found herself passing a grand, imposing building set amid trees in its own small grounds. She might have guessed it was the head office of some old, select merchant bank, or an exclusive hotel, but coming from the many small windows she could just hear the refrains of musical instruments. Looking at the sign above the tall wooden entrance doors, she read that it was the Royal Academy of Music, founded in 1822.

She stopped walking, poignantly realising that that was where she was supposed to be now – the Royal Academy of Music was the college to which her private tutor had always urged she must aspire, and where he had often predicted, in his inflated way of speaking, she would one day arrive and triumph.

She walked on, turning off the major road and down towards the park, already able to see the perimeter railings. A little way inside the park, she chose to sit on a bench beside an ornamental pond, where she ate her food, petitioned by two ducks and one goose. Should she go back to see if Robert had returned? she wondered. No, she'd try phoning him from the tube station, she decided.

Midway between the park and Harley Street was Regent's Park Underground station. From a call box just outside it, Jennifer phoned Robert's office, and learned from Jeremy that Robert still hadn't returned.

'He probably wants to be alone with his thoughts for a while,' said Jeremy.

'Maybe,' said Jennifer. 'Could you ask him to ring me at Yvette's when he gets back?'

Leaving the call box, Jennifer descended the station steps and bought a ticket for Holloway Road from the vending machine. Riding a stainless steel lift down to platform level, a drunk old man in a cheap suit told her she was the prettiest girl he'd seen all day, but she should wear something more feminine than that "yeti coat".

It was darkening-over by the time she emerged on to Holloway Road. The rush hour had begun, and at the tube's exit she felt like a salmon battling against rapids. Nearing Yvette's street door, she saw that the cat was outside again, crouching low and nervous. Recognising her from some paces distant, it arched its back and meowed, and scampered in ahead of her once the door was open.

Inside the flat, Yvette had her favourite wrap-skirt lifted high to examine the red scar on her milk-white hip.

"Ello, Jennifer,' smiled Yvette, kissing Jennifer's cheeks. 'No!' she shouted when she saw the cat.

'Why not?' argued Jennifer. 'You can't just throw it out.'

'Steven doesn't like cats,' replied Yvette, trying to corner the animal.

Jennifer's expression showed she could scarcely believe what she had heard. 'He's not even here now!'

Yvette produced the same face she had pulled in response to Jennifer's reaction to hearing the story of her scar: a sullen yet reluctantly yielding look. Leaving the cat alone, she resumed examining the legacy of her previous relationship.

'You're back from work early,' remarked Jennifer, to diffuse the tension.

'Took the afternoon off,' said Yvette. Continuing to look at her scar, she decided, 'I'm going to 'ave a tattoo over it tomorrow.'

Jennifer's comment was no comment.

'Yes, a tattoo,' said Yvette, making her decision final.

'Don't suppose Robert called at all?' asked Jennifer, taking off her coat.

'No,' answered Yvette, letting her skirt fall into place. 'What are you doing tonight? Are you seeing 'im?'

Jennifer sat on the sofa. 'Doesn't look like it.'

'Steven's taking me for a meal and then we're going to see a film,' announced Yvette. 'I'll be staying at 'is place tonight. You don't mind, do you?'

'No, I don't mind,' answered Jennifer, aware that she sounded downbeat.

'You won't be sad on your own?'

'No. Why should I be?'

But Jennifer did feel sad once she was alone. It was not the solitude, however. It was a sense that things already seemed to be coming apart at the seams. A sense of looming disappointment. Or maybe she was just pessimistically imagining it? she questioned.

Later in the evening, curled up on the sofa with the cat, the issue

552

of her future began to trouble her. She had so far failed to investigate college options, but was not sure whether that was a bad thing or a good thing. Perhaps the college decision had been born out of vague desperation? Perhaps it would be better to wait for something more appropriate to come along? Maybe working for Robert and Jeremy would prove to be it?

When she next looked at the clock, it was approaching midnight. Since Robert had still not called, she fed the cat, and made the sofa her bed.

2.23
Revenge

They were still wearing their ceremonial robes. Simon was holding the weighty Empathy Device, and by the light of the candle Carl was holding, Albert lifted the latch and opened the master door of Deepdale Hall. Outside, the waning moon glowed through softly weeping clouds. Inside, earthly tears were being shed.

'We'll see each other again, though, won't we, Master?' said Simon emotionally. 'When the Golden Millennium begins, old age will be conquered, and eventually I'll graduate to other planets as the same person I am now, won't I?'

Standing under the Gothic arch of the doorway, looking out to the weakly moonlit forecourt, Albert answered, 'That's right, Simon. If you do your work here first, one day, maybe a million years from now, we'll meet again. And you too, Carl.'

'Stay a bit longer, Albert,' entreated Simon.

'Yeah, Albert,' said Carl, 'don't go yet.'

'I have to go now,' said Albert. 'There's little time to spare. The spaceship is due in an hour, and it's over half an hour's drive to their landing site in the Lake District. It won't wait for me. Earth is insignificant in the great cosmic scheme of things.'

'Let us come with you,' implored Simon.

'No, Simon. I've told you, you can't come. You're not ready.'

'I mean just to be with you on the car ride. We won't go near the spaceship. Promise.'

'No, Simon.'

'Please.'

Albert turned to face him. 'Goodbye, Simon.'

'Goodbye, Master,' said Simon, choking with emotion.

'Goodbye, Carl,' said Albert.

'Goodbye, Master,' said Carl. 'Take care.'

Except for the ever-present gripping sensation in the pit of his stomach, Albert felt nothing. Not even impatience. Stepping out into the drizzle, he walked to his car, crunching gravel under his feet.

'Master!' called Simon urgently, scurrying after Albert, struggling with the cumbersome weight of the Empathy Device.

Cupping his hand around the candle, Carl followed Simon. ''Ere, Simon,' he advised, 'careful with that device thing.'

Reaching Albert, Simon anxiously asked, 'What about the combination for the Empathy Device?'

Stopping halfway between the house and his car, Albert said, 'I've written it in an envelope, Simon. The envelope's hidden inside my mattress.'

'In your mattress?'

'Yes, Simon. You'll find it easy enough.'

'But we can't go into your room because of the spiritual shield.'

'I've deactivated it, Simon. My room is safe for you now. Don't lose the combination. The Golden Millennium depends on you doing my work.'

'No, I won't lose it, Master.'

'Only activate the device when the Third Satellite is in orbit,' Albert reminded him. 'If anything goes wrong and you miss the date, wait for the next date. You know the dates for the next thousand years, so don't worry. Never tell anyone about the device or the project or me. Not even the Orthrium leader. You two are the only people who can ever know. The technology's too powerful to be revealed.'

'I understand, Master. No one will ever be told.'

'Do you understand as well, Carl?' asked Albert, fixing him with a look, observing that he too had become tearful. 'Never a word to anyone until the Empathy Device is working and the world is peaceful and safe.'

'They'd 'ave to torture me, or worse, before I'd grass,' declared Carl.

'Godfrey bless you,' said Albert.

'Master,' said Simon, in a worried voice, 'what if Phil's ghost comes back?'

'Don't worry, Simon. He can't harm the Empathy Device now. It's spiritually shielded.'

'Could he hurt me?'

'No, Simon. Not while Godfrey is in your heart.'

Albert turned, and walked the final steps to his car.

'Goodbye, Master,' called Carl.

Simon could contain his emotion no longer. Putting the Empathy Device down, he ran to Albert, falling to his knees before him. 'Don't go, Master. Please don't go. I love you.'

Carl ran to Albert too, losing the candle flame along the way.

'Simon, I have to leave,' said Albert, with one hand on the car door handle. 'I'm no longer of this world. I've changed. My time here has come to an end. Even if the Golden Millennium were never to arrive, I could not stay. My spirit has seen too much.'

He opened the car door.

'Please, Master,' begged Simon as Albert got into his car.

Albert closed the door and locked it. Before starting the engine, he lowered the electric window. 'Don't ever make the gatekeeper leave his cottage. He's spiritually linked to this site. I can't explain more, it's too complicated. Let him live in his cottage as long as he wants, and look after him. But don't ever let him into the grounds. He might find the body.'

'Yes, Master,' wept Simon.

The window went up, the engine started, the lights shone, and gravel crunched deeply. Proceeding at a stately pace, Albert drove into the woods. Simon remained kneeling in the veiled moonlight, watching the car's lights sink deeper into the obscuring trees, then seeing the misty sky beyond the estate acquire a thin, milky illumination.

Eventually, when no relic of Albert remained to be seen, Carl said, "E's gone then, ain't 'e?'

'Yes,' murmured Simon. 'But we'll see him again one day. Somewhere.'

'Yeah. One day.'

Simon got to his feet. Walking back to the house, he picked up the Empathy Device.

'Mebbe we won't miss 'im so much once the device thing gets workin' on us?' suggested Carl.

'Hopefully,' said Simon quietly. 'Hopefully.'

'Champion stuff, that crystal energy. Can't wait.'

Once inside the house, Simon placed the Empathy Device somewhere he believed it would remain hidden from any intruder, then he and Carl went directly to Albert's bedroom, the route now lit electrically. Examining the mattress revealed a slit in its side. Exploring the slit revealed an envelope. Opening the envelope revealed a single sheet of paper. Unfolding the sheet revealed... sabotage.

On the sheet of paper, the numbers 1 to 13 had been written. Below each of these numbers was a *burn hole*, each of which had evidently destroyed another number: *the secret positions for the rods*. And below the burn holes, singed into the paper was the message: *Revenge from beyond the grave you put me in, brother.*

Frantic, Simon held the paper up to the light. Nothing. Not a single burnt number could be read. He tore the envelope wide open, but nothing else was inside.

'What's up, Simon?' asked Carl.

'Phil's ghost,' answered Simon, pale with worry and fear. 'He's destroyed the combination.'

'Y'kiddin'?'

Simon began tearing at the slit in the mattress, widening it enough to accept his arm.

Nothing.

'We've got to catch him up,' said Simon, running out the room. 'Come on.'

'Catch who up?' asked Carl, pursuing Simon down the steep steps leading from the bedroom. 'Albert?'

'Yes, Albert. We've got to get the combination from him before the extraterrestrials take him away.'

Hampered by their robes, they ran through the corridors of the house. Once he fully understood the exigencies of the situation, Carl, fleeter of foot and more acrobatic on the stairs, spurted ahead, and had the cab's engine running by the time Simon made it outside.

'Faster!' urged Simon before they'd even left the forecourt.

Carl drove through the woods as fast as he dared. Once on the public road, he flogged the sluggish diesel engine to its limit.

'How long since he left?' asked Simon desperately. 'Ten minutes?'

'Longer, I reckon. Fifteen.'

'Pass me the road atlas.'

Studying the map, Simon realised that at Rookhope, Albert would have had two choices of direction, but both would eventually put him on the A689, which by now, whatever route he'd chosen, he should already be travelling on. 'Left here,' he said, when they reached the Rookhope junction. But, studying the map further, he saw that in about twelve miles, the road west divided. One fork led to Carlisle; the other to Penrith.

Albert would most likely have taken the Penrith route into the Lake District, Simon desperately decided.

With the engine sounding overworked, and the cab tilting on bends, it seemed they were speeding over the Pennines, through the drizzle and mists. But cars would sometimes overtake them, to Simon's dismay. Consequently, before they'd even reached the road's big divide, he was becoming resigned to the fact that, unless Albert had been delayed by something unforeseen, they were not likely to catch him up. But they had to try, he knew, and they pressed on until Penrith, and then on further still, by random choice, to the shore of Ullswater.

'It's no use,' conceded Simon, looking despondently across the vast, eerily moonlit lake, 'he'll be in space by now.'

'Yeah? Y'reckon?'

'Has to be. He said they were picking him up in an hour, and that was over an hour ago. We might as well head back.'

Carl pulled up, swung the cab around, and they drove back to Deepdale Hall. But along the way, their spirits improved when they realised that all they had to do was try different rod positions on the Empathy Device until the lights showed it was working. Then, Simon advised, they should quickly move a rod again to quell it until the Third Satellite was in orbit, for only then would they be able to operate it secure from hostile detection.

That's what they'd do, they decided.

Returning to the house, Simon and Carl retrieved the Empathy Device from where it had been hidden, and scrutinised it. Then Simon began trying combinations at random, watched by Carl.

'Y'need a system, I reckon,' advised Carl after some minutes, 't'make sure y'don't keep trying the same combination.'

'You're right,' said Simon. 'Let's think about it over some food.'

'Pity Phil's dead. Were a marvellous cook, weren't 'e?'

'He was,' agreed Simon, 'but evil.'

'Too right,' said Carl, taking his robe off to prepare for kitchen work.

After they'd eaten, dressed in their *Not Long Now* T-shirts, Simon and Carl sat down near the fire in the big room, with the Empathy Device on a table before them. The fire warmed their sides. Candles on the table provided the preferred illumination for their sacred work.

'Remember,' said Simon, 'as soon as the lights on top light up, move one rod one position. I think it should be safe if it only works for a moment. Foreign armies wouldn't be able to trace it that quickly.'

'We could hide it somewhere else afterwards,' suggested Carl.

'Yes, that's good thinking, Carl. That's what we'll do. Hide it somewhere far away.'

Over their food, they had decided that the best system for trying combinations would be to set all the rods to their lowest positions, then pull one out in increments, then move another one a notch, and repeat. Now they were set to begin. Pushing all rods in, Simon moved the first rod through its thirteen positions. Then he reset it, and moved the second rod up a notch. Then he moved the first rod through its thirteen positions again, and back to base. Then he moved the second rod up one more notch, and moved the first rod through its thirteen positions again.

Albert had supposed something like this would happen, and inside the Empathy Device, the rods connected to heavily greased cogs, among other components. Simon's arm would wear out before the components would, Albert had gauged.

It was only after several minutes of systematically moving the rods that even the smallest fraction of the enormous number of possible combinations began to become clear to Simon. But, assisted by Carl, he persevered, becoming more and more disheartened as the night wore on. Assiduous in their efforts, it wasn't until night became grey morning that they began even vaguely comprehending the full scale of the task ahead of them.

'This could take monfs,' Carl had taken to saying.

Finally, too tired to go on, Simon stared at the rods, slowly recognising that it might take *years*, not months.

Going to his bedroom to sleep, he wept quietly in despair.

2.24
Sexy

Albert had not gone west to the Lake District. Once beyond the gates of Deepdale Hall, he'd sped along to Rookhope, where he'd taken a minor road that led *east* to Stanhope and the A689. And upon joining that A road, at a slower speed he'd continued eastwards, toward Durham City.

Still headed for Durham City, driving along, he felt no sense of success, or even relief. He felt nothing at all, except tense in the pit of his stomach — like his body was anxious, but his mind was somehow detached.

It was Ron who had taught him to drive, but he'd never taken his test. So, although his car was taxed and had a current MOT, he had no driver's licence and hadn't even been able to think about insurance. But all he had to do was get to Rebecca's, and within ten minutes now he'd be there. Under the passenger seat, hidden carefully enough within the upholstery to survive any routine police search, was his *Not Long Now* T-shirt. Inside this folded and rolled-up garment were three hundred fifty pound notes and thirteen diamonds.

All the roads were familiar now. He was back home. Somehow, now that he was rich, he could face seeing his friends again, and it seemed like he'd been away a long time.

It was nearly ten o'clock when he arrived at Rebecca's house. The household's two cars were occupying the short drive, but he noticed Ron's car parked on the street nearby, and pulled up behind it. First thing he did after switching the engine off was to retrieve the rolled-up T-shirt and its fantastic contents. Still wearing his robe, he entered the house without ringing the bell, using the key Rebecca had given him. Closing the door behind him, he went directly to the living room, lit only by the light of a small television and the red glow of a simulated coal fire. Rebecca, Ron and Sarah were on the sofa, with Ron in the middle, all vaguely staring at a suitcase opposite — Albert's own suitcase. His suitcase seemed to have replaced the television as a point of focus, except for Tony, who was using the suitcase as a stool, sitting on it to watch the television, with his back to the door.

All heads except Tony's turned to look at whoever had come in. Seeing Albert standing in the dim doorway, wearing a golden robe and clutching a rolled-up T-shirt, Ron was the first to speak, observing dryly, 'So you're still alive, then?'

Albert appeared nonplussed. 'Why shouldn't I be?' he returned in a subdued, uncertain voice.

'Ask the girls. They were painting melodramatic pictures.'

Albert looked at Rebecca. 'Hello,' he said quietly.

At first too thrown by the sight of him in a golden robe to speak, in a voice that was little more than a murmur, Rebecca eventually said, 'Hi.'

She leaned over to switch on a table lamp.

Looking at Sarah in the improved illumination, unsure how she would react to him, Albert gave her a limited twiddly finger wave.

Fazed, Sarah twiddled her fingers back. 'We were worried you might have topped yourself. You're supposed to be broken-hearted, after all.'

'Yeah, living one,' said Ron accusingly, 'deem yourself a poet?'

'I am broken-hearted,' said Albert, remaining in the doorway. 'I've just learned to live with it.'

'Shallow,' accused Ron.

'Quick learner,' returned Albert, slowly.

'Hello, Albert,' said Tony, with a downbeat lack of enthusiasm and without turning around.

'Hello, Tony.'

'Where've you been, Albert?' asked Rebecca.

'Can't tell you.'

'You've turned gay, though, haven't you?' said Ron.

In his oddly retarded state, Albert found Ron's comment unfathomable, and his expression showed it.

'The dress,' explained Ron.

The robe. Albert looked down at it. He'd become so used to it, and was so numbly preoccupied, he hadn't realised he was still wearing it. Or rather he did know he was wearing it, but it didn't seem important or unusual. 'It's my uniform,' he said. 'I've got a job.'

The job claim clinched it: Rebecca was certain Albert was not quite his usual self. 'Are you all right?' she asked.

'No. I've got a feeling that won't go away.'

'That's your gayness,' stated Ron, getting elbowed in the ribs by both Rebecca and Sarah.

'I'm not gay. I've got a job, that's all.'

'Vicar?' wondered Ron.

'Higher,' said Albert.

'Bishop?' wondered Sarah.

'Higher. Much higher.'

'Pope?' tried Rebecca.

'Higher.'

Shrugs and blank looks indicated that Albert's inquisitors couldn't think of any transvestite job in the world higher up the career ladder than Pope. Finished guessing, they stared at him, framed in the doorway, wearing a fancy golden robe.

'You've flipped, haven't you?' said Ron, delighted. 'You've finally gone wacko. Told you you'd go mad one day. It was that E that pushed you over the edge, wasn't it?'

'I'm not mad. I've got a job, that's all.'

Ron stood up to patronisingly beckon Albert further into the room. 'Come on, we'll take you to the mental hospital. Put you in the gay ward.'

Rebecca pulled Ron back down, then sought to raise her husband's interest. 'Tony,' she said petulantly, 'we think Albert's gone mad.'

Tony reluctantly looked over his shoulder for a moment. Observing Albert in his robe, he concluded, 'Yep. Totally bonkers. Take him to my hospital. Put him in the gay ward.'

'I'm not gay,' said Albert. 'I've just got a job, that's all. I'm not mad, either.'

Ron took his mobile from his shirt pocket. Pretending to dial a number, he said into the phone, 'Hello, Gay Helpline? ... Yeah, hi. It's about a friend of mine. He's acting really suspiciously ... What's that? ... Yes, all the signs are there ... Yes, that too. Long and golden it is ... You'll send someone over to take him away? ... That's good ... Ten minutes? ... Right. Thanks. Be careful, he's wacko with it. He'll have the strength of ten hairdressers.'

He put his phone away.

Getting up off the sofa, Sarah went over to Albert. 'Are you all right?' she asked.

'You owe me ten grand,' demanded Ron, suddenly remembering.

Albert ignored Ron, but addressed Sarah. 'Any word from Jennifer? Is she all right?'

'She's all right,' said Sarah. 'She phoned. She's in London. She's living in some French woman's flat.'

'Did you give her my letter?'

'I told her about it on the phone. She said she didn't want to see it, but I sent it to her today anyway. She should get it tomorrow.'

'Tomorrow,' murmured Albert.

'Hopefully,' said Sarah. 'I'll ring her tomorrow if she doesn't call me first. I don't want to appear like I'm hassling her.'

'I'm sorry,' said Albert. 'I'm so sorry.'

Ron pitched his oar in. 'Don't blame yourself, Albert.'

'Why not?' Albert came back. 'It was my fault.'

'I know it was,' agreed Ron. 'I meant don't blame yourself when there's other people who can blame you a lot better. Sarah's aunt, for instance. She wants to kill you. I said I'd help, but now you've turned gay, she could probably handle you herself.'

Looking shamefully at Sarah, Albert again expressed his remorse. 'I'm sorry. I'm so sorry.'

'It's okay,' said Sarah, giving him a quick hug. 'Good to see you again.'

'What about Sarah?' asked Albert, talking to Ron over Sarah's shoulder, looking like he was numbly expecting the worst reply. 'Is she pissed off with me?'

'Sarah? That was her who just hugged you — recognise? It's traditional to return hugs, by the way.'

'Albert, come and sit next to me,' said Rebecca, shoving Ron off the sofa.

Sarah led Albert to the sofa. Smiling a concerned smile, Rebecca sat him down on her left, and Sarah, in turn, sat on Albert's left.

'You're acting a bit weird, Albert,' said Rebecca. 'Are you all right?'

'No. Never felt worse.'

'What's the matter?'

'I've got a feeling that won't go away. I'm not mad though. You'd have this feeling too if you'd done what I've done.'

'Why've you got a dress on?'

'I'm not gay. I've got a job.'

Displaced from the sofa, Ron occupied an armchair, from where he asked, 'Ever thought of doing it competitively?'

'Doing what?' asked Albert.

'Being gay. You could win medals, you. Represent the country.'

'I'm not gay.'

'You are. Just admit it, then you'll feel so much better. Isn't that right, Tony?'

'Certainly is,' answered Tony, without turning around. 'Repressing all that intense gayness must be doing him damage most everywhere.'

Ron had more to say. 'You're deluding yourself because of your madness. You think you're sitting between two gorgeous chicks, holding a T-shirt on your lap and wearing a butch lumberjack shirt, when in fact you're sitting between two sailors, holding a pink purse and wearing a sparkly dress. You've got a stupid pudding basin haircut too — we all meant to tell you about that before, but we never had the heart.'

Looking at Ron, Albert said, 'Thanks for bolstering me. Anyone else want to stick the bolster in?'

Still looking at the television, Tony raised his hand to say something, but Ron beat him to it. 'You're ugly, too.'

Albert delved into the folds of the T-shirt on his lap. 'Do you want this or not?' he said, producing a diamond.

'Want what?' asked Ron.

Albert tossed it to him. 'It's your redundancy payment. It's worth around four hundred thousand pounds.' He delved into the T-shirt again, pulling out a wad of fifty pound notes held together with an elastic band. 'And here's the ten thousand for your broken stuff.'

He lobbed the money to Ron, who became instantly dumbstruck. Tony turned around.

'Thought you'd want one too,' sneered Albert, lobbing a diamond to Tony, who immediately scrutinised it.

Rebecca and Sarah were also dumbstruck, particularly after Albert gave them a diamond each.

'What are they?' puzzled Tony alertly.

'Badly cut diamonds,' answered Albert, 'but worth a fortune.'

'It's real!' gasped Sarah. 'Feel how cold they are. Real diamonds feel cold. That's why they're called ice.'

'The money's real too,' said Ron, stupefied. 'Where the fuck did you get ten grand from?'

'Told you,' said Albert, 'I got a job.'

'Did a job, more likely,' said Tony.

He was beginning to get better, realised Albert. He could feel his usual self returning, and the tenseness in his stomach easing.

'Albert,' snapped Rebecca, while the others continued to gawk at their gems, 'what have you been up to?'

'I got a job,' he said, taking another diamond out of his T-shirt and handing it to her. 'Here's one for Jackie.'

'Albert!' she screeched. 'Stop it.'

'Okay. I'll keep the rest for myself.'

Ron looked up from his diamond and money. 'How many more have you got?'

'Eight.'

'Eight!' screeched Rebecca.

'And each one worth four hundred grand?' asked Tony suspiciously.

'Around that figure.'

'Why are they all shaped like pyramids?'

'Can't tell you.'

Ron, Sarah, Rebecca and Tony all looked at each other, none of them knowing what to think or say until Ron took the lead: 'Well done, Albert,' he said simply.

'Yeah, well done, Albert,' said Sarah, in a similarly understated manner. She tried to hand her diamond back, but Albert indicated he wasn't interested in its return, leaving her looking uncertain. 'You're really giving it to me? Why?'

'I'm constantly impressed by your choice of sister.'

'But I barely know you, Albert.'

'Lucky you.'

'Albert!' shrieked Rebecca suddenly. 'Where did you get them?'

'Really can't tell you,' said Albert.

'Then we can't accept them,' said Tony firmly, proffering the return of his diamond and gesturing Rebecca to return hers.

'I'll have it,' said Ron, snatching Tony's diamond. Holding his hand out to Sarah and Rebecca, he said, 'If anyone else is moral or chicken or confused, just pass them this way.'

Sarah and Rebecca were as yet unwilling to part with their gems.

'What have you been up to, Albert?' asked Tony, in a low, serious, disapproving voice.

'What have I been up to? Remember you saying I had one of the most cunning minds ever devised by nature? Well, these diamonds were acquired with that cunning running at full tilt. No one will ever even be sure they're gone. There's reasons why I can't tell you more, but trust me on it: no one will ever know they're missing.' He took another diamond out from the folds of his T-shirt and offered it to Tony to replace the one Ron had taken from him. 'Worth more than your puny house.'

Tony looked at the fortune within his reach... deliberating... 'I'd be crazy to,' he decided. 'Too much to lose. You'll all end up in prison.'

'Suit yourself,' said Albert, returning the diamond to the T-shirt. 'Negotiate with Ron if you change your mind.'

'Albert!' cried Rebecca complainingly. 'Tell us where you got them.'

'Ron,' said Albert, 'tell her to shut up. No more questions. The diamonds aren't hot. They never will be. No more questions from anyone except to ask my advice on how to sell them. Serious: they'll have to be sold according to my directions, even though they're not hot. Can't say more.'

'Why can't you say more?' demanded Rebecca.

'Shut it, Rebecca,' ordered Ron, 'the lad's done well.'

'Yeah, shut it,' said Sarah, 'four hundred thousand times.'

Rebecca gazed at the two gems in her hand. 'Fuck me, Albert,' she breathed, 'you go away penniless, and come back rich in under a week.'

'In a dress, though,' reminded Ron.

'I like his dress,' said Sarah. 'He looks sexy.'

'You'd tell any man with a bunch of diamonds on his lap he looks sexy,' said Ron.

'True,' agreed Sarah.

'I'm rich,' murmured Rebecca, staring at her fortune.

'So am I,' murmured Sarah, staring at her own fortune.

'Where did they come from, Albert?' murmured Rebecca.

'The next person to ask me any questions about the diamonds forfeits theirs,' proclaimed Albert. 'And I mean it. Just fucking trust me about them. And don't tell anyone else about them — important. So long as there's no publicity, no one will know they're missing. Ever.'

Rebecca looked into Albert's eyes. 'Tony,' she ordered murmuringly, 'open the emergency champagne and put some music on.'

Though he grumbled, Tony compliantly provided champagne, but refused to have anything else to do with celebrating the "heist", as he called it. Furthermore, he swore everyone, even Rebecca, to promise to keep his name out of it when the police came. He never saw any diamonds; he never heard about any diamonds.

Using surgical spirits, he cleaned his prints off the one he'd touched.

And after tonight, he ordered, the gems were to be gone from his house.

Although Albert remained more subdued and slower in manner and response than normal for him, and much, much more subdued than the occasion would demand, he drank a glass of champagne and did his best to appear celebratory. But the initial surge of cork-popping excitement soon subsided, and now he was sitting quietly on the floor, with his back rested against the sofa. Tony had gone into the kitchen. Sarah and Rebecca were on the sofa. Ron was sitting at the dinner table, in a kind of trance, beholding his money and diamond, and the diamond he'd lifted from Tony. Ron's face now bore much the same expression that Albert's had the very first time he saw Jennifer's photograph: awe; love; desire; regret; passion — all mixed into one. And there were other, fleeting, facial nuances as yet unknown to lexicographers, those elusive nuances that throughout history have sent poets running for their quills and painters running to their canvases. To the despair of those same poets and painters, such elusive nuances have always defied perfect artistic crystallisation, redirecting the frustrated poets to bawdy taverns, and the tormented painters to gunsmiths.

'So what are you going to do now that you're rich, Albert?' asked Rebecca, although she didn't expect to hear the answer, for she was on her way out the room.

'Let's all go to Iceland,' suggested Sarah enthusiastically, leaning forward to tap Albert's shoulder. 'You'll love it, Albert. The aurora is amazing. Everything's amazing. It's like another planet. Volcanoes. Glaciers. Hot springs. I hardly had time to enjoy it when I was there. And Ron was at work most the time.'

'Yeah, I wouldn't mind going back,' said Ron, putting his fortune aside and bringing out his joint-making paraphernalia. 'Ivor was a top geezer.'

'Yeah, Albert, you'd get on with Ivor,' predicted Sarah.

'You barely know me,' Albert reminded her.

'No, you would,' she insisted. 'He was really clever and imaginative. He was always coming out with interesting theories and things, wasn't he, Ron?'

'She's not lying,' said Ron, already working on his joint.

Sarah continued. 'Like when he took us to see the aurora and he started going on about sending a spaceship to the stars, but then a faster spaceship would catch you up two hundred years later... oh, no, that's not it. Shit, the champagne's got to me... Yeah, sorry, forgot to mention that he thinks we could all live for ever soon because of medical science.'

Sarah continued relating Ivor's scenario, but her voice fell away from Albert's attention. Prompted, it had suddenly struck him that the fruits of cutting edge biological research might now be his to buy. Soon — surely soon, he was certain of it —, when stem cell research evolved into actually growing new organs and limbs and replacing diseased brain tissue, and when ordinary cells became subordinate to the will of science, never dying yet never turning cancerous, then a person with enough money could buy lasting youth. It hadn't dawned on him till now, but he might well be one of the first immortals — he still had over three million pounds worth of gems in his possession.

Life might be worth getting started on after all.

'Fuck,' he breathed, inaudibly.

'Here you go,' said Ron, standing over Albert.

Albert looked up to see that Ron was offering him a pipe, already lit. Sarah had stopped talking, and was patting the sofa to entice Ron to sit beside her. With a fire gently warming him, a fortune in his lap, and a champagne glass in one hand, Albert accepted the pipe. He drew deeply on the psycho-active smoke, and, putting the pipe aside, rested his head back against the sofa, gazing softly upward. With his unusual sensitivity to dope, he felt the universe gently expand. The music — a Beatles album — became clearer and more beautiful. The fire's softly flickering glow on the ceiling became deeper in hue and saturation. Time subtly dilated.

Rebecca had gone upstairs, and now, above the music, Albert heard her footsteps creaking the ceiling, becoming louder. Suddenly, the anguished feeling inside of him that had begun to ease became overwhelming. Frightening. He sat up straight, looking forward, looking at the fire. There was a suspended sense of... he didn't know... something bad. Galumphing noises — only Rebecca running down the stairs.

'Tony still in the kitchen?' complained Rebecca upon entering the room. 'What's he doing in there?'

'He's distancing himself,' said Ron, lighting his joint. 'He thinks we've turned into gangsters.'

Crossing the room, Rebecca noticed Albert's stiff posture. 'What's the matter, Albert? You looked spooked.'

'Nothing's the ma—'

He dried up. Within a pattern of shadows in the simulated coal fire, he'd suddenly begun to see the smashed, bloodied face of Phil, and felt his own face burn red with guilt and shame.

'What's the matter, Albert?' asked Rebecca again, now sounding confused and concerned. 'Why's your face gone all red?'

Albert couldn't answer, for he was listening in astonished shock to the Beatles: he had begun interpreting each line of lyric so that it became a personal condemnation. Not only the full lines, but elements of the lines, too. It was all a perfect analysis and judgement, stunningly clever. He wasn't hearing things that weren't being sung, just finding new meaning in the familiar words. And there was no effort or delay involved: in a literal instant, his mind was twisting what it was hearing to make attacks upon him. Some of the interpretations even relied on cryptic references and word play as cunning as a Times crossword.

Part of his mind had turned traitor. A powerful part.

'Albert, what's the matter?' asked Sarah, leaning forward.

Rebecca knelt on the floor beside him. 'Are you all right, Albert?'

'No,' he murmured, staring transfixed into the fire. 'I'm not all right.'

'Tony!' yelled Rebecca. 'Come here. Now.'

Eating a sandwich, sounding and looking unenthusiastic, Tony came in from the kitchen. 'What?'

Rebecca pointed anxiously to Albert. 'Albert's gone funny.'

'Albert?' mumbled Tony. 'What's wrong with him?'

'Fuck knows,' shrugged Ron, leaning forward to peer at Albert. 'I gave him a pipe, then that — all spooked and freaked and God knows what else.'

'He's had a smoke?' asked Tony rhetorically, going over to Albert. Kneeling beside him, continuing to feed his sandwich into his mouth, he enquired, 'What gives, Albert?'

Albert looked at Tony, but reddened deeper, and turned away, holding a concealing hand to his face.

Taking another bite of his sandwich, Tony, sounding only mildly intrigued and sympathetic, diagnosed, 'A genuine cannabis psychosis — cool.'

'Told you he was gay,' said Ron.

2.25
Bender

Despite the noise of the impatient morning traffic, Jennifer was sound asleep on the sofa — dreaming, Yvette could tell. Having just arrived home from spending the night at Steven's, Yvette was being as quiet as she reasonably could be, treading softly around the room to find her things before leaving again for work.

The cat was following her, but she paid it no attention.

A cupboard needed to be opened, and it made noise. 'Bonjour,' said Yvette brightly and musically when Jennifer stirred.

'Bonjour,' returned Jennifer, sleepily.

'I 'ave to get ready for work. Sorry about waking you.'

'It's all right. It's your flat.'

'But it was your dream, and I broke it,' returned Yvette. 'Were you dreaming? Your eyes were moving so fast.'

'I was,' said Jennifer, sitting up. 'I was playing violin.'

She realised it was her first violin dream for... for years.

'A letter's come for you,' announced Yvette, smiling and presenting an envelope.

Jennifer recognised her sister's handwriting. Putting it aside to read later, she slipped her feet into sandals, and shuffled to the bathroom, dealing with the cat's litter tray on the way.

'Making toast and marmalade,' called Yvette after her. 'Do you want some?'

'Yes, please.'

Presently, in the kitchen, Jennifer was putting food out for the cat while Yvette put food out on the table.

'What should we do tonight?' asked Yvette.

'Can we go dancing again?'

Yvette erupted into a grin. A personal triumph is how she looked upon Jennifer's transformation from demure to pleasure-seeking in only five days. 'Of course we can,' she answered, doing her amusing gangling arms dance. 'But first I see Steven after work. Let's meet in the same club we did last time.'

'Okay. What time?'

'Nine,' decided Yvette. 'That'll give me plenty of time. Wait where we were sitting when we first took the E.'

'Okay.'

Once Yvette left for work, Jennifer took a bath, spending longer in the water than usual. After her bath, she sat down with some coffee to read the letter from her sister, but the envelope contained only the letter from Albert that Sarah had spoken of, forwarded to her unsolicited. Discovering this, she was annoyed at the liberty. She'd moved on now. She was with new people, and didn't want to have to think about the complicated mystery that Albert had been.

But she read it anyway.

> *Dear Jennifer,*
>
> *Please excuse me the necessity of writing you this letter, but there's so much I have to say to you before I can rest tonight ...*
>
> *... Whatever paths we take in our separate futures, I wish you every happiness, although I fear that without you, my own path shall forever darken.*
>
> *I'll be forever sorry,*
Albert

By the time Jennifer reached the end of the letter, there were tears in her eyes. Beyond being moved by Albert's expressions of love, loss and remorse, she was concerned to learn of the bad time he had had on his first E trip after he'd gone looking for her. She could imagine how upset she could have felt if something emotionally wounding had happened to her on her first trip.

Much of the complicated mystery that Albert had been was now solved for Jennifer, and she, too, like Sarah, regretted many of the misgivings she had had about him. But there was no thought of going back. Reading the letter, she was moved by sympathy, not yearning. It did cross her mind that things would have turned out different had she gone to Ron's party, but the past was the past, she resolved.

She was worried about his reported disappearance.

Resisting a desire to read the letter again, Jennifer took what was left of her coffee to the window, where she stood watching the cars and people. Even though the sound of the heavy traffic met with little resistance from the glass pane, the flat still felt oddly quiet. Oppressively quiet.

The television remote was on the widow sill. Suddenly snatching it, she pointed it and conjured up Jerry Springer. She quickly vanished him, switching to a schools programme about the Romans in Britain.

Looking at the remote, she was struck by how it was like magic. She had no real idea how it worked. She remembered her father saying how, when he was a boy, he could take most any household electrical device apart and eventually understand what the components were and what they did, but everything was becoming a black box secret now. Science, she thought, had first sought to explain the world, now it seemed to have made it impenetrable and magical.

Finishing her coffee, she left the window. Sitting on the sofa, vaguely watching the television, she thought about what she could do with the daylight. She would shop for food, she decided, but knew that wouldn't take long, for there was a mountainous supermarket just down the road.

In ten minutes, she was ready to go out, returning half an hour later with four carrier bags of groceries. Once she'd put the shopping away, she rested on the sofa with a snack and another coffee. Looking at the answering machine, she saw that no messages had been left. Dialling 1471 informed her that no one had even rung, let alone left a message. She replaced the receiver, hoping Robert would call before she was driven to call him. But when noon approached, and he still hadn't considered her feelings, or perhaps just hadn't got out of bed, she reached for the phone again.

'Hello, is that Jeremy?'

'Yes. Jennifer. How are you?'

'Okay. Is Robert up yet?'

'Well, yes and no,' said Jeremy, offering a temporary puzzle in a voice that sounded displeased. 'Yes, because he's just returned after yesterday's disappearance. And no because he's collapsed on the office floor.'

The remainder of the conversation told Jennifer that Robert had apparently been drinking without pause all day yesterday, and all night too, fortified by cocaine, and the inevitable crash had come upon his morning return. He was now effectively unconscious on the floor, said Jeremy. Hearing this, beyond her concern for her new friend, Jennifer was also concerned for her money. Still not very clear what it actually was that Robert did to earn his living, she knew that whatever it was, he couldn't do it if he was lying in a stupor.

She proposed that she should go to the office straightaway to do what she could to get Robert back on track, and the suggestion was gratefully received. But by the time Jennifer arrived in Harley Street, Robert had recovered enough to answer the intercom.

'Oo's that?' he asked in a squawky comedy voice. 'Oo's that down there calling us up 'ere?'

'Robert? It's Jennifer. Are you all right?'

'Jenny! Come on up!'

The lock buzzed, and Jennifer pushed open the heavy door. Robert was waiting for her at the top of the stairs, outside his office door, with a wet grin that didn't look too far from lunacy. He put his arms around her, giving her a tight hug. 'How are you doing, Jenny?'

He smelled of booze, fags and unwashed clothes.

'Better that you,' answered Jennifer, with an edge to her voice.

'Yeah? Just you wait a few minutes.'

He released her from his arms and went into the office, going directly to the kitchen.

'Robert, you totally stink of drink,' said Jennifer, following him into the cramped kitchen, which she discovered to be a museum for half-eaten take-aways and unwashed cutlery, plates and cups. Only one small area of work surface remained uncluttered, where Robert was preparing something with his back to her. Over his shoulder, through the serving hatch she could see Jeremy engaged in what appeared to be an earnest conversation on the telephone.

Adopting the voice of a smashed Dudley Moore in *Arthur*, Robert protested his sobriety. 'Stink of drink? 'Ow come? I've only 'ad one little'un. Thirty big'uns, but just one little'un.' Grinning, he looked at Jennifer, but saw no evidence that she was amused. 'I think you need cheering up,' he decided playfully. 'I know, let's have sex. I've got loads of coke left. Sex and coke, that's what it's all about. Let's go to bed.'

'*You* should go to bed,' said Jennifer. 'You look terrible.'

'Feel great though.'

Robert returned his attention to doing whatever it was he was actually doing on the Formica work surface, which Jennifer observed now involved bicarbonate of soda carefully pinched from a can. Then it involved a cocaine wrap taken from his pocket.

'What are you doing, Robert?'

'Washing some coke. Makes it purer. Do you want some? You paid for it.'

'Robert, please don't take any more. Go to bed. Can't you see what's happening to you?'

Robert ignored her, and she became resigned to watching him as he continued his work.

Jeremy came into the kitchen. 'Robert,' he said, too earnest, troubled and resolute to acknowledge Jennifer yet, 'we've got to start selling on the new book soon.'

'We can't,' claimed Robert, continuing with his task. 'Not until we replace Mark.'

'We can. We can make a start at least. We can sort out the sales pitch and do some of the groundwork.'

'Did you manage to speak to Mark?' asked Robert.

Jennifer suspected that Robert's enquiry was simply a diversion.

'No,' answered Jeremy. 'He doesn't answer his phone or return my messages. I think— What are you doing?'

'Washing the coke. It makes it purer. Trevor showed me how to do it. It gives an amazing hit. It's like a mental orgasm. Me and Trevor were smoking it all last night.'

'You're making crack, Robert,' said Jeremy sternly, 'that's what you're doing.'

'What?' protested Robert. 'No I'm not. I'm just washing it.' He turned around and offered Jeremy a small pipe made of silver paper. 'Have a go. Might cheer you up a bit.'

Jeremy suddenly knocked the crudely-fashioned pipe out of Robert's hand, and it landed at Jennifer's feet.

'What did you do that for?!' cried Robert in a high voice, getting down on his knees to salvage what he could.

Jeremy was angry, even though he didn't suit it. 'It's crack, Robert, you fucker. The most addictive drug there is.'

'It's not,' argued Robert, innocently. 'I'm just washing it.'

'Please don't take any more,' requested Jennifer, uselessly.

Robert pushed her foot away so he could rescue the spilled contents of his pipe.

Jennifer had seen enough. With Robert still on his knees, she turned and left, and he let her go without a word or a look.

Containment

After a night of systematically trying combinations on the Empathy Device, and realising they'd only made the smallest dent in the task, when the sun came up, Simon had gone to bed tearfully despondent. But upon waking in the afternoon, a grim, devout resolve overcame him. If years were needed, then years he would give, he'd decided. He would give up years of his life, if necessary, to trying the remaining combinations. And although he couldn't now proceed with his business plans for the Deepdale Hall, he would not have to relinquish the sacred property, for money would never be a problem: Albert had insisted he limit the expenditure on the diamonds, leaving him adequately funded in case something unforeseen arose.

Wise Albert, he thought.

When Simon announced his steely intentions, Carl pledged to stand by him.

'Got t'get that energy goin', ain't we?' reasoned Carl. 'Magic stuff.'

'Yes,' agreed Simon. 'We'll never experience the New Age again unless we're prepared to devote our lives to doing Godfrey's will.'

Shifts. They would do it in shifts, they decided. While one rested, the other would work. This work pattern would not be broken until those lights came on, as they had done for Albert, to show that the combination was right. And they would pray to Godfrey, as well. Pray always for help and guidance and the strength to go on.

There would be no centre for New Age studies, Simon advised Carl. They had to devote all their time to unlocking the combination. And since, by Albert's wise order, only they were allowed knowledge of the device, it was up to them alone. They alone would know and keep the world's greatest secret, and, unsung, would endure tedium in the name of Godfrey and the Golden Millennium.

They were a match for it, they vowed.

So Simon drew up a rota for cracking the Empathy Device combination: fours on, fours off for each of them, day and night. And they would work on it in Albert's turret bedroom, which seemed a fitting place. And they should wear their robes when in there, decreed Simon, to show respect for the holy shrine and the sacred task.

Simon donned his robe to begin the first four-hour shift. Taking the Empathy Device up to the turret room and settling down to his work, he was still unaware that thirteen variable positions on thirteen different rods gave three hundred trillion possible alignment combinations. Moreover, he was unaware that to run through all thirteen variable positions on thirteen different rods would take nine million years of trying different combinations at the speedy rate of one per second.

2.27
Still Mad

The morning after Albert's return to Durham City, Rebecca and Tony were having breakfast in their pine kitchen while Albert sat in the living room. He'd spent the night on the sofa, but hadn't slept, or even put his head down. Nor had he eaten anything since going ga-ga on the dope, for when the dope wore off, he'd remained ga-ga.

He still couldn't look people in the eye.

Almost fully dressed for his day's consultancy work, Tony was eating at one end of their rectangular kitchen table. At the table's other end, however, gazing at two gemstones cut to pyramid shapes, Rebecca was wearing only a dressing gown and slippers — she had phoned work, claiming sickness.

'Jesus,' complained Tony, continuing the theme of the morning, 'he turns up with the haul from some heist, and you think he's a hero. I want those things out the house by the time I get back this evening. And his. I'm serious.'

'Don't be so boring,' said Rebecca, continuing to find the gems a greater visual draw than her husband's face.

'You'll know about boring when you're in prison, wife.'

Rebecca put the gemstones into her dressing gown pocket.

'Anyway,' she said, 'never mind about the diamonds, you have to help him.'

'Bollocks to him,' declared Tony, indiscriminately buttering a toasted fruit scone and somehow getting some in his wispy beard, which he wiped away with kitchen paper after Rebecca petulantly pointed to it. 'I used to offer to help him, but he just took the piss.' He received a rebuking look from across the table, which elicited a more considerate and professional attitude. 'He's having some kind of guilt crisis, unleashed by the cannabis after God knows how many years of depression.'

'I'm not depressed,' called Albert drably from the living room, 'I'm melancholic.'

Remembering that Albert could hear them, Rebecca and Tony lowered their voices.

'Guilt about what?' said Rebecca quietly. 'That's what I want to know.'

'Well, just a wild guess, but hijacking that pile of diamonds might have something to do with it.'

Rebecca went to pour herself a coffee from a percolator. 'That can't be it,' she decided, returning to the table. 'He said no one will ever even know they're missing. It's got to be about Sarah's sister. He was knocked for six over her running off, wasn't he? And he kept saying sorry to Sarah, didn't he? What do you think?'

'What do I think? How should I know? The mind's a fucking funny thing. Especially his. And he's keeping perfectly tight-lipped, isn't he? Anyway, going mad's the sanest thing he's ever done.'

'Tony, help him,' entreated Rebecca.

'Help him yourself,' retorted Tony, 'you're his moll now.'

'Tony!' snapped Rebecca.

'Oh, don't worry about him,' grumbled Tony, 'he knows he's gone loopy. He's not going to go out and do crazy things, like think he can paint the Forth Bridge or something. He's going to stay in and work everything out. He'll think his way out of it on his own. It might take him months, or years, but he'll pull through. He's not like the feckless cases I see every day. He ought to be pleased, really. Who knows, once he gets this out of the way, he might even be a better person for it? It can be a privilege to go mad. He's in the hidden rooms at the moment, having a good look around.'

'Privilege?' challenged Rebecca. 'Haven't you seen him in there? He hasn't closed his eyes all night. He's tortured.'

'I know that,' said Tony, bending to put his shoes on.

'So help him.'

'I'll write him a prescription for something to help him sleep,' conceded Tony, grudgingly.

'No you wont,' insisted Rebecca. 'You're not stuffing him full of sedatives. You'll help him properly.'

'Bollocks will I,' said Tony, leaving the table to go into the living room. 'You help him if you're so keen.'

Still in his golden robe, Albert was sitting uneasily on the sofa, staring at the floor when Tony came into the room, followed by Rebecca. The Beatles album that had been playing when he'd gone mad was now on low-volume repeat play.

'Ay-up, nutter,' said Tony jauntily as he lifted his jacket from the back of a chair.

'Ay-up, Tony,' returned Albert quietly, his troubled gaze remaining directed at the floor.

'Still mad?'

Albert gave a small, sorry nod to confirm his condition. 'Loco. The Beatles have been putting the boot into me all night.'

'The bastards,' said Rebecca.

'Don't blame them,' said Albert. 'I deserve it.'

Rebecca stopped the CD.

'Put on that Paul Simon CD over there,' suggested Albert. 'See if he hates me too.'

While Tony put on a flamboyant tie, Rebecca put on *Graceland*. 'How's that?' she asked when the music came on.

'Not good,' admitted Albert, two seconds after the vocals began.

Rebecca turned the CD off, and stood near the fire with her arms folded.

'Hey, Albert,' said Tony, now pulling his briefcase out from behind the sofa, 'if you stop being mad any time today, could you fix our fridge? It keeps making the milk freeze over.'

Albert looked toward the ajar kitchen door, and to the fridge beyond. 'I'll try,' he said quietly.

'Nice one,' said Tony. 'We might as well get some work out of you while you're feeling guilty.' He lobbed a biro at Albert. 'Isn't that right, fruitcake?'

The biro hit Albert's face, and although he had seen it coming, he hadn't dodged, or even flinched.

He stared at the floor again.

'Tony,' rebuked Rebecca, picking the biro up and returning it to her husband, 'don't bully him just because he's vulnerable now.'

'Can't think of a better time,' said Tony.

He threw the biro at Albert again. It struck his head.

'Albert,' complained Rebecca, 'don't let him pick on you. It's not right. It's you that picks on him, remember? Stick up for yourself.'

Slow to respond, Albert said, 'Why should I defend someone I don't love?'

'Because I want you to defend someone *I* love,' answered Rebecca.

Staring at the carpet, Albert visibly coloured.

Now ready to leave the house, Tony kissed Rebecca goodbye, reminded Albert about the fridge, and went off to work.

Once Tony was gone, Rebecca went to work on Albert.

'Come on, get up and take that dress off,' she ordered.

Continuing to look at the floor, Albert slowly stood up to pull the gown off over his head, leaving him in the shirt that was a present from Jackie.

'Now,' said Rebecca, 'for the first time ever, tell me honestly and properly how much you love me, have always loved me, and probably always will love me.'

'No,' said Albert to the floor, 'it's a curse being loved by me. It'll bring horrors. Cramps, too.'

'Albert,' she snapped, 'stop joking for five minutes, and tell me you love me.'

'The minute I stop joking is the minute I'll need a straitjacket.'

Rebecca slapped Albert's face. 'Tell me you love me — *now*.'

'You mad bitch!' he complained, employing a defensive cringe to protect himself from further assault. 'What did you do that for? I'm supposed to be the nutty one.'

'It's therapy,' said Rebecca.

Albert rubbed his stinging cheek. 'Therapy? Not in this century it's not. I swear I'll therapy you back the very first day I stop being mad.'

'Good. Now tell me honestly you love me or I'll therapy you again.'

She raised her hand offensively.

Cowering and holding his arms over his head, Albert said, 'I love you, Rebecca. I really do love you. But I'd love you even more if you stopped hitting me.'

'And I love you too,' returned Rebecca plainly. 'Now look me in the eyes and tell me you know I love you.'

'Don't love me, Rebecca,' he said, his voice sinking to a grave murmur. 'I'll be bad for you.'

She slapped him again — hard, and on top of the first slap. 'Tell me.'

Albert winced and cringed. 'Okay! Okay!'

'Tell me now.'

Albert looked Rebecca in the eyes. 'Rebecca, I know you love me.'

His face began burning with shame, and he turned away.

'Thank you,' said Rebecca. 'Sorry I had to hit you.'

Albert sat on the sofa again, staring bleakly at the floor. Although his blushing subsided, one cheek remained red from the slaps. 'Rebecca,' he said quietly and apparently earnestly.

'What, Albert?'

'You know you just said you loved me?'

'Yes.'

'Lest I somehow make a fool of myself, does that include bedroom love?'

Rebecca smiled tenderly. 'No, Albert. Now please, please go upstairs and get some sleep. You look exhausted.'

Albert did go upstairs, but couldn't sleep. Lying on his back, staring at the dim ceiling in a feeble, drifting state, it seemed that every bad thing he'd ever done in his life was returning to haunt him. The gripping feeling of anguish in his stomach had become worse than ever, and he wondered if he'd ever be able to eat again. His mind teemed and churned with incidents he'd thought long forgotten: kids bullied when he'd been a child himself; cruel words spoken. And Peep. He began torturing himself over Peep. A cat had died because of him – could he ever forgive himself that? Maybe he should devote the rest of his life to cat welfare?

And the face of Phil he'd conjured in the fire's flames hung appallingly before his inner eye.

A child began screeching in the street, and it tore through Albert. It sounded to him like the prolonged, agonised, slowly fading scream his mother had made after dropping the electric fire into her bath water. It *became* that scream.

As the day crept imperceptibly on, there was no let up in his internal torment, only enlargement. His own mind had become his severest critic and most tireless prosecutor. What time was it now? he wondered when it began to feel like he'd been lying alone with his stinging thoughts for an age upon an age. He could tell through the closed curtains that the light outside was fading, so it had to be around four or four-thirty, he reasoned.

Voices. He could hear voices. Rebecca and... *Jackie. Jackie was downstairs.* He had to apologise to her for being so... so insensitive. And had Ron been right? *Had* he been leading her on? He had, surely. At best he'd been negligent; at worst, callous. He began frantically formulating the things he needed to say to her, but collapsed in the endeavour when he heard someone coming up the stairs.

Someone tapped on the door, but he didn't respond.

More tapping.

Albert remained silent, but the door opened, and, tentatively, Jackie came in, dressed in her work outfit. He looked at her, and tried to speak, to gush his sentiments, but couldn't produce a word. She turned the light on, and he burned with shame. Pulling the duvet over himself, he hid like a tortoise, hunching up in the centre of the bed.

'Oh, sorry, Albert,' she said, 'I couldn't see if you were in this room. Too dark in here.'

'Hello, Jackie,' said Albert anxiously, finding he could talk while concealed.

'I hear you've gone mad,' she said, with some amusement in her voice.

'Demented.'

'Yeah?'

Jackie sat on the side of the bed, looking at the duvet hill that was Albert.

'I also hear you've done mysteriously well for yourself?' she said.

'Very well. Rebecca's got your cut.'

'We'll talk about that later. Have you really gone mad, Albert, or are you playing a game?'

'Mad as a hatter.'

'Yeah? What's it like?'

'It's... interesting... and scary. Maybe I'll be mad for the rest of my life. That wouldn't be any picnic.'

'Don't suppose it would,' agreed Jackie. 'Rebecca said you were up all night staring at the fire. Did you sleep well today?'

'Yes,' he lied.

'Come downstairs then,' she suggested. 'We're about to eat. Tony'll be back soon.'

'Not yet.'

Jackie patted the hill that was Albert, and gently repeated, 'Come downstairs.'

'No, Jackie, I can't.'

'Do you want me to bring something for you to eat up here?'

'No, I'm not hungry.'

580

'Sure?'

'Jackie...' said Albert, quietly, preparatorily.

'What?'

'I'm sorry.'

'What for?'

He hesitated. 'Anything you think I should be sorry for. Anything and everything.'

Jackie was silent until she philosophically sighed, 'Not that much, really, Albert.' Getting up off the bed, she told him, 'You know where to find us.'

When Jackie left the room, Albert emerged from under the duvet, and began worrying that he should be fixing the fridge for Tony. It was surely just a thermostat problem, he figured. He *had* to fix it. He couldn't *not*.

So, a little later, when he heard Tony return, he steeled himself, and got out of bed to see to the fridge.

2.28
Reunion

After leaving Robert on the floor, Jennifer had begun to wish she hadn't been so temperamental. Yes, he had maddened her, but she'd really wanted to shake him, not walk out on him. Besides, she reminded herself, twenty thousand pounds of hers was invested in him — which was beginning to prey on her mind more and more — and she should have remained in the office on that account alone.

Now she was back in Yvette's flat, and the afternoon hours were already dragging. The temptation to phone Robert was strong, but she resolved to wait until he called her. When the phone rang just after four o'clock, she was sure it would be him, gushing contrition, but it was Jeremy, calling to apologise on behalf of "the company", even though Jennifer now knew it was not an incorporated company, but a simple partnership. As well as apologising, Jeremy told her not to worry about her investment because they'd soon be back on their feet. 'It's looked this bad before,' he said, 'but we always pull through.'

When she asked how Robert was, Jeremy told her he'd gone out again after she'd left, but he didn't know where.

Although pleased to have been called, Jennifer derived little financial reassurance from Jeremy's grave optimism. Also, she was now even more worried about Robert than before. But it was all beginning to feel like some oppressive drama in which she, strangely and almost dreamlike, was merely mechanically playing out her part while also impassively observing from a distance. It was all beginning to feel unalterably scripted, too.

Not long after the call, she went to cook something quick and easy, which she ate at the kitchen table, absently looking at the photographs pinned to the fridge door, photos which went back to Yvette's early childhood. Taking a coffee into the living room, she sat on the sofa, and the cat settled on her lap. She began thinking about Albert's letter, and retrieved it. She read it, then read it again as the day dimmed around her, until it was almost too dark to see the words. No tears were engendered this time, but it was a long while before she felt inclined to switch on a light.

Despite sitting through what at any other time she would consider a good selection of programmes on television, the evening hours passed slowly for Jennifer until she suddenly realised she'd have to hurry if she was to be on time to meet Yvette at the club. Quickly looking through the clothes she'd bought in Camden, she chose to wear purple velour flares with a loose red top. After seeing to her face and feeding the cat, she put on the coat her aunt had given her, rather than her "yeti coat", and rushed out to begin what she remembered as being a ten minute walk — left down the road from the flat for five minutes, then left again for about another five. She soon saw that her memory was true: left off Holloway Road, in the distance, she spied a small queue, and above the queue, a familiar sign.

She joined the queue, which diminished quickly. Paying her entrance fee and leaving her coat with an attendant, she bought a drink and went up to the balcony area to look for Yvette. But Yvette wasn't there, and neither was she dancing down below, as far as she could see, and she could see the heads of every dancer.

Drifting around the circular balcony, avoiding the lingering gazes of the E'd up young men, Jennifer kept watching for Yvette. Eventually, although unsure how long she'd been waiting, she began to suspect Yvette wouldn't arrive at all, and the more frustrated she became over her absence, the more annoying the repetitive, thumping music became to her undrugged ear.

She decided to try scoring some E herself.

'Can you point out who I can buy some E from?' she shouted into the ear of someone who looked like they should know.

'That geezer down there with the yellow shirt,' shouted the young man back. 'Don't buy from anyone else or you might buy shit.'

Five minutes later, Jennifer had two E's in her palm. This time she a took whole pill, keeping the other for Yvette, should she arrive. Fifteen minutes after ingestion, she suddenly thought she might be about to vomit, and rushed to a toilet where she was immediately sick into a basin. But it hadn't really felt like her puking, inasmuch as there was no sensed physical discomfort. And once done, she felt well again — better than well. So she rinsed her mouth and went out to dance.

Very soon, through the sea of faces on the dance floor, she saw Yvette coming to her, smiling hugely and rushing with outstretched arms to greet her.

Jennifer returned the smile and greeting.

'Sorry we're late,' shouted Yvette into Jennifer's ear. 'Steven wanted to watch something on television.'

Jennifer now saw that Steven was behind Yvette. He was a tall man in his middle twenties, with shoulder-length streaked-blonde hair and tanned, developed muscles. He smiled little, and had yet to say anything Jennifer had considered amusing or intelligent. She raised her hand to acknowledge him and mouthed "hi", and he returned the gesture before beginning a small but serious dance.

'I've already got an E for you,' shouted Jennifer into Yvette's ear. 'I've just done one.'

Yvette shook her head disapprovingly. 'No, I don't do that any more,' she shouted back. 'It's bad. You shouldn't need it to 'ave a good time. Steven never takes drugs.'

Surprised and confused to the point of disorientation, Jennifer looked at Yvette and saw an unyielding yet sullenly embarrassed expression. But Jennifer's consternation was short-lived. Now angry, she took out the remaining pill and blatantly swallowed it in front of her companions, receiving a look of cynical rejection from Steven.

Steven then prompted Yvette into dancing with him, which she began at once.

Jennifer resumed dancing, at first near Yvette, but when Yvette began bumping and grinding with Steven, she moved away to her own space. When other dancers obscured her from her companions, subject to a sudden surge of pique, she left the floor, and then, after retrieving her coat, the club.

Outside the club, walking past the queue for entry and seeing the smiles and hearing the laughter, Jennifer was touched by an anxious sense of disconnection, the very opposite of what the E had given her on her first trip. Moreover, there seemed to be a sinister, mocking motive to the laughter and smiles that surrounded her.

It was the just the drug and her distressed state of mind, she told herself. Just the drug.

Once away from the club and its queue, she paused to allow herself to settle. Looking around, the traffic and pedestrians had a kind of quiet stillness to them. Looking up, the clouds were sombre and dramatic, like on the Dales, but strangely low. Moreover, the brooding, tumultuous sky seemed... personal. On the Dales, she was a small element in a vast landscape under an indifferent, wilful sky. Here, she was under a sky that knew her most solemn thoughts and secrets. But she didn't feel threatened or overwhelmed. Looking up, she saw... a sacredness. 'Like music,' she murmured. Then her eyes shuddered, and a wave of... a wave of *feeling* passed through her.

584

Her trip was deepening, she realised. The first pill alone had been double the dose of her first experience, now the second pill seemed to be adding its effect.

She knew she had to move on before someone approached her. It would happen. Some sleazy guy would notice her. She began walking, but didn't know where to go or what to do. Not back to the flat while she was still affected by the E — Yvette might turn up there with Steven. But she was yearning for familiar company. She wanted to be with Robert. She wanted to be with Robert like he'd been when she'd first met him less than a week earlier.

Holloway Road was ahead, and she could see a telephone. She would ring Robert, she decided. Becoming aware that she was almost running now, she made herself slow down. Reaching the booth and lifting the receiver to her ear, the dialling tone sounded faint and remote, and at first she thought there was a fault on the line, but then attributed it to the E.

Her call went unanswered.

Leaving the booth, she stood on the street, anxious and undecided. Coming along the road was a black cab with its *For Hire* light on. It seemed to present itself — to exist — just for her. She flagged it down, and asked to be taken to Camden, where she was dropped at the French restaurant. But Robert wasn't there, she discovered, so she walked a few minutes to the Mexican bar, but he wasn't there, either.

Outside the Mexican bar, she again tried to phone him, and again her call went unanswered. She flagged another cab, having remembered the tapas place. However, when the cab turned off Marylebone High Street into Paddington Street, it looked deserted... and darker compared to the other streets. Jennifer had the impression, for a moment, that the street was an ominous cave of sorts.

'Just here, thanks,' she said to the driver, who pulled up on the left, fortuitously right beside the steps leading down to the tapas place. She hesitated, having doubts about whether to get out the cab at all. The restaurant might not even be open so late, she worried.

'Have you got the time?' she asked the driver.

'Just gone quarter to eleven, darlin'.'

Not even eleven yet. She peered down to the barred basement window and saw a gentle, warm light that, to her drugged eye, seemed... loving.

She got out of the cab, and heard mellow jazz guitar coming from the restaurant, which ended when she was paying the driver.

Descending the steep stairs to the basement door, she felt sure Robert would be inside. A slim woman in a smart business outfit came out just as she was about to enter, and smiled at her in passing. Turning her head to watch her pass, Jennifer's eyes shuddered, and another wave washed through her.

She stepped into the restaurant, and the first sight to register was the gently smiling face of Denise, the Brazilian waitress, wearing her white blouse and black skirt waitress outfit.

'Hello,' said Denise. 'How are you?'

'Have you seen Robert?' returned Jennifer, with stress in her voice.

Denise became more serious. 'Robert?' She made a butterfly in flight gesture. 'Here before, but gone now. Where, I do not know.' Seeing the disappointment on Jennifer's face, she appended, 'But sometimes he comes back later. Why not wait for him?'

'Can I?'

'Of course,' said Denise, her usual smile returning.

'But I'm not very hungry.'

'Don't worry, you can just have a drink. The musician will play again soon. He's very good. You will enjoy him.'

Jennifer looked around, and observed that all the tables were occupied. Her petty predicament must have shown on her face because Denise, with amused, gentle exasperation in her voice, said, 'You can sit at the bar!'

Jennifer sat on a stool at one end of the short bar. Near her, a red semi-acoustic guitar was plugged into a small amplifier, along with a microphone on a stand. Already, she felt warm, and undid her coat. It was the E, she decided, making her more sensitive to temperature variations.

Denise asked her what she'd like to drink, and she requested a white wine, which was promptly served.

'Oh, thank you, Denise,' said Jennifer, sounding deeply grateful.

Denise smiled warmly. 'You are very welcome.'

Jennifer began counting money, but Denise said, 'I'll start a tab for you, okay?'

'Okay,' agreed Jennifer.

Sipping her wine, Jennifer realised she had no real thirst for it in any quantity. However, the diners' talk had begun sounding like a lulling hum, and even if she were to learn now that Robert would not appear, she would be happy to stay, stay where she knew at least one person's name.

The door beside the bar opened, and Anna appeared, carrying

food — looking harried, Jennifer thought. Smiling, Denise took the plates from Anna, who went away again. Watching Denise as she moved between the tables, Jennifer became captivated by her soft beauty and grace. Sometimes Denise would glance back, and dedicate a smile to her.

Hearing a click from the amplifier, Jennifer turned and saw a pale, tall, thin man in his late thirties, with gaunt features and long brown hair, tied back. He was slipping the guitar strap over his head while pulling a stool in position with his foot. Sitting on the stool, he moved the microphone closer to him, and switched it on. 'It's me again,' he said modestly. 'This next one's one of mine, so if you don't clap at the end, you'll hurt my feelings. I wrote it after a love affair, which also hurt my feelings.'

His long, bony fingers splayed out over the fretboard, and, at a soft volume and with a mellow tone, he began playing, at once impressing Jennifer with his musicality.

'Looking for Robert, I hear,' Jennifer heard someone behind her say. She turned and saw Mike, the restaurant owner. Beads of sweat were on his brow, and his white shirt was wet under the arms. He was opening a bottle of wine for a customer, but looked too tired to be working. By appearance, he needed two long night's sleep.

'Do you know where he's gone?'

'I do, Jennifer. A private bar in Brewer Street.'

'Where's that?'

'It not too far. Off there myself soon. We can share a cab if you want. I can sign you in to the bar.'

Jennifer hesitated. She was comfortable here now, and was enjoying the music. 'Okay,' she said, in a voice that gave away her misgivings.

'Give me ten minutes,' said Mike, before disappearing through a door behind the bar.

Mike was back in much less than ten minutes, just as the guitarist was ending his piece, which Jennifer applauded. When she raised the matter of her tab, attempting to settle it, he told her it was on the house, without asking the sum. After speaking briefly with Denise, he gestured for Jennifer to follow and paced to the door, going quickly up the stairs to street level. Catching him up, Jennifer felt uncomfortable, like she was a child again, tagging along behind one of her school teachers.

At once feeling the chill of the night, she buttoned her coat.

'You've brought me luck,' said Mike, putting an arm out to stop an oncoming cab. 'Usually have to walk to Baker Street to find a cab this time of night.'

In the cab, they sat at opposite ends of the bench seat, Jennifer on the left. The heater was blowing hot, and she undid her coat, sitting with her legs crossed at the thigh. Mike began complaining about the pressures of running a business, and Jennifer found herself pondering his accent. Geographically, it was neither here nor there to her ear, but she came to realise he spoke like John, who'd been born and raised in Nottingham. Perhaps, she now thought, Nottingham was like some hub around which the country's wilder regional accents spun, counterbalancing each others' opposing tones.

'I tell you, it's murder owning a bar,' he said. 'Constant hassle. If it's not the customers, it's the staff. You don't want a job, do you? Denise is leaving.'

'I've never done bar work.'

'Don't worry about that. There's no secret to it.' He paused, then tentatively asked, 'Have you done an E?'

Worried to be admitting to taking drugs to someone who looked as old as she remembered her father, Jennifer responded, 'Does it show?'

'A bit.'

'Good?'

'Lonely,' she confessed.

'Lonely? Someone as beautiful as you? You are beautiful, Jennifer.' Jennifer's reply was in a quiet, uncertain voice. 'Thanks.'

'Very beautiful,' said Mike.

Moving closer to her, he tentatively kissed her cheek. Then his hand went on her crossed thighs.

'Take your hand away, please,' said Jennifer, sounding like she was enduring immersion in an icy bath.

Mike's hand remained on her thighs. 'You're so beautiful,' he breathed, now kissing her neck.

'Stop it,' said Jennifer. 'Stop it now.'

He continued kissing her neck. 'What's the harm? You've done an E, I've done some coke. You said you're lonely — let's enjoy ourselves.'

His hand began to work its way in-between her thighs, but she squeezed tight. 'No,' she said firmly, but his hand became more determined. 'No!' she yelled, pushing him away. 'Driver, stop.'

The driver stopped the cab at once, and turned to his passengers. 'What's up, love?'

Jennifer was already opening the door, and didn't wait to answer the cabbie before getting out on to the narrow street that was bustling with pedestrians. She began walking off.

Mike slid over to the open door, leaning out. 'Jennifer, get back in. I'm sorry.'

Jennifer spun around and screamed, 'No! Piss off!'

Dozens of heads turned to look at the scene, and Mike closed the cab door.

Once around a corner, Jennifer began to feel utterly wretched. All she wanted was a friend tonight. She wanted to hold and be held by a friend. She continued walking, with no destination, feeling so distressed and lonely she was jealous of the couples she was seeing. Hundreds of couples on their way from, or to, a happy night out.

She stopped, arrested by an illuminated sign inside an open doorway across the street:

BUSTY, EIGHTEEN-YEAR-OLD MODEL UPSTAIRS

The sign was familiar. She must have been on this street before. Now she remembered: it was opposite the bar where Robert had shared his cocaine with the Rolling Stone. And there was the bar, just a few steps away. But there was no chance of Robert being there, she understood, since he was supposed to be in some place on Brewer Street. But maybe he'd moved on? she hoped, considering his fondness for spreading his drinking.

She approached the bar's entrance. Arriving just ahead of her, coming from the opposite direction, a young man who wouldn't have looked out of place in Darlington town centre on a Friday night peered into the open door and decided to enter, but a doorman inside stepped in his way.

'Private party, mate,' said the doorman, who Jennifer believed not to be the same one she'd seen on her first visit.

'Cunt,' muttered the young man as he went away.

Jennifer's heart sank, thinking Robert would probably not be there if there was a private party in progress.

'Feeling upset, luv?' asked the doorman when he saw her standing outside.

'No,' mumbled Jennifer. 'A bit. Something just happened. Nothing.' She was about to ask if he knew Robert and if he was inside, when he stood aside to permit her entry.

'Don't look so sad on the way out, luv,' he joked, 'or the place'll get a bad name.'

Upon entering, Jennifer saw no evidence of any party in progress, but thought no more about it. She was only thinking about finding Robert. She looked all around downstairs, but saw only strangers. Going upstairs, as the room came into view, she saw not Robert, but Mark, wearing the same light-coloured jacket he'd been wearing the first time she'd seen him here. He was sitting on one of the low two-seater sofas, looking morose and sullen, as if he were at odds with life. Beside him was a young woman with short ginger hair who appeared comparatively joyful.

Avoiding being seen by Mark, Jennifer turned around on the stairs and left the bar. Outside, she walked to the busiest end of the street, but with no idea where to go from there. The E was still strong, and she didn't want to go back to Yvette's yet. Maybe she should take a cab to Brewer Street? But then what? She didn't even know the name of the place where Robert was supposed to be. And besides, Mike would be there.

She had a thought. A clear, strong, compelling thought. She could persuade Mark to help Jeremy and Robert. After all, the argument that had led to his leaving had apparently been over her. It was her duty to try to make things better.

Deliberately giving herself no time to reconsider, she returned to the bar at a brisk pace, and was again allowed unchallenged entry.

Looking up from his low sofa, Mark recognised Jennifer at once. 'Hello, Jennifer,' he said, downbeat, like she might be bad news, his cheerless, moon-like face appearing worried.

'Hello, Mark,' returned Jennifer quickly.

The ginger young woman beside Mark gave Jennifer an unreciprocated smile.

Pulling his hair back over his head with both hands, Mark looked gloomily around the room, resignedly sighing, 'So where's Robert?'

'He's not with me. Can I ask you something?'

'You can ask me anything you want, Jennifer. It doesn't matter now.'

Jennifer came straight out with it. 'Will you help me help Robert? Teach me how to run the business? How to make the books you do?'

Mark balked. 'What? Are you mad? Tell them to find someone else, then run for your life.'

'They tried someone else. Someone called Penny.'

590

Mark pointed to his companion. 'This is Penny.'

'Hi, Jennifer,' said Penny, smiling at the farce.

Jennifer was perturbed. A feeling that something sinister and conspiratorial was afoot took hold of her, and she shrunk back half a step. No, nothing sinister. Just a coincidence.

'But it's my fault,' she blurted to Mark.

'What?' exclaimed Mark, nervously amused by her passion, and colouring slightly.

'Why you left,' explained Jennifer. 'You had an argument with Robert about me.'

Mark drew in a deep, stressful breath and lent back in his seat, putting his hands behind his head for a moment before picking up his bottled beer. 'That's not strictly true. It wasn't even an argument. I'd just had enough of him. The thing with you was just the last straw.'

'What was wrong with me staying overnight?' demanded Jennifer, in a state of perplexity. 'It's his room.'

'Nothing was wrong with you staying overnight,' answered Mark, 'but I had to listen while he took Mike on a victory tour.'

'Mike who owns the tapas restaurant?'

'He doesn't own it,' corrected Mark, 'he manages it. And he's going to be sacked soon, I happen to know.'

Jennifer was no less confused about her involvement in Mark's departure from Robert's life. 'What do you mean a victory tour?'

'A tour of your stains on the carpet and the bed. It not the crudeness, it's the falseness of the bloke. Perpetual falseness.'

The full, disorientating treason struck Jennifer: Robert had been boasting of his sexual conquest of her to the very man who'd just forced unwanted attentions upon her, triumphantly showing him where her period blood had stained during the sex they had had.

Observing Jennifer to be deeply wounded, Penny took her arm. 'Sit down,' she said sympathetically.

Numbly obeying, Jennifer sat on the sofa opposite Mark and Penny, across the low table bearing their drinks. Hurt and confused, she looked into Mark's eyes with a dazed, searching expression.

'Don't worry, you're not the first,' muttered Mark resentfully. 'Most every month he finds some lost soul and does a cheap emotional guru job on them. Never fucks them the first night, so they think he's a saint. A few weeks later he's done with them, and they come asking me what he's really like. Sometimes they end up back with him again for a while, and they tell him what I said about him. I'd had enough of all that, thank you.'

The E seemed to surge, but only to worsen the emotional storm in which Jennifer felt herself adrift. It was all becoming like some strange, dark dream. She seemed somehow detached from the surreal events being played out around her, but also at the centre of them, inclined to believe something insidious and manipulating was afoot.

Vaguely aware she was warm, she mechanically unbuttoned her coat. 'He was so plausible,' she murmured. 'So caring.'

'Believe me, Jennifer,' said Penny, 'Robert throws his arms so easily around people because it means nothing to him. Absolutely nothing. He's giving nothing away.'

'That's right,' agreed Mark, adding, 'He once told me he always wears a mask, and can make people believe anything he wants them to believe about him. Like I was going to be impressed or something.'

'Do yourself a favour, Jennifer,' advised Penny, 'forget him.'

'I've lent him twenty thousand pounds,' revealed Jennifer in a faint voice.

Mark nearly sputtered his drink. 'Twenty grand!' he said in a high voice. 'You lent him twenty grand?'

Penny lifted her jacket off the floor. 'Good time for me to leave, I think.' She kissed Mark's cheek. 'Bye, Mark. Bye, Jennifer. Sorry about your troubles.'

'Keep in touch,' said Mark to Penny as she left.

'Will do,' she called back from the stairs.

Mark turned to Jennifer in earnest astonishment. 'Why did you lend him twenty grand?'

'For his business. They said they'd pay me thirty back in a few months.'

'No they won't,' stated Mark. 'They'll never have money again. It's doomed. I kept telling them that. Money's owed all over the place — sixty grand to the VAT alone. They never do any selling any more. Even if they get their shit together and manage to start a new project without me — and I don't see how, considering they never even got their heads around e-mail — they'll —' He suddenly looked troubled and concerned. 'Did you sign anything linking you to the business? How did you give them the money?'

Slow to apprehend the questions, Jennifer answered, 'No. Nothing signed. I just transferred money to Robert's account.'

'When did this happen? After I left?'

'Yes... The other day.'

Mark thought for a moment. 'Transferred to the business account or Robert's personal account?'

'Personal, I think. A Barclay's account.'

'Yep, his personal. You're on your own, then.'

Jennifer stared at him, slow to understand the situation. 'They were worried you might be able to get at it if it was in their business account.'

'Would have been your best hope,' said Mark. 'Get him to give you it back before it all goes up his nose. Demand it. Tell him you'll inform the police about them unless they give you your money back.' He paused. 'The whole business is bullshit, you know that?'

'You mean about them exaggerating things?'

'Exaggerating? The books never go *anywhere*. There's never any official backing. The only people who see copies are the advertisers themselves.'

Jennifer's expression revealed a lack of comprehension.

Sitting forward, Mark went on. 'Look, it's like this. A title for a book is made up, say like *The Regional Health Authorities Review*. Robert and Jeremy phone up health industry companies and pretend to be working on behalf of the Health Authorities. They tell them they're on an approved supplier list, and persuade them to take out expensive adverts, saying the book is official and will be sent to every doctor and health manager in the country. So a stethoscope manufacturer thinks their advert is going to be seen by tens of thousands of important medical people. It's not. Only a few books are printed to send to the advertisers themselves. There's no distribution. And there's no official backing at all, only lies.'

'So it's fraud?' murmured Jennifer.

Mark sat back. Now, he sounded resentful, even ashamed. 'Yeah, it's fraud. Wasn't meant to be when I set the business up, but it soon went that way. I'd had enough of that, too. I'd rather be poor than go on doing that. But the worst thing about it was the self-denial. Woe betide anyone who spoke the truth in that office. It was all right for Jeremy. In his woolly-minded way he actually believed it was all worthy stuff, brainwashed by Robert's compliments. But I was expected to act in the charade, too.' His voice became low and bitter. 'Never been good at accommodating other people's delusions. It's one thing being in a fucking gang of muggers, but its another when the gang insists between itself they're fucking charity workers.'

Jennifer's gaze had sunk down, and she was staring at the table with a strange look on her face, as if she were internally drifting away on some dark tide. Mark, now that he had finished explaining, complaining, confessing and unburdening, viewed her uneasily.

'I've taken two E's,' she murmured, seemingly to herself.

'Jesus,' reacted Mark, sitting forward. 'Shit. Wish I'd known. Sorry, Jennifer. Thought you were a bit... Do you want a drink or something?'

'I want to go home,' she murmured fadingly. 'I want to go home.'

'Okay,' said Mark, at once standing up. 'Come on, I'll see you into a cab. Have you got money? I'll lend you it if you haven't.'

Jennifer looked up at him, at first appearing to be in a state of insensibility. 'I've got money.'

She stood up, and Mark led the way out the bar, looking over his shoulder at times to assure himself she was still following him. Once on the street, he yelled and waved to an approaching cab. Turning to Jennifer, who was now standing beside him, he asked, 'Stupid question, but are you all right?'

The question seemed not to have registered, and was not repeated. The cab drew up in front of them. Mark held the passenger door open, but Jennifer didn't climb in. She looked at him: a strange, spectral look. 'Come with me. I don't want to be alone. I've taken two E's.'

'I know you've taken two E's,' said Mark.

'Please,' said Jennifer, her eyes pale and sincere, bewildered and beseeching.

'Nah,' said Mark, shuffling in discomfort. 'It'll end in trouble for me. It always does. I'm out of it all now.'

'I've taken some ecstasy,' said Jennifer.

Mark deliberated, then relented. Stooping, he clambered into the cab, and Jennifer followed, sitting on his left.

'Where to?' he asked.

'Holloway Road,' she answered, but thereafter sank into a state of apparent deep abstraction, staring at the flip-up seat in front of her, unresponsive to Mark's single attempt to draw her into conversation.

Later, when the cab was in virtually stationary traffic, waiting to join a main road, Jennifer was still staring at the flip-up seat, but in a vague voice, she said, 'He assaulted me.'

'Robert?' asked Mark incredulously.

'No. Not Robert. Not really. His friend, Mike. Sexually assaulted me.'

'Oh, Mike. Shit. Sorry. Are you —'

Having at last been able to turn on to the main road, the driver slid his glass screen open, and spoke over Mark. 'This is Holloway Road, mate. Whereabouts?'

Jennifer looked out the window, and a resolve seemed to suddenly possess her. 'Here. Right here. This is it.'

Leaving the line of traffic, the cab pulled into the kerb. Jennifer saw no light on in Yvette's flat. With her hand on the door lever, she looked at Mark. 'Will you come in and help me carry some things out? I'll have you dropped anywhere you want after.'

'What kind of things?'

'A suitcase... and some bags. I'm going to move into a hotel.'

'What? How long will it take?'

'Ten minutes. Less.'

'Okay,' said Mark, but not sounding happy.

Jennifer opened the door and hurried out, oblivious to the driver's need for payment.

'Can you wait for us to come back?' Mark asked the driver.

'If you pay me first.'

Mark handed him a twenty pound note.

'That'll keep me here a while,' said the driver. 'I'll toot if you're too long.'

The telephone was ringing as Jennifer, accompanied by Mark, let herself into the flat, but it stopped right away. Although wary of Mark, the cat loped to her, rubbing against her legs, but she ignored it.

'Feeling any better now?' asked Mark.

'Yes,' said Jennifer, looking preoccupied and serious. She took off her coat, laying it over the back of the sofa. 'I'll get my stuff from the bathroom first. I won't be long. I haven't got much here.'

While Jennifer was absent, Mark wandered around in an unsettled manner. Noticing a photograph on top of the television, he picked it up for closer examination.

Holding a half-full carrier bag, Jennifer returned. Standing in the middle of the room, tying the bag's handles, she looked at the cat. 'I'm taking the cat,' she announced. 'Will you help me with it?'

'Whose flat is this?' asked Mark.

'Yvette's,' answered Jennifer, retrieving her suitcase from behind the sofa. 'Robert's French friend.' Glancing at Mark, she saw that he was looking at a photo of Yvette and Peter. Then she remembered. 'God, I'm sorry,' she said, pausing in her task. 'I wasn't thinking. I should have told you. It's all right, she's out clubbing. You can leave now if you want. Thanks for bringing me back.'

'Not as sorry as me,' muttered Mark, looking at the photo in his hands. 'I had to go and meet the one I couldn't forget, didn't I?'

'Is it that bad?'

'Couldn't be worse. Might as well have died the day I first saw Yvette. Better than this miserable life sentence.'

'Maybe you just don't know her well enough?' offered Jennifer.

'I know her,' muttered Mark. 'I know Peter, too.'

'She's got a new boyfriend.'

Jennifer had spoken without thinking, hoping to ease Mark's obvious hurt, but she could see at once she had failed.

'Yeah?' returned Mark. 'Why does that hurt me so much? It shouldn't make any difference, should it?'

'Don't you have a girlfriend yourself?'

He shrugged. 'I'd only be lying to her if I did. I've told enough lies in my life.'

A key entered the door, which opened. Yvette came in, hand-in-hand with Steven, who was wearing a thick, heavy jacket. Mark knew it made no real difference to him, but seeing Yvette with a new boyfriend wounded him badly.

Yvette's face became instantly angry when she saw Mark.

'What are you doing 'ere?' she said brutally, unhanding Steven and stepping toward Mark.

'Leaving,' returned Mark.

'I asked him in,' said Jennifer. 'I'm leaving too.'

'What are you doing with my photo?' Yvette challenged Mark.

'Nothing,' said Mark, going to put the photo back where he'd found it.

Yvette turned to Steven and said, 'Get 'im out. Robert says 'e's weird. I 'ate 'im now as well. Really 'ate 'im.'

'Sling y'hook, pal,' ordered Steven, slipping quickly out of his bulky jacket.

Mark told Jennifer he'd wait for her on the landing, to help her down the stairs with her bags when she was ready. Stepping out the flat, he received a threatening glower from Steven.

Jennifer wordlessly resumed her packing while Steven stood guard by the door.

'Where are you going?' asked Yvette disapprovingly. 'Robert's?'

'Fuck Robert,' returned Jennifer, stuffing her new clothes into carrier bags.

''Ow can you say that?' challenged Yvette.

'Oh, open your eyes.'

'Yvette,' said Steven sternly, 'thought I'd told you to get rid of that fucking thing?'

He was looking at the cat, which had just come out of hiding.

'I did,' protested Yvette, at once trying to catch her pet.

'LEAVE IT!' shouted Jennifer, so loud that Yvette and Steven were jolted. 'Leave it,' she repeated, but quieter. 'I'll take it. You don't want it.'

Heavy thumping began on the ceiling, and Steven looked up. 'What the fuck's that?'

'The woman upstairs is complaining,' explained Yvette. 'She won't stop for five minutes now.'

Looking fearful, Mark stepped into the flat. 'What's going on?' he asked Jennifer. 'What's the noise? Everything all right?'

'Oi!' exclaimed Steven aggressively. 'We told you to fucking get out. Now fuck off.'

Steven stepped toward Mark and added physical impetus to his order, but Mark pushed his arm away. Instantly, Steven viciously set upon him, headbutting him, then unleashing a flurry of five or more punches before his victim even had time to fall. And when Mark did hit the floor, Steven danced clear like a boxer, keenly assessing the damage and further opportunity for attack.

Jennifer shrunk back in fright, horror and disbelief.

Mark quickly managed to make it to all fours, lurching unsteadily for the door and escape, but he received a gratuitous, stomping kick to the body that made Yvette flinch, and left him lying face down. Slowly, woozily, he dragged himself to a corner near the door, where he slumped down, with his shoulders and head against the wall. His eyes appeared ten gallons drunk. Blood was running freely from his nose, over his chin and down on to his light shirt, so he appeared to be wearing a glistening red tie. More blood was seeping from a torn ear.

Transfixed by shock, horror and stomach-gripping fear, Jennifer could barely react. She looked to Yvette, but Yvette assumed her sullen aspect, the aspect which Jennifer had learned spoke her resentful awareness of self-fault. The ceiling was still being thumped, and Jennifer watched mutely as Steven pulled a chair into the middle of the room and made return thumps.

'Shut up you fucking mad whore or I'll come and sort you out too, you slag,' he bellowed upward. In response, the thumping became violent pounding – jumping, it now sounded like, so hard the ceiling could be heard cracking. 'You fucking cunt bitch,' he roared.

'No, Steven,' reproved Yvette, with an intolerant weariness in her voice. 'Just let her finish. Get down.'

Mark began crawling out the door, while Yvette, acting as if nothing grotesquely untoward had happened, took off her jacket and went to the kitchen.

'Yeah, fuck off, cunt,' snarled Steven after Mark, stepping off the chair.

Still barely able to react, Jennifer went to Mark, now crouched on the dim landing. 'I'm all right,' he said as she knelt beside him. 'Leave me.' His jaw didn't seem to work properly any more, and his laboured words were close to unintelligible. He struggled to his feet, belligerently shaking off Jennifer's numb attempts to assist, and went down the stairs, stooped and leaving a trail of blood drips.

'I'm sorry,' she murmured.

Watching Mark descend, Jennifer's drugged eye began seeing her surroundings as dark, sinister and claustrophobic, and the pounding on the ceiling reverberated in the stairwell like some maddening, nightmarish headache.

Yvette's telephone rang. 'Ello?' Jennifer heard Yvette say, in a voice subdued and tense, but straining to sound normal. 'Ello, 'ow are you? ... Yes, she is. She's just outside.' She appeared at the door. 'Jennifer, your sister's on the phone.'

Jennifer looked at Yvette, but appeared to understand little.

'I've made coffee,' added Yvette, in a voice that fell away, and she went back into her flat.

Stirred into numb action, Jennifer went downstairs to look for Mark. The street door was open, and she found him outside, leaning against the window of the laundrette under Yvette's flat, bent over a small puddle of blood.

'I'm sorry,' she murmured, standing beside him, placing a hand on his back.

'I'm all right,' he groaned, slowly straightening up.

Blood was still dripping from his nose, and he pulled his shirt out from under his belt to hold to his face. Slowly, Jennifer reached to touch Mark's cheek, wiping blood on to her hands and transferring that blood to her own face and clothes while he woozily watched in benumbed confusion and disquiet.

'Oi, Jennifer,' called Steven from the window above.

Jennifer looked up and saw Steven holding the cat out at arms length, wriggling and struggling in his unfriendly grip.

'Take this fucking thing with you,' he said, dropping the animal

598

to the pavement.

The cat landed heart-stoppingly hard next to Jennifer, but immediately ran off, heedless of direction. Where it had landed, she saw something. Picking it up, she confirmed it to be a tiny, bloodied, broken tooth. Uncomprehendingly, she looked up to the window again and saw Yvette close the curtains. She stared at the tooth resting in her palm, then turned back to Mark, but he was not there. Hearing an engine start, she saw the cab that had been waiting drive off with Mark in the back.

Nothing felt real any more. *She* didn't feel real – didn't feel like she was part of the world around her, and the world around her was a dark, grotesque carnival. She saw the cat run behind some roadside rubbish bags, and went to pick it up, but it darted away from her, on to the busy road, where it at once received a glancing blow from a vehicle. She winced, and winced again when the following vehicle ran directly over it, bursting it. Then vehicle after vehicle reduced it to a thick slab of mince and fur while she stood helplessly by. Finally, oblivious to the traffic, she stepped out into the road to rescue the cat's remains, causing drivers to brake hard and angrily blare their horns, anger which quickly became bewildered concern.

Holding blood, guts, fur and bones to her bosom, oblivious to the stares of pedestrians, Jennifer went back inside, closing the street door behind her. She carried on up the stairs and into Yvette's flat. The woman above was still jumping, and Steven was in the middle of the room, glaring up at ceiling. Seeing Jennifer, he barked, 'You going to answer that phone or—' His words tailed off when he saw that she was carrying the cat's oozing remains, and blood was smeared over her face and clothes. 'Fuck me,' he breathed.

Yvette appeared, carrying a bowl of soapy water, and saw Jennifer standing by the door.

'Oh my God,' she murmured, halting and staring. 'Is that my cat?'

Like some pale, tragic apparition, Jennifer looked at Yvette but seemed to see beyond her, to some other world. Then she looked at the telephone, and moved toward it, watched wordlessly by Steven and Yvette. She slowly, carefully, knelt down, and with the pulped cat in her lap, picked up the receiver off the table.

'She's lost it,' said Steven, unsympathetically.

Yvette adopted her sullen look, and placed her bowl of soapy water down. Squeezing out a cloth, she began scrubbing the carpet where Mark had bled.

'It was me,' murmured Jennifer.

'Yeah, go on, get more blood on the carpet,' muttered Steven to Jennifer before picking up and putting on his coat. Going over to Yvette, who continued to scrub, he said, in a voice that betrayed some uncertainty and nervousness, 'You'll ring me tomorrow, then?'

Without looking up from her cleaning work, Yvette sullenly and quietly answered, 'Yeah, okay. Bye.'

Standing over Yvette, Steven deliberated a moment, began to stoop to kiss her, hesitated, then walked out the flat, leaving the door open, which Yvette reached for and closed.

'I'm not seeing 'im any more,' she said, in her subdued voice, continuing her cleaning as the pounding on the ceiling went on.

*

Still wearing the shirt Jackie had bought him, Albert was sitting in a corner, clutching a small velvet pouch Rebecca had given him earlier. The Beatles were again criticising and judging him while he studied one of Tony's psychiatry textbooks, open on his lap, searching to understand what had gone wrong with his head.

Jackie was present, but about to leave. She knelt down beside him. 'Any luck yet, Albert?'

Colouring slightly, not raising his eyes from the text, he quietly said, 'Far as I can tell, I'm a manic-depressive, passive-aggressive, submissive-assertive, moralistic-libertarian, narcissistic self-loather. Small wonder my life's a mess.'

Jackie smiled, and ruffled his hair before standing up. 'Got to go and meet my boyfriend. I'll see you soon.'

When Jackie left, Albert emptied the velvet pouch on to the carpet beside him, and stared at his collection of diamonds, which Tony had still not managed to have banished from the house — Tony, in fact, had resorted to more or less banishing himself instead, going off to visit his parents on the Isle of Wight for the weekend.

Continuing to stare at his gems, Albert knew he could reasonably dare to consider them as representing a significant addition to not only the quality of his life, but also the quantity. He could invest in a bio-technology company, and be among the first to benefit from the nature-defying discoveries.

Ron was lighting a joint. Albert wondered whether he would have been all right had he not drawn on that pipe last night. Would he have gone ga-ga the very next time he got stoned? Or was it because bad things had been so fresh in his mind? Or was he simply due to go ga-ga anyway, never mind the dope... or Phil? He would never know. Never know. And would he ever feel comfortable again? He feared not. He could reasonably dare for extended life, but that life would be a poisoned one, and his sparkling riches now appeared to him like some taunting, mocking irony, placed in his possession only because they were of no use to him, or rather he was of no use to them.

'Jennifer?' queried Sarah. 'What's all that noise going on?'

When Albert heard Sarah say Jennifer's name, realising who it was she was calling, he became tremulous.

'It was me,' murmured Jennifer, in a voice strange to Sarah.

'What was you? Is there something wrong? Why did it take you so long to come to the phone?'

'It was me,' murmured Jennifer again.

'Are you pissed or something?'

'I've taken some ecstasy,' murmured Jennifer.

'You don't sound very ecstatic.'

Jennifer fell silent, and Sarah now became deeply worried.

'Jennifer? Are you there? Jennifer? Jennifer, if you're there, Albert's here. He's back. Do you want to speak to him?' Receiving no reply, Sarah turned desperately to Albert. 'Albert, speak to her. She's taken some E.'

Albert glanced nervously at Sarah, and shook his head. 'Can't.'

'Albert,' demanded Sarah sternly, 'speak to her. She's freaking out or something.'

'So am I,' said Albert.

'They died because of me,' said Jennifer, but Sarah didn't hear properly.

'What? What did you say?'

Jennifer fell silent again.

'Wait there,' said Sarah to Jennifer. Bringing the phone to Albert, Sarah made him hold the receiver, lifting it to his ear.

As if having resolved some internal struggle, Yvette stopped washing the carpet and went over to Jennifer, who looked at her without seeming to perceive her presence. Tearful now, she took the bloodstained telephone from Jennifer's hand and spoke to the caller.

'You 'ave to come,' she said.

'Jennifer?' asked Albert nervously.

'No, Yvette. Someone 'as to come.'

'What's happened?'

'Never mind. Let me talk to 'er sister. Quick.'

With a fearful look, Albert offered the phone to Sarah, who

took it and heard Yvette's unspecific, subdued explanation and call for assistance while Ron and Rebecca gathered around her in concern.

'Okay, tell Jennifer we're on our way,' said Sarah, once she understood a small part of the seriousness of the situation. 'We're leaving now. We'll keep calling along the way. We'll be there in around four hours. For God's sake, don't let her leave your flat.' She put the phone down, and picked up her coat. 'My sister's had some kind of breakdown. Who's coming to London with me?'

Ron immediately picked up his coat too, but Albert remained on the floor, nervously observing the earnest pre-departure activity.

'Come on, Albert,' said Sarah, 'you too.'

Albert looked at her, and shook his head. Feeling himself burning, he held a concealing hand to his face, and looked down.

'Come on, Albert,' said Ron.

'I can't,' said Albert, 'I've gone mad.'

'Bugger that. Come on, hurry.'

'You don't understand,' said Albert, shamefully.

'Albert,' said Sarah, ready to leave, 'she'll want you there. I know it.'

'I can't,' he said guiltily. 'I've gone mad.'

'So has Jennifer, by all accounts,' returned Sarah, 'so come on.'

Glancing up from his low position, Albert felt an intimidation. Displeased people were towering over him. He felt like a small child again.

Sarah knelt beside him, causing him to colour up anew. 'Albert, remember me telling you that after meeting you, Jennifer stopped feeling so bad about feeling bad, the way you joke about feeling melancholy?'

'I remember.'

'Well, maybe she won't take being mad so seriously with you around, joking about how you've gone wacko too.'

Falling silent, Albert struggled with his inner opposition. He couldn't even contemplate leaving the house, let alone going all the way to London. It was beyond the shattered remains of his confidence.

'I can't,' he said. 'I'm with the fallen.'

'Albert!' snapped Rebecca, flipping the psychiatry book off his lap and pulling him up by the hair, 'stop being a self-absorbed, introspective, poetic wanker and go with Sarah. Jennifer needs help.'

'All right, all right,' he desperately acquiesced, wincing with the pain Rebecca was inflicting. 'I'm going.'

Only minutes later, he was in the back of Sarah's car, about to join the southbound motorway. Ron was in the front passenger seat. It was past midnight, so the traffic was light, and was mostly northbound. They would make good time, Ron predicted, especially if they didn't stop to pick up the dodgy-looking hitchhiker on the roadside ahead holding up a sign for London. Ron began entering Yvette's number into his mobile while Sarah drove with a worried, preoccupied look. There was an air of quiet but steely purpose, which Albert could sense but couldn't imagine he was making a contribution to. He was of no use at all, least of all himself.

When they passed the hitchhiker, Albert suddenly realised it had been Joe, and felt guilty about leaving him on the roadside.

'We should go back and pick up that hitchhiker,' he said quietly.

'Bollocks,' said Ron. 'He looked a bit weird.'

'I know him,' murmured Albert.

'Yeah? Who is he?'

'A poet I met the other day. He won a prize. We should go back and get him.'

'Don't be mad,' said Ron, 'we can't turn back now.'

Ron was right: they were already slipping on to the motorway.

'We've got another poet to worry about first,' said Sarah.

'You calling Albert a poet?' challenged Ron. 'You've gone as mad as he has.'

'No, my sister. I used to call her The Poet.'

'Oh.'

'Maddened not mad,' murmured Albert, too low to be heard, recalling how, after all his trials, Joe had finally understood that he was not mad, but had been maddened. Was that his own condition? And could that now be the condition of Jennifer? Was it the eventual condition of all poets: to become maddened into crippling self-doubt and paralysing, incredulous astonishment by... the often routine, everyday madness of others? Joe had been maddened by communion with the lady he named the Antichrist, who could cheerily tell a thousand ruinous lies to conceal a single bland truth. And he himself, on top of all his previous trials, had been finally maddened by a murder cheerily committed in his own name for the sake of the madness of religious belief, an astonishing madness banally embraced in one form or other by most every living person.

Wordsworth had got it wrong, Albert realised: poets don't become mad, they become maddened. One way or another, they become maddened. Either by the drip, drip of the world's banal lunacy, or prematurely by some sudden flood of lunacy.

And what of Jennifer? wondered Albert. What had maddened her? He would find out. He would find out and show her that she was true while whatever world she had fallen into was false.

'Can I put some music on?' asked Sarah, and without waiting for any expression of consensus, she pushed in the CD that was already half-loaded. 'This is the one you copied for me the other week, Albert. I've worked out some of the cello parts. I'll play along to it one day for you.'

Albert had given Sarah a copy of his favourite album: Nick Drake's, *Five Leaves Left*, with its lush, orchestral arrangements. But tonight he expected the vocals to trigger trains of cheerless, self-accusing thought, as the Beatles' lyrics had so successfully managed the previous night. The music began, and Mr. Drake's mellow, breathy, flutey voice sang of "*a troubled cure, for a troubled mind*", but no self-accusing thoughts arose, only a clear command to himself to do as Sarah wished: to be a troubled cure for Jennifer's troubled mind. To do anything and everything in his power to bring her peace of mind would be his life, a life he would be content to live.

The end